# THE HERACLIAD

## THE EPIC SAGA
## OF HERCULES

RICHARD BERTEMATTI

ISBN: 978-0-9903027-1-1 (paperback)
Library of Congress Control Number:  2014939856

Published by Tridium Press

www.bertematti.com

*Uxor mea, familia mea:*
*Amor ac deliciae meae, mundus meus, vita mea*

THE HERACLIAD


*I sing of Heracles, Zeus' son,*
>*By far the best of men.*
*Born in Thebes fair-dancing*
>*To lovely Alcmenè.*
*On order of Eurystheus his lord*
>*He wandered o'er lands and seas,*
*Suffering violence as he went*
>*Performing noble deeds.*
*Atop snowy Mount Olympos*
>*He lives now happily;*
*And as his wife he now enjoys*
>*Neatly-ankled Hēbē.*

*Hail, lord, son of Zeus!*
*Make me rich and virtuous!*

>Homeric Hymns 15-
>'To Heracles the Lion-Hearted'

# CONTENTS

# PROLOGUE

After Perseus the Gorgon-slayer accidentally killed his grandfather Acrisios, he was ashamed to inherit the throne of Argos. He therefore approached his great-uncle Megapenthes, king of Tyrins, and asked to exchange kingdoms with him. Although Perseus then took control of Tyrins and neighboring Midea, he decided to found the stronghold of Mycenae further north on the Argolid plain.

While residing at Mycenae, Andromeda bore Perseus five sons: Electryon, Sthenelos, Alcaios, Mestor and Heleios; and one daughter, Gorgophone. Electryon, who inherited the throne after his father's death, in his old age fell into conflict with Pterelaos and his sons, descendants of Mestor, who hailed from the Taphaic lands off of Acarnania. These Taphians, called also Teleboans, sailed to the Argolid to lay claim to Mycenae. When Electryon refused to relinquish any share of his kingdom, they stole his cattle. A fierce struggle ensued between the sons of Electryon and those of Pterelaos, in which all but one were killed on each side. The remaining Teleboans managed to flee with the cattle, and on their way homeward entrusted them to Polyxenos, ruler of the Epeians.

Learning of the death of all his sons, save the youngest, Licymnios, Electryon resolved to make war on the Teleboans. In his absence, he entrusted the kingdom to his nephew Amphytrion, son of Alcaios, as well as the care of his beautiful daughter Alcmene of Midea, enjoining him not to touch her until he returned. It so happened that shortly after Electryon departed, Amphytrion learned the whereabouts of the missing cattle, and agreed to pay the king of the Epeians a large ransom for them. On hearing word of this, Electryon returned, demanding how Amphytrion could keep privy a transaction involving his own property. Amphytrion, thinking he had done the High King a favor, became so annoyed that he threw a club at one of the cows that had had strayed from the herd. Redounding off the bovine's horns, the club flew toward Electryon, striking his head and killing him instantly.

Electryon's brother Sthenelos in the aftermath seized control of Mycenae, Tyrins and Midea from Amphytrion, who had a right to Perseus' ancestral realm from his father Alcaios, and banished him. Taking his betrothed Alcmene and her brother Licymnios with him, he fled to Thebes, where he was purified by Creon, son of Menoiceos, who had assumed the throne after the murder of Laios. There Amphytrion wed Alcmene, while Licymnios married his sister Perimede. The chaste and pious Alcmene would not, however, admit Amphytrion to her marriage-bed until the murders of her brothers were avenged. Amphytrion therefore prepared to march against the Teleboans, hoping for Creon's assistance. The latter, however, first asked him to rid the territory of Thebes of a pernicious vixen from Mount Teumessos, sent there by Dionysos. As a ward against greater mischief, the Thebans were reduced to exposing to her one of their sons each month. Amphytrion, knowing that this fox was fated never to be captured, visited Cephalos in Attica to persuade him, in return for a share of the Teleboan spoils, to lend to the hunt his dog, Lailaps, fated to always capture whatever it pursued. This dog Cephalos' wife Procris received from Minos and brought it back from Crete. The chase for the Teumessian vixen caused such an intolerable paradox that the very fabric of nature would have been bruised had not Zeus intervened and turned both beasts to stone: the hound about to catch its prey; and the vixen ever escaping by a hair.

With his allies, Amphytrion sailed off to fight the Teleboans; but he could not capture Taphos since Pterelaos wore a golden lock of hair, given to him by Poseidon, that rendered him invincible. When his daughter, Comaitho, saw handsome Amphytrion as he lay a distance away at anchor, she fell in love with him; and thinking to do him a service, she plucked the golden hair from her father's head, causing his death. Amphytrion was then able to complete the conquest of the islands.

Meanwhile Zeus, father of men and gods, had been observing these events with interest; for no mortal woman of great beauty ever escaped his notice. With his wife Hera preoccupied with one of her own intrigues, he came down from Mount

Olympos, and transforming himself into an exact likeness of Amphytrion, visited Alcmene with the glad tidings that her brothers had been avenged (in this, at least, Zeus was truthful, for the true Amphytrion had just accomplished that). As proof, he presented her with an ancestral goblet of the Teleboans, a gift of Poseidon, which Amphytrion had selected for himself from the spoils, and Zeus had appropriated for his ruse. Overjoyed, Alcmene allowed him into her chamber, and there Zeus enjoyed her inordinately by tripling the length of a single night. Knowing that this union would produce a most especial offspring, Zeus wished not to rush. He, therefore, ordered the Sun to unyoke his team and cease his diurnal ride across the æther; the Moon he commanded to slow her advance on the heels of day; and Sleep he enjoined to keep men in thrall so they would lose track of the time. All on earth remained drowsy and knew not the frolic of the god. As the long night came to a close, Zeus looked at the sleeping Alcmene, her white arms resting at her side, and her bosom rising gently with each breath, and said: "Today I have conceived a son; and he shall be the savior of gods and men." He then returned to Olympos, assuming once again his terrible form.

In the morning, as Dawn with rosy fingers touched heaven's rim, Amphytrion returned in triumph, and marching into his bedchamber to greet his wife received less of a reception than he had hoped. Alcmene soon grew weary of hearing him recount his exploits; for she had heard the same narrative the night before. "We hardly slept," said she. "Why do you repeat again what you have already told me?" Confused by her remarks, and seeing the Taphian goblet already in his wife's possession, Amphytrion called for the aged and blind seer Teiresias, the wisest man in Thebes, who told him immediately that he had been cuckolded by the king of the gods.

After nine months Zeus, in the company of the male gods on Olympos, boasted that the mighty son he had fathered, the last by a mortal woman, destined to rule the Argives, was about to be born. Hera, after eavesdropping at the door, on a pretense invited Zeus into her chamber, and after plying him with nectar, the divine drink of the gods, made him confirm by an oath that any son born before nightfall to the House of Perseus, would become High King of Mycenae.

At once Hera called for Eileithyia, goddess of childbirth. "Fly to Mycenae and ensure the son of Nicippe, wife of king Sthenelos, is born first," ordered Hera. Eileithyia did as she was bidden and hastened Nicippe's pangs so that she pushed out Eurystheus, son of Sthenelos, at seven months. Thessalian witches, meanwhile, she sent to Thebes to delay the labor of Alcmene. One of them squatted cross-legged at Alcmene's door, her clothing tied in knots, and her fingers locked together. A handmaiden of Alcmene, fair, golden-haired Galanthis, noticed the crone, and thinking something foul was afoot, ran from the birth chamber to announce, untruthfully, that Alcmene had just given birth. In surprise, the witch sprang up, breaking her binding spell. At that moment, Heracles, originally called Alcaios after his grandfather, was born, followed by a twin brother, Iphicles. Galanthis laughed on hearing the babes' cry, proud of her deception. The witches, although they had accomplished their commission, were much less amused. Seizing the girl by her hair, they cursed her and turned her into a weasel. Faithful Galanthis continued to roam Alcmene's house after that, although the poor girl was no longer much noticed.

When Amphytrion told Alcmene what he had learned from Teiresias, she fell silent with astonishment. Who was she that a god—Zeus himself—would wish to visit her? She looked at her children, sleeping peacefully at her breast, and grew fearful of Hera's jealousy. In her heart she knew that the firstborn, though smaller than his twin, was the one divinely sired. She became so obsessed with the threat of Hera's displeasure that she decided, against all maternal instinct, to expose the newly-born Heracles. At least in that way, if Hera wished him punished, no harm would come to her other son; at the same time, if he was truly the son of Zeus, then surely the god would not allow anything to happen to him. If she had decided wrongly, however—woe betide her! One early morning, she tightly swaddled the babe, and leaving Iphicles in the care of a handmaiden, took little Heracles to a field outside the walls of Thebes beyond the Neistan gates. There she laid him down on the soft grass, and sitting by him for a moment, with the breeze gently caressing them, she wept over her helpless boy. Three times she tried to walk away, and three times she returned, ready to take him back into her arms. At last she kissed his little face and left him.

Unbeknownst to Alcmene, a giant, golden eagle flew high overhead, and seeing the child, darted upward, piercing the clouds, and arrived at the side of the throne of Zeus. This splendid creature was Zeus' messenger, ever at his side, adopted when it first appeared to him as a sign of good omen at the eve of the war against the Titans. On hearing what Alcmene had done, Zeus was not at all worried, for he knew that his grandmother Gaia, the Earth, would cushion his son's form on the dewy grass; and he knew his old grandfather Ouranos, the Sky, would not allow him to get too hot. And so, with a sparkle in his eye, he conceived a humorous plot. He called for his favorite daughter, Athena. Tall and marvelous, her white skin lambent with divine light, she entered the hall, greaves on her legs, a golden corslet about her breast, and her high-plumed helm held ready at her side. She bowed slightly before her mighty father, inquiring whether he wished her to carry forth his awful ægis. He looked down at his gray-eyed daughter with amusement, for from the moment, after suffering a terrible headache, his head split open and out she sprang full-grown and full-armored, she was ready to do battle; and yet she possessed a most gentle side, delighting in handicrafts and husbandry, the taming of horses and the culture of city life. He had her put away her accouterments, and beckoning her close, whispered in her ear what he wished her to do.

Somehow, Athena convinced Hera, who had much to do that day, to accompany her on a casual stroll. They ended up near Thebes, where Athena spied a baby on the ground, quietly sleeping to the warbles of bluejays and finches coming from a nearby grove. "Why look, dear Hera—what a stout little boy! Who could have left him there?" Athena, acting surprised, stooped to pick up the boy, who, awaking, began to smack his lips. "His mother must have been daft to abandon him," she said. "He must be famished. Hera, you have milk—give the little one suck!" Without a thought Hera, who had raised many children of her own, bared her breast and took the child in her arms. Little Heracles, however, latched on to her with such force that Hera cast him from her, and in the process a spurt of milk dashed across the sky and formed the Milky Way; some say, however, that it was formed long before that, but in a similar fashion, when Zeus was forcibly weaned by his mother

Rhea.

As Athena laughed merrily at her expense, Hera, guessing now the identity of the child, and that he would become immortal from ingesting the divine milk, stomped off with revenge on her mind. Athena took up the child again and in the form of an ordinary maiden entered the city. She arrived at the house of Alcmene and remained in the courtyard while the lady was informed. Alcmene had spent the rest of the day secluded in her chamber, the curtains drawn, sitting in the dark, her mind heavy with the thought of her crime. How was she to excuse it to Amphytrion when he returned? When a servant entered to announce the visitors, Alcmene's heart leapt within her. She rushed to the courtyard and saw the child she had exposed. Was her crime discovered? Alcmene, seeing the goddess's divine light spilling from under the hem of her garment, dropped to her knees in fear, with head bowed low, expecting a dire punishment. Athena laughed, bid her rise, and handing her the babe said: "Here is your son; rear him well!" In a flash Athena was gone. Alcmene, trembling but thankful, hugged the child and smeared him with kisses.

After that Alcmene held both her children close, and watched them grow into pudgy infants: especially little Heracles, for he was the stoutest of the two. One summer night, when they had reached ten months of age, she gave them their nightly baths and fill of milk. Then she laid them, as in a cradle, on a large bronze shield in a figure of eight that Amphytrion had brought back from his campaign against the Teleboans, under a fleece coverlet, and rocked them until they feel asleep, cooing: "Sleep sweetly and lightly, my babes. Sleep, sweethearts, brothers, good children. May heaven bless your slumber, and in the morrow your awakening." Carefully shutting the nursery door, she retired to her own chamber, where her husband, weary from the day, already slept.

At midnight, when the house was darkest and quietest, two monstrous snakes with azure scales, sent by Hera, slid into the house. Along the cold marble floor they writhed forward on their bellies, eyes glowing with an evil light. Reaching the nursery, they reared their ugly heads above the rim of the shield, hissing and spitting out deadly venom. Iphicles was first to awake, and seeing the serpents ready to strike with long, hideous, moist fangs, screamed and kicked off his blanket in an agony to flee.

In the next room, Alcmene heard the frightened cries of Iphicles, and seeing a pale light shining under the nursery door, roused her husband: "Arise, Amphytrion! I cannot stir from fear. Do you not hear the cry of Iphicles?—for surely it is him. And that brightness—as if it was day: are you sure it is the dead of night? Something dreadful must be happening!" Amphytrion jumped out of bed, and not bothering to put on his slippers, grasped his sword; and, calling his servants for lamps, rushed into the nursery.

There sat Heracles, who had not uttered a sound through the ordeal, holding the bristling snakes in the grip of his soft tiny fingers. As he strangled them to death, he crowed with delight. When they fell limp, their unnatural light extinguished, he threw them to the floor at Amphytrion's feet. Amphytrion had no doubt now of Heracles' sire; and neither did Alcmene. She took up the distraught Iphicles, stiff with fright, and tried to sooth him at her breast. Amphytrion laid Heracles back beneath the woolen coverlet, and in no time he fell fast asleep.

At dawn, after the cock had crowed thrice, Alcmene sought Teiresias and told him of the prodigy that night.

"Tell me, wise one, what this means," she begged. "I must know for sure, once and for all, if he is the son of Zeus. If so, what is his destiny? Tell me all, whether joy or sorrow is in his future and ours."

The aged prophet, given the gift of augury by Zeus himself, consulted his inner sight and responded: "Be of good cheer, Alcmene, for you have found favor with God. Your son will be the greatest of all men. He will perform mighty deeds in the service of humanity, and undergo many labors, never to be forgotten unto ages and ages. His life will contain both glory and great suffering, for Hera hates him; it was she who sent the serpents to destroy him. In the end, however, he is destined to join the company of the gods, giving hope to all who wish to follow in his steps. And by the sweet light gone from my eyes I swear that women, as they card their wool in the evening, will celebrate the name of Alcmene in song. Now, my lady, you must do this: strew your hearth with dry furze, thorn and brambles. At midnight—the very hour they chose to slay your son—burn the serpents upon the smoldering wild wood. In the morning, send a maid-servant to collect the ashes and take them to a river-cliff, where she must scatter them and return without looking back.  Then purge the entire palace with brimstone and sprinkle spring water, mingled with salt, from a wool-wound branch.  After all this is done, sacrifice a wild boar to Zeus.  The child will then be safe, until the time comes for him to embark on his destiny."

Alcmene did as she was instructed, ready to share with her glorious son in the exquisite joys and exquisite sorrows that Fortune had in store.

# BOOK I

## IN THE MIDST OF LABORS

### 1

On his birthday, Eurystheus, High King of Mycenae, forgetting about Heracles, abandoned himself in a grand celebration to which he invited all the chieftains of the Argolid. Midway through the festivities, his youngest daughter Admete appeared and began to dance in whorls of violet-colored flounce and glittering veil, enrapturing the guests as she twirled on petal-soft feet. Concluding before her father's throne, she looked up at him with the depths of her limpid eyes and breathlessly said: "Will you grant me anything I wish?" Eurystheus was so pleased, and his judgment so impaired by wine, that he lifted her veil, caressed her blooming face, and promised her anything, even half his kingdom. "It is said that the terrible god Ares gave the gift of a golden girdle to the queen of the Amazons," said Admete. "I very much desire to possess it." Eurystheus, taken aback, rued his rash oath as his herald Copreus entered to announce that Heracles, after four months and a day, had returned with the savage mares of Diomedes. Eurystheus betrayed not his twin feelings of rage and astonishment at hearing the news, but smiled placidly at Admete, promising to grant her caprice. Bowing before her father, she hid her glee at the success of her scheme, for she guessed that Eurystheus would certainly entrust Heracles with the insuperable errand.

Heracles, who had driven the mares across the mountains, through Emathia and Thessaly, into Boetia, down the Isthmus, and up the long, walled passage to the imposing gates of Mycenae, above which arched two artfully carven lions of dark limestone, gaily painted and  inlaid with eyes of precious stone, waited with subdued impatience for Eurystheus to come see for himself.  The king could not at first believe that the mares, now docile, were those that belonged to Diomedes and ate man-flesh; and, in an offhanded way, accused Heracles, who took no evident notice, of mischief.  After much reassurance from Heracles, Copreus found the nerve to approach and examine the chariot, upon which intricate designs, identifying it as a royal Thracian vehicle, were embossed in gold.  Eurystheus then publicly dedicated the prize to Hera, ignorant of the havoc that the Cretan bull he had not long before released had caused at Marathon.[1]

Dismissing Copreus, Eurystheus directly ordered: "My daughter made an unusual request of me today, Heracles, and it seemed fitting to pass it on to you as your next Labor.  You must strike out for the world's end and capture a sacred girdle from the Amazons."

After some pondering, Heracles said: "Unlike my previous Labors, what you ask of me now I cannot do alone.  Give me leave to assemble a company for this purpose."

"Gods forfend that the mighty Heracles should need assistance!" jauntily pronounced Eurystheus as he departed, the wine keeping him in rare good humor.  Just then a lad kicking up dust ran up the long ramp.

"Heracles!" panted Iolaos.  "Do you think so little of your friends?"

"How so?" asked Heracles with a sheepish pout.

"You abandoned me in Crete," muttered Iolaos.

"That I did!" roared Heracles merrily, upheaving his young nephew and kissing his face and neck.  "I couldn't bear to bring an end to your amusement.  How did good king Minos treat you?"

Iolaos beat at his shoulders until Heracles put him down.

"One of his daughters, Phaidra, kept me virtually a prisoner," complained Iolaos.  "She wanted to see me try my hand

---

[1] The mares were driven to Mount Olympos and released.  In time they were killed by wild beasts, but not before they foaled others of their kind.  This stout breed, it is said, survived until the time of the Trojan War and afterward.

at bull-leaping, and so I was forced to practice every day for her sport whether I wanted to or not! I can hardly feel my bum; and more than once I nearly killed myself on the horns. I was only able to escape with Theseus after he stove the Cretan ships."

Seeing Heracles quirk his brow at the mention of his young cousin, Iolaos knew better than to delay an explanation.

It happened, Iolaos related, that Androgeos, a son of Minos, was killed by jealous competitors from Athens while on his way to Thebes to participate in the games held in honor of king Laios. When Minos, who had been offering a sacrifice to the Graces on the island of Paros, received the news, he put an end to the flute-playing and threw down the garland from his head; and after completing the sacrifice, assembled his fleet and sailed to Attica. He first besieged Megara, hearing that some Megarians were also involved in the plot against his son. But the Athenians, secure in their high stronghold, were not sorely affected. Minos then prayed to his father Zeus for vengeance, upon which plague and pestilence fell upon the city. Unable to bear it any longer, the Athenians consulted the oracle at Delphi, which instructed them to do whatsoever Minos asked of them. After sending a delegation to Minos to inquire what would satisfy him, he ordered, in requital for Androgeos' death, that the Athenians were to send seven youths and seven maidens every nine years to Crete. He would not divulge the consequence of the offering. The first contingent, chosen by lot, was sent immediately, and as they never returned, the worst was guessed. It was rumored that he trapped them in the Labyrinth, an intricate structure of intersecting passages built to house the Minotaur, the horrible offspring of his wife Pasiphaë and the white bull that came from the sea, which Heracles had captured. They then starved to death wandering around the maze, or were devoured by its awful denizen. After nine years, cries of lamentation were again heard in Athens, as mothers and fathers clung to their children boarding the black-sailed ship, never to see them again. When the third time arrived, the citizens had had enough. They petitioned king Aigeus to save their children; but he could do little, and fretted over incurring their displeasure for exempting his son Theseus, who had lately arrived in the city, from the tribute. But it was said that Theseus was actually the son of Poseidon, who lay with his mother Aithra, daughter of king

Pittheus of Troizen, on the little island of Sphairia on the same night she married Aigeus, after being instructed to go there by Athena in a dream. Aigeus, who had gone to Troizen to consult the wise Pittheus about an oracle concerning his inability to father an heir, returned to Athens, but not before burying his sword, shield and sandals under a rock. He told Aithra that if she bore him a son, on reaching manhood he should try to move the rock, and taking the items he found, visit him at Athens. This Theseus did, and after many adventures on the road to Athens, by which he cleared the Isthmus of the brigandage that had multiplied during Heracles' absence in Thrace, arrived there.

A certain witch, who after arriving in Athens and curing Aigeus of his infertility took up with him, sensed the identity of the handsome young stranger before Theseus had revealed himself to Aigeus. Feeling her position threatened, she convinced Aigeus to send Theseus on the dangerous mission of capturing the Bull of Marathon—the very bull Heracles had brought back from Crete. Like Heracles, he wrestled the bull into submission and brought it back in triumph to Athens, where he sacrificed it to Athena on the Acropolis.

The witch continued to poison the mind of Aigeus, making him think that Theseus had arrived as a foreign agent to threaten his throne. He thus agreed to her scheme to envenom Theseus, for she was an adept at poisons. While Theseus sat at meat, she placed a tainted cup before him and waited for him to drink. But when Aigeus saw Theseus wearing the very sword he had left for him buried under the rock, he recognized his son and heir, and dashing the cup from Theseus' lips, saved his life. The witch was banished from Athens for her impiety.

With the doomed ship lying at anchor under a black sail, waiting to transport the latest victims to Cnossos, Theseus nobly stood in the assembly, feeling the pain of his fellow citizens, and volunteered to go. King Aigeus, wracked with grief, took him aside with pleas and tears but could not dissuade the ardent youth, who assured him that he would return after putting an end to this cruel business. Taking the ill-fated youths and maidens to the temple of Apollo at Delphi, he there offered for a safe return an olive branch twined with white wool. The oracle instructed him to make Aphrodite his guide and protectress; and for this reason he sacrificed a she-goat on the seashore, which, by a miracle became a he-goat. The last words Aigeus told Theseus were these: should he return, he was to hoist a far-shining white sail.

While the sorrowful ship clove the Cretan sea, Minos, who had sailed to personally collect the tribute, could no longer restrain his amorous desires. Approaching Periboia, one of the Athenian maidens, he touched her white cheeks and would have gone further had not Theseus stood up for her defense. The sailors were astonished at his boldness; while Minos, surprised by his presumption, asked who he was to question him. Theseus replied that though he recognized that Minos was a descendant of Zeus, he also could claim divine parentage as a son of Poseidon; and that further outrage would lead to an armed struggle. Minos in anger called upon Zeus to present before all a sign of divine favor. Thereupon a searing white bolt of lightning flashed from the clear sky and like a whiplash nicked the whitecaps. "See you Father Zeus' gifts to me," said Minos. "Now prove yourself a son of Poseidon! I will cast my golden signet ring into the sea. Boldly enter into your father's house and retrieve it." Theseus, without a hint of fear, stripped himself and from the stern leapt in behind the ring. Minos, astonished, ordered the ship hove to; but the wind, blowing astern, still drove it along a fair distance, to the dismay of the young Athenians, who shed tears for their rash defender. Minos waited in apprehension, scanning the depths for an impossible sign. At last, dismissing Theseus as a bold but quixotic adventurer, he ordered the sailors to drive on. But as the sail bellied once more, one of the maidens cried out, seeing dolphins frolicking in a ring. And in the midst of them appeared Theseus, wearing on his head a wreath of dark roses. Pulled aboard, he presented Minos with his ring.

The arrival of the ship proved a spectacle for all the Cretans, Iolaos among them, who crowded about the docks for a view of the victims. With Iolaos were the daughters of Minos, one of whom, Ariadne, was stricken by the work of Aphrodite with admiration at the sight of Theseus. Meeting him later in secret, she proclaimed her love, promising her help in exchange for being taken back to Athens. Theseus agreed. She presented him with a magical ball of thread that Daidalos had left her, which, when one end was tied to the lintel, would unravel itself within the involute

Labyrinth to the innermost rooms where the Minotaur dwelt.

That night, Minos locked Theseus and the other Athenians in the Labyrinth. Instructing his friends to remain by the entrance-way, Theseus tied the end of the thread to the lintel, and dropping it on the ground, watched the clew roll onward of its own volition. He followed it, watching it get smaller and smaller, until he came upon the den of the sleeping Minotaur. The monster, half-man, half-bull, could certainly inspire dread in even the heartiest warrior; but Theseus, unshaken, jumping on him, wrestled him to exhaustion, and then pummeled him to death. Rolling up the thread into a ball again, Theseus easily found his way back.

Ariadne, waiting at the door, freed the Athenians, and leading them to the harbor, stole with them aboard their ship. Iolaos, alerted to the escapade by Phaidra, joined them, longing for home. The alarm sounded; but the ship, helmed by the skillful Nausitheos of Salamis, slipped into the dark night, evading the Cretan fleet.

"And so, concluded Iolaos, "we landed at Dia, where, for some reason, Theseus deserted poor Ariadne. They say that Dionysos appeared to him in a dream, and falling in love with Ariadne, demanded her for himself. But he did not wish to talk about it for the rest of the journey back to Athens, even though he knew I was your nephew, and he admires you above all other men. Even sadder, Heracles: as we neared home, Theseus, perhaps out of grief over Ariadne, neglected to replace the black sail with the white, as he had promised his father. The old king, who would climb the Acropolis every day and spend long hours there with his eyes fixed on the horizon waiting for the ship to return, cast himself down from the rocks when he spied the black sail, his heart broken."

Heracles mutely shook his head at the conclusion of Iolaos' tale, feeling pity for Theseus' ill-fortune, but joy at the feats the young man had already accomplished. He had last seen him many years before while dining with king Pittheus in Troizen. As he entered the house, he shook off his lionskin and threw it upon a stool, where it lay as if alive. Seeing it, a group of children ran away shrieking—all except seven-year old Theseus, who, snatching a little axe, prepared to fight what he thought was a wild beast that had made its way inside. Heracles took this all in jovially, commending his little cousin for his bravery. From that day, Theseus resolved to follow in Heracles' footsteps.

"We must pay Theseus a visit," said Heracles. "He will certainly like to join our expedition to the land of the Amazons."

❧

Iolaos drove Heracles northward toward the Isthmus Road, made safe by Theseus. Heracles had long had it in mind to do that himself, but none of his Labors had yet led him into Attica. He remained content, nevertheless, to hear of Theseus' exploits, recounted on the flight from Crete, recognizing the excellent training the young man had undoubtedly received in virtue and chivalry. Once they passed the broad city of Corinth, and its looming, colossal citadel of rugged rock and green scrub rising above them, another hour put them on the road, which would take a day to cross. Not having to worry about robbers and ruffians lurking in the rocky heights, Heracles could sit on the car floor and consume a whole leg of mutton that Iolaos had cooked up for the journey. As he stood to throw away the bone, Heracles was captivated by a sky so blue that it pained his eyes; and, down below, by the blackness of the plunging rocks into a sea that seemed an unbroken continuation of the sky. Heracles flung the bone several bow-shots away into the placid gulf. He claimed to hit a lapwing square in mid-air; but Iolaos, whose eyes were sharp, doubted his boast.

After sunset they made camp near Eleusis, and in the morning drove on. Where the road rounded the small cape to turn south toward Athens, they could see the mighty city while yet afar, with its massive palace sitting upon a great plateau, nestled within sheer cliffs, glowing like plated electrum against the rising sun spilling between the mountain-peaks. As they approached the city walls, which stretched across the Attic plain down to the sea, Heracles took the reins from Iolaos. Seeing from a distance the dust kicked up by the horses, the bowmen on the battlements nocked their arrows, and the soldiery waited patiently, javelins ready, to challenge the newcomers.

The captain of the guard recognized that the massive man encased within the lion's pelt could be none other than Heracles, and remembering Theseus' orders, cried out to his wardens to open the gate. They swung the doors open in haste, for Heracles seemed to have no intention of stopping. He drove the chariot at full speed inside, only then reining in the horses, sending a knot of soldiers scrambling to avoid being trampled. The captain rushed down from the walls and saluted him by knocking his spear-haft against the boss of his bull-hide shield.

"Hail noble Heracles!—for surely it is you," cried the captain. "The king expects you."

"King?" said a puzzled Heracles. "I do not know the king; tell me, has that boy Theseus become your king now?"

"Most assuredly," said the captain. "Upon the death of king Aigeus, his only son has assumed the throne."

"The king is dead?" asked Heracles, and then declaimed with vigor: "Long live the king!"

At this the soldiers within earshot up and down the long walls thrice knocked their spear-hafts against their shields.

"You will find lord Theseus at his father's funeral games," said the captain. "My men will escort you."

Heracles thanked him, and handling the reins back to Iolaos, sat on the car floor until two outriders arrived to lead them up the walled ramp to the city. They passed through an upper gate into the city proper, where the road led through the market-place to the cypress-tinged slopes of the Acropolis upon which the royal palace stood. In its shadow, south of the public square and the law courts, spectators ringed an open field. In their midst the competitors tried their hands at casting quoits and javelins; wrestling and boxing; archery and sword-fighting; running and jumping; and also at musical contests to determine who could sing the sweetest with his lyre. Many of these events were held at the barrow of Aigeus over which the Athenians had strewn wind-flowers and anemones.

Theseus sat forlornly upon a high wooden bench observing the boxing contest. It would have been his own specialty to box or wrestle, but he felt much too saddened to participate in the games, unable to forgive himself for his father's death.

A hush fell over the spectators, and the participants ceased their athletics as Heracles and Iolaos rode into their midst. Theseus looked up, and just for a moment forgot his grief. Before him came the man he most admired in the world. At night his dreams were colored with the hero's exploits; and during the day, he strove to continually emulate Heracles in all things. It was therefore to his utter surprise that Heracles came near and bent his knee before him. Theseus quickly jumped off his seat, and grasping Heracles' forearm, around which he could not fully wrap his fingers, lifted him up.

Theseus said: "I must needs bow to you, Heracles! Today there stands no greater in Athens!"

"I am but a man," said Heracles cheerfully; "and you find yourself lord of the greatest city in Greece, noble cousin."

Grasping Iolaos' shoulder, Theseus said: "You must know, Heracles, that Iolaos was being molded into a great bull-dancer. I almost dissuaded him from coming with me, knowing the loss it would prove to the culture of Crete."

"Crete can keep its bulls—and its dancers!" muttered Iolaos.

Theseus rejoined with a laugh: "Now that you're here, Iolaos, I am tempted to add a bull-leaping contest to these games; but it being a sport dear to Poseidon, performing it here in Athena's city would prove heretical."

"Well, then Theseus, what event is left for me?" asked Heracles.

"I'm afraid that the games are near their end—this being the last day—and there is probably no one who would dare compete against you," said Theseus. "I would be honored, however, if you would serve as President of the Games."

To this Heracles assented, and took a seat next to Theseus to watch with great interest the remaining competitions; but he could not keep himself from jumping into the all-in wrestling contest, at which all the challengers bowed out, afraid to face him. At the conclusion, Heracles awarded the victors their olive-wreaths. Then over the barrow of Aigeus he assisted in further sacrifices until late in the evening, when the fires of the holocaust sent spires of black smoke up into the porticos of the stronghold.

Theseus invited Heracles and Iolaos up to the palace. In the guest-rooms, surrounded by wall-paintings of gods and illustrious men, they were bathed, oiled and dressed by the palace women. Theseus met them on the main terrace, from where they could see a bright new moon crowning the dark mountains to the north. They ate and drank as Heracles recounted his adventures to the wondering Theseus, who had heard of them here and there, but now delighted to learn them from Heracles himself.

Heracles was no less amazed at hearing recounted the fullness of Theseus' heroic deeds from the moment he left Troizen, for Theseus was an average-sized youth of no great musculature, although his hands were large and his limbs long, and in grappling he was unmatched. In this art his intellect and skill made up for his lack of brawn: since he intimately understood the kinematics of the body, he knew how to use an opponent's weight against him. In this way he was able to overcome countless brigands, most much larger men, for big men predominate among the ruthless. On the Isthmus Road, on the narrowest part where one can see the Corinthian gulf on one side, and the Saronic Gulf on the other, he was waylaid by the savage robber Sinis, who made a pretense of needing help in bending pine-trees over until their tops touched the ground. As the unsuspecting victim assisted, Sinis would let go, and the tree would hurl him off into the air. Or else, he would bend two nearby trees down toward each other, and then tie the victim's arms to each, so that he was torn in half when the trees were released. Sinis, nicknamed the 'Pine Bender', was so strong that he could do such things; but Theseus, after a long struggle, overcame him, and served him up to his own cruel and peculiar torture.

Near Eleusis, Theseus met with another miscreant named Cercyon, who not only robbed his victims, but challenged them to a wrestling match, killing them in a final move. Theseus happily accepted the challenge, and killed him by fighting close to the ground, and attacking his knees. He finished Cercyon off with the brass-bound club he had taken from Periphetes, a dangerous cripple near Epidauros, and the first of the brigands he overcame on his journey.

But the story Heracles most enjoyed involved Sinis' father, Procroustes, who lived on the roadside between Eleusis and Athens in a shack with two iron beds, one short and the other long. He would treat wayfarers hospitably, and invite them to stay the night. If they were tall, he would conduct them to the short bed and force them to lie down upon it. Since their legs would stick out, he would cruelly hack them off until their bodies fit. If they happened to be of short stature, he laid them on the short bed and hammered their limbs until they expired from agony. Theseus skillfully brought Procroustes under submission, and, laying him on the short bed, pruned the part of his legs that protruded.

Heracles asked to see Theseus' brass-bound club to compare it to his own. The heft felt the same, even though his was longer and more knotted. He handed it back and said: "I had hoped to find you under better circumstances, so I'll understand if you turn down my request. My next Labor is to reach the country of the Amazons in order to fetch their chieftain's girdle. For this I'll need ships. Can you outfit me? I promise to return them in one piece."

Theseus knotted his brows and crossed his arms. "Heracles, even a great man like you cannot possibly go against an entire nation—of fierce women, no less," Theseus said. "You'll also need some stout volunteers to accompany you."

"Of course—I have no doubt that I can find good men in Athens," said Heracles. "I had thought of asking you to join me, but this seems an inopportune time."

"True," said Theseus quietly, looking down in dejection. "My father has just died; I am but weeks on the throne; the city is threatened by the Pallantids;"— he suddenly looked up, his face aglow—"but I would still follow you, Heracles, to Hell if you asked me."

Heracles let out a roar of delight. The two men embraced. Heracles said: "My quest shall be successful then. Iolaos shall sail with us. Can you invite Peleus, who won the wrestling contest?"

"He shall come," said Theseus. "His brother Telamon is also in Athens. Do you know him?"

"Telamon of Aegina?—of course! Together they are like the famed Tyndarids in their stoutness and nobility," said Heracles.

The next morning Heracles strolled down to the Phaleron, the great port of Athens, to look at the ships. It was mid-summer, and soon the season for sailing would be past. He found three Phoenician galleys that pleased him, square-sailed and single-masted, that could seat twenty men each. These ships Theseus impressed into his service, paying the master handsomely, and promising to return them promptly. Heracles passed on the existing crew, small men from Tyre and Sidon, and decided to gather his own, so the call went out for volunteers. As word got out that Heracles was in the city, the people forgot their grief over Aigeus, and men lined up eagerly by the quay-side, hoping to join the expedition. Heracles also felt the ships needed some reinforcement, and so ordered the topsides recaulked, and had a wickerwork shield, covered with leather, installed over the gunwale to withstand the spray.

Heracles made the volunteers perform certain acts, like run up the long walls to the city and back, or fight among themselves, in order to discover the best and bravest of them. Those that passed the initial challenges had to sit on the thwarts and pretend to row for hours with a half-oar. He did this to see who would tire easily. He had just about filled the number of the crew when a commotion erupted in the market-place. A man dressed in leather breeches, red buskins and a jerkin trimmed with gold came running toward Heracles, pursued by soldiers. He threw himself on the ground and grasped Heracles' knees.

"Heracles, savior of men!" he pleaded. "Preserve me!"

"How now?" said Heracles, surprised. He pulled up the man as the soldiers came to a stop not far away, their swords drawn, unsure of what to do. One of them spoke up: "If you know this man, Heracles, then you know he's the craftiest thief in all Greece."

"No, no!" pleaded Autolycos. "You have the wrong man. I am not *that* Autolycos, son of Hermes, who dwelt on Mount Parnassos. I am Autolycos, son of Deïmachos. I hail from Thessaly."

Heracles felt like playing a jest. "He is a crafty fellow!" he told the soldiers. "If you believe he is that knave you speak of, come take him."

"Has wine and time dimmed your memory, Heracles? Was not the other Autolycos one of your tutors? I am hardly half his age!" said Autolycos, dropping again to his knees.

"Yes—I suppose he is correct." said Heracles to the soldiers. "You have the wrong man. Leave him with me."

The soldiers looked at one another, sheathed their swords and walked off.

"I am leading an expedition to plunder the Amazons and my crew is still three men short. Will you join me?" Heracles asked.

"Need you ask?" said Autolycos, dusting off his breeches and smiling broadly with the thought of gain; and then inserting his fingers in his lips, he let out a piercing whistle. "My brothers Deilion and Phlogios will come also."

The two brothers, who had been hiding in the crowd, approached to greet Heracles. Being stout young men, they were readily accepted. His crew complete, Heracles retired to the palace, where he feasted with Theseus for several days more.

2

At day's first light, spectators thronged the royal port, from the seashore to the gaps of the colonnade fronting the portico of the precinct of Zeus and Athena, wherein their bronze statues stood overlooking the Phaleron. Heracles took a starboard oar by the helmsman; while Theseus took the master's seat, for Heracles would not hear of him chafing his hands in rowing. When the hawsers were unhitched from the mooring stakes and thrown aboard, Heracles began to heave his oar and off the flagship went a bit unevenly at first, for none could match the heft or strength of Heracles.

They steered southward down the Saronic Gulf, keeping several bowshots from the shore, and fighting a northeast wind that served no purpose this side of the peninsula. Theseus prayed to Poseidon that the same wind would prevail on the other side of the Attic cape, pouring out a libation into the sea. Heracles had dedicated the voyage to Zeus, hoping that he would restrain Hera from causing mischief, although generally she had little power over the seas.

They made good headway down the coast, passing through the narrow channel between the small rock of Phaura and three-tongued Cape Zoster, whose bulging rocks seemed from a distance like ships moored in array. South of there a stretch of stone pines scented the air with their resinous aroma. At noonday, with the sun beating down on their unprotected heads, they reached the towering Sunium promontory, where a temple to Athena gleamed at the peak. A cozy harbor lay at its base, where some of the men wished to stop and refresh themselves. But the wind was still favorable, so Theseus ordered the sails hoisted. All took a hand to raise the mast, setting it down into its crutch, hoist the yard, and unfurl the white sail, which immediately bellied with the brisk breeze from the southwest. As soon as they began to round the headland, however, the breeze died down, and they were left becalmed in the water.

Telamon told Heracles: "We have been at sea half a day, and already the men complain of blistered hands and sore bums. We can take to the oars again, travel up to round Euboea, and then cross the sea, hoping the wind turns more favorable by then. But I am inclined now to cross the sea at the narrowest point that we may always remain within an hour or two of land. I feel already a southeasterly wind abrewing, and it would make no sense to fight it. Let us run before it and stop at one of the friendly islands of Minos for the night."

The proposal pleased Heracles, since he neither wished to stop, nor push his men too hard on their first day. The winds blew astern, and carried them as far as the island of Cynthos, where the oars stirred again the waters. It was decided by unanimous consent to stay the night at Paros, one of the larger islands, for it had safe anchorage, and was more hospitable than the sheer cliffs of its neighbors. They continued their strokes, listening to Theseus string a song on the lyre, as darkness fell upon them, and a bright new moon rose from the southeastern horizon.

For only a short while did they lose sight of the twinkling lights of settlements on the islands around them. The sea then turned black and cold in every direction; and the men rowed silently and piously, exerting themselves with the thoughts of a hot meal and rest somewhere ahead. Autolycos gave a cry when the marble edifices of Paros shone in the distance, as bright and white—even at night—as if aglow from some internal combustion. The ships settled into a small bay free of rocks. Above them stretched Paros, the principal city, spread out over rising, fir-fledged hill-slopes dotted with olive groves and orchards. They dropped their anchor-stones and went ashore with aching arms and stiff legs. Two of the crew volunteered to fetch water, while the others lit a fire and gathered around it, wrapped in their sheepskin cloaks. Heracles asked Theseus if he wished to accompany him on a night-time hunt, but Theseus wished not to venture into the island, since Paros was allied with king Minos, and there was no telling if Minos still pursued him. Heracles went off by himself, and when he returned, with a she-goat across his shoulder, he found the camp all in alarm.

Peleus had seen a frog jump into the fire, and thinking it an ill-omen, sought to account for his comrades. After searching for those who tarried long in fetching water, he found them dead in a ravine. Before he knew it, several men jumped from the bushes to attack him. Peleus fought them off and ran back to the camp, where the rest rallied to his assistance. They captured the four attackers and held them for Heracles.

"Who be these?" asked Heracles, looking at their faces in the glow of the campfire. Theseus explained that they were minor sons of Minos who had settled at Paros: Eurymedon, Chryses, Nephalion and Philolaos. (The island was ruled by Alcaios, son of Androgeos, another son of Minos.) Minos' sons had run into the two men at the ravine, and inquiring who they were, discovered that Theseus was with them. After murdering them, they then plotted how to attack the camp and capture Theseus for affronting their father. It was then that Peleus had surprised them. On hearing this Heracles grew so enraged that Chryses, greatly fearing the coming wrath, took to his heels. Heracles rushed to Iolaos, who kept his bow and quiver, and nocking an arrow, shot the son of Minos as he ran up the road to the city. Then he took up his club and dispatched the others with single blows.

Heracles' companions stood around mutely, shuddering at the sudden bloodshed, some fearing that the ghosts of the dead men would come and haunt them. Peleus assured them that he found the two crewmen lying face-down, and so their ghosts had not seen him as he passed; and that the four sons of Minos paid a just price for their crimes. Theseus tried to pacify Heracles, but the latter's eyes still flashed fire, and the veins of his bulging neck seemed ready burst. Theseus found such extreme wrath troubling: a blind, chaotic, ineluctable fury, as terrifying in its inhumanity as a scene of carrion-crows feasting on the dead.

King Alcaios came down the road at the head of his retainers and the leading citizens of Paros. He was young and stout, with a Cretan's long dark hair and smooth face. He formally hailed Heracles, having noticed his stature from afar and rightly guessing that he was the leader. But as he drew near and saw the slain men in a heap, horror arrested him.

"Are these my uncles lying in the sand?" he cried out, kneeling down to look at their faces.

"They are four sons of Minos," said Theseus, stepping forward. "They killed two of our party, and for that Heracles dispatched them."

"Heracles?" asked Alcaios, looking diffidently up at the hero. Getting to his feet, he returned to the safety of his retainers. "I am Alcaios, grandson of Minos. These my uncles settled here, much against my wishes, for I have little to do with my grandfather (except to pay him tribute, for he rules the seas) or the rest of my family, being instead loyal to the memory of my great-granduncle, the wise and noble Rhadamanthys, who possessed Paros when out of jealousy he was driven from Crete."

Theseus let out a slight breath of relief and said: "Then I feel no qualm in identifying myself."

"The slayer of the Minotaur?" asked Alcaios when he heard the name of the famed Athenian. "I count any deed against the tyrant Minos as worthy of my greatest admiration, and that impossible task most of all."

Heracles, whose intense anger had somewhat subsided, and now only simmered, said: "We came as strangers to your island, expecting hospitality, and were met instead with violence. As a result, I now have two empty bench-seats on my ship. I am on an important mission and my crew must be at full strength. I demand, therefore, requital for my lost sailors, or I will besiege your city, and when I have taken it, raze it to the ground."

Alcaios was horrified by the threat. He consulted with his men, and returned an answer, saying: "My uncles were ruffians, and deserved what they received at your hands, Heracles. I will lose no sleep over them. I am very sorry for this business, however; and to make you whole, this is what I propose: take any two Parians as your slaves. I invite you into the city to look around and decide."

Heracles thought a moment, and then nodded his head, pleased with the suggestion. He said: "I accept your offer, king Alcaios. I choose you as my slave. And for my second choice—that fellow there, of noble bearing, who looks like you."

Alcaios, turning white, looked over at the man Heracles had pointed out. He said: "I certainly wish to honor you, Heracles, but I am the king, and that is my brother Sthenelos. Surely—"

"I will entertain no further discussion, or I'll think again of taking your city," said Heracles, his agitation now gone and his countenance restored to its usual jovial flush. "I promise to return you both to Paros when the job is done. Be here in the morning. We sail at dawn." Sthelenos, looking forward to an adventure with such a leader as Heracles, raced back to the city to burnish his four-plumed helmet with scarlet crest.

In the morning they breakfasted on barley-bread soaked in undiluted wine, as well as on some figs and olives which king Alcaios had brought for them, for he feared Heracles and wished to ingratiate himself with him. There was little he could do but obey Heracles' summons. Paros was not fortified and possessed no soldiery, relying instead on Minos for protection. And since, by his own design, he maintained an unsteady diplomacy with Crete, there was no time or opportunity to summon assistance against the mad Tyrinthian.

They waited some hours for a favorable wind, and then weighed anchor. After clearing the bay they shipped the oars and raised the sails. Heading northeast, they soon sailed past fair Dia, largest of the islands of Minos. Theseus stood at the stern looking out at the fertile island as they left it astern. He had tears in his eyes, which he tried to hide from Heracles, who had come to sit beside him.

Theseus did not wait for Heracles to inquire the reason for his sadness. He said: "Had it not been for Ariadne, fair daughter of king Minos, I would not be alive today. It was she who assisted me to escape the Labyrinth, for which I promised to take her with me back to Athens. We fled Crete and came to Dia, where the people treated the daughter of Minos like a goddess, not knowing yet how we had affronted her father. We were entertained by the king and queen of the island in high fashion: the queen attired Ariadne from her own wardrobe, anointing her with fragrant attar. We slept that night in the royal palace, and free of cares loved one another. But I had a troubled sleep, and in a dream Dionysos offered me a ripe pomegranate in exchange for Ariadne. I did not deduce the meaning of the dream until the next day, when a great commotion drew us to the seashore. A spectacular red-sailed ship arrived, with vines twined up the mast, and ivy encircling the rigging. Women, young and old, wearing the masks of beasts, danced and sang on deck. They came ashore, waving their ivy-entwined staffs topped with pine-cones, and their music seemed to drive everyone mad; for soon the whole populace joined them in their wild dances, while jars and skins of wine passed hands freely. Behind these Mainads came a tall figure, dressed in a scarlet tunic and crowned with an ivy chaplet. Little horns grew from his head; his face was painted white, with black circles around his eyes; and his lips were stained scarlet. I did not believe this was Dionysos until he ran into a thicket and out emerged a lion that roared mightily. The reverse operation occurred, and out emerged the god in human form again. He took a flute and ran off into the hills, with his wild women following. The women of Dia peeled off after them. Someone took the hand of Ariadne and pulled her away. I tried to follow, but was so jostled about that I soon lost sight of her. The youths who had sailed with me to Crete found me; but they were drunk, and expected me to rejoice with them. At last I saw no harm, and followed them into the woodland, climbing the mountain to where the snow first covered the ground like rime. The youths left me to pursue the maidens, for they were running about half-naked like does chased by wolves. The madness of the god gripped me somewhat, though not a drop of his vinous poison had yet touched my lips, and I thought only of Ariadne and her white arms and pendant breasts breathing honey. Through the mad wood I rushed, the thickets filled with cries of pleasure or pain: for who can tell the difference? Then, in a dell of lush turf, surrounded with cornel-trees thick with berries, I saw Ariadne embraced. I stared, abashed, only a moment, and then forced myself to tear away. I do not believe Ariadne saw me; and it was the last time I saw her. After the revelry subsided, I gathered Iolaos and the others, and we sailed away."

"No matter," said Heracles; "let us turn the ships about and land there a moment. I will wrestle with Dionysos for your woman."

"She is pledged to him now; and I am certain she is there no longer, for the god likes to travel the world with his Mainads and his wine," said Theseus gravely. "And so to this sore place have I arrived: both my father and my lover are no more. To think, as I left Crete, that I thought myself happy!"

"To the happy, such a blow is great," observed Heracles. "But the unfortunate think little of such things since he ever dwells in misery. That is why I say a man should not count himself fortunate until he breathes his last, and has weathered the storms of Fortune. But take heart in my example: you are not the only one at odds with a god. Hera has hounded me since my birth. She turned me mad; and now I must perform these Labors. Like me, you have chosen the hard path. You could have remained comfortably in Troizen, yet you lifted the stone and recognized your destiny. In this journey of ours there will be grief and sorrow, and some joy at times. We must all accept the lot we have been given; and remember that we strive not against gods, or even men, but against ourselves."

Theseus looked out until Dia grew small and was swallowed by the foamy grey.

෯

They crossed the open sea and threaded through the Scattered Isles, landing on the little island of Patmos when they could row no more. They rested there an entire day, and passed the time hunting or in games. Iolaos, however, had to tend to Alcaios, who suffered from terrible sea-sickness. Iolaos administered to him wormwood, which in the area grew without gall. Briefly they stopped at flowery Samos, for two of the sailors hailed from there and wished to see their families. Hugging the Ionian coast, they continued northward, blessed with clear skies and light winds, stopping at Lesbos to enjoy its famed wine

They remained in Lesbos until evening. Theseus advised Heracles that they should enter the Hellespont that very night. "We sail with warriors in unmarked vessels," he said. "It would be best not to be noticed by Troy's coast-guards, or they will detain us until we pay the passage tax."

Sthenelos added: "I sailed once to Phrygia on a diplomatic mission. If the winds are favorable, and our arms ready, we can certainly get past Troyland and up the length of the strait in a single night."

"But at night any keen observer on the coast would be able to see our white sail," said one of the two Samians.

Sthenelos responded: "It will not be possible to use oars alone to passage the Hellespont. The strait is long, and the current rushing down from the Sea of Marmora is strong. Imagine a drinking-horn—I mean the fluted Cretan kind—poured from aloft: you would not be able to quench the flow coming down the pike. It is even worse on the other side, for there you have the outflow of an immense sea pouring down the Bosporos."

"Let us paint an owl on the sails—the sign of Athena," said Theseus. "If they do notice us, they will see we come from Athens, and leave us be, since my father had friendly relations with the Trojans."

It was agreed to paint an owl on the spare sail with stain from the ship's tar-pot, which they hoisted after stopping for a day at a sandy cove on the eastern part of Imbros. Heracles grew heartened that the winds turned westerly, and so all bent to the oars under the cover of a waning crescent moon obscured by white clouds over Thrace. When in the distance they could see the white cliffs of Cape Hellas, the northern lip of the entrance to the strait, Peleus suggested they muffle the oars with strips of old cloth. As they rounded the headland, they were nearly spun around by the biting current of the Hellespont. "Port the helm! Put your backs into it now, men!" cried Heracles, leading the way with prodigious rowing, while the helmsman wrestled with the rudder to keep the keel pointed into the current. The wind shifted slightly and hit them hard abeam, bringing rain and breaking waves over the gunwale.

It seemed as if the ships would scud toward the Trojan side, when the wind suddenly broke, which allowed them to regain the Thracian coast, where the current was weakest and smoothest. A south-westerly wind picked up just in time. The oarsmen worked as if entranced, while keen-eyed Autolycos, up in the prow, called out if they came too close inshore, where rocks could destroy the ship, or veered midstream, where their efforts would be retarded. They made less progress than they had anticipated due to the inclement weather, which was perhaps the reason why they did not encounter any other ships in the channel, Trojan or otherwise. When the sun broke at their backs, coloring the white sail orange and slowly opening vistas that had hence been in darkness, they were nearly twenty leagues past Ilion and out of its territory. The exhausted oarsmen clamored to stop, and so they anchored near Sestos, where they refreshed themselves from a cold stream. Alcaios sacrificed a ram to Poseidon, praying loudly that he would not abandon them for the remainder of the journey up the strait, and adding quietly that he should be especially vigilant to return him and his brother back to Paros of the white marble rocks.

For the next two days, the wind fixed north-eastwardly. When it finally veered to the south-west, they cast off again and struggled up the remaining portion of the strait until they broke into the Sea of Marmora late in the afternoon with the red, dying sun overwhelming their eyes. Sthenelos raised a cry when he saw the island of Proconnesos, which, because of its abundant marble deposits, could be compared to Paros. It is the largest island in the Sea of Marmora, not counting Bear Island across it, which is really a peninsula. They harbored there for a night, building two large fires of driftwood. The air was much colder so near Thrace.

The next day dawned bright and gusty, with winds rolling in from the direction of the Thracian cliffs. As the men were breakfasting, Sthenelos pulled Telamon, Heracles and Theseus aside. "The next challenge will be the Bosporos," he said. "The heavy waters of the Axine Sea roar down that crooked strait, making the ingress much more difficult than the egress. At the end of the final curve of the Narrows lie the twin rocks called Sympleglades. These clashing rocks seem unrooted from the sea floor, and rush upon one another at random times, crushing whatever vessels are between them. Many good ships have been lost in that passage; but it is still navigable in certain seasons, as the Trojans have proven. Wait until the rocks clash, but not too close, for the mighty waves generated will engulf us. As soon as they move apart, let us bend to the oars to make the final crossing. We will have perhaps a quarter-hour to pass through unscathed."

When a south-westerly wind began to brew, the men left Proconessos behind and made for the Narrows. Sthenelos kept at the helmsman's ear, to guide him. He had never navigated past the Sea of Marmora, but had been briefed on the dangers by king Phineus of the Thynians. The current ran most swiftly in the middle of the channel, while on the edges counter-currents mitigated the danger of jutting, awash rocks. The ships held to the eastern side, gliding in and out of eddies to propel forward. The strait narrowed or widened at every turn, causing them at times to lose the wind and row with greater alacrity. As they sailed past the final bend, they noticed the shore was thick with driftwood. When one of the sailors, recognizing the danger ahead, cried out to Zeus to save them from the clashing rocks, the rest grew agitated. Heracles asked Theseus to sing a song to calm the men. Moving midstream after rounding the eastern headland, they came into view of the Cyaneian Rocks, one on either side of the Narrows: two massive, craggy, black rocks that seemed to float freely on the agitated sea. Through the thick mist they appeared to glide toward one another, the waters around them foaming and hissing, and rising in tempestuous waves pouring between them. "Bring her under the lee of that beetling point!" cried Heracles, pointing to a small cove between projecting rocks under the shelter of the Thracian cliffs. They made for the shoal, waiting for the rocks to crash into one another.

"Look! Autolycos cried. "A ship is at the lip of the rocks. I think they shall not make it!"

Indeed, a small vessel appeared through the mist between the rocks, its oars cycling furiously like birds' wings. The ship was nearly clear of the crags when it suddenly lurched and with a thunderous crash its stern snapped like it was made of twigs. The ship immediately wheeled about in the irresistible current, spinning like a top, and broke up in the midst of the towering waves that raced down the channel.

The men aboard Heracles' ship sat breathlessly watching the disaster and hearing the cries of drowning men through the roar of the turbulent waters. Heracles was the first to bend his oar, calling on the rest to row for dear life. Birds once again flew upstream as a hopeful new light entered the channel. They moved midstream, where the current was strongest, still backed by a good wind, as pieces of the wrecked ship raced past them. They were about to pass within the hissing waters between the rocks when Autolycos spied a man overboard. But there was no time to stop. Peleus rushed to the foredeck, extended a boathook , and, displaying some fine strength, hauled him up like a catch of tunny. By then the ships were midway between the rocks, and huge hacking waves hitting them abeam, indicated the rocks were on the move again, although they could not see anything clearly through the mist on either side. For love of that distant vision of open water ahead, every oarsman followed through with desperate stroke. They broke out with little time to spare, and did not stop until they rounded the eastern headland.

They beached the ships as soon as possible on a sandy spit. The man they had rescued was named Dascylos, son of king Lycos of the Mariandynians. He had been captured by Bebrycian pirates for ransom, for the violent Bebrycians were always at war with the Mariandynians and the other peoples along the littoral. Dascylos offered to guide the ship to his father's realm, where they would be welcomed. After a day and a night of rest and refreshment, they set out again, rounded Cape Calpe, and sailed upland, passing the mouths of several large rivers. Dascylos directed them to round another headland, and to anchor beyond it in a bay nestled between sheer, tree-fledged cliffs, where they found Lycos, the chief city of the Mariandynians. Leaving half their men to guard the ships, Heracles, Theseus, and the rest followed Dascylos into the city, which was renowned for the beauty of its orchards and gardens. King Lycos welcomed them warmly, indebted to them for the rescue of his son. He took particular interest in Heracles, with whose exploits he was acquainted from travelling bards, although he had considered most of them mere legends. But one look at the towering hero convinced him that all the tales were true. He prepared for them a lavish banquet, replete with every delicacy. He ordered his stewards to bring out the best and most aged jars of wine. He assembled all the best poets, dancers and musicians of his realm for the night's entertainment.

Before entering the banqueting-hall, where two dozen couches were arranged in a half-circle, the guests were garlanded and their heads arrayed with ribands while young boys washed their feet. Merry and refreshed, they filed into the refectory. Although the Mariandynians were of Thracian stock, king Lycos spoke the language of his guests perfectly, and was a great admirer of Greek customs. He therefore wished to hold a grand drinking-party, in the Greek fashion, after the meal. This seemed most fitting, for it was known, after all, that viniculture began on the southern coast of the Axine Sea, where grapes first grew wild. From there wine reached Greece by way of Crete, whose people were pioneers in many things.

Firstly, a cup of herbally infused wine passed from lip to lip. Then, after filling their trenchers with generous portions of tender sucking-pig, steaming table-fowl, heaps of tunny, pilchards and dolphin-meat, chunks of mutton and goat-meat, they ate to bursting, then settled back on their couches, nibbling chickpeas, until attendants brought in ewers and basins so that they could wash their hands.

Out of politeness, king Lycos reclined on the rightmost couch.  He had expected Heracles to take the leftmost seat of honor, but the latter declined, yielding it to Theseus.  Instead, he took the couch beside that of Lycos, who was pleased with the arrangement, for he wished to be close to the hero.

The tables were cleared.  The dogs moved about devouring the scraps.  Stewards, working in pairs, brought in large, almost unwieldy, bell-shaped wine jars, filled to the brim with the finest wines of Thasos, Chios, Lesbos and Rhodes, which they placed in the center of the room.  One of them dipped a bowl in the wine and deposited it into a libation cup that was passed around among the guests.  Once in Lycos' hands, he spilled from the cup a few drops of the unmixed wine in honor of Dionysos, and sang a dithyramb, with the assistance of a chorus of dancing girls; which displeased Theseus on account of Ariadne; but, as a good guest, he sat and listened to the following without displaying a bitter countenance:

Chorus:
*We sing now of Dionysos, son of Semele*
*How he appeared by the shore of the sea.*

King:
*A ship came swiftly 'cross the bounding main*
*Filled with men bent on some foul gain.*
*They signaled one another to behold*
*He who stood clothed in purple fold.*
*Thinking him the son of heaven-nurtured kings*
*They sprang ashore to do a devilish thing.*

Chorus.
*They took hold of the Thrice-born Son of Zeus*
*And cruelly girt him in a noose.*
*But no withes would hold his feet and hands;*
*Yet this went unnoticed by the surly band*

*Save the brave helmsman, good of soul*
*Who by divine light was in the know.*

King:
*'Madmen!' cried he, running from aft to lee;*
*'Know you not who this lad be?*
*He must be Zeus or Apollo of the silver bow,*
*Or else Poseidon who lays the mountains low.*
*Does he not look unlike mortal men,*
*Or has the foamy spray confused your ken?*
*There is no ship that can hold this man—*
*Let us then leave him upon the jutting strand,*
*Lest he stir up angry winds and squalls*
*That'll cast our ship against the rocky walls.'*

Chorus:
*The master laughed: 'The madman is you who believe*
*Those tales! Hoist the sail, and hawsers unreeve;*
*Mark the wind and set us on our course,*
*While him I interrogate by force.*
*This boy is no doubt Cyprus-bound,*
*Or Egypt, or some land unfound.*
*In the end he will speak of all his wealth,*
*And we'll take hold of it by stealth.*

King:
*The helmsman did as he was told,*
*Steering back into the spanless cold,*
*While Dionysos sat smiling in the bows*
*Knowing men could not a god o'erthrow.*
*No sooner had land been left behind*
*Than wondrous sights showed them a sign*
*That a divinity among men now dwelt,*
*And was making his presence felt.*

Chorus:
*First a sweet and fragrant wine,*
*Thick and dark from the sacred vine,*
*Ran down the boards from end to end*

*And to the ship a heavenly odor lent.*
*Next an ivy-plant twined about the mast,*
*And silver vines from the halyards cast.*
*Then garlands 'round the thole-pins sprung;*
*While from the oars fruity clusters hung.*

King:
*The pirates, scared out of mind,*
*Bade the helmsman steer the ship to land.*
*But from the bows a fearsome roar now came:*
*Behold: a dreadful lion with yellow mane*
*Sat where Dionysos had once been;*
*The handsome lad was nowhere to be seen.*
*As if these marvels did not the sailors scare,*
*Amidships appeared too a ravening bear.*
*And when the lion upon the master leapt,*
*O'erboard went they of all hope bereft.*
*Into dolphins was each man transformed*
*Their human shapes into animal deformed.*
*Save the helmsman, who was spared*
*From the fate his kinsmen shared.*

Chorus:
*Hail, child of fair-faced Semele!*
*He who forgets you cannot sing sensibly.*

All congratulated the king for such a sublime production; even Theseus gave up grudging applause. Next, each man threw dice to determine who was be the lord of the feast. Iolaos and Alcaios tied with treble sixes and so they threw again and the lot fell on Iolaos, who, discomfited, looked to his uncle.

Heracles said: "Before my nephew can perform his duty, we must first discover the consensus here among us. I can only speak for myself in this, but I am certainly ready at any hour for a hearty bout of deep drinking. And do not let the soft beginnings of a beard on Iolaos' face fool you—he already has quite a head for tipple."

The room was evenly split between those who wished to drink hard and those that did not. King Lycos sided with the latter, for he wished to discourse with Heracles with a clear mind. It was finally decided that each man would drink only as much as he wished. For this purpose Iolaos instructed the stewards to mix the wine with three parts of spring water chilled with mountains snow. While the cups were being filled, the piping-girls began to play a gentle tune. The guests first drank in honor of Lycos for his hospitality, and then the cups were filled again. It was the job of Iolaos to keep his eye on the filling and emptying of the wine jars.

"Since we will remain light on the wine, it must needs we be heavy on the brain," said Alcaios. "What shall we discuss? Perhaps Heracles can mesmerize us with some philosophy?" He said this because he was still bitter with Heracles for removing him from Paros against his will, and wished to make fun of him.

"I hold this philosophy," said Heracles: "while no mortal is happy all the time, the blessed gods are always."

"We are most happy now!" cried Autolycos, draining his cup and then holding it out for more.

"Be thankful when things go well," warned Heracles. "At any moment your fortune can turn."

"The gods cannot be always happy," said Telamon. "Does not Zeus vex Hera when a beautiful woman catches his eye? And the Smith, did he not assume a grotesque shape after being cast from Olympos and crashing like a lightning-stroke on Lemnos? And they not only have their own problems—they have to contend with mortals, who blaspheme them, or forget their sacrifices, or commit other sacrileges."

"I do not think the gods are concerned with us," said Peleus. "Why should those immortal beings care for the worms that crawl about the surface of the earth—here one day and gone the next?"

"Of us all, Heracles, the son of Zeus, is best suited to answer the question," said Theseus.

Heracles said: "It is best not to think too much on the gods, for our mortal affairs seem enough to occupy our time. In my youth I wanted nothing more than to see the face of Zeus."

"And have you seen it?" inquired Alcaios.

Heracles, scowling, said nothing.

"Some philosophers say that attachment breeds only discontent, and that to be truly free and happy one must care for nothing at all." said Dascylos.

"I disagree," said Heracles. "Is there no happier man on earth than one who shares his bed with a beautiful wife, and whose children like olive plants surround his table? I was once that man. But fickle Fortune saw my happiness, and, encouraged by some god (whom I shall not mention again), turned to cast me down into utter misery. At times—as this—my mind becomes distracted from the pain and horror I carry with me at every moment. O! I see the atmosphere has turned somber. I apologize for making my problems yours. Iolaos, you are failing in your duties! Beckon these attendants to bedew with frequent mizzles our small cups that levity may return to this fine drinking-party. And be not tardy, excellent host, in supplying us with larger drinking vessels."

Iolaos did as he was told, and then reclined to observe his uncle with admiration; for though Heracles lived with pain in his heart, he tried always to maintain a sunny disposition in order to avoid offending his friends.

"Allow me to propose the next topic of discussion," said king Lycos. "Let each man state that thing he most prizes. I am eager to hear what you Greeks claim as best worth having."

Autolycos answered first: "To me wealth is the greatest possession, for it can provide all other good things. We have two kings here who can attest to that fact."

"Perhaps so," said king Alcaios. "But as you can see, all of my wealth could not stop that bull of a man from kidnapping my brother and I."

"You are not imbibing enough, Alcaios, if you do not yet cherish our company," said Peleus. "Give that man more drink!"

"Riches cannot buy happiness, brother," said Philogos, to whom Autolycos replied cheerfully: "True enough—but it can rent it a while!"

A troupe of dancers and acrobats danced and tumbled, eliciting applause for their acrobatics. When they were done, one girl sat at the harp and played so sweetly that not an eye stayed dry among the guests, each reveling in memories cooked up by the plaintive strings.

"Hear, hear!" cried Theseus, at the conclusion of the harp-song. "I see clearly now what is most important. It goes by the name of Beauty, and takes many forms, such as the beautiful sounds created by her fingers. Is not the soul stirred to goodness by beauty? It seems that all men seek the good, and the good by necessity must be beautiful."

"But why should the good be beautiful?" said Alcaios. "The beautiful is not always good. Take the example of the Gorgon. By all accounts she was most comely, yet at the same time a horrid and evil monster."

"Do you not place Beauty in the company of Goodness?" asked Theseus.

"I do not," said Alcaios. "Beauty is no quality in a thing itself. It exists merely in the mind that contemplates it."

"That cannot be," said Delios. "Only a madman would find no beauty in the blossoming flowers of springtide or the swelling fullness of the autumn harvest."

"Such things merely give men pleasure, or they please men by their suitedness," said Alcaios.

Said Heracles: "I intended to listen quietly to this disquisition, knowing well that any man can be my master in intellection. But either wine is going too quickly to my head, or I misheard you, Alcaios. Do men take a pleasure in a thing because they judge it beautiful; or do they judge it beautiful because it gives them pleasure?"

"The former, I'd say," said Alcaios.

"And how is it, then, that two men can agree that a thing is beautiful if beauty is nothing, as you say?" said Heracles.

"It must be by some common custom."

"And from whence comes this custom?"

"I do not know for sure."

"Tell me, is Beauty not manifest in the order and symmetry of disparate things? A man may walk by a pile of stones, but look twice at a well-formed wall."

"True," said Alcaios.

"But do you also judge the light of the sun to be beautiful? Or the color of shining gold?"

"Of course they are beautiful."

"But these things are devoid of parts. So which is it? Is Beauty found in the multiplicity or in the unity of things?"

"In both, I suppose."

"But how could something be both wet and dry? Or cold

and hot?  It must be that Beauty is inherent in a thing, and not in its accidents, for it to have beauty both in its whole and its parts."

All marveled at Heracles' words, for his head and eyes were small in proportion to the rest of his body; and the lower part of his forehead projected somewhat, giving him an obtuse appearance. Yet now his wine-flushed face shone with sagacity, as if he had released an inner wellspring of knowledge kept hidden from the world.  The truth was that he had been tutored for a season in rhetoric, philosophy and astronomy by Cheiron in the wooded fastness of Mount Pelion.  But being more interested in boxing and wrestling, he did not give those subjects the attention they deserved. Everything he had learned, however, he kept locked safely in his head, ready for use should the situation demand it.

Said Lycos: "Now I am most eager, Heracles, to hear about your famous Labors.  Will you not tell us?  But begin, if you please, at the beginning, that we may have all the facts concerning you."

3

Heracles looked at the eager faces around him, intent on hearing some good story. With wine making his lips nimble, Heracles began his tale:

"Very well; as you wish to know how I have cut my way through the world, I will indulge you. At the beginning, you say? Then know that I was born smaller than my brother Iphicles, but soon surpassed him in all things under the solicitous care of my mother Alcmene and the guidance of my father Amphytrion. My tender years were spent tutored by the venerable Centaur Cheiron, along with other princely children, upon Mount Pelion in Thessaly, learning letters and the ways of nature. When I grew older, Amphytrion taught me to drive a chariot, and how to avoid grazing the wheels when going around the turn-posts. Castor, exiled from his homeland, taught me horsemanship and fencing; and the use of sword and javelin, and how to marshal a company and lead troops into battle. One of Hermes' sons, the famed thief Autolycos, instructed me in wrestling. That man had so grim a look about him when fighting that none ever dared challenge him. Eurytos of Oechalia, a grandson of Apollo, taught me archery. In this skill, particularly, I have excelled above all men.

Although at first I played sweetly on the lyre, I became a bit clumsy with the delicate instrument as my hands grew bigger. Eumolpos of Eleusis was my teacher in this discipline. One day Eumolpos was absent, and Linos, a son of Apollo—whose normal duty was to teach me literature—took over the musical lessons. I wished not to deviate from the way I had been taught by Eumolpos, and striking what Linos felt to be a false note, received buffets for my stubbornness. In a flash of anger, where thought came later, I jumped up, and not knowing yet my own strength, struck Linos so hard with the lute that he fell dead. I immediately regretted what I had done, and in vain tried to revive my teacher, shaking him and crying out for assistance. Growing afraid for myself, I ran off to hide in a secluded grove. The crime was soon discovered, however, and I was brought back to the palace under guard.

I was put on trial for murder. My parents, sitting near me, anxiously watched the proceedings. The case against me seemed secured until, in my own defense, I quoted before the court a law of Rhadamanthys justifying resistance to an aggressor. So persuasive was my argument about the inalienable right of self-defense that I was acquitted. Amphytrion, worried that I would commit further crimes of violence and anger, sent me away to tend his cattle on Mount Cithairon where I might learn to master my temper There I remained until my eighteenth year, dressed like a rustic, sleeping under the stars, and to increase my strength lifting a  bull-calf every day until it was fully grown. By then I measured in stature four cubits and one foot. Contrary to what you might think, I was then generally abstemious during the day; and for supper liked to eat only roast meat and barley-cakes.

One day, as the cattle grazed along the foothills, I sat upon a rock pondering my destiny. I wondered if I would remain a cowherd all my life. I was still tormented by Linos' death: the grievous result of my unchecked temper. I felt good for nothing. After a glance at the cattle to make sure none had strayed too far, in weariness I dropped my head in my hands. Looking up again, I thought my eyes deceived me. Two women walked up the hillslope toward me. One was dressed in a simple white gown and a goodness and wisdom emanated from downcast eyes on a modest and gentle face. The other, her cheeks artfully rouged, came gaily dressed in bright fabrics, with jewels and gold around her neck and wrists. She walked boldly ahead of the other, assured of herself, glancing all around her with cunning eyes as if extracting admiration from the world. She was the first to draw near to me, saying: 'Young man, I see you are here pondering what path of life to follow. I invite you to follow me—and you will have the easiest and most pleasant life among men. All your days will be spent in leisure, eating, drinking and making merry. There will be no place for toil or dangers, only enjoyment. Let others do the hard work— you rest and be refreshed! Happy you will be all the days of your long life.'

Thinking to be visited by goddesses or nymphs, I asked her, 'What is your name?'

'I am called Pleasure,' said the woman; 'but my enemies have other names for me.'

By now the other woman had come up. I sensed that she was high-born and loved her for the truth and modesty that reflected in her eyes.

'Young man, I know of your fine breeding, and how you have learned all the skills you will need for the path I hope you take,' said she. 'I will not stand here and deceive you with sweet words and promises of pleasant things. The gods have decreed that nothing good in this life can be got without hard labor. If you wish to enjoy the fruits of the earth, you must sow and reap. If you wish your mind to dwell on lofty things, you must direct it so, controlling all your passions. If you wish to be strong, you must master your body, fearing not labor and sweat. If you wish to be remembered, you must serve others. Only in the service of gods and men will you achieve greatness. Do not be misled by my companion, who is better known as Folly and Vice. Her path is broad and there are many who take it. Mine is narrow and there are few who find it. I am named Virtue. Follow me and experience true and lasting happiness, not the fleeing joy of fleshly pleasure.'

'Don't listen to her,' the first woman said. 'My way to happiness is short and sure. Hers is long and hard, as she's admitted herself.'

'Make your choice,' said Virtue quietly. 'Her way leads to pleasures that can never satisfy. Only by noble deeds and virtuous living can a man achieve true happiness.'

It did not take long for me to decide. I resolved to follow the hard road wherever it might lead, shunning pleasure and ease. 'I choose your path, noble lady,' said I to Virtue. 'Instruct me now on how to set foot upon it.'

'You have chosen well,' said Virtue, as Vice turned away sullenly. 'Your journey begins—now!'

A roar such that shook the very rocks swept across the valley. I looked, and lo! a great tawny lion, as large as a horse, leapt amidst the farthest-straying cattle. I sprang to my feet, and with a roar of my own, ran to protect the herd. The lion, interrupted in its bloody repast, fled.   I resolved to hunt the fell lion down, considering it noble Virtue's first task.  I rushed back to gain her blessing, but she and her companion had vanished.  At once I left my father's cattle with other herdsmen and, unarmed, set off.

I spent a day and night seeking the lion in the woods of Cithairon, but it proved elusive.  This lion, it turned out, had another lair on Mount Helicon, sacred to the Muses, at the base of which lies the city of Thespiai: thus some called the beast the Thespian Lion.  I then headed to Mount Helicon, thinking I would have greater success there, but stopped off first at Thespiai for a meal.  On seeing such a strapping, lusty youth, the king there, Thespios, took an immediate liking to me and invited me into his house.  There I lodged for fifty nights while I spent the days hunting for the lion.  Thespios had fifty daughters, and wishing grandchildren as stout as I, caused them, one after another, to spend a night with me.  As it was late and dark when I took each girl to bed, I could not very clearly identify her, and so thought I was enjoying the same one each night.  But one of the fifty refused me, and her father condemned her to remain a virgin.

After scouring the mountain, rich in wild-strawberry bushes, I tracked the lion to a dark and foul-smelling cave.  I knew I had found the right place from the piles of crushed and half-eaten bones.  I looked around for a suitable weapon, and spotting a young wild-olive tree, I uprooted it, ripped off the boughs and made myself a stout cudgel.  As I finished, the lion emerged from its cave, and uttering a mighty roar, sprang at me.  I rushed forward and met the beast head-on, swinging my club and striking the lion's poll with such force that it collapsed with limbs splayed and never rose again.

As I returned from the hunt, my olive-wood club balanced on my shoulder, I encountered two Minyans from Orchomenos on their way to Thebes.  I struck up a conversation with them; but when I learned the point of their errand, my eyes flashed fire and my anger smoldered.  Some years ago, during a festival of Poseidon at Onchestos, Clymenos, the king of Minyan Orchomenos, was killed with a stone flung by a charioteer of Menoiceos, father of Creon, regent of Thebes.  The king's son, Erginos, led his army in an expedition against the Thebans, defeating them.  As part of a treaty, confirmed by solemn oaths, he despoiled them of armor and weapons and demanded that the Thebans pay an annual tribute of one hundred heads of cattle for twenty years.

'Indeed," said one of the heralds scornfully, 'our lord Erginos was certainly clement in settling for cattle instead of chopping off the ears, nose and hands of every man in the city!'

On hearing this insult, I could no longer control himself.  I dropped my club and crossed my arms.

'So you have come for your tribute?' said I.  'Begone! return to your master with this year's bounty.'

With this, I overpowered them and cut off their ears, noses and hands.  Tying their extremities around their necks with cords, I sent them back ignobly to Orchomenos.  When king Erginos received his mutilated subjects, he was so wracked with rage that he sent a missive to Thebes, threatening war for this outrage unless I was delivered to him.

King Creon of Thebes found himself in a bind as worse as when the Sphinx held sway.  I was beloved in the territory of Thebes for having rid them of the lion.  If he did not give me up, however, Thebes would be burned.  When word of the Minyan demand reached him, I told Creon not to fear.  Rousing the men of the city to fight for their freedom, I led them into the temples and tore down the votive offerings of weapons and armor from captured spoils.  I assumed command of all willing to fight, teaching them the use of weapons and tactics of battle.  With me stood Amphytrion and my brother Iphicles, eager to prove himself.  As we set out, an oracle declared that success in the war could only be achieved if the citizen of most noble descent consented to die for the people.  All looked to the famously-descended Antipoenos, but he refused to take his life.  His daughters, Androcleia and Alcis, did so in his stead, and were later greatly honored.

With their demand unfulfilled, the Minyans took up arms and marched against Thebes, making it as far as the plain by the Sanctuary of the Great Gods, where I ambushed them at night and took their chariot-horses.  Leaving most of the Thebans to continue the attack, I reached the coast and stopped up there two large limestone tunnels through which the river Cephissos emptied into the sea, turning the great Copaic Plain into a marsh.  By this, I hoped to prevent the advance of the Minyan cavalry, forcing the fight to move upland.  The strategy worked, and with the greater mass of the combatants fighting in the hills, with a small force I descended on Orchomenos and tore down the gates. Amphytrion fell fighting by my side.

'Father!' cried I, cradling his body in the midst of the battle.

'Alcides—my son,' said Amphytrion, beholding for the last time my face, streaked with blood and sweat, and daubed with the first flush of a beard. 'There is something you must know for certain. Your true father is not I, but Zeus himself. You were born as the sun entered the Tenth Sign amidst prodigies and wonders.'

I thought I misheard the faint words of my dying father amidst the clamor. 'But you are the only father I know—the only one I have loved,' said I.

'And I have loved you as my own son,' he replied.

And so Amphytrion breathed his last. Mourning him, I moved his body to a safe place until I could later give it proper burial, and joined my comrades in sacking the city. When the Minyans had been completely defeated, I compelled them to pay a double tribute to Thebes. On my return there, still reeling from Amphytrion's revelation, I dedicated an altar to Zeus and a stone lion before the shrine of Glorious Artemis. In gratitude for saving the city, Creon gave me his eldest daughter Megara in marriage and appointed me protector of the city. Iphicles was rewarded with the hand of the youngest daughter; his first wife Automedousa, who bore him a son, having recently died.

Megara came to live with Alcmene and I in the house of Amphytrion. How easily I was bewitched by the radiant daughter of Creon! I strove to be an attentive and dutiful husband. I liked to lie with her on the terrace, observing how the golden moonlight dabbled her tawny hair. Over time she bore four sons in close succession: Therimachos, Creontiades, Opitos and Deicoön. I grew rather proud of my boys and planned for them bright futures. I taught them what I had learned in my youth, especially how to fight and take command, wishing to instill in them honor and bravery. Iphicles, who lived nearby, sent me his oldest son Iolaos, along with two more children from his second wife, to be tutored. All the children, therefore grew up together, and loved each other as siblings.

I went often to the temple of Zeus on the highest point of the city, by the seven-gated wall, to make offerings. I wished above all to make the acquaintance of Zeus, my real father, hoping that the king of the gods would descend and show himself to me. But he never did. One afternoon, however, as the sunlight waned through the colonnades, a woman, her head draped by a cowl, appeared from the shadows. She seemed to be merely a suppliant, and so I paid her no mind. But at the noise of a strong wind sweeping the sanctuary, I happened to look behind me, and swore I spied, as the woman seemed to vanish, a pair of merry grey eyes and a glint of armor through the open folds of her cloak.

At midsummer, when the days were long and sweet, Megara held a feast to celebrate my return from a campaign against Pyraechmos, king of the Euboeans, and ally of the Minyans, who had been guilty of oppressing his own people. As a warning to all tyrants, I ordered him tied between two colts, which, set to run in different directions, tore apart his body. Afterward, his corpse was left unburied beside the river Heracleios, where it is said a neighing sound arises whenever horses drink there.

We dug pit to hold a roaring fire for roasting oxen. Iphicles with his wife and children attended, as well our sister Laonome, born to Alcmene last of all, with her husband, the Lapith Polyphemos, and their little son Hylas, a bubbling boy of two that could have rivaled Ganymede in his beauty; and also Licymnios and many of my friends.

After we ate and drank our fill, I gathered the children to engage them in various games and martial exercises. While Iolaos contented himself at quoits with his brothers, seeing who could cast the farthest, my four sons practiced at archery and sword-play with the palace children. I had planned a brilliant future for each of them: one was to rule Argos; another was to succeed at Mycenae; the third was to lord it over Boetian Oechalia; and the last was to reign at Thebes. The Alcaids, as they were then called, would have the choice of the finest royal brides from the great cities of the Greeks.

Seeing how content the children appeared at their exercises under the warm sun, I retired to a hill, a wineskin at my lips, to watch; and thanked the gods for my good fortune. But my thoughts were not entirely free of misgivings. Although I was greatly honored as Thebes' protector, waging war against Creon's enemies, I resented having to serve as another man's vassal. And for Amphytrion's crime, I still lived in exile; when, as a Perseid and grandson of Electryon, to rule the Argolid was my right.  But on that throne sat Eurystheus, whom I hated, considering him a craven pretender.

Now, I imagine that Hera, guiding her chariot through the air back from her beloved Argos, spied me and detested my contentment.  Drawing the reins with trembling arms, she raged: 'Am I inferior because I am the wife of Zeus?  Does he alone have the right to hate, as when he squeezed the groaning clouds and loosed the fountains of the earth to destroy that first race of men?  How can the son of Alcmene rejoice while I am mocked?  Intolerable!  Though I am forbidden to kill him, I am not prevented from engorging him with bitter gall.'  She raced to earth and summoned the Fury Allecto from deepest Hell, that lover of bloody crimes, to do her foul bidding.

I passed the day consuming wine.  Megara, recognizing my proclivity for excess, ordered the servants to ignore my summons for more.  Yet I clamored for the sweet juice, and received all that I wished.  When it was time for a sacrifice before the altar of Zeus to purify me of the blood I had recently spilled in battle, I stumbled to where my wife and children stood in holy silence.  As my eldest son was about to dip a lighted brand in holy water, an abrupt change came over me.  The grim daughter of Night, hovering before me in a foul mist, had plucked a black snake from her writhing hair and tossed it into my breast, where it burrowed deep into my heart to spread through my senses the flaming poison of a madness fresh from war and slaughter.  I heard voices around me, and strange moans.  Gripping my head, I tried to shake off the unwanted sounds; but they grew louder, and more vile.  I heard a multitude of cries, and clashing steel, and stomping feet.  With a madman's laugh, rolling my bloodshot eyes, foam oozing from my mouth, I cried: 'Why sacrifice before I have slain that usurper Eurystheus?  T'would be double the work to kindle again this purifying flame.  Father, 'twas better that you died than live with the shame of exile from your own land.  Soon as I bring hither the head of that weakling, I'll finish these rites.  Spill the water!  Give me my bow.  To Mycenae I'll go.  I'll need too crow-bars and pick-axes to level those Cyclopean walls.'

Then I made as if I mounted a chariot, and with an imaginary goad excited imaginary horses.  Those who watched me felt both fear and amusement, and said to one another: 'Is he making sport of us, or is he mad?' I ran off to my house shouting vile threats against my cousin. I returned with my great bent bow and quiver, spilling arrows as I fumbled to sling it across his back. Alcmene caught me by the arm, sensing the worst. I thrust her aside and took aim at my children, thinking them the sons of Eurystheus. In fright they dashed madly about, seeking refuge behind the altar or the pillars, or beneath their mother's skirt. With outstretched hands Megara cried: 'What are you doing, Alcides? Do you mean to slay your children?' And all joined her in supplication. I paid no heed, and first hunted Creontiades around the pillars until, coming face to face with him, I shot the boy through the heart, boating: 'Here lies Eurystheus' son dead at my feet!' Deicoön, who had taken cover with Opitos behind the altar, emerged to throw himself before me when he saw he was next within his father's aim. 'O father, slay me not! I am your child—your own son!' I struck him with the bow and crushed his head. Opitos now thought to run, but with an arrow I sent him sprawling to the dust. Two sons of Iphicles were next victims of my unerring aim, and afterwards were thrown into the fire. My youngest son, Therimachos, I tore from Megara's arms, and urging him to flee, picked him off from a fair distance. I then turned to Megara, thinking her Eurystheus' wife; but Iphicles bore her away to safety. As I nocked another arrow, a heavy stone came flying: from whence I knew not, although I thought I saw Athena in her plumed helm standing near. It struck my breast and drew from me him all wind and sense, so that I fell to the ground as if asleep.

Awaking, I found himself bound fast with cords to a pillar of the house and guarded by Creon's soldiers. With bleary eyes and labored breath I tried to make sense of my circumstances. I saw wailing servants scrubbing at stains of blood.

'Why do I lie here, frapped like a ship with tackle?' I yelled, straining against the cords. Seeing Alcmene coming near, I said: 'Mother, why do you weep and veil your eyes from your own son?'

Alcmene dismissed the guard. She stood over me, her face contorted in anguish, her tears bathing her white cheeks.

'My child!' she wept; 'yes—mine still, despite all your misery.'

'What is there so sad that you weep, mother?' I asked.

'Your own eyes would see should your senses be restored.'

I could not remember anything. I once more took in the scene of evident tragedy.

Alcmene, raising her arms, cried in anger: 'Zeus! Do you not see these deeds of Hera? Her jealousy has outdone us.'

Alarmed, I asked: 'What? Am I a victim of her enmity? What have I done?'

'Behold!' she lamented. 'There lay the corpses of your children.'

I trembled. 'What?' spat I. 'Who has murdered them?'

Alcmene could hardly say the words: 'You—by your own hand.'

Speechless, I wailed like a wild boar tormented by the hunters' lances, which, wounded runs off to fight death in some covert.

'And Megara?' I cried.

'She, at least, escaped your madness.'

'Woe! Horror! Why do I sit here still alive? Free me that I may leap from some sea-facing cliff, or burn myself in fire, or plunge a sword into my breast to avenge in me my children's blood!'

I roared in anguish, and by my exertions burst asunder the knots that held me. Seeing a cloak cast off nearby, I took it to cover himself. 'Let me veil my head in darkness,' said I; 'for I cannot atone for the evil I have done.'

The soldiers, swords drawn, rushed back. Alcmene urged restraint, pleading to be left alone with me, stating that Anticyreos had cured my madness with a dose of black hellebore. As the soldiers once more retreated, she knelt beside her trembling son. She reached for my hands, but I would not surrender them.

'This is certainly Hera's work,' she said. 'O my dear son— none other will ever bear a greater share of suffering.'

Then, throwing back the cloak from my head, Alcmene entreated: 'Remove this mantle from your eyes. Show the sun your face.' Grasping my face and knees, reaching again for my hands, she cried as great tear drops anointed my bloodied fingers: 'My child, restrain your savage temper. Mix not your own blood with those of your children, joining woe upon woe.'

'Mother, fly from my pollution!'

'If I share your misfortune, what is that to me? Let your curse come on her who bore you.'

'I am resolved to die, mother.'

Alcmene burst into a fresh flood of tears.

'Are these truly the words of Alcides?'

Beating my head, I said: 'Remember, I am the son of he who killed your father. When the foundation is badly laid, the house will be cursed. Zeus—ah, Zeus, my alleged father!—he begot me as a butt for Hera's hate. Let her rejoice, thumping heaven's floor in a wild dance. But what shall I do now? In happy Thebes I cannot remain. Wherever I go, they will leer and say: "Is that not the son of Zeus who murdered his own children? Plague take him!" This is the end I foresee. Therefore it is best I am seen no more, for what right do I have now to live?'

Alcmene slapped me across the face, showing me an ire I last witnessed when as a boy I ever misbehaved.

She said: 'I will never counsel you to die rather than endure your suffering. There is no man alive immune from misfortune, nor any god. The poets sing how they unlawfully intermarry and inflict violence upon one another—and yet they still inhabit Olympos despite their crimes. What makes you think that you—a son of man—can kick against the pricks of fate while they do not? Leave Thebes in compliance to the law. Seek a sovereign willing to cleanse you of your bloodshed. Fight, son, fight! Stormy winds do not always blow so strong.'

I took my mother's hands and kissed them. I said: 'You need not mention the poets' fictions. The gods, as far as I know, want not and dwell in supreme happiness. Yet, I will hearken unto you. I will not take my life, lest I be branded a coward and bring shame upon our house. He who does not temper his frail nature against the vicissitudes of Fortune is no better than a dog. I will go into exile.' As a tear for the first time in my life sought to escape my eye, I remarked: 'Give my children due burial, since the law forbids me. Tell Megara that I lament the poor return I gave for her love and care. Remain in Thebes, mother, and do not think to forever cling to sorrow and bitterness. Land of Cadmos, weep for my children, and for me!'

I left Thebes that very hour. An utter desolation filled my soul and wracked my body with powerful convulsions of grief. To lose my dear wife and children—and by my own hand! Mercifully, I could not remember what I had done. Although I blamed Hera for my madness and its consequences, I could achieve no relief from my bloodguilt.

Day and night circled each other, and neither sleep nor the promise of a new day ended my grief. With the lovely visage of Megara floating before me, and the laughter of my children still in my ears, I went as a suppliant to Thespios, who purified me and allowed me refuge in his city. Yet my guilt continually consumed me. I rejected all comforts and fellowship. The day came when I could no longer endure my anguish. Before the cock's crow I took up my club, and left Thespiai to head north across the mountains to Delphi, where the gods were bound to answer."

4

"It was said that Zeus once sent out two mighty eagles, one to the East and the other to the West; and where they met marked the center of the world; and Zeus laid a stone to mark the place. A great earth-born serpent, the Python, was raised to guard it. The location—Delphi—on the southwestern spur of Mount Parnassos, near a gorge and spring and overlooking the gulf, was later coveted by the god Apollo, who wished to establish thereat an oracle. He used his golden bow for the first time to slay the Python, and let the ancient creature rot in that holy spot. A temple to the god was built there; and where the spring flowed under it, upon a rocky cleft from which divine effluvium rose, Apollo established his priestess to utter prophecies.

I resided at Delphi until the appointed day when the oracle was in session. After leaving an offering I confided my question to the priests on the temple porch, who then retreated inside to the sacred apartment where the Pythia sat motionless upon her high tripod, her eyes shut, wrapped in the mists rising from a chasm beneath her. The attendants, ready to translate the Pythia's ecstatic utterances that only they could interpret, were surprised when she, before they even divulged the question, cried out most uncryptically: 'Phoebos Apollo has decreed that he shall no longer be known as Alcides, but shall take the name of Heracles, since from his good works among men he will win imperishable glory. And as penance he must henceforth reside at Tyrins, and serve Eurystheus for a Great Year, performing ten Labors as he sets before him.'

On hearing the oracular response from the priests, I became furious, for I had despised Eurystheus since his youth. Yet I could not oppose the will of Zeus in the matter. I spent many days wandering the woods of Mount Parnassos, still haunted by the loss of my family; until, willing to do anything to purge my defilement, I agreed to abase himself before one I considered an inferior, as the oracle had commanded.

I took the road southward; and as I neared the Isthmus to cross into the Peloponnese, a young lad ran toward me calling my name. It was none other than Iolaos there, my brother Iphicles' eldest son, who had been searching for me. Surprised and delighted, I embraced him in my stout arms, not having seen him since that terrible day. Even after the death of his brothers, Iolaos still loved me; and, growing into manhood, wished for nothing more than to follow me and share in my adventures. I tried to dissuade him from such a road, lauding his parents and extolling the virtues of an ordered city life. But Iolaos persisted, and would not leave me alone.

'Very well,' said I; 'you shall be my shieldbearer should I go into battle; and my charioteer should I grow tired of walking. Did I not train you myself in such things? But even more you shall be a companion in my Labors, reminding me of my former life of joy, and sustaining me in my present life of penance and sorrow.'

And so I settled at mighty-walled Tyrins, not far from Mycenae and Argos, situated on a long hill on the arid plain. I moved into the royal palace, abandoned since the ancient days of Megapenthes, son of Proitos. A few old domestics still remained, spending their days sweeping the tiled floors and wiping the dust off the faded paintings that adorned the walls of the great hall. Being a descendant of Perseus, I was welcomed by the people as Tyrin's rightful lord. I remained there only a few days before setting out with Iolaos to begin my servitude to king Eurystheus.

At midday we arrived at Mycenae. The city rose on a rugged height upon the Argeian plain, recessed between two lofty summits. Any traveler nearing Mycenae would have marveled at its massive walls, nearly two rods thick, fortified by the Cyclopes for Perseus, as in olden times they had constructed Tyrins for king Proitos. Proitos had a twin brother, Acrisios, with whom he was ever at odds, even from within their mother's womb. After the death their father Abas, lord of Argos, they fought several battles over the kingdom. Proitos, defeated and exiled, sought the aid of Iobates, king of Lycia. From him Proitos received not only military assistance, but also his daughter, Stheneboia, in marriage. Proitos, assisted by Lycian troops, returned to the Argolid and established the fortress of Tyrins upon a rocky hill, compelling his brother to share the land with him.

Acrisios, ruling Argos, married Eurydice, daughter of Lacedaimon, the king of Sparta. No male issue came from the union; only a daughter, Danaë. When from an oracle he learned that Danaë would bear a son destined to kill him, he imprisoned her with her nurse in an impregnable brazen tower without doors or windows. Zeus, who loved her, visited her, dripping as golden dew upon her virgin lap. By this she conceived Perseus. When Acrisios heard the sound of Perseus playing, he brought her forth and questioned her about the child. Not believing that he was the offspring of Zeus, yet fearing the possibility, he locked mother and son in a chest and cast them to the sea. The chest drifted for many days and nights, borne by the waves, until it washed ashore on the island of Seriphos, where it was found by Dictys, whose half-brother, Polydectes, ruled the island. But the king, seeing Danaë, developed a passion for her. It was he who sent Perseus to fetch the Gorgon's head, for he feared Danaë's mighty son.

The great doors of the Lion Gate, of thick, iron-banded wood, were opened for me: I was expected, since a dream had warned Eurystheus of my arrival. Of premature birth, thin and skulking, with a head too small for his crown and feet too big for his shoes, he was a man who surrounded himself with the trappings of power—strong guards and sycophants—but who lacked the force of courage and conviction radiated by truly great men. A slight tremble coursed through his frame when from his right-walled throne he saw me enter the great hall; yet his fear turned to delight when I, bowing slightly in inarticulate formality, repeated the oracle of Apollo delivered through the Pythia, which words confirmed his dream and gave him the elusive confidence of the weak-hearted.

'Well Heracles—is that your name now?—what a fine brute you turned out!' he said insolently. 'You should have kept to your first profession, although I hear that lion proved more than a match for you. Ha! I think you have given me an idea for your first task. Before that, however, you must swear a solemn oath that you will serve me without condition, and that you will never threaten me or my kingdom, as you did your own family.'

My face grew flush with anger, yet I maintained my composure and said with measured words: 'I am here by heaven's decree, lord Eurystheus. I will do as you as you say.'

Eurystheus regarded me for a moment, and taking confidence from his ring of guards, descended from his throne and twice circled me, a look of disdain in his eyes.

'See there over the great hearth, upon the columns and around the walls of this mighty hall, the bones and pelts of beasts my fathers hunted,' said he. 'Another terrible lion lurks in the north, in the mountains near Nemea, ravaging the land. No man can kill this beast, it is said, for its hide cannot be penetrated, neither by iron, bronze nor stone. Bring me this lion, that I may add its pelt to the prizes of this hall.'

Iolaos swallowed hard on hearing this daunting task, and glanced apprehensively at me. I returned a gameson wink, instilling confidence back in the young man. I lifted the club off my shoulder, and brought it down into my palm with such a force and sound that Eurystheus started in fright.

'I thank you, lord Eurystheus,' said I with a laugh, 'for granting me this first challenging adventure. There is no question now that you will work me very hard during my indenture. As you can see, I appear as a simple rustic. I carry this little club, and this bow serves me at times. But in order for me to accomplish this task, and the others you will command, I will need also some hunting-nets, and a good chariot.'

Eurystheus dispatched attendants to outfit me with all I required. I do not think he as yet contemplated my demise, since I could prove useful in riding his realm of pests and bringing him glory as the initiator of good deeds.

When all was ready, I left Mycenae with Iolaos at the chariot reins. Not long on the road, we stopped off at the town of Cleonai, on the verge of the Nemean valley, to find lodging; for I knew, if descriptions of the beast were accurate, that it would take some time to track down. We came to the house of a poor day-laborer named Molorchos.

'Tell, me good man, if you know the whereabouts of the fearsome lion that lurks in this vale,' said I.

'Aye, I know it,' said Molorchos sadly; 'for my only son, not two years ago, was tending our sheep there by the foot of Mount

Apesas, when the lion jumped on him and carried him away. O that the gods took pity on a poor old man left childless! My son was no doubt devoured, and his bones left to blanch, unburied, near a noisome cave.'

'I know how it is to lose a son—in a worse way than you,' said I; 'but I shall avenge your son when I find this lion.'

'You seem likely to do it!' said Molorchos. 'Are you a god, or the son of a god? I've never seen such a stout, bold, broad-shouldered fellow.'

'Why—he is Alcides of Thebes,' said Iolaos.

'That name is known from Athens to Argos, it seems,' said Molorchos. 'I would be honored to have the great Alcides—as well as any of his friends—as my guests in my little hut. Come, eat and refresh yourself. I shall kill for you my only ram.'

'Forbear!' said I. 'After I depart, wait for me thirty days. If I do not return, sacrifice the ram to me as hero; otherwise, we shall honor Zeus the Savior.'

For this first Labor, at least, I wished Iolaos to stay safely with Molorchos. Iolaos agreed with reluctance, only on the condition that I admit his assistance on my next task. Equipped with my trusty bow, a quiver full of sharp arrows, a short sword, and my club, I entered the sprawling valley of Nemea in search of the lion. Born of Selene, Titan goddess of the moon, it was said to have fallen from the sky and landed upon Mount Tretos. Others said that the lion was the offspring of Typhon, the last of the Titans defeated by Zeus, and Echidne; or even of the Chimaira, but no one was certain. Not finding anyone to direct me, since the inhabitants had either fled or been devoured by the lion, and not locating any tracks, I spent several days searching the slopes of Mount Apesas above Nemea, where it is said Perseus first sacrificed to Zeus. After that I ascended Mount Tretos to continue the hunt. One evening I came upon a den in one of the rocks, strewn about with bones. The cave had two mouths, one a little higher than the other. There I spied finally the object of my quest: an enormous tawny lion—larger than the one I had faced on Cithairon—heading back sluggishly to its lair, its coat and chin spotted with fresh blood. Secreted in a brake, I very quietly nocked an arrow and let it fly; it hit its mark against the lion's massy flank, but rebounded harmlessly. I set another arrow to the string, pulled it to my ear, and with unerring accuracy sent it whizzing directly into the lion's chest, but with the same result. The lion, taking no notice of the arrows, headed into its cave to settle in with full stomach for the night. I now drew my sword and crept after the lion, thinking that a double-edged blade of hard bronze would surely do the trick. As the lion turned to see who disturbed it, I struck, but the sword bent against the impenetrable pelt. The lion, finally feeling threatened, roared so loudly that rocks fell from the precipices above. Leaping about and rearing on hind legs, it took a swipe at me as I ducked and reached for my club. Swinging it with might and main, I struck the lion square on the crown. The wood shattered instantly into pieces; but the lion felt the mighty blow, and was left dazed. Shaking off the ringing in its ears, it let out another roar before fleeing into the darkness of its cave.

I looked down ruefully at the stump of the splintered club, still gripped tightly in my hands. I cast it aside, ran up the slope to the other cave mouth, and strung a net about it to prevent the lion from running out of that end. Knowing that no weapon I possessed could aid me, I ripped my cloak, wrapped the shreds around my arms, and entered the lower cave, prepared to subdue the lion by brute strength. The cave, growing darker with every step, snaked into the mountainside. I proceeded slowly and cautiously, my ears attuned to every sound. When I could hear the lion's heavy breath and the dripping of its fangs, it proved too late. The lion, its keen eyes adapted to the darkness, sprang upon me. But I battled to stay on my feet, seizing the flowing mane to ward off the snapping maw. Battered about the back and shoulders by the lion's sharp claws, and feeling its hot breath against my face, I grasped the fore-legs, pushing the beast down until, leaping aside, I was able to vault on its back. Now, wrestling an animal is little different than wresting a man, assuming one could steer clear of claws and fangs; and so from that point forward I exercised an advantage over my adversary, for I am unequalled in wrestling prowess. Pinning the lion's hind-legs with my feet, I thrust one arm under its fore-leg, raising it up. Bringing my other cloaked arm under the lion's neck, I gripped hands under the lion's throat and reared back with all my might. Man and beast plunged downward in the darkness as I tightened my grip. The lion, smothering me under its bulk, struggled viciously, feeling itself strangulated.

Breaking my tight hold for a moment, the lion twisted its head and snapped off a bit of one of my fingers. Despite the intense pain, I renewed my stranglehold and with groans and fearsome roars of my own held the lion's head in chancery until its thrashing stopped.

I released the carcase, kicking it aside to unpin my arm. After binding up my wounded hand, I felt an overwhelming weariness, and using the lion's haunch as a pillow, fell asleep in the cool darkness of the cave.

I awoke the next day from a long sleep. Gripping the lion's fore-legs, I dragged the carcase outside, where I hoisted the enormous lion across my broad shoulders and walked back to Cleonai. Along the way I stopped to pluck some wild parsley to a make a crown for my expected sacrifice.

A month had passed since I went off to hunt lion. Molorchos, remembering his duty, was preparing to offer his only ram as a funeral sacrifice for me. Iolaos stood by him, grim and silent, unbelieving that his great uncle was no more. Just then, Iolaos looked up, and over a hill saw me bounding with the great tawny lion on my back, its mane wafting in the breeze. Iolaos let out a cry and ran to meet me, amazed at the size of the animal I carried.

'Stay your hand!' I cried to my host, dropping the heavy carcase. 'It is to Savior Zeus that we will sacrifice, who gives good things to all men.'

And so Molorchos, full of joy, brought the ram to a turf altar, where he sliced its neck, and allowed the blood to drip. Molorchos skinned and cut it apart, and setting the rump-slices between two pieces of fat, lay this and the bones upon the fire. The smoke rose heavenward as a savory aroma for Zeus. When the offering parts had been burnt, we took the fleshy cuts of meat and roasted them on spits, and sat down to a hearty meal."

5

"Before quitting Nemea, I cut himself another club, stouter than the first.

The lion proved too big to carry in the chariot. I sent Iolaos ahead back to Mycenae, while I bore the lion on my back across the plain. At the pass to Argos, I procured a mule and sent it back to Molorchos in gratitude. Iolaos, meanwhile, informed Eurystheus that I presently returned. In addition, reports came in from every town I passed that the carcase of the Nemean Lion was being delivered to Mycenae. Yet, nothing could prepare Eurystheus for the sight of the enormous beast dropped on the stone floor before him. Thinking the beast had come alive, he leapt off his throne and cowered behind it. When laughter at his discomfort rang around the hall, he grew angry, and forbade me from ever entering the city again with his booty. He no longer desired the lion's pelt; and so I carried the carcase outside the city walls and for a time pondered how to flay it, for nothing could penetrate the skin. At last, employing the lion's own sharp claws, I stripped off the hide and made myself this covering of impenetrable armor.

Eurystheus now hated me more than before. Hera herself, no doubt, put a thought into his head for my next Labor, for she hoped to bring about the demise of the bastard son of Zeus. This was to destroy the Lernean Hydra, a monstrous water-snake reared by her own design, when she foresaw the day Heracles would walk the earth. This creature came forth also from Echidne, the mother of many such monsters. It lived in a deep and forbidding swamp at ancient Lerna, on a narrow strip by the sea not far from Argos, where unwary travelers perished.

We arrived at the edge of the marsh, and looked out into the misty, reeking morass filled with ancient, gnarled trees webbed in vine. It was said a way to the underworld existed beneath the bottomless abyss of a dark pool, which Dionysos traversed to recover his mother Semele

'They say that of the Hydra's many heads, one of them is immortal; and by its noxious breath can instantly kill men!' observed Iolaos with trepidation. Iolaos drove around the swamp, until we found a stretch of firm ground. Leaving the chariot there, we made our way inside on foot looking for the triple spring at the source of the river Amymone, where the Hydra was believed to have its lair. This river derived its name from one of the daughters of Danaös who was loved by Poseidon. A fountain gushed forth whereat she drew the god's trident from a rock.

Beyond a small lake we came to a grove of gigantic plane-trees, where the river formed from numerous springs bubbling forth from under the rocks. In a deep hollow, half-submerged in the pooling waters, beneath the enormous roots of a plane-tree, I perceived a disturbance. Guessing that we had chanced upon the Hydra's lair, I bade Iolaos to start a fire; and then taking branches of gorse, tied them lit to my arrows. These I shot within the cavity formed by the arching roots, one after the other. The streaks of flame trailed through the mists. Presently a horrible hiss emitted from the hollow and the murky waters churned. Out slithered the Hydra—a sight so terrible that Iolaos' knees buckled under him. While swimming through the brackish water it resembled a long, monstrous snake; but as it neared us out came one head, then another, until its hulking mass reached the muddy bank and rose from the sedge to tower above us. It stood on four legs, like tree trunks, and whipped the water with a long tail. From its enormous, scaly, barrel-like body ten serpent heads waggled on long sinewy necks. Holding my breath, I rushed toward the monster, battering apart the nearest heads with my club. To my astonishment, however, the ruined necks simply snapped upward, and like sudden boils on seared skin, out popped new heads in replacement! To make matters worse, a monstrous yellow crab—as large as a milch-cow—scampered out from the swamp and bit me on the foot. 'Not fair!' I cried. 'Now it's two against one.' In a rage, I crushed the crab with a single blow of my club. 'Iolaos, set the grove afire, that we may rid ourselves of these pests,' I commanded. Iolaos, regaining his courage, lit a fagot in the flames, and ran about setting the neighborhood on fire. Then, in a flash of inspiration, he rushed to my side while I was still vainly crushing heads, and burnt and seared the bloody neck-stumps. This operation ceased the natural regeneration of the heads. Delighted, I finished off the rest of the Hydra in due course, and with my sword cut off the immortal head, which had kept aloof during the battle, finally putting an end to the monster; this head, however, continued to hiss and snap at us. I therefore buried it under a large rock on the road to Elaios so it would no longer prove a nuisance to anyone. Returning to the carcase, an idea struck me. I pulled the slimy mass from the water by two of its necks, disemboweled it, and dipped the tips of some of my arrows in the blood and steaming gall. I reasoned that if even the breath of this creature was so pernicious, that its blood would surely be a powerful toxic. With arrows thus envenomed, from which the least wound would prove fatal, we returned to Mycenae."

## 6

"King Eurystheus listened intently to the report of my conquest at Lerna, but kept his eyes averted from me in my bristling lionskin, that I wore as a cowl, with its paws tied about my neck in a reef knot. The very sight of me, methinks, excited terrors in his mind. He would rather have been done with the whole business, had not Hera constantly, like an irksome gadfly, pestered him in dreams, instructing him on how to extend his cousin's trials.

Announced the king: 'There is in Arcadia a hind, with brazen hooves and golden horns, and sacred to the immortal huntress Artemis. Some say that it is actually a stag, but I do not know. What you must do is bring me this hind alive. Capturing it, after battling lions and snakes, I hope is not beneath your abilities, Heracles.'

Taking no affront, I jovially said: 'O king! I have heard of this creature's great size. What will you do when I bring it hither, and freeing it, it enters to gambol about your spacious throne-room?'

A din of mirth filled the hall, which the king cut short with an impatient wave of his arm. In scheming silence he watched Iolaos and I, with merry hearts, depart.

It was said that while the divine daughter of Leto was yet a child, she saw five magnificent gold-antlered hinds grazing by the river Anauros in Thessaly. These creatures were the fleetest of their kind; but Artemis proved the swifter and pursuing them, caught four of them in sequence and harnessed them to her chariot. The fifth hind eluded her, fleeing into Achaia, and then further to Arcadia, where it sometimes roamed free about the hill of Ceryneia, near the river Cerynites where it issues from the mountains. There Artemis left her, pleased at the keen instinct of the beast, and forbade anyone to molest her on pain of her displeasure. Although

Hera had put it in Eurystheus' mind to send me after this beast, he was slow in realizing the wisdom of the errand: if beasts and monsters were not enough to slay Heracles, perhaps the rage of some rash god could prove sufficient. Who better to play this role than the chaste Artemis, goddess of the hunt and of the moon, who, unlike her twin sibling, could often be cold and cruel.

I began my third Labor in the early autumn, while yet the waning summer spread its heat across the vast and mountainous stretches of Arcadia. Iolaos drove me to the town of Oinoe, on the border of Argolis, near Mount Artemision, where Artemis had on a peak of that range a great sanctuary. Iolaos remained there while I set out on foot in search of the hind, which I foolishly believed would not prove difficult to capture. A fortnight later I returned and sat down with Iolaos to a meal of roast spring lamb and barley-bread. As we ate, I described to Iolaos that I had seen the magnificent animal resting in a thicket on the mountain, the sun twinkling on its gilded horns, and had tried to entangle it in a net, but the powerful hind broke through. I pursued for many a night and a day, but could never get near her again, so crafty did she prove.

'I would so like to see this hind, Heracles,' said Iolaos. 'Perhaps between the two of us we can capture it?'

I lifted my face from my trencher, my eyes twinkling, and said: 'You shall see her, my dear Iolaos, I promise you that. I must trap it myself, however; and with the least force, for I must not hurt it and anger the goddess of Oinoe. I can't have two goddesses mad at me! I fear this task will last long, so there is no use for you to remain here. Return to Tyrins and wait there.'

In the morning, after Iolaos' departure, I piled stones to form an altar, secured a goat from a passing herdsman, and sacrificed to Artemis in propitiation. After burning the thighbones rolled in fat, I consumed the roasted meat and proceeded back into the wilderness.

My instincts were not far off. My skills as a hunter were strained to their utmost. I pursued the hind all through Arcadia, up into the snowy mountains and deep down into the shaded valleys. I would track the dappled doe by the deep prints of its brazen hooves. But no sooner would I draw near, than the hind would escape me again. I would catch tantalizing glimpses of moonlight twinkling on the horns, passing swiftly through the pines-boughs or across the high grasses. At times I was tempted to draw my bow, although I wondered if the hind would prove swifter than my arrows.

I laid traps, digging deep, thatch-covered holes. I ran her into gorges and to cliff edges. I set nets and other contrivances— yet all in vain. The wily hind always eluded me. Long days and sleepless nights I simply waited, perhaps dug into some hole, or perched high upon a tree, hoping to cross her path. As many times as I found her trail, I lost it again. I followed her through the central uplands, across mighty rivers, north into Achaia. And then, in the midst of winter, I pursued the hind high into the snow-matted mountains. For a spell, wrapped tightly in my lionskin, beard glistening with frost, hands and feet numb from the cold, eyes blinded by the snow, I considered giving up the enterprise and turning back. Memories of my children restored my resolve. Though I could never bring them back, I was prepared to expend my very being to expiate my awful sin. Onward then I trudged, alone—for it is sometimes in the arena of solitude that men must do battle. Despising hunger and frost, I kept alive in my mind a precept of wise Cheiron: 'To master the world, first master yourself.'

The hind eluded me further, and missing its forage-land, fled back the way she came. It had been a year of relentless pursuit. I pressed on, however, beyond the limits of mortal endurance, and almost trapped her on Mount Artemision, where I found the hind asleep under a tree. Bursting from its hiding place, the hind fled into the heights of Arcadia, and then descended to the river Ladon. I had had enough. I did not want to risk another circuitous pursuit through Pelops' land. As the hind bent its head to drink, I bent my bow and pinned its forelegs together. The arrow passed cleanly between bone and sinew, and drew no blood. The doe fell forward, desperately kicking with its brazen hooves, unable to run any longer. I fell upon it, and pulling the head down by the horns, trussed its limbs. Hoisting the struggling bulk across my shoulders, I said: 'Of all my Labors, I shall recall you most of all, Cerynitis, for in your innocence you have caused me the greatest effort.'

At that moment I think Artemis and Apollo, hunting in the pine forest, saw me transporting the deer. As Artemis recognized her favorite pet, she grew wroth, and bent her gleaming bow, saying: 'Look what that impudent man has done—treating my sacred hind that way. I'll teach him! One dart and he'll regret being born!' At this the patient Apollo stayed her hand and said: 'Sister, do you not know who that is? It is none other than Heracles of Tyrins. Go see what's he's about. I'm sure he has an explanation.' Strong-voiced Artemis relented. Wearing the shape and attire of an Arcadian maiden, the divine radiance of her bronzed limbs muted for mortal eyes, she dashed across turf to intercept me.

Having now, reaching my target, forgotten every trial scaling the mountain haunts and crossing untrodden meadows, I hardly felt the virgin goddess tugging at my load.

'Stop there! Do you not know that hind is sacred to the Mistress of these woods?' she cried. I turned, surprised at the unexpected company.

'I beg your pardon,' said I humbly, not certain who addressed me, whether a nymph or the goddess herself in disguise. 'I have hunted this hind for a year and day at the behest of king Eurystheus of Mycenae. I mean no harm to it.'

Artemis knew of my Labors, and her anger subsided. She patted the beast and it licked her hand. 'Show the hind to your master, but be sure she remains unharmed, or risk the virgin goddess' displeasure,' she cautioned. 'And when you are done, return her hither, where she is pleased to dwell.'

She left me and I continued on my way.

Eurystheus grew so fearful after suffering a nightmare in which I hunted him across the wilds of Arcadia, and catching him, bound his arms and legs like a pig ready for the roast, and sticking an apple in his mouth, carried him back to Mycenae across my shoulders, that he ordered his smiths to construct a brazen storage jar large enough for him to hide in! This he caused to be buried in a courtyard of the palace. He posted a sentry on the topmost battlement to be on the lookout for me, and to signal an alarm should I appear on the plain. This the sentry did, reporting excitedly that I carried the largest hind he had ever seen, its gilded horns gleaming in the sun. Eurystheus jumped into the jar and closed the lid behind him, but not before entrusting orders for my next Labor to his plump herald, a son of famed Pelops and Hippodameia, a fugitive from Elis whom he had purified for murder.

I reached the gates of Mycenae as the breathless herald rushed out to meet me. I stopped when I saw the guards hastily shut the gates after him, shifting a bit the weight of the twitching beast on his back.

'Hail, most noble Heracles!' called he, in awe and fear before me, while trying his hardest to maintain an official demeanor. 'I am Copreus, herald of king Eurystheus—'

"What say you your name?' I blurted.

'Copreus, said I!' stammered the herald. 'The king is indisposed, and has sent me to inspect your prize, as well as inform you of your next Labor.'

My cheeks bulged and I turned red with merriment as I tried my best to suppress a hearty laughter, for the name Copreus meant nothing less than 'Dung-Man'. Now I love a good jest, and never let go of an opportunity to playfully chide others, but I prefer to do so only with those I either know well enough and like, or know well enough and hate. It is impolite to make fun of a stranger; since, not knowing the context of a remark, he could end up needlessly offended.

'Well, Copreus, here it is,' said I, inclining one shoulder so that the hind could affright him with her kicks. Copreus jumped back to avoid the knock of the brazen hooves, which sliced the air like a smith's swift hammer blows. 'Does the king want to see for himself?'

'No—that will be all with that,' said Copreus quickly, making an annotation on his tablet. 'My lord now has another task for you.' He cleared his throat and continued: 'A mighty boar ravages the land about Mount Erymanthos. You are commanded to capture that creature and bring it back—alive, as you did with this hind.'

'Humph! That is no ordinary boar,' said I. 'I have heard that district is sacred to Artemis, as is this hind. She'll surely be angry at me now! But if I must, I must.'

Copreus, relieved at my disregarding attitude to what to him would have been an impossible chore, wiped his brow and turned toward the doors. I followed, but the gates remained shut.

'The king reminds you that you are forbidden to enter the city with these wild beasts," said Copreus deferentially, thinking I would feel slighted.

'Very well, Dung Man,' said I, feeling that by now I knew the man.

Feared throughout northern Arcadia, the Erymanthian boar was exceedingly large and fierce, with bloodshot eyes and white, gleaming, crescent-shaped tusks as long and broad as those of the legendary oliphant. It hid in the thickets on Mount Lampeia, and foraged across the cypress-covered ridges of Mount Erymanthos and down to the region of Psophis, attacking man or beast with impunity. No young men hunted in those forests, nor maiden ran barefoot in May Day reverie, for fear of the monster. Mount Erymanthos takes its name in this wise. Erymanthos was a son of Apollo who once caught sight of Aphrodite bathing in a clear spring. This goddess, so affronted that a mortal saw her naked form without her permission, struck Erymanthos blind. The poor lad wandered up and down the mountain, his eyes in darkness, calling out for his divine father. Apollo heard him, transformed him into the boar in question, and loosed him in a grove where Aphrodite liked to meet her mortal lover Adonis. One day, the wife of a Cyprian king boasted that she was more beautiful even than Aphrodite. The goddess, whose sole duty is to make love, and whose prerogative is in the domain of beauty, earthly or divine, avenged the insult by causing a certain outrage between her and her father. In wrath her father pursued her, and would have struck her with his sword had not Aphrodite, in a moment of pity, changed her into a myrrh-tree. The sword cleaved the tree and out fell the infant Adonis. The boy was so beautiful that Aphrodite snatched him up, hid him in a chest, and entrusted him to Persephone, Queen of the lower world. Persephone grew curious after a while, and opening the chest, saw the lad, and kept him. Aphrodite raced to the dark depths to demand him back. Zeus finally settled the dispute between the goddesses of love and death. Adonis, who had by now grown into a handsome youth, would spend part of the year with Aphrodite, part of the year in the underworld with Persephone, and the last part by himself, for all men need some time away from the company of women. The wily Aphrodite, however, beguiled the youth to spend all his time with her— for what mortal could resist her? It is said that the aggrieved Persephone then alerted Ares about this in order to make him jealous, for he also lusted for Aphrodite. Ares changed himself into a wild boar and gored Adonis to death. From his blood anemones sprang as his soul descended to Tartaros where Persephone waited. But Aphrodite gained the upper hand again, by persuading Zeus to decree that Adonis would finally spend only the gloomier months in the lower world, and the gay spring months with her. It is said that the drops of sap shed by the myrrh-tree are for Adonis.

On my way through Arcadia, in a sunny glade by the river Ladon, near the place I had captured her, I loosed the hind and allowed her to run off, thus fulfilling my promise to Artemis. The goddess was satisfied and left me alone. I watched the beast skip through the undergrowth until I could no longer see the glimmers off its golden antlers, then sat on a rock to think up a plan. The boar was to be the second beast I had to catch alive, but I knew this hunt would prove quite different. The hind, though dangerous in its own way, was not a predator whose belligerence I had to consider on its own merit. A wild boar was a different matter. It would be a violent pursuit. Once cornered, should I use too little force, the beast would try to gore me; but should I use too much force, I could risk killing it. I had to exercise a balance in which I had little practice, since I oftimes failed to appreciate the enormity of my own strength. And so with a prayer I tightened the quiver-thongs about my back and repositioned bow, scabbard and satchel so as not to impede my ambulation, and set off northwestward.

I headed into the woods of Mount Pholoë, planning to cut across into the next valley, where began the range of snow-capped Erymanthos that divide Arcadia from Elis. The area around Pholoë is a known haunt of Centaurs. If you have never seen one, most possess a man's head and shoulders attached to a horse's body. Others are a whole man, with half a horse growing from behind. I knew to be careful, for though the Centaurs did not generally interfere with men, they did not like to be bothered in their mountain fastness. Although Centaurs as a whole are wild and lusty, the one Centaur of my acquaintance, Cheiron, is intelligent and civilized. He taught me logic, rhetoric, the arts of healing, and how to read the stars. 'Young Alcides,' Cheiron once advised me, 'decide no suit between men, until you have heard both sides first.'

I followed a pass through the rocky heights of the mountain, noticing hoof-prints on the ground here and there; and though I saw no Centaurs, I could sense they spied on me from secret places, for they were furtive. Keeping my olive-wood club at the ready, I descended a gorge ringed with caves, and was crossing up the other side when I heard someone hail me. A Centaur, his chest bare against the winds, stood on a ledge waving. I approached him warily.

'I recognize you by your lionskin, sir.' said the Centaur. 'You must be the champion Heracles. I am called Pholos. Come into my den, and allow me to entertain you.'

I glanced about me to make ensure that I was not walking into a snare. Centaurs were not known to be treacherous, save when intoxicated. This Centaur, however, seemed in full possession of his wits.

'Come right in, sir,' said Pholos, hospitably taking my weapons and gear, and laying them aside. 'Allow me to prepare a meal for you. And with it I have some fine drink.'

'I thank you then, Pholos' said I, feeling welcomed. 'I have been busy with my work, and have not had a chance to eat. And I am famished!'

Pholos started a fire at the entrance of the cave, and roasting some meat, set it before me; but he preferred to eat his raw. When we had eaten our fill, Pholos went back into the darkness of his cave, dug about a bit, and came back bearing a great store-jar from which he brushed black earth.

'Four generations ago, Dionysos came among us, and gave this cask to a certain Centaur, telling him he must keep it until the man Heracles should pass by. And so some of us have kept watch for you that we may please the gods in all they say.'

'Then bless the gods!' said Heracles jovially. 'I am that man!'

'I fear one thing, however,' said Pholos. 'Centaurs keep all things in common, especially wine, of which we hardly partake, for it inflames us immeasurably. If I am found out that I have shared this with a stranger—'

I countered: 'Let us retreat into this cave, you and I, where we won't be seen, and enjoy this good draught. In any case, I promise to defend you against all enemies.'

And so Pholos opened the cask, and straightway the cave was filled with the sweet fragrance of the strong old wine. We drank it neat, and I was sure I had never tasted such good wine in all my life.

'The last time I saw your kind, I was a lad, sent to Mount Pelion to learn from good old Cheiron. Tell me if you know of him,' said I, reclining on the ground against the wine-jar.

'Of course I know Cheiron!' responded Pholos, the wine exciting him. 'He moved down to Cape Malia after being driven from Mount Pelion by the Lapiths.'

Aroused, I said: 'Pray, tell what happened.'

'Did you not hear?' responded the Centaur. 'A summer ago, Peirithoös, chieftain of the Lapiths, took Hippodameia, daughter of Atrax, to wife. His good friend, a certain Theseus of Troizen, attended the wedding celebration, along with the Centaurs of Mount Pelion; for the Lapiths and the Centaurs are cousins, both being descended from Ixion, a lord of Thessaly. Wine flowed freely that day within the house, and when the Centaurs caught the fragrance, they pushed away their milk bowls, and ran in to fill their throats from the wine-jars. Taking wine unmixed with water maddened them, and they began to overturn the tables where the guests were seated. The boldest among them, Eurytion, lusted after the lovely bride, his blood running hot, and, taking her by the hair, dragged her off. I fled; but the other Centaurs, emboldened, followed suit, and claimed those women and girls from the Lapiths they found agreeable. Theseus led the rescue, saving Hippodameia and the others who were taken, and rallied the Lapiths to the offensive. The fight lasted until nightfall, with many Centaurs and Lapiths killed in the struggle. But the Centaurs suffered the worst, and Theseus and Peirithoös drove them from their ancient home on Pelion to Mount Pindos. After some time, the Centaurs regrouped and renewed their conflict with the Lapiths, who fled hither. But the Centaurs pursued them, expelled them, and made this region their stronghold. Old Cheiron, unable to stomach the violence, and finding it difficult to return to his ancestral home, retired to Malia.'

By now the strong odor of the hundred-year-old wine had wafted out of the cave and reached the nostrils of other Centaurs living nearby. Not all of them knew of Dionysos' ancient instructions, and grew angry that a communal drink was being consumed without their knowledge or participation. Armed with rocks, uprooted pine trees, firebrands and axes, such as are used to slaughter oxen, the Centaurs rushed to Pholos' cave. While enjoying the strong wine in moderation,—remembering the god Apollo's wise axiom[2]—I heard the commotion and jumped to my feet. Before I could reach my weapons by the cave entrance, two large Centaurs, Ancios and Agrios, burst in. Arios swung an axe, but the axe-head struck the rocky ceiling and his swing was impeded. I took the opportunity to bring my fist down on Agrios' nose, followed by a swift kick to his midsection, where the horsey part began. As Agrios' front legs buckled, Ancios fell in behind him bearing a log. I caught the tree by the roots and stripping it out of the Centaur's hands, swung it back toward him, thrusting one massive equine body into the other and casting them both out of the cave. Meanwhile, the terrified Pholos hid in a fissure, marveling at my awesome strength in contending with creatures possessing the swiftness of horses, the strength of two bodies, and the wisdom of men. Any other man would have already been unmatched.

I uttered a roar of anger, which, magnified by the cave, ringed the mountain like a roll of summer thunder. As the harrowing cry gave the attackers without some pause, I managed to take up my bow and quiver and shot several arrows out of the cave in quick succession, each reaching a mark. The Centaurs, seeing their friends felled, quickly lost heart, and fled. I emerged from the cave, an arrow drawn to my ear rather than my breast for greater force, and picked off the fleeing Centaurs one by one. They fell climbing the ridge, or fleeing into caves, or running down into a gorge. So numerous were they, however, that many more rushed at me, rearing and lashing out with their horsy fore-legs. I thrust my bow aside, took up my club, and repelled them, breaking many heads and backs. Then securing some firebrands dropped by the attackers, I lit some of them on fire, so that they galloped howling off the cliffs.

Centaurs climbing to higher elevations now flung down great boulders. I once again took up my bow and let fly the deadly darts, dispatching the closest ones first, and then concentrating on those farther away. 'Mother!' cried the Centaur Malanchaites, raising his arms to the sky after an arrow penetrated his belly. 'Do

---

[2] On Apollo's temple at Delphi was written: "All things in moderation."

not leave us helpless against this wild man!' Their mother, the cloudy Nephele, heard them from the upper air, and sent down a heavy rain, which made the ground slippery for me and loosened my bow-string, but had no ill-effect on her children, who went about confidently on four legs. Without sign of fear or distress, however, I continued the counter-attack, wiping the rain-water from my eyes to ensure the accuracy of my aim. I pursued the Centaurs up and down the mountain, until returning to the vicinity of Pholos' cave, I prepared a final arrow for a lone Centaur heaving a rock over his head, about to launch it. The arrow passed through his neck and into the knee of another Centaur who appeared on a hill behind him. The rain fell down so thickly that I could not tell one Centaur form another, but coming closer I howled in grief, recognizing the graying hide and flowing beard of Cheiron, whom I had accidentally wounded. Cheiron had come up all the way from Malia to visit his friends, and found ill fortune instead.

I ran to his side, broke off the arrow-head and drew the shaft out of the wound. The Hydra's deadly venom, however, had begun infecting Cheiron's body, causing him immeasurable agony. I carried him to Pholos' cave, and applied to the wound vulneraries that Cheiron himself drew for me from his satchel. It was no use. Cheiron's wound was incurable; yet being immortal, he could not die. Mad with grief, cradling the head of my old teacher, who bore me no ill-will for the accident, I called out for Pholos, but no response came. Cheiron pointed out the body of Pholos, fallen over one of his brothers at the mouth of the cave. It so happened that before I had broken off pursuit, Pholos had come forth from his hiding place to bury his brothers. Pulling an arrow from a corpse, he marveled at how such a small thing could kill creatures of such size; but the arrow slipped from his hand and landed on his foot, after which he died instantly from the Hydra's poison.

I buried my friend, and now the mountain bears his name. With a heavy heart I collected my gear and left Cheiron in the cave, since he did not wish to be moved.

Descending to the valley on the other side of Mount Pholoë, I crossed the cypress-shadowed wilderness and reached the river Erymanthos, which flowed down; and from a ridge fell into the Alpheios from the south, at the very border of Elis and Arcadia, a river called the Diagon. I climbed the ridge, looking to ford this river, and there was accosted by one Sauros, who seemed like a beggar but was really a cruel bandit who did mischief to travelers, stealing their belongings and killing them by drawing. Seeing through his ruse, I played the role of a meek pilgrim, and when Sauros tried to rob me, with one hand I flipped the robber headlong off the ridge and into the water, meeting him a fitting punishment. One good thing came from the encounter. I gained possession of Sauros' hand-cart, which I planned to use to convey the boar back to Eurystheus. The ridge now bears the name of Sauros, and his tomb is situated there.

With winter closing in, I wasted no further time and began to hunt the boar about the foothills of Mount Erymanthos. After locating it, I watched the enormous beast daily in order to learn its habits. After feeding, the boar liked to frequent a certain thicket, where it slept during the day. I sought to trap it there, and so rousing it with loud shouts and great noise, the boar sprang forth, its tusks gleaming. Narrowly avoiding a goring, I failed to trap him, and so had to pursue him up the mountain. An idea then entered my mind, which I carried out with great success. I waited for a good snowfall, and ran the beast into a snowdrift on the heights, from which it could not dislodge itself. Bearing the biting wind and cold with fortitude, I jumped on its back, and bound it tight with rope. Heaving the stinking bulk onto the hand-cart, and applying even more rope to secure it, I began the long trip back to Mycenae."

## 7

Heracles, dissatisfied by his little wine-cup, requested a drinking-horn, which he drained before continuing: "Despite the express orders of king Eurystheus, the stout gates of Mycenae could not withstand me when I rammed the boar-laden hand-cart through and handily entered city. We proved a great spectacle as I wheeled the boar[3] through the market-place; the children especially marveled at the hulking, snorting, kicking mass of fur, out of which those terrifying tusks projected from underneath unblinking blood-shot eyes. I stopped at a fountain to refresh himself, and then continued on my way up to the palace, hindered by no one; but midway I stopped to listen to a herald addressing himself particularly to those of Minyan stock, exhorting the best among them to join in a quest to the far-off kingdom of Colchis. With my appetite for adventure whetted, I left the fettered boar outside the market-place; and instructing some citizens to alert Eurystheus, I went to speak to the herald, from whom I learned that I was to report to a certain Jason (who, as it turned out, had also been tutored by Cheiron after my time), who under the auspices of king Pelias of Phthiotis, was organizing the expedition to sail in the early summer.

When Copreus found me, I led him to where I had left the boar, which whined horribly, foaming at the mouth, and blinked its eyes. Copreus, making an annotation in his tablet, said: 'For your next Labor, my lord Eurystheus commands you to clean out the cattle-yard of king Augeias of Elis.'

-------------------

[3] Eurystheus would not agree to emerge from the jar and see the boar for himself, so terrified was he even of its snorts. He ordered it cast into the sea, where it swam to Italy. It is not known who dispatched it, but its prized tusks were preserved in Apollo's temple at Cumae.

Now I minded not at all to carry out heroic and dangerous duties, but I felt being ordered to perform such humiliating work an activity beneath me, and guessed Eurystheus ordered so out of spite for having to hide from me. I shrugged my shoulders, however, and muttered some quip about the curious circumstance of being ordered to clean up dung by none other than the Dung Man, for I now felt no qualms about calling the herald that when I wished. But as I walked away, Copreus enjoined: 'I neglected to add, most noble Heracles, that you must perform this task in a single day, and without assistance.'

I now employed Iolaos to drive me back through Arcadia and into the fertile land of Elis to the northwest. At seeing a vast multitude of kine milling around a lake, I asked an old herdsman working there if they were the property of king Augeias; and if so, what was the extent of his pastures. The old man stopped his work and gladly answered: 'By all means will I assist you, sir, since I fear the vengeance of great Hermes o' the Ways against all who deny any traveler due guidance. His flocks feed not altogether; but range from the sacred river Alpheios to the vineyards of Buprasion. But the herds, I'll have you know, do not leave the honey-sweet grass around this mere of the river Menios, and range as far as where the stream goes running again through thickets of wild-olive and the sanctuary of Apollo o' the Pastures. In that place we laborers have our quarters.

'Yea, the whole plain belongs to wise Augeias, the wheatfields and the vineyards alike, where at the end of summertime the vintners come. But pray tell me, sir, what errand has brought you? Do you seek an audience with the king himself, or one of his officials? I say—you certainly cut a fine figure, sir; aye, I dare even call you a son of an immortal.'

'I have business with the king,' said I. 'Lead me to him.'

'Surely, some god watches o'er you, sir,' said the old man. 'He'll be at the yards for sure, he and his noble son Phyleus. Why, 'twas only yesterday he came down himself to survey his possessions. By the gods, kings in their hearts are like other men: they have to often see their wealth to make sure they still have it.'

And as we came near the vast enclosures, a multitude of dogs surrounded me with a great clamor. The herdsman with harsh words and the threat of casting stones scattered them, all the while rejoicing that the cattle-yards possessed such good defenders. 'Great Zeus!' he exclaimed for the sake of appearance, 'what inconsiderate beasts the gods have given men! If they were any brighter, and better knew the difference 'tween friend and foe, no other beast could claim greater honor; but such is not the case, and they're nothing but noisy swaggerers.'

At the sound of the evening bells, when the Sun's fiery steeds beat a path to the westward, cows and sheep in the thousands came shambling home across the pastures like fleecy clouds driven by a strong north wind which, piling into one another, appear to have no end drifting through the vast æther. Lowing filled the fields as the cattle settled into the byres, where farmhands descended with their milking-pails and the yearlings jostled to draw their dams' sweet warm milk. I marveled at the enormous number of beasts, at the size of their yards, and at the inordinate mounds of filth that choked the byres and sheepfolds: these had not been cleaned in thirty years, the herdsman told me, affecting the entire district with a noisome stench, and sometimes pestilence. When rain drew some of the dung away into the surrounding pastures, it caused the ploughmen great consternation.

The cattle of Augeias were immune to distempers and prospered continually, producing females more often than not; to remedy this, the king kept three hundred white-legged, bent-horned bulls and two hundred red bulls at the ready. To protect the herds against wild beasts he employed twelve large swan-white bulls consecrated to the Sun. When the mightiest of these, called Morning Star by the herdsmen because of its exceeding brilliance, spied my tawny lionskin, it bellowed and charged at me. But I, leaping aside, caught its left horn with strong hands and drew its neck downwards; and while I held the snorting bull thus at bay, the muscles of my arms stood as in a heap. Augeias and Phyleus had by then arrived to make the rounds of the farmstead. They called their herdsmen to take control of the impassioned bull.

Phyleus said to his father: 'There came a man from Argos, an Achaian of sea-facing Helice, not long ago, who told us that he had seen an Argive slay a dreadful lion, whose den lay beside the grove of Zeus at Nemea. A scion of Perseus, he said this lion-killer was. Only one man could perform a deed like that; and by that lionskin he wears it is evident that none other than Heracles of

Tyrins honors us with his presence.'

Augeias, a young, well-fed man evidently accustomed to a life of ease, attended to my proposal. 'Yes, your heard me aright,' said I, neglecting to mention that I was in service to Eurystheus so as not to add to my humiliation. 'I shall clean your byres in a single day. Of course, the work will be quite demanding, and so I wish for a substantial reward.'

'And what might that be?' asked Augeias.

'I ask only for a tithe of your cattle,' said I, since I considered that so much wealth could not rightly belong to ten men, or much less one.

Augeias did not wish to be impolite, but he could hardly suppress a laugh. Members of his retinue, however, showed less restraint, until my glower dispelled their mirth. Augeias thought for a moment on the matter, then seeing no harm in offering such a magnanimous reward for a task that he believed could not possibly be accomplished within the time allotted, agreed to the proposition. I asked for Phyleus to witness the agreement. The youth happily agreed to do so, despite a stern look from his father.

After Augeias returned to Elis, I walked around the cattle-yards uttering curses over the impracticable task of cleaning them in a single day. Iolaos could offer no ideas as to how I was to accomplish the task, except to hand me a basket. I commenced to remove the filth in it, until, overbore with hopelessness, I sat down wearily.

A certain Elean ploughman, Menedemus, son of Bounias, disgusted for many years by the inordinate amount of dung, suggested that I clean the stables by diverting a stream. Iolaos laughed at this proposition, but I thought deeply on it and sent Menedemus off to organize a work party of his countrymen. While they with shovels and mattocks delved a deep trench along one wall of the cattle-yard, I began to carry out the principal part of the plan. On my approach through Elis I had noticed the many tributaries and streams of the Alpheios and Peneios rivers that crisscrossed the land. I took with me some Elean volunteers to the bank of the river Manios, a tributary of the Alpheios that ran through the city of Elis, and there assisted them, by delving and damming, to direct its course. We worked all night, into the next day, with me piling great stones to create a new channel to the opposite wall of the stable-yard, where I made a breach in its foundation. Once the first trench was completed, I rent the wall there for an outlet. Returning to the weir at the Manios, I knocked loose the stones of the sluice.

Water raced down the artificial channel and poured into the yard through the first breach, and in due time washed away all the filth out of the second breach, from where the torrent spread through the sheep-folds and pastures, until all was deposited into the swales of the Peneios.

King Augeias himself came out to inspect the work I had performed, and, though thoroughly astonished, returned to the city in a foul mood, for I did not fail to remind him of the reward he promised to pay me. But when Augeias learned from Copreus, who had arrived at Elis to verify the completion of the Labor, that the work had been ordered by Eurystheus, he decided to forgo payment for what he thought should have been an unpaid service. In this his nephew Lepreos, founder of the city of Lepreon in Arcadia, agreed, advising the king to shackle and imprison me instead. When I vigorously protested the decision on the moral ground that a workman, regardless of the circumstances, was always worthy of his wages, Augeias denied ever promising a reward and agreed to submit the matter to arbitration.

When the judges were seated, I called on Phyleus, who testified against his father, telling the court that I was in the right and his father in the wrong for not carrying out what he had promised. In a rage, before the judges had even time to adjudicate, Augeias banished his son from Elis and forbade me from ever entering his realm again. Phyleus retired to Doulichion and settled there.”

## 8

"And thus that Labor concluded. Eurystheus, secure within his storage jar, ordered Copreus to waste no time and send me off on my next task.

'Near the city of Stymphalos in Arcadia there is a lake that is infested with numerous man-eating birds, sacred to Ares,' said Copreus. 'You are commanded to remove them.'

'By Hera's teats!—the birds of Ares!' I exclaimed. 'I'll have angered all of Olympos before this business is said and done  But if I must, I must.'

Lake Stymphalis lies in a dark valley, in the depths of shady woods.  I arrived there at dusk, with the rolling clouds red and ominous, as the chariot of the Sun descended into Ocean beyond the land of the Ethiopians.  The fearsome birds of Ares, with beaks and claws and wings of bronze, feasted on the flesh of men and beasts.  They had flocked to the dreary marsh after being scared off by wolves from their home near Orchomenos in Boetia.  They are the size of cranes, but resemble ibises: with beaks more deadly, straight and sharp, and able to pierce a man's cuirass.  They rose on occasion in a great flock from the swamp, stamping out the sun as when locusts fill the air and bring darkness to the eyes of men, and killed their prey with a deluge of brazen feathers.  Descending afterward on the carcases, they consumed the flesh.  Noxious ordure they also dropped upon the ground, blighting the crops. These fearsome birds, nestling in their coverts, I observed from the edge of the morass.  I tried to shoot them down with arrows, but they were too numerous.

I could not draw closer, for the marshy ground gave way under my weight.  I laid aside my bow and prayed to Athena, whose presence I often felt: 'I call on you, dearest of the Immortals, who sprang from the head of Zeus, as I wish good ideas would spring

from mine.  You have seen me try to disperse these cursed birds—
if they can be called that—in vain with my arrows.  Yet they mock
me, flittering about with irksome trills, going here and there, but
remaining unmoved from their nests.  They cannot reach me here
with their darts, but neither can I do much with mine, so numerous
are they.  Tell me, you who always have an audience with the great
immortal King—what can I do?'

I crossed my arms and stood immobile for some time, my
brows furrowed in thought.  Iolaos, finding it strange to see a man
of action in such a state of irresolution, suggested that we pay our
respects at the ancient shrine of Stymphalian Artemis, whose image
was of gilded wood.  The likenesses of the fierce birds were carved
below the roof of her temple, along with maidens having clawed
feet, resembling Harpies.

On returning to the lake, I hatched an idea to frighten off
the birds.  'I will climb yonder peak,' I explained to Iolaos, 'and
make such a bruit that you will see the marsh cleared before the
night descends fully upon us.' I sent Iolaos to fetch me the largest
bronze rattle he could find, which he procured from Amphidamas,
prince of Tegea.  Alone I then climbed a spur of Mount Cyllene
overlooking the swamp.  With my mighty hands I vigorously shook
the rattle.  The strident noise, echoing through the lowland like the
clatter of troops in battle, so alarmed the birds that they rose in a
large black cloud of fluttering wings and raging darts.  The ensuing
shower of metallic feathers would have maimed me had it not
encountered my impenetrable lionskin. At once I took up my trusty
bow, and with keen sight loosened my shafts, by which many birds
fell from the sky

When Copreus reported to Eurystheus that I had indeed
cleared the Stymphalian marsh of the man-eating birds, showing
him a brace of dead birds which I brought back as proof, the king,
sullen and depressed, jumped back into his jar.  He sat there in the
dark until a notice adventitiously arrived from Crete.  He crawled
out and gleefully called for the herald with instructions on where
next to send me.  Since my Labors thus far had been confined to
the Peloponnese, Eurystheus thought of a way to magnify his fame
abroad as a great benefactor by having me capture a savage bull that
reportedly terrorized the island of Crete; and if in the process the
bull did away with me, he considered it so much the better.

With Iolaos I embarked on a ship from the harbor at Nauplia, After days of rough weather, we marveled at the sight of the island, rising from the wine-dark sea like a frosted emerald, with its rugged, wood-covered mountain range extending across its long breadth.

The harbor of Cnossos teemed with ships bearing perfumed olive oil, sheep's-wool and flax, wheat and barley, fish, saffron, red safflower, figs, famed silphium and beautifully painted jars and other pottery in which the Cretans specialized. Warships stood ready to defend the island kingdom against all aggressors. The Cretans enjoyed the distinction of being the first nation to have a navy: so secure did they feel that they had never bothered with land fortifications.

The sprawling, gleaming palace of king Minos lay not far from Cnossos in the valley of the river Amnisios, surrounded by hills wooded with oak and cypress trees. The river, coursing through Cnossos on its way to the sea, had its sources on Mount Ida, the loftiest of the island's peaks. At his birth, Rhea secreted the infant Zeus in a cave on the snow-crowned mount, where nymphs ministered to him, feeding him honey and milk from the udder of the magical goat Amaltheia. Now, certain Cretans say that they can also point out Zeus' tomb; which makes them liars, since how can the Father of Heaven ever die?

An armed escort conducted us through the paved avenues of the palace, marked everywhere with images of the royal double-axe carved in relief or incised on door and walls. After traversing a bewildering maze of corridors, we arrived at the spacious central court, paved with colored tiles, where rows of plane-trees shaded gushing fountains and decorative fish-filled ponds. Galleries of short, inverted, vermillion-painted columns—wide at the top and narrow at the bottom, unlike those used in Greece—surrounded the courtyard. They were constructed from the trunks of cypress-trees and mounted on porphyry pedestals with rounded capitals painted blue.

After some time, king Minos entered the courtyard. Plump and short of stature, with curly black locks, a jutting, square-cut beard and eyes darkened with ground galena in the manner of the Egyptians, he clapped hands, jingling with golden bracelets and rings inlaid with sard and chalcedony, to dismiss his guards.

'Having heard of your exploits for some years now, I am greatly honored to receive you, hero of Thebes,' said Minos resoundingly, walking around me and examining my magnificent physique not very well covered by the lion's pelt.

'Mighty lord Minos,' I acknowledged with a respectful nod. 'I have been sent by king Eurystheus of Mycenae to assist you with the matter of the wild bull.'

'I see,' said the king, walking briskly to a door. 'Come with me: we must talk in private. Who is the boy?'

'My nephew Iolaos,' said I.

King Minos clapped his hands again and immediately young women appeared bearing baskets of flowers and garlands, one of which they placed on Iolaos' head. 'Take our guest Iolaos to the baths,' the king commanded. Iolaos, markedly pleased, departed with them sheepishly. I followed the king into an anteroom on the west side of the court, and then through two double-doors into a small throne room. Minos sat on an alabaster seat, flanked by frescoes of two crouching gryphons, across from a lustral basin and directed me to take a seat beside him on a gypsum bench.

'The bull,' said he with an air of resignation, 'runs wild, terrorizing my subjects, and no one has been able to stop it. I will tell you the provenance of this beast; but you must never mention what I say to anyone else, Heracles, for few—by my own design— know the real story. I have spread the rumor that the bull is the same that carried Europa to this island. Of course, the story was that Zeus, falling in love with her while she gathered flowers in a Phoenician meadow, changed himself into that bull, snow-white and exuding a divine fragrance; and by breathing forth a crocus from its mouth enticed her to climb upon its back; but few mark the inconsistency, thinking these ancient legends rightly shrouded in mystery. But I will tell you the truth, since we both come from Zeus (my grandfather was the great Minos of old, born from Europa after her rapine).

'On succeeding my father Lycastos to the throne, I was a young man intoxicated with power. Celebrating among my friends, I uttered rashly that the gods would surely answer whatever prayer I made to them. So dedicating an altar to Poseidon the Earth-shaker on the strand, I prepared the lustral water and the barley, and prayed that a bull might emerge from the sea ready for sacrifice.

No sooner had I finished speaking than a monstrous bull, as white as driven snow, leaps from the sea and swims ashore to where I stood. The bull shook the seawater from its hide, pawed the ground, and bowed its neck that I should pet it. The bull was so spotless, so gentle, its horns sharp and dazzling, its haunches as well-muscled as your own limbs, that I could not bear to slay it and taint the hide with its blood. I ordered it brought to the palace, washed, garlanded and fed, while I found another bull for the altar.

'I grew very fond of the white bull and kept it as a pet in the courtyard, where it slept under the trees and drank from the fountains. After wedding Pasiphaë, for fear of offending her delicacy, I loosed the bull to graze on the gentle hill-slopes outside palace. All was well for a time, until Poseidon remembered my sacrilege and wrought his revenge. He poisoned the mind of Pasiphaë with detestable thoughts as she sat each day at her window to watch the bull forage, causing her to burn for it. Not finding a way to satisfy her awful lust, she turned to that artificer, Daidalos. By his demented cunning he built a marvelous simulacrum—a mechanical heifer skinned in real animal hide in which Pasiphaë could hide. In that contraption she allowed the white bull to cover her. The horror, Heracles! You see why I wished to discuss these matters in private. From that foul sin was born a strange creature, part man, part bull, which I had to confine in a special prison—the Labyrinth—when it grew to crave human flesh.

'After Pasiphaë had union with the bull, it turned savage, and ran off to scour Crete, burning orchards with its breath. They say it now haunts the region about the river Tethris. I have already sent several hunters to capture it, to no avail. And I cannot destroy it for fear of offending Poseidon.'

'I will capture the bull!' I exclaimed. 'But king Eurystheus wishes me to bring it back to Mycenae.'

Minos said, relieved: 'You can do what you will as long as you do not harm it. And you shall have whatever assistance you require.'

'That won't be necessary,' said I. 'This task I must carry out alone.'

'As you wish,' said Minos. 'Tomorrow you may begin; but today, you are my guest; and we will feast.'

I joined Iolaos in the mosaic-floored baths, consisting of

several rooms under high-groined vaults.  One was a cold room, and another a hot room with a double pool into which fresh water poured from terra-cotta pipes and heated underneath by a wood burning hypocaust.  Even the latrines ran continuously to wash away the filth!  King Minos gave us a tour of the rest of the palace.  Over a thousand interlocking rooms covering nearly three hectares, housed not only the royal quarters, but the entire administrative and economic centers of the government.  Brightly colored frescoes decorated every wall, depicting ruddy men engaged in athletic feats, or fishing, and milk-white women gathering crocuses.

That night we feasted inside a cavernous dining-hall, dipping into trenchers heaped with an abundance of food: chines of beef, sun-dried grapes, roast ewe with capers, stewed octopus, thyme-honey from the palace's own extensive store-rooms, cheeses of all types and innumerable fish and sea-fowl. Entertainment came in the form of dancers and young, agile men leaping over small bulls.  Cretan raisin-wine and the fermented honey-drink called mead flowed freely, but I drank little, wishing to get an early start the next day.  Iolaos I left to the cruelties of the vine, knowing that the best way young men learn moderation is in occasional excess.  I retired well before midnight, carrying the slumbering youth to his bed.

When Dawn, clad in her saffron robe, began to diffuse her light, extracting the vivid, moist greens and browns of the cypress-covered mountains, taking with me only a rope, I rode out to a valley cut by the river Tethris, flowing down from the mountains south of Cnossos. On the opposite bank I caught sight of the bull's hoof-marks, and tracked it inland to a fertile plain whose crops the ferocious beast had long burned up or trampled.  I kept to a safe distance, watching it day by day, learning its habits, and waited until it knelt to rest under a clump of oaks at midday.   I meant to approach it stealthily from behind, but the bull, alarmed, ran off.  I kicked my mount and sped after it until we were abreast, then jumped off the horse and onto the bull's back. The mighty beast, blowing smoke from its snout, shook me loose, gained some distance, and then circled around ready to attack. After pawing the ground and snorting flames in anger, the bull charged toward me. Leaping aside, I reached out to grab its horns.  But I was no match for the instantaneous force of the bull's mass, and was dragged backwards with the horn-tips piercing my shoulders. Digging ankles into the earth, I regained a foothold and with groans pushed back until I could arrest its stride. The fierce bull bucked and kicked and scorched me with desperate breaths, but I held fast to the horns, driving the head ever downward, trying to wrestle it to its knees. Man and beast fought, each relentless in its designs, until late in the day, when the bull finally buckled, exhausted, and its foam-flecked snout dug into the ground. Affixing a knee against the bull's neck, I released a hand to wipe the thick sweat from my eyes and proceeded to hobble it.

Minos sent slaves with large Cretan hounds to assist in securing the bull. They affixed on it a nose-ring and halter, and by a stout chain and a long staff tied to the ring I pulled the bull to the harbor, from where by ship I took it to Mycenae. Eurystheus, alerted to my coming, from a tower watched me lead the magnificent white beast up the mountain road, as children ran alongside trying to touch its bristly flanks and the people threw down palm fronds and spruce boughs on the ground, yelling "Hail Heracles!" The king grew jealous at the acclamation directed at me, since he hardly stirred the people to such passion.

I came to a stop before the Lion Gate and called for Eurystheus. Copreus emerged, sighing in wonder at the black smoke puffing from the bull's snout.

'I am losing count, Dung Man,' cried Heracles. 'How many more Labors are left me?'

'Is this the beast that aggrieved the Cretans?' asked Copreus, seeing how the bull appeared docile under my stern control. 'You have mastered it well enough, noble Heracles.'

'What shall I do then—release it?' said I, making to unhalter the beast. The people who had thronged around us grew alarmed and scattered.

'Desist!' implored Copreus. 'The king will decide its fate.'

'Very well,' said Heracles. 'If I have acted to the king's satisfaction, I believe I have earned a day's respite before my next task.'

'There is no rest yet for you, Heracles,' said Copreus. 'My lord has received reports about the cruel Thracian king Diomedes. He keeps four mares tethered with iron chains in his stable, and feeds them the flesh of strangers to uphold their savagery. The king orders you to end this terror by capturing the mares and bringing them hither.'

Afterward, Eurystheus came down to examine the beast I left tethered at the gate. He could not, because of its beauty, bring himself to kill or sacrifice it, and instead ordered its release, thinking it appropriate to declare: 'Mighty Hera! I, king Eurystheus, lord of Argolis, the land you love and protect, do dedicate this bull to you. Grant us good fortune!'

But Hera, loathing a gift that glorified me, drove the bull to Sparta by causing horn-flies to harass it, where it increased in savagery. From there it roamed into Arcadia for a time, and then across the isthmus to Attic Marathon, where it spread as much terror as it did in Crete until the coming of Theseus."

9

"Thinking to save a day from the long voyage ahead, I crossed Argolis on foot to the town of Epidauros; but I had to wait there more than a week to find passage on a Thracian-bound merchant ship.  During that time I hewed himself another club from a wild olive-tree I discovered by the Saronic Sea and had the tip bronzed by the local smith to increase its durability.

The ship took its customary route around Attica and then up the Euboean channel.  Rounding Cape Cenaion, where stands a notable temple of Zeus, we sailed across the mouth of the Pagasaian Gulf and through the narrow strait separating the headland of Euboea from the cliffs of Magnesia.  From there the ship turned to the northeast, passing through the strait by rocky Sciathos, and hugged the mainland coast as far as Casthaneia, from where, after laying at anchor for three nights to wait out a storm, the sailors braced the sail full to the yardarm and, with prayers to Poseidon and Aphrodite Casthanitis, embarked into the open sea.

A month and several ports of call along the three peninsulas of Chalcidice later, we landed on the well-wooded Thracian coast, opposite the island of Thasos, where shepherds came to sell us mutton.  I received two yearling lambs at no charge, for the shepherds trembled at my glowering look.  On the rocky beach I built an altar and sacrificed to Zeus, praying for the success of my current Labor.  After I had eaten my full, and rested a while under a crop of myrtle-trees, I sewed myself some leggings from lambs' fleece, the wind being more bitter there; and after securing directions from the sailors, headed off to find the city of Tirida, which was not far.  They begged me not to go, saying the natives there, the Bistones, were a wild tribe who disliked strangers, but I knew that already.

It was said the Thracians were the largest nation in the

world (after the eastern Ethiopians). They were divided into various tribes, all savage in their own ways, which could never be united under one ruler, on account of their belligerent personalities.

When I came knocking at the city gates, my brass-bound club on my shoulder, I was admitted without delay. King Diomedes, a son of Ares, never turned away strangers: their visits ending up always permanent, for the Bistones would eventually round them up and kill them for sport, feeding some of them to Diomedes' wild mares.

I was brought before Diomedes, a savage-looking old man covered in animal skins and tattoos like my old Thracian nurse. He lived with his many wives in a large wooden house on a hill in the center of the city, surrounded by his footmen. Introducing his wives, then sending each away with a pat on the buttocks, he explained that when it came time for him to die, a great contest would be held to determine which of his wives he had loved the most. That one would be eulogized, and then her relatives would slit her throat. She would then be buried with her husband, while the other women would mope for being rejected from such an honor. Feasting on boiled meat and sucking beer through a barley-straw, I listened attentively, while at the same time inwardly condemning the evil custom.

'You may have any of my virgin daughters tonight, if you wish, Heracles,' explained Diomedes. 'I have six of them at home still. Most of my sons I have sold away to other lands, lest someday they grow and plot against me. But if any are born from you, him I will honor as a grandson of the gods, although we ourselves worship only those whom you call Ares, Dionysos and Artemis.'

'I thank you for your kind offer,' said I, feigning a gracious disposition. 'But, since I cannot long stay, I'd rather have a look at your mares—you have four, I believe—for they are the talk of my homeland.'

'The wishes of my guests are never denied,' said Diomedes, a bit suspicious. 'My groom will show you the stables. But do not get too close to them, Heracles, for they are a bit on the wild side.' He said this as a pretense only, for he intended that I meet the same fate as all other strangers to his realm.

A youth was fetched; and when he came before us, a look of recognition marked his countenance at the sight of me; but the groom, saying nothing, only bowed to the king and waited for me to follow. In the courtyard, the boy, looking nervously about, led me under the eaves of the stable door. Turning to me, the boy said: "Do you remember me, sir? I am Abderos, son of your friend Thromios."

Taken by surprise, I exclaimed, when I finally recognized him: 'How now? You mean Thromios of Opian Locris? Are you that lad who, grasping my knees, rode about on my shins in the house of Ceyx?'

'Yes; the same, O mighty Heracles! I hoped you would remember me,' said Abderos trembling with hope.

I laughed and said: 'Of course I do! But when I saw you last, you were knee-high to a wine-jar. How did you arrive here?' Sadly, Abderos explained: 'On a trip to Chios with my father, our ship was attacked by pirates. I was sold to the Trausians, who then traded me to the Bistones for some golden lynx-skins. King Diomedes took a fancy to me on account of my skill with horses, and made me a groom to those awful mares. Heracles, you must save me from this place! I wish just to return to my home in Locris. The mares terrify me. See how they have maimed me.' Abderos held out his left hand, which was missing three fingers.

I patted Abderos on the head and said: 'I will rescue you, lad. But first, prove useful to me. Tell me: are the mares guarded?'

'They need no guard,' said Abderos.

'Very well,' said I. 'Then do this: prepare for me Diomedes' chariot, and have it ready at the rear of the manger.'

'What is it you intend to do, Heracles? Steal the mares? It is not possible,' said Abderos. 'They obey no man except the king, and only after they are sated—with man-flesh! Yet he has never bridled them, nor hitched them to his chariot. They are kept chained to their bronze mangers—the only thing that can hold them. In any case, even you are in danger if you remain here, for no doubt the king will try to kill you and turn you to fodder.'

'Fear not, Abderos,' said I cheerfully. 'Just do as I say. What is impossible for men is possible for Heracles!'

Abderos took heart and ran off to fetch Diomedes' chariot. I entered the stable-yard dragging my club behind me. The four mares, larger and lustier than stallions, with shaggy, unkempt manes reaching to their hooves, chained apart from the other animals on the far end, reared and snorted when they saw me, rattling their fetters fiercely. Their troughs were covered in blood and gore and bones littered the ground up to their fetlocks. I could not even approach them, so fierce was their aspect, akin to the wildest of beasts. This task could prove the hardest of all, I imagined, for not only did I have to drive out these intractable horses, I had to do it under the nose of an entire nation of barbarians. I looked about me at the other animals, cowering in their pens, and selecting a fat calf, killed it with my club and flung the carcase among the mares, of which they made short work, ripping and gobbling up its flesh like carrion-birds. I then thought I could approach them, calmed somewhat by their filled bellies. The mares, however, still reared, and extended their mouths to chomp at me with their grinding teeth. And so I swung my club carefully, using just enough force, and knocked one of the mares senseless: the legs buckled and it fell to the ground gasping for breath. Judiciously swinging again, I brought the club down on the polls of the others. All now subdued, I jumped in the midst of them and covered their heads with feed-sacks. As I finished, the first mare I had struck revived, and rearing up blindly, struck me in the chest with its front hooves. I fell back onto the dust, the wind knocked out of me. The mares now were solely engaged in trying to shake off their coverings. Sneaking behind the stalls, I unhooked their iron chains one by one from the posts around their bronze troughs. With the ends of the chains in one hand, and the club in the other, I drew out the reluctant mares. When they resisted, I yanked at the chains, pulling their iron collars roughly. When they attempted to trample me, I kept them at bay with my club. In such a fashion, I dragged the mares out behind the stable-yard, where Abderos waited with Diomedes' chariot. In astonishment Abderos watched how I broke off the chariot's iron central pole, and after threading the ends of the chains through it, twisted it in my bare hands into a circle. This I attached to the chariot's prow.

'Quickly, Abderos, pull off the sacks!' I shouted, mounting the chariot and jerking back the chains. Abderos, fast and nimble, unmasked the mares. Able now to see, and feeling less secured than in their stalls, they darted wildly forth, nearly toppling the chariot from their misdirected thrusts. I pulled back on the two middle chains to control the course, and lashed the mares to equalize their efforts. 'Come on, boy!' I cried, afraid to leave Abderos behind. The youth ran behind the chariot, and jumped aboard just as we flew past the front of Diomedes' house. Rousing the Bistones to action, Diomedes seized a spear, mounted another chariot and led the pursuit.

I had no trouble bursting through the town gates. When the guards saw the fierce horses tearing like a storm toward them, they ran from their posts and left the postern wide open. As we raced across the plain, stones struck the chariot-rail, hurled by slingers closest in pursuit. I released my grip on the chains, passed the lash to Abderos, urged him to keep at the horses with alacrity, and readied my bow. I picked off the nearest slingers and archers. The sea lay ahead. But the Bistones were too numerous to fight, and I would have ended up trapped on the shore. Taking control of the chains again, I veered the mares westward toward higher ground, wound past giant rocks, dove across a plain and down into a hollow, and then back up into low hills across from the sea cliffs. For a moment out of Diomedes' sight, I reined in the mares on a knoll behind the shelter of a clump of boulders. The animals seemed content simply to snort and shake their foam-flecked chins, their fierceness whelmed by weariness and exertion. Leaving Abderos with the mares, I raced up a defile at the base of the rocky coast and discovered an ancient moss-covered sea wall, built of large stones, battered by wind and waves. Over the top the sea-spray exploded, meaning the tide was high. I could hear now a smattering of hooves in the distance. In another moment, Diomedes appeared on a nearby hill. Laying aside my club, I applied my shoulders to the sea wall and began to push. As flesh pressed against stone, nothing at first seemed to happen. Pushing more and more, my teeth clenched, my sinews threatening to burst beneath the skin, I began to shift the massive stones: ever so slightly, but enough for the brine to trickle through cracks with each smashing breaker. I paused for a moment, took a deep breath, and renewed my forceful assault. The water now poured over me as the top stones shuddered. I backed off, knowing the structure was now weak and would not hold long. Climbing out of the defile, I taunted the Bistones, who rushed into the low-lying plain after me. Then a great wave, as high as the sea cliffs, rolled toward shore. I dropped to the ground as it broke against the rocks, smashed apart the sea wall, and poured down the defile. In moments the raging water, free of its age-long impediment, cascaded into the plain. Hardly had the waterfall abated, when another roller brought more water flooding into the hollow. Diomedes and his men found themselves stuck in a marsh. Scrambling to reach higher ground, they drove their chariot wheels into the muck and had to leave the cars and horses behind. I picked off a number of them with arrows as they scrambled up the hills-sides. The rest, losing their spirit to fight, ran off. Keeping Diomedes in sight, I raced around the forming lake to apprehend him, for ending his life was not part of my instructions. Stunning him with a tap of my club, I carried him back to where I had left Abderos with the mares. But, coming near, I feared the worst: for the mares, pulling the chariot behind them, had wandered some distance; and I could not see Abderos. Dropping Diomedes, I ran after them and discovered, to my horror, their continued repast on the half-eaten corpse. In fury I drove them off; and, lamenting that I seemed to bring nothing but evil to those around me, gathered the remains of the tender youth in my lionskin. I thought to kill the mares; but when I heard Diomedes awakening and calling out something in the rough Thracian tongue, I returned to his side, picked him up, and threw him under his own mares. The beasts, not quite sated with Abderos, attacked their new living meal with vigor: in little time they tore the king apart and ate up every last morsel. Afterwards, a remarkable change came over the mares. They ceased their crazed manner and grazed mildly. I approached them cautiously, but they paid me no mind, and allowed me to stroke their blood-specked backs. Consuming the flesh of the man who had taught them to violate natural law appeared to pacify them completely.

I fetched some timber from a nearby copse, and after building a pyre upon the knoll, to which I added pine-brands to make it blaze, I burned to ashes what remained of Abderos. Upon the bones and ashes I piled earth to form a barrow. Bidding farewell to my young friend, I mounted the chariot, secured the chains, and lashed the mares into a spirited trot.

Rather than pursue me, the Bistones, who as savages were naturally obsequious and subject to whomever was strongest and most powerful, declared me their new king. I left them a measure of civilization by instituting games in honor of Abderos, holding all of the usual contests except horse-racing. A town developed in that place, which the natives called Abderia. And when these things had been accomplished, I departed."

## 10

Heracles would say no more about himself to his spellbound audience, nor entertain any questions. Instead, he pressed Lycos for any information that would prove useful on their journey.

"You are fortunate, Heracles, that your course does not take you about the northern seaboard," said Lycos. "There dwell various tribes of the Scythians, whose habits are not only strange, but evil and unjust. The Taurians, for example, sacrifice to their gods those who have been shipwrecked, or any Greeks they take at sea. When a Taurian overpowers an enemy, he cuts off the head, brings it home, and impales it on tall wooden stake higher than his chimney. Beside them dwell the Man-eaters—perhaps the vilest of all races of men. They have no conception of justice, nor of any other civilized traditions. The roam about, wear skins and furs, and eat human flesh. Between here and the land of the Amazons you will find equally savage, but less inimical, peoples. Neighboring us to the east are the Henetians, whose country abounds with wild she-mules. Then come the surly Paphlagonians, who only treat those kindly that trade with them. Passing several capes you will come to the outflow of the Thermodon. Here is the plain of Doeas, and nearby are the three cities of the Amazons.

"I will tell you now what I know of the warrior women. It is said that they are the children of Ares and the naiad Harmonia, who wedded him in the glens of the Acmonian wood. At first they lived beside the river Tanais far to the north, called first Amazonius but now after the name of the son of an early queen, Lysippe. Having offended Aphrodite by his love of war and scorn of matrimony, he became afflicted with an incestuous passion for his mother. Rather than yield, he flung himself into the river and drowned. Thence the miserable Lisyppe led her people round the

Axine to their present location.

"They are a rather inhospitable people, rude and insolent, devoted only to war, without justice or mercy. I therefore fear for all of you in this enterprise, seeing that you are small in number (yet the equation is balanced somewhat since you have Heracles with you!). They allow no men among them, except that once a year they company with the savage Macronians in a midway place. In this way they reproduce. The girls they keep, while the infant boys are given back to the Macronians, except for some which motherly instinct compel to keep among them. But they break the arms and legs of these hapless children, and return them to the Macronians before they learn to speak, or else they must be put to death. It is said that the Amazons sear off their right breasts, for while they are young their mothers, using a red-hot irons, mutilate them so that as adults they are unhindered in using the bow, and have greater strength in their pulling arm. Although I have never seen one of these virago women, I have seen pictures on vases and such, where they are drawn with both breasts, so this may be a mere legend. They have always two sovereigns—presently Hippolyte and Orithya—who by turns conduct wars or remain home to defend their borders."

King Lycos offered Heracles his son as a guide to travel with them as far as the Thermodon. In return, Lycos asked of Heracles a favor. He needed his assistance to put an end to the hostilities between the Mariandynians and the Bebrycians to the south-west, who liked to cross the Sangarios River to harass them. Heracles gladly promised to do what he could on his way back from Amazonia, since he felt well treated by his host.

11

They rested all the next day from their long repast and on the third waited on the beach for a favorable wind. It did not come until the sun had nearly set, and so they waited another night, returning to the palace to retire. The next morning a westerly breeze held steady, and after revictualling their ships from Lycos' storehouse, set sail once again. Dascylos sat with the helmsman, helping to guide the flotilla through the choppy waters of southern coastline. They made good progress, taking to the oars only for several hours to speed them along when the wind had slackened. That night, Dascylos pointed them to a rocky patch in a shallow gulf, and there they anchored.

At dawn they sailed onward, late in the day rounding Cape Lepte, which juts out precipitously into the sea. Dascylos urged them to sail on past the next cape, protected by dark reefs, until they came to a stretch of beach in a deep gulf. They ran the ships ashore and retired for the night, building fires of driftwood.

The next day they bore down on their oars, for the wind abandoned them, making for the next promontory, near which the mighty Halys River strikes with white spume the headland rocks, pouring in a great torrent down to the sea. Dascylos told them that around the next promontory lay the Thermodon; and that the Amazons would surely be observing the seacoast. But they still had yet another half-day's travel. As the sails bellied once again with a north-westerly wind, Heracles decided to waste no further time. They rounded the jutting headland and sailed into the sluggish mouth of the Thermodon. They lay anchor by the shore, where the grassy lowland sloped gently to the bay, and disembarked fully armored. Heracles wrapped himself in his impenetrable lionskin, slung his bow across his back, and supported his great club on his shoulder. A half-league further up, beyond some brushy hills, they could see a fortified city, protected by tall palisades on all sides; and in the distance the hazy blue silhouette of a sprawling mountain range enclosing the entire plain. The headwaters of the Thermodon are there, and mighty streams branch out in all directions over the fertile plain, creating marshes, but coalescing into a single outflow at the lowest and most narrow point.

The men saw not a soul—only wild horses grazing on the hills. Heracles bade Iolaos and Theseus to accompany him to Themiscyra. His intention was to enter the city peacefully, as his own herald, for he could not guarantee the safety of any other in this foreign land. No sooner had they begun their march, than a wild shrieking rose from beyond the high brush shielding the beach. From the uplands rode a tight squadron of Amazons on brown broodmares, crying out in a terrifying manner. They separated as they came close, surrounding Heracles and the men in a half-circle, hemming them against the ships. They were all tall and manly, with long hair flowing out beneath their helmets, riding without bridle or saddle. They wore deerskin trousers in the manner of the Scythians, dark-red buskins and short, furry jerkins, over which some wore a sort of narrow leather cuirass. Each carried swords, knives and a small crescent-shaped shield at their belts; and all held a bow at the ready, for they were able to ride and shoot at the same time.

Heracles, caught in surprise by their swiftness, hardly had time to unsling his bow. One of the female warriors, keeping a nocked arrow pointed at Heracles, rode forward, and called out to him in a crude, guttural tongue. She was taller than the rest, and her red hair matched the color of her buskins.

Heracles raised a hand, slowly passing his bow to Iolaos beside him. "I do not understand your speech," he said, raising the other hand in a sign of friendship. "But I wish to meet your queen Hippolyte," he continued.

At the sound of the name, the Amazons looked one to the other. Each now abandoned their designated targets and focused their weapons on Heracles. Then Dascylos, who had disembarked only to stretch his legs a bit, intending to remain with the ship, came forward and addressed their commander, Melanippe, in her own language. He exclaimed that the man before them was the mighty Heracles, who had been sent to their land by the gods on an important errand. He spoke falteringly, for his knowledge of the Amazonian tongue was imperfect, but with enough clarity that Melanippe ordered her warriors to relax their aggressive postures. She responded that Heracles alone should accompany her to the city, and that none other could leave the bay on pain of death. Heracles accepted the terms, untied the sword from his belt and slung off the lionskin. At the sight of his uncovered physique some Amazons gasped. Melanippe uncoiled a rope, tied a noose at one end, and threw it to Heracles, indicating that he should walk behind her secured at the neck, keeping the rope-length between them. Heracles, growing impatient, thought for a moment of yanking the rope to pull the red-haired Amazon clean off her mount. He thought better, however, and complying with the request, set off in tow with them.

The Amazon guard followed a course near the shoreline, passing several watch-towers hidden in tall thickets. They turned up a coastal road toward the gates of Thermiscyra. There were no other settlements about. All of the Amazons lived in their high-walled cities. When the gates were opened, a dozen warriors ran out bearing javelins with bronze points, forming a corridor through which they passed. As Heracles entered the city, women in the market-place dropped their wares and children stopped their play. All stared in wonderment at the giant man—a rare sight among them. At the end of the main street a stockade surrounded the royal house, temples and various administrative buildings. Melanippe unhorsed and alone led Heracles up the steps into the palace. Queen Hippolyte presently appeared, treading gracefully toward them with long strides. She was taller than Melanippe, nearly reaching Heracles' chin in height, with short reddish hair streaked at the temples with gray. She seemed near fifty years old, but her face was still beautiful and taut, and her lively bearing seemed that of a much younger woman. Her habit consisted of a short tunic, secured at the waist by a girdle, so that it barely reached the knees; a long-skirted jerkin, flat sandals laced up her long legs, and a hooded mantle. For jewelry she wore hoop-rings in her ears and arm-bands in the form of serpents; and on her head rested a circlet adorned with a half-moon. Her ample bosom indicated that Lycos' story was apocryphal after all.

Melanippe drew down on the rope fastened around the

neck of Heracles to compel him to bend, but it was as if a child had pulled on a bull's halter. Heracles snorted, and then of his own will dropped to one knee, bowing before the queen. When he looked up he found her observing him rather admiringly, walking around him as if she examined a prized steed. Melanippe spoke to her; but the queen said nothing. She went to recline on couch, dismissed Melanippe with a fillip, and beckoned Heracles to approach her.

Heracles, removing the noose from his neck, rose, but remained where he stood.

"By the looks of you, you are either a Phrygian or a Greek," said Hippolyte haltingly, but precisely. "Although a man of your size I have never encountered."

Heracles was surprised she spoke his language so well, and relieved he would not need to call for Dascylos.

"I am honored, most illustrious Hippolyte, to be in your presence," he said. "I am Heracles of Tyrins, a chief city of the Argives."

"Heracles—the name is familiar to me," said Hippolyte. "Are you the son of a god?"

"Zeus is my father," responded Heracles.

"Do not speak the name of any male divinities," advised the queen. "They are not welcomed in our land. We worship only Bendis, mistress of the moon and hunt. To lord Enyalios our father we also pay honors, and him alone."

"But Zeus is the chief among gods," said Heracles. "Does he not also deserve honor?"

Hippolyte laughed. She said: "Did you not know that Zeus was last-born of your gods, and that he suckled on a divine goat while Bendis, full-grown, hunted in the mountain fastness?"

"I wish you no disrespect," said Heracles; "and will speak no longer of my gods."

"You are polite for such a brutish-looking man," said Hippolyte. "You are also fortunate to be standing here. The only men who ever see the inside of our city are prisoners caught in war. Those we sell as slaves or put to death. You must therefore excuse my sister Melanippe if you felt ill-treated. If you please, come hither. Stand before me."

As soon as Heracles took a step, his trained ears detected the slight warping sound of bending bows. He glanced behind him at Amazon guards ready to cut him down at the first sign of danger to their queen. He proceeded cautiously. Hippolyte smelled of heather, ox-hide and other wild things. She grasped a massive hand, losing her hand in his, and then passed light fingers over the rock-like muscles of his forearms and thighs.

Looking up into the eyes of the towering figure, she asked: "Why have you come, Heracles?"

"I am here on the orders of Eurystheus, High King of Mycenae," said Heracles. "He has sent me to bring back your girdle, said to have been a gift from Ares."

"You speak the truth: Ares gifted the girdle to my forbearer Marpesia for her service, for she extended our realm across the Tanais into Thrace, and across the Thermodon and the inaccessible mountains into Phrygia and other parts of Asia. But I must ask— how do you intend to gain possession of my girdle? I am told that you came on ships filled with armed men."

"I am not one to lie or mince words, noble queen," said Heracles. "It was my intent to make a polite request. But, should you deny me, I am prepared to lay siege to your city and seize the girdle by force."

"Such frankness and honesty in a man is as common as a rose-bloom in winter," said she, hiding the gravity of her thoughts. With her sister Orithya, who had pledged to preserve her virginity to the end of her life, engaged in war abroad, only a small number of warriors remained to defend their city against the strangers. "While I doubt very highly that a few men will risk taking on the entire Amazon nation over a war-belt, I might consider simply giving it you, Heracles. But first you must consent to be my guest and accompany me on a hunt this afternoon."

"I will most gladly consent to that," said Heracles. "And what of my friends? They wait for me at the ships."

"I will send word to them of your safety," said Hippolyte. "But they must remain where they are as long as you are here. I cannot risk causing scandal among my people by allowing any more free men into the city. Our laws and customs are ancient, and I cannot alter them."

Hippolyte called for her attendants, who fitted her with buskins, changed her into a hunting-cloak, and set a tall-plumed leather helmet on her head. Leaving the city by a postern gate, they were joined by several warriors and another of the queen's sisters, Antiope, similarly red-haired and youngest of the four chieftains: a fair, slight maiden blessed with unadulterated femininity. Heracles was given a horse and an ashen bow that, compared to his own, seemed like play-thing in his hands. Led by fleet-footed hounds, they drove across the fertile plains where gazelles leapt, chased home by a coming storm. Heracles, although he was less skillful in negotiating both bow and horse at once, awed the Amazons with his uncanny accuracy. One by one the graceful beasts fell; only a rare arrow missed its mark. From the field the riders plunged up the cool mountain-slopes, the air pregnant with mist from the wandering strands of the Thermodon, racing toward the sea with churning, foam-flecked waters. They hunted birds and hares and a she-boar until the gloom settled among the pines and the hounds wheezed in weariness.

There was no dearth of palace women willing that night to bathe the rippling body of Heracles. A fortunate few washed him in warm water, spread soothing oil across his vast limbs, and attired him in clean linen. He was escorted to queen Hippolyte's chamber, where he dined with her on the roasted flesh of the hunt, along with wild salads and steaming clumps of sheep's cheese. Her apartment was sparse, more befitting a warrior than a queen. In an ante-room stood a shrine to the goddess Bendis. She seemed to Heracles very much like Artemis in appearance, and he wondered whether it was not the same goddess in different forms. The queen spoke of the long history of her people, now divided into a confederacy of several tribes. They kept mostly to their own affairs, except in war-time, when the tribes could be counted on to unite for a common cause. Heracles recounted his Labors thus far: his battles and journeys far and near. When the evening star waxed bright, chasing away the lesser stars, she invited him to lie upon a tiger-skin before the crackling fire of a hearth, and there held his head to her bosom, caressing his thick and curly beard. Although he did not intend to bring up the matter of his children, the queen could not miss how he often spoke in a melancholy tone, and cajoled him until he revealed all to her. It seemed to her that a sob or two escaped him, but it could have been the hissing of the fagots in the fire.

And so for the next three days, Heracles hunted and

feasted in the company of Hippolyte, who, for the first time, dared to consider another man her equal. It seemed she could not bear to be away from him. She kept Heracles by her day and night, as one keeps a beloved pet. Like the odor of strange flowers, or as the savor of a strange fruit, was Heracles to her. She forgot to recall Orithya.

On the fourth morning, Heracles woke warmed under a pool of sunlight from a high casement. When the sun moved off, he curled up the tiger-skin around him and called out for a drink. The palace women ran in bearing platters of barley-bread and cheese, and a flagon of icy river-water. After refreshing himself, he lay face-down upon the queen's bed and called for one of the women to knead his body with oil, still sore from the previous days' hard riding. One woman entered abruptly, shooed the others out, and approached Heracles, who was expecting a pair of light hands to squeeze muscles. Instead, a strong hand slapped his buttocks. A familiar voice accompanied the blow, saying: "So this is how the mighty Heracles spends his days now! Indolent, and in the care of women!"

Heracles turned about and sat up with a start, grabbing the stranger by the collar. "Theseus!" he cried. Theseus dropped the fold of the mantle covering his head. His beardless youth had allowed him to sneak into the city and pass as one of the Amazons.

"We grew worried about you, Heracles, having not received word since you left us." said Theseus. "But I see you're not any worse for the wear."

"I am still in the process of securing the girdle, foolish lad," said Heracles. "Do you not know what will happen if you are caught?"

"If I could make it out of the Labyrinth," said Theseus, "I can certainly find my way out of here. But can you complete your Labor?—that is the question. It appears you are not trying very hard!"

"You of all people should know that at times brain surpasses brawn, and charm prevails over threats" said Heracles. "Hippolyte, though an Amazon, must be wooed like any other woman. She has promised, in any case, to give me the girdle. Tonight, I am sure she will deliver it."

"She will give it to you just like that?" asked Theseus

"Let it never be said that there is not more to Heracles than meets the eye," said Heracles proudly.

The door opened suddenly. Theseus barely had time to cover his head before Antiope walked in to inform Heracles that the queen awaited him for another day at the chase. She glanced at Theseus, squinted her eyes suspiciously, and then left. Theseus stood there dumbly.

"What is it, man?" asked Heracles, rising to dress. "You seem as if you've been transfixed by the vision of a god."

"My eyes would not tell the difference," said Theseus. "Who was that fair maiden?"

"Antiope, the queen's sister," said Heracles. "Would you like me to make an introduction?"

"Nay, Heracles, not at the moment. I fear the type of caress an Amazon would give me," said Theseus. "In sooth, I have never seen a lovelier woman. She reminds me of Artemis of the Golden Shaft, light and lovely. Is she swift of foot? How is her speech? Is it soothing like an Arcadian breeze? Does her hair trail behind her like a swallow's tail as she rides her swift steed?"

Heracles laughed and said: "It appears that the spry son of Venus has found his way to this cold northern land. Although the queen is as old as my mother, I too am strangely warmed by her touch and delight in the feeling of her breath upon my neck. These Amazons are bewitching to us hard men. But now hie yourself away, Theseus, before you are discovered. I plan to join you back at the ships on the morrow."

That night Hippolyte fulfilled her promise by presenting Heracles with her girdle: a wide, jewel-encrusted baldric that glittered in the firelight. But as they reveled in each other's company one last time, rumors were already circulating around the city that Heracles planned to kidnap the Amazon queen. It began with one old crone in the market-place; and as is the case with women everywhere, the gossip quickly spread like a wildfire. When some in authority sought the crone, she could not be found, for it was none other than Hera, who came down from Olympos to forestall Heracles' success. The goddess humbled herself to assume an old, bent form; and with a few choice words of malice started the frenzy. The outrage reached the palace, where Melanippe, not willing to take any risk with her queen, assembled the royal bodyguard and hastened toward the queen's chamber.

Heracles, garbed comfortably in one of the queen's gold-spangled robes, sat up when he heard the clamor. A pounding at the door followed, with Melanippe asking for admittance. Heracles, confused, snatched the queen's sword from above the bed and held the point to Hippolyte's neck, saying: "What treachery is this, O queen? Have you grown weary, and now wish to dispose of me?" Hippolyte, as confused as Heracles, and for the first time fearing for her life at his hands, cried: "I know not what is happening! Allow me to answer the door. It is my sister. I shall soon discover the cause of this disturbance." "Nay," said Heracles. "I shall answer the door myself, and cut down any who try to enter." Leaving the queen on the bed, Heracles jumped to the door. He unlatched it and caught Melanippe, the first to rush in, in the crook of his arm, disarming her by squeezing the air from her body until she stood listless. Hewing the air with sword strokes, he kept the other Amazons back. Learning from them the cause of the uproar, Hippolyte in vain tried to convince her sister of the misunderstanding.

"They think you are to kidnap me," said Hippolyte, trying to approach Heracles. He kept her back at sword's length. "I have naught to do with this! You must believe me. Did I not give you the belt? You were free to leave, to return to your ships. One more night with you was all I wished. Already a stigma marks me for what I have done. But I love you, Heracles. My subjects get to company with men each year, but not their queen. It is beneath her, they say. You alone I have found worthy to share my bed."

"Your sweet words prove no comfort to me," said Heracles in dismay, for he felt his affection betrayed. "Were I not Heracles, these cruel women would have hacked me to pieces in your own bed. Trust women and trust deceivers! Bitch, I should kill you where you stand; yet your loveliness stays my hand. Your sister I will take me with me as surety as I make my way out of the city. If you love me as you say, do your best to control these Harpies, or I swear to you there will be more bloodshed this night than the daughters of Ares have ever witnessed."

Dragging Melanippe with him, he roared at the throng that

now crowded the doorway. Fearing for their commander, they allowed him to pass, but soon encircled him with gleaming swords and piercing daggers. One Amazon swung at him, but Heracles parried and clove with such force that he burst the other sword to pieces and hacked the woman through the collar-bone. He rushed now like a stampeding boar through the group. Bodies, weapons and armor flew aside like leaves in the wind. Remembering the way to the postern gate, he bounded down steps and corridors, Melanippe hanging from his arm like a child's doll. Once outside, arrows landed at his feet. He flung his sword at the archers atop the palisade. The blade, twirling and hissing through the air, hewed them like a scythe through tall wheat-stalks.

A rider, running a second horse beside him, approached, calling his name. It was Theseus, with his lionskin, bow and quiver.

"I see you've overstayed your welcome!" cried Theseus. "Are you now ready to depart?"

"More than ready," said Heracles, draping the limp Melanippe across the spare horse and climbing on behind her. An arrow struck Theseus' mount in the croup, giving it impetus in flight. Heracles kicked his horse hard to gain some distance, and then turned to speed some shafts into the air. Bodies fell off the city wall, landing upon the Amazons who now streamed out of the city like enraged bees from a beehive. Heracles kicked his steed again and off into the night he sped.

A flock of water-fowl, flying back to its favorite marshes, would from above have seen a curious sight. A wedge of smoking torches spread across the Thermodon plain in pursuit of two lone riders. Theseus was the first to make it back to the ships, his mount nearly collapsing under him. He rallied the men to prepare for battle. Next Heracles arrived, and entrusted Melanippe to Dascylos on the ship. Then bending his great bow he began to douse the torchlights in the distance before he could even see the faces of those who carried them. The horsed Amazons tried to form a line, but Heracles caused them to retreat under the threat of arrows that never missed their mark. A great host on foot now rushed in from the sides, and met Heracles' companions in grim combat. Heracles lay down his bow and took up his brass-bound club, and with mighty swings crushed heads and bodies until he had swept the vanguard from the field. The Amazons, not expecting such fierce resistance, fell back beyond a hill.     As soon as Antiope came among them, she took command, and led another attack, wishing to overwhelm the strangers with their numbers.  They rushed forward swiftly, discharged their arrows and darts, and then retreated with parting shots, vaulting on the back of their horses and shooting, to the terror and astonishment of the Argives, over their shoulders. At their flanks, other Amazons rushed onto the beach, followed by more horsewomen bending their deadly bows.  They would have succeeded in crushing Heracles' band had he not felled the tempestuous Aella, for there was none other as fleet of foot.  But the arrows of Heracles outran her, and she fell to the dust.  At the sight of such a renowned warrior stretched dead on the field, the common ones fell back, afraid of the savage Tyrinthian.  But Antiope gathered the most stalwart to her side, and rallied them. The first to ride forth was Prothoe, armed with a spear.  Seven times she had won in single combat, and none could defeat her. Heracles let fly a shaft, but she caught it on her half-moon shield. She spurred her steed and at full speed loosed her javelin.  It flew true to its mark, but Heracles had by then taken up again his club and swatted the missile from the air like an impatient shopkeeper slaps down a fly about to land on his victuals.  Undaunted, she withdrew her sword, and was about to close the distance between them when a spear from Telamon's hand pierced her breastplate, the bronze tip sprouting from her back with a spurt of blood. Down she fell as darkness closed over her eyes.

One after the other the bravest rode out against Heracles, and he dispatched them without mercy, including Phillipis, who lasted not long in her first conflict; Eriboea, who her bravery misled into thinking that she could face Heracles without assistance; and Celaeno, Eurybia and Phoebe, companions of Bendis in the hunt, who, despite their skill, could not land even one arrow on their mark: Heracles cut them down as they stood abreast.  After them Heracles slew Deianeira, Asteria, Marpe, Tecmessa and Alcippe, who had sworn to know no man all the days of her life.  He cut her days short, his anger now doubled at the realization that he had forgotten to take the girdle with him.

Amidst the cries and shouts, the clash of arms and the thunder of hooves, Heracles heard a singular wail.  Looking across the melee he saw a noble form riding tall on a white charger.

Hippolyte, wearing her glittering baldric, its jewels emblazoned with the moonlight, from which depended a silver scabbard inlaid with ivory and a bronze double-edged battle-axe, looked about in agony at her fallen sisters. When she espied Heracles, wrath overbore her. She pulled a spear standing upright from a dead warrior's back, and swooped down upon him. Jumping aside, Heracles evaded her spear-thrust, and with a sweep of his club splintered her horses' legs. It staggered down on its haunches, pitching the queen forward. She rolled quickly to her feet, and crouching like a lion, circled Heracles, her lance couched in the curving horns of her splendid shield. Heracles' breath left him at the sight of such a magnificent warrior. In her tight-fighting corslet and golden greaves she dazzled his eyes like a lightning-bolt through a rainstorm.

With eyes casting sparks beneath the brow of her golden-plumed helm, Hippolyte uncoiled her sinuous form to cast her spear. Heracles had only a moment to present his shoulder to the relentless shaft. The spear-point, impelled by fury, drove through his lion's pelt. Heracles, spun backward under the ponderous force of the throw, felt his flesh pierced. But the lance, not allowed to go deeper, dislodged and fell to the ground. Heracles bloodied his fingers on the gash, marveling at the only weapon that had ever managed to penetrate his natural armor.

With a withering war-cry, Hippolyte closed on Heracles with her battle-axe. Heracles took up a discarded shield and arrested the blow. Hippolyte, unable to dislodge the axe-head, drew her sword and in a flurry of hacks and slashes sought to end Heracles' life. He parried each blow with his buckler, until, overtaken by battle-fury, he went on the offensive. Wrenching off Hippolyte's axe, he swung it downward. She raised her half-moon shield, but it broke asunder under his mighty axe-stroke. The axe-head bit through her cuirass and struck her left breast. With blood dripping down her silvery legs, she staggered about grasping at her wound, and then fell face down.

"Woman, this is a fair price you pay for your treachery," cried Heracles. "Not even Ares will save you from my hand." Roughly turning over her sprawled body, Heracles wrenched off her gleaming helm, releasing a mass of red-gold hair. Seeing again her full and lovely face, the same which, warmed by the hearth-fire, gazed upon him as he told her his stories, he was straightway gripped with remorse. She breathed heavily, and a tear slid down her cheeks grimed with dust and blood.

"Will you kill me, Heracles, and take what was freely given you?" said Hippolyte, still defiant. "I ask for no quarter. Only free my sister Melanippe, still in the bloom of life, that my people may still have a queen."

Heracles groaned, saying: "Hippolyte! What madness has overtaken us? I see now no treachery in your eyes, only our shared sorrow at such needless bloodshed. I sense the hand of cruel Hera in this mess. Call off this ambush, I pray. I shall free Melanippe back to you."

Hippolyte pounded weakly at his chest, saying: "How dark a day for the Amazons when Heracles trod our shore." And then with a sigh she closed her eyes in death. Heracles wearily shook his head. He stripped her of her glittering belt and lifted the limp body in his arms. "Queen Hippolyte is fallen!" he bellowed as Amazons massed around him, too late to defend their regent. "Let us end this useless struggle. Go bury your dead, and we shall bury ours."

Antiope, at that moment battling Theseus, was the first to withdraw from the fight, leaving the latter panting after her, marveling at her prowess, handsome figure and dexterous limbs. Melanippe, freed from the ship, joined her comrades, who settled behind a range of hills while the dead were retrieved from the field. After the grieving Amazons, bearing their queen with her armor and weapons (other than her battle-axe, which Heracles kept), returned to Themiscyra, Heracles took an accounting of his companions. Twenty-nine still lived. The majority had been slain, including Sthenelos, who fell in full armor while bravely fending off a group of Amazons trying to set fire to the ships. His brother Alcaios knelt beside the body, weeping bitterly and cursing Heracles under his breath. Six had deserted, running away down the coast when the battle became heated.

Pyres were built of brush and driftwood, and the bodies set upon them. They danced about the pyres, clashing their arms, and then set them afire. When all had been consumed, save the bones, barrows were heaped over the common grave. But Alcaios would not consent to leave his brother there and took with him the bones and armor, of which the four-peaked helm with blood-red crest still glowed golden among the embers.

Heracles decided it would be quicker to return on foot to the Mariandynians. With him went Autolycos and his brothers, Dascylos, Iolaos, Peleus, Telamon and Alcaios. Theseus and the rest remained with the ships, laden with spoils and captured Amazons. They clasped hands to wish each other well. Once a fair eastern wind swept along the coast, they raised sails and pushed off. Theseus sighed as the headland of Amazonia was lost from view, vowing someday to return and fetch Antiope for himself.

Those who chose to follow Heracles soon regretted their decision. Staying close to the rugged coast, he marched them upwards of seven leagues per day, stopping only to sleep for a few hours each night. When he did not drink, Heracles needed little sleep. In Paphlagonia, Phlogios fell ill. As Heracles would not wait for him to recover, he left him in the care of the local inhabitants. Autolycos and Deileion remained behind with him; they did so, however, in foul spirits, thinking themselves abandoned. As they neared Mariandyne, Alcaios could no longer bear to carry Sthenelos' armor, and so they buried him beyond the river Callichoros, heaping over his remains a huge barrow. Arriving back in Mariandyne exactly seven days after he set out, he found that King Lycos' brother Priolas had been killed by the Mysians. Heracles competed in the funeral games, boxing against the local champion Titias. Although he did not set out to hurt him too badly, he knocked out all his teeth and killed him with only a few jabs. Regretting the accident, Heracles not only aided Lycos against the Bebrycians, whose ruler, Mygdon, he killed, but he also subdued the Mysians, Phrygians and Bithynians, driving them almost to the Bosporos. The land recovered from the Bebrycians king Lycos renamed Heracleia in the hero's honor.

12

With the enemies of King Lycos at heel, Heracles, along with Peleus, Telamon and Alcaios of Paros, took to sea from the Bithynian harbor on the Sea of Marmora. The second day found them sailing down the Hellespont, a quicker route going out than in. They passed a few Trojan ships near Dardanos, but the sea-lane was clear after that, which seemed odd so near the great city of Troy. As they came near the mouth of the Scamander, where the churning waters poured into a large bay forming a natural harbor, Iolaos cried out amidships, trembling with agitation. All looked to where he pointed, and in the distance, from the jutting crag of a rocky islet in the bay, a white form seemed to undulate like the sail of a far-off ship. At first no one could make out what it was they looked at, until Peleus informed them of the unlikely opinion that it was a person who seemed stranded upon the rock. Heracles asked the helmsman to approach the shore. The crew grew abashed and astonished when it was clearly a poor maiden, stark naked save for the jewels around her neck, wrist and ankles, that stood there chained to the rock. Her long, honey-hued locks, wet with spray, covered her modesty. The steersman was afraid to get too close to the islet, for dark rocks were awash all around it. On Heracles' orders, the ship hove-to within shouting distance. Heracles called out to the maiden, but she came cross so faintly that her words could not be heard against the howling wind and crashing tide.

Heracles asked Iolaos: "What could be the meaning of this strange sight?"

"It seems she has been abandoned there as a sacrifice to some god," said Iolaos. "You see how the tide is rising, and the waves will soon mercilessly engulf her."

"I cannot believe any god would demand such a thing." grunted Heracles, beginning to strip down to his leather codpiece.

"We shouldn't interfere, Heracles!" implored Alcaios. "If she is meant for a god, you will bring down his wrath upon us."

"Let Olympos boil over, for all I care," said Heracles. "I will rescue that poor girl."

Heracles leapt over the gunwale and splashed into the sea with such force that a wave valuted in the air and mizzled the crew. He swam to the islet and climbed onto the slippery rock. The maiden, weeping uncontrollably, cried out for mercy. Heracles found a path that wound up the side of the crag, approaching the girl on its sloping flat surface. Lowering himself down to the ledge where she was bound, he comforted her with kind words as he gripped for support the iron ring to which her manacles were chained above her head. The rapid, pounding surf jetted against their bare bodies.

"Maiden, how came you here?" asked Heracles, testing the strength of the manacles.

"I am Hesione, left here by my father, king Laomedon," said the maiden. "O! hurry! before the sea monster comes for me! But how, without tools, will you break my bonds?"

"My hands are tools enough," said Heracles. Grasping each side of a brass wristlet around the seam, he pulled savagely until it snapped. In another moment, he had unclasped the other. Hesione collapsed into his arms, too weak to support herself after her agonizing imprisonment. Grasping her shivering, naked body with one arm, he climbed back down to the base of the rock. Despite her protests, he pulled her into the water, swimming on his side while holding her up above the waves. In this laborious manner they returned to the ship. They were pulled aboard and Iolaos wrapped Hesione in his blanket. Heracles threatened the sailors for their leering.

The ship entered the broad bay, landing by a sand-bank, beyond which the plain of the Scamander stretched green and brown and interspersed with low hills and shrubbery. Not far, upon a hill, Troy stood behind its massive stone walls. They made camp, building several fires. At one apart, Hesione warmed herself and ate ravenously while caressing her sore wrists. She was afraid to return to her father. Heracles promised to take care of the matter as soon as he learned all the details. And so this is the story she told him.

With Troy, the ambitious Laomedon sought to build the grandest city on earth, with walls to surpass even the giant-wrought walls of Tyrins and Mycenae. When Apollo, passing through Phrygia, saw thousands of men in exhaustive labor, drawing up massive stones by means of ropes, pulleys and machines never before seen among men since the dawn of the Egyptian race, he grew envious and wished to be a part of the enterprise. Likewise, Poseidon, watching from the swollen deep, developed an interest in the project and joined Apollo in taking human form. They presented themselves to the king as laborers and stone-smiths. Laomedon, who had men enough in his employ, at first turned them away; but he eventually relented, promising them payment in gold if they proved valuable. No better hire had the king ever made, for while Poseidon labored at the walls, Apollo tended the king's cattle on the wooded slopes of Mount Ida. When the walls of Troy were raised in a twelvemonth, Laomedon wondered about the pair of disguised immortals, since it was said that stones raised themselves and tools did their work outside of human hands. Yet, when it was time to deliver due compensation, the haughty king kicked them out and sent them away empty-handed, claiming that he never promised any reward and threatening, should they protest, to bind them in fetters, cut off their ears, and sell them as slaves to a foreign king. Apollo in his fury sent a plague upon the city. When the sickness ran its course, Poseidon unleashed an even more exacting punishment. He released a sea monster to ravage the Trojans. At certain times it would rise up from the depths and destroy ships, or kill those who made their living by the seashore, or snatch the farmers who tilled the fertile plain contiguous with the sea.

The terrorized populace pleaded with Laomedon to arrange an end to their misery. He therefore sought answers at the oracle of Zeus the Thunderer, which lay between Sigeum and Cape Rhoeteum. The advice received was horrid to his ears: to assuage the god, he needed to expose for the monster his daughter Hesione on the seashore. Laomedon refused to do this; instead he pleaded with the Trojan nobles that it was more proper from them to sacrifice their offspring, even trying to force one Phoenodamas to give up one of his three daughters, whom he had kept at home under the circumstances, while all others had sent their children away for safety. Finally, when it became clear that the present evil was solely the fault of Laomedon, it was decided that none other than he should be made to suffer. At the urging of Phoenodamas, lots were cast at the assembly and the black pebble fell upon Hesione, which indicated the propriety of that conclusion. Unable to delay the inevitable any further, Laomedon himself rowed Hesione to the islet and chained her to the rock, afterward returning sorrowfully to the city.

Heracles persuaded Hesione that she had no reason to fear in accompanying him to the city since it was his intention to slay the sea monster. But he wanted first to have some words with Laomedon. Along with Iolaos, they crossed the plain in view of the imposing city, encircled by a massive limestone circuit-wall with flanking towers and brick ramparts. Unlike Mycenae, built on a mountain, Troy spread across the plain from a commanding hill, crowned with a vast palace complex on its looming citadel.

At the Scaean Gate, bronze-plated double doors as tall as poplars, and flanked on one side by the great square tower of Ilion, they encountered Laomedon on his way out of the city, for he had been alerted about the rescue of his daughter. He fell upon her neck with many tears, imploring her forgiveness for acting out of necessity. Filled with joy, he invited her benefactor up to the palace, where a feast was held in Heracles' honor. Afterward, as they strolled along the terrace, Heracles noticed two peerless snow-white horses grazing and prancing in the field below. They treaded so lightly that it seemed they floated over the turf.

Heracles asked the king: "If I destroy the sea monster, will you gift me those beautiful mares?"

"How can I refuse anything to the man who saved my daughter and now offers to save my people?" Laomedon said after a moment of pensive silence. "But I must inform you that what you ask of me is no light matter. Those horses were given to my grandfather Tros, father of Ilos (from which this land, Ilion, took its name), by Zeus himself in compensation for the abduction of his son Ganymedes. It so happened that the boy radiated a divine beauty and the ruler of gods and men fell in love with him. Taking the form of a great eagle, Zeus swopped down one day upon the plain and snatched him. It is said he was installed in Olympos as Zeus' cupbearer, filling his cup with the sweet nectar. The horses are immortal and matchless in grace and beauty. They can run like the wind over standing grain and over water, so my father told me. You therefore drive a hard bargain, Heracles, in asking me to part with those sacred animals. But for the love of Hesione, I agree to your request."

Loving horses, Heracles was well pleased. From Laomedon he learned as much about the sea monster as he could: its size, shape and habits. It was not known when it would strike again. Heracles retired to a guest room to doze a bit, wherein he could also meditate, and afterward returned to the king ready with fresh ideas. First he ordered a high wall to be built near the place where the monster was last seen climbing onto the shore. Then he asked for a suit of armor. As no armor existed to fit his prodigious size, Laomedon ordered his best armorers to construct a new set immediately. Heracles was measured, and soon the foundry grew loud with activity.

The first attempt at building a wall ended in disaster. The monster appeared suddenly and snatched up the workers one by one until none were left. It took several days to find masons courageous enough to continue the construction. When Heracles went to inspect the work, he prayed to Athena for her blessing, and dedicated the wall to her.

When the wall was finished, Iolaos drove out Heracles fully armored. He wore a heavy, golden cuirass, embellished with the curvatures of his pronounced musculature, the two plates hinged on one side and laced on the other, held firm by iron bands over his shoulders; long greaves of shining bronze; a helm after the Corinthian style, constructed of a single piece of adamant fitting closely at the temples; and the glittering shield—the shield!—was like none other ever seen among men—the very work of Hephaistos it seemed. Its entire face shimmered with enamel, white ivory, gold and yellow electrum. On its orb hung concentric circles of deep-blue sapphire; in each zone cunningly wrought scenes breathed with life. For its boss the horrid face of Fear held place, worked from adamant, staring backwards with eyes that glowed afire; its snarling mouth was full of teeth; and above its brow hovered fearful Strife. The next band showed Fate and her dread work among men: clothed with a garment red with blood, she carried from the tumult a wounded man, a hale man and a dead man, glaring and gnashing her teeth. Then one could see the heads of twelve frightful snakes, which seemed to snap their black jaws at every agitation of the shield. Boars and lions, with glaring eyes, were also there depicted, their bodies locked in bloody struggle. Ares, lord of war, had his place, standing in his chariot, urging men into battle with his bloody spear. Nearby came Athena, wearing a golden helm, and shaking the awful ægis upon her breast. Beyond that were pictured the company of the gods on high Olympos, in whose midst the son of Leto played a golden lyre while the Muses could be heard spinning sweet songs by the cunning capture of the wind through the whorls of the relief. A pleasant scene followed, depicting a rippling sea wrought of tin, filled with silvery dolphins swimming and devouring fish. One could almost see the waves hitting the shore, upon which a fisherman seemed poised with his casting net. Exquisitely wrought was now the figure of Perseus, whose carved form did not seem to touch the shield, but float above it, flying through the air with the aid of his winged sandals carrying the awful head of the Gorgon in a bag of silver at his back. At his heels nipped her dread sisters, hissing and spitting, the glaring snakes bristling on their heads. The widest band portended a scene of future horror. In a shifting tapestry, men fought one another in pitched battle, some defending their city and others attempting to sack it. They rattled their spears and swords, rushing one upon the other like enraged lions, bringing upon themselves bloody ruin and destruction. One could not be but moved by the figures of wives and daughters upon the city's towers, crying and tearing their tender cheeks, while old men gathered at the gate supplicating the deathless gods. And in the midst of strife the cruel Fates, daughters of night, rushed to the fallen, eager to drink their warm blood as it spilled on the hard-packed earth. Grasping them in their claws, and gnawing them in their fangs, they sent their wretched souls to Tartaros; and after sating their hunger, cast their bones behind them as refuse before moving on to another unlucky victim. By them stood Death lowering, pale, knobby-kneed, shriveled with hunger, teeth foul with mold, with blood dripping from his cheeks. Around the rim the Ocean Stream beset the marvelous shield-work, over which life-like swans soared and the glossy water teemed with fish.

Armed with his bow, a heavy falchion, a short spear and a

long, heavy steel-tipped javelin, Heracles made camp by the wall and remained there in vigil day after day while Iolaos brought him food and drink.  On the third day, Heracles said: "Hero Iolaos, beloved of all men, only you have been a faithful companion in all my struggles.  Even when monsters threaten us, you do not shy from doing your uncle service."  He said this because Iolaos would remain with him as long as he could, whetting his weapons and poring over the scenes marvelously carved on the shield.

Warned suddenly by the gasps and cries of the multitudes of Trojans who amassed each day on the high ground by the city, Heracles climbed the rampart to look out at the sea.  In the distance a patch of water bubbled and hissed.  "Begone, Iolaos!" cried Heracles, rattling his spear to spur the chariot team away.  Soon a long black shadow glode beneath the water, leaving a trail of white foam as it headed toward the shore.  Heracles did not see the monster until it reached the foreshore, when its head rose out of the water like a plume, as when a boiling subterranean current breaches a weak part of the earth and bursts forth with a thunderous roar.  The sea serpent opened its gigantic mouth showing three rows of jagged teeth, as long and thick as oar-shafts. From their midst lashed out a triple tongue, spewing venom down on the clear water.  Its eyes flickered as if with fire and from its snout hissed a spray of foam.  It slithered onto the shore and rose up to more than half its height, spreading its golden crest and blotting out the sun.  The bloated, mold-green body, long and scaly, with vestigial clawed limbs uselessly grasping, rippled across the sand in great arches.  Although stationed at a safe distance, the Trojans ran for their lives in terror.  But Heracles stood firm upon the wall, and arching his great bow, assailed  the horrid form.  The arrows struck the hard scales as pebbles a mighty tree-trunk, glancing off and leaving the monster unconcerned.

The huge-bodied serpent, deprived of its usual morsels, spied Heracles in his gleaming armor.  Straightway for the wall it snaked.  Compacting its scaly coils in undulating knots, it sprang upward, bending its long body into a bow, ready to drive downward upon its prey.  But Heracles grasped the short spear, reared back and propelled it with all the strength in his body.  The shaft sped to its mark, driving deep between two coils on the monster's neck. With blood spurting from the wound, the serpent roared in pain;

with its great maw it snapped the spear-haft away, leaving the iron point embedded in its flesh. Twisting and writhing, now more from anger than from anguish, the serpent lashed its tail against the wall, bursting apart the mortar and bringing down the stones in a dusty heap. Down tumbled Heracles; and if not for his armor and exceptional constituency, he would have perished in the fall. Heracles struggled to his feet, holding his shield and long spear ready against the snapping jaws that roared toward him. He thus held the monster in check, exposed to the pestilential breath that issued from the horrid maw. Thrusting now his spear between the rows of teeth, he wounded the monster anew. Snapping its head back, the sea serpent ripped the javelin from his hands and with a bite smashed it to pieces. Uttering a fierce war-cry, Heracles unsheathed his sharp-edged falchion and ran forward to hack at the monstrous bulk. With a single ripple of its scales the serpent dislodged the hero, leaving him sprawled on the ground. Seeing the opportunity to put an end to the defender, the serpent brought down its head flat to the ground and with frightening speed slithered toward where Heracles lay, the scales hard as iron scraping the ground. Then, unhinging its jaws and opening them to their largest extent, the monster engulfed Heracles, swallowing him up in a single gulp before snapping shut its mouth with a clang that resounded through the plain. Twisting about, the serpent plunged back into the sea. Those still watching the struggle from the city walls saw the dark coils writhing beneath the waves, and then saw the serpent no more.

Iolaos mounted the chariot and raced out to the beach, leaving behind a trail of dust under the hard-charging hooves of the horses. He pulled the reins and in desperation jumped off the car while the horses still galloped. He tumbled into the trench left behind by the monster and then staggered into the swell while crying out for his friend. At the ebb he fell to his knees, his face in his hands, and wept. The shield of Heracles lay beside him.

All of Troy mourned for the valiant hero; but more because they lost their best hope of salvation. Peleus, Telamon and Alcaios, not knowing what next to do, waited for ships to return from safer harborage so that they could leave Troas behind them. King Laomedon consulted again the oracle of Zeus, but it returned silence. He locked himself in his palace, deathly afraid of the people's murmurings; for all had lost hope and waited for the monster to return as if for death itself. The nobles called again for the revival of the original plan. The king put them off as long as possible, but on the third day decided to leave Hesione once again upon the rock. This time she did not resist, but as a favorite lamb culled reluctantly from the choice flocks, allowed herself to be led to the shore.

Iolaos waited mutely on the beach, unable to accept the death of Heracles. He prayed to Athena, whom he knew watched over him. No answer was returned, save the cry of the gulls as they dotted the ashen sky. He turned to see the procession approaching the shore. A throng of Trojan women, veiled in black, marched ceremoniously, weeping, beating their breasts and clawing their cheeks. In their midst sat splendid Hesione in a long, billowing garment. Behind her rode Laomedon: a gaunt, dark figure, aged beyond his years.

But lo! far off in the water a dark mass rose to the surface. Iolaos watched intently as the tide brought it slowly toward the beach. In little time, the massive, hulking carcase of the sea serpent lay on the shore. The women in Hesione's procession ran off shrieking, for though the monster was plainly dead, its grotesque head and bloated, slimy, putrid, malodorous carcase elicited even greater horror. Suddenly, as Laomedon danced for joy at being delivered from the monster, a coil of the carcase shuddered. The king fell backward from fright. Scales burst apart like chain-armor sundered by a spear thrust. The tip of a falchion broke out from the monster's belly, followed by a hand ripping and twisting the unyielding caul and sodden skin. After a bout of furious hacking from within, Heracles burst out dripping blood and slime like ambergris, and entangled in long thin umbles. "I thirst!" he cried before collapsing on the sand. He was unhelmed—and had nary a hair left on his head and face!

It took six horses hitched to the royal chariot to carry Heracles in his armor back to the palace. Despite the ordeal, he was sanguine. He craved only water and sleep. When he was well enough to appear again before the king, he explained how, after being swallowed, he lived inside the belly of the monster for three days and nights. First he had to fight other dangerous creatures the sea serpent had swallowed whole from the deep, dark waters. Then he had to hack through layer after layer of the tough viscera, carve up the oily liver—which ultimately killed the serpent—and then break through the hard skin and plate-like scales. His hair fell out in the intense heat of the monster's innards.

Laomedon feasted Heracles and his companions for four nights in his hall, during which time the Trojans went out to see the rotting hulk of the monster and marveled, esteeming Heracles as the greatest man in the world. Over these encomiums Laomedon grew envious, fearing that the Trojans would prefer Heracles as king. Even Hesione had fallen in love with her benefactor, despite his odd appearance, although a light beard had begun to grow and his head bristled with new hair, and wished to leave with him. Laomedon therefore organized a great hunt for Heracles on the slopes of Mount Ida. But when Heracles and his men returned, Laomedon barred the Scaean Gate against him. Heracles demanded a reason for the unmerited affront. Idaios, the royal herald, addressed Heracles from Ilion's tower, accusing him of moving the city in a conspiracy against the king on account of his great popularity. Heracles, filled with wrath, would not even countenance the accusation, and demanded the promised mares. This Laomedon refused, even against the entreaties of his equitable son Podarces, claiming that as the divine mares were his to begin with, he could do with them as he pleased. At this Heracles cried: "False and unworthy king, do you withhold from me my just reward, and recompense me evil for good? I swear by the gods, that as I have just delivered Troy from great calamity, I shall deliver it again to the pestilence of war and death." Laomedon felt no tinge of trepidation at his threats, so confident was he in the strength of Troy's walls.

## 13

Heracles appeared so sullen that the Bithynians sailed off; and no other ship, save a Thracian vessel, allowed him passage. Along with Iolaos, Peleus, Telamon and Alcaios, he landed first at Thracian Ainos, near the mouth of the River Hebros. There he was entertained by King Poltys, a son of Poseidon. But his brother, Sarpedon, insolently mocked Heracles for his bald head. He was also angry that Heracles had killed his father's sea monster. Heracles kept silent so as to not insult his host, but as he sailed away, he heard Sarpedon yelling insults at him from the beach. He strung his bow and let fly an arrow at the impudent fellow, wishing only to put fear in him by nicking his ear. But the wind slightly veered the shaft and it pierced him through the eye, killing him instantly.

Next they came to the island of Thasos, which had been settled by Phoenicians who sailed from Tyre with Agenor's son Thasos in search of Europa. Thracians had arrived from the mainland, attracted by the gold mines on the island, the largest of which was situated on the eastern side, facing Samothrace. There was continual strife between the two groups. The Thracians envied the Thasians, who paid no taxes on their crops and derived two hundred talents annually from the mines. The Thasians begged Heracles for assistance, believing him to be an incarnation of the Phoenician god Melqart because of his great size and strength. Heracles therefore organized them, helped them to subjugate the Thracians, and expelled the latter from the island. Alcaios, still grieving for his brother, and weary of the fighting and sailing, stayed behind. Heracles entrusted the administration of the island to him.

Heracles sailed on and arrived at Torone on the southwestern edge of the heavily wooded peninsula of Sithonia, one of the three fingers of Chalcidice that extend into the sea. On the long beach of thick yellow sand he was challenged to a wrestling match by Polygonos and Telegonos, sons of Proteus, an Egyptian who had settled in Thrace. Heracles was always in the mood for a good grappling bout, but the two jumped on him simultaneously, seeking to do him harm. After a bit of a struggle, for they were as sneaky and slippery as their grand-sire, Heracles killed them.

At the Thessalian town of Meliboea, Heracles parted company with the sons of Aiacos, since he wished to complete the journey home on foot. With Iolaos as his shield-bearer, Heracles crossed Thessaly, and then passed through Boetia. Coming near Thebes, Heracles greatly desired to visit with his mother. By now he had grown back all of his hair, and his beard was once again thick.

Alcmene lived still in the house of Amphytrion, on the left of the Electrian gate, and was still honored greatly by the people. Heracles' old Thracian nurse, Geropso, seeing him in the courtyard, would have cried out in delight had not Heracles hushed her with a finger to his lips. He crept to his mother's apartment and found her sitting at her warp-weighted loom, carefully teasing the white wool into a long garment while humming a gentle tune that he remembered from his infancy. He stood at the doorway unseen, contemplating the tall woman with dark eyes who seemed charmed with the gifts of Aphrodite. From her fine hair, the color of fired bronze, held together at the nape by a gold filigree ornament, to the jewel-clasped sandals on her delicate white feet, she seemed not to have aged at all since he saw her last before the madness struck him. It was said that she surpassed the tribe of womankind in beauty, height and wisdom; all of these things seemed true.

Heracles leaned too heavily on the door, and the hard wood groaned under the weight. Startled, Alcmene turned to look. Seeing her son, she dropped her heddle rod, sprang to her feet, and ran into his arms. She sighed and wept, unable to form words. Heracles bent his head, burying his face in her fragrant hair, as he did as a child. As she kissed his face and neck, he felt warmed by a mother's love, as boundless as the Ocean Stream.

"Dearest son," said she, leading him to the couch. "My heart is near to bursting with joy now that I see you again with my own eyes—so often have I dreamed of this day! Let me look at you. Your hands are rough and calloused. This finger! and these scars upon your shoulders—what have they done to you, my boy? Listen to me!  A mother always sees her swaddled child, no matter how big he is!  What brings you here back to your mother?  Are your Labors complete?  Iphicles keeps me informed as well as he can, but I only imagine where your adventures take you from day to day."

Heracles responded: "I am only passing through on my way back to Mycenae, mother.  I had to go afar off—to those wild women called the Amazons—to fetch a little thing for Eurystheus. But as I saw the marble heights of Thebes gleaming in the sun, the thought of you gnawed my heart.  I was afraid how you would receive me."

"You will always find me here, Heracles," said Alcmene.  "I spend my days at the loom, thinking of times past and wishing only for your happiness.  Have you seen Megara since—"

"I cannot face her—not yet," said Heracles, his breast heaving with a heavy heart.  "She hates me, and rightly so; but I am trying, dear mother, to atone for my awful deeds."

"She does not hate you, Alcides," said Alcmene; "but her grief has changed her.  The world becomes a different place when you are left bereft.  All the beauty that is life—the rising sun, the odor of springtime, the warmth of an embrace—these seem to vanish like the dew of morning.  Had I not other childen, I would want an end to my days. When you are ready, Megara will be waiting."

"And tell me, mother," said Heracles with knitted brows. "Has Zeus ever come to you again since the night I was conceived?"

Alcmene, blushing, replied: "Why do you ask?  Am I not already the most blessed among women for bearing his son?  Does Zeus need again to humble his majesty?"

"I often wish that I could see my sire face to face," said Heracles.  "Were I a common man, there would be no basis for my desire.  But since I have been given such gifts as of only mortal men can dream, I would think that he has some better purpose for me."

"You do not need to see the blessed gods to be the man you were born to be," said Alcmene.  "See how the world is already a better place because of you, cleared of dangerous beasts and evil men.  That is your purpose, Heracles. Men everywhere are inspired by your fortitude, temperance, prudence and sense of justice. It has been so since you were a child. You were a bit impetuous, but always of a noble heart. Amphytrion used so say of you: 'He is a hard-headed boy; but let him be and he will find his way.'"

Heracles took her slender hands in his and kissed them. She called for a pot of the lentil broth he so enjoyed, and he ate while telling her of his adventures. That evening, he took his leave (she wept only after he had left for fear of offending him, crying to Zeus: "Why did you afflict my son Heracles with such a restless spirit?") and continued to the house of Iphicles. Through a window he saw a joyful Iolaos showing Iphicles his Trojan shield before the warm hearth-fire, and could not bear to interrupt. He felt Iphicles never forgave him for killing his sons, as well as robbing from him the affections of Iolaos. So he left Iolaos with his father and mother for a much needed rest after sharing in his Labors, and left the city. On the springy turf within an oak grove he lay to rest, watching the starry heavens until the wheeling Bootes' Wain was lost in the wake of the morning star.

Queen Hera paced to and fro across the brazen floor of her palace on high Olympos. Dark-colored birds—crows and ravens—continually brought her news about the son of Zeus whom she detested, as she hated all of the illicit offspring of her husband. Heracles had survived already nine superlative feats at home and abroad: and so Hera pondered how next to ensure a certain death for him. She remembered that in the far uncharted west of the world there lived the strongest mortal alive—yes, stronger even than the mighty Heracles. He was named Geryones, the son of Chrysaor, ruler of the misty land of Tartessos, rich in gold silver. He owned a herd of red cattle, tinged by the sun's waning light. What if Heracles was commanded to bring the herd back to Mycenae? Hera delighted in the audacity of her plan. The task would involve an endless number of hardships, any one of which could result in grave injury or death. She knew that as long as she did not kill him outright, she could not be accused of breaking her oath to Zeus All-Seeing. Securing her chamber door by the secret lock known only to her, she called out for a Dream to serve her.

"Go," said she to the wispy Dream hovering before her, "and enter into the mind of Eurystheus as slumber douses his eyes. Tell him that Heracles will soon return from his latest assignment no worse for the wear. He therefore must send him out on his most exacting Labor yet to fetch the cattle of Chrysaor, wealthiest of all kings, which he pastures in far-off Erytheia, sacred to me, in the great Ocean beyond even the most westerly spur of the world. He must acquire the cattle without either demand or payment and bring them back to you. This surely will be the end of this son of Zeus: for even if he survives stealing the cattle, the journey back will prove dolorous, so will I plague him along the way, besides the natural dangers from evil men and wild beasts, pathless ways and forbidding mountain ranges, he will encounter. Allow him no rest; send him immediately. Burden his mind with the strain of yet another adventure that will take him far from home for months and years. Heracles, you see, is like a blind man groping in the dark. The fool does not know that all of his struggles are for naught. He will never find the peace he seeks, even after saving half the world." The Dream nodded and flew off, straight out of a window, and down from the snowy peaks of Olympos. Across the Thessalian plain he sped, teeming with wild horses with their thundering hooves, across the River Spercheos, grazed Mount Parnassos mantled with laurel, then continued over Orchomenos, thick with flocks, until he reached King Eurystheus behind the strong walls of Mycenae. The king had just retired, nestled comfortably in his bedclothes, thinking of how long it had been since Heracles had gone: that death had probably, happily conquered him at last. His throne was safe now, and no blood was on his hands: for the ghost of Heracles would never be able to find him from such a faraway place. Then just as the mind falls away into the abyss of sweet slumber, the Dream, taking the form of Sthenelos, his father, appeared next to the bed and relayed the message sent by Hera. Waking in disquietude, the king waited for Dawn in her all her loveliness to grace the sky, hoping that the news of Heracles' imminent arrival was merely a passing nightmare's vagary.

Heracles that very day arrived. As he waited in the great hall, Admete, daughter of Eurystheus, hesitantly came forward to take Hippolyte's girdle from him. As soon as she had entered the hall, she saw that the thing in Heracles' hands was not the delicate girdle she imagined, that symbol of the Amazon's virginal ideal, but a broad baldric stained with sweat and blood. Her disappointment faded somewhat when she beheld closely the golden buckle and precious jewels inlaid in the tough leather. Thanking Heracles, she ran off with it, quickly, peeking abashedly once behind her. When Eurystheus saw his daughter in possession of the girdle, he turned ashen-faced and locked his door. Summoning Copreus, who at that moment sat at breakfast—and who tarried not in obeying his lord's summons, hastily slipping into his herald's robe—Eurystheus informed him of Heracles' next errand, and dispatched him to the main hall. Heracles smarted at not seeing the king, feeling that after such a long and arduous journey, his presence before the hero was warranted. Yet Copreus flattered him with gracious words in the manner of a herald, who learns his art from Hermes messenger of the gods, and soothed his spirit up to the point of divulging his next Labor.

Perhaps Heracles should have been prepared for the craftiness of king Eurystheus. After being sent afar on his longest and most dangerous Labor yet, Heracles had imagined that the tenth and final one could not be any more outrageous. He had been ready for anything as he returned triumphantly with the Amazonian prize, but seeing his mother and brother again made him long for the warmth of the hearth-stone and the quiet and pleasurable company of family as he used to know it. For an unguarded moment he thought of Megara: of the way he used to lie in her arms on their wide four-posted bed; while his children, fresh from the morning, ran in to pile upon him. But reality showed now a grimmer face, and he knew that never again could he regain those precious moments. Weary of the endless hardship, he wished to dispense with his mental anguish. But there was still much of him required, however, as he soon learned.

Copreus relayed the message to Heracles as he had heard it hastily from Eurystheus, leaving nothing out. Yet the instructions lacked detail on how to reach the kingdom of Chrysaor at the bounds of earth; or how Heracles was to accomplish the feat of fetching his cattle. At that time few sailors dared venture far across the Sea, and much less beyond land into Ocean.

Heracles surrendered to Copreus Hippolyte's gold-spangled robe, but kept her battle-axe for himself. The belt and robe

Eurystheus deposited at the Heraion, the great sanctuary to Argive Hera perched on a mountain terrace overlooking the plain between Tyrins and Mycenae.

On his way to Tyrins, Heracles raised his eyes and prayed:

"Hail!  Father!  Most High!
Lord of Dicte, King of the sky,
Guide me in days ahead
Where to the world's verge,
And the Ocean's star-lit edge,
On a perilous quest I'm led.
Athena was first at Perseus' side,
To swell his strength and pride,
When to torrid Libya he hied
To hunt the Gorgon's scaly hide;
From Hermes: an adamantine scythe,
And sandals to give him flight.
The Gray Ones were plunged in night
When he snatched their only eye.
Only from Hera have I gifts:
Madness and misery, boundless and swift;
Of mankind by awful deeds bereft:
I dare not hands to heaven lift.
Grant me, mighty Zeus, a sign
That thou make my orisons thine."

At the conclusion he saw an eagle circling, and then flying away into the west.  He took this as a propitious sign.  For this task he needed experienced sailors who knew the seas, and there was no better place to organize such an expedition than at Crete.  He sent word to Iolaos at Thebes, who returned to Tyrins in the company of Iphicles and Telamon.  The son of Aiacos had parted with his brother after an argument, and was on his way back to Aegina; but on hearing that Heracles was again on the move, he could not pass up another adventure.  Heracles nearly wept when he saw his brother, and wanted to embrace him, but held back for the sake of manly dignity, and also because he did not know how Iphicles would receive him.  For a long time Iphicles stared hard at him. The death of his two children was still raw in his heart, and he could not see past the madness to the man. Heracles noticed the anger in his brother's face, and extending his hands said: "Brother, when we were young, our father Amphytrion called for me when he needed strength, but you when he needed wisdom. I resented you when I was banished to the mountain-slope. You stayed behind, continuing to enjoy vittles from the table and our mother's tender caresses. Yet in our childhood I never ceased being your keeper, saving you from the wild beasts and lifting you from the swollen rivers as we spent our days in the wild wood. I can never bring back to the upper air the children I took from you. With you I share this greater pain, for I killed my own children, and a greater number of them. They also I shall never see again under the light of the life-giving sun. Come with me now: share in my struggles that you may see how I daily pay the wages for my sin. Forgive me, brother. Let us walk this wide world together once again." Heracles bowed his neck in humility. Iphicles looked at Iolaos, overwhelmed that his own son had shown more compassion than he; and seeing the mountain of a man weighed down with contrition, he laid his arms around his brother's neck and wept. The two embraced for the first time since that dark day. But deeper things still gnawed at his heart.

When Iolaos heard Heracles speak of Crete, he said: "Do you not recall how you killed the four sons of Minos on Paros? King Minos will not receive us as kindly as he did the first time. And besides, what if princess Phaidra drafts me back into the fraternity of bull leapers?"

"A good point, Iolaos!" responded Heracles. "But the sons of Minos were first at fault, and proper justice was meted out to them. It seems to me that Minos was ready to rid himself of them, for why else would they take refuge on Paros under an admirer of Rhadamanthys? I will take my chances in Crete in order to gather a crew of the best sailors for this present assignment. As for you Iolaos, did you not tell me that Theseus, on his journey to Crete, disguised two of his men as women? Take you then the same disguise! Your hair is already long, and hardly a beard grows on your face. Wrap yourself in a mantle, veil your face, slip some sandals on your dainty feet and anoint yourself with fragrant oil. The disguise will carry you far!" All laughed at the good-natured taunts of Heracles; even Iphicles, who with a finger poked his son in the ribs. Iolaos did not appreciate the jest, but after further consideration, considered the prospect of renewed bull leaping a greater evil than the insult to his manhood, and so went off to the market to find women's clothes.

They took passage on a Cretan ship at Nauplia. A knot of soldiers, present on every Cretan merchant ship above a certain size as a safeguard against pirates, eyed them suspiciously, but did nothing to stop them. From the sailors, Heracles learned that Minos was ready to send his fleet against Athens to revenge himself on Theseus, as soon as the ships the latter stove on his escape were repaired, for they had blocked up the harbor of Cnossos. Knowing this disturbed him somewhat, for he did not wish it known that they were boon companions, and neither that Theseus should come to harm, since the Cretan navy was the most powerful in the world.

They made land first near the outflow of the river Charadros, which watered the Thyreatic plain at it southern extremity, one of the most fertile plains of the Peloponnese. The coastal strip, nestled between the spurs of Mount Parnon, was lush with grains and grasses, waving in the breeze like a green and golden sea. They did not stay very long. The barbarous Cynurians kept watch from their huts on the eastern slopes of the mountain and sometimes attacked visiting ships. They were one of the most ancient tribes of Lacedaimonia, believing their ancestors had sprung from the earth, as the Athenians did. But there was no doubt that they were of Pelasgian stock, smaller and darker-hued than the Greeks.

Assisted by a northwesterly breeze, they sailed on, but a headwind caught them not soon afterwards. The waters off the coast grew choppy, and not wishing yet to head into open sea, they turned in at one of the small capes of Brasiai that project gently to the sea. There a dispute arose between the Cretans and some local townspeople, who believe, unlike the Cretans—holding the opinion of the Argives—that when Semele bore Dionysos to Zeus, Cadmos put her and the godling into a chest; and they say the waves washed them up there. The people interred Semele with honors and brought up Dionysos. That is the reason they changed the name of their town, which used to be called something else, to its present one, on account of the waves washing up things. Furthermore, they say the tragic Ino, in her wanderings, came there and became a nurse to Dionysos. This idea was at least accepted by the Cretans, but when some demanded proof of these claims, they were shown a grotto where Ino allegedly suckled the divine son of Semele. On a promontory under which they harbored, they found four bronze statues, each not more than a foot high, with caps on their heads. None could explain who these were, except one of them looked like Athena. Heracles laughed at them since they were so puny.

As the sun grew red around the mountains, and the starry darkness crept upon them from the east, they sailed into the fine natural harbor of Zarax, a town of wattled houses built on a promontory. The harbor, on its northern side, provided a peaceful anchorage protected by cliffs, and was accessible through a narrow inlet. They saw none but fishermen with their nets. Some Cretans made a fire and slept on the beach; but Heracles and his companions slept on the ship, rocking gently in the cove.

When morning came, they weighed anchor and continued on. The rising sun to clarboard was bursting through the clouds, and the rosy fingers of Dawn reflected crimson against the white sail. All hands manned the oars against a headwind: the struggle turned some minds to wish to land briefly at Epidauros. The people there say they are descendants of Epidaurians from the Argolid, who, landing on the Lascanian shore on their way to the island of Kos, were visited by dreams and omens, chiefly involving a snake they had brought with them, which escaped and slithered into the sea. The captain, saying that he was behind schedule, would not acquiesce, and ordered the galleymaster to push on. The last stop they made before heading into the open sea was at Nymphaion harbor, on a southern bulge of the peninsula, just west of Cape Malia. There the sea lane was thick with ships since the weather was clear and the waters, normally treacherous, flowed with unusual calmness. King Minos ordered all ships returning from the Peloponnese to lay offerings there at a standing statue of Poseidon. From a spring in a cave close by the sea they also filled their water-jars, for the harbor at Zarax was ill-watered and they wanted to be prepared for the most precarious portion of their journey.

Leaving the rocky headland of Cape Malia behind them, they plunged on into the wide blue-black sea. When the rocky tips of distant Cythera were lost from sight, they raised sails and prayed to Poseidon for a safe journey. They did not ship their oars, however, so as to make Crete before dusk. Iolaos, despite having twice made the trip, kept his back to the mast, peering out in all directions in the hope of spotting the small, midsea island of Aegilia. At last, with the red sun dipping into the western horizon, crimsoning the waters like the spilled blood of sacrifice, they spotted the bold snow clad summits of the White Mountains of Crete and all hearts lifted. Then a sailor up in the crow's nest cried he saw a line of dark-blue sails with red devices off to the west. The captain rushed to the foredeck to peer with his own eyes. Soldiers surrounded him, speaking excitedly among themselves; but since they spoke Cretan, neither Heracles nor his companions understood; save Iolaos, who had picked up a word or two during his sojourn on the island. They said, Iolaos believed, that the royal ships of king Minos were leaving Crete. As they drew nearer they could see now the king's galley, larger than the rest, with the figurehead of a bull, riding the waves in the center of the flotilla. Heracles for a moment grew concerned that they sailed after Theseus. He was ready, if necessary, to slay the soldiers, commandeer the ship and ram Minos' vessel. The bearing of that action on Theseus' safety, however, was doubtful; and it would assuredly result in his death and that of his companions. Iphicles, perhaps knowing what ideas passed through his brother's head, gripped his shoulder in a cautionary manner. Then, happily, Heracles realized the ships were heading in a north-westerly direction; and what sailed did not seem to be the bulk of Crete's navy, only a royal entourage. He felt pleased that he had not acted rashly.

After furling the sails, they threaded their way through the ships crowding the river-mouth of the port of Amnisus and moored by a long, high wharf. Gaily-dressed gentry mixed with laborers on the quay-side, a general tumult running through the crowd. The soldiers debarked first, and joined a waiting contingent. As they conversed, they looked shipward up at Heracles, who, gathering his companions (Iolaos having donned his disguise under the ridicule of the sailors), led them down the plank. One of the captains began to walk toward them; but when he saw Heracles heave his massive club across his shoulder, he turned to other affairs. They heard pure Greek now, as well as Cretan mixed with Greek, and soon learned the cause of all the excitement. The artisan Daidalos, whom Minos imprisoned in the Labyrinth for his role in Theseus' escape, had managed to make his way to the rugged coast with his son Icaros, from where, it was believed, he mysteriously procured a ship and fled the island. Upon hearing of this, Minos grew so enraged that he determined to go after Daidalos himself: for although he wished to keep Daidalos in perpetual punishment, he did not want any other city to enjoy the marvels born of his mind and hands. Daidalos was chiefly responsible for much of Crete's thalassocracy, having designed a special mast, yards and sail that could propel a warship through any type of wind and water. It would have been disastrous for Crete had he offered his services elsewhere.

Iolaos thought he saw princess Phaidra carried upon a litter near the royal quay, and not fully trusting his disguise, hid squarely behind Heracles. Heracles was relieved that Minos had gone off and that he had been able to arrive on Crete unmolested. He lost no time in preparing for the expedition, sending Iphicles and Telamon off to secure a ship while he tried to form a worthy crew of those who knew the sea. Heracles, however, stood out by his uncommon size among the small-statured Cretans, and soon a curious, gibbering crowd of onlookers surrounded him. He was recognized immediately by his club and lion's mane, and hardly anyone failed to remember the great favor he had done Crete by ridding it of the marauding bull. Here and there among the crowd, however, some angry voices rose. "There is the man who killed the sons of our king!" cried one who came running. The notice spread like fire, and the people began to murmur. In response, the captain of the guard made his way back to the ships, leading his soldiers heavily armed with long spears and bucklers. Seeing them, Heracles growled, and cutting for himself a swath through the mass of bodies surrounding him, prepared to meet the challengers head on. Just then three bare-headed royal courtiers, bejeweled and wearing colored loin-cloths, breathlessly intercepted them with solemn deprecations. Behind them servants walked solemnly but quickly, bearing a large litter on their shoulders. One courtier parted the purple fringed curtains and flipped the corners upward. Within reclined a fair woman with long, golden hair, crimped and studded with gems, flowing from beneath a wide bonnet. Her tight bodice lay open to the waist, exposing half a pendulous breast on each side;

and her flounced, lace petticoat, ringed around the hem with bells and pomegranates, flared out from her narrow waist down to her ankles. She tapped the side of the litter with her scepter, and the bearers crouched to lower it.  Dropping one foot wrapped in a chamois boot, then another, she stepped out from the litter and walked toward Heracles between a corridor of awed Cretans, who bowed deeply and remained so.

"I am Queen Pasiphaë," said she, crossing her white arms. She was evidently of Greek blood, so much taller and fairer was she than her subjects. "I did not have the pleasure of meeting you the last time you were in Crete, although when I learned what you did I was sore vexed: for I dearly loved the bull you took away.  Your nephew—his name I forgot—remained some time with us.  Has he returned with you?"

Heracles glanced about him but could not find Iolaos, who had slipped into the crowd when he saw the queen's litter approaching.

"Mighty Queen, it was not my intention to deprive you of your sacred bull," said Heracles, bowing before her. "I was ordered to bring it to Mycenae by king Eurystheus of the Argives, and he was no doubt compelled by some oracle to make me do it.  I am but his slave, and am sent about the world to perform various deeds and bring him back exotic gifts.  Had I known the bull of Crete meant so much to you, I would have defied even the heavenly powers to allow him to remain.  But in my task I had the blessing of king Minos himself, who told me the bull was a nuisance and responsible for many outrages.  I am happy to report, at the very least, that it runs now free and happy on the plain of Marathon, munching on new grass and coupling whenever it desires."

"Then tell me, Heracles, your business here." said Pasiphaë. "You find us at a very unsettling time.  First that young Athenian kills my son Asterion and escapes, and now my lord goes off suddenly in a pursuit.  Britomartis preserve us!  Have you any knowledge about these things?"

Heracles answered: "My lady, I know nothing about that Athenian you speak of, and I shall not speak ill of him since the Furies will surely take their share.  I only wish upon you a greater fruitfulness that you may replace the son you lost.  As for lord Minos, I pray that the gods deliver him pursued quickly into his hands, whoever he may be. I have returned to Crete due to the excellence of your ships and the great skill of your mariners in the hope of organizing an expedition to help me accomplish my next Labor from king Eurystheus. I ask your leave and blessing, O Queen, to do that."

Pasiphaë tapped her scepter against her forearm, signaling her servants to bring up the litter behind her. She was helped inside by her courtiers. Before drawing closed the curtains she fluttered her dark eyes at Heracles and announced he was free to do as he wished, with support from the palace, as long he did one thing first: he was to rid the land around Cnossos of bears, wolves, snakes and other dangerous creatures. This was to be his penance for stealing from Crete her sacred bull. Heracles, taking Iolaos with him, ranged the forests and wooded foothills and destroyed so many injurious creatures that to this day Crete remains free of them. When he returned to the port city a fortnight later, fortunate to have escaped the hot Cretan sun by hunting in the cool shade of the wood, his companions stood ready to depart in a sharp-keeled ship. Telamon and Iphicles had assembled a fine crew that included thirty stout oarsmen, mostly Cretan, but also of other nations; a sun-burnt Egyptian helmsman named Thamuz; and a Phoenician master with a falcon nose who claimed he had once sailed to Hesperia for tin. A native of Argos joined them also: handsome Antores, an erstwhile acquaintance of Heracles, who had fled from his city for siding with Athens in some dispute.

14

After Daidalos, by his artful contrivance, built a mechanical bull so that Pasiphaë could consummate her unnatural passion, king Minos, fearing Poseidon, dared not kill the offspring. And instead of immediately punishing the artifex, he ordered him to build the Labyrinth as a prison for the Minotaur: a maze from living rock so intricate, with winding paths that doubled back and tricked the eyes that it seemed not even the builder himself could find a way out.

Ever after Daidalos lived in fear of Minos. When Theseus was imprisoned in the Labyrinth, and Ariadne, falling in love with him, implored Daidalos for assistance, he did so grudgingly, and against his better judgment. He gave her a clew, with which Theseus could find his way out of the maze by tying one end of it to the entrance-gate, and unwinding it as he made his way through the dark corridors. Afterward, by winding the thread back up, he could easily find his way out. Minos was so outraged by the brazen escape of Theseus and the death of the Minotaur, whom he had come to value as a tool of his power, that he imprisoned Daidalos, and his son Icaros, born to one of his slaves, in the very structure the craftsman designed: for, after all, there could only have been one man in Crete wise enough to help Theseus escape.

Now Daidalos was of the Athenian royal family, being the son of Alcippe and Metion, the son of Eupalamos, the son of Erechtheus. He lived at Athens, from whence his fame spread through the world. He honed his skill first with statuary, being the first to open the eyes and the feet, and to extend the hands, which for stability had always been carved close by the sides. His sculptures of wood and bronze were so life-like that bystanders would long gaze at them, expecting them to speak or blink their eyes. Indeed, some of his statues could move on their own, or speak, and how this was done remains a great mystery. He worked also in white stone, which he preferred for figures of the gods. It is said that he invented those tools so useful to craftsmen: the axe, the plumb-line, the gimlet and mucilage to fasten together disparate things. He tried to take credit also for the saw; but that implement, however, was invented by his nephew Talos, son of his sister Polycaste, whom he took as his apprentice when the boy, merely twelve years old, came across a serpent's jawbone; and using it to cut a stick in two, copied the same design in iron. He followed this marvel with a refinement to the potter's wheel, whereby the potter could turn it by a pedal underfoot, as well as the compass to mark out circles. Daidalos soon grew acutely jealous of his nephew, and leading him to the roof of Athena's temple on the Acropolis on the pretense that he wanted to show him the sights of city, pushed him over the edge so that the boy fell headlong onto the jutting rocks. Tortured by guilt and remorse, he rushed down and carried off the corpse in a sack, thinking to bury it secretly. Challenged by some citizens, he announced that he had collected a dead serpent according to the law. In this evasion he was not altogether untruthful, for Talos was also of the royal line of Erechtheus, who was descended from Erichthonios. When Athena one day visited Hephaistos' workshop, wanting to fashion some arms, the latter, having been abandoned by Aphrodite, burned with desire for her. He chased Athena, and catching her after much effort, for he was lame, he tried to have union with her. The virgin goddess, outraged, pushed him away, causing him to spill his seed on her leg. Repulsed, she wiped away the seed with a piece of wool, which, after she had thrown it to the earth, engendered Erichtohonios. Athena took the child, and wishing to make him immortal, reared him in secret. She placed him in a chest, entrusted it to Pandrossos, daughter of earth-born Cecrops, the first king of Athens. When her curious sisters opened the chest, they beheld a snake coiled up next to the babe. Driven mad by the Athena they cast themselves from the Acropolis.

But there being bloodstains on the sack, Daidalos was apprehended and tried for murder. Found guilty, he was banished from the city. Talos was buried where he had fallen, his soul flying off in the form of a partridge; and his mother hanged herself. The Athenians later built a sanctuary beside the Acropolis to honor her. Daidalos settled in Attica, but hounded by the people, fled across the sea to Crete.

One of Minos' slaves, Naucrate, bore Daidalos a son, Icaros, who with him Minos entombed in the Labyrinth. Having entrusted to Ariadne the clew for her lover's benefit, Daidalos found himself and his young son hopelessly lost within the maze's winding ways. Sheer rock faces surrounded them at every turn. High above, they could see only strips of blue sky through the impending boughs of dark ilex, or the twinkling massing of stars at night. Settling down in despair, Daidalos looked at his son in grief, remembering the cruel murder of his young nephew, close in age. As the gloom deepened, he noticed the feathers strewn around him, dropped by countless birds crossing over the twisting caverns. He glanced upward to see a skein of geese pass overhead, flapping their wings in formation, bellowing their cautious cries. His devious mind revived. "Take these feathers up, my son," he cried. "Bring them all to me!" While Icaros gathered the downy quills, of all colors and sizes, Daidalos collected the wax from spent candles. With his materials assembled, he set to work. Melting the wax on flat stones whenever the sunlight spilled over the high walls, he used it to weld together the smaller feathers. The larger ones he tied together with threads unwound from his own clothing. From thin dead branches he constructed frames on which to affix the feathers, and in time constructed two pairs of wings, a large pair for himself and a smaller one for Icaros. Having keenly studied the structure and mechanics of birds' wings, he made the artificial ones articulate precisely, imitating nature down to the proper alignment and position of the quills. He practiced first by himself, running to and fro through the narrow corridors while flapping his wings, until he could lift his body from the ground. Then he taught his son to do the same, and the student soon surpassed the teacher in dexterity. "Dearest son, we will soon take to the air," said Daidalos when the day had come to attempt escape. "But heed my warning: neither fly too high lest the sun melt the delicate wax of your wings; nor fly too low when we are over the wide sea, lest the surging spray weigh your feathers down." He helped his son with the downy gear, and then slipped on his own, heeding the boy to follow him closely. Running swiftly and flapping earnestly down the longest and widest pathway he could find, their heavy bodies grew lighter than air and up they soared through the craggy chasm. The sprawling Labyrinth lay below them like an exposed honeycomb. Daidalos marveled for a moment at the breathtaking brilliance of his own design, then looked back to make sure his son still followed. But as they neared the northern shore, Daidalos, old as he was, realized, in the face of the endless sea stretching before them, that he could not much longer strain his desperate arms. With a cry of despair he stopped his flapping and tried to glide down to where land still welcomed him, certain his son would follow. Tumbling roughly into the shingle, he spied a wavering speck against the sky and cried out for his son, but to no avail. The boy, exulting in his new-found power, flew higher and higher until he joined in company with the birds. But the bare heat enveloped him. The hardened wax gave way and fell in droplets from his pinions. His feathery frame unraveled and down he fell at twice the speed of his ascent. Daidalos watched helplessly from the beach as his son plunged afar into the dark waves, resulting in splash of white foam, as when the dead, leafless branch of an overhanging tree, dislodged by the wind, falls into a river and is carried away by the rippling water. The father tore his shirt in grief, and defiled his head with dust. A partridge alighted on an ilex branch above him and twittered felicitously.

From the Cnossian heights, Pasiphaë's spies spotted the intrepid father and son; the queen was still solicitous for the obliging craftsman. She ordered her servants to find Daidalos and bring him succor. They hid him in a village on the coast until he could devise another means of escape. After the slaying of the Minotaur, Minos kept all ships under military guard; and all vessels in or out of the harbor were dutifully searched. Daidalos therefore decided to build his own ship, smaller and faster than any of the rest. Pasiphaë had her bodyguard—all loyal men from her native Colchis—supply him whatever materials he needed. It was not his own preservation which motivated him, but faith that his son had survived the fall and, driven by the sea, had taken refuge on some small outlying rock. And so Daidalos built two small ships, one he would steer, the other—strangely, wondrously—that could sail itself. He devised a new type of sail, improving on the design he had given Minos, to lie across a specialized frame of yardarms that could be articulated in any direction to catch and manipulate the wind for propulsion. When ready, he launched first the mechanical automaton in a northwesterly course, while he himself sailed northeast toward where Icaros plunged, after seeing the fleet of Minos take to sea in hot pursuit.

## 15

The pious Iphicles sacrificed two bleating ewes: one to Apollo for the disembarkation and the other to Poseidon for a tranquil sea and favorable winds. When such a one blew from the south, the sailors took to the benches and rowed smoothly out of the harbor. They raised the mast into its crutch, tightened the forestays, and unfurled the sail. With a bellied sheet the ship cut the waves, leaving mountainous Crete astern.

They stopped first at Aegilia, mid-way between Crete and holy Cythera. The Dog Star had appeared a fortnight before and the sun now beat mercilessly upon their heads. The rocky island afforded little shelter, and so they did not long remain there. By nightfall they arrived at Cythera, nestling into a natural harbor. Great breakers pummeled the coast, jostling the ship around its mooring; they had to haul the ship deep into the sand, securing her with shoring timbers. As that work took the better part of the night, the crew rested until morning around their campfires. As Dawn in her saffron robe hastened from her bed, an astonishing site left the rising sailors bewildered. Half of a clam-shell, as large as a hide-bound shield, lay on the beach. Half the men believed it was the very shell upon which Aphrodite, born from the foam, washed ashore. After pouring libations to the Goddess of Love, and rubbing themselves with myrtle and rose petals from a nearby combe, they pushed off. Heracles found the treacly odor emanating from the men distasteful, but there was nothing he could do about it. He had examined the shell and found it quite an ordinary, albeit unusually large, natural specimen.

The next few days proved uneventful. Winds abaft held steady and the days were clear. Crossing a wide gulf, they struggled around the peninsula of Messenia, deeply indented with many coves and rocky harbors. The Phoenician master intended to drive on toward Zacynthos, in keeping with their westerly direction.   But as they left the mainland astern, the sky grew dark in the north and the breeze abated, portending a storm.   As they sailed on the darkness overtook them, with great blue-black clouds crowding the sky, until they could not discern between day and night.   The rain fell in heavy, lashing sheets; the winds rolled the waves under them so that one moment the prow seemed ready plunge into the swirling abyss, and the next leaping to touch heaven.   Mingled with the deluge came lightning flashes and long-sounding thunder that seemed to rattle the timbers under their feet.   Through all this the dusky helmsman kept himself lashed to the tiller, although he could not know where the fierce storm carried them.   For two days the ship, surrounded by a constant darkness, was buffeted by the unruly sea. At last mountains rose in the distance, and the shining Pole Star irrupted through the dark cloudfront. The men strained at the oars, making for landfall, where they could find mercy from the heady billows.  Before them stretched a long island, broken up by narrow channels.  The shipmaster immediately recognized it as Sphacteria, and directed the ship around it, where they would find sandy Pylos[4]; it was possible to cut through the channels only in calm weather. Once behind the island, which acted like a jetty, they were protected from the winds and violent breakers, and could enter the deep bay of Pylos in relative calm.  After securing the vessel to the mooring-stakes, the exhausted crewmen shuffled onto the quay and ran off to find shelter.  In the morning, with the sky as clear as if nothing had happened, they came back to examine the ship.  The storm had torn away planks from the hull port-side, several oars were lost, and parts of the vessel needed to be re-caulked and tarred.  As they had lost their tar pot, some men went into the port-town, located up a gradual slope on a promontory, to buy another; while others sought additional timber to repair the ship or construct new oars.   The coastland, however, seemed devoid of good trees, covered instead in clumps of gray-green sage, yellow broom and other shrubs that

---

[4] Several towns with the name Pylos claim the honor of being Nestor's city, including Pylos in Elis and Pylos in Triphylia. The prominence of Messenian Pylos, with the most spacious harbor of the Peloponnese, makes it the likely candidate.

grew from every orifice of the limestone protruding from the thin, red soil. The island protecting the harbor appeared well-wooded, but the master did not want to risk sailing the ship again until repairs were made. Heracles, therefore, taking Antores and Iphicles with him, headed inland toward the city proper, which they could see rising in the shape of innumerable white buildings from the rocky heights, to find some stout timber. But as they moved up the road, they saw a procession coming down to the beach by another way, marching in holy silence, leading twelve black bulls that had never know a yoke, their glossy hides twinkling in the sunlight leaping from the bay. They stopped, divided into groups, and dug shallow trenches or heaped rocks and sticks into cairns to prepare for the sacrifice. Overlooking them, lying on a couch covered in soft grey fleece, an old man, greatly advanced in years, age pollarding his head into nothing more than stringy white beard, offered counsel to eleven stout men and one youth who sat around him like whelps around a hoary lion.

"That must be Neleus, lord of Pylos," announced Antores. "Around him sit his twelve sons. It would do us well, Heracles, to approach and greet him, so that we may join in the sacrifice to Poseidon."

"Did not Iphicles already pour libations to Poseidon?" said Heracles doubtfully. "And see what good that did us? Leave any hope aside that prayer can turn the decree of the gods. Nevertheless, let us avail ourselves of their hospitality while the ship is repaired. See how they are firing up the pits. Soon they will roast the delicious flesh, and we end the poorer for not being pious."

King Neleus was the son of Poseidon, who ravished Tyro, the daughter of Salmoneus and Alcidice, on the banks of the river Enipeus. Tyro, ward of her cruel stepmother Sidero, who murdered the two sons she bore to her uncle Sisyphos, had fallen in love with the river-god; but Poseidon noticed him spurring her advances, and taking his form, decided to avail himself of Tyro's affection, consoling her afterward with the knowledge that she would bear twin sons. Tyro, however, out of shame exposed the children, and they were found by a passing horse-herder. One boy was named Neleus, and the other Pelias, since his face was marked with a black-and-blue bruise after being kicked by a brood-mare. Tyro later married her uncle Cretheus, who founded the city of

Iolcos. He took the boys as sons. After Cretheus' death, Pelias seized the throne and exiled Neleus, who, arriving in the land of Messene, founded Pylos. There he married and raised one daughter, Pero, and twelve sons: Tauros, Asterios, Pylaon, Deïmachos, Eurybios, Epilaos, Phrasios, Eurymenes, Evagoras, Alastor, Nestor and Periclymenos. The last became a conjuror.

As the three Argives approached over dunes of red sand, Nestor, the youngest son of Neleus, left his seat, and ran to greet them. Heracles marveled at the fluency of speech that poured from the young mouth. Taking Heracles by the hand, Nestor led them to his father.

"What? Heracles you say?" said Neleus, his frail eyes squinting up at them. "Are you a priest of Hera? We are all lord Poseidon's men here. Come hither, Melampos, you leech, don't let these men just stand there. Bring the cup of offering and put it in their hands. Let that one in Cretan garb have it first, for he is no doubt a devotee of the Earthshaker."

Melampos, wearing a gold-embroidered cape, entrusted a two-handled goblet to Antores, while an attendant poured in a little wine. Antores spilt the wine on the ground and prayed for Neleus and his sons, for Pylos, and for success on their journey to the lands of the west. The cup was likewise passed to Heracles and Iphicles, who parroted Antores' prayers before requesting a full measure of the sweet rich wine.

The old king burnt the first of the offerings: the shoulder-blades wrapped in fat and drizzled with wine. The smoke rose in winding coils, a savory odor for the god. The choicest fleshy parts were roasted on spits, and everyone had their fill. The king then asked Heracles what was his business. Heracles recounted his Labors, ending with the present one. Neleus thought he was spinning tales and laughed him to scorn, calling his latest adventure foolhardy at best. The ire of Heracles rose, filled as he was with hot meat and wine; but Melampos, the royal physician, took him aside and begged forgiveness for his king, who, though old, was still savage in his ways, reared as he was on mare's milk. Now this Melampos was not, as some believe, the Minyan, brother of Bias, who dwelt with Neleus for a time at Pylos. That Melampos was considered the first mortal endowed with the power of prophecy and the knowledge of haruspicy, as well as the first to practice the art of medicine. He also brought the worship of Dionysos to Greece. After leaving Messene, he ruled in Argos.

Melampos confidentially beseeched Heracles to take him along. He had spent his entire life at Pylos and was eager to see the world. Heracles remarked that the man's shoulders were broad, so he could row or fight if needed, but his hands were soft and his look studious. Heracles demurred and changed the subject.

After three days the ship, plugged with dripping beeswax and newly tarred, rode high in the harbor. The last crewman ashore unhitched the hawsers, coiled them around his arm, and threw them over the gunwale. As soon as he climbed the ladder aboard, oars dipped into the water. As the ship pushed off, they heard a cry. Melampos ran along the quay waving his arms, begging to be taken aboard. The ship lay now beyond reach, gliding out of the deep broad bay. Melampos unclasped his cape, stripped to his breech-clout, and plunged into the blue water. As swiftly as a dolphin he swam under the waves until he reached the ship, and then came up near the stern. Heracles threw a rope down at him and pulled him up, happy to see such drive and ambition.

From there fair winds carried them westward. It was the shipmaster's intent to stop off at the Strophades, but the helmsman, miscalculating their course, passed them leagues on their larboard. Not wishing to circle about in open sea, the crewmen bent at their oars, making for Zachyntos, until a tailwind relieved their labor, and they entered the harbor in the deep of night. The beach, surrounded by vertical walls, was covered by sea turtles burying their eggs in the sand. The men fell instantly upon the helpless creatures, ripping them open to pull out and cook the meat and tripes and immature eggs, while the fins they boiled for stew. They slept well that night amidst the discarded carapaces. Heracles, to guard the ship as usual, slept on a blanket spread out on the quarter deck.

Next they came to rugged Ithaca, grounding the ship high on the beach. The harbor there was deep, affording good shelter from the wind-lashed waves. As soon as they rested and revictualed the ship, they rowed on toward Drepane, the land of the Phaiacians. Since king Alcinoös was a kinsman of Sisyphos, and thus of Neleus, Melampos raised a fuss about stopping there, thinking word would get back to Neleus of his disloyalty. And so they continued up the strait instead, stopping briefly on the coast of Epirus. Heracles there organized the men in games of wrestling, running and jumping, thinking it would be beneficial for their worn muscles. It was a fine land, gently sloping, full of trees well-watered by springs.

A howling north wind kept them beached for two days. At the first break, they rowed beyond Drepane, making sail and turning westward as they neared the cliffs of Ceraunia in order to take the shortest route toward Hesperia, known also as Ausonia, a land only the master, the helmsman and one or two other crewmen had seen. At midday, from seemingly open sea, hazy blue hills rose up from the horizon, and then a low coastline frothed with white spray. The wind died and the canvas slackened. The men shipped oars and took their meal, looking wistfully at the land of the west, wondering what new sights awaited them. Refreshed, and with bellied sails once again, they furrowed the waves, following the coastline south to disembark at a narrow rocky strip to the lee side of the Iapygian promontory. That night they feasted well on the wild goat of the nearby craggy hills, courtesy of Heracles, who went off with his bow and came back bearing three kids across his shoulders.

The new day saw them crossing the wide bay of Tarentum. Hearts warmed anew when in the distance dim land appeared above the sea. The bold and rocky Lacinian headland, the termination of a branch of a great mountain range that forms the backbone of Hesperia, did not appear very inviting, and so they pressed to double another promontory, behind which opened a wide but shallow gulf. Mountains, densely forested, formed an impenetrable wall to their north. That night they disembarked on the western side of the gulf, where the rocky shore seemed less dangerous, and the hills-slopes, carpeted in wild-olive and purple vines, reached to the sea.

A fortnight after leaving Crete, they rounded the toe of Hesperia, jutting out boldly into the sea, for the whole land was said to be shaped like a buskin. The headland seemed so rugged, with crescent-shaped ridges running down it like a spine that Iphicles jested that at least one of its thrusting promontories be named after Heracles. Far across the waters none could miss Mount Etna, its crater-top glowing with fire and belching black smoke, displacing the fleecy clouds with inky blackness. And to their north, up a narrow strait, they could hear fearsome breakers pulverizing stones and crashing on thrusting reefs. The current seemed to pull them hither. "Row for your lives!" roared the Phoenician captain. "At the end of that narrow channel rise the crags of Scylla, and across it the whirlpool of Charybdis. Woe betide us if we're pulled into their lair!" With their hearts pounding and sweat bathing their limbs, the crewmen churned the waves, guided by the fiery mountain in the distance. Even Heracles took a seat, relieving the weary men, applying his massive arms to the stroke. As they neared Sicania, the waters grew thick with ash and floating white pumice, like the barley beer Egyptians drink through a straw.

At a natural harbor, wide and free of winds, they beached the ship and streamed out into the sand, weary bodies falling where they willed. When they awoke night had fallen. A mist seemed to cover the land, blotting out the moon and stars, with only the pulsating red flame at Etna's crown beckoning their eyes, like a lighthouse fire, which pierces the fog to allow ships safe harborage. Under their blankets the men huddled, listening to the low, distant rumbling of the fiery mount, under which it was said the snake-limbed Giant Encelados lay buried, felled by Athena's spear in that primeval, titanic struggle for supremacy. His awful breath boils forth in molten rock and thick smoke, and as he rolls from one side to the other in his discomfort, the whole land groans and shudders.

When rosy dawn burned away the shadows, and sweet dew sparkled on every limb, the men awoke to find that the island seemed rather pleasant, with soft meadows along the shore, and nearby a poplar-grove with fresh water bursting from a grotto. Bleating goats heckled them from the hills. This time no man surrendered his hunger to Heracles, but each one took up his spear or bow, and fanned out into the tree-covered island. They returned with plenty to eat and joyously feasted before their ship. When the master saw the sailors, their bellies full, prepared once again to stretch upon the strand, he roused them up, pointing a trembling finger at the woods. He said: "There live the Cyclopes, they say, fearsome giants with a single peering eye on their brows. They neither sow nor harvest, trusting only to the gods, who make their land pregnant with golden wheat and barley, and vines overweighed with grapes. They are lawless, and fearless, and kill any man who comes upon them. I do not know if they frequent the coast, but I do not want to be here to find out. Therefore let us push off and continue our journey." The sailors grumbled that they were being overworked and had not yet seen any reward for their labor. Such indolence raised the ire of Heracles, who stomped among them, dragging his club behind, leaving a deep furrow in the ground. Without a word from Heracles, the crewmen ran to the ship in fright.

They made several more stops down the coast that day, past fat marshlands, and then rounded the island rock of seagirt Pachynus, the extreme southeast corner of the island. From it and two other pointed promontories, the land bore also the name of Trinacria, since it had the shape of a triangle. But a violent wind sweeping down the western coast kept them at bay, forcing them to take shelter in a rocky cove. There they passed the night in misery, for there was nothing to eat or fresh water to drink, except for the provisions they had on board. As soon as the winds died down, the ship took to the waves again staying close inshore, coming around a headland as dawn burst behind their backs. There, through thick smoke, they saw an astonishing sight. In the harbor of the city of Inycum, ships burned with all-consuming fire. Most hulls were eaten down to their keels, but on a few vessels one could still see the melting paint of the prows. The Cretan sailors cried out in dismay, identifying the flotilla as that of Minos himself, the same that Heracles had seen sailing off the day he arrived in Crete. The Phoenician master urged caution, wishing to sail well-past that point. But Heracles, ever curious, compelled them to anchor up-wind from the burning ships, where he could disembark and investigate. Alone, he came ashore, and from a high point watched the Cretans sitting on the beach helplessly before their torched ships, surrounded by rings of well-armed Sicani. There had been a skirmish that left many corpses upon the sand. Heracles took the road up to the city's mighty ramparts. Before the gates swords clanged and spears flew between the Cretans and the Sicani, who overwhelmed the invaders. As it seemed every Cretan would be cut down, Heracles ran into their midst, taking up a fallen shield, and pushed back against the Sicani, with every swing of his club felling them by the dozens. A cheer rang from the Cretans, many of whom recognized the lion-maned hero. Heracles drove the Sicani back into the city. As the Cretans pressed on behind him, Heracles turned on them also, threatening to crush their heads if they came any nearer. Thus he stood before the two camps, preventing any more fighting between them. "Send me your leaders!" he cried. A short Cretan and a tall Sicani came forward. "These barbarians have killed king Minos and burned our fleet," said the Cretan admiral. Heracles turned to the Sicani captain, who responded: "They came here looking for Daidalos and threatened war upon us if king Cocalos did not deliver him." Heracles warned them to desist from fighting further while he went to the palace to speak to Cocalos, from whom he intended to get the complete story of the present conflict.

As Heracles approached the king's house, a spear flew at him from the parapet, which he caught on the shield he gripped in his right hand. Pulling out the quivering shaft, he sent it back from where it came, transfixing a Sicani through the chest. The shield Heracles now took under his arm, and coiling himself, cast it like quoit, dislodging the rest of the defenders from the roof. He burst through the doors, demanding to see the king. Thinking him sent by the Cretans, the palace attendants scattered and hid. Heracles stormed through the house until he found the king's chamber, and entering there, saw Cocalos, Daidalos and the corpse of king Minos upon a bier.

Daidalos, who resided still at Athens as Heracles fame began to spread, recognized the stalwart hero and commended him to the king, a kindly man who seem befuddled at all that had occurred. He took them into the banquet-hall, where plates of heaping food and bowls of wine were brought for Heracles; and as he ate, the king spoke thus: "I am a Greek, Heracles, as you can see by my fair skin and hair. I came to this land in my youth, and came to rule over a portion of the swarthy Sicani, teaching them an alphabet and building up this fine city with its tall, strong buildings and walls. Recently, this man Daidalos came to us from Crete, claiming sanctuary as a fugitive. I took him under my protection and soon marveled at the skills with which the gods have blessed him, for it seemed that whatever he touched took on life. Just the other day I hear a fleet had sailed into our harbor. It was that of king Minos of Crete. I welcomed him with all hospitality, treating him as befitted a great lord. He explained that he had been searching for this man Daidalos from city to city, and asked me pointedly if I knew where he was. I did not want to implicate my new friend, so I lied to him and told him I had never heard of him. Minos then laughed and seemed to change the subject. But he presented me with a large sea-shell, explaining that he wished to pay a reward to anyone who successfully passed a linen thread through its whorls, from one end to another. I had never tried this myself, and thinking it an easy task, essayed to do it. I wetted the end of the thread with spittle, twisted it taut between my fingers, and spent quite a long time at it, but could not accomplish what he demanded. I asked him to give me some more time. After the king retired to the guest-room, I brought the shell and thread to Daidalos."

Then said cunning Daidalos: "The task seemed to me impossible at first; but after deliberating on the matter, I found an ant and yoked it lightly with the thread. I spread a bit of honey on the tip of the shell, and then allowed the ant to wind its way up the spiral in search of the food, taking the thread with it. What labor a man could not do, the industrious mite accomplished in little time."

The king continued: "This very morning I presented the shell to Minos, his task accomplished, and expected to be given a large reward. Instead, Minos' face grew flush, and shaking his bejeweled fist cried: 'Lo! I have found the rascal at last! For who else but Daidalos, with his shrewd mind, could find a way to do this? Surrender him to me now, I order you, or it will go ill with you.' At this I grew deathly afraid, for king Minos did not seem to me a man with whom one wanted to tangle. I admitted Daidalos' complicity and asked for some time to search the city, claiming he had fled. He agreed, saying he would go take a warm bath in the meantime. While I sat in my chamber, not knowing what to do, something foul brewed above the guest rooms. My daughters, whom I love more than life—precocious though they are—upon hearing the danger facing Daidalos, hatched a plot not to lose him, since they had become rather fond of the beautiful toys—dolls with moveable limbs and eyes that closed when they were reclined—he had made them. And so they boiled water, and as Minos sat in his bath, poured it into the cistern so that it fell upon him, scalding him to death. I swear that I had no knowledge of this dastardly plot! But there is nothing I can do about it now. When the Cretans heard that Minos was dead, they marched up to city. I told them it was an unfortunate accident—that he had tripped on a rug and fallen headlong into a caldron of boiling water: this was not far from the truth. The enraged Cretans, suspecting foul play, then attacked us. My people, however, beat them back to the shore, and burnt their ships. I sit here now, once king of a peaceful kingdom, and now staring destruction in the face: for when the rest of the Cretans hear of this, they will ferry over their entire army against me."

"And why was king Minos in such hot pursuit of you, Daidalos?" asked Heracles, although he already knew.

"I cannot hide anything from you, Heracles," said Daidalos. "Something in you compels me to lay open my heart. Perhaps it is your earnest, beady eyes; your mouth, generous but grim; or those brows, twice knitted like Father Zeus', who, when he shakes his ambrosial locks, all heaven and earth follows suit. It was I that helped prince Theseus escape by entrusting to king Minos' daughter a simple trick. For this act of kindness I, who was at once so highly favored in the Cnossian court, fell into disrepute. Minos imprisoned my little son, pride of my old age, and I in the very Labyrinth I built. I then contrived a most ambitious means of escape. How I rue the day that plan came into my head! I fitted my son and myself with artificial wings. We took off and cleared the beetling heights of the maze. But how foolish was I to think that such gossamer things could carry us far over land and sea! I fell, exhausted, upon the beach. My son, still propelled by youthful strength, made it farther, out over open sea where the tumbling waves clamored for him to join them. Fly not to close to the sun, I admonished him, nor too close to the sputtering brine, lest either pull you down. And as I saw him soar, foolish youth, like Phaëthon when he disobeyed his father's words and rode the flaming chariot and untiring horses too close to earth, until woods blazed and the mountain-tops melted, and Zeus put an end to his insolence with a single thunderbolt, down my son plunged like a seabird slipped from the talons of a cruel kite, and with a splash his body was lost to me forever. I mourn him still, even more so when I think his shade wandering the cold banks of Styx, alone and unburied."

Heracles carried the corpse of Minos out to the Cretans, who wept over their fallen king and lamented that they were now cut off from their homeland and had nowhere to go. At the insistence of Heracles, Cocalos ordered the Sicani to welcome them, give them their women for wives, and allow them to live peaceably among them. When the Sicani saw the honor with which the Cretans buried their king, they repented of their aggression and allowed the Cretans to settle where they wanted. Some of them built the city of Minoa further up the coast, while the rest settled inland. Daidalos later built for Cocalos the city of Camicos, along with an aqueduct to provide it fresh water from mountain springs. It was so impregnable that Cocalos moved his royal residence and treasures there. When a temple to Aphrodite was erected at Camicos, the body of Minos was sepulchred in its center. Afterward, however, nearly all of Crete emptied out in an expedition against king Cocalos to avenge the death of Minos. The huge army besieged Camicos for five years. Unable to capture it, and driven off by hunger, they left, but were forced by storms to land at Messapia. With their ships smashed, and with no further hope of returning to Crete, they built first the city of Hyria, followed by others, until they forgot they were Cretans.

Having thus brokered a temporary peace between the followers of Minos and the Sicani, Heracles returned to the ship with provisions and gifts from Cocalos, including a bronze tripod, gold and silver talents, swords with jeweled pommels and lambskin cloaks. The crewmen fell into arguments when dividing the gifts. Heracles took none of the treasure for himself, except that he placed the tripod in the bows, where, once a favorable east wind allowed them to embark, he sat to watch the foaming waves peeled back by the beaked ship.

The helmsman set course for the small island of Cossyra, roughly halfway between Sicania and the coast of Libya. It was barren and devoid of fresh water, but offered secure harborage at its northwest corner. They set out from there a day later, expecting a full day's voyage until the first of many stops along the Libyan coast to the uncharted lands of the west.

As they neared land the next night, guided by the Lesser Bear, a series of strong southerly wind gusts shot up the strait, yawing the ship around several times, pushing them back toward where they had come. Heracles, jumping to the helmsman's side, applied his mighty arms to the tiller, holding it steady, while the men rowed against the towering waves. From the deep sea combers sped toward them like horses at full gallop, washing over the deck and spreading terror. Heracles felt the tiller suddenly grow slack in his hand—the rudder had broken off! For two days the ship pitched and rolled at the mercy of the unyielding sea. The men bailed futilely, barely able to keep up with the many leaks afflicting the vessel. They knew their end was to founder midsea and drown, or be broken on a rocky shore. Finally, all they could do was brace themselves, or cower under their benches. When they could spot the thrusting reefs awash, dark and jagged, some men despaired and jumped overboard, risking their lives to the hacking waves. Only Heracles stood tall at the bows, his arms wrapped around the forestay. He looked back at Iolaos cowering in the arms of Iphicles and felt helpless. Witnessing the dark, swirling sky and the yellow half-moon in a bed of stars, he acknowledged how puny he was in the face of nature's fury. He himself did not fear to die; but his heart ached for his brother, his nephew and his friends who risked all for him. Again, he seemed to bring misery to those around him. He thought that the storm was another work of Hera, and that perhaps by jumping into the sea he could propitiate the goddess and spare the ship. But if prayers did not alter the mood of the gods, why should sacrifice—or anything else? Then he thought of all his Labors, and their cause, and that all would inexplicably be for naught if he brought an end to himself. There was still so much work to do. His work on earth—whatever value it had—was his salvation: he had to finish it. Whatever ill misfortune wrought, he knew one could only meet it by valor and endurance.

The ship rode high upon the swell, and then dropped prow first into a watery chasm so rapidly that men and gear tumbled afore. As the vessel came out upon the next crest, a gigantic wave, like a mountain, came rolling astern in one final heave. For only a moment did Heracles glimpse the dark, forbidding landmass below them.

When Heracles awoke he was lying face down on a vast sandbank under a parching forenoon sun, the low tide sucking at his immovable form. After coughing forth water and sand, he pushed himself to his knees to look about. The ship, sundered on a rocky spit, lay in the shadow of a cliff far up the coast. From that point downward, the seashore was littered with timber, tackle, gear and men. Heracles, feeling oddly weak, stumbled across the sand to the nearest man. But he was drowned, finally released from the sea as the tide receded. "Iolaos!" cried Heracles, looking desperately for the lad. He found him lying near the ship. Heracles raised him in his arms and shook the youth until he coughed forth water and opened his eyes. Heracles embraced him with such vigor that Iolaos feared his ribs would crack. Antores joined them, and all three roused the survivors. In all, twenty-two men lived through the shipwreck, including Melampos, Peleus and the Egyptian helmsman. Of those that perished, some were found washed ashore, including the captain, who lay crushed in the ship's wreckage. The sea claimed the rest. Iphicles and Iolaos recovered as much as they could from the ship's lockers, including weapons, armor, cloaks, sodden barley-bread and dried meats. Heracles recovered his club, bow, quiver, as well as the mighty shield and sword from Troy. The rest gathered what had washed up on the beach. Some wine-jars were still intact, but all the stores of fresh water were lost.

After they ate and drank all but the contents of two wine-jars, they gathered the dead and laid them in a file on the beach. Despite the intense heat of the sun baking their brine-bathed skin, they donned whatever armor they could secure, covered the dead bodies with driftwood, and danced around them three times before setting them afire. The flames soon roared from the steady sea-borne wind. When only glowing bones and ash remained, they raised a barrow over them.

All around them lay foreboding wilderness. Beyond a line of sand-hills, mountains hemmed the shore from one edge of sight to the other. The men sat about listlessly under the hot sun, their strength sapped from the ordeal. Finally, the Egyptian Thamuz, his dark skin gleaming, stood and said: "We have no doubt, by the mercy of all-seeing Ra, reached Libya. There before us appears to be Cape Hermaium jutting far out into the sea. We, therefore, are not in such a bad way, since we have been spared the low-lying, sandy stretches to our south and east, beset along the coast with salt-marshes and quicksands, and inhabited by strange nomads and savage tribes. For example, south of us lies Lake Tritonis, and around it live a people called the Auseans. At their annual festival each year they divide their maidens into two groups. Armed with sticks and stones they fight each other in honor of the goddess you call Athena, sometimes killing one another. Further down the coast dwell the Makai, who shave the sides of their heads and wear the middle in a long bushy strip, like a cockscomb. Next to them you'll find the Gindanes, whose women wear as many leather ankle bracelets as the men with whom they have companied. The Lotus-eaters are their neighbors, living on nothing but sweet lotus-fruit, similar to that of the date-palm. Further east, Nasamones have their territory. These people have the curious custom of sharing their new brides with all their friends. They also produce nothing of their own, relying instead on the riches of shipwrecks given to them by the Syrtes. Now, beyond the coast lies a wilderness teeming with wild beasts, and then comes the desert, interminable, in which no one who enters ever returns. Between these two extremities live various other peoples, such as the Garamantes, whose eat snakes and lizards, and whose language is unlike any on earth, sounding like the screeching of bats. I know more about those parts of Libya than I do what lies to our west. I have only heard that the inhabitants are no longer nomads, but plough the land. They say also that in the wilderness live headless beasts with eyes on their chests; but I am inclined to disbelieve this."

Then said Heracles rousingly: "Up with you, men! Our long journey has only begun. We must continue toward the setting sun. I need to find the cattle of Chrysaor, and nothing will dissuade me."

"I will follow you, Heracles," said the Egyptian, "as far as my legs will carry me. But if we continue westward down this barren and mountainous coast we will perish from the heat and thirst  We must try to skirt these mountains, travelling a bit inland first."

Ignorant of the terrible hardships ahead, and beguiled by the greenery of the mountain fringe, the suggestion was accepted by all. Gathering all they could carry with them, they marched far down the coast until the long ridges melted into forested hills and scrubland where they happily plundered the fruit-trees. But beyond this, to the west, they faced  dry, high plains ringed with desert. Having come that far, they had no other recourse but to plunge into the sands, keeping the sun before them and hoping to arrive again at shady woodlands. But once swallowed up in the yellow, sun-burnt waste, and having finished the last of the wine, despair gripped the men. A hot, southerly wind blew on them incessantly, spraying their eyes with grit and drying their lips and tongues.

When the wind abated, a worse thing occurred.  In the distance a grim shape coalesced from the heat and sand, taking the form of a giant hollow serpent, rising into the air and then descending on them.  The Egyptian knew it was but a desert mirage, formed by sluggish arid air, just as clouds can take familiar shapes on humid days.  The monstrous phantasm dropped on the ragged troop, chilling the spine and filling each man with terror.  Even Heracles, thinking a monster attacked them, swung his club wildly at the quivering mass of heavy air until it broke in pieces, pouring down around them and vanishing like fog dissipating at first light.

Night found them deeper into the desert, with no hope of ever reaching the end of it.  The men huddled in their blankets and cloaks, burrowing into the sand to escape the grim cold that enveloped them as completely as heat did during the day.  But the warmth of their bodies produced a plague of serpents, which trailed silently toward them through the dust.  These were born, they say, from Medusa's throat, which Perseus clove with a curved blade when he sought the Gorgon in the uttermost parts of Libya. Holding up his golden shield, which safely bore the monster's dangerous visage, he approached her in her slumber among the relics of her stiffening gaze; and with a single stroke, guided by Athena's hand, dislodged the snake-locked head.  As he flew with it through the æther on Cyllenian sandals, the burning earth drank the venom of the dripping gore and caused nature to beget its deadliest crop.

The first to perish was a young Cretan, who bitten a giant Hæmorrhois, began to dribble from every orifice with blood.  Not far from him, another suffered the dry Dipsas' bite, which parched the very moisture from his body, so that with burning thirst he dug futilely through the sand after some hidden stream, and finding none, ran off raving into the night, never to be seen again.  A third fell prey to the Prester, which exudes scorching vapors from its mouth.  The poison putrefied his blood, and his face and body became distended, swelled with suppuration, until no one could recognize him as he died in agony.  Melampos did his best to treat the afflicted, marvelously sucking out the poisons with his mouth and administering whatever remedies at his disposal, including the yellow sap of hog's-fennel, mandrake-juice to relieve the pain and the spittle of those who had fasted the longest, which is a sure antidote against asp bites.

The following day, with the unmitigating sun directly overhead, men began to drop in the sand, unable to continue marching across the undulating, interminable sand dunes. Only Heracles trudged on, a model of endurance, the sand sucking at his legs and making difficult even his long stride. On reaching the summit of a sand-ridge, he looked down in astonishment at a flat, stony plain sprinkled with shrubs and palm trees. A solitary spring twinkled at the base of the ridge. He cried out to his friends what he had found, his booming voice echoing through the dunes. Iphicles only laughed, thinking Heracles deceived by a mirage. Heracles dismissed the others with an impatient wave and disappeared down the other side of the ridge. When time passed and Heracles did not reappear, Peleus, bothered by the serpents that slithered toward them from all directions, led the rest of the men up the ridge. Seeing the oasis, they cried and danced for joy, then tumbled down the sand. Iolaos found a copse of date-palms, and shunning the fruit scattered at its base, found the strength to climb the shortest tree. He brought down a handful of sweet, ripe dates for all to eat.

After they had eaten and refreshed themselves, the men were reluctant to leave the shade of the palm trees. When Heracles threatened to kill those who wouldn't follow him, almost a dozen men fell at his feet, beseeching him for mercy and kindness. Their captain explained that they had followed him this far, through storms, a shipwreck, and now near death in the desert; and thus he had no reason to impugn their loyalty. They merely wished to be relieved of their present service, since they thought they would never see their homeland again and desired, not having wives or children, to make a new start of things in this place. Heracles was not all pleased by their proposition since he was down to half the men from when he started, leaving him at a disadvantage should greater challenges arise later in the quest. Yet, he never wished to become an oppressor, and thought that men everywhere should be free in their service. He called for a show of hands as to who would follow him and who would stay, and only one other cast his lot with the schismatics. Heracles then magnanimously fetched great white stones, and began to assemble for them a crude enclosure where the men could sleep safe from wild beasts. Thus he laid the foundations for the future city of Hecatompylos, so called because it came to have a hundred gates.

The Egyptian assured Heracles that another day's march westward would bring them to a more hospitable wilderness. And so the crewmen who followed Heracles bid farewell to their friends and left them. That night the pale moon rose above the horizon, limning the distant dunes in blue haze. They continued on for several more hours, afraid to settle for a moment because of the abundance of serpents writhing through the sands. The ground then sloped higher, and grew harder and stonier, and soon they passed again into wide shrubland. Before they knew it they were enclosed in wooded hills.

The next morning, the tramping of hooves awoke them. They looked up to see horsemen clothed with leopard skins. Although armed with javelins and daggers, they appeared to present no threat, being merely curious. Melampos was the first to approach them, speaking to them in all the dialects he knew. But not comprehending him, the horsemen looked at one another in confusion. Then through various gestures Melampos came to an understanding with them, and informed the others that they should follow these natives to their village. Heracles reluctantly agreed, walking behind the rest to keep an eye out for ambush. The horsemen led them past the hills and fields of rich black earth crowned with wheat, vineyards and olive orchards, to a large settlement of round wooden houses with thatch roofs. These people—the Masylians—welcomed them, bringing them out bread, baskets of fruit and platters of meat. The Egyptian partook of all except the cow meat, since in Egypt the people abstain from such in honor of Isis. After they had eaten their fill, their headman invited Heracles, the largest man among them, to company with his young daughters. Heracles, not to appear disrespectful, entered their dwelling but did nothing untoward with them, except throw them up in the air like infants or balance them on his shoulders in feats of strength, so that they giggled; and their father the king, listening at the door, was satisfied. The visitors remained in the village for three days, during which they forgot their hardship. On the fourth day the Libyans supplied them with small horses and donkeys to carry their wares. By then Melampos had learned much of their speech. He was told to expect several more tribes of ploughmen like them as they continued their journey, and to beware of bears and other wild beasts in the woods. But what lay in the extreme west no one could tell him. Melampos found no evidence of any diseases among the Libyans; they seemed to be the healthiest people he had ever encountered.

Beside the Masylians dwell the Masæsylians. At this time, being at peace with their neighbors, and enjoying the fruits of midsummer from their fields and orchards, they welcomed Heracles and his followers, but not as warmly as the Masylians. Heracles procured a chariot from them after helping them construct bows out of ibex horns.

Leaving the Masæsylians, they passed through thick woods and grassland teeming with antelopes, gazelles, camelopards and wild rams. Lions watched them from their lairs in the rocks but did not venture forth. They hunted the wild game. In one place they marveled at oliphants lumbering around waterholes and spraying water from their snouts. At night they kept a fire ever burning, and a careful watch, lest panthers, hyenas, or asps creep toward them.

They came next to the land of the western Ethiopians. As they passed through the midst of low hills, they were pelted by rocks. Looking up they saw what seemed to be little hairy men who mocked them with piercing cries. The natives they met explained that these were not men, but creatures called monkeys, which they hunted and ate with great relish. The western Ethiopians, like the Masylians, took great pride in their grooming, assiduously cleaning their teeth and pairing their nails. They also cultivated bees, which produced honey in great abundance. Heracles, who liked to eat barley-cakes with honey, was astonished to discover that these people also learned to produce a substance from wheat and tamarisk that so tasted like bee honey that he could not tell the difference.

After a ten day march Heracles and his followers encountered a stronghold high on a hill. It was the first walled city they had seen since arriving in Libya. While the rest made camp hidden in the woods at the edge of the plain, Antores mounted a horse and rode up the city. When Antores did not return that day, Heracles, Iphicles, Peleus and five others, in full armor, rode toward the city. As they did so, the gates opened, and out raced horsemen, fanning out down the steep hill in a cloud of dust. At once

Heracles gripped his bow and, as soon as he was close enough, let fly a shaft at the nearest of the attackers. Heracles spurred his mount, and galloping to his fallen victim, discovered that it was a woman—though with little of the feminine in her appearance—dressed in leopard skin, who lay in a crumpled heap, his arrow protruding from her neck.

A spear flew by his head, rousing Heracles from his distraction. He turned, bent his bow, and shot another arrow, killing a second warrior. He thought: "What is this—another race of Amazons?" Cupping his mouth, he called for the rest of his followers, who raced their steeds out of the woods and engaged the attackers in battle, killing their horses to force them to fight on foot. In response, foot-soldiers rushed out of the city to assist their struggling cavalry. Although outnumbered, Heracles and his followers fought fiercely, and overcame the women, since they wore no armor, save snakeskin greaves and spaulders, nor had edged weapons; only a surfeit of manly vigor carried them. The women withdrew finally into the city, and released Antores, sending out with him an envoy to sue for peace. She, like her brethren, possessed fine muscular limbs, but was shorter of stature than an Asian Amazon, darker of hue, and wore close-cropped hair.

Heracles listened in astonishment at what Antores learned during his confinement. Antores explained that this tribe was ruled by war-like women, each of whom served for a fixed period in the army, all the while maintaining their virginity. When their period of service expired, they married and had children, but remained still in service over civil matters. The men, meanwhile, spent their days cooking and cleaning about the house, just like housewives. They served neither in war, nor in the government; they possessed no rights of free citizens even, but had only the responsibility of rearing children. When a girl was born, the right breast was seared with red-hot irons to atrophy it, reasoning that such feminine appendages would only be a hindrance in battle.

Heracles then questioned the envoy, convinced that her race was related to the Amazons along the Axine, whom the majority of mankind believed to be the only such people; but the envoy knew not that name, saying that it was a term invented by foreigners. Their tribe was ancient, she said, living first on an island in Lake Tritonis. There, on a ridge of land running out of the marsh, they built a city called Cherronesos, from whence they spread out and subdued the nomad tribes to the east of the marshes. Their greatest queen was named Myrine, who with thirty thousand foot-soldiers and three thousand cavalry, marched west and defeated the Atlantians. But in the process they came to blows with the savage Gorgons, whom they subdued for a time, until Perseus arrived to slay their queen Medusa; after that the Gorgons were heard from no more. Myrine crossed into Egypt, allied herself with Horus, who ruled Egypt at that time, and waged war against the Arabians. The Syrians fell next to these Libyan Amazons, and they continued subduing the peoples of Asia, including the Cicilians, the Phrygians, and other races around the region of the Taurus. Her success was checked by Mopsos, who had been exiled by Lycourgos, king of Thrace: it was he who once chased off the nurses of Dionysos, so terrifying the god that he leapt into the sea. Mopsos, allied with Sipylos the Scythian, killed Myrine in single combat on the Scamandrian plain, routed her warriors, and forced them back in defeat to Libya, where they found their principal city destroyed by an earthquake and underwater. The few that remained moved westward, building their present city and forgetting much of their former glory.

Heracles thought on the matter, and considering it unnatural that any more nations be under the rule of women, took the envoy hostage and laid siege to the city, calling on the henpecked husbands of the Amazons to rise up and acknowledge him as their liberator. This they did, and throwing off their aprons, rushed out and brought their wives under submission, stripping them of their war-gear and whipping them until they ran around nearly naked and crying for mercy. Heracles also ended the abominable practice of searing the breasts of baby girls, so that the next generation developed into buxom women and forgot their war-like ways. The entire world thereafter, save one or two enlightened poets, forgot that there was such a people as the Libyan Amazons; from whom, it is not unreasonable to suppose, the better-known Asian Amazons inherited their fame.

Continuing on, the land turned arid, with only gnarled trees here and there, and blasted by the hot south wind. Heracles and his companions then encountered a stretch of salt flats. They tried to go around it, but a day's journey in each direction brought no end to the white expanse; and so they wrapped their heads in their cloaks and passed through it on foot, leaving behind their horses, and taking only the pack-asses, which could stomp through the hard ground with greater perseverance, better handle hidden quagmires and require less water, than their larger cousins. A fortnight since leaving the city of the Libyan Amazons, they arrived at foothills spread through a wooded upland of broad conifers and dried ravines. Ahead of them the mountain ranges that girt them branched off together to the northwest, forming an impenetrable jumble of steep peaks.

Between the hills ran deep and narrow canyons littered with great rocks fallen off the rocky hillsides. Above them beetling crags shadowed dark caves. No beasts or birds seemed to inhabit this gloomy hinterland. Not a sound reached their ears, save the howling of the winds through the defiles. The men peered up nervously at the dark spots on the hillsides, thinking that pairs of red eyes watched them. Thamuz reckoned they had travelled over seventy leagues since they had set out from the coast, and, if they followed the mountain range northward, they would reach the bounds of the earth and the edge of Ocean.

As twilight fell, Heracles decided to make camp, not wishing to continue lightless through the dangerous maze of rock. They settled around a stream where they filled their water-jars. One man climbed the hillside, wishing to find the source of the water while there was yet light, and soon vanished among the rocks. As they feasted on dried antelope meat taken from the Libyan Amazons, and sang songs around the fire, they quite forgot about their friend until a piercing scream chilled their blood. "To arms!" someone cried, and all reached for their swords and spears. Heracles pulled a burning fagot from the flames and sought to pierce the crags with light. A dark mass tumbled downward, landing by the fire: horrid headless remains; mangled, bloody limbs; bones broken and protruding. More men brought firebrands to Heracles' side, sending shadows to flight, and revealing, perched on a ledge, a monster that from horror nearly blinded the eyes. The creature, on its haunches like a lion about to leap, shared with mankind a general shape, but nothing more. Great leathery wings fluttered around a body covered in colorless serpent scales; the hands and feet ended in grasping claws; and on the pale, horrid face, partly concealed by seaweed-like hair, a long lolling tongue scoured a pair of yellow, protruding fangs. As the accreting flames brought more to light, one could see that the rocks around the monster bore the weathered shapes of men and beasts! "Gorgones!" cried one of the men, at which the rest dropped to the ground in terror, shielding their heads in their arms. Heracles without fear thrust the brand higher so that he could face his foe in all clarity.

"I see a familiar face upon that shield!" hissed the Gorgon Stheno, seeing the shield of Heracles blazing forth at his feet. "Do the gods that rule over all hate us so, that now they send another Perseid to torment us? For you are Heracles, are you not, descended from that cruel man who hunted down and slew our sister Medusa? Although we were first herded into these lonely wastes by the Tritonian women, and then crushed a second time by Perseus, we still manage to hear at times what is discussed in high Olympos; are we not also of divine parentage, having come from the loins of Phorkys, the last of the three sons of Pontus, and Ceto? A son of Zeus, we hear you are; and benefactor of mankind involved in strange Labors. Go, then, on your futile errands. We prophesy also: and I see only a cruel and lonely death for you, scion of the Gorgon-slayer. Away with you, and bother us not. If you do, we will sweep down; and although we have no power, as our sister did, to turn you to stone, we will tear you with our claws and devour you with our teeth"

Thus said Stheno, raising a cloud of dust under her beating wings. But before she could rise, a long lance launched by Antores from behind Heracles whistled through the air and struck the Gorgon's armored breast, but bounced off, clattering back down the hillside. Steno grinned hideously. Her mocking laugh was echoed by her sister Gorgon, Euryale, on the other side of the gorge. "Heracles, you have kept your companions ill-informed!" cackled Stheno. "You should know full well why it was Medusa who Perseus sought to kill." Euryale, from her hidden den, answered: "Of us three only she was mortal—and no mere mortal may destroy us!"

With curdling cries swooped the awful sisters. Heracles' followers, fleeing in utter panic, were swept up and crushed like rabbits in eagles' talons. Heracles raised his shield, against which the bulk of Stheno struck with such force that he was thrust off his feet. Confusion filled the gorge: the screams of dying men; darting flames; the hideous winged shadows of the Gorgons crossing over their heads. Still on the ground, Heracles reached for his bow, fitted a sharp arrow, and pulled until the bow strained and he could feel the arrowhead press against his thumb. The bent bow groaned under the tension, but he held it rigid, waiting, watching the stars from beside the scattered brands. When he noticed the stars obscured by the dark bulk of a Gorgon flying high in preparation for another assault, he released the missile. It blasted upward through the æther and reached its mark. The barb cut through two of Euryale's overlapping scales and pierced the immortal skin, holding fast in her belly. The wound welled with thick ichor—not golden, as that of the blessed gods, but green and fetid. Knocked off her windy course, the Gorgon spun in the air and dropped quickly in a heap. Heracles jumped to his feet, grasped a sword, and sought the fallen monster. All around her, where drops of her blood had fallen, vipers and scorpions grew spontaneously and scurried off. As he towered over her, Euryale, grasping the protruding shaft in one clawed hand, cried: "Do not consider this a victory, Heracles, or a deed beyond the pale. The High Ones have allowed you to spill my blood by your unerring aim, but nothing more. My life cannot be taken by a mortal, even a son of Zeus." Hissing, she snapped her toothy snout at Heracles, but could not reach him. Despite her asseveration, however, she felt the strength of her limbs ebbing from her. Heracles swung his blade and sliced off the head. The trunk fell over, a swarm of noxious creatures budding from the bubbling, severed neck.

At once Stheno ferociously fell upon Heracles, landing roughly with her pincered feet on his shoulders, trying to lacerate and maul him. The impenetrable lionskin saved his life, affording Heracles the opportunity to grasp the Gorgon by a wing and wrench her off his back. Cast against protruding rocks, the monster lay still momentarily stunned. Heracles pounced on the fiend, clipping her leathern wings under his feet. "What my forebear Perseus began, I shall finish," said he. He raised his sword and brought it down on Stheno's crown, slicing the head apart through its awful mocking lips. As with her sister, asps, engendered from the gore, pullulated in the yawning gap. Heracles gripped both heads by their stringy hair and cast them far away from him into a deep cleft. In this way Heracles destroyed the race of the Gorgones utterly.

Those who had fled for their lives into the dark passes returned. Heracles eyed them darkly, muttering what an otiose gaggle accompanied him. Averting his gaze, they went about gathering the dead. In the morning they heaped pyres and collected brushwood with which to burn the bodies. After dancing around the corpses thrice in full armor, wailing and beating their swords against their bucklers, one of them lit a flame. They stood around until their fallen comrades were reduced to ashes and charred bone. Then they buried them, heaping a cairn above the grave. Peleus hunted down a wild ram, which they sacrificed, pouring the blood upon the stones. Of the original mariners, there were now less than twenty left.

As the afternoon drew on, Heracles led his companions out of the gorge to the edges of the mountains, littered with boulders and jagged rocks. From there they entered a sheltered valley of thick pine and cypress trees. As night fell, distant thunder rumbled, followed by cool rain: the first to touch their faces since their arrival. After passing the night huddled in their cloaks under the broad evergreens, each man quite forgot the waterless terrors of the desert. The morning rose gay with birdsong. Melampos found a hive in the hollow bole of a shea-tree. As he did not know how to safely extract a comb, the Egyptian showed him how to flush out the bees with smoke. The extracted honey was of excellent taste and quality, and a useful balm for parched, sunburned skin.

Deeper into the mountains, cut by deep ravines and pocketed by shady hollows, they climbed. Keeping a northerly course, they left the forests behind and clambered through bare, mossy rock. After many days, the group emerged into a clearing bathed with the erubescent light of a spectacular sunset. They stood on the bald, flat top of a promontory. Around them spread an illimitable blue sea. Across a narrow strait a tall, black mountain peak, mantled under a layer of dense white clouds, faced them. Together the two extremities were known as the Pillars of Atlas. Heracles looked to the west and saw nothing but endless, wide-ridged Ocean, mottled by pools of sunlight streaming through the clouds. Not a throat was moist, nor an eye unmoist, by those who beheld such savage beauty. They had reached the uttermost part of the world.

As the sun gave its flame back to the nearer stars and the Pleiades grew bright behind the receding day, Heracles, looking up at the boundary between light and dark, saw there a swift luminary riding the ebbing sunbeams. He climbed a rock for a better look. Lower it flew, precipitously down toward their quarter of the world. Heracles now made out, on the arc of heaven, what seemed like a luminous chariot pulled by winged horses. "My bow, Iolaos, quickly!" cried Heracles. Iolaos ran to him with bow and quiver, ignorant of what Heracles had noticed in the sky. Perched upon the rock, one mighty leg before the other, like two stout oak-trunks, he nocked an arrow and pulled back to the feather, aiming the arrow-point at the glittering car. He said under his breath: "If only I could reach you, Sun-god, with this missile: I'll punish you for the never-ending heat you have cast down upon our heads." But Helios, who knows and sees all things on earth and heaven, caught sight of the brazen Heracles from his high-flying car. Spurring his steeds with lash and goad, he turned off his usual mid-way course, and, affronted, flew down swiftly toward the lofty spur, ignoring the very advice he gave his son Phaëthon, who long ago presumed to ask his father for the chariot reins to prove for himself his divine parentage. Because Helios swore an oath on Styx, which he had never seen, that he would grant whatsoever his son asked, and so could not deny him even so futile a wish, he bowed his bright head three times and with grieving heart allowed Phaëthon to approach his flaming car. He said: "No one save I, not even the lord of Olympos himself, has the power to control this chariot and these fiery steeds chomping at their golden bits. But if you must do this, I advise you that the first part of the journey is steep. When you reach mid-heaven, you will be as high as the stars; do not look down, lest your heart tremble and you slacken your hands on the reins. For the final part of the course you will descend rapidly, and it is there that you must exert your utmost control lest you plunge headlong into the waters. But why, my son, did you wish for so hard a thing? I could have given you anything else you asked. Did you imagine your journey will lead you to pleasant groves with abundant fruits, or the golden palaces of the gods, or even stately temples filled with gifts? Instead there lurk dangers that make even my ancient heart quake!  There is a horned Bull along the way, snorting fire.  Beside him stands the Haimonian Archer, then a roaring Lion, and a Scorpion sweeping all before it with its venomous tail; across, the Crab awaits, reaching out to snatch you. And you must not forget the steeds, nearly uncontrollable when fresh from their stables.  Their breasts are filled with fire, and steam gushes from their snouts.  I beg you relent: see me full of concern! A bane you ask for, instead of a blessing.  Do not do this—let your choice be wiser!"

But Phaëthon would not relent.  When Dawn opened wide her purple gates and the evening star left his watch in the sky, Helios anointed his son's face with fire-proof unguent.  He gave the foolish boy some final advice: "Follow my well-laid tracks.  Keep the middle course that the earth and sky may share equal warmth, or else either side will burn.  Spare the lash, and keep the reins: the steeds, fed on ambrosia, will propel you on their own, so strong are their fire-laced limbs."

As soon as Phaëthon proudly mounts the car, the impatient horses flap their wings and dash from the golden palace.  Feeling their weight light, however, the team turns wild and leave their accustomed track.  Phaëthon, panicking, not even knowing the horses' names, unwisely—and in vain—lashes their steaming backs. On all sides Phaëthon is hard pressed with the threatening figures of savage beasts.  The chariot is borne along unknown ways like a rudderless ship before a gale.  Phaëthon looks down from the dizzying height, ignorant of the distance he has travelled, or how much of the westward expanse he still needs to cross.  He drops the reins and grips the car rim white-knuckled.  The horses, feeling the lines slack against their backs, rush now, unrestrained, where their savage natures take them.  Like levin-light that fills the sky, some of it piercing the clouds and the rest striking the ground, the chariot climbed high into the sky, searing the clouds and igniting thunderheads, or else dropped near earth, turning the green meadows into white ash.  The seas boiled; the streams evaporated, the mountain-tops were rent with fissures.  Naiads wept, in terror fleeing their vanishing springs and fountains.  The Nereids plunged deeper with the fish to avoid the scalding waves.  Hamadryads, Meliads and Nymphs left their beloved oaks, ash-trees and pines to the flames.  The cities of men perished in vast conflagrations.  It is said that Libya became a desert then; and the Ethiopians turned black, for their blood rushed by the heat to the surface of their skin. The air choked with black smoke and whirling ash.

Then Earth, shielding her brow, implored the lord of Heaven for aid. Zeus, feeling the paving stones of Olympos turn hot, and seeing the smoky darkness climbing the peaks of the sacred mountain, bent back with a thunderbolt and cast it at the wayward chariot, meeting fire with fire. The yoke is split; the horses, loose, scatter in terror. The chariot bursts apart. Phaëthon, in a long trail of flame, plunges headlong into a mountain lake, which hisses and roils at receiving his seared body.

But Helios controls his descent, so that his chariot does not again bring catastrophe upon earth. The white-hot incandescent car cools down to an orange luster, then to the color of burnished bronze. The fiery steeds rear and canter, but obey their master, their cycling legs slowing to a measured trot. Only Heracles, it seems, could clearly see the form of the god. The rocks melt. The failing day seems to revive. Heracles sees his followers scatter down the slopes in terror to hide under rocks and in dens, unafraid of the wild beasts laying there. Some rush as fast as they can into thickets, or crawl to the bottom of fissures. Only Heracles stands firm against the coming onslaught, never loosening his shaft, knowing the futility of such an act.

The immortal hooves touched down not far from Heracles. Helios drove them around, first in a wide circle, then coiling inward by successive passes as they slowed, before bringing the chariot to a stop. The force of heated wind and the rumbling of the mountain peak pitched Heracles from where he stood, casting him down to the dust. Head down he lay for a moment, overshadowed with brilliance. With hands shading his eyes he dared to look up at hooves like black marble and the milk-white pasterns of the snorting horses. They were surrounded by a wall of flame, rising from the deep groove the chariot wheels had cut circling the mountain-top.

Heracles rose on one knee, his eyes growing accustomed to the intense radiance. He saw four impossibly large white horses, with feathery wings sprouting from their backs. Their eyes glowed red, steam rose from their nostrils, and sparks flew every time they chomped their bits or shook their clanking bridles. The two trace-horses were secured by golden ropes, while the two middle ones were tethered to the yoke on a long pole of gold set with light-reflecting hard chrysolite and jewels. The enormous, luminous chariot sat on an axle of gold securing golden-rimmed tires around a ring of silver spokes.

"There now Pyrois, Eous, Aethon and swift Phlegon! Not yet have we reached your pasturage under the western skies, where you feed not on common grass, but on ambrosia, and refresh your weary bodies from the daily toil," said the divine driver, stepping off the car. He was twice as tall as Heracles, with long powerful limbs clad in golden armor under a purple robe. A glittering circlet wreathed his white locks; and a white beard framed a broad, ancient, effulgent face. He crossed his arms and with deep-set brows under a radiant aureole said: "Up with you, mortal! You dare aim at me when I am far; face me now that I am near—if you can." Heracles, for once feeling weak-kneed, straightened his frame to face the Titan. He could see nothing else save the prodigious form towering over him.

Said the son of Hyperion: "Those few times I dared venture this close to earth, I hid my true form, lest Clymene be consumed by my glory. Likewise for Circe and Leucothoë I diminished my splendor, although their deity would have shielded them from destruction. But now I stand undimmed before what I think is a man, and yet he lives! But you are more than a man, are you not? Nothing is hid from me. O, that rascal! Now I know why he bade me hide my face for three days. Not long afterward I saw an infant left lying in a stony field. He grew to manhood battling wild beasts and freeing men from fear. As a man he has ranged this wide world performing brave deeds that astound even my ancient eyes. He fears nothing, and no one: not even I, who was before even the Olympians. Yes—he is the greatest of all the mortal children of Zeus. I see the same restless spirit as Cronides; the same ardor burning within you; the same courage and strength in your right arm. This once I will forgive your wonted brashness, Heracles; although my first thought was to kill you, as your father once killed my son, felling him by his mighty thunderbolt. Yet such had to be, or else my rays would have nowhere to shine had heaven and earth been dissolved. Tell me, then, what brings you so far from your homeland? I have seen you crossing the wide deserts and barren wastes, although I know not why you do so."

Heracles, overcome by the intensity of the Titan's radiant countenance and the pulsating heat of the celestial chariot, staggered back toward the outcropping from where he had dared to threateningly aim his bow, bracing himself against it with head askance.

"Lord, forgive my foolishness," said Heracles contritely. "You shine on the just and the unjust, as you must; but for a moment I thought of nothing else but the tormenting heat you have afflicted me with each day. I set out from Crete seeking the land of Erytheia. Shipwreck cast me in these lands: but it is there, across the sea, that I believe I must go, and I don't have the wherewithal to do it."

Helios thought a moment, and then his face beamed with mirth. He said: "Fortitude I value in men and gods above all, especially in one who would dare challenge the invincible Sun. Because you still live before me, there is more here than meets the eye. I shall reveal a thing to you unknown to mortals. After traversing the sky I reach my other palace far off in a land on earth-girding Ocean that no man or god has ever visited. There my horses crop in lovely meadows and drink their fill from snow-waters tumbling down the mountain-sides, thawed by a perennial spring. Then as night covers your world and sweet slumber closes the eyes of men, I board a golden vessel, constructed by Hephaistos, and sail around the underside of Ocean, back to my principal palace in the east, from whence I issue forth again each morning to drive the shadows off with splendor. That is the secret, Heracles, of how night turns into day—a thing only imagined by your poets, but now revealed to you. In the morning this vessel I shall lend to you to convey you to Erytheia. One full day you may have it, but you must return it to me at the hour of dusk. Only you, Heracles, may ride in it. I shall entrust it to one of the sea-gods, who will deliver it to you down by the seashore. In the same way shall you return it after you have reached your destination."

Helios mounted his chariot, lashed his steeds, and took to the air in a whorl of flame, rising high, challenging the luminosity of the waxing moon. In moments the last bit of day fell behind the western horizon, quenched by the edge of the dark sea.

Heracles lurched from the blighted patch where he had

faced the god, blinded in the sudden darkness. A strong breeze scattered the remaining fire that swathed him, allowing the bravest of his companions, returning from their hiding-places, to see that the hero was still alive. Antenor approached first, then Peleus. Iphicles and Iolaos followed, carrying Heracles' sword and shield. Heracles shook like a man rising from frigid waters, and his lionskin was steeped with sweat. Those around him marveled that his hair and beard shone white with a strange radiance. Melampos brought him a water-jar, which Heracles tipped over his head. He shook off the water and sat, his thoughts filled with the meaning of his brush with divinity. His companions pressed him about what had occurred, for they saw nothing more than Heracles suddenly struck by lightning, and then shrouded by dense smoke and flames. Heracles kept a holy silence. At last he rose and instructed his followers to remain on the mountain while he climbed down to the coast to await the gift of Helios. "Where I am going, you cannot come," said he. At once, Iphicles retorted: "We have followed you all this way, brother, and now you wish to abandon us?" Others added their dissent by their murmurs. Heracles stretched his hand and said: "What I do now, I must do alone; but I promise to return for you. After all, I enlisted you to assist me: who now wishes to disobey my command?" None answered him. Iphicles walked off in a sullen mood, jealous that Heracles continued to be favored in life. Although Alcmene tried to extend her love equably toward him, who ever lagged Heracles in size and gallantry, Amphytrion left no doubt as to which son he preferred. Iphicles, though intellectually superior to his brother, therefore grew up tainted with jealousy and spite. He suffered greatly when Heracles was chosen over him as priest of Ismenian Apollo for a year. Only the best boys of noble families had the honor of being designated Laurel-bearers, for they were crowned with wreaths of sweet laurel. Amphytrion was so pleased that he dedicated to the god a bronze tripod, which can still be seen, remarkable for its age.

Heracles rose before dawn while his companions still slept. He looked over their still forms like a shepherd counting his sheep. He unstrung his bow and secured it at his back beside his quiver. His shield he left, not wishing to disturb Iolaos, who slept on it. With his brass-bound club resting on his shoulder, he made his way down the mountain, his path guided first by the thin moonlight, and then by the nascent light of the new morning breaking up the forest mist. Hours later he emerged into foothills that sloped down to the sea at a narrow strip of sand and rocks frosted with white spume.

Heracles walked up and down the short beach, looking out at the landmass on the other side of the channel, wondering if the land of Erytheia lay nearby. The two towering promontories on each side of the strait stood like pillars guarding the edge of the unknown. After a while he grew hungry and climbed back up into the hills to look for berries. When he returned he saw grounded on the beach a vessel such as he had never before seen. It had the appearance of an enormous caldron or goblet of orichalc, lenticular in shape, with a length exceeding one hundred royal cubits and half that as wide. It rose six cubits high to a rim curled outward in scalloped petals like a lotus flower. Carved in relief all around were the seas and all the lands of the world, covered by a representation of the sky, wherein day and night revolved. Above this, embedded in a sidereal band, could be seen six constellations, with the other six wrapping around the sea-facing side. The wrought sea held fish and dolphins and whales; blue-haired sea-gods lorded over them, while green-haired Nereids sunned themselves on rocks. The land teemed with cities and men and beasts, mountains and trees, rushing rivers and trickling streams. Much of the ancient workmanship had lost its luster in the lapping brine, and was now covered in barnacles and sea-moss.

Heracles walked around the vessel seeking for a door, wondering how it's vast size and ponderous form could float, much less propel itself, without any visible mast, yards, sails or stays. As he passed a hand over the carvings, he felt the bowl-like vessel shudder, and saw seams of light appear around a detaching flap that, with whirring of internal gears, ponderously lowered itself to form a gangplank. Inside, the vessel's surface appeared smooth, except for a horizontal flange encircling its diameter. In the very center stood a stanchion supported on a tripod.

Heracles pitched his club and bow through the gangway. Applying a shoulder to the vessel, he tried to push it into the water. His feet dug deep into the sand; and his arms and back strained like never before. When the vessel slid forward a foot, Heracles relaxed the pressure, breathed deeply, and then bent his back again. Another foot it shifted. Heracles groaned but would not relent, his hands and shoulders and the nape of his neck incised by the carvings. Finally the waters received the vessel, freeing it from the foreshore. Heracles vaulted inside. The door swung close behind him.

Standing on the flange, Heracles could see over the vessel's rim. The tide carried the strange ship outward, but the current set it slowly spinning about. Heracles could see no evidence of a tiller or any other naval apparatus. It seemed to drift aimlessly, with a bias toward the open sea: an odd behavior for a preternatural vessel. Heracles muttered a prayer to the Sun; and when that seemed to have no effect, called upon Zeus, Athena and the other gods for assistance. The vessel still seemed to float listlessly, whirling around its axis.

From where he stood, Heracles could see a gap at the top of the stanchion. A thought came to him that was so strange, he laughed at himself. But sensing no other alternative, he jumped down to the flat bottom, removed his lionskin, and attempted to affix it to his club, looping the jaw over the broad end of the club and tying the hindpaws around the grip. He then climbed the tripod until he could reach the top of the stanchion, and inserted the narrow end of the club in the hole so that it stood upright. Immediately the makeshift sail bellied with a southern wind. Heracles held one forepaw steady, bracing his new sail, or turned it slightly to capture the shifting breeze. The vessel stopped rotating, righting along its major axis, and sailed across the strait. But midway, the winds roiled the sea; the waves, rocking the vessel, propulsed it toward the watery expanse. Heracles, alarmed and indignant, strung his bow and aimed an arrow down at the rising billows, crying: "Desist, mighty Ocean! If I feared not to aim above, I fear less to aim below."

The waters calmed and a southeast wind pushed the strange vessel beyond the mouth of the strait and up along the rugged coastline of the facing mainland. Heracles, not knowing where the island of Erytheia was situated, trusted in the favor of the gods, and the giant golden goblet to convey him there. He imagined that the legendary kingdom of Tartessos, ruled by Chrysaor and his three mighty sons, lay somewhere along the coast of the mainland. Stealing the cattle would not be the principal challenge. Once in his possession, he had to somehow get them back overland to the

Peloponnese, battling the three mighty sons of Chrysaor and prevailing along the way against sundry dangers and hardships. For that very reason he had raised an expeditionary force in Crete. Finding himself alone, a small bit of doubt for the first time weakened his resolve.

The great mountain ranges of the southern coast of Hiberia gave way to long stretches of white sands, alluvial plains, and heady bluffs clothed in greensward. Small fishing villages came and went, but no settlements of consequence appeared. Then ahead, what at first seemed to be a broad cape turned out to be the southern spur of an island separated from the mainland by a long narrow channel. The headland, at first flat and covered in flooded pools and banks of sedge, rose steadily into gentle hills intercalated with pleasant meadows. Winds and waves conspired to ground the vessel in the marsh. With a mechanical hum, the door dropped and Heracles stepped out into a morass thick with seaweed. Wading through the rushes he reached firmer ground, and continued walking across the plain, hoping he had reached Erytheia. He climbed the nearest hill and looked down onto a haymeadow, thinking how pleasing cattle would find it to feed among the lovely tall sunflowers. Beyond the field more green hills dotted the landscape. Heracles searched his satchel for the last of the berries and some dried meat, accompanying his meal with his last bit of water. Still hungry, he crossed the plain and climbed a taller hill farther inland, called Abas, stopping at a grove of olive trees. After eating his fill, he reached the top of the mount for a better view. A single red cow grazed at the foot of the slope. The rarity of cattle of such uniform color, like the hue of sunset, convinced Heracles he had at last reached his destination, although he wondered where to find the rest of the herd. He strained to listen; and sure enough, as the wind died down, he could hear happy bellowing from beyond the opposite hillside. Rubbing his hands together in satisfaction, he was about to bound down the slope when the sound of two deep growls arrested him. He turned quickly, club at the ready, expecting to see a pair of dogs behind him. His eyes shifted upward to take in a monstrous two-headed black dog, from snouts to tail as long as an Egyptian crocodile and as tall as an ass. The beast began to bark at him furiously, each head darting in and out in quick succession, resting back on its haunches ready to leap. Forestalling the attack,

Heracles, soundly gripping his club in both hands, raised it high above his head and rushed against the monster, bringing the massive end of his weapon down sharply where the two shaggy necks joined. The crunching of bone from the single blow turned the harsh barking into a quick whimper before the dog fell lifeless. From the shoulder of the hill Heracles now saw more cows appear from behind a knoll, led by what appeared to be a giant herdsman. He was of such stature that he could keep two cows abreast to either side within the reach of his arms. The herdsman searched about in alarm, having heard the ruckus of the two-headed dog, calling "Orthros! Orthros! Where are you? What have you found? Is there someone come to destroy our peace?" Spotting Heracles, he furiously bounded up the hill toward him, his stride so wide that Heracles did not have time to arm his bow. As the herdsman aimed hands as large as palm fronds to buffet him, Heracles swung his club upward, like a boxer delivering an upper cut, and propelled the giant's oversized jaw bone up into his brain so that he tumbled lifeless back down the hill, like a poplar, which caught in a violent windstorm heaves to and fro until it cracks and falls. Heracles, who had not expected so quickly such a strange and unruly welcome, remained wary, searching out the countryside for other foes. Besides more shambling oxen entering the meadow, for the moment no other threats appeared. Down the slope he went to gather the cattle, the majority of which grazed in a wider field behind the knoll. There were also oxen, yearlings and calves in the herd, all tawny and straight-horned. In all there must have been close to five hundred heads: powerful, broad-browed, loud-bellowing, not encumbered with too much fat or flesh, but neither lean nor weak.

Another, smaller, herd of cattle, these black-skinned and belonging to Hades, grazed on a nearby slope. Menoitios, a daimon invisible to Heracles' eyes, tended it. Seeing Heracles, Menoitios grew alarmed and sped across the island to its northern end as fast as lightning bursting from one dark cloud strikes another. There, in a small house overlooking the sea he found Geryones sharing a meal with his green-haired mother, the Oceanid Callirrhoë. Geryones, a monstrosity born with three bodies conjoined at the waist, was as gigantic as as his neatherd, but built like a mountain, with three pairs of rock-hewn limbs. He turned one of his three heads to Menoitios, taking corporal form on his arrival.

"Lord Geryones," called Menoitios. "I see a stranger among your herd. He is no doubt a cattle thief!"

When Perseus slew the Gorgon Medusa, and her fermenting blood spilled upon the sand, from her pains she birthed the winged horse Pegasos and the giant Chrysaor. Wandering over the sea the latter came to Hiberia and founded Tartessos, becoming a great and wealthy king. From his union with Callirrhoë, whom he loved when he saw playing in the sea, came Geryones and snake-tailed Echidne.

Geryones, springing to his feet, said: "Who is it that steals my prized cattle? Is he man or god?"

"I do not rightly know," said Menoitios. "He has the appearance of both, wears a lion's pelt, and carries with him a brass-bound club twelve forearms long."

At his words Callirrhoë grew pale. She grasped Geryones and said: "I know him, my son! He is Heracles, puissant son of Zeus. Long ago I dreamed that he would someday come to do you harm. Oh—do not go! Let him take your cattle if he wishes. I shall find you more to tend."

Geryones, not yet considering his mother's entreaties, said to Menoitios: "And what of my herdsman Eurytion, or his man-eating dog Orthros, kin to Cerberos, guardian of the underworld—are they not defending my property?"

"I fear the worst, lord Geryones," said Menoitios. "That mighty man has killed them."

Shaking with anger, Geryones said, "Fetch my helmets! Lace up my cuirass at the sides. Bind up my greaves!"

"Remember your daughter, tender Erytheia," said Menoitios; "and your parents: your dear mother Callirrhoë who clings to you, and Chrysaor, loved by Ares for his prowess. Her tears make me repent of telling you. You are no doubt a prodigy: the most powerful man on earth; but only death can be the lot of him who strives against this Heracles."

"I cannot die, mother; is that not so?" Geryones asked Callirrhoë, but she returned only silence.

Grasping three spears in three hands, Geryones said: "Do not with talk of chilling death try to frighten my manly heart, nor beg me any more to endure the outrage of larceny; for if I am by birth immortal and ageless, so that I shall share in life on Olympos, then what is harm is there to endure the reproaches of Heracles and to watch my cattle being driven off far from my pastures; but if, my friend, I must indeed reach hateful old age and spend my life among short-lived mortals far from the blessed gods, then it is much nobler for me to suffer what is fated than to avoid death and shower disgrace on my parents and all my race hereafter. I am Chrysaor's son! May this not be the wish of the blessed gods concerning my kine."

As Geryones tried gently to pull his mother from him, she groaned: "Unhappy woman, I, miserable in the child I bore! Miserable in my sufferings! I beseech you, Geryones, if ever I offered you my breast—O, how I rejoiced to see you at your dear mother's side, gladdened by your feasting at my paps—listen now, and stay with me. I shall call on the blessed gods for help, while you remain in safety."

Geryones could no more be detained. With his broad shield before him, and three ashen spears ready in one hand, he went forth from his homestead. Callirrhoë rushed to the seashore to implore heavenly aide. Her prayers reached the gods in assembly on high Olympos. Zeus alone, terrible in his aspect, did not wish to intervene in order to give all advantage to Heracles. No other gods took sides save grey-eyed Athena, who spoke to her uncle Poseidon, driver of horses, saying: "Come now, remember the promise you made, and do not try to save Geryones. Listen to our Father in his wisdom and hold your hand." She singled him out because Poseidon, who had fathered Minyas of Orchomenos, on Callirrhoë, was determined to come to her aid. But remembering the oath of all the gods concerning Heracles, he also desisted. Only Hera, sulking, pretending she had to leave the assembly for one reason or other, flew down from Olympos to see what aid she could render Geryones, sensing her last best chance to ensure Heracles' destruction.

Geryones marched with all his stout legs across the island in a third the time it would have taken an ordinary man. He came upon Heracles by the river Anthemous, still rustling the herd. Heracles, resisting the temptation to slaughter one of the cattle, had instead caught some coneys, and eaten them cooked over a fire. In the meantime the kine, no longer under any control, had scattered over the island  From the top of a hill, Geryones rattled his spears on his shield, and his mouths cried out in unison: "You there—recreant thief!  Is this what men do in another's house?—steal his property and consume his things?  If so, then I am glad I have lived far from such an evil lot, here alone."  Heracles, for a moment unsettled by the sight of the towering triple-bodied freak with horse-hair plumes shaking atop each helmet, dropped the lionskin from around his shoulders and responded:  "I take it that rather than the sons of Chrysaor being three, he is three-in-one!  I admit that for a moment you made my knees knock, you gruesome thing. But your advantage is now gone."

Geryones thrust his three spears into the ground.  "My fearsome aspect gainsays my true nature, Heracles," said he. "While my father lords it over men in the land yonder, and delights in his battles, I have sought a peaceful and bucolic life here at the spur of the world, where the setting sun blankets all in crimson.  You should see the beauty of it!  These cattle of mine I tend as if they were my children.  Did you know that when I make cheese I must first mix the milk with a large amount of water, on account of the fat?  Or that the milk of my flocks yields no whey?  And who but I could know that these poor creatures would choke to death within fifty days, unless a vein is opened and they are bled?  Not the thief who comes once in the night knows these things, but the herder who cares for them each day.  But if only there is a bit of justice in this world, my right hand shall lay low any who wish to harm me or my own."  With this he pulled one upright spear from the ground and launched it with such force that its massy tip glowed hot as it sped through the air.  Heracles barely had the chance to jump aside; the spear-point nicked his shoulder as it passed where had had stood.  Heracles, defenseless, for his weapons he had left by the riverbank, sought to shield himself behind the heifers; crouching there gripping his bleeding wound, he called out: "If only you would give me these cattle of your own accord, all would be well, and you would have no reason to think me flagitious; for I am forbidden to ask or take payment, you see, by the terms of my assignment.  I ask you, therefore, to come down, and let us discuss this like men."  Geryones, certain of victory, grasped his two remaining spears and like a spider scampered down to the plain. While he did so, Heracles continued to scurry from behind one cow to another until he could reach the riverbank.

Hera now appeared beside Geryones, visible only to his eyes, and said: "Take not your many eyes off Heracles, son of Chrysaor. He is a man not to be trusted in an open fight. Spear him from a distance, if you can, and stay out of reach of his man-crushing club. Do not let him arm his bow withal, or else he will pierce you with his deadly arrows. I shall stay by your side until you make the dark earth his bed."

Geryones, encouraged by the goddess, advanced with resolve. But his mother, arriving nearby, called to him one last time, saying: "Strength wins victory, my son, for sure—but not this time. Do not listen to her, hateful and white-armed. Obey me, instead, my child." Geryones looked to his mother, and for a moment longed to smell the fragrance of her locks. But the Queen of the gods showed her a Gorgon face, and Callirrhoë fled in fright.

Meanwhile Heracles, deliberating with himself whether to attack Geryones by stealth, or face him honorably in open fight, decided, given their inequality, that the latter choice afforded him greater odds against the mighty man. Crouching by his weapons, he gave up any pretense to honor by devising for him a bitter destruction. Attacking with the club would have been futile, for it seemed like a twig against the giant. He went for his bow instead, as Geryones let fly another shaft. Heracles leapt aside, once again narrowly avoiding certain death. He landed by some rocks, and taking the largest in his hand, curled his arm and at the giant cast it swiftly. The stone passed over Geryones' shield, which he kept in front of his chest, and struck the brow of the central head with such force that it dislodged the helm. Geryones dropped his shield to grasp his bruised head. Heracles fitted an arrow to his bow and released it hastily from the cord. Unbeknownst to him, Hera had stooped before Geryones to pick up his shield, and the arrow pierced her right breast. With a cry of anguish, she fled and returned to Olympos. Geryones, full of blind rage, rushed toward him, spear trained for a killing thrust. Heracles pulled out another arrow, this one fouled with the blood and gall of the Hydra. As Geryones closed in, Heracles loosed the desperate shaft. Although ill-aimed, and launched obliquely, it reached its mark, thrusting into Geryones's exposed brow, cutting through flesh and bone. Sticking out from his head, it stained with gushing blood his breastplate and big-boned limbs. Then he dropped his head to one side, as a poppy, which with weary neck, bows its head when weighed down with springtime rain, and, spoiling its tender beauty, suddenly sheds its petals. Geryones fell first to his knees, and then dropped on his faces, his armor clattering as it struck the ground.

Heracles took up his club and cautiously approached the fallen hulk. He prodded one of the heads with his foot, which appeared like a child's next to the massive helm. When the lips on another head suddenly moved, Heracles swung down his club and dashed the head into the earth. Heracles then leaned on his club as he contemplated the giant lying dead among his kine, not knowing whether to thank Fortune or some other god for directing his envenomed shaft. It seemed to him a shame that a man so gifted with such a prodigious frame should not have proved victorious. He felt remorse that he had come to steal the cattle simply at the whim of the cruel Eurystheus. "One could hardly be the benefactor of mankind if one went about treating innocent people in an insolent manner," said he to himself. "I shall ever remember you, mighty Geryones." At the same time he felt conflicted at the thought that perhaps it was a natural right that the superior and stronger should lay claim to the possessions of the weaker and inferior. Not being able to reconcile his sense of justice with what seemed to be the course of nature, he spent the rest of the day raising a huge barrow over the giant, which appeared like hummock from a distance. In time two trees grew there, such as have never been seen before. They appeared a cross between the pitch-tree and the pine-tree, forming a third species; and blood dripped from their bark, just as gold does from the Heliad poplar.

With the light waning in the hills, and the island awash in a crimson gloom, Heracles marched the red cattle to the shore, where the vessel of Helios stood motionless, and its surface lambent with the lustrous twilight, as when a caldron glows evenly over a flame. He hastened to ferry the herd to the mainland, so that he could keep his promise to Helios and return the vessel. With their hooves trampling through the muddy reedbed, he drove them three abreast into the divine ship until it filled to capacity with the lowing beasts. Heracles once again braced his shoulder against the vessel's rounded side and pushed. Although the barque was now immensely heavier, it did not sink lower in the water; and being almost wholly afloat, slid off with surprising ease. Heracles boarded as the door swung shut, climbed atop the flange, and there waited as the waves carried him the short distance to the mainland.

The vessel rode into the wide delta of the Tartessos River, which rises deep in Hiberia from mountains rich with silver, and empties into a broad gulf. Pushed along by the outflow, it floated southward into the marshy lowland along the coast teeming with cormorants, finally came to rest at a sandbar at the lip of an estuary. When the door fell open, Heracles pounded the walls with his club to alarm the cattle, which hastily poured out to the riverside. The moment Heracles stepped off, the door swung shut, its outline once again inhering into the vessel's delicate fretwork.

Finding that the cattle could not stray very far since they had been cast on an islet bounded by the river and its tributaries, Heracles decided to make camp and pass the night. He heaped up stones from the stream-bed for an altar, and slaughtering a calf which had become separated from its mother, burned the thigh-bones wrapped in fat in honor of Helios. Then he feasted by the fire and fell asleep.

Heracles awoke to find the strange and ancient vessel gone, having been pulled back into the sea during the night, returned by Ocean to its rightful occupation. He roamed the islet assembling the cattle, and then marched them across several streams crisscrossing the lowland. Keeping to the riverside, he came across fishermen, who told him of the double mouth of the river, and how a harbor-city of Tartessos lay between them, while the city proper lay further up beside the northern river branch. Heracles could now see broad, round single-masted Phoenician galleys with square red and white sails sailing up the river, towing behind them dinghies tied to outriggers. Not wishing to come across Tartessians who might recognize Geryones's cattle, he drove the cattle southward into the uplands, where broad bright fields of soft grass detained the hungry animals. He hoped to find a pleasant dell in the hinterland where he could for a time leave the cattle, while he set out to secure a ship to rescue his companions stranded in Libya.

As he rounding up the cattle once again, he saw a band of men marching across the field. Thinking himself discovered and the army of Chrysaor after him, he nocked an arrow and held it ready. "Hail Heracles!" cried out one among them, and a familiar voice it was!  Antores greeted him again, and Heracles roared with delight.  Soon he was surrounded by the men who had travelled with him across the Libyan sands.  Peleus explained that they had spotted Phoenician ships heading toward the strait, and hastily descending the mount to the seashore, made a ruckus until one of the ships turned landward and rescued them.  They were on their way to Tartessos, where the intrepid Phoenicians, alone of all peoples, traded native Tyrian purple, a dye derived from the shell of a sea-snail, along with spices and frankincense from Arabia, for tin, gold and copper.  As the ship made its way up the river, Iolaos saw the herd of red cattle crawling along the countryside like a swarm of beetles.  They asked the captain to disembark, and were rowed ashore in the small trailing boats.

Melampos showed him a map on papyrus furnished to him by the Phoenicians, who advised them to travel by way of the southern coast of Hiberia on their route eastward to Greece, where they would find hospitable Phoenician settlements; for the interior plains were arid and bleak, and filled with savages.

As his men assembled the cattle, Heracles left them for the high promontory at the farthermost edge of land and sea, overlooking the unfathomable Ocean and the strait to Libya.  There on the bare, windswept crest, to mark the westward limit of his journey, he erected two pillars; and on them, as a warning to sailors, he incised:

## NOTHING FURTHER LIES BEYOND

It became considerably easier thereafter to drive the cattle, since Heracles posted his men in a ring around the herd to contain and protect them from wild beasts.  It took many days to climb out of the river basin onto high table-land rimmed by mountains, where the corralled winds blew fiercely.  Moving southward at a slow pace with their shambling charges, they descended into treeless valleys bordered by rocky, limestone spurs.  The land then rose again in the face of another mountain range surrounded by vast forests and shrubland.  These they skirted for the sake of the cattle, following valleys deeper among the high, snow-crested peaks until they began to think they were walking in circles and would never reach the coast. Heracles forbade the men to slaughter the cattle, fearing that he would have nothing left to show Eurystheus. The men therefore hunted black boars and deers in the woodlands and picked wild figs. In a certain district they came across a grove of what appeared to be golden-colored apples. None had ever seen or tasted the sweet, round fruit, but Melampos thought them sacred to the gods and advised against consuming them. But the men would not heed him, and gorged themselves even on the peelings. When he also warned them against eating beans, they paid no more attention to him. Heracles, however, from curiosity asked him the reason for the proscription, and Melampos replied cryptically that eating beans was the same as eating one's parents. Rather than press the matter, Heracles judiciously left the man to his scruples. A more rational reason to avoid beans, he thought, was that they invariably produced flatulency, unless eaten on the first of June, with bacon.

Following the winding valleys carried them into the heart of the mountains, where they hunted for level passes. Through a deep gap overshadowed with gloomy pines, they came finally to an overlook and the seaboard opened below them. They marched across the plateau until the slope turned gentle beneath their feet, and descended down to a fertile coastal plain. From there they could see a large settlement hugging the seashore, with familiar Phoenician ships anchored off the coast. Leaving the cattle grazing on the plain, they came among the Phoenicians, who received them kindly and supplied them with provisions. Many of them were so impressed with Heracles, who reminded them of Melqart their god, that they gave up all to follow him.

They continued their journey through the plain, so hot and humid, with moist breezes from the sea, that Heracles more than once held himself in check so as not to renew his hostility with the sun-god. Along the way they stopped at whatever towns came by, and at each Heracles gained more followers. He also procured wagons, hitched to the bulls and horses, to carry supplies for the growing band. One town they found to have been settled by Sicani, who hearing of Heracles' acquaintance with just king Cocalos, joined him almost to a man, taking their wives and children with them. By the time he reached the marshy delta of the River Ebros, which flows from one end of the country to the other, Heracles' army and baggage train extended nearly eight stades long. They found a passage through the watershed by a dry lakebed hoary with salt, and continued onward to higher ground, arriving at another Phoenician town situated on an elevation around which a river flowed and emptied into the sea. The wine in this place was most excellent, rivaling even the best each man had tasted from their own countries.

An impenetrable wall of mountains rose before them. The lofty range, capped with eternal snow, seemed to grow out of the sea toward heaven and extended north and west as far as the eye could see. To reach the mountains they had to cross an immense plain embroiled in thick fog, even under strong sunlight. The mountain chain naturally divided Hiberia from the lands of the Celts, and extended from Ocean to Inner Sea for a distance of three thousand stades. Certain Celts who joined Heracles knew the country, and informed him of the few passes that would accommodate the cattle. To reach one, Heracles turned northward until the seacoast was far behind them and the ground rose gently into the foothills.

The pass led them to leafy summits where lofty waterfalls thundered from on high, creating mountain streams of glacial water that meandered through pine-clad valleys surrounded by precipitous granite cliffs. At times rain fell heavily, and the air grew comfortably cool as it swept down the snow-speckled aerial summits. Heracles had never before seen such breathtaking, rugged beauty; and in the early mornings, when the sun first showed its face from behind the peaks, he climbed the highest rocks to fill his lungs with the alpine air and take in the sublime and terrifying grandeur.

On the northern slopes the land grew wild and barren. Bearded vultures and golden eagles flew from peak to peak hoping for a repast. After a long descent they arrived at a flat, rocky meadow carpeted with short grasses and clumps of lichen. There the cattle milled about while the great host rested. Descrying springing ibex on the steep-wooded slopes surrounding them, Heracles strung his bow, eager for a hunt. As he searched through the gloomy pine forest, he came across a meandering mountain stream. He knelt to drink, bringing the water up to his mouth so as to remain vigilant. Scanning the trees as he drank, he thought he saw a white form flitting through the wood. He splashed through the stream, nocking an arrow as he ran. Drawing close he saw that it was not a beast he pursued, but a maiden, tall and fair, who looking back at him, filled the wood with her laughter. Sheathing his shaft and hanging his great bow across his back, he continued the chase, wondering who she was who toyed with him. As she ran the breeze blew through her garments, laying bare her limbs; and her long rose-colored hair fluttered behind her. She came to a stop at last, unable to run any longer. Heracles could have easily overtaken her, but he deliberately slowed his pace, delighting in her beauty while in flight. With her back to a spreading fir, she eyed Heracles suspiciously. Keeping a distance from her, Heracles cried out: "Who are you maiden? A nymph and keeper of these woods? You have no need to fear Heracles of Tyrins." The girl pulled up her garment to cover a bare shoulder. "I am Pyrene," said she. "Do you not know that you hunt unlawfully in the royal woods? I shall tell my father about you, Sir Heracles, and he shall bind you up to the highest peak as prey to the vultures," she added in a playful way.

Heracles said: "And who is your father that he claims to rule these rain-swept mountains?"

"He is king Bebryx," said Pyrene; "and this is the country of the Bebricians[5]."

"Well, princess Pyrene," said Heracles, his heart feeling strangely a-flutter, "I deem myself your prisoner. Conduct me to your king, as I would like to have a word with him."

Pyrene walked off, glancing back demurely at Heracles to see if he would follow. He marveled that this young girl evidenced, while all alone, no fear of encountering a fearsome stranger in the woods. She led him up the slope to a high ridge overlooking a broad valley, and there a city covered the hills, black smoke rising from the rooftops.

King Bebryx, a rough man of uneven temper, who ruled also the lands to the east of the mountains from his stronghold, listened to the charges brought against Heracles with some amusement, for his daughter's childish ways served to calm his savage nature. After making her case, delivered with frequent

---

[5] These Bebricians were of no relation to the Bebrycians of Thrace, whom Heracles came across on his quest for the girdle of Hippolyte.

sidelong glances, full of innocent coquetry, at the accused, he dismissed her with a wave; but she went instead to sit beside his chair, hiding behind the folds of his robe, from where she could watch Heracles. Under normal circumstances, king Bebryx would have had an intruder quartered. From his scouts, however, he knew of Heracles' army camped nearby, and did not wish to provoke any threat to the peace of his kingdom. He therefore welcomed Heracles, plying him with abundant food and so much sweet wine that he became fuddled more than usual due to the thin air of their high altitude. Heracles retired that night to the guest-room, his head wreathed with myrtle, and fell fast asleep on a black bear's soft hide. He dreamed that he ran anew after Pyrene through the pine-woods, his heart aching for her and his brow fevered with deceitful love. "O, why do you run from me?" he cried after her swift form. "I shall not harm you! See my brawny arms can be gentle." He caught her, bringing her lithe body against his. For a moment he was back at Thebes with Megara in their garden, wrapped in the scent of marjoram and thyme.

Heracles awoke, startled, unsure of where he lay. His fingers held a strip of garment smelling of wild blossoms and pine. Putting no stock in the vagaries of dreams, he returned to his slumber. The next day, as he feasted again with the king, an old crone entered the hall and fell down weeping at the king's feet. She was Pyrene's old foster-nurse, who came to nervously report that she had not seen the girl all day. Pyrene would go each morning to play in the woods, but never failed to return by midday for her bath. King Bebryx, alarmed, ordered her found. As the night was coming on, he knew that wolves, bears and lynxes with shining eyes would leave their dens to hunt; and so he grew afraid. Heracles stepped forward, offering his assistance, and at once left the manor-house.

Heracles scoured the wooded slopes while there was still light. When twilight mantled the forest with gloom, the lack of visibility inspired desperation. On reaching the stream where he had first seen Pyrene, an awful realization came over him. Recalling his dream with uncommon clarity, he fell to his knees buffeting his head. The strip of garment! Heracles ran savagely to the spreading fir. There he stopped, his blood running cold. On a bed of cones lay another part of Pyrene's garment, inked with blood. Heracles discerned tracks through the undergrowth. He followed them to a cave not far away.  In that bear's den he found Pyrene.  Bringing her forth, he laid her down gently.  Pale, filled with grief, he called her by name and the mountain-tops shook with the force of his cries.  All the cliffs and haunts of the wild beasts echoed back: "Pyrene! O Pyrene!"  Had he the full intelligence of his awful deed, he would for his crime have jumped from the highest crag.  But the gift of Dionysios was merciful, keeping him deceived.  He never knew with certainty that Pyrene had entered the guest-room while he slept, curiosity and the flush of youthful, confused inclination compelling her; that the creaking floor-boards under her feet aroused him; that he reached out in the darkness and grasped the soft, white arms; that, swirling in the madness of drink, he passionately handled her.  Breaking from his grasp, Pyrene fled into her beloved woods in shame and dread of her father's wrath. There, at the very spot where they had first spoken, she lay down weeping, informing the dark forest of her secrets, stretching out her hands for aid to the trees that had so often given her comfort; there the wild beasts found her.

The torn and bloodied rags of her dress he took back to the king, concealing from him that he had found Pyrene and buried her remains in a moonlit clearing.  Promising to leave Bebryx a tenth of Geryones' cattle, he departed for his encampment, leaving the Bebricians to their sorrow.  Along the way he pondered many things.  Whether from lust or madness, he understood that he was as dangerous to his friends as to his enemies.  He wanted to blame the wine, so beneficial to men, as a curse to him; but he recoiled at the thought that a man could not learn to control all his thoughts and passions.  If he could pummel his own body, subjecting it to strict discipline and strenuous activity to augment his strength, how could he not likewise bring his own mind and heart under control? Cheiron had taught him that nothing exterior to the mind can ever affect it unless allowed through willingness or weakness.  Why then did he do what he did not want to do?  It was clearer to Heracles now more than ever that his greatest Labor—greater than anything Eurystheus could impose—was to master himself.

He considered also on the nature of the short and feeble life of mankind.  He thought:  is it all to be born; to eat and drink; to love or hate,—and then to die and descend to the undergloom as shades, twittering in the dark?  What hope was there for those not favored by the gods?  It was said that the virtuous and heroic spent eternity in the bright meadows of Elysion, where it is ever spring and no sorrow enters.  He had to know if such a thing was true; if those he had loved were in that place, reposing in flowery groves. He pledged to scour, before his end, every part of the world to discover the secrets of the gods.

Heracles, still suffused with sorrow, slept apart, away from the dying camp-fires.  Iolaos, in the morning finding him, aroused him and the two breakfasted in silence, since Heracles did not wish to reveal to him his recent misfortune, afraid to lose the love of the youth even for a moment.  Iolaos, familiar with all of the moods that afflicted his uncle, dared not press him.

As he had promised, Heracles set apart a tenth of the cattle and left them milling on a hill as a secret propitiation for his transgression.  Wagons were hitched and in a long line his followers went on.  The end of the pass drew near, descending steeply to a low-lying plain cradled within the rocky spurs of the foothills. Heracles could have headed southward, continuing along the coast of the Inner Sea; but he wished to prolong his journey until he could perform some benefaction, as if deeds, good or ill, could balance themselves.  The quest for greater wisdom also spurred him; and since a new and unknown land opened up before him, he could do no less than satisfy his curiosity.  He encountered first the spuming falls of a river that flowed northward, beginning somewhere in the mountains through which he had marched.  At a little town hard by one side of the river the people informed him of the barbarity of their overlords, who killed strangers for sport.  This cruel practice he put to an end, along with a general lawlessness to which the inhabitants were disposed, vanquishing the savage tribes he came across, which was no small feat, since he had at the same time to protect the cattle.

Although separated into numerous tribes and nations, the Celts derived all from the same stock and possessed the same physiognomy: tall of body, lean-muscled, with pale skin and blondish hair, made even more so by washing their hair in lime-water.  Great numbers of those he freed joined him, until one could not easily determine where the train of his army came to an end. With such a continually expanding mass of people, animals and booty, Heracles deemed it wise to diminish the size of his host lest it became unmanageable. Traversing the breadth of the land and coming to a lofty hill surrounded by mountains and sitting between two streams, he founded a city that he called Alesia to commemorate his travels. The Celts to this day call it the mother-city of their whole country. While the city was being built, Heracles was visited by Galata, a Celtic princess, who like her countrymen, was exceedingly tall and lovely. The gifts with which nature had endowed her, however, produced a haughtiness that frustrated any man who tried to woo her. But on seeing Heracles, she was stirred by his manly prowess and the superiority of his features. With the consent of her parents, she eagerly shared with him her affection; and from the union came a son, Galates, who, on reaching manhood, subdued a large tract of his country. He called his subjects Galatians after himself.

Heracles then turned his army southward to explore the length of the land. After many days they arrived at the swollen river Rhodanos, which, rising in alpine heights, expands into mighty streams as it flows northward through Celtica, dissecting the land with its foaming waters. Horses could ford the fierce current, but the cattle recoiled in terror. Heracles ordered rafts to be built, secured by cables, and when the cattle refused to step even on these, he had them covered in soil. In this way, by small steps, all were ferried across. It was not long before this fluent land offered up another waterway, a confluence of the Rhodanos called Druentia, which filled all with trepidation. Its current was not only fierce, but carried on its back boulders and tree boles uprooted from its headwaters in the mountains. Brave men tried to cross it, but soon regretted trusting the river's tricksy fords, which unexpectedly swelled from the waters' shifting channels. It seized them and carried them off, whirling them about with all the detritus, so that they perished miserably. There was little to do but boldly face the river's raging course, for they found themselves hedged between it and its parent. Heracles walked the length of it from end to another to locate the highest point, where, just shy of it, he assisted his stoutest men to cast in rocks to create a sieve. The barrier held back for a time the largest fragments, so that, by a similar contrivance as before, men and beasts could be ferried across to the other side. The enterprise, however, proved fraught with peril, for every time the weir crumbled, the spate swept off whatever was in the water at the time. Through great hardship, and after many days, the crossing was completed, but not without occasion for great mourning over the loss of life and equipment.

From the river the column advanced toward the sea, for Heracles wished to resume the coastbound route back to Tyrins. Along the way he was harassed by the natives, who tried to raid some of the cattle and supplies by night. As their pestering was inconsequential, and time precious, he organized no effort to fight them, but kept his followers at a steady march, stopping only to allow the cattle to feed. Although he was both amazed and peeved at the belligerence of the tribes, and crushing them would have been a worthy effort, his heart was set now on finishing this final Labor and achieving freedom from Eurystheus' service.

Passing into the land of the Ligurians, whose domain extended westward to a greater extent at that time, he became the target of an organized resistance. The Ligurian tribes, an ancient people unlike the Celts or Hiberians, but similar to them in their mode of life, and who wore their hair long, lived in scattered villages on either side of the mountains, as well as within them. They were small of stature, but nimble and vigorous from the constant exercise of extracting something useful from the soil, since their land was stony and fruitless: it could be said they quarried rather than tilled it. Both men and women were inured to hardship, for they worked side by side cultivating their niggardly plots. On seeing the great host of Heracles, with all the cattle, descending toward them, they renewed alliances amongst themselves and assembled an army. As Heracles organized his own forces to meet them, sending horsemen to the front and expanding the rearguard, two sons of Poseidon, Ialebion and Dercynos, who had been warned in a dream of Heracles' coming, attempted the bold act of stealing all the cattle, impulsed by the god to take revenge for the sorrow Heracles had brought upon Callirrhoë. Heracles, who felt he had labored hard for the cattle, thought their wholesale thievery a great injustice and killed them. The Ligurians, meanwhile, attacked, driving Heracles' army, untrained for such an intense struggle, to the banks of the Rhodanos. But Heracles, vaulting on a horse, rallied his horsemen against the Ligurians, who, mounted on dwarf-horses and mules, were no match for the racing stallions of the lowlands. The battles continued day after day, with the hardy mountaineers retreating—led by one Ligys, brother of Ialebion—and then returning later in greater numbers. Heracles and his main force made a stand on a broad, round plain by the mouths of the Rhodanos, a hundred stades from the sea, which was strewn with stones in such profusion that it seemed they had at one time rained from heaven. There Heracles, exhausted and wounded, knelt down nearly in tears. He had run out of arrows, save a few still tainted with the Hydra's blood, which he did not wish to waste even in the face of possible defeat. He feared an inglorious end to the whole enterprise. But looking at the stones, which were the size of a man's fist and had rough edges, and seeing how the Ligurians were excellent slingers, he encouraged his soldiers to imitate them. Along with them, he took up discarded slings, and arming them with rocks, rushed against the enemy casting the deadly projectiles. The Ligurians, lightly armed and seeing their own weapons turned against them, were put to flight in great numbers, so that those that remained abandoned the hostilities for the time being.

Heracles took some of the Ligurians as prisoners, offering to accept as guides in exchange for their lives. To this they heartily agreed, for they often had no qualms about shifting their loyalties if the situation so demanded. They advised Heracles that he should abandon the idea of continuing his journey along the coast, since the mountains extended completely to the sea and offered no easy passage. It was better to head a little more inland and find a way through the Rhipaian Mountains, where he had a better chance of getting all his cattle across. Not realizing that this had never before been attempted, Heracles marshaled all his forces and advanced toward the mountains through open country, reaching the foothills without encountering any further opposition from the local tribes. As the mountains loomed nearer, many of his followers, whether from strain of battle or fear of what was to come, abandoned him. Those that remained, although familiar with rumors and reports, were not prepared for the reality that invaded their sight. Before them the mountains, merely the western spur of that great and impenetrable range that marked the northern extremity of the known world, towered like an unholy excrescence of the earth, as high above the ground as perhaps Tartaros was below it. The towering peaks, lost in clouds, swirling with hail and hoarfrost, engulfed in impenetrable ice that never thaws, extended past steep faces impossible to climb. Spring did not invade there; an eternal winter always held reign, filled with every wind and storm capable of bringing misery to man.

Heracles took stock. After releasing from service those who had brought their wives and children, encouraging them to return to their homes or to settle nearby, he was left with two thousand fighters, a third of them on horseback. Assembling the core followers who had come with him from Crete: Antores, Peleus, Iphicles, Melampos, Iolaos, and Thamuz, he tried to lift their hearts by recalling the adventures they had been through together, as well as the glory of surmounting the challenges that lay ahead. In little time, he told them, their journey would end, and nothing would be left but the memories of hardships endured and triumphs won. These mettlesome captains, in turn, rallied the rest, until all were eager to begin the crossing despite the ever-present apprehension inspired by the dreadful, frozen heights, on whose peaks Gryphons were said to build their eyries.

As soon as they made some progress up the lower slopes, which as of yet afforded an unconstrained and  pleasant climb, the local tribesmen, who had been observing them from their crude huts and castles upon the rocks, planned to bring destruction upon them. The Ligurian guides remained silent; but the Celts who were loyal to Heracles disclosed the danger. Heracles therefore ordered a halt at the foot of the pass and sent them forth as spies. Because they shared much of the language and customs as the wild mountain men, they learned that these held the pass only in the daytime, retiring to their homes at night when the air grew cold. So Heracles turned the matter over in his mind and the next morning ordered his troops to march further up the defile, just shy of where the enemy waited like patient carrion-birds. The tribesmen watched them all day, and not finding an opportunity to successfully attack the fortified camp, dispersed that night. After having many more watch-fires lit than normal, Heracles led a force of agile fighters to occupy the cliffs above where the tribesmen had been stationed. At dawn the next day the main body continued up the pass. The mountain men began assembling at their usual stations. Looking up, however, they saw themselves pinned to their positions by those having the coign of vantage.

Heracles' stratagem held only a short while. As the pass

climbed higher, it became narrower and uneven, and flanked by precipitous drops. The barbarians, seeing an opportunity, began to cast down stones. The sudden attack served to throw the main body into confusion. There was so little space for movement, and such a rush to get out harm's way, that horses and pack-animals slipped off the edges into the flanking gorges. Seeing the sorry state of things below, Heracles rushed his men down from the heights, routing out along the way the enemy ensconced in the rocks. Pressed between fighting men on both sides, the tribesmen gave up the struggle and fled. After order was restored to the main column, it was able to advance unmolested through the narrowest portion of the pass between sheer cliff faces. Beyond that point they came to a village belonging to the tribesmen. They seized it easily, for it was nearly empty of men, containing only women and children, and secured much grain and livestock. Some of the wild Celts with him petitioned to take the women and kill the male children, but Heracles forbade them since such unconscionable acts contravened all human decency.

For the next four days the march continued without issue. The pass still wound through the lowlands dotted with hamlets, but none of their inhabitants ventured out to threaten them. As the track climbed higher, they reached the treeline, where extensive patches of oak, beech and ash-trees covered the slopes. These virgin woods soon gave way to impenetrable forests of fir and spruce, forcing Heracles to scout out detours that carried them up trackless ways to fearsome heights. On the tenth day Heracles reached the top of the pass, where in a wide grassy area fringed with wildflowers, and where trees no longer grew, he pitched camp and rested for two days, allowing stragglers to catch up and providing needed rest to men and beasts alike. Above them loomed the bitter snow-capped peaks; the cold breathing from there discomfited them, especially at night when the northwest wind howled down from the heights, bedewing their faces with moist snowflakes.

If anyone thought the worst was behind, he soon regretted harboring that opinion. Soon after resuming march, the snow began. Flurries turned to a thick, relentless snowfall, covering all in a white blanket that made a monotony of vision. The entire host trudged on, exhausted, with uneven footsteps through the frozen muck. The next day the sun rose high and bedeviled the frozen peaks, so that, through a narrow track, with precipitous walls on every side, the thawing snow fell down in vast sheets, burying the tail end of the column in an avalanche. The mountain savages, minding the confusion, saw one more opportunity to inflict injury. Emerging from their caves, their faces covered with filth and their hair matted with dirt, so that they projected a fearsome aspect, the savages nimbly descended sure-footed through hidden paths and familiar snow-drifts, and attacked with wild ferocity. Where before the snow-covered ground, treacherous though it was, shone with a pristine beauty; it now ran hot with thawing rivulets of blood. The fighting continued into the next day, with the enemy focusing all their energy on the flanks, trying to split the column. Heracles made his way to the back of the column, where he helped to dig out the buried rearguard, and leading them in a charge, pushed the enemy back up the slopes, where archers and slingers could pick them off. After nightfall the fighting fell off, with only small skirmishes here or there, until the surviving tribesmen gave up the struggle and disappeared back to where they came.

With the morning light the carnage was terrible to behold. Men and beasts lay sprawled up and down the path, and through the narrow byways, on snow dyed crimson. Heracles howled for Iolaos until he found him, covered in others' blood, and embraced him tenderly. Melampos tearfully reported that their Egyptian helmsman had perished in the battle, along with most of the remaining Cretans. Heracles had charged them to protect the red cattle, and they died doing so. All now waited on Heracles to take command, but he was sullen and tormented, and walked off by himself until he was but a distant speck on the white landscape. Antores sought to follow him, but Iphicles held him back, saying: "Leave him be. He rightly feels the pain of his failures. See into what misery he has led us, simply for some kine which he deems of more importance than men."

Peleus, in charge of the horsemen, helped to reform the column, and led it onward in the descent. Meanwhile Heracles, his shoulders bowed, climbed to the edge of a rocky precipice. Below him spread a vast landscape thick with low-lying clouds and fog and the black crowns of scattered ridges. Heracles looked back at his followers winding slowly down the snow-clogged defile, and sighing deeply, said: "Great Zeus, thy will be done! I ask nothing for myself, for I believe that what each man does will shape his fortune. But If I am indeed thy son, grant me this request: save these who have followed me willingly across the world. I have retrieved the cattle of Geryones as I was ordered, and should I perish on these frosty peaks, bring my companions safely to Greece. Consider, then, my Labors complete. Preserve the life of all in this company, great or small, that they may seek out their homes or establish new ones, and end their days in tranquil peace, remembering that they once served Heracles, the benefactor of mankind."

Thus he prayed. As Heracles gazed at the sea of mist, by degrees the clouds broke, and he saw revealed a deep and endless verdant valley, couched between the distant edges of two faded mountain ranges. Down its length ran the blue ribbon of a mighty river, fed by numerous tributaries, turgid with snow from mountain torrents melting in summer's wane. Since embarking across the mountains, for once his heart lifted; and hope, the greatest thing possessed by men, invigorated his weary body and renewed his courage. He waited for his forces to reach him, and gathering his captains, pointed at the woods and fertile plains below, lifting their spirits by the knowledge that, after a descent shorter than the ascent, they would cross through to that happy land.

The descent on the Hesperian side of the mountains proved indeed shorter, but correspondingly steeper. The pathless track grew narrow, slippery, and flanked by precipitous drops. If one man or beast stumbled, the rest slipped down with him in a confused jumble, sometimes over the precipices, so that as many lives were lost on the way down as were lost on the way up. But as there was nowhere to go but forward, the whole company marched on until progress ended at the edge of a narrow cliff from where it proved impossible to continue. Heracles, with the rearguard, went up the column to determine why they had halted. On seeing the sheer drop, he looked around for another avenue. But the pass had to be abandoned, and a new one discovered. So he led them down an adjacent slope, opposite the lee side, where a recent snowfall had covered the old snow underneath. But no sooner had the multitude of feet and hooves trampled through the shallow layer of fresh snow than their track became the bare ice beneath. The heavy cattle and the mule-train weighed down with gear broke through the ice and were left there affixed and unable to move. Heracles at once ordered the column to turn back to the ridge, from which they had not made much progress. After spending the rest of the time clearing an area of snow and rescuing trapped beasts, they pitched camp for the night. The next morning Heracles surveyed the scene with fresh eyes, but he could think of no easy way to get down to the well-watered valley that beckoned them like land to sailors lost at sea. Iphicles came forward, and having earned his living as a stone-cutter after the death of Amphytrion, described a method of making the slope traversable, to which Heracles listened dubiously because of the immensity of the undertaking. Heracles did not entertain the plan until the next day, when it came evident that everyone would starve if they remained any longer stranded on the ridge. Save for butchering the red cattle, no other means existed to procure sustenance. So Heracles asked Iphicles to carry out the task he proposed, which was to cut through the ice and rock of the slope face to carve out a serried track that would provide adequate foothold. For the next five days every available hand busied himself in the labor. Trees were cut and hauled up from the lower slopes, since the terrain where they encamped was bare; these were rolled down into an immense pile of timber, which, with help from the wind, was lit on fire. The roaring flames melted the ice and heated the rocks, and as the conflagration progressed down the mountainside, bouts of continuous condensation and solidification shivered them. With mattocks and pointed weapons the men followed, chipping at the frangible granite to reduce the declivity. After the track was sufficiently hewn, they were able to abandon the ridge and descend to where meadows and oak forests abounded. The beasts were put out to pasture. Heracles counted the cattle of Geryones one by one, finding happily that the hardy herd had not suffered an appreciable loss. Yet it still pained him greatly that so many lives were lost in the crossing, and those who lived were left squalid and savage-looking and covered in filth. He let the men rest as long as they wished, and after three days of recuperation the descent resumed to the sunny foothills where they captured and ate mountain hares and ibex, and drank from cold streams, and rejoiced at seeing butterflies.

They followed the course of the river westward through woods moist with mist and loud with the rushing water. At a certain point they came across a marble slab embedded in the riverbank. Tall and graceful poplars grew around it. Though covered in the mire and cracked with age, those who came near saw engraved on the stone in ancient and unknown characters:

NEARBY PHAËTHON LIES, WHO DARED TO DRIVE
HIS FATHER'S CHARIOT; THOUGH FAILED, HE TRIED.
AND IN HIS FALL HE GAINED
THE DEATH OF ONE SUPREMELY BRAVE.

The learned Melampos could make out the name of Phaëthon in the epitaph. After consulting with their Celt guides, Melampos concluded that the river before them was the legendary Eridanos, where it was said Phaëthon, the son of Helios fell from his father's flaming chariot. Filled with excitement at the discovery, he sought eagerly for a lyre, and sitting on a rock, narrated the somber story. He sang how Phaëthon fell like a star, leaving a coruscating trail through the sky, into a deep lake, where the river's god bathed his smoke-blackened face, and nymphs consigned his torched body to the ground. Helios, ill with grief, hid his face for one whole day, although the flames Phaëthon had kindled on the earth prevented a decline into total darkness. Frantic Clymene sought her son over the earth until she found his grave by the headwaters of the deep-eddying Eridanos, but could do nothing but wet his tomb with her tears. Her daughters, the Heliads, soon arrived to mourn their brother, tearing at their breasts, and lying night and day by his tomb, calling out to ears that would never again hear. For four moons they filled the wood with their piteous cries until Phaëthusa the elder felt her ankles stiffen; and Lampetia, trying to help, found herself rooted to the ground; and a third sister, tearing her hair, clutched only leaves. The others cried out as wood grew about their legs, or their arms became long branches. Bark began to sheath their lithe bodies, until all that was left were mouths crying for succor. Clymene can only race from one tree to another, pressing her lips against theirs, or tearing at the bark to free her daughters. Blood drips, as from wounds. "Stop, mother," say the Heliads. "You tear at our bodies; farewell now. We shall ever remain by our beloved brother, shielding him from sun and rain." Bark closed even over their mouths. Their tears flow still, and hardened by the sun, drop as amber from the branches. As proof of the truth of the tale, Melampos reached a hand into the stream and pulled some nuggets of the fulvous resin, which, for medicinal use, he deposited in his satchel.

They passed from the woods into the wide lowland plains, travelling alongside the river, crossing its many affluents flowing from deep mountains sources or draining from lakes above the valley basin. Another great mountain range crowded their view ahead, almost contiguous with the one that they had crossed. The Ligurians they had taken prisoner begged to be released to their countrymen, who also populated that side in a wide swath of land down the coast. From his great heart, Heracles did so, since they had shared in the same sufferings. They repaid him, however, with guile, telling him that the Apennines were impassable this far north. Since the geography of the land was imperfectly known outside of the native tribes, Heracles saw no reason to disbelieve them. In addition, his forces, remembering the hazards across the mountains, were not at all eager to repeat so soon the experience. Heracles, therefore, led them southward until they came near the coast, where olive trees began to take the place of mountain pines and larches, and, rounding a broad bay, proceeded down a high and narrow coastal strip ringed by hills. From the land of the Ligurians they passed into that of the Tyrrhenians. It was not known from whence these peoples sprang; whether they were native to the land, or consisted of Pelasgians who swarmed there across the sea, or were derived from Maonian colonists. They had a language and customs unlike any those of any other nation, and liked to build their settlements on hills, the steeper the better, which they surrounded with thick walls. They mined and commerced in iron and copper. Heracles kept well clear of their hill-forts and pasturelands, so that he was able to pass through without engaging them.

From there they encountered the river Albula as it made a great bend westward: a natural demarcation between the Tyrrhenians and the Umbrians to the north, and a colony of Arcadians who settled east of it. This river, turbid, rapid, irregular, and having a yellow and muddy hue, seemed to present an insurmountable obstacle to Heracles' weary followers. Heracles had them therefore pitch camp by the riverbank, while he himself drove the cattle onward, searching for a place to ford it. Downriver, at another bend, he found a place where sediment had collected, raising the riverbed into an islet which divided the river, and there drove the cattle before him as he swam. Finding on the other side rich pasturage on a plain between the left bank and a ridge of hills, and unsuspecting of any danger, he let the cattle graze, while he, weary from a habitual lack of sleep, lay down on a grassy bed to sleep.

In the morning Heracles awoke refreshed, and the world seemed bright and new to him. He breakfasted on the crumbs of barley-cakes from his satchel but could not find anything to drink, repulsed by the river water's insalubrious complexion. Forgetting his thirst for the moment, he rounded up the cattle, with the intent of securing them in a vale he saw farther south amidst some low, wooded hills while he waited for his comrades.

Knowing the tale of the herd, since he grew accustomed to count them each day from an obsession over the great hardship it took to procure them, it took not long to notice that some of the finest kine, four bulls and four heifers, were missing. He searched up and down the plain, driving the cattle before him, reluctant to leave any out his sight. On a marshy plain between two hills rifled with freshets he noticed hoof-marks in the mud. They led into a forest surrounding a third hill, called Aventine. There, hard by the river, he found a cavern under the mount, its entrance sealed by a great slab of rock. Above the doorway hung skulls and rusty arms, and before it bleached bones littered the ground. Every track, noticed Heracles, led from the cave, and none toward it! Bewildered, Heracles knocked upon the door with his club so that the skulls rattled and fell. As no answer came, he prepared to drive his herd away from so strange a neighborhood. Just then he heard a bellowing from within the cave; for the stolen cattle heard the lowing of their companions outside and answered them, as they are wont to do. Heracles, entertaining now no doubts, and recognizing thievery and artifice, struck the door again with the intent of breaking through it. But his great knotted club splintered and cracked against the hard rock. Studying the door, he found it cunningly wrought, resting on hidden groves, so that it could slide upward like a portcullis. Bracing his shoulders against it, he heaved and began to raise the slab. But with a crack and a clatter of chains from within, the door slid from his hands and dropped, effacing the little progress he had made. The sonorous laughter of the beastly thief Cacus, terror of the Aventine wood, passed through the door after he had broken the tackle that animated it. He was the son of Hephaistos, and as skilled as his father in mechanical arts. While Heracles had slept by the riverbank, Cacus, going forth to perform his nightly mischief, came across the cattle, and attracted by their beautiful chestnut coloration, stole some of the most splendid ones, dragging them backward to his cavern by the tails to throw off the trail.

Heracles, not only robbed, but perceiving the added injury of being mocked, seethed with anger. With sighs and groans three times he tried again to lift the stone, but it would have taken ten yoked oxen to move it. Three times he tramped about the hill, looking for some other ingress. Weary, but with his anger still black, he descried a thin column of black smoke from a crack on the hillside, where a flinty outcropping arose on all sides sheer, covered with the nests of carrion-birds. Heracles climbed the mount, bracing himself against rocks and tree roots. Then digging his heels into the crack, he pressed his back against the left-leaning rock. Rocking back and forth he loosened it, and ripped from its roots, it toppled over in a thunderous, rocky avalanche, bursting asunder the side of the hill, exposing the shadowy den of Cacus to the light, as if the earth, riven from some cataclysm, brought to the open the gloomy netherworld. There stood the beastly Cacus, shaggy from head to foot, of huge frame and grim countenance, looking up with peaked eyes and trembling like a shade thrust into daylight. "I see you now, worm!" cried Heracles exultantly; "and I accept your invitation." He rained down stones and heavy boughs on the entrapped thief; but taking with him a firebrand, Cacus fled into the dark recesses of his sprawling cavern. With a leap Heracles cleared the chasm and landed on the grotto floor, filthy with bones and debris. On one side he saw the stolen cattle tied and safe, and on the other tunnels filled with smoke, for Cacus had set fires as he fled. Heracles plunged into the thick smoke, and with black soot blinding his eyes, relentlessly sought Cacus throughout his vast underground domain. With flames on every side, and billowing smoke plunging all into night, Heracles staggered with outstretched arms, ready to grip the fulsome thief. At last Cacus, himself overcome by the fire and black cloud, fell to the ground. Heracles, close behind, stumbled over him. There in the gloom they fought strenuously; even in his weakened state Cacus matched Heracles in strength. Round about they tussled in the filth. Cacus cut Heracles with jagged, broken bones; and Heracles, his hand reaching a cudgel, battered in the giant thief's face. "Help me, comrades!" cried out Cacus to his neighbors. "A stranger has broken into my home and is doing me violence!" Heracles crushed his jaw so he spoke no more, and Cacus, vomiting blood and smoke, nearly gave up the struggle. Then Heracles held him in a knot and strangled him until his eyes nearly popped from his head.

Coughing, his lungs aching for want of clean air, Heracles found his way through the roiling fumes back to where sunlight penetrated, dragging the misshapen bulk of Cacus by the heels. He stopped a moment for a salutary breath, then yoked the four bulls to the chains and balances by the door. Their combined brawn tore the rocky slab from its grooves, further dispelling the darkness from the lair. He led the lost bulls and heifers to the herd and said: "Cattle of Heracles, go: my club's last labor, twice sought after by me, twice my prize; sanctify the cattle-market where you end up with your deep lowing and may your pastures become a famous gathering place."

After immuring Cacus under boulders, he purified himself down by the river, washing off the gore and filth, and streaked his face in mud to confuse Cacus' ghost.

Still parched with thirst Heracles ranged about, seeking a stream or fountain, when he heard girlish laughter from a grove where the trees formed a shaded circle. In its center stood a ruined hut, lit by aromatic fires burning myrrh; and a poplar's spreading foliage, home to singing birds, overshadowed it.

Heracles rushed there, and standing before the door said: "O you, who linger in the grove's sacred hollows, open your shrine to a tired man. I hear the sound of refreshing waters within, perhaps from a clear and cold fountain—but a handful of it would be enough for me." The laughter ended abruptly at his words. Heracles, distressed that whoever was inside put sacred rites over the welfare of a human being, continued: "Good goddess—or whoever you may be—have you not heard of he who slew the Hydra? Or chased the gold-antlered hind for a whole year? Or travelled to the end of earth for the cattle of Geryones? I am he—

Heracles! Allow me entrance; o, how this land, blessed with beauty unparalleled, scarcely seems opened to me. Even if it is to Hera you sacrifice, bitter as she is against me, she would not shut her waters from me. But if any of you are afraid of my face, or the lion's pelt about my shoulders, or my hair blanched by the Libyan sun, I am the same who once dressed in soft clothes and passed my time in king's houses, eating fine foods and playing with little ones."

At length the door cracked open. An aged priestess, her white hair tied with a purple ribbon, stood before him and said: "Stranger, avert your eyes and leave this sacred grove; by doing so you will remain safe. The altar guarded in this lonely hut is prohibited to men, and sacrilege is avenged by our laws. The gods will grant you other waters to quench your thirst. This one flows only for womankind."

Heracles, cross at his ill treatment, and ignoring the warning, with one push burst the door from its hinges and rushed past the priestess to the sacred fount bubbling from a rock. He bathed his head in the life-giving waters and drank deeply, leaving a trickle. The horrified priestess and her younger acolytes fled in terror. When he stepped out shaking the water from his shaggy face, he found himself surrounded by a crowd of herders, ploughmen and other local inhabitants. Although a few ill-informed individuals shook their fists at him, accusing him of open murder, the rest stood before his gigantic form in awe, rejoicing that he had rid them of Cacus, reviled for his villainies. The poorer among them, collecting laurel branches, wreathed crowns for him and themselves, dropping at his feet and worshipping him, seeing in him something divine. Before he could say a word, the crowd parted to admit a young man into their midst. He was Evander, who ruled the Arcadian colonists more by his personal ascendancy than by the exercise of kingly power. Slight of build, yet prodigious in his intellect, he was the son, as was supposed, of Hermes by Themis, and Arcadian nymph, while she was married to Echemos. At her instigation, Evander killed his father; and this began a civil war in their city Pallanteum. The winning side banished Evander, and he led a colony from Arcadia to Hesperia in two ships. They came to dwell among the Aborigines, a people believed to have also come from Arcadia, who had dispossessed the ancient Umbrians and Sicels after their migration. They were governed by Faunus, the son of Picus, who was the son of Cronos the Titan, called there Saturn, if such can be believed. Dethroned by Zeus, Cronos took refuge in Hesperia, where, finding the people crude and contemptible, scattered across the mountains, without knowledge of husbandry or agriculture, taught them these things, and gave them laws necessary for a civilized life. He so blessed the increase of their livestock and the yield of their crops, that they lived without care, simply taking of the earth's abundance, drinking honey and milk, their limbs never wracked with age, but ever dancing and laughing, and finally, when the time came, drifting off in death as in a sleep. But later generations forgot such advancements, and retreated back to their former bestial ways.

Faunus, who adopted the cruel and perverse practice of sacrificing strangers to Cronos, nevertheless kindly received Evander and his people, considering them kinsmen, and giving them all the land they desired. But as they were small in number, they chose a hill near the Albula, by the inspiration of Themis, who was a prophetess, and there built a town which they named Pallanteum in honor of their mother-city in Arcadia. Their town they adorned with all the buildings to which they had been accustomed; including, since they were very pious, a multitude of shrines and temples. They first erected a shrine to Pan, the oldest of all divinities and haunter of Arcadian woodlands, in a large cave under an embowered hill. In return for their hospitality, Evander and his mother taught the rustic Aborigines the use of letters, and performed music for them on lyres, flutes and harps, since the latter knew only the shepherd's pipes; and promulgated laws and all things necessary for the public good, introducing arts and culture where none had existed for a long time.

Evander first questioned some local herdsmen to find out what occurred, and seeing that Heracles grew impatient, inquired of him directly. Heracles responded curtly, saying only that he would say no more until he had supped, charging the nation with atrocious hospitality. A woman in the crowd accused him of violating the sacred spring, but she was shouted down, for the priestess was the wife of Faunus, and most resented that she still practiced archaic rites within their ambit. Evander, impressed with a sense of Heracles' greatness and raw power, invited him to his residence. Heracles followed him into the town, which had grown all around and up the wooded hill like a caracole. Evander felt a bit ashamed at the modesty of his house, thinking Heracles would develop a low opinion of him. Evander's kingdom was yet small and weak, and he had little riches. Heracles said not a word as he entered, stooping to cross his threshold. Evander made ready for him a couch of scattered leaves under a woolly fleeceskin, and had food and drink brought out. When Evander learned the hero's name, and things concerning his father and his country, he cried: "Heracles, son of Zeus, hail! My mother Themis, who speaks truth in the name of the gods, spoke your very name not a fortnight ago! She prophesied of your coming, and that you will be raised to heaven as a god because of your virtue, and that here a shrine will be dedicated to you that will stand for ages, one which a future nation—the most powerful nation the world will ever know—will call their greatest." Heracles looked deeply at Evander, at first thinking him a blandisher, until he could not disregard the sincerity in the young king's speech and manners. He grasped Evander's right hand and said: "Well met, sire! I myself will fulfill your mother's prophecy by building this altar. There sacrifices can be made to me as a hero now, and later, if what you say comes true, as a god!" The latter part he added as a jest, since he could not believe a man could become a god; but Evander started up earnestly, ready to commence. Just then they heard a commotion nearby: angry shouts and the clash of arms. Both ran from the house. Heracles' followers poured in from all sides, resisted by butchers and bakers, fullers and shepherds, and Evander's small defensive cohort. When Peleus saw Heracles was safe and sound, he rode through the midst of the disturbance to separate the parties.

With peace made between the two groups, Heracles made good on his proposal. Early the next morning, he heaped stones for an altar near the market-place and selected the most beautiful of the red heifers for sacrifice. Evander, meanwhile, appointed members of two prominent families to assist him, charging them to present themselves promptly. Heracles, recalling the insult at the fountain, accepted only the men among them, and not the women, saying: "This great altar, dedicated to my herd's recovery, will never be open to women's worship so that my thirst will never go unavenged." The family of the Potitii arrived first, bringing the heifer, its head encircled with ribbons and garlands, to the altar.

There they washed their hands and grabbed handfuls of barley grain. Raising his arms, Heracles gave thanks to Zeus while the barley was cast onto the altar fire. Heracles then cut a few hairs from the heifer's head and added them to the flames. Then holding the animal over the altar, he slit its throat so that blood laved the altar stones. The Potitii next skinned the carcass and butchered it, piercing the umbrals with forks and roasting them over the fire. After they consumed these delicacies, members of the second family, the Pinarii, suddenly arrived. They joined in the rest of the banquet, but from that time onward it became the rule that, due to the disgrace of arriving late, none of the Pinarri would ever eat the entrails of a victim when presiding over that rite. As the common people pressed around the altar clamoring for a look, Heracles took pity on them and entertained them with a grand feast, butchering for them several more of the plumpest cattle. He also distributed a tithe of all the booty he had collected on his campaigns, making sure even the poorest among them received something.

Heracles remained at Pallanteum well into autumn, when the mornings dawned crisp and cool, and the foliage burst forth in wild color. Yet the weather remained mild close to the coast. The red oxen grew fat foraging the dewy grass of the glades. Many of Heracles' followers, enchanted by such a fertile land, so bounteous in all things man could desire, wished to settle there. Antores took an Arcadian wife, and Melampos grew enamored of young virgin. He composed many poems for her, and was highly esteemed for his skills as a physician. He started the practice of recommending his patients bathe in springs of hot water, which were numerous, and by this many bodily infirmities were healed. Heracles had union with several women, including the priestess Rhea and the youngest daughter of Evander, Lavinia, whom her father eagerly introduced to him, hoping to mix Heracles' glorious blood with his. Long after Heracles left them, Rhea bore him Aventinus in secret on the Aventine hill and Lavinia bore him Pallas; but the latter died before he arrived at puberty. Heracles also unwittingly had union with Fauna, the wife and sister of king Faunus of the Aborigines. She was the priestess who barred his entering the sacred spring. And it happened in this way.

Evander took Heracles to show him the breadth of the land. It was evident that no other country in the world was more blessed with good things.  Temperate weather; good, arable land; copious timber from the wooded hills; broad, sunny meadows; an abundance of beasts for hunting; sea-fish innumerable; orchards bursting with fruit trees; vineyards yielding succulent grapes: all of these blessings were attributed to Cronos since, being more ancient than the Olympians, he had greater power to grant mankind everything sufficient for happiness.  One day as they were returning from a hunt, they saw the people excitedly rushing to a hill abutting the Albula, called the Cronian in honor of the god.  In all seven hills encompassed the domains of the Aborigines and the Arcadians.  There, on a bare, rocky eminence king Faunus, surrounded by white-clad priests, prepared to fling two old men into the river.  When Heracles demanded to know the reason, Faunus, with a narrow, sallow face like an old goat's and white hair coiled above his head in the shape of horns, answered: "Do not interrupt our ancient annual ritual, O Heracles; for an old tradition enjoins us to 'cast into the water of the Tuscan river two of the people as a sacrifice to the Ancient who bares the sickle.'  We do so as a thank-offering to He who of eld trod these very glades and continues to shower us with his munificence."  Meanwhile the two old men who were to be sacrificed trembled and held out bound hands to Heracles in supplication.  Heracles said: "I have heard of this god, a bloody and vicious one, since with a sickle he unmanned his own father.  He seems no different than the gods of Celtica, who also demand the abomination of human sacrifice.  Travelling through these lands I have put an end to such practices where I have found them, as I shall do so here.  Release these men and go your way, and never again perform this despicable rite."  Faunus pointed a bony finger at Heracles and said: "A minion of Iuppiter has no say here in the Saturnian land.  Since Evander tells me you claim to be his son, a worthier sacrifice will you be.  Long ago Iuppiter overthrew Saturn, and now that act shall be avenged.  Seize him and cast him over!"  When the priests laid hands on Heracles, he shook them off like a horse shakes raindrops from its back, and picking up Faunus with one hand, flung him over the edge of the precipice.  With a cry he hit the yellow flood and was carried away, where he drowned ere he reached the sea.

The Aborigines rose up in fury, more at the desecration of their ritual than the murder of their king, fearing that in anger the god would repent of his beneficence. Heracles appeased them by teaching them a new way to perform the sacrifice. He erected an altar on the hill and had them construct effigies of men from bulrushes, complete with bound hands and feet and clothes. These were to be thrown instead into the stream. The people thought well of this, and the practice has continued to this day. Later the ancient roots of this ritual were forgotten, and it was believed to have started when one of Heracles' followers who remained there, pining for his home in Argos, wished at his death to be thrown into the river so that his remains could somehow reach the shores of Thessaly. But his son disliked this charge, and burying his father, cast an effigy of him into the river instead. The truth of the matter, however, has been well documented.

One night shortly thereafter, while Heracles lay slumbering in Evander's house after a night of feasting, Faunus' wife and sister Fauna, after having painted her cheeks red with alkanet root and rubbed spikenard between her withered breasts, entered surreptitiously and lay with him. She detested the man, but learned in a dream that he would father a great people. Being childless, she thought her spring had long died up and had little hope the prophecy would come true through her. But she later miraculously bore Latinus, who succeeded to the kingdom of the Aborigines when he became of age. It was supposed that he was the son of Faunus, since she never revealed the truth of his conception.

While Heracles and Evander one day drank with Cacius, a notable citizen who lived on the hill called Palatine, and whose house one reached by an elegant stone stairway, certain Tyrrhenians arrived to collect tribute from Evander. Evander meekly submitted, sending someone to collect it from the treasury. But Heracles cast the delegates out, ordering them never to return and interrupt their drinking bout. They left with dour faces, promising a sorry end to the matter.

When the rumor of war reached his ears, Heracles organized his troops, along with large numbers of Aborigines and Arcadians. The men had grown soft from many months spent idle, their stomachs filled with venison and sweet dark wine, but Heracles had them grease their swords and pointed lances, and retie the ox-hides of their shields. Meanwhile, Evander prepared to defend the walls of his settlement at the foot of the Palatine. Long stakes, hewn from stout oaks, sharpened and hardened with fire, the Arcadians affixed along the riverbank, and behind commenced to dig a trench; and with the mass of displaced earth, a rampart.

Skilled in war, ever ready for battle, the Tyrrhenians in their high-walled cities flung open their gates and out thundered two-horsed chariots, columns of spearmen, and horsed troops, among them a young and ruthless officer, Mezentius. When the Arcadians saw the swirling dust kicked up by columns of enemy soldiery streaming across the plain, felt the earth trembling under their tramping horses, and heard the trumpets sound in alarm, panic gripped their hearts.

Evander, emboldened by the aid of Heracles, called his troops to order, trotting his warhorse up and down the riverbank. But the common people held back in fear, having never yet faced such a well-equipped foe; even the wild Celts, with their natural ferocity, were not accoutered as these. From head to foot, the Tyrrhenians were encased in armor, and each man had with him two lances, a great round buckler, and at their sides whetted swords. They possessed also the advantage of chariots, the first peoples to employ them in the region. Heracles rightly saw the peoples' dismay, and grabbing a colored pennant, carried it to the highest point on the riverbank. There, high on his horse, he cried: "Countrymen and proud friends! Men of Achaia and Crete, Ligurians, Celts, Aborigines and Arcadians! We are here to strike a blow for freedom—freedom from fear and tribute! No people should be ruled without consent, forced to give up the sweat of their brows and the gifts of the earth to foreign kings. Work now to break these bonds of slavery, and fight for the sake of your ploughlands and vineyards, fisheries and pasturages. Although now you are some divided in language or race, I foresee that someday you will be united as one nation on these banks, occupying the seven hills, and masters of your destiny. See how I share all hardships with you, and pledge my life to your struggle." At these words all cheered in consent. Heracles rode to Evander, placing himself under his command. Evander called for his captains and divided up the host.

The Tyrrhenian chariots and horsemen drew up aslant across the river to establish a ford across the water, by which the mass of their foot-soldiers gained the other side. Heracles led the first sortie, taking position atop the ramparts to harass by arrow and deadly lances the attackers as they tried to cross the defensive ditch. But, like a flood, the Tyrrhenians, far outnumbering Evander's countrymen, overwhelmed the ramparts, forcing Heracles to pull back. Evander, the scales of his fitted cuirass glowing red in the dawnlight and his legs shod in golden greaves, led his main force in a direct charge against the middle of the enemy rush. The two sides confronted each other in a forest of bristling spears. Through their midst Evander led his cavalry, crushing the Tyrrhenian footsoldiers under his fiery steeds, until the ground choked with blood and armor. Peleus and Heracles, meanwhile, attacked the flanks, keeping the pulsing enemy troops confined to a narrow track of the plain, preventing them from spreading around to the undefended hills around Pallanteum.

Mezentius, who was later to gain the throne of Tyrrhenia, but lose it from his tyrannous cruelty, spied Evander in the tumult. Gripping his heavy lance, he reared back on his mount, and let the deadly wood slice the air. But vigilant Acoetes, armor-bearer to Evander, lashed his horse, drawing blood from the flanks, and in time interposed his shield before his beloved master. The force of the spear thrusting through his targe ripped him from his horse, and left him pinned to the ground. Evander, turning in surprise, saw Mezentius bearing down on him. Raising his gleaming sword, Evander met him in a clash of steel that staggered the troops, like birds scattered from their perch at the burst of a sudden thunderclap. Mezentius—younger, stronger and massive in his armor—hacked at Evander's oblong shield and tight-linked mail until the latter's horse quivered under the battering's weight.

A Tyrrhenian chariot, overwhelmed by the Albula's furor, as if the river-god, offended, could no longer abide the violation of its tumultuous flow, was suddenly swept away, breaking the cordon that allowed safe passage. A mad scramble ensued as the remaining attackers sought to reach the eastern bank. The welter of desperate horses and churning chariot-wheels distracted Mezentius, allowing Evander to interleave sword-blows of his own before Mezentius snapped his reins to gallop away to the riverside, where he attempted to reform the squadrons. Heracles once again assembled his men at the top of the rampart, and heaving or rolling down great stones, rained death down on men and horses, crushing plumed helms and wrecking chariot-poles.

Evander, charging through a thicket of quivering spears, dealing death to his left and right with his untiring blade, reached the hill of his beloved town. From walkways atop the high palisade and from the flanking towers the defenders looked down for hope and guidance from their leader. With shouts he encouraged them to hold firm, but to prepare stones, arrows and caldrons of boiling oil in case the enemy neared the walls, although he saw how the Tyrrhenians seemed held in check: their foot-soldiers hemmed in from every side, like a flock of sheep corralled by a few barking hounds, and their cavalry unable to surmount the rampart. But then the clangor of brazen trumpets chilled him to the marrow. Speeding around the hill, emerging from the underbrush, he froze in his tracks. Through the valley, from the direction of the Aventine, another army stirred the black dust. He recognized the standards of the Latian tribes: the Rutulians, who often harried them, confining them to their side of the river; the Laurentines, proud in holding the first place among the Latians; the Praenestines, ruled by Erulus, whose mother, the Sabine goddess Feronia, endowed with three lives and three sets of weaponry; and even the Daunians, kin and allies of the Rutulians, from the eastern coast. Evander dispatched Acoetes, urging him to fly in search of Heracles to inform him of the new threat; for now Evander faced the grim prospect of war on two fronts. Then turning his horse about, he returned to the thick of battle, where he gathered his chief officers and two-hundred horsemen. His Aborigine auxiliaries, and those countrymen who had lost their mounts he urged to burden themselves with discarded arms and form in lines, enjoining them to prepare for a desperate fight on foot, which was against their custom. With one last look at his beloved city, harried on all sides by the threat of steel and fire, he led his cohorts into the quaking valley. When Erulus saw him, he rode out from his troop on his richly caparisoned horse, and taunting him said: "How far from home you find yourself Evander! What god or madness led you to leave cold Arcadia, replete with springs mewed by hidden chasms, to dare establish a beachhead in our sacred land, hemmed in as you are by fiercer foes than helpful allies? You behold from your high walls, soon to be the surfeit of Vulcan's appetite, the ruins of Janiculum, built by no less than blessed Saturn himself, but now overgrown with tangled leaves and bristling with underbrush, the haunt of wolves and screech-owls; so shall your town be this day when proud Ausonia washes away the foreign filth accreted on its shore."

Evander held his tongue in check, but not his anger. He organized his soldiers, forming first a line of overlapping shields, and behind them ready pike-men. In a third row the archers massed, their bowstrings burdened with fletched shafts. At his command they aimed for the clouds and released a shower of wood and iron, which fell like hail from a clear day on the advancing Latian columns. Down fell numerous of their van, pierced through eyes and necks or gaps in armor. Solid pikes now formed a bristling fence, dealing painful death to all who dared breach it. From behind it whizzed out lances, unstopped by shield or cuirass. The armies now closed in, man against desperate man, with the Arcadians fighting more fiercely since those who struggle for the sake of their wives, children and possessions, though fewer in number, fight with greater heart. From the Aventine to the Palatine hills flowed a new tributary of the Albula, mixing red with the yellow flood. Evander, first among princes, led his cavalry left and right, bringing sudden death to Latians in the flanks or the rear; or else, arraying his equestrians like an arrow-head, pierced the center of the enemy formation. But the waves of Latians would not subside, and soon Evander was pinned to the slope leading, through leafy forest, to Pallanteum's postern gate.

Heracles by a single arrow slew both driver and warrior of the first chariot to the reach the level field. Seeing now the walls of Pallanteum under siege, he vaulted in the car and spurred the horses with voice and lash. Like a tempest he thundered up the well-worn paths, cutting a swath through enemy ranks toiling to make some breach into Evander's home. Cowering under shields against the stones and burning brands falling from above, they hardly knew what great force rushed against them, like men at sea swept from their thwarts by a sudden gale.

Evander and his forces pushed back against the Latians, holding their ground until the day waned and the faint moon first appeared. By then the Arcadians, outnumbered ten to one, had spent nearly every bit of strength and blood. Evander once more found himself retreating up the hill, threatened on one side by

Erulus, and on the other by Iapygian Daunus, son of Lycaon and a fellow Arcadian. Tearing off his damaged helm, he turned his face, dripping with sweat and blood, to view in horror the black smoke rising from the great towers he built with his own hand. Thinking the city lost, he leaned wearily against his horse's neck to observe, in the gathering gloom, his brave countrymen fighting to the last. His mother's prophecies and all the omens of earth and sky, now seemed empty delusions. Thinking to muster his troops and cohorts together, whatever was left of them, for one last stand, he placed to his lips the delicate horn, cut from a roe-deer, he carried at his belt. And as he blew and filled the forest with the dire wail, the very trees around him shook and the ground rumbled. Heracles, with his Trojan shield blazing crimson from the sun's dying embers, drove from one side into the fray, leading a great number of chariots behind him; and from the other side of the hill, Antores mirrored the charge into the valley. Heracles, after aiding the defenders at the walls, called on his men to seize the chariots from the Tyrrehnians still trapped at the riverbank, for most of the fighters had continued on foot, leaving their drivers in the lurch. By killing the drivers and seizing the reins, they were able to secure a fair number of cars for the offensive.

The Latians, panicked by battle cries and the thunder of hooves, broke ranks, and a disorder reigned on the darkening battlefield. After learning from Acoetes that the city was safe, save for one part of the wall that fell prey to flames, Evander assembled his troops and pressed the rout, while Heracles, on reaching the rear guard, closed in. With nowhere to go, the Latians fought savagely at close quarters. Erulus was the first commander to break past the chariots, fleeing with his squadrons. Seeing this, Evander pursued him across the silent countryside to the very walls of Praeneste, where he cut down the front rank, and reaching Erulus, thrust his sword through his ribcage so that he toppled off his horse. Amazingly, Erulus regained his feet and cast one of his spears, which clove Evander's horse through its armored snood. Landing on his feet under his collapsing horse, Evander retorted with a spear-cast of his own. The spear-point ripped through the center of Eurulus' shield and struck through the belt, invading his belly cavity and making mincemeat of his innards; but he winced as if only slightly vexed though black blood streamed down his legs. As he was about to cast the second of his three spears, Evander rushed at him bearing his sword in his right hand, and in one stroke stove in helm and head.  This time the king of Praeneste fell and rose no more, his monstrous triple life spent in a single day.

⁓

Wishing to get a head start before winter set in, Heracles took his leave of Evander, taking with him only two-hundred of the best fighting men, including his brother, Iolaos and Peleus.  The rest, which included handsome Antores and Melampos, he left as a garrison, settling them around the Cronian Hill, three stades to the north of Pallanteum, in case hostilities brewed anew among Evander's neighbors.  These maintained their own government for a while, but eventually adopted the laws and manner of life of the Aborigines, until in time any differences between them were effaced.

Having committed themselves too far down the coast, no other choice existed but to continue by a southerly route to a point where they could double the mountain spine.  So from the Albula Heracles drove the cattle of Geryones before him.  Within two days they passed through the Phlegraian Fields, a region as close to the horrors of the underworld as could exist in the open air. Covered with hissing fumaroles and pools of boiling mud, the land appeared blighted and blasted, streaked with yellow tuff and jagged rocks, like a primordial battlefield.  With noxious vapors swirling round their feet, they hastened to pass through as quickly as possible.  The Aborigines who accompanied them mentioned to Heracles the purported existence of an underworld entrance beside a small but unfathomable mere called Avernus, sacred to Persephone and Hecate, which filled a crater at the top of a steep and precipitous height, surrounded by dark and shaggy woods.  At once Heracles' curiosity was aroused and he left his company to discover it, much to the dismay of the native guides, who believed that any living thing approaching the lake would be overcome by its mephitic exhalations.  As proof they pointed out that no birds dared fly above the lake, and those that did quickly perished.

Heracles climbed through Hecate's gloomy wood until he reached the lake, rimmed with steep hill-brows all around, wrapping the whole enclosure in shadow. A blue miasma floated above the surface of the water, flickering over the marshy bank under the bending leaves of dropping willows. He stopped his nose against the stale and heavy air, suffused with sulphurous fetor. One end, where the crater-side rose highest, was perforated with a hundred caverns, some large and some small. He thought he heard a movement at the mouth of the largest cavern, and approached. As he looked into the dark opening a pale form suddenly appeared before him, driving him a step backward in surprise. A woman dressed in scarlet, on her head a chaplet of laurel, her hair gray with age, but her face still strangely comely, stood before him. She seemed not at all surprised, but smiled approvingly, and retreated back slightly into the shadows.

Her voice came forth as if echoing through the honeycomb of grottos, saying: "Mightiest of men, what seek you here in Apollo's sacred shrine? Are you lost upon your way?"

Heracles sought to come closer, but she raised a hand in warning. Heracles bowed and said: "I know not whether you are a goddess, or merely a woman favored by the gods. But youth and age seem in you strangely commingled, and your august dignity leads me think there is here something of divinity. Know you who I am?"

"I do," the woman said; "and I shall tell you who I am: no goddess that you should bow to me, but a slave to the god. I am Deiphobe, called also the Sibyl. Endless life was offered me in return for Phoibos' love. A bribe he sought to give me, asking me whatsoever I wished to have. I pointed to a heap of dust and said 'As many particles are there, so shall the number of my birthdays be.' But foolish me!—I should have asked for long youth to match my long life. This he deigned to give me if I sacrificed my virtue, but again I refused, longing to remain unwedded and alone in my solitary glen. Seven centuries have I passed here, and three are left before my days equals the count of those grains of sand, growing ever older every day, faltering in my steps, my limbs wasting away until I dwindle to a tiny thing fit for a jar. But my voice shall never fade: so have the Fates decreed."

"Then you know all things, holy priestess," said Heracles. "Tell me, where is the entrance to the land of the dead? I was told it is hereabouts."

"Are you mad to wish to descend to the undergloom before your time?" asked the Sybil.

"I long to see my dear children again," said Heracles.

"There, across the mere, on that yonder slope thick-set with trees and briars, is a yawning cavern from where these deadly vapors pour.  It is there," said the Sybil.  "No living man has ever entered or returned.  You shall be the first, son of Iuppiter;—but not now, and not here. The realm of the dead has many mouths hidden in the dark places of the world.  No; long after you shall come another who will pluck the golden bough and be allowed admittance to Acheron's overflowing bank."

"I shall pluck that golden bough," said Heracles.  "Only show me where to find it."

For a moment, the Sybil's face came full into the daylight at the threshold of the cavern.  A look of horror covered it.  Her lips trembled and her eyes shone wildly.  "The god comes!  He comes!" she cried, and tearing at her hair, shook all over in ecstatic frenzy. As she disappeared from sight it seemed a thousand raving oracles sounded at once from the pockmarked slope in strange and diverse tongues; and a pale light shone from the cavern.  The Sybil's voice irrupted the cacophony, clear but distant and in its strident tone barely human.  Heracles stepped further back in tense wonderment at the divine possession.  From the darkness the Sybil chanted:

> *"Ancient gods conspire*
> *And son o'erthrows his sire*
> *To end the glorious age*
> *With bloody war and bitter rage.*
> *Until the Twelve sit on their thrones*
> *Of shining gold and precious stones.*
> *They fear the mighty coming forth,*
> *Sprouting madly from the earth.*
> *Gift of her who bore them all,*
> *And now machinates their fall.*
> *Father plants another son*
> *Before they all become undone.*
> *He tempers him by mighty deed;*
> *Of him that day will they have need.*
> *In heav'n shall he make abode*

*After one last labor yet untold.*
*He'll rive the darkling gates of Hell,*
*And harrow the fields of asphodel.*
*But too the Twelve shall fade away;*
*Even he shall molder where he lay;*
*But the light will shine anew,*
*Wrapp'd in flesh and bone and thew,*
*To illume the minds of men,*
*And bring the glorious age again."*

Then the preternatural light faded and it grew quiet in the murky dell. Heracles looked back across the lake and through the effluence saw the infernal cave, a dark patch within the trees. He started on the path toward it, and then hesitated, remembering the words of the Sybil. At another time and at another place would he descend.

Returning to his men, Heracles said nothing about the Sybil or the entrance to Tartaros, saying he had found nothing but a somber lake and some broken cenotaphs, by which perhaps the funereal legends began. By doing this he waylaid the curiosity of his men and compelled them to go onward. But they came to a dead end, a rough peninsula surrounded on all sides by water. And so they turned back, hugging the western shore, until they arrived at a little bay where hot springs bubbled forth. The shortest way forward, along a low narrow stretch between the sea and another lake at the bight of the bay, lay bestrewn with boulders and deep ditches and washed over by the strong tide. He was preparing to turn around when some men came forward with armfuls of fresh oysters that they had found at the lake, which they described was nothing more than a briny, shallow lagoon, beyond which rose lake Avernus. The other men grew hungry for such delicacies, and while some more were sent to collect more oysters and other shellfish, Heracles had the rest construct a causeway along the strip. They built up a level sandbank, about eight stades long, wide enough to pass their wagons through, and massed up a dyke to protect against the waves. By this road they easily passed on.

Moving southward, Heracles founded two coastal settlements in the shadow of hump-backed, black-topped Mount Vesuvius, presiding over rich farmland all around it.

Near what is now Poseidonia, the people welcomed the hero with baskets of roses, which had the peculiarity of flowering twice a year, in spring and winter, and were unsurpassed in fragrance. They also showed him a rock celebrated for a certain ancient occurrence. There once was, they said, a certain hunter whose prowess was unequalled. It was his practice to dedicate to Artemis the hands and feet of the animals he hunted, nailing them on trees. One day, after killing a wild boar of exceeding size, he said, as though disdaining the goddess: "The head of this boar I dedicate to myself." As was his practice, he hung the head on a tree that grew beside the rock. But the air being warm at midday, and his limbs weary, he lay down to sleep beneath the tree. But as he slept, the thong holding up the head broke, and it fell upon him and killed him. Heracles considered his ending a just comeuppance, not for the contempt shown to the goddess, but for wantonly breaking a habitual practice.

The verdant Apennines continued shadowing them to the westward as they proceeded, looking for a break in the mountain chain. It was not until they reached Rhegion, where they found a colony of Chalcidians, that the mountains finally terminated, extending low hills to the coast. Since Heracles had marched his company hard after leaving the Phlegraian Plain, he allowed them a deserved rest. Weary himself, he went apart to a grassy knoll by the banks of the Halex river, at the border between the regions of Rhegion and Epizephryneian Locris, where it passed out of a deep ravine, and there lay down to sleep. But being much disturbed by the noise of crickets, he prayed that they would disappear. Evidently, his prayer was granted, since to this day the crickets on the side of Rhegion are mute, while those on the Locrian side continue to sing. It is conjectured, however, that this is a mere legend, and that the real reason for this is that the former side is so densely shaded that the crickets, always wet with dew, cannot expand their membranes to make their peculiar sound; while on the latter side, the abundant sunshine ensure the membranes remain dry and ready for articulation.

Heracles slept soundly until awoken by Iolaos, who was in great agitation. He reported that one of the bulls, bellowing and bucketing, had broken loose from the herd, and raced away toward the sea. Heracles hastened back to camp to investigate. By now he knew all the herd well, and realized that the bull that escaped was the most magnificent one of the group, thick-barreled, deep, dark roan in color, and possessing curving horns twice as long as the rest. Eyewitnesses added that it had madly leapt off a promontory, splashed into the sea, and swam away across the narrow strait toward Sicania, a distance of about a league. Cross at losing such a kingly specimen of his breed, Heracles, accompanied by Iolaos, boarded a boat and was ferried over to the island, hoping to find the bull.

Arriving at the other side, Heracles inquired of the natives whether they had seen the animal thereabouts. As they spoke their own language, and did not understand that of Heracles, they relied on his mannerisms to decipher what he meant. Thinking he referred to a calf, not a bull, they called it a *vitulus*. From that word Heracles called the land he had traversed Vitulia for the first time.

Not at all disheartened, Heracles and Iolaos continued their search, traversing the length of the island along its northern coast, until midway they found some inhabitants who had seen a large sodden bull along the way. After many days, for Heracles would never abandon something to which he put his mind, they arrived at the territory of the Elymoi in the extreme west of the island. There a splendid city covered the slopes of a lofty hill, surrounded by a fertile plain. From a hill Heracles observed the herds that milled about, and among the cattle, by a crooked olive-tree, he noticed a bull strangely checkered in white and red. "Nature is bound to astound us with its power of creation," said Heracles to Iolaos; "but never have I seen such an odd pattern on an ox. Let us take a closer look." They descended to the plain and waded in among the cattle. Even Iolaos recognized Geryones' bull, now docile and happily foraging. Its lustrous red coat had been spattered with ceruse to disguise it. Heracles tied a cord about its neck and was about to lead it away when herders ran over crying in alarm, declaiming that a thief was trying to do away with their king's cattle. Heracles tried to explain to them that he was only reclaiming his own property, passing his hand over the back of the bull to show how the applied coloring came easily off. They would not even consider his argument, and ran off to the city to alert the authorities. Heracles had not made it out of the plain before king Eryx and his men-at-arms intercepted him.

"Stay, thief!  Do you not know what a grave crime you are committing?" cried the king's lieutenant, Entellus, who was as large and shaggy as king Eryx, except that he had hair on his enormous head, while the latter went about with a bald pate.

"As I tried to explain it to the herdsmen hereabouts," said Heracles, "this bull belongs to me.  It escaped from my herd on the mainland, swam across, and shambled its way here."

"You are either lying or you're mad," said Entellus, fearlessly sidling over to where Heracles stood.  "Either way, you are mistaken, and it will cost you dearly."

King Eryx cleared his throat and said: "He speaks the truth in part.  The bull did wander in among my possessions, and seeing how lovely it was, I wanted to keep it for my own.  In case its rightful owner came about snooping, I disguised it with white markings.  But it seems that owner has found it after all.  Tell me, sir, how did you—if indeed the bull belongs to you as you say—come into possession of it?  I have never seen the like, so ruddy and with horns as long as my arms."

"So you know that I speak honestly," said Heracles, "I will tell you its provenance.  The bull belonged originally to Geryones, son of Poseidon, who lived on the westernmost part of the world. I, Heracles, was tasked to carry off his cattle by the king of Mycenae.  I am under orders to obey him, and can do nothing else."

"So you have more creatures like this in your possession?" asked Eryx eagerly.

"Yes: a numerous herd with the same red hide," responded Heracles.

King Eryx clapped his hands.  "I propose a contest.  Defeat me and I shall surrender the bull.  Lose, and I keep it and the rest of the cattle." he said.  His utter confidence came from his prowess in boxing and wrestling, being undefeated in both.  In addition, since he was the son of Aphrodite, he thought himself immortal.

"Very well," said Heracles, equally as confident in himself. "I accept your challenge.  What do you propose?"

"A wrestling match, perhaps?" said Eryx.  "Or shall we box?"

"Let us do both!  And why not add throwing the quoit, archery and chariot-racing also?" said Heracles.  "Surely, such stakes for which we wager deserve the greatest exertion possible."

"Pardon, but the stakes do not seem very high for me, since I have little to lose in comparison," said Eryx.

"My intent is to even out this disparity," said Heracles, looking about the meadow. "Why not stake your rich ploughland against the bull in addition?"

"What?" laughed the king. "My land has greater value than these beasts, however marvelous they are."

"True, if it were that alone," said Heracles, his broad chest heaving with a feigned sigh. "Should I lose the cattle, I will not be able to conclude my Labors, and thus lose my reward."

"What happens to you is of little consequence to me," said Eryx dryly. Entellus took him aside to advise him to dismiss Heracles as a simpleton and maniac. Heracles, guessing what passed between them, interposed: "As you said, I must defeat you utterly, in every contest." King Eryx, thinking it impossible for Heracles to win every match, accepted the terms.

Not long afterward clarions sounded from the city wall calling the citizens to assemble in a nearby valley: a grassy plain, surrounded by winding, woody hills that took the form of a natural arena. There the elders sat in the front rows on raised seats, while the commoners crowded eagerly behind, ready for an entertaining spectacle. When king Eryx took the field a great shout rose from the crowd, for they expected him to crush bone and spill blood by his marked strength. But when Heracles walked in, the people grew silent, murmuring amongst themselves as to the identity of the impressive champion, and wondering whether their king could withstand him. For the first event the two men took their place at one end of the field, and coiled their bodies to cast the quoits. Heracles cast the farthest on all three attempts, with king Eryx not far behind him. Following this, attendants set targets in the ground, tall broad stakes on which they depended round white wooden shields with red circles at the center painted in madder. Eryx, no great archer, did not begrudge Heracles the victory, who placed three successive arrows in the dead center of his target, peeling apart each previous shaft in turn. At first the people were afraid to cheer for Heracles, but by then a clear assent rose in favor of the stranger.

For the third event, the two-horse chariot race, Eryx was certain he would snatch a victory since he maintained lusty stallions in his stables; while Heracles was given a team of unkempt geldings. Posts were set to mark out a clear course around the field and the two men stood high, side by side, in their chariots awaiting the signal. When it came, Eryx bolted out first. He reached the turning-post with Heracles hot on his heels. But Heracles roared at his team, and beat them savagely with the lash. Fire then seemed to enter them and they surged ahead, overtaking Eryx at the first post. They continued in this way, one falling behind, and the other jumping ahead, until their horses, frothing at the mouth, could run no longer. Seeing that Heracles' team had stopped slightly ahead, Entellus ran out, pulled the ear of one of Eryx's horse, and pounded its head with his fist in the hope of reviving him. They would not budge, however, and Heracles was declared the winner by a head.

King Eryx did not allow the string of defeats to discourage him since he felt absolute certainty about winning the boxing match. Heracles was without a doubt stronger than he, but the king was lighter and quicker on his feet, which for victory in boxing is paramount.

A sandy pit was prepared in the center of the arena while the contestants rested and refreshed themselves. As they entered the ring, Entellus ran forward and threw Eryx's enormous and fearsome gloves onto the sand. This he always did to strike terror into the king's opponents. The gloves were stitched from the hide of seven oxen, weighted down with lead and iron, and appeared stiff with dried blood. When Entellus was certain that Heracles had gotten a good look at them, he tied them on Eryx's hands, twisting the thongs around his wrists. Iolaos came forward with a pair of light sparring-gloves, the only ones he could find. Heracles said nothing untoward, although he thought it rude that Eryx failed to offer him a like pair. At the same time, he thought it was best not to weigh down his hands, seeing that now they were perhaps more evenly matched: Eryx gaining strength and power from his gloves, and Heracles gaining speed and dexterity without them.

Eryx threw down his cloak and bared his giant limbs and taut sinews. Likewise, Heracles untied his lionskin to reveal his own rampant body bristling with cresting muscles; his massive joints and thick limbs; the hard contours of his bones and sinews; his well-rounded shoulders and broad, corded back; and his heaving, thrusting chest. Even Entellus, no slouch he, marveled. At the signal the fighters approached one another with arms extended, and commenced lightly sparring in order to feel out the skill of the other. Lighter of foot, Eryx was the first to make a serious move, diving down and then coming up swiftly with an upper-cut. Heracles drew his head back to avoid the blow and countered with a jab that narrowly missed his opponent's head. The two men separated a bit and circled each other cagily, like facing lions about to spring. Heracles now stepped in, chopping downward with his powerful right arm. Eryx sidestepped easily and came around with a left hook against Heracles' ear. The blow from the heavy, leaden glove, coupled with his own unchecked impulse, made Heracles almost trip over his heels. At ring-side, Entellus acclaimed his master, while Iolaos shouted encouraging words at Heracles. Heracles shook off the ringing in his ear and ran in offensively jabbing with his right, landing one or two glancing blows. Eryx, slightly younger and lighter of bulk, hammered at him, ambidextrously striking chin and nose, then belly and flank, until Heracles, his face bleeding and swollen, could do little but keep his arms drawn in protectively. It quickly became apparent to Heracles that Eryx took to boxing with the singularity of an artist, careful in his footwork and studied in his striking. Heracles, accustomed more to all-in fighting, felt constrained and unable to adopt the same finesse. He therefore held out, jabbing or hooking here and there to keep Eryx engaged, until the latter, with all his shifting and fancy movement, began to weary. This took about an hour. His gloves now felt heavy. His timing grew imperfect. Heracles came out of his protective posture, like a snail, sensing the end of a danger, emerges from its shell to continue slithering on, and gave Eryx a powerful blow to the kidney. He followed up with a right hook that clipped the tip of the chin. Eryx, stunned and crazed by his loss of advantage, closed in with an upper-cut, and then clinched Heracles, trapping his arms. Heracles spun out, stepping left around Eryx, and raising his right arm, brought down his fist with devastating result. The blow caught Eryx on the temple and flattened him to the ground.

The heart of Entellus sank as he ran into the ring to revive Eryx. Heracles lingered near to be certain he did not kill the king, and sighed in relief when he saw Eryx stir. With one of his eyes beginning to swell shut, Heracles retreated to his corner where Iolaos stanched his blood and gave him water to drink.

Entellus begged Eryx to abort the final event and return the wayward bull to Heracles. The king gave it serious thought, but decided against doing so, once again filled with a foolish optimism that he could best Heracles at wrestling. The contest adjourned until the next day to give the opponents a chance to rest and heal. That night Eryx acted the perfect host. He feasted Heracles until the small hours. At noon, the people assembled again in the valley; but they were silent now, with not a cheer or hoot emanating from the crowd, only a nervous chatter.

Heracles and Eryx met again at the sand-pit. Slaves came forward to rub them with oil. The sun glistened on their naked bodies. Eryx was eager to begin, but Heracles first asked Entellus to clarify the rules. There was to be no intentional hitting or kicking, nor breaking fingers, and neither gouging of eyes nor grasping and pulling the genitals. The winner was the first to score three points. One could win a match by pinning his opponent to the ground; by throwing him outside the wrestling-pit; or, by compelling him to concede defeat, indicated by raising a finger.

After wrapping their hands in rawhide thongs, under which was inserted a patch of sheepskin for wiping away sweat from the eyes, they circled about, and then thrust themselves into a clinch. Once again, Heracles proved the stronger, and moving from an overhook to a pinch grip, drew Eryx off his feet and cast him outside the sand-pit. For the second round, Eryx nimbly slipped out of Heracles' attempt to clinch him, and coming up behind him, put him in chancery. Heracles easily broke the hold, but before he could perform an offensive move, Eryx grabbed and locked his right arm at the elbow, forcing Heracles to take a knee to avoid the pain that came from the maneuver. Heracles wiggled this way and that, but Eryx held firm, keeping constant, painful pressure on his joint, sweeping him around in order to push him lower to the ground. Heracles knew full well the intentions of his opponent, but he could do little to escape the simple, precise and powerful hold, designed to keep even a larger and stronger opponent at bay, as a tiny bit can control a horse, or a rudder a sea-vessel. While Heracles lay prone, Eryx jumped on his back and tried to strangle him, anchoring himself around Heracles' waist with his powerful legs. Heracles first tried to dislodge him by forceful moves. When that failed to break the hold, Heracles slipped a hand into the crook of Eryx's elbow to ease the pressure on his neck, and then gripping his forearm, slowly pulled Eryx onto his shoulder. With a mighty heave, Heracles rolled Eryx. As Heracles tried to pin his back to the ground, Eryx clung to him with great vehemence to avoid defeat, like an octopus to a rock that is suddenly revealed in the ebb; but Heracles eventually prevailed and scored another point.

After a long period of rest, in which a desperate Eryx wept in the arms of Entellus, lamenting his foolishness at agreeing to such an arduous contest for such high stakes, the opponents met a final time. Eryx, aware now of Heracles' favored moves, wrestled him dexterously, matching his size and strength, as in the boxing bout, with his own skill and swiftness. Eryx did not remain long in any grappling posture, opting instead to throw Heracles as often as he could with foot-sweeps; yet he could not pin him down. The two men struggled until nearly sunset. Heracles found it admirable that Eryx did not resort to striking below the hip-bone, biting or casting sand in his eyes, as fighters sometimes do in frustration. At last, Heracles escaped a poor joint lock and swiftly threw Eryx on his hip. When Eryx tried to roll away, Heracles pounced on his back and wrapped his forearm across his neck. Eryx tried valiantly to break the choke-hold but could not. Feeling his head lighten, he knew that he had to but extend a finger to end the bout. As his eyes bulged from his head he thought he saw a vision of his mother Aphrodite descending in a cloud. She smiled lovingly on him. The sight of her surpassing beauty and the smell of her golden, ambrosial locks made him forget himself. He went limp in Heracles' arms. The sight of the beaten king seemed to flatten the entire crowd, as when a roiling rainstorm pummels a field and levels the crops, so that in the morning the farmer finds all the grain stalks bent backwards.

With tears in his eyes, Entellus cried "His majesty is dead!" after he had expended all attempts at resuscitation, at which the elders wailed to see that their lord was not immortal. Eryx's body guard rushed in to surround Heracles. In his defense, Heracles protested that the king failed to give any sign of submission; and that, in any case, death was also a valid indication of defeat. Despite his grief, the fair-minded Entellus agreed to both points and released Heracles from any retribution. Heracles returned with Iolaos to the palace, since he had squarely inherited the kingdom, and gave Eryx a lavish funeral, holding Games for several days, at which he presided, robed in the king's purple cloak embroidered with golden pine-kernels. As the Elymoi were an obsequious people, Heracles was given every honor, even as a god, since the commons thought that only one god could defeat another. Even Eryx's daughter Psophis submitted to Heracles, and becoming pregnant, bore him two sons: Echephron and Promachos. These two, on reaching manhood, left Sicania and settled in Arcadia at Erymanthos, which they renamed Psophis in honor of their mother, a city that lies securely between the wide river of the same name on its eastern side, and another river torrent descending through a deep ravine on its western, while the northern face is protected under a steep hill. There they built a sanctuary to Erycinian Aphrodite, similar to the one found on the eastern tip of a great crag on Mount Eryx.

At the conclusion of the funeral Games, Heracles magnanimously announced in the hearing of all that he would turn over the kingdom back to the people until such a time as one of his descendants should appear among them and demand it back. This very thing happened many generations later. With Iolaos he left the Elymoi, driving the bull along with several fine heifers from the herd of Eryx to keep it company. It came into his mind to pay a visit to king Cocalos at Inycum to see how he fared. Travelling down the coast to the borderland, he found, at the edge of the brackish river Halycus, a town built by some of king Minos' stranded men, which they named Minoa in honor of their late ruler. He tarried there for two days and then turned inland, thinking that a visit to Inycum would prove too great a detour. Crossing the breadth of the island midway they came to a remarkable and lofty hill, perhaps even a mountain, coiffed with a circular table-land, surrounded on all sides by wooded, precipitous cliffs. At its summit few seemed to live, since only a dwelling here or there could be seen through breaks in the trees, with scattered hearth-smoke winding up into the upper air. All around the hill the land heaved with wild ruddy wheat, despising the cold winds and frost brought in by the night. Heracles marveled at the fecundity of the island; for from one end of it to other he saw nothing but fertile fields, wild orchards pregnant still with fruit and flowery meadows swelling in the errant breeze. As they walked around the base of the mount, the gleaming columns of a temple, perched high on a crag, came into sight. Heracles was curious what divinity, who had so copiously showered upon the land such a multitude of blessings, was worshipped there. As they sought a way up the rugged slope, they heard the sweet notes of a flute and turned back. Near a gushing cascade, sitting on a rock, a young shepherd gaily played a syrinx. So sweetly did he play that his wooly sheep pranced about the clearing where they milled; and none dared to stray.

At the conclusion of the song, Heracles stepped forward and said: "Good shepherd, you play most divinely upon those pan's-pipes. Tell us, your name and that of the god who has breathed in you such skill. Perhaps that sanctuary hither belongs to him?"

The shepherd jumped down from the rock. He was a young man of twenty, peerless in beauty, his brow bound with laurel and his slender form wrapped in a foxskin cloak.

"I am Daphnis," said he, hanging his pipes to his belt. "If you see aught worthy about me, it is because I hail from Hermes, and my mother is a nymph of the Pergusan wood, or so I am told by my foster-mother. I play by the favor of Paean Apollo, who taught me in the chirping of the birds, the trickling of the stream, and the wailing of the wind. In this land, however, none is worshipped more than the Goddess; it is her shrine you see there balanced on the rocks."

"Goddesses there are many," said Heracles with a laugh. "Leave song and riddles behind, and speak to us plainly."

"Strangers, I see," said Daphnis, noticing the red bullock of Geryones coming around a bend. "One may speak here of the Goddess, or the Goddesses, with all confidence, friend. It is Demeter and Persephone, beloved of all, to whom I refer."

"The rape of Core—do you know the tale? Are we not close to the spot from whence she was taken?" said Iolaos, tense with excitement. "My school-teacher, an Athenian, claimed it occurred not here but at Eleusis. I have heard others say at Colonos, or Arcadia, or at Boetia; but each teller wishes to aggrandize his own city."

"Since I have no city to call my own, loath as I am of

joining the madding crowd, you may believe me when I sing to you the true story," said Daphnis. "I have in my store plenty of honey in the comb, sheep's cheese and barley-bread. Sit and eat while you allow me to practice my skill, for I consider myself a poet first and a flutist second."

He led them to a small grotto where he kept his vittles, and spreading them out on the level grass, invited Heracles and Iolaos to recline and eat. Taking out his syrinx, he blew a few notes by way of introduction, cleared his throat, and began to sing softly of things from a younger world.

He sang how when the earth-born Gigantes strove against the immortals, Zeus, with his thunderbolt, cast in the forges of the Cyclopes, smote vast Typhon and heaped Sicania upon him; his head lay under Etna's weight, which with every groan expurgated fire and black smoke. So too as he tried to roll the fathoms of earth from his ensnared limbs, whole mountains and cities swirled with him. The rocks fractured and chasms formed where once stretched meadows or quiet valleys. The son of Cronos, the second Zeus, the lord of the underworld—he who should not be named—feared lest his gloomy realm be exposed to the light of day and the poor shades become discomfited in their timeless existence. Mounting his iron chariot, he lashed his black chargers to ascend in a rare show to the upper world where he could examine if the foundations of earth were still sound. As he roamed Sicania he was seen by Erycinian Aphrodite from her temple on the sacred mountain. Quickly she called for her impious son, Eros, who though seeming like a babe, wearing still his breech-clout, he was really the oldest of the gods, and the most mischievous. Sitting him on her knees, the fragrant goddess tells him: "Gird your quiver about your shoulder and grab your little bow, my son. Select the sharpest and truest arrow you have and ready it for that gloomy wanderer there, that lord of many. Already we are despised in heaven—Artemis follows Athena in cold virginity; shall we leave this third part of the world bereft of my greatest blessing? I feel pity for him, so grim of aspect and dread in shape. He was given the most despised of Cronos' inheritance, deprived of life-giving light, roiling with flames and sulphurous ash: an empty abode, hideous, full of horror and despair, without so much as even a child's laugh to sprinkle it with joy. See, he flies by that stream-fed vale where Demeter's daughter is fain to disport. If we do not act now, she too will remain among the palsied ranks of the unwed. Let them be bound together in love." At once the little godling mounted the air and flew unseen to a place of ambush. As Hades sped by he loosed at him a golden shaft. The lord of the dead felt a pinprick in his cold heart turn into suffocating fire. It was then that he saw Persephone in the company of Ocean's daughters treading the grass to her favorite place; and he loved her. Brooding and confused, he returned to his dark lair. As much as he tried to cast Persephone from his mind, immersing himself in the affairs of his gloomy empire, he found he could not eat or take that divine sleep enjoyed by the gods. Summoning the son of Maia, the only one of the gods equipped to travel between the lands of the living and the dead, he tells him: "Tell the Thunderer: never have I contested the empery I was given. I complain not when the gods feast together on the bright heights of Olympos, or gather on the sunny ridges of Ida to share the cup of nectar as Apollo plucks his lyre. I say nothing that Poseidon beds his bevy of naiads when he wishes, or that you yourself find your own sister not enough to fill your pleasure, but consort with other goddesses and even mortal women! You do as you please, and now your children fill heaven and earth. Good for you! Now, indulgent brother, grant me only this. I wish to take Demeter's daughter for my wife. I love her and her alone, and will share dominion over the vast leagues of the dead with her: a greater realm than yours! Refuse me and I will burst the gaols where the primeval monsters dwell. All Hell shall vomit forth darkness over earth and heaven, so that not one of our blessed kin will find escape."

Hermes, trembling, rose skyward on his winged sandals, glad to quit the dark abode. Hearing his brother's demand, Zeus went apart by himself to ponder the predicament. If he refused, Hades would unleash chaos on the world. If he agreed, he would never hear the end of it from Demeter; and rightly so, since what parent would wish their child bound to such a fate? He decided, therefore, to take the diplomatic route and neither approved of the marriage, nor opposed it. Hermes reported this to Hades, who grew pleased, taking Zeus' indecision to mean he could do as he wished.

Quickly Hades dons his black armor and terrifying helm,

plumed high with carrion-bird feathers, and calls for the Furies to yoke his team. They bring from grazing by Cocytus' banks the fierce Orpneaus and swift Aethon; and from the dark meadows of Erebos glorious Nycteus and Alaster, favorite of the dark lord's steeds. These stand ready before the gates, chomping at their bits, ready to pull the black two-wheeled chariot on its rapturous errand.

Not far from lofty Henna (sang Daphnis) is a deep pool called Pergus, overspread with white swans and shaded from the sun's heat by leafy woods. There grows the pine-tree, the favorite of mariners; the hard cornel-tree used for implements of war; the oak, beloved of Zeus; the cypress to shade the sepulcher; the beech-tree filled with honeycombs; the laurel to augur the future; the elm, clothed in vines and creepers. Within this grove of everlasting Spring a fair meadow hosts Persephone and her companions, the daughters of Ocean, as they play and gather into their baskets and laps the red roses, the blue hyacinths, the purple violets and all manner of sweet-smelling flowers. Demeter's pride, girt in an embroidered blue dress secured with a brooch of jasper, decks her head with a rose coronet and sweetens her breath with marjoram. Others, like bees buzzing about after nectar, despoil the glade of crocuses and hyacinths and wreath necklaces of white privet and lilies. In this happy way they pass the morning while the sun melts the dew and the blossoms preen with freshness.

The friends spread throughout the meadow, singing and laughing, eager to surpass one another in their gathering. Persephone, seeking the loveliest flowers, strayed farthest of all to where a marvelous narcissus grew. A hundred golden-yellow blooms sprouted from its stem; and the sweet odor enraptured one to heaven. As she reaches out both hands to pluck the prize of her pursuits, the ground trembles with an ominous roaring. Underneath the keeper of the shades sunders the deep-rooted rocks, opening passages where there were none before, hurtling his chariot to meet the light of day. He tunnels through the earth as enemies beneath the barren field of a city under siege, until at last they break forth within the walls to everyone's terror and chagrin.

And so near the narcissus earth devoured earth, and from a wide chasm Hades erupted, lashing his hard-breathing steeds reluctant to face another beamy day. Black smoke and dust follows in his wake, rising up, spreading, and hiding them in darkness.

Those nymphs who came near now flee, and there is no one to help Persephone as she is snatched away, crying out in terror for her mother. In her rapine her dress tears and the flowers she had gathered in her lap fall; in her innocence the loss of them left scattered doubles her grief.

In vain she cries and pleads, beating her soft arms against Hades' cold armor, her hair streaming as she's borne away. Hades says nothing as he rides the wind, seeking for swifter re-entrance to his realm, until her entreaties temper his indurate heart. Wiping her tears with the edge of his billowing cloak he tells her: "Dearest Persephone, cease your anguish and sorrow. Where we go you shall be Queen of a vaster realm alongside a husband not unworthy; for I possess that third of the world that is illimitable, with its own mountains and rivers and vast meads of asphodel where dwell the blessed. An endless host will you command whose numbers ever grow. Kings, bereft of all good things they had in life, shall at your feet fall destitute in death. You shall pass judgment on the evil, and grant rest eternal to the good. Only Hera will be your rival, for you shall play the same role in Hell that she does in Heaven."

Persephone, unconsoled, resigned herself to quiet sobs, trying in her final act to behold deeply one last bit of the green earth and blue sky, hoping against hope that someone heard her cries or witnessed the crime. Only one dares to intervene: the nymph Cyane, who standing in her pool, recognizes the daughter of Demeter and cries: "No farther shall you go, unloved Plouton, with your unlawful cargo! You act against the maiden's will; she would rather be wooed than ravished." Hades sees her stretching out her arms to bar his way; in wrath he smites the pool with his scepter. The limpid waters divide to the floor, which splits wide in another cavernous chasm. Hades needs not lash his steeds any longer: they know the new passage returns them to their funereal stables. In a moment the black chariot carrying the sweet damsel plunges into the abyss. The shades below tremble as they see their dark sky pierced by an evening star more glorious than that of the empyrean. The darkness vanishes and the eternal murk dispels before the glorious face of the Goddess. For the first time the wailings cease; the torments end; the judgements are suspended; and even those wandering in Elysion's fields are reminded that their blessed state is but a pale reflection of true glory.

Cyane, in anguish over Persephone and the violation of her fountain, deliquesced in her tears and her divine form disappeared into the pool.

But lo! Demeter did hear her daughter's anguished cries, since what mother fails to detect her child's slightest whimper wherever she may be in the house, even in the thralls of deepest sleep. Over land and sea she roams, coming at last to Sicania, where round Henna she saw the flowers strewn, dropt from her daughter's lap, and the deep ruts of the chariot wheels. Up Etna's slopes she ranges to where Zeus laid the foul spoils of the monsters' war. In a wood dense round Etna's summit his bloody shield hangs beside the flayed Gigantes' skins and death-masks frozen in horrid looks. Their bleached bones and stinking sloughs still smoking from the rain of thunderbolts, bends down the branches. And higher than all the trees stands a pine stout enough to bear the arms of the Giant-king Encelados. A quiet sanctity cinctures this grove; and none have dared since time primeval to disturb it until Demeter comes hither with an axe. Two cypress trees she carelessly hews until their foliage lies in dust. From these she fashions torches to last many a night. Climbing to the mount's fiery brim, treading the molten rocks where no mortal can, she dips their oily heads into cresting waves of the Phlegeton until two new bright flames blaze, and those from a distance think that Etna's cone has once again convulsed in fiery splendor. "Where under wide heaven shall I find thee?" the anguished mother cries, her face burnished in the torchlight. "As every mother hopes: I thought to carry festal torches on your marriage day, not these through long and awful night. You were my only joy, my sole possession, the true evidence of my fruitfulness. Now I am reduced to misery and shame—can the gods be also the sport of fate? If so, then shall the entire world suffer! From it I will withdraw my tender succor. Rain shall no longer fall to water the ploughed fields. The dew shall no more moisten the thirsty stalks. The seed shall shrivel and die where it lies, even as my aching heart has shriveled to a stone." Her curse takes hold first round Henna's field where the joyful flowers withered. Everywhere she ranged in futile search the drought and famine followed.

For nine days she wandered over the parched earth wrapped in a dark cloak, her golden hair darkened by a mourning mantle and her brightness diminished.  Neither nectar moistened her tongue nor pure water touched her body.  None could give her news.  As the tenth day dawned, mysterious Titan-born Hecate left her cave and met the mother at a crossroads.  From her cave she had heard Persephone's cries but could see nothing; yet she knew who did.  She takes Demeter to see Helios as he touches down in the West, ready to stable his steeds in the earth-circling vessel back to his eastern palace. Watchman of gods and men, he tells her the awful truth, yet enjoins her to be angry at none but Zeus, who by his diffidence encouraged the rapture.  "Yet, goddess, lay aside your grief and put off your loud laments.  After all, Hades—your own brother—is no unworthy suitor."

Demeter, wracked with a more terrible grief, nurses incalculable hatred toward her sovereign brother, and no more joins the Olympians in their feasts and conventicles.  Instead she reduces herself to a beggared state, and in the guise of an old woman, friendless, bereft of children and years, wanders listlessly, all hope of seeing again her daughter, shut up in the unknown confines of the nether gloom, extinguished.  She reaches the environs of Eleusis, where she sits forlornly by the Maiden's Well, in the shade of an old olive-tree.  Out of pity for the well-watered orchards and the bright-hued flower-beds she stays her curse this once.  There the daughters of lord Celeus come to draw water in pitchers of bronze.  The eldest, lovely Callithoë, lays her down her vessel and addresses the cloaked divinity: "Dear old mother, who are you and why are you here so far from the houses of our city, in whose shaded halls dwell old women like yourself, and young ones too, who would welcome you with open arms?"  Demeter, admiring their beauty, as of goddesses in the blossom of their girlhood, told them how she had been taken from Crete by pirates, how she had escaped them; and, wandering alone and destitute, came hither. "And may the gods bless you with husbands and children, dear maidens, if you take pity on me.  Show me where to go; no burden shall I be in that household, for I will work cheerfully at such tasks as befit my page.  I can nurse new-born babes in my arms, keep the house tidy, or teach the younger women to card wool or ply the spindle."

Callidice, loveliest of the sisters, replied: "Look no further than our own house!  Come with us; our mother Metaneira shall welcome you. She has lately born her only son, the fruit of her maturity, who came to us only after many prayers. If you would fain to nurse him, and to raise him to his youth, all women will envy you for the gifts our mother will grant you."

Demeter nodded her assent. Joyously the maidens filled their pitchers and went off to give their mother the news. Metaneira invited the stranger without a second thought. The sisters sped back to the well, springing down the path like does in springtime. To their house they conducted Demeter. Metaneira, sitting by a pillar, holding her little son Demophoön to her bosom, straightway rose from her couch to offer her seat. But Demeter silently sat upon a lowly stool, refusing all comforts, until Iambe, a girl of the palace, by sport and coarse jets, brought a smile to her downcast face. When Metaneira offered her a cup filled with sweet wine, Demeter refused the draught, asking instead for water mixed with meal and sprinkled with a little pennyroyal. Metaneira prepared the cup as instructed and gave it to the goddess, who grew well-pleased. As she drank, Metaneira observed her and remarked: "Grandam, your appearance is at odds with grace I see shining in your eyes. You seem nobly born; yet you have submitted to the will of the gods, as all must. Since you are here now, I will give you what I can; only take my son as your own that he may grow strong under your loving hand." Demeter stretched out her arms, saying: "May the gods richly bless you, noble lady. As you wish, I shall nurse the child at my breast. In my arms he shall be safe from any witchcraft, and the bellyache or toothache shall not come near him, for I know many charms against such banes of childhood." She then took the swaddled babe in her arms and loved him as her own. Thenceforth Demeter anointed him by day with ambrosia; in the after-noon she breathed on him her divine breath as he napped upon her sweet-scented bosom; and at night she secretly lay him like a brand in the midst of the hearth-fire so that his mortal part could slowly burn away and only the divine remain. The boy thus grew strong, and seemed like a god in his agelessness and beauty. But one night Metaneira, grown curious of the charmed development of her son, kept watch. When she saw Demeter about to commit again the boy to flames she cried out and struck her hips. Demeter, caught in her goodly work, withdrew the boy from the hearth and in wrath cast him to the ground. "What fools you mortals be!" she ejaculated. "You know not what harm you bring. I was to make your son as the Immortals—ageless, deathless; as my adopted son, I would have given him every honor. But by the black waters of Styx, he will not now escape the mortal lot of suffering and death. Only, because he slept in my arms, will he have fame everlasting. Behold—I am that Demeter who brings good things to men. Build me a temple where I shall teach the people my sacred rites and numinous mysteries, and sorrowfully pass my endless days." Demeter let drop her ragged cloak. Her form grew in stature. Her aged looks gave way to eternal beauty and grace. Her divine body effloresced into a searing brightness that lit the house as with lightning. Once more her golden hair, cinctured by a glorious nimbus, tumbled down her shoulders; and a fragrance emanated from the folds of her garment. In swirl of luminous mist she was hidden from their eyes.

Metaneira, speechless, stood frozen, forgetting her son left wailing on the floor; until his sisters, awoken by his cries, rushed from their beds to the still radiant chamber. One took up the child; another rekindled the fire; a third looked to their mother. Altogether they essayed to console the child, washing him and singing him lullabies; but, lacking in the skills of his former nurse-maid, they could not comfort him at all.

At dawn lord Celeus learned of what transpired. At once he ordered a temple to Demeter built and filled the altar with the gifts of the earth. Demeter took her residence in the sanctuary's innermost chamber where she continued to nurse the grief in her heart, pining for lost Persephone. For the kindness of Celeus and his house, she continued to spare Eleusis from the dreadful consequences of her woe while the rest of the world she plunged into want and misery. The ox pulled the plough in vain over the desiccated ground, while men broke their mattocks harvesting stones. The barley died upon the stalk, or else choked on the thorns and thistles. The orchard-trees withered; and the vines, once fragrant and pendulous with purple grapes, perished under black frost. Zeus could no longer ignore the cries and petitions of mankind. He sent first fleet-footed Iris to implore Demeter to relent and return to the company of the gods. Other gods he sent, one after the other, bearing costly gifts for his downhearted sister; but she remained unmoved. Finally Zeus sent their ancient mother

Rhea to beseech her, thinking Demeter could not refuse her. The latter only replied that she would never again set foot on Olympos, or allow a seed to sprout, until she beheld again the lovely face of her daughter. Encouraged, Zeus once again sent Hermes to parley with the grim ruler of the dead, commanding him to release Persephone for the sake of mankind, since if men perished and no more were born, not only would the gods on high miss their gifts and sacrifices, but the world below would soon become bereft of new tenants. Hades relented, dissimulating regret at losing Persephone. A short time before he saw Persephone wandering about Elysion's meadow, where grew a lone pomegranate tree. The bright red flowers and bursting fruit stood in contrast to the endless fields of ghostly asphodel. Persephone, drawn to the tree as a bee seeks the most brilliant petals, with a trembling hand plucked a single fruit. Breaking it open, she extracted and ate but seven sweet ruby seeds; she could indulge herself no more.

"Go now, Persephone, back to your mother," said Hades to her as his iron chariot was made ready for her departure. Persephone sprang with joy beside Hermes, who took the car's heavy reins and rescued her from the dark pit. Neither sea, nor glens nor mountain-peaks could slow the deathless horses until they arrived at Eleusis before Demeter's temple. Demeter came forth. Persephone leaped from the chariot and ran to her, tears of joy streaming from her eyes. They stood a long while in rapt embrace. But Demeter's heart felt heavy with some premonition. Still holding her dear child she said: "Tell me, Persephone; hold nothing back! Did any food pass your lips while you dwelt in the lower world? If not, you will never be separated from the mother who bore you and whose love for you cannot be contained in all wide earth and heaven. But if so—alas!—then by ancient law you must return to where you were taken, for the darkness under the earth now claims you."

Persephone needed say nothing. The dismay in her eyes conveyed the awful truth. Their brief joy turned to grief, and they embraced again, commiserating with one another. As Persephone in obedience readied to mount the infernal chariot, noble Rhea, sent by Zeus, arrived to invite mother and daughter back into the company of the gods. The wise Father commanded that for a third part of the year Persephone should dwell with her lord in the lower world, but for the other seasons she could remain beside Demeter. "So it is said; so it shall be," said Rhea. "Now relent, daughter of mine, and bless the ground with fruitfulness again that mankind may live."

And so, sang Daphnis, while Persephone is with her mother, springtime bursts upon the earth. The land heaves with fruit and flowers. The rain runs swollen through the furrows, and soon the soft green shoots appear. These grow and ripen into golden grain which is reaped and gathered into threshing-floors to be made into life-giving bread. But when it is time for Core to descend into the dark places, rime covers the fruitless ground, a chill wind blows, and the seed lies hidden as if dead; and men huddle in the darkness, mourning with Demeter, awaiting the months of warmth and brightness. And so it is through the cycling year.

No longer was Persephone that fair maiden gaily gathering flowers in the blooming meadows with brow undimmed by care or worry. When she takes her place beside her grim consort in their gloomy realm, she knows duty as its infernal queen. Yet with joy she looks for her release, when again she may walk beside her mother through flowery vales and fields covered with the ripening grain. Even then she has memory of where she must return, so that in her joy ever contends with sorrow.

Daphnis rested his fingers on the lyre strings, concluding softly:

> *When the taper of life burns low,*
> *And you bow your head in grief,*
> *Remember she who ever dies:*
> *Core, whose time is brief.*
>
> *Through autumn's decay and gloom*
> *She's subject to th'infernal king;*
> *Then returns with greater purpose,*
> *In the freshness and verdure of spring.*
>
> *As the seed hiding in winter's reign*
> *Rises new-born in the furrow,*
> *So you go down into the grave,*

*To rise resplendent on the morrow.*

Daphnis unstrung his noteless lyre and said: "Dear friends, I must be off. The bleating sheep mark the day's waning, and I must go gather them into their pen where safe they'll sleep from wild dogs and wolves."

"Before you go, good shepherd," said Heracles, "tell me one thing. How can a man a die and yet live?"

"Since I am but a simple poet," said Daphnis, "seek Eleusis and the mysteries of Demeter. I hear that happy is he who has seen these mysteries. But those who have no part in them go down hopeless into the darkness and the gloom."

Daphnis took up the remaining crusts into a basket and returned them to his store. Singing a hymn to his father Hermes, he gathered his sheep and led them away over a rise. Heracles thought long about the two sorrowful goddesses, who alone of all the deathless gods were acquainted with grief, and of whether the life of a simple seed through harvest and frost, an allegory of such high hope, could be instructive of such a monumental mystery as death.

Such thoughts and plans, however, fit ill at the present time, when all Heracles wanted was to drive Geryones's cattle onward to Mycenae. He tickled the downy chin of Iolaos, who had fallen asleep at this breast, to rouse him and said: "Rub sleep from your eyes, lad. We still have much ground to cover." They gathered the bull and the cows and continued across the island until the waning horns of the moon appeared distinct in the darkening sky. They passed the night sheltered in a thicket.

At the site of present Syracuse on the eastern shore of the island, the natives led him up a rushing stream lined with reeds to the sacred spring of Cyane, which had a dark chasm beside it, down which Hades carried away Persephone. Not far away on a small island, they explained, bubbled another fountain called Arethusa after the nymph who was pursued by the river-god Alpheios. She dwelt across the sea in Achaia; and one day, tired from the chase, from the Stymphalian wood she came to dip her naked body into a crystal-clear stream shaded by silvery willows and poplars. As she swam she stirred the waters, and with it the river-god's heart, who saw her and desired her. Without her robe, left pendent on the other bank, she fled over plain and mountain, past Orchomenos, frigid Erymanthos and Elis; all the while seeing her pursuer's unrelenting shadow. At last, on her last breath, she called out to Artemis, goddess of the hunting-nets, to help her servant and armor-bearer. The goddess heard and wrapped her in a cloud of mist, around which Alpheios circled, calling her name. Arethusa though hidden, felt fear like a lamb encircled with wolves. Sweat drenched her limbs, dripping off into a pool about her feet. In no time her body changed into a stream of water, escaping the protective mist in thin rivulets. When Alpheios saw in the waters the one he loved, he essayed to conjoin his waters with hers. Artemis delivered Arethusa by reaving the earth, so that she plunged into the dark chasm and came out in an unknown land. As she passed beneath the earth she saw sad Persephone sitting on her unwanted throne. This she related to Demeter, beseeching her to forswear her disaffection with the land that delivered her.

Heracles spent a long while meditating by the fountain, dwelling on the Two Goddesses because they were, in their continual sorrow, so unlike the other blessed ones. His heart enlarged with so much veneration for them that he fetched a bull, killed it with a single head-blow, and as a sacrifice plunged it into the clear waters of the spring. Henceforth the natives sacrificed each year a bull in the same manner and held festive gatherings in commemoration of the rape of Core.

Those native Sicani, who under king Cocalos had resented making peace with the Cretans, meanwhile had infected their compatriots in the interior with hatred of all strangers. When these heard that Heracles was making the circuit of the island, they organized an army and marched against him. Heracles found ready volunteers among the Siceloi, who controlled the eastern portion of the island and resented the invasion, and met the attackers on the fertile plain of Leontini between the two streams. These ran red with blood as the Sicani were routed as far as the city of Agyrium in a day's time, suffering tremendous losses.

Heracles and Iolaos retired to Agyrium, situated atop a steep and lofty hill, to rest after the battle. The residents, however, afforded him no respite. Night and day they honored him for his heroic exploits and for freeing them from the threat of the Sicani with splendid sacrifices and a week-long festival. The idea spread to treat the hero on equal terms with the gods since, besides his military successes, he was the subject of an astounding miracle. On his way up the city he took a road which was all rock, and yet the bull of Geryones left hoof marks in it as if it was wax (in a similar way Heracles left a footprint at Pandosia once he returned to Ausonia that was much revered, and on which no one dared tread.)

"You see, Iolaos," said Heracles, "how these good people treat me as a god, paying me divine honors. Do you think such a thing appropriate?"

"That I do not know!" said Iolaos.

"It seems to me," said Heracles, "that men find themselves in the same state from their last day forward as they were before their first day."

"And what state is that?" asked Iolaos.

"Where were you before your birth?" Heracles inquired.

"Nowhere, I suppose," said Iolaos.

"Then where shall you be after you are dead?" said Heracles.

Iolaos, confused, said: "But what of the souls of the dead received by the underworld?"

"What are these souls?" said Heracles. "Of what are they formed? Without material bodies, how do they see, or hear or touch?"

"The gods know!" said Iolaos.

"If so," said Heracles, "why do they not tell us? These must be vain imaginings by which we relieve our terror of the last day."

"Then I do not wish you to die," pled Iolaos, "if there is no hope beyond the grave."

"Death is nature's boon!" said Heracles. "If it is pleasant to live, how can it be pleasant to cease living?"

"Then let us die together, since I never want to be separated from you," said Iolaos.

"Alas, I cannot even find comfort in death!" said Heracles, affably gripping Iolaos' neck with a hand. "With you in the bargain, Iolaos, how then can I leave you and surrender to the grave? Am I not Heracles? I tell you: I will forge my own immortality in the crucible of my Labors."

"Then, perchance, when you become a god, will you raise me up also from the realm of shades?" asked Iolaos.

"Yes Iolaos; and we seem to participate even now in that coming immortality, since prodigies abound and we are showered with honors wherever we go," said Heracles. "So let them sacrifice to me now, no longer as a hero, but as a god, if they so please. May the gods not punish me further for my forwardness, although I need nothing from them. Let them witness that, trusting in myself, I have achieved all things."

"But your sorrows, Heracles—will they cease when you dwell with the deathless gods?" asked Iolaos.

"Did you not hearken to that poet?" said Heracles. "As the Two Goddesses suffer still, so shall I join their company, and serve as an example of longsuffering to men. Do you love me, Iolaos?"

Iolaos cried: "I do!"

"Then, after I have left this world," said Heracles, "gather my children, from wherever they may be."

In gratitude for the devotion of the people of Agyrium, Heracles dug before the city a lake, four stades around, which he called after himself. He also had molds made of the bull's tracks in the stony ground, distributing these to adorn their temples. He dedicated to Geryones a sacred grove of plane-trees; and likewise to Iolaos, for whom, promising to share with him his divinity, he ordered annual honors, sacrifices and athletic contests. The residents developed the habit of letting their hair grow long from birth in honor of Iolaos, until they received certain omens in their sacrifices. The sacred precinct of Iolaos came to be held in such awe, and such sanctity pervaded it, that young men lost their speech, becoming as dead men, who failed to perform the necessary rites. Once they vowed to do aright, however, their malady left them.

Returning to the site of Syracuse, Heracles hired a boat to return them and the bull to the mainland. He found that a large number of his company had deserted him while he was making the circuit of Sicania, thinking he would never return. Peleus maintained order among those remaining and kept Geryones's herd unmolested. The returning bull seemed happy to be again amongst its kith and kin.

From there they drove the cattle up the eastern coast on the other side of the mountains, arriving in the territory of king Lacinius at the southern extremity of the gulf. This ruler refused him any hospitality. Heracles, who prized neighborliness highly, to vex him let the cattle stray across his pastures, enclosed within a forest of tall pine trees. Lacinius sent out spies to find out more about his obstreperous guest. Learning of his strained relation to Hera, he churlishly commenced building a magnificent temple to her adjacent to the forest, at the extreme point of a bold headland, formed from an offshoot of the central range, jutting over the sea. When he heard the masons at work, Heracles went to the site to find out what was going up; and on learning to whom the sanctuary was dedicated, collected the cattle and left the region in disgust. The temple was completed long afterward and had no peer in fame or sanctity.

A short way up the coast Heracles passed the manor of Croton, a grandee of that region, who treated him, in contrast with Lacinius, with the utmost courtesy. Croton was a man advanced in years, but who still retained in his mind an image of his youthful vigor. He asked Heracles to join him in heaving stones to prove his strength. Croton easily raised three stones, each progressively larger. But as he held a fourth stone, the heaviest yet, above his head, he tottered. As Heracles tried to steady him, his grip weakened and stone crushed his head. Heracles was so aggrieved that he organized for his kind host a magnificent funeral and erected a grand sepulcher on the banks of the Aesar. As he committed Croton's corpse to the grave, he felt light-headed and was compelled to announce to the people of the place that at a later time someone would found a city bearing Croton's name. The very thing he prophesied happened after his deification, when a certain Argive, Myscelos, claimed Heracles appeared to him in a dream and ordered him, under threat of terrible punishments, to lead a colony to Sicania. Of this request he was sore afraid, since the laws of his country proscribed a change of fatherland. Fearing the vision of the god more, he made ready to move his household and belongings; but rumor of this spread and he was tried in the law-court. The accused appealed to Heracles, who he considered responsible for his alleged crime. When the time came to cast lots to either condemn or free the prisoner, all the pebbles that were dropped in the urn, by all admittance, were black; yet, when the urn was overturned to count them, they came out white! Freed, Myscelos went his way and fulfilled the oracle.

Heracles resolved to make no further friends or enemies during the remainder of the journey. He drove the cattle the rest of the peninsula, across the gulf to Iapygia, and then for many weeks followed the coast clear to the head of the Cronian gulf. Skirting around it, he led his company down into Istria and then though rugged and mountainous Illyris as the frost of winter fell on them. They hastened through the valleys, ringed with endless tracts of spruce and pine, with soft snowfalls following at their heels. Arrived at Epidamnos on the coast, Heracles found a certain Dyrrachos, the son-in-law of the king, who was responsible for adding a dockyard there called after himself, in war with his brothers. Heracles aided him in battle, forming an alliance with him for a portion of his territory, but accidentally killed his son Ionios. After raising a barrow for him, Heracles threw the body into the sea so that it would bear his name.

As they passed into Epirus, they turned inland, since the coast consisted of rugged and lofty mountains ruled by robber-tribes, with few traversable valleys. Near an extensive plain they arrived at the sacred oracle of Dodona, the oldest and most celebrated of all shrines, in the land of the Molossians. It was at first devoted to the Mother Goddess, called by the Epirots Dione, until Zeus took residence there. When Heracles questioned the elderly bare-footed priestesses in the oak-grove as to whether Dione was simply another name for Hera, at which he would have moved on in disgust, they assured him she was a much older, and better-behaved, divinity who was simply Zeus' temple-associate.

As Heracles spoke to the women, the priest of the place, dressed in rough hemp tunics, with long, matted unwashed hair, and dirty feet, came over to entice Heracles to question the oracle. When he offered them a red yearling calf as a gift, they looked askance at it until he explained from whence it came. They then took it eagerly and conducted Heracles to the sacred Oak in the center of the grove beside a spring, where, in the hollow trunk, three black doves made their nest. Heracles asked them when and how his end would come. The priestesses proceeded to put their heads to the heart of the Oak to listen to the cooing of the doves, while the priests ran around the grove, rustling the tree-leaves along the way. The copper vessels depending from the branches clanged together like wind-chimes and produced long discordant tones.

The hierophants then congregated to whisper among themselves, until a priestess stepped forward to deliver the words of the god. She approached Heracles solemnly, in a cloud of incense, and said: "Savior Zeus says: no man alive may kill Heracles."

At Dodona Heracles remained for a day to satisfy those among his company who wished to consult the famous oracle, such as Peleus, who was told he would produce a son of great renown, peerless in bravery, and a conqueror of cities. In the market-place of the village, whose meager and unkempt appearance belied the stature of the sacred precinct, Heracles saw a tall handsome fellow wearing a closely fitting leather tunic and a mantle of leopard-skin around his shoulders to keep off the rain. His fair, braided hair rested across his shoulders. He had come in from the grove trailing a long branch of oak. A look of cognizance came between them, although neither remembered ever meeting the other. The young man, however, looked away in a haughty fashion. Heracles, undismayed, blocked his way and asked where he had gotten the branch, thinking that he had torn it off the Oak of Zeus.

"I am Jason, son of Aison," said the man. "This branch did indeed come from the sacred Oak, but it was given to me as a good omen by the priests."

"You seem a rough, yet refined fellow," said Heracles. "You smell of woodland pine and mountain marigolds, and your hands grasp the branch in the manner of javelin throwers, but your nose is straight and your bear yourself with undue dignity. What endeavor of yours would require such an inordinate blessing from the gods?"

"I ask you, sir, not to pester me with any more questions," said Jason warily. "I am very busy and must be on my way."

Heracles obstinately crossed his arms and replied: "You have now the misfortune of arousing the curiosity of Heracles of Tyrins."

"Heracles!" said Jason, his mood suddenly altered. "I guessed from your size and gear that it may have been you. I count myself fortunate to make your acquaintance. We both share a deep bond, for I too was reared at the feet of the good Centaur Cheiron; and he taught me much about you."

Heracles clapped his hands for joy and wrapped one burly arm around Jason's neck.

"I greet you as more than a brother, then, since those pupiled by Cheiron form a small and exclusive fraternity," he said. "And how is Cheiron? Tell me that he yet lives? I saw him last on the threshold of death—alas, pierced inadvertently by one of my own poisoned arrows when I was fighting off a mad troop of his kin."

"He cannot die," said Jason sadly. "In pain he remains, resting in his homely cave. I left his tutelage not long ago, on achieving my twentieth-year."

"Now that I am no longer a stranger to you," said Heracles, "tell me what this branch business is about? I would be chagrined to be left out of some important doing."

Jason explained that, to take his rightful place as king of Iolcos, he was in the process of organizing an expedition to fetch the Golden Fleece, an artifact currently in possession of Aiëtes, king of Colchis, on the far side of the Axine Sea where the indomitable horses of the sun are stabled. He had travelled to Delphi and then to Dodona to seek the will of the gods, and was rewarded by a branch of the sacred Oak that he was to make a part of the ship he was building for the quest.

"It was of you I heard speak in the marketplace of Mycenae! Alas, I've been away too long to follow through," lamented Heracles. "I would still like to accompany you. I made a similar voyage not long ago, as far as Amazonia. It is a long and arduous journey, full of dangers at every turn. I can no doubt be of service."

Jason remained silent for a moment, rehearsing in his mind the words before he spoke them. He could not ask for better than having the redoubtable Heracles among his crew; but he was just starting to make a name for himself and did not want to be overshadowed by the famous hero.

"Well, as I said," stammered Jason, "this will primarily be a Minyan enterprise."

"I am not a Minyan, and the Minyans perhaps consider me still an enemy from sacking Orchomenos in my youth; but I bear no grudge, as I hope none bear any toward me. Surely you can find a place for me and some friends, possessing no less bravery than I, should they wish to participate? I speak of Peleus of Aegina; as well as my brother and nephew. You have whetted my appetite for further adventure and I will not take no for an answer."

"First place will go to Minyans, but I will be certain to reserve a seat for you," said Jason, overcome by Heracles' enthusiasm. "We assemble at Iolcos in the spring."

At the banks of the Arachthos river they parted company after a small disagreement as to which way eastward to take around the Pindos range. Jason, at the suggestion of his traveling companion Iphitos of Phocis, who had entertained him when he arrived at Delphi, followed the river-valley northward, aiming for a known pass; while Heracles, at Peleus' insistence, continued southward, crossing the river, and skirting by the foothills. Days later they reached the land of the Dolopians, where Heracles spent the night in the wilderness. While in the middle of soothing sleep, Heracles awoke to learn that the cattle had run off. Hera, who had not yet taken her vengeful eyes off the hero, had sent a pesky warble-fly to molest the cattle, driving them all willy-nilly. Heracles was somewhat relieved that only half the cattle went missing, the rest carefully guarded by astute Molossian hounds that had been impressed into service during the time in Epirus. He at once called Iolaos to prepare his chariot and rode off alone into the night.

Heracles found and gathered most of the cattle in the immediate vicinity. Some of the herd, however, wandered across the Thessalian basin and clear into Thrace as far as the river Strymon, in which, unjustly blaming the river-god for his troubles, he cast great stones to make it unnavigable. He managed, after months of relentless pursuit, to gather most of the missing cattle, although a few remained scattered and became the progenitors of the wild Thracian variety.

Heracles expected to deliver the cattle to Eurystheus at Mycenae with no further incident. After rejoining his friends, they crossed the length of Epictetus until they reached Trachis on the Maliac Gulf. There Heracles paid a visit to his relation Ceyx, a nephew of Amphytrion and lord of Trachis, who was as yet unmarried. After three days in Trachis, they proceeded down to Boetia, where Iolaos and Iphicles returned to Thebes, and came to the Isthmus. At its narrowest part, however, as the company passed through a gully, a giant brigand named Alcyoneus appeared above them hoisting a massive rock. Without warning he dropped it on them, crushing no less than twelve wagons and killing double that number of horsemen. The giant, who towered nine cubits to the top of his pointy head, aimed a smaller rock  at Heracles, who had rushed from the front of the column where he was driving the cattle.  With one swing of his club, Heracles stopped the missile in mid-air, but in the process thunderously splintered his cudgel.  As the fearless Alcyoneus descended from the ledge, laughing as if he faced no danger, Heracles bent his great bow and the music of the bowstring rang out.  Alcyoneus, his neck pierced, rolled down to Heracles' feet.  As the giant tried to rise, blood gurgling from his nose and mouth, Heracles hove the first stone that had caused so much destruction, dyed in the blood of his followers, and flattened Alcynous under it.  One could still see that very stone where he left it.

On the Argeian plain, Heracles divided the booty accumulated during the long journey, keeping nothing for himself, and dismissed his loyal company.  Copreus the herald came down to inspect the cattle of Geryones, walking among them with his secretary close behind taking note of their number and condition. "Hail Heracles!" said Copreus at the end of his inspection.  "The king did not expect you to ever return from this latest expedition, although I personally had no doubt you would." Heracles waited by the chariot.  Copreus poked one thin cow in the ribs and said, "They seem certainly to be the famed cattle of Geryones—a little worse for the wear, however."

Heracles said: "Will king Eurystheus come out to see them? It has been eight years and one month since I entered his service.  I have performed all my Labors and am anxious to be dismissed."

"I am afraid the king is not here," said Copreus.  "He is about the Argolid on business.  When he returns he will no doubt notice them milling hereabouts."

"Very well, Dung-man.  Release me that I may attend to other matters," said Heracles impatiently.

Copreus sighed deeply.  "Noble Heracles, despite the king's disaffection for you—you should hear the excoriations with which he fills my ears!—I personally have nothing against you." Copreus, heading back to city, turned to say:  "It is therefore with great regret that I must inform you that you cannot be yet dismissed from service."

Heracles felt he did not hear Copreus clearly and asked him to speak up.

"I said—you are yet under thrall to king Eurystheus," called Copreus nervously, quickening his pace.

"How so?" said Heracles, feeling the anger rise in him like the flaming streams bubbling within Etna. "You must be mistaken. I have completed the ten Labors. First I killed the Nemean Lion, then—"

"You can take it up with the king, Heracles," said Copreus. "I am merely his messenger. Remember when you cleaned the stables of king Augeias? Because you engaged in that task only after demanding recompense, and with the help of others, my lord has decided to discount that Labor. And remember when you hunted the Lernean Hydra? We learned your nephew Iolaos assisted you; and so king Eurystheus has dismissed that Labor also, since he did not give you permission to utilize outside help. In light of these, you have only completed but eight of the ten Labors, and have two yet remaining."

"Gods blind me!" exclaimed Heracles. "Tell me you jest, Dung-man!"

"I do not!" said Copreus. "King Eurystheus instructed me to tell you, should you return, that for your next Labor you are to bring back some golden apples from the garden of the Hesperides—a handful will do."

"Garden of the Hesperides?" cried Heracles. "Where in unholy Tartaros is that?"

## BOOK II

---

## THE GOLDEN GLEECE

### 1

From all over Greece the bravest and most prominent of men made their way to the city of Iolcos at the summoning of Jason, son of Aison, under the auspices of king Pelias. Heracles tarried through the winter at Tyrins, resting from his arduous expedition after the cattle of Geryones, and then, at the first sign of spring, prepared his chariot for the long trip to Thessaly. He found little use in being overly concerned with his continuing servitude under the unjust and pedantic Eurystheus, since he could do nothing about it. More Labors would wait for his return. Word of the quest to Colchis had spread through Greece, whipping all the young, ambitious princes therein into frenzy. Heracles felt no less stirred by the prospect of another grand undertaking, one to a side of the world he had not yet adequately explored (since the journey to Amazonia took him only as far as the Thermodon); and one in which he could participate without duress. Under compulsion or not, he needed constant work and adventure to keep his mind free from troubles and headaches. As for the apples of the Hesperides—he did not even know where to begin. He hoped that contact with other adventurers gathering at Iolcos would provide him some useful intelligence. Peleus agreed to join him there, as well as Iphicles, who promised to also bring Iolaos.

As Heracles passed Mycenae, he could see long columns of black smoke arising behind the citadel. At that moment, to spite Heracles, king Eurystheus was offering up blazing hecatombs to Hera from the cattle of Geryones, praying for her cooperation in his eventual destruction.

The organization of the expedition after the Fleece came in this way. To Athamas, a Boetian king and son of Aiolos, was born Phrixos and his sister Helle, by his wife, the cloud-nymph Nephele, under the influence of Hera. Secretly in love with the mortal Ino, daughter of Cadmos and Harmonia, he took her also as wife, inspiring Nephele to return to the gods in humiliation. In her just complaint before the heavenly court, she demanded the death of Athamas, which was not granted, since his due for his lack of fidelity was a great multiplication of misfortunes. Meanwhile Ino, discontented with her lot as his chosen wife, nursed a hatred in her heart for Nephele; but especially for her two children, Learchos and Melicertes, whom Athamas loved deeply, even more so than her own issue. She therefore hatched a plot to have them killed to prevent them from inheriting their father's kingdom. After the harvest was reaped, and the time for the autumn sowing came, she convinced all the women of the land to remove the barley-seed from the jars of the temple-precincts, where they were heaped, and to parch them before their hearth-fires under the ruse that that this had been divinely instructed to ensure a bountiful harvest. The women did so, unbeknownst to the men, and in the morning returned the seed to storage. Their men later plowed the fields, planted the seeds, prayed for rain and waited. Not one green blade split the furrows; only weeds proliferated through the barren glebe. After many weeks of hopelessness, the people feared to starve that winter, and marched to Orchomenos to beseech the king. He could think of nothing to do save seek an answer from the Delphian oracle. When scheming Ino witnessed the messengers returning with an answer, she sent them bribes that they should report the words of the oracle as being this: "O king, the gods in their anger have blighted the harvest. To end the dearth, you must sacrifice your son Phrixos to Laphystian Zeus." When Athamas heard the dire pronouncement, his heart split. He remained locked in his palace, brooding, while the people, hunger gnawing at their bellies, demanded the death of his firstborn in accordance with the vatic pronouncement. When he could hold out no longer, he called his son Phrixos, and holding back his tears, asked him to bring back from the royal fold the choicest of sheep for a sacrifice in which he was to assist. The lad, just turned sixteen, took his sister and inseparable companion, Helle, to the place where the black-faced sheep shambled. It did not take them long to make a selection, for from the sheepfold emerged a tall and stately ram, with great curving horns and a curious purple pelt, as if dyed with murex, glittering with gilded ringlets. The ram boldly nudged at Phrixos until he led it away. As they approached Mount Laphystios, rising above Orchomenos, the ram turned its face to Phrixos, opened its lips and said with the voice of a man: "I am not the sacrifice, dear boy; but you. Heed my words, and do carefully as I say; for I was sent by your mother, whose immortal love overshadows you like a cloud. When you lead me to the altar, and the slaves approach with the laver and the bowl of barley, and the sharp knife hidden in a sleeve, jump then upon my back. Help your little sister also. I shall carry you both to safety." Too astonished were Phrixos and Helle to respond. Phrixos indicated his obedience with a nod. When they arrived at the designated place, a wide grove on a shoulder of the mount, all was ready. Athamas, unable to bear the sight of his son, looked away as the slaves brought over the ram, tied ribbons around its horns, and held the wooly head down in preparation. With a groan, Athamas embraced his son and said: "It is the will of Zeus that you die this day upon this holy mount, my son. Lay upon this cold slab and close your eyes." At once Phrixos knew that the ram spoke truth. Seeing the glint of the sacral knife in his father's hand, Phrixos leapt upon the ram, reaching out for Helle to join him. With their tender hands caught in the clinquant rings, the ram vaulted and took flight, soaring eastward far and high until it presented but a speck against the blue sky.

Over land and across the wide sea flew the golden ram, on its back the children buffeted by fierce winds and clouds pregnant with rain. Phrixos urged his little sister to hold dear, not knowing when or where their journey would end. Helle, however, could no longer bear the dizzying heights. Her feeble hands fell slack. She slipped from the ram and fell as they swept past the sea and came over that long and narrow strait, now called the Hellespont after her.

Phrixos in anguish saw Helle fall, her gown fluttering, as the white flowers of the cornel-tree shed by a springtime breeze. More than once he thought to join his sister in certain death, but the voice of the ram encouraged him to persist. To the far ends of the world the golden ram conveyed him, landing at last in the misty land of Colchis where the Sun stables his fiery steeds. King Aiëtes, who despite his wariness of strangers, since an oracle portended his death at the hands of a foreigner, kindly received Phrixos, hoping for divine favor. In gratitude, Phrixos sacrificed the ram to Zeus and offered its Golden Fleece to Aiëtes, who hung it on an oak tree in a grove sacred to Ares. In return, Aiëtes offered him his oldest daughter Chalciope in marriage.

As for Athamas, his ruin was not yet complete. After the flight of Phrixos and Helle, Hera drove him mad on account of Dionysos, who, born to Semele, was hid in his house disguised as a girl. During a hunt, Athamas transfixed Learchos with an arrow, confusing him with a deer. Ino boiled her remaining son alive in a caldron of water, and then, with the caldron in her arms, leaped to her death into the sea. Banished for the murder of his son, Athamas fled Boetia after inquiring at Delphi where he should settle. The oracle returned that he should settle where wild beasts welcomed him. Wandering northward to the Thessalian wilderness he came upon wolves devouring a pack of sheep. His presence scared the wolves away from their repast. Recognizing the portent, Athamas settled there, calling the country Athamania. Athamas married a third time, to one Themisto, who bore him two sons. It is said that she, after unwittingly killing her children, put an end to herself.

After the death of Cretheus, another son of Aiolos, the founder of Iolcos and ruler of Phthiotis, the mantle should have gone to his son Aison; but instead, his half-brother Pelias usurped the throne. Pelias and his brother Neleus were sons of Tyro and Poseidon, as has been previously related; and Tyro was married to her uncle Cretheus. From a prophecy Pelias learned that he would be killed by a descendant of Aiolos since he had incurred the enmity of Hera when he murdered hard Sidero at her altar; and so ordered put to death all of the children of Aiolos he could reach. Meanwhile Aison had fled with his wife Alcimide to the wilderness, where a son, Diomede, was born to them. Pelias, who had spared his half-brother for their mother's sake, wished to show no such pity for their newborn son. When he arrived at their rustic house, he was met by a great lamentation. Aison, who reported the child still-born, had secretly sent the babe away to be reared by the wise Centaur Cheiron in the fastness of Mount Pelion. Under Cheiron's care, Diomede grew and waxed strong in spirit. He ate fruits, roots and brown honey; and the meat of the wild stag that he learned to hunt with spear and bow; and drank from cold mountain springs. He learned from Cheiron to sing, to make music on the harp, to dance delicately, to run and wrestle. At night Cheiron would explain the movement of the stars that filled their eyes. With other companions fostered by Cheiron, the lad learned the value of duty and loyalty, bravery and the bonds of sacred friendship. Still, not knowing his own circumstances, he wondered what right had he to live in Cheiron's cave among so many sons of kings and illustrious men.

When Diomede had grown to be a goodly youth, tall and comely, with bright, unshorn locks rippling down his back, Cheiron walked with him through the leaf-strewn paths he knew so well and revealed to him his true lineage. "That glorious city by the sea, visible from these cloud-girt ridges, is your heritage," said Cheiron on the eve of departing to his fateful encounter with Heracles. "Soon you will go there to avenge your father and wrest the throne from the usurper. Because you will rule prudently and justly, and set all things aright among men, no longer shall you be called Diomede, but Jason shall be your name."

Jason listened in astonishment. As Cheiron did not afterward return for a long time, the eager youth bid farewell to his companions and descended his mountain home into the cool shade of the pine trees. He settled on a farmstead and tilled the land as a hireling until, hearing that Pelias planned to celebrate a great festival, started for Iolcos. Halfway there he came to the river Anauros, and there, on the bank, found crouching a crone begging to be helped across the torrent. Jason, who learned from Cheiron equal parts courtesy and pity, bravery and fierceness, offered her his broad back. As he ferried her across the wintry waters, he remarked how heavy she felt for such a slight old woman; the old crone only laughed and tapped his head to hurry him along. Midway the purling waters, inflamed by the melting snows of Pelion, made Jason almost lose his footing in the muddy river-bed, which retained one his sandals. Reaching the other bank, sopping and aching from the struggle and burden, he put down the old woman gently; but when he turned to face her, she was vanished from sight, leaving a few peacock feathers where she had stood. Cheerful at such an auspicious omen, believing he had been favorably visited by no less a personage than the queen of the gods, he boldly entered the city.

In the meanwhile, king Pelias was making ready a sacrifice to Poseidon in the market-place. Hearing a murmur among the people, who gossiped among themselves when Jason appeared among them, wondering if the stranger was Apollo, or Ares, or one of the sons of Poseidon for his beauty and grace, he left the altar and rode into the crowd in his mule-car. Seeing Jason, wrapped in a leopard-skin cloak, and carrying two spears, one for throwing and one for thrusting, he stopped, afraid. Despite the youth's uncommon appearance, with his golden hair, princely mien and splendid limbs clothed in Magnesian garb, the sight of his unshod foot filled him with apprehension: for another oracle had warned him to beware of a man who appeared one-shoed.

"You there," said Pelias, trying to hide his sudden fear with disdain. "What is your name and lineage?"

Jason approached and said gently: "Who I am I shall tell you presently."

Pelias, taken aback by the unmannered response, snorted heavily. Looking down at Jason's bare foot he asked: "Tell me, stranger, what you would do if by an oracle you knew a kinsman was out to kill you?" Jason thought a moment, and then, as by divine inspiration he felt these words leave his mouth: "I would send him off on such an adventure, so full of perils, that he would find it difficult to return." It was Hera who instigated the words since she hated Pelias: not only for slaughtering Sidero at her altar, but also for thereafter omitting her in his annual sacrifices.

"Indeed!" said Pelias. "Such an exercise would be accepted by only the boldest of men—you perhaps? Or mayhap your boldness, bordering on insolence, is due to your ignorance of where you are or who I am."

"By your costly garbs and bejeweled fingers you seem a man of authority," said Jason.

Pelias introduced himself and asked Jason to reciprocate, but still the latter demurred, saying: "Lord Pelias, I will undertake any task you lay before me. Only, if I do so and succeed, you must surrender the throne, which you hold unlawfully, to me."

Pelias looked about him nervously, since a crowd had

gathered, hanging on every word exchanged between them. He dismissed Jason with a wave and said: "Enough prattering! Even were you to succeed in plucking a hair off Zeus' chin, I could not yield to you the throne of Iolcos, since only a Minyan may sit on it. My half-brother Aison, though aged and infirm, lives still, and when he dies, the throne, which I hold in regency, will pass to me; and I when I die, to my son Acastos."

"Nay," said Jason. "I am the rightful heir among the children of Aiolos, to whom Zeus awarded this kingdom. I am Jason, son of Aison—better known to you, uncle, as Diomede."

Pelias dared not question him further in public. He warmly placed an arm around Jason and led him to his mule-car. Once they had trotted up the road a bit, Jason showed him his purple swathing-clothes as proof of his identity. Seeing them, Pelias wept, declaiming how glad he was that Jason had been spared during the turbulent time of his ascendency. He wished to lodge the youth at the palace; but Jason asked to see his parents first. Pelias drove him to the lonely house, where the aged Aison wept on his bosom, and his mother Alcimide, carrying in her arms Promachos, a son born in her old age, swooned for joy. Aison's brothers, Pheres and from Messenia Amythaon, hearing the news, arrived soon afterward. For five days they feasted in joy and contentment.

Aison tried to dissuade Jason from claiming the throne, fearing that Pelias would surely decide to kill him. Jason did not wish to offend his father, but felt it necessary to correct the injustice committed against him in Pelias' unlawful rule. To the palace Jason hurried, and when he stood before Pelias said to him: "Uncle, do not think that I come here desiring to choose gain over righteousness. We are both reasonable men, and I have no doubt that you have acted up to now in my father's best interest, with all due attention to the good of this realm. Although you cannot ignore the laws of polity and succession, given us by the gods for the common weal, we should not fight one another and tarnish the memory of the glorious antecedents from which we spring. You may keep all the cattle and sheep, and all the land of their herbage from which your wealth derives. I ask only for the scepter and throne where Cretheus sat of old, dispensing justice and beloved of his people."

Pelias shook with rage. His mind sought vainly how to rid

himself of Jason. To do so openly was not an option: his appearance was now well known throughout Iolcos and beyond, since even his princely uncles and cousin came to see him. No wars raged to which he could send him to fight; and Heracles of Tyrins had made monsters scarce. There was yet the angry sea, he thought, and its never-ending perils.

"It shall be as you say," said Pelias mildly, no frown clouding his face. "First however, do me this noble service. You have heard how Phrixos, sprung from the blood of Athamas, escaped from his immolation to Colchis by the frozen Phasis upon a golden-fleeced ram. In a crime unimaginable to us who love peace and civility, and eschew cruelty and violence, the unmerciful king of that land, Aiëtes, slew him as he sat at banquet holding the wine-bowl. This I know!—the trembling shade of Phrixos himself interrupts my sleep with lamentable complaints: his bones lie unburied still in that foreign land. He bids me, night after night, as I lay in febrile state and fearful of the shadows, to give his bleached bones proper burial and to bring back the Golden Fleece as expiation for Athamas' sacrilege, which has brought down Zeus' wrath upon our house. If only my limbs still possessed the strength they once had, even now you would be seeing me return in triumph, restoring that sacred treasure to our temple wall. Nor is my son yet ready for the strain of empire, or the bloody exploits of war. But you, noble Jason, I sense possessed of an indomitable will. You indeed are worthy of such a task. Far greater, I can tell, do you wish to imbibe among your comrades, even if death were the price, the magic potency of valor, instead of remaining by your mother's side in a savorless and riskless life. Achieve the quest, and I swear that the throne of Iolcos will be yours."

For a moment Jason regretted the rash suggestion that ignited the proposal. He could see through Pelias' dissembling: that the usurper wished nothing more, at best, to discourage him and force him to abandon his ambition; or, at worse, to devise his ruin and death by sending him on a fool's errand to the ends of the earth. Even if he possessed Perseus' winged sandals, or could ride the dragon-pulled flying chariot of Triptolemos, the task to fetch the Fleece—if it even existed—seemed almost impossible. Then the incident at the river Anauros came to mind and he took heart. In his inmost mind he prayed to the Queen of Heaven for her aid in crossing the seas, and to Pallas for protection against the dark unknown. He parted from Pelias, who pledged to finance the voyage, while Jason agreed to organize the enterprise.

The first to join the crew was Pelias' son Acastos. He told Jason: "Despite my father's disapproval, I am ready to sail with you. Let no one think me indolent or cowardly; my heart is pledged to you, friend and cousin." Jason did not try to dissuade him, thinking his company would ensure that Pelias would not in some way try to sabotage the expedition. He then sent forth heralds to all the principal cities of Greece to proclaim the quest, and valorous men began to stream into Iolcos. To seek the guidance of the gods, Jason first visited Delphi, where the Pythia apparently gave him a favorable utterance, although he was not completely certain since her words came forth cryptically in her chewed laurel-leaf ecstasy. Then he sailed to Athens, where he sought an audience with Theseus, since none could profitably ply the waves without the blessing of that famous city. Theseus itched to accompany him, but he was presently beset by troubles with the Pallantids, who formented revolution. "I feel trapped here," he told Jason, "like a shade in Tartaros. Nevertheless, I will offer you any support I can. I will send letters at once to Troy to ensure for you a safe voyage through the Hellespont. Have you yet readied a ship?" When Jason responded that the vessel had not yet been built, Theseus laughed and called for Argos, son of Hestor, the best shipwright of Athens and a devotee of Athena. Argos, ordered to build the swiftest and most elegant war galley to ever cross the sea, packed his tools and left for Iolcos at once. "And if Heracles of Tyrins joins you, give him my greetings," said Theseus as Jason left. From Athens Jason made passage through the Gulf of Corinth, up along the coast of Epirus and into the wide estuary of the Thyamis to Dodona, where he was given a branch of the oracular oak-tree as a holy thing to build into the prow of the ship. He also there encountered Heracles, as has been related; but he intentionally failed to honor Heracles with the mention of Theseus, so as to not grant him much importance.

2

When Jason arrived back at Iolcos, the building of the ship was well underway. At the foot of Mount Pelion Argos found sufficient tall pine-trees for the planking, which he cut and trimmed, and floated across the bay to the ship-yard of Pagasai. From there his builders cut and smoothed the logs into planks and steamed them over fires, molding them to the correct curvature for strakes. Argos then sought for the stoutest oak-trees for the frame, a broad straight one for the keel and curved larch and plane-trees for the ribs. When these were fitted together into a long, narrow hull, the strakes were fastened in single pieces from stem to stern, fitted carefully edge to edge in the carvel fashion using mortise and tenon, and dowels to secure them, with the seams sealed with hot beeswax. The frame, inside and out, was daubed with boiled tar to make it waterproof.

The mast was cut from a single oak-tree, twice the length of the ship, which could be fitted in a crutch midship, and supported by a forestay from the bow and three backstays to the sternpost. Employing an innovation of his distant relative Daidalos, Argos ensured the square white sail could be swiftly furled to the spar by means of cables and a pulleys. Fifty oar holes were cut around the vessel and fitted with bronze oar-locks and leather thongs to hold the oars in place. Two large steering oars were fitted to the stern to either side of the raised helmsman's seat. To the prow, curving upward to a massive carved ram's head, was fitted the oracular timber from Dodona.

Iphitos, son of Naubolos, a skilled painter, decorated one side of the prow with lively scenes of river-nymphs and sea-gods, and the other with images of fighting Centaurs and Lapiths, with bowls and chairs and pitchers flying among the fighters. But above these images, near the ram's head, two great red eyes were painted:

the eyes of Athena to guide the ship through the murky darkness of the deep.

When Jason saw the long ship, he thought it the most handsome vessel ever to grace the waters. Nothing like it existed, not even among the Cretans or Phoenicians, who were renowned seafarers. Although it could seat fifty men, its narrow beam promised to make it fast, light and nimble; yet its construction was strong enough to withstand the choppiest seas and the strongest gales. Argos grew so proud of her that he demanded to sail with her, as did Iphitos. Jason honored the master shipwright by naming the ship *Argo*.

Young men of all stripes streamed into Iolcos throughout the winter and spring, lodging in the palace and feasting in the hall of Pelias. Soon there were too many, Minyans and otherwise, to consider; and when Pelias began to complain to Jason that his stores were growing barren and his hospitality strained, Jason tasked two eminent sea-men, Tiphys son of Hagnias, of Boetian Siphai; and Ancaios of Tegea, son of Lycurgos (or, as some said, of Poseidon) to cull from the eager crowd the least qualified. Those who were not already practiced oarsmen were made to row in hollowed-out boats around and around the bay. Half the men left after being subjected to that exercise, claiming they were not built for such work. Others Peleus examined for their martial prowess, engaging them in horse-races and mock battles with wooden swords. After returning to Aegina from fetching the cattle of Geryones, Peleus and his brother Telamon conspired against their half-brother, Phocos, whom they envied since he excelled them in their military games, and was always their father's favorite. Phocos was born from the sea-nymph Psamanthe, who turned herself into a seal to avoid the further embraces of Aiacos. According to Peleus, Telamon threw a quoit at Phocos. According to Telamon, it was Peleus who dispatched him. Whatever the case, they hid the body in the woods. When the fratricide came to light, Aiacos banished them from Aegina. Telamon fled to Salamis, to the court of Cychreus. But he returned to Aegina a short while later, positioning himself on a mole off the harbor since he was forbidden to set foot on the island, from where he loudly declaimed his innocence. But his remonstrations failed to move Aiacos, and so Telamon returned to Salamis, where Cychreus gave him his daughter Glauce in marriage.  As for Peleus, he became a wanderer, finally arriving at the fortress of Phthia, where king Eurytion purified him of the murder.

✑

By early summer, those few destined to win immortal fame on the *Argo* had risen to the top of the assembly, as cream in milk fresh from the dugs, bound together in the bonds of friendship, and ready to face any danger in the hope of glory.  Still, Jason worried that the benches of the *Argo* had not yet been filled.  Pelias was beginning to lose confidence that Jason could organize the expedition, and deprive him of the opportunity to get rid of him without incurring blood-guilt or appearing treacherous toward such an illustrious band of heroes.  He set a firm day of departure, the first new moon after the rising of the Pleiades, under the pretense that it came from priests at the shrine of Laphystian Zeus.

When the day arrived, Jason went morosely to his father's house, where he found Aison, ill and sick at heart wrapped in the coverlet of his bed.  His mother Alcimede no longer held her tongue in check, but opened her mouth and her heart with these words: "If only on that day, when I heard king Pelias give the awful pronouncement, I had left this life and all its cares, so that you could bury me, my son.  Instead, it is I who will be left alone, longing for you, twice cruelly separated from me, the first child for whom I lost my maidenhood, thinking you forsaken on some Scythian shore, lashed with breakers under a leaden sky and truculent winds forever wailing.  Is that a mother's reward?"  Thus she said, collapsing in his bosom, and drenching his hair with her hot tears, like a lonely young girl falling upon her grey-haired nurse, weary from the reproaches of a stepmother, who must spend her life in misery and robbed of all joy.

Aison, who had kept quiet through his wife's keening, rose on his bandied legs, his shoulders bowed with age, and tried to relieve his son's discomfort, saying: "If only I had the strength of my younger days, you would see me clinging to the *Argo*'s sternpost, ready to jump aboard and join you in the rowing. But if I cannot go with you, at least my prayers will, some of which have already graciously been answered.  A ship filled with princes sails forth,

257

with you, dear son, its captain. Some day you will return bearing the Golden Fleece upon your shoulders and I will be here pridefully to receive you, as my glory gives way to yours." But he spoke wistfully, knowing that his own fate was sealed the moment Jason departed.

But no decision had yet been made as to who was to captain the *Argo*. Jason said nothing to dispel his father's assumption, hoping that, despite his ignorance of seamanship, he would be the natural choice. He embraced his mother while he felt his father's arm about his neck.

"Please mother, do not abuse yourself with grief," said Jason, sounding more confident than he felt, "since your tears cannot prevent whatever Fortune has in store. Instead, take courage that I sail under favorable oracles, and in the company of renowned men. Both of you of remain here quietly with my brother and your servants, out of the way of Pelias; and know, father, that I will surely return to avenge you."

Jason left them to their mourning and passed through the broad avenues of the city, where the other heroes had that morning progressed in the glittering array of their armor like bright stars beyond the clouds. The people acclaimed him, and mourned for him, saying: "Would that Phrixos and his ram had perished also in the sea's dark waves! Alcimide, you would have been spared such misery. As for Aison—t'were better for him to have already been wrapped in the sere cloth of death under the black earth, oblivious to this terrible labor."

The aged Iphias, priestess of Artemis, crossed his path to kiss his hand and utter words of prophecy that burned in her breast. But as the people pressed in, Jason did not notice her, and so he passed on.

At the broad beach of Pagasai Jason found his comrades sitting on the lowered mast, folded sails and cordage. Argos, dressed in a long cape of bull's-hide covered in dark hair, rose to greet Jason, who gave him the order to launch the ship. The crew stripped to their breech-clouts, laying their clothes in a heap on a flat rock just out of range of the waves. Under Argos' direction, they wrapped a twisted cable around the ship, pulling it taught on both sides, so that the planks would not burst their bolts in the force of hitting the water. From the prow to the sea they then dug out a channel a bit wider than the *Argo*'s beam, hollowing it out as they proceeded deeper than the bilge. Into the channel they dropped smooth, heavy logs so that a level platform extended from the rollers upon which the ship's flattened bottom already lay. Tiphys climbed aboard and reversed the oars through the oar-holes, so that the ends projected a cubit beyond the sides of the ship. Each man took his place behind an oar, and at Tiphys' direction, heaved with their arms and chests, pushing forward to shift the ship off its base onto the new set of rollers. After a moment's intense effort, in which the men groaned and grunted while Tiphys shouted orders as to where the greater force was needed, the ship's hull creaked and commenced to slide forward. Continuing their exertion, their feet dancing and sinking in the sand, the men pushed forward mightily. With a shout on both sides they got the ship to slide on its own; with a rush it almost toppled them. Smoke rose as the stout keel scraped over the rollers. "Steady!" cried Tiphys. "Don't let her get away from you!" The men between the oars now dropped away and wrapped their arms with the frapping cables, pulling back to slow the ship's progress. With a plash the prow slid into the water, the rest following, until the ship rode confidently in the shallows. Argos watched his creation with apprehension as Tiphys looked about for leaks. Since none were found, Argos had the men reverse the oars and tie them to the thole pins, step the mast, and load the stores.

As they completed their tasks, a commotion arose from the crowd that had gathered at the beach to watch the launch, turning into sustained sounds of wonder and acclamation. From their midst, walking along the coast road, appeared Heracles in the company of a man and a youth so handsome that more heads turned to marvel at him than at Heracles. From the beach, Peleus was the first to recognize the newcomer. He jumped up and down, waving his arms and calling "Heracles! Heracles!" Erginos of Orchomenos angrily drew his sword, remembering his defeat by Heracles when he attacked Thebes. When Telamon saw this, he reproached him saying: "Do you not know who that is, hot-head? Yes, I've heard your bitter stories, poured out over too much wine. Forget your past grudges. You will have as your comrade the greatest man who ever lived, skilled in war and every other thing that will be of use to us. Put your sword away before you cut yourself, and thank the gods that Heracles has arrived in time." With this, Telamon ran off after his brother Peleus.

Jason, who had been heaping stones for an altar, turned to look and his heart sank. His fear of being overshadowed, after so much hard effort, momentarily clouded his judgment. But he thought better and ran off, outstripping Peleus and Telamon, to be the first to welcome Heracles.

"Hail and well met, master Jason!" said Heracles, giving Jason his right hand. "You have got yourself a splendid ship there. Never quite seen one that long and thin, but it looks like it will do; and you must know best. I see I have cut it close. You weren't going to take off without me? Even when I said I would come? What of my brother Iphicles and my nephew Iolaos, are they here yet? In any case, I've brought some more relatives. Have you room for all of us? This is my brother-in-law, Polyphemos, married to my only sister Laonome.; and this handsome boy is his son Hylas. The last time I saw him he was knee-high to a dormouse. I recruited them as I passed through Thebes. Look what a splendid boy he's grown up to be, with his bubbly white cheeks, curved scarlet lips, bright locks and tender chin unshaded yet by any down—looks a bit like you, doesn't he? But don't think him a milk-fed babe. He's swift, fights well, and can carry my shield easily enough. He makes his father proud. I love him to death and wish to make him my squire if Iolaos doesn't mind. Where is Iolaos? I do not see him."

By then Peleus and Telamon arrived at his side, panting. It was a merry reunion until Heracles was told that neither Iphicles nor Iolaos was among them. He doubted them and ranged up and down the beach looking for Iolaos until he came across Augeias of the Eleans, who crouched behind the platform from which the *Argo* had been launched, pretending to rid his sandals of sand.

Heracles remembered him at once and said indignantly: "You have done me a grave disservice, not only for refusing me my a reward after doing the good work of cleaning out your filthy stables in one day, but also in tattling about me to Eurystheus, resulting in a lengthening of my Labors."

Augeias, far from the safety and comfort of his court, answered contritely: "It is indeed very good to see you, Heracles. I must however, take issue with your accusations. As for your first point, it was not I, but a lawfully appointed court of inquiry that was ready to decide the matter. Because you came to me unsolicited and acquitted yourself in bad faith, it seemed most just that any contract between us be rendered null and void. Had you told me at the outset that you came at the order of Eurystheus, perhaps matters would have taken a different turn. As to your second point, I was content, after your departure, to let the matter rest. But as Eurystheus sent a messenger to inquire about the task he had imposed on you, I could do no less than provide the High King with a full and accurate report. If I have caused you grief by my actions—all done in good conscience, mind you—there is little now that I can do about it except share with you the joys and pains of our coming expedition. I am perhaps the wealthiest of all men here assembled, and greatly wish to behold the glory of the Colchian king and the land he rules, where our common father, the Sun, keeps his horses stabled."

Displaying an unconventional mildness under the circumstances, Heracles nodded his head with a grunt, by which sign Augeias thought that the air had been cleared between them. But every time Heracles saw Augeias in his unsoiled linen tunic; his cloak of Phocean purple, embroidered in gold; and the bulging money-sack hanging ostentatiously at his waist, he recalled his resentment and entertained thoughts of vengeance. As the ship had been loaded and victualled, he sat on a log to wait for Jason.

Jason called the crew together. As he did not want to be considered a laughingstock by a brazen show of presumption, he resigned himself to the certain expectation that Heracles would be chosen captain over himself. With a resolute countenance shaded with specious goodwill he addressed them: "Friends, as our ship is ready to sail, it behooves us to set off at once while the breeze blows to our advantage. It is true that I have up to now organized this expedition, sending out word and bringing together such a gallant group of brave men. Yet, I have no skill in navigation, and it does not always please me to order men about. Choose therefore one from among you to be your leader on land and sea. There are many here who boast being a god's progeny, such as the most excellent Heracles, who is without equal among us."

While all turned eyes to Heracles and shouted their assent that he should lead them, Jason sat down silently with downcast eyes. Only Erginos did not agree with the rest, muttering under his breath that only a Minyan should be appointed to lead a Minyan enterprise, although only thirteen Minyans counted among the crew. From where he sat, Heracles extended his right hand and said: "Let no one offer me this honor, as I do not consent; and I forbid any other to stand up or be nominated. There is the man who brought us together. Jason, and no other, shall be our captain."

Quiet words circulated among the Argonauts as they considered the matter, for Jason was still a youth; but none dared to contradict Heracles and so most joined in a chorus of enthusiastic assent. Jason, elated, rose to his feet and said: "You honor me in giving me charge of this expedition. While we wait for my father's neatherds to bring the offering, let us build an altar to Apollo of the Embarkations, whose oracle promised that he would show us the right paths of the sea if we would only begin our journey with sacrifices and feasting."

The men brought down great stones to the water's side and there completed the altar, upon which they spread branches of dried olive-wood. Aison's slaves in the meantime brought two choice oxen from his meager herd, which the younger Argonauts unyoked and dragged to the altar while others made ready the lustral water and barley-meal. Jason came near and said solemnly: "Hear me, lord Apollo, who dwells in Pagasai and the city of Iolcos. When I visited your oracle, you promised to be our guide and to bring this expedition safely to its conclusion. Be with us now, and be our help in all challenges that confront us. Guide our ship as we sail away and some day return to our native shores, keeping us all safe. As many as return will be the count of the bulls we will slay on your altars at Delphi and Delos. As for now, come, Far-Darter, to receive our sacrifice as we embark. Let me loose the hawsers as you command; and may a gentle breeze carry us over a mild sea."

As he concluded his prayer, Jason cast a handful of barley-grains at the oxen along with a sprinkle of the lustral water. The oxen, skittish to be brought so near the heat of the altar-fire, shuddered their massive bodies and tried, snorting and kicking, to wrench their horns, tied with blue ribands, away from the hands that held them. Heracles, who was quite hungry, picked up his club and crashed it down on the poll of one ox. Its heavy body sagged and dropped immediately on the sand. Ancaios of Tegea, son of

Lycourgos, dressed in the skin of a Manalian bear, frowned upon such a crude slaughter. He grabbed his whetted double-sided axe and in one clean stroke sliced the neck of the other bull, right through the tough sinews, so that it fell over its own horns. Idmon, son of Apollo, and an augur, came forward to collect some of the blood in a bowl to pour over the altar. After this, the men set to flay and cut up the steers, chopping up first the god's portion, which they wrapped in fat, and burned on spits. Jason, who, from his life in the wilds of Pelion, showed himself inferior to none in animal butchery, then poured on the roasting meat a libation for Apollo. A second cup he spilled in honor of Poseidon, into whose extensive domain the Argonauts would soon plunge. He prayed silently that none but the god would hear: "Lord of the sea, you who with a nod can churn the ocean to foam, hear my prayers and be kind to your servant. Know that I chart a path through your waters at the command of Pelias, who no doubt has contrived to bring me and my friends to ruin on this perilous journey. I beg for your mercy and justice. Receive us with your waters, bearing up in safety this shipload of noble and kingly men."

Meanwhile, as the moist gobbets of bull-flesh roasted in the flames dancing through the grate, Mopsos, son of Ampycos—but thought to be son of Apollo for his skill in soothsaying—stood at the shoreline swaying as in a trance. He wore a flowering white robe that reached to his buskins and a curious helmet adorned with laurel leaves from the banks of the river Peneios. He moaned and the others crowded around to hear him. "What is it I see?—none other than Poseidon, arising from the sea! Was he summoned hither, or was his anger aroused from our daring? He calls together the maritime gods, who clamor for him to defend against us divine law. But Hera herself arrives to implore her brother for mercy! And there is Athena, our advocate by her words. Behold—the sea gods have yielded! O!—but I see more. Who is that carrying a silver pitcher, his hair covered in wet rushes? I see fierce bulls belching flames from their nostrils. There also lies the spangled Fleece amidst laurel-trees. What now? A woman, covered in the blood of her children, flying through the air in a chariot drawn by winged dragons!" Mopsos stopped, looking about him at an audience benumbed by his dark visions.

Idmon, coming from the altar, where he had been

examining the entrails, looked back to see the smoke of the sacrifice spiraling upward in dark columns.  Finding in it some good omen he said: "Nay, I see how our voyage will fare.  It is the will of heaven that we return here with the Fleece, but not before facing countless trials and being weighed down with the burden of grief.  Have courage, friends, and despise not the struggle that will bring us in the end the loving embraces of fathers and mothers welcoming our return."  Tears ran down his cheeks, which his companions thought were born of joy; but he had long before divined also his own fate in the hobbling flight of a magpie, which was to perish on a foreign soil.

"You see," Jason said, "how the augur's words forebode for us a happy ending if we all invest this enterprise with all the courage and strength we can muster.  Forget that it is Pelias who sends us forth; this business is of the gods.  It is the task Zeus has both set before us and blessed.  Let us trust in his wisdom to see us through our trials.  In the meanwhile, let us enjoy this last night at home in feasting and sweet fellowship."

The crew made couches of leaves and soft seaweed on the shore and reclined in rows as the midday sun passed on to cast the ploughlands in the shadows of the rocks.  Great trenchers brimming with meats and viands passed from hand to hand, while servants ladled off cups of rich wine from decorated wine-bowls.  All afternoon they passed in riotous story-telling, as men enjoy doing over good food and drink.  At twilight they built fires which shone in a line along the beach, while out in the harbor the sea returned only darkness.

Idas, son of Aphareus and brother of Lynceus, a savage man ever full of scorn and ready with coarse jokes, on seeing Caineus, son of Coronos, daintily wiping his mouth, said: "Is that not he who was once a woman?  The same happened with that Theban seer Teiresias, who they say went from one to the other and back again, and afterwards was struck blind from a wager of the gods' gone sour.  Once, walking on Mount Cithairon, he saw a male snake mounted on a female snake, and striking them with his staff, killed the female.  As soon as he did so he grew paps and hair on his loins, and became a woman.  Seven years afterward, he saw two other snakes together; killing the male snake this time, he was turned back into a man.  Meanwhile, Zeus and Hera, discussing which sex experienced the most enjoyments, called Teiresias before them, to whom they posed the question. Having experienced both sides of the issue, he sided with Zeus, who contended that women held the advantage by their insatiability. Hera was so cross that she struck the old bugger blind."

Coronos came to his son's defense, saying: "You are mistaken Idas. It was my father whom you describe. He fell in battle against the Centaurs. Nestor, you were there."

Nestor, wise and eloquent even in his youth, spoke up saying: "I was; as were others of our company, including Mopsos and Peleus. That the elder Caineus was once a woman is nothing compared to the marvel of his inviolability; for his flesh could repulse barbs and spears, as a mountain-face scorns the hailstorm."

The Argonauts unfamiliar with that story clamored to hear more saying, "Tell us, Nestor, how was he conquered?"

Nestor said: "With all respect to Coronos, let me begin the tale with Caenis, daughter of Elatus, most beautiful of all the Thessalian maids. Even Peleus there, among many others, was a suitor; but she refused to be bound in wedlock. Once, while walking along the lonely seashore, Poseidon saw her and burned with love. While ravishing her, he asked her to make any request, which he would not deny her. 'I ask never again to suffer such injury as this: make me no longer a woman,' said she. Poseidon honored her petition and the change took place even as she spoke, so that her last words came forth in a deep tone. Besides that, the god made the new man invulnerable to spear or sword. Rejoicing in his new sex, Caineus went off to roams the fields of Thessaly, engaging for many years in manly and noble exercises.

"Now, the brave Peirithoös married Hippodame, inviting his cousins the Centaurs, to recline at tables in a tree-shaded grotto; there was no further room at the palace for those curious half-men. The princes of Thessaly were all there, and I among them, and the palace resounded in a noisy clamor. As the bride entered, escorted by a crowd of matrons and young wives, the nuptial song, accompanied with the smoke from the wide hearths, rose to the crossbeams. As our eyes beheld the fair Hippodame, we praised Peirithoös for his fine taste, and then all but sealed the coming doom with our kind words. For, at a window, Eurytos, most savage of the Centaurs, had been jealously watching the proceedings; and filled with drunkenness and lust, since Peirithoös did not stint the Centaurs their portions of wine, which they madly drank unmixed—this Eurytos whistled for his companions and then burst into the hall, overturning the tables, and dragging away Hippodame by the hair. The other Centaurs now barged in, and took this maid or that matron, as it fancied each, so that it seemed like a town, from the sound of womens' shrieks, was being sacked.

"Up rose Theseus, crying: 'What madness has engulfed you, Eurytos, to this vile deed? In attacking Peirithoös, you have injured also me!' He said this, for as you all know, Peirithoös is his boon companion. He struck at Eurytos and rescued Hippodame from his horsy embrace. Eurytos, turning on him, tried to beat the hero's head with his fists. Theseus took up an antique mixing-bowl, inlaid with rough carvings and figures, and hurled it at Eurytos' face. He fell backward, his hoofs kicking at the earth, while from his crushed face poured out wine and brains mixed. Enflamed now in greater measure by blood and death, the other Centaurs cried 'To arms! To arms!' and wine-cups and flasks, before aids to the banquet, became deadly missiles in their hands.

"One Centaur, Amycos, galloped forth from the inner sanctuary with a chandelier hung about with glittering lamps. Rising on his hind legs he brought it down upon the Lapith Celadon, crushing his skull and shattering the bones of his face. His eyes from their sockets leapt and his nose ended up lodged in his throat. Pelates saw this, and tearing the leg from a maple-wood table, dispatched Amycos with two blows. The first drove his chin into his mouth until he spat out his teeth afloat in blood; while the second released his shade to Tartaros.

"By now the fight had spilled outside the house. Gryneos, with awesome strength, wrenched up a smoking altar, fire and all. This he hurled into the midst of the Lapiths, crushing Broteas and Orios. Exadios repaid him with the votive antlers of a stag hung from a pine-tree. With the double branching horn he gouged out the Centaur's eyes; one orb clung to the tip of the horn; the other rolled down his beard suspended in its vile jelly.

"Rhoetus next whirled a burning brand of plum-wood from the ruined altar, striking Charaxos on the temples and setting his golden hair aflame, as a field of autumn grain consumed from a lightning-stroke. One could hear the scorching blood hissing in his wound, as when a smith takes in his pincers a glowing bar of iron and plunges it into a tepid pool. Charaxos, shaking the fire from his smoking locks, tore from the ground a threshold-stone, and heaving the terrific weight on his shoulders, tried to cast it on his foeman. Missing Rhoetus, it landed on his comrade Cometes instead, seeding the earth with his crushed bones. Rhoetus rejoiced, and renewing the attack with the fire-brand, succeeded in cracking Charaxos' skull, so that his bones made soup with his brains.

"Rhoetus would not relent. He next killed the young Corythus, whose cheeks had just darkened in soft down. Seeing this, Evagros cried: 'What glory do you get from slaying a boy?' Rhoetus responded by pushing the flaming stake down his throat. He turned on Dryas next, but Dryas turned to pierce him with a stake. The Centaur groaned, pulled the stake from the wound where neck and shoulder meet, and limped away covered in blood. Not all Centaurs there joined in the impiety. Pholos and Melaneos fled, as did Abas and Asbolos, the augur who had vainly urged his friends to avoid the battle. When Nessos, though guilty of slaughter, tried to join them, Asbolos told him: 'Fly away! for you the bow of Heracles is reserved.' What say you about this, Heracles?"

Heracles, munching on a side of beef, was not paying much attention.

Nestor continued: "Through all the commotion slept Aphidas stretched on his side upon the shaggy skin of an Ossean bear: his hand still loosely held the cup of mixed wine. The Lapith Phorbas saw him, and taking up his javelin exclaimed: 'Mingle your wine with Stygian waters!' and drove the iron-tipped shaft into the Centaur's neck, exposed as it was from his head thrown back in sleep. From his wounded throat the blood poured into the wine-cup he still grasped.

"There was Aphareus, with arms wrapped around an oak-tree heavy with acorns, swaying it back and forth to tear its clinging roots from the ground. Peirithoös, seeing him thus engaged, let fly his spear, transfixing his human torso to the trunk. The Lapith slew also Lycos and Chromis, as well as Helops, whose skull he pierced from the right to the left. Dictys, fearing the carnage inflicted by Ixion's son, ran unheeding off a cliff, impaling himself with all his animal weight on an ash-tree's top.

"Aphareus, seeing his comrade's bitter end, and wrenching a rock from the mountain-side, fell under the force of Theseus' oaken club, his arm smashed to splinters. Theseus then leapt on the back of stalwart Bienor, who never bowed to a man's weight, and digging his knees into his ribs while gripping with left hand his long mane, laid waste to his head and face with the gnarled club. To death Theseus also sent Lycopes and long-bearded Hippasos; tall Rhipheus and Thereus, who could catch bears alive in the Thessalian hills. Demoleon at last sought to check the hero's success. He tore up an old pine tree by the roots and hurled it at Theseus; but the latter ducked in time and the tree struck instead Crantor, reaving his shoulder and chest."

Peleus mournfully exclaimed: "My poor armor-bearer Crantor, who I took from king Amyntor of the Dolopians! I well remember that day when I hurled my ashen spear at that double-natured fiend and it stood there quivering in his ribs. Tore it out he did, but left the fatal point embedded in his lung. Desperately he reared and struck me with his hooves, but my shield and casque preserved my life. I delivered my thrusting-spear deep through his shoulder, piercing his breast. And remember, Nestor, how before that I pinned the right hand of Dorylas, who charged me with a pair of bull's horns dripping blood, to his forehead; and as he stood there, blood pouring and crying madly, I ruptured his belly with my sword so that his entrails tumbled out; and as he staggered forward, they entangled in his hooves and burst, until he fell to the earth on the empty cavity of his belly."

Amphiaros interrupted, saying to Nestor: "The tale, though interesting, waxes long: and you still have not told us how Caineus fell."

"Yes; yes," said Nestor. "Bear with me a moment longer and I shall tell you what befell Caineus. First, however, let me not forget Cyllarus, whose double form cannot preclude me from praising his beauty. Imagine the finest statue that our gifted artists carve: such was his human form. His face, affording a pleasant glance, was just touched with a golden down, and golden hair flowed to his shoulders. Even his horse-shape was perfect, with a back so broad and comfortable, and bold chest so swelling with muscles, as to delight even the horse-tamer Castor. All over he was as black as pitch; but his legs and tail were white as the snow. Of all his kind only Hylonome captured his heart, the most beautiful of the Centaur maids, who by her preening won him. One heard she liked to straighten her long locks with a comb and twine rosemary or violets or roses in her hair; and sometimes also white lilies. Twice each day she bathed her face and body in a brook that flowed from the wooded height of Pagasai. In their love they wandered together on the mountain-sides, and rested within cool caves. That awful day they together fought us fiercely until Cyllarus fell under a spear thrown from an unknown hand, pierced where the chest rises to the neck. Hylonome held his dying body in her embrace, caressed the fatal wound, and by her lips on his sought to contain his fleeting breath. When she saw he was dead, she uttered some words (which the din of battle prevented me from hearing) and thereupon fell upon the spear that killed Cyllarus, dropping on his breast, and perishing together with him in her arms.

"I also cannot forget the Centaur Phaiocomes, wrapped completely in the hides of six lions, with his log that two yokes of oxen could hardly budge. He struck Olenus with the trunk, crushing his head, and causing his brains to ooze from every cavity of his face, as curled milk seeps down through oaken withes. As the fiend tried to despoil his victim, I thrust my sword deep into his groin. Teleboas then wounded me—see I show you the scar, still fresh; but I killed him also, and Chthonius as well. Oh, what use is there to continue detailing that great struggle?"

"Lest my comrades think me only an augur," said Mopsos, "I too had reason to glory that day."

"Why yes," said Nestor. "You slew the daring Hodites, did you not, nailing his tongue to his chin, and his chin to his throat, with your spear?"

Coronos said: "Allow me, noble Nestor, to now describe the deeds of my father and so satisfy the curiosity of these hearers, putting Idas to shame for his insolent remarks. You and Peleus, and any others here in attendance that day can testify to my words. My father Caineus had slain five Centaurs when huge-limbed Latreus rushed in, freshly girded with spoils, and armed with his Emathian lance, sword and shield. Haughtily clashing his arms in the sight of both camps so as to get everyone's attention, he taunted my father for once being a woman, ordering him to give up warfare and return to his distaff and wool-basket. In response, Caineus heaved his spear and struck Latreus on the side, where man and horse met. Howling with pain, Latreus struck Caineus with his lance, but it redounded in his hand. He thrust at my father with his sword, and even tried to swing at his flank, but the blade glanced off the skin as off marble and shattered into slivers. As Latreus stood there amazed, my father exclaimed: 'My turn to try your body with my blade!' and plunged his sword downward behind the Centaur's shoulder-blade, to the hilt, twisting it about to put him to a miserable end.

"The other Centaurs, beside themselves at seeing their mightiest comrade vanquished by my father, in vain attacked him with every weapon at their disposal. My father continued unharmed. Then one of them cried, 'What shame! How is that we of two-fold strength cannot make a dent in that so-called man? We must be what once he was! Rouse yourselves, then, and let us heap stones and tree-trunks and mountains and crush out his stubborn life.' The first was he to snatch up a tree, felled from a recent storm. The others followed, ripping up great stones and trees until Pelion lost its shade. They buried Caineus as they planned, until he could hardly move or breathe. To the bitter end he shook that towering mass by his exertions. Some guessed he was borne alive to the subterrene Pit, but Mopsos denied it, saying he had seen a golden-winged bird rise from midst of the pile."

"I saw it too, circling round on fluttering wings," said Nestor. "'Hail, Caineus, glory of the Lapiths: once its greatest hero, now a bird without likeness!' was the cry of Mopsos. Disgusted at seeing one overcome by so many, and with our wrath enlarged by grief, we went on the offensive. We slew half our foes and set the rest to flight, ridding Pelion of its double-formed inhabitants."

Idas, unbowed by the deflection of his insult toward Caineus, looked about to see who else might be the victim of his acrid tongue. Sitting near Meleager was one Argonaut, whom he had never before seen during the long process of their assembly, wrapped in a deer-skin cloak. Beneath the wide brim of an Arcadian hat, Idas could see the tip of a hairless and delicate chin. He was about to make some scurrilous remark when Jason caught his notice, sitting by himself, evidencing a look of despair in pondering the awesome task set before him. Turning to him, Idas said loudly and scornfully: "Son of Aison, tell us the plan you seem to be churning in your mind.  Go on: tell us all what your young brain conjures.  Are you overpowered by fear?  It is fear that confounds cravens."  He drew up his spear, twirled it in his fingers, and jabbed its broad point into the air.  "Witness my daunting spear, with which, above all other men, I achieve glory in battles.  Not even Zeus can strengthen me more than this!  As long as you have Idas with you, no challenge shall elude us, not even if a god opposes us.  Know what a great help you have with you in me."  Wrenching a flagon of unmixed wine from a passing boy, he raised it to his lips and imbibed until his dark beard ran with purple rills.  The others, noticing his brutish behavior, clamored at him from their seats, making Gorgon faces or pushing out their palms at him with five fingers extended.  Idmon reproached him: "Wretched man!  You will bring destruction on yourself with such talk.  Has the wine swelled your heart to your ruin, emboldening you to mock the gods?  There are better words you can use to encourage a comrade—if that is what you do—but you speak now with callous recklessness.  Such bluster did the sons of Aloeus, who overmatch you in valor, direct against the blessed gods as they piled Ossa upon Pelion to reach Olympos; and, powerful though they were, they were no match for the arrows of Leto's shining son."

Idas burst out laughing at this reproof.  Filled with scorn, he cried: "Tell me, prophet, if the gods will also do to me as your father did to the Aloadai?  You won't escape my hands if your vision turns out baseless!"

With these words he flung his cup at Idmon, preparing to pounce on him.  Seeing this, Admetos, son of Pheres, drew his sword in defense of his nephew, whose mother was his sister Antianeira.  Lynceus came to his brother's side, ready to run Admetos through with his spear. Bloodshed would have ensued had not their companions, Jason at the front, restrained the combatants, rebuking them forcefully for their silly dispute.  Tempers, seduced by wine, would have simmered on longer had not sweet sounds sprinkled them with calming dew.  Orpheus had arrived tickling the strings of his tortoise-shell lyre, which he improved by increasing the number of strings to nine, in honor the Muses, one of whom, Calliope, was his mother. With a smooth bald head under his fox-skin cap, gentle demeanor, and dressed in narrow trousers with an outer tunic tied at the waist, he seemed out of place among all his lusty companions. He was fetched by Jason from his home in a cave at the foot of Mount Olympos at the insistence of Augeias, who would not have sailed without him for two reasons. First, he thought Orpheus, by his music and song, could assist in pacifying the barbarians encountered on their expedition, since—it was believed—even the animals lost their feral natures and skipped along behind him when he performed; and second, because Orpheus had spent time in Egypt learning their secret lore, from whence the Colchians were believed to have come. At first Orpheus declined, loth to leave the serenity of his rustic life. But, as he had dedicated himself to the service of mankind, he agreed to be the ship's coxswain, since he possessed a weak constitution and could not row for long. His disposition at that time was still cheerful, having not yet known the loss of Eurydice.

When Heracles saw him, he wondered if this Orpheus was the brother of Linos, the music teacher that in his youth he had thoughtlessly brained with his lyre.

Orpheus, taking a seat, lifted his divine voice, coated with the Muses' sweet honey, and sang how in the beginning all was without form, and void; and there was only deepest darkness.

Out of the darkness emerged Chaos. All things whirled as in a wind: a boundless, unordered mass of atoms. And it came to pass that the mismatched seeds of all the elements came together in their own way. The heavier separated from the lighter. Ethereal fire, lightest of all, rose upward to form heaven, while earth fell downward by its own weight; and between them settled the air. Water streamed down to the lowest place, and there held the land together.

The Earth was alive, and she was called Gaia. To cover her she gave birth to Uranos, the starry sky. Then she bore the mountains by herself, and the forests with their lonely glens, and finally the stormy Sea. Drinking the rain Uranos sprinkled upon her, she begat Briareos, Gyges and Cottos, three giants, each with an hundred hands and fifty heads. Next she bore the one-eyed Cyclopes who liked to build massive walls and work as smiths at the fire. Uranos hated these monsters and cast them deep under the earth in the pit of Tartaros. It is said that an anvil, falling through a cleft in the earth, would take nine days to reach it. Uranos thought he could produce a better brood of children, and so fructifying Gaia again, caused her to produce the race of the Titans. Of these the youngest, and craftiest, was Cronos. But Uranos hated also this offspring, fearing the loss of his power to them, and hid them in dark caverns away from the light of day. Grieving for her children, Gaia called upon Cronos, and giving him a sickle of gray adamant, instructed him to wait in ambush for his wicked father. As night fell and Uranos spread darkly above the earth, Cronos sprang from his hiding place and with a stroke of his sharp sickle severed his father's genitals, casting them behind him. Uranos, weakened, was pulled down by the rest of the Titans and imprisoned in Tartaros. They appointed Cronos as their chief, and he took ownership of heaven. But soon he too feared to lose his power, and imprisoned in Tartaros all of his siblings, save his sister Rhea, whom he took as wife. He also spared some of the Titans' children, such as Atlas, who by his enormous size, could prove useful; and Prometheus and his brother Epimetheus, since the former amused him by his cleverness, and the later by his dullness. Uranos, however, from his confinement whispered a prophecy, carried upward by Gaia through the hard-packed earth and hissing forth in sulphurous springs, that a son of Cronos would do to him as he did to his father. When Cronos heard the warning, he determined not to let any of his own children live, and so swallowed each whole as soon Rhea bore them, one every year.

And thus he consumed first Hestia, then Demeter, Hera, Hades and Poseidon. By the time Rhea bore her third son, Zeus, she could no longer withstand this wickedness. She entrusted the swaddled babe to Gaia, who understood her plight very well. She carried him to the island of Crete far from land, and hid him in the steep cave of Dicte on the Aegean hill. There two ash-tree nymphs tended him and nourished him with goat milk. So that Cronos might not find him neither in heaven, nor on earth, nor in the sea, his crib was hung upon a tree. The nine dancing Curetes guarded the infant night and day, clashing their spears upon their shields to counter the his cries. When Cronos got wind of Rhea's latest birth, he searched for her and angrily demanded the child. She meekly passed him what appeared to be a swaddled babe, but in reality was a stone tightly wrapped. Swallowing the stone up, Cronos was satisfied and went on his way.

Upon reaching manhood, Zeus sought out his mother and

twith her hatched a plan for vengeance. Rhea convinced Cronos to accept Zeus—in disguise—as his new cupbearer. Zeus poisoned his cup, causing Cronos to vomit forth first the stone, then Zeus' siblings. Incredibly, they had matured quite nicely inside Cronos' belly, and came out fully grown. Zeus led them in a war against Cronos, who countered by freeing the other Titans. Captained by the formidable Atlas, the Titans resisted Zeus for ten years, until Gaia prophesied victory to her grandson only if he took allies from those first monsters imprisoned in Tartaros. And so Zeus freed the Cyclopes and the hundred-handed ones, who, in gratitude, came to his aid. The Cyclopes forged thunderbolts for Zeus. For Hades they made a helmet of invisibility; and for Poseidon a mighty trident. Aided by the three hundred-handed ones, who could lob a multitude of stones at once, Zeus and the New Gods soon routed the Elder Gods, and defeated them. Cronos and most of the male Titans Zeus imprisoned behind the unscaleable walls of gloomy Tartaros, save Atlas, who was meted perhaps a stiffer punishment: for eternity he was to hold up heaven's vault upon his shoulders. The female Titans Zeus spared for the sake of Rhea and Metis, for whom Zeus lusted.

Wise Prometheus sided with Zeus during the war, and afterward was left free with unbounded leisure to pursue wisdom and the arts. His favorite activity was to mold things from mud, and to breathe into them so that they lived and walked about or flew as high as clouds. Until this time the earth had only brought forth creeping things, and no higher beasts existed until Prometheus made them. He then had an idea to make creatures similar to the gods, and formed the monkeys. They did not look quite right, and so he shortened the limbs, sheared off excessive hair and lobbed off the tail, and soon man walked upright upon the earth. He delighted in his new pets and taught them many useful things. But there was one thing they lacked—fire, which Zeus derived from the blazing bolts of the Cyclopes. One day Prometheus asked Zeus for a bit of it, but Zeus refused, impressed not at all with the race of men who still lived in caves and ate their meat raw. Prometheus realized he had to procure that divine substance at all costs. With a giant fennel-stalk, he stole up to Mount Olympos, where the gods had made their abode. He cut it in half, and passing by the hearth where a fire always burned to keep the Olympians warm on those hoary heights, lighted one end. When the fire smoldered in the pithy middle, he joined the sticks together again and returned to earth to pass the fire to his creatures. Armed with the most prized possession of the gods, men could cook and keep themselves warm. In addition, Prometheus taught them how to bake pottery, fire bricks and melt metals to make tools. Men soon left their caves, built dwellings, and enjoyed the advantages of a civilized life, practicing the useful arts and sciences that Prometheus taught them.

When Zeus witnessed the flashes of flame filling the earth, he knew Prometheus had robbed him to benefit mankind. So angry he became that he shook his head pendent with golden locks, and with it Olympos rumbled. Summoning Prometheus before him, Zeus promised him a terrible punishment, and the destruction of all men. "Nay, Father, stay your hand," said Prometheus. "Firstly, you cannot take away a gift an Immortal has given, so men will now always have fire. Secondly, you cannot destroy mankind, for from that brood will one day appear the savior of gods and men." "How so?" asked Zeus. "Tell me all you know and perhaps my wrath will be abated." But Prometheus would say no more. Cruel Zeus ordered Hephaistos to chain Prometheus with unbreakable fetters to a high crag of the Caucasus Mountains. "There you will lie forever, by day tormented by the searing sun; and by night freezing from the wintry blasts," said Zeus. "Moreover, a vulture will gnaw at your liver; yet each day your liver will grow back anew, ready for a repeat of your agonies."

But Prometheus, seeing the happy future, knew his torment would end at the appearance of the Deliverer, born to a mortal woman from divine seed. He therefore bravely bore his punishment through the long ages, filling the haunted heights of his mountain prison with his cries, so that men feared to come near.

Orpheus ended his song. The men still leaned forward, their ears straining, their minds enraptured, as if by magic, in the peace that spread from Orpheus like the warm light of a fire. Augeias asked him to reveal the identity of the promised demigod, since he styled himself a son of Helios. Others, such as Castor and Polydeuces, sons of Zeus by Leda, wondered also if Orpheus' prophesied of one of them. "I shall not say," said Orpheus; "for I cannot reveal the mysteries of the gods. Only know this: he is among you, but only for a short time."

Lastly they poured libations to Zeus on the lingering flames of the sacrifice and then reclined on their seaweed couches to watch the dying embers of their campfires. Sweet sleep stole over them, and each man dreamed of what would come.

As Dawn spread over the world her saffron-colored robe, a sharp landward breeze awoke Tiphys. At once he roused Jason and his comrades, enjoining them to make haste to go aboard and ready the oars, thinking that a southerly wind was cooking. The first to climb aboard was Mopsos, who standing by the prow veined with the Dodonian branch, proclaimed that it groaned in passion for the departure. The men then drew lots to determine their positions on the rowing benches. The middle seats, however, were left to Heracles and the mighty Tegean Ancaios on account of their size. Idas, who had been observing the ship floating on a even keel until Heracles stepped in, called out to Mopsos: "Did you not hear the *Argo* speak, Mopsos? She is refusing to carry Heracles because he is too heavy!" The others did not join Idas in his fit of laughter, keeping their eyes on Heracles in case his displeasure had been aroused. But Heracles only cried: "Well met! Well met!" and laughed along at his own expense.

After pulling in the cables, the men took their assigned seats, sliding their weapons and gear beneath their benches and hanging their shields from the gunwale to shield them from the spray. Jason, standing in the bows, poured out libations of rich wine into the calm waters of the gulf, looking at the wooden western flank of Pelion, clothed in chestnut and maple, oak and beech; and at Iolcos, his homeland, where he had embraced his aged parents. He turned his eyes away as he wept silently.

As Jason raised his sword to cut through the last hawser beholding them to the shore, a cry arose from his companions. Down the beach ran Acastos, holding up two javelins and with a shield bouncing at his back. Acastos splashed into the water and climbed up the ladder to join the crew. Jason's heart gladdened to see him, since he had thought the prince's words of joining him had been idle talk. Acastos had publicly mentioned to Pelias his desire to join in the quest. Pelias wholeheartedly agreed, not wishing to raise in Jason or the others doubt about his sincerity toward the mission. He planned, however, to detain him at the last minute on some pretext. Acastos pretended to have forgotten the whole thing and went out to hunt with his courtiers. Leaving them on Pelion, he retrieved his shield, which he had hidden under a rock, and ran without stopping to the ship.

When the boatswain Echion, son of Hermes, had inspected the rigging and the supply of cordage, and had stowed away the anchor-stones, he gave the word; and Orpheus, sitting on the bow-bench, tuned his lyre and began to play a rhythmic sound. The men grasped their oar-handles and to the music pushed and pulled so that the sea on either side of the ship churned with foam under the assault of the sweeping banks of oars. The *Argo* slowly pulled away from its mooring and glode into the dark waters, leaving a white path in its wake. The people of Iolcos crowded the beach, watching the ship, glittering with shields, until in its offing it seemed to dwindle and disappear.

With powerful strokes the men propelled the ship across the gulf of Pagasai. Under the steady hand of Tiphys, who mastered the rudder like a horseman handles a bridle, and the direction of the oar-masters, Zetes and Calais, they rounded the curving western spur of the Magnesian cape and passed out opposite the Posidium promontory. As the winds still held, Tiphys cried: "Make all sail!" and the men, after stowing and locking their oars, raised the tall mast into its crutch, pulling tight the stays to secure it. The sail they raised and unfurled, belaying its cables to the bollards so that the fabric stiffened against the wind. Speeding now past the headland of Tisaia, Orpheus added his sweet voice to his music, hymning Artemis, Protectress of Ships, who haunted the wooded peaks of the peninsula, ever watching over Haimonia as she busied herself with her maidens in the chase.

Jason, looking over the side, saw fish leaping about the biting prow. "It is true what they say about you, Orpheus son of Oiagros!" he laughed. "Even the animals are seduced by your song. The fish follow us as when a flock of sheep, their bellies filled with grass, follow to their stalls behind the shepherd playing shrilly on his pipe."

Those who offered thanks to the gods for such an auspicious beginning soon rued their gratitude. As the island of Sciathos came into view out of the haze of the western horizon, the sea began to seethe from conflicting winds. The east wind commenced the tempest, smashing huge billows against the hull, while the north wind joined the chorus, bringing with it black clouds and turbulent squalls. The proximity of the mainland, normally a relief to sailors, proved a curse, impelled as the vessel was, rocking violently, toward certain destruction on rocks and hidden reefs. "Pray to your father Boreas that he may spare us for your sakes!" begged Peleus to Calais and Zetes, blue-haired twins and sons of the North Wind; but his voice was lost in the noise of raging elements. Others blamed Idas for his impiety. Heracles remained silent, staring at his club and quiver at his feet, useless now. With every yaw it seemed the yardarm caught up crabs from the sea. The rocky beach loomed closer with very stroke of lightning. Nauplios, who, as a veteran sailor had been trusting in his father Poseidon, suddenly cried: "Have courage, friends; for all is not lost. Nearby is the tomb of Dolops. It is clearly his shade that has whipped up this terrible storm, so that we may not pass by without reverencing him. Let us all agree to go ashore and offer sacrifices." As soon as the shipmates, clinging to one another, consented to his words, the winds died down, the clouds parted, and blue sky, laced by a rainbow, covered them.

They moored close to the beach at Aphetai, turning the prow seaward, and went ashore. Only those native to the region had known about Dolops, thought to be a son of Hermes, although none, not even Nauplios, could say anything about him. They located a mound nearby, covered in anemones and shaded by cypress trees, which they took to be Dolops' sepulture, and that evening killed and burned sheep in his honor. They found the wind against them in the morning, and so took to repairing the leaks and the tattered sail. For two days they waited until Dolops released them by sending a southerly wind.

Pushed on by a steady breeze they left Sciathos in their wake, skirted around Cape Sepias, and proceeded close to the shore to where they could see the clouds drifting past the peaks of well-wooded Pelion. There, on its crown, amidst the mountain-ash, those of the Argonauts who had been tutored by the Centaur Cheiron recognized the dark outline of the cave from where he dispensed justice and freely shared his wisdom of the arts and sciences. Jason remembered fondly his dancing lessons; Peleus, his training with sword and spear; and Heracles, the mildness with which the old Centaur corrected his impatience when he could not master a lesson on the first try. Alone of all the Centaurs, only Cheiron, gravely ill from his envenomed wound, yet unable to die, was allowed to return by the Lapiths to his grotto in the fastness of Pelion: even as the Argonauts sailed he was being carried hither from the cave of Pholos, that he might pass his unending days in the comfort of his leafy home.

With a rising offshore wind they reefed the sail and once more hacked the waters with their oars. Tiphys had them row long into the night, wishing to make progress as far up the coast as possible before turning at Casthaneia at the foot of Pelion where chestnut-trees abounded. They built fires, refilled their water-jars, and feasted on mutton procured from local shepherds.

As Meleager sat eating his meal, his bench-mate, the Argonaut wearing the Arcadian hat, bearing a quiver and a light bow slung around a shoulder, came to sit beside him. The Calydonian prince had not yet found the opportunity to introduce himself, as he was a quiet and conscientious young man and ever under the watchful eye of his uncle Iphiclos, his mother's brother. He had always kept his head down as he rowed, in which position the sight of the delicate feet and toes of his comrade, dressed in golden sandals with straps wrapped high up the slender but tight calves, had uncomfortably stirred his heart.

Idas too had been curious about this newest Argonaut since the night they disembarked. As Meleager washed down his meat with a bit of wine and turned to his companion with some amiable words, Idas snuck up behind and yanked off the broad hat. Meleager gasped as he looked upon a freckled face too maidenly for a boy's, and at the same time too boyish for a maiden's face. Her hair was cropped short like a man's and she wore a tunic, but, as she stood, her shapely buttocks illumined by the firelight could not be mistaken, except by Idas, who joked: "What dark magic is this, Periclymenos? Did you fail halfway in transforming one of us into a woman? Or is she related to you, Coronos? If your father went one way, why not the other? I would say she is a woman, if it was not for the look of her chest, which is as flat as a washing-board."

The others now came around, some chattering in wonder, while others declaiming the pecancy of a woman having stowed away among them. The woman would no longer be silent. She reached behind her back and pulled off the linen strip she had been using as a brassiere, and her bosom filled the front of her tunic like a bellied sail.

"Were my bow handy I would put a quick end to your unkind jests, Idas," said she, glowering at the brother of Lynceus. Jason pushed through the crowd to see about the commotion. "Atalanta!" he cried. "Did I not refuse you from joining us?"

"You did, Jason, although you thought nothing of keeping the spear I gave you as a gift when on your way to Arcadian Tegea to recruit Ancaios," said Atalanta, looking defiantly at all the leering faces.

"You know the reason, Atalanta," said Jason. "I do not doubt you could hold your own against any of these men. I only fear the bitter strife that would develop should the men fall in love with you."

Atalanta responded: "You know I hold love and marriage in disdain. I follow the virgin Huntress in this regard."

"You are correct, Jason," said Augeias. "Send her away. Already I see Meleager flush with affection."

"Let us keep this slattern for sport," said Idas brusquely.

On hearing this Ancaios of Tegea shouted: "Watch your tongue! If anyone touches her, he will answer to me." His brother Amphidamas, as well as Cepheus their countryman, joined him in this resolution.

"Very well then," said Idas, moving off so as to avoid a confrontation. "At the very least let her stay for the sake of Palaimon, who is lame in both feet from a brush fire, walks about with a staff, and is in need of a helpmeet."

Palaimon found this suggestion most agreeable, until he realized it was only more tomfoolery as the others laughed at his expense.

Meleager stood boldly beside Atalanta, drawing sighs from his companions, for side by side they seemed as glorious as Leto's shining children. Meleager's bronzed body rippled with muscles: a younger version of Heracles he seemed; and his companions had no doubt he would have surpassed them all had Heracles not been among them.

Meleager said: "Friends, I see you are all of different opinions concerning Atalanta. I can only say that, as bench-mate through our journey thus far, she has never once flagged at the oar, or complained one bit about the work. Allow her if you please, to continue with us."

When some clamored to hear her story, for they had heard that she had once killed two Centaurs who snuck into her cave to ravish her, Atalanta began: "I was born in Arcadia, to Iasos son of Lycourgos, who, since he wished only sons, exposed me on Mount Parthenion, by the side of well and at the entrance of a cave. There, Providence sent a she-bear, who had lost her cubs, to suckle me, until I was rescued by a passing band of hunters. I grew up in the wooded mountains, under the guidance of Artemis, living a hardy and chaste life, unafraid of wild thing and toil, skilled in the hunt. There is little that is different between me and you, except my sex; but even among the gods the female divinities are by no means inferior: by the force of their characters even the Father of all is sometimes moved."

Jason was about to set the matter to a vote, when Iphiclos son of Phylacos, his maternal uncle, who, due to his age, refrained from rowing, but came along to dispense advise and sustain morale, said: "Comrades, I must inform you that Atalanta should be no stranger to us. Her mother, I'll have you know, is Clymene, daughter of Minyas, who in her old age Iasos took to bed in order to dip his toes in our royal lineage. She is thus not only a niece to the son of Lycourgos, Ancaios, and related to Amphidamas; but she is also an aunt to your captain."

Admetos, learning that she was his half-sister, loudly proclaimed that, as a Minyan, she had first right to be part of the expedition. Jason suspended the vote as unnecessary, and gave her the right hand of fellowship. Meleager then invited her to hunt the moonlit slopes of Pelion with him. They went off and did not return for a long time. Only Heracles saw them return, since he could not sleep from dyspepsia.

At the appearance of the morning star, while Dawn in her saffron robe still lounged in her celestial bed, the *Argo*, followed by an unsteady coastal breeze, cast off under the broad swings of the oars. They ran on past Meliboia, cautiously watching a storm brewing off the coast, then raised sails by Eurymenai in the shadow of the yellow peaks of Mount Ossa, covered in a light scattering of spring snow, from where a misty breeze carried them to the outflow and rich delta of the swift river Peneios.  The Peneios is the chief river of Thessaly, watering through its many affluents the fertile ploughlands and expansive plains where horses graze, from its birth in the Pindos range to its debouche into the sea.  Mopsos and Idmon, as well as Orpheus and other companions devoted to Apollo wished to disembark to visit Apollo's shrine in the vale of Tempe on the right bank of the Peneios, which formed a wide, deep gorge extending from Ossa in the south to Mount Olympos in the north: a misty valley surrounded in places by wooded slopes and towering cliffs.  It was there, Orpheus sang, that Apollo, smitten by Eros' love-shaft, had chased his first love Daphne, daughter of Peneios the river-god.  Fear sped her flight, while love gave him fleeter wings of desire.  As the hunter almost catches the hunted, his breath hot on her neck, she reaches the turgid river at its steepest descent, where the steam rises like clouds to the treetops, and cries out to her father for deliverance.  At once the nymph is transformed.  Her hair changes to leaves; her slim body grows wide and rough; her feet elongate into roots; her arms, spread in supplication, become boughs.  When Apollo reaches the stream's bank he sees only a fragrant laurel-tree; but leaning against the trunk, he feels inside the beating heart of his beloved.  He takes the glossy leaves to adorn his hair and lyre; and ever after victors in the games are crowned with laurel garlands.

They were running for the shore when a strong western wind bellied out the sail.  After consulting with Tiphys and Argos, Jason decided it was time to leave the coast and, taking vantage of the breeze, venture seaward across the Thermaic gulf.  As they left the mainland astern, they could still see, for a great distance, the lofty ridges of Mount Olympos, whose principal snow-capped summits of pale rock, bathed in sunbeams, rose above thick clouds and mist into serene blue sky.  Its eastern extremity extended down to the mouth of the Peneios, broken by deep, wooded ravines, and encircled by thick bands of beech, oak and plane-trees.  All hands kept their eyes on the mountain as they sailed across the stretch of open sea, awed by its undiminished grandeur.  At dusk they could still see it, framed in a fiery red nimbus; and as night came the milky moonlight reflected from its highest peak like a beacon.

In the dead of night, surrounded by darkness, loose meteors flashed through the whirling constellations.  The sailors peered about them, fearing the starry omens, as travelers look this way and that while travelling by night on an unfamiliar road. Then a rocky landmass appeared ahead of them, which for a moment confused Tiphys. Sharp-eyed Lynceus, climbing up the mast for a better look, reported that it was not an island; but, from its numerous settlements, possibly Phlegrai, the westernmost of the three headlands of Chalcidice. Tiphys confirmed this from the position of the Pole star behind him, which ever remains fixed.

"Heracles, is that not the place you fought the Gigantes?" asked Hylas, bringing Heracles a cup of water to drink.

"Why, my boy, who has filled your heads with silly stories?" said Heracles, laughing.

"Then who was it, Heracles, who dragged the Giant Alcyoneus across the border of Thrace since he could not be defeated while on Phlegraian soil?" asked Oileus, son of Hodoedocus.

"How should I know?" said Heracles. "Did not such things happen in dim antiquity? I am not yet even forty years old. The only foeman I knew by that name was a ruffian I fought on the Corinthian Isthmus on my way back to Mycenae with the cattle of Geryones—and though of great size his spattered brains showed me he was no more than a man. If anyone knows to what this fool refers, let him speak."

Orpheus called from the bow: "I will tell what I have learned from wise men in my travels. When the Olympians defeated the Titans and imprisoned them in Tartaros, their mother Gaia was so angered that with swollen womb she ripped open Phlegrai's side and out burst the Gigantes, twenty-four in number. These creatures, of immense size and strength, covered in hair and slithering about on dragons' tails, cast great rocks and flaming trees at the blessed gods to destroy them. Now, the gods possessed an oracle saying that they could only defeat the Gigantes with the help of two demigods. When Gaia learned of this, she searched the earth for a special herb said to make the Gigantes invulnerable. To forestall her Zeus ordered the sun and moon not to shine, and under dim starlight searched the secrets places of the earth, plucked the herb, and brought it safely to Olympos. Athena, meanwhile, he dispatched to find the mortal helpers This is where, I believe, the mighty Heracles became inserted into the story, for the legend of the war against the Gigantes is derived, no doubt, from ancient Babylon, where a similar tale is told. There the gods enlisted the help of the god Marduk to decide the civil war between the new and primordial gods. Marduk, ready with his bow and arrows, too makes use of an herb: in his case to counteract the poison of the sea-monster Tiamat.

"To continue: Zeus called together the immortal council and exhorted them with these words: 'Deathless army, dwellers of the sky, witness how the Earth spans a new brood to conspire against us. Let us give back to her as many dead, so that her mourning might last through the ages, as she weeps by as many graves as the number of her children.' As a signal for battle, trumpet blasts echo from the storm-clouds. Heracles, if I may so call our counterpart to Marduk—whoever he was—felled first the eldest of the Gigantes, Alcyoneus, with his arrows; but as he derived strength from his native soil, the monster recovered as soon as he had fallen. On the advice of Athena, Heracles laid his hands on Alcyoneus and dragged him beyond the bounds of Phlegrai, and there he finally perished of his wounds. As soon as he returned to the scene of battle, the Giant Porphyrion, filled with lust, ripped at Hera's robe to ravish her. At her cry, Zeus brought down the Giant with his thunderbolt; and Heracles dispatched him with an arrow. Gigantic Ephialtes then came charging. Both Apollo and Heracles took positions, and pulling back well-fletched arrows on taut bowstrings, shot him through the eyes, one arrow for each. The other demigod, Dionysos, and Hecate, also joined the fray. Dionysos killed Eurytos with a blow of his *thyrsos*; while Hecate dispatched Klytios with her searing torches. Ares urged his Thracian steeds into the fray, lancing two-bodied Pelorus in the middle where the two serpents' tails joined to the Giant's torso. Seeing his writhing victim, Ares rode his chariot across the boundless limbs until its wheels spun in pools of blood. Athena, with the Gorgon's head affixed to her glittering shield, only had to present herself before her foes. Pallas immediately turned to stone; as did his brother Echion, for daring to gaze at the deadly talisman. Palleneus, averting his eyes, rushed at the daughter of Zeus, nigh missing her with his sword-thrust. She countered, striking his chest with her sword; while his serpent tail froze into stone, so that one part of his body perished by a weapon, while another from the

Gorgon's glance. Even lame Hephaistos lent assistance, impaling Mimas with missiles of red-hot iron from his smithy. Seeing themselves routed by the glittering Olympic host, the remaining Gigantes fled. Athena by her power ripped Sicania from its sea-bed and buried Enkelados under it. Polybotes fled through the sea, pursued by Poseidon, who tore off a chunk of Cos and threw it at him. That piece is now the island of Nisyron. Hermes, wearing Hades' cap, invisibly swooped down to kill Hippolytos. Artemis did away with Gration while the Fates, armed with bronze cudgels, did in Agrios and Thoon. The rest Zeus picked off with his thunderbolts. All the while Heracles ranged about, executing those in their death throes with his arrows. The bodies of the earth-born Gigantes turned into those hills and great rocks, which their mother, in pity, clothed with trees."

"Gigantes or not," said Augeias with a yawn, "let us stop here for the night. I hear the bleating of tasty sheep far up on those hills."

"I am curious," added Butes son of Teleon, "to taste the local honey, which I hear is of great quality; although, I can safely say, not as good as that from my hives on Hymettus' flowery slopes. There bees like only the wild thyme, and from it make a deliciously piquant, decidedly less viscous honey, of a mottled amber color."

Nauplios said: "The sky is clear, the wind still holds, and no tinge of red, to portend foul weather, colors the moon's delicate horns. I say we eat aboard and continue sailing through the night."

Jason and Tiphys agreed, to the chagrin of the other companions, who wanted to, at the very least, stretch their stiff legs. The sailors ate bread with a cup or two of wine, and then, as time passed, overcome with sleep, settled down as best as they could. Nauplios, accompanied by Samian Ancaios, relieved Tiphys at the helm.

The *Argo* kept a steady course through the night, skirting by Phlegrai's hills and then out beyond Cape Canastraeum. They passed the uninviting headland of Sithonia and by dawn came within the shadow of Mount Athos on Acte, the easternmost promontory of Chalcidice. The sun rose neatly and golden out of the water, warming the sailors' faces to a pleasant awakening. Ancaios roused Tiphys, who again took the helm. The crew breakfasted and by a loud clamor compelled Jason to let them land.

As it would be a long haul before the next stop, Tiphys indulged them, carefully steering the ship inshore through the choppy and dangerous waters surrounding the tip of the peninsula, past the rocks, and to quiet place at the end of a ravine. The huge cone of Mount Athos, the highest point in sight, pierced the sky with its naked crest, its slopes completely covered in dark, evergreen forest.

## 3

They remained at Acte only a short time while Hylas, carrying a bronze pitcher, sought for water. Heracles walked off, under the pretense of stretching his legs, but returned with two suckling lambs he had taken from an unattended sheepfold. He was prepared to offer their owners something of value for them, but the native Pelasgians, on seeing him bound over a hill balancing his club from one end on his hand, fled in terror, and Heracles did not so much as see the dust whirling at their feet. The lambs were hastily consumed. Although Heracles could have easily eaten both, he was content to keep for himself only a sheepshank and a liver, leaving the rest to his friends, who had not tasted meat since leaving Casthaneia.

On they sailed with the wind abaft, but blowing more weakly as the hours passed. At dusk the sail flagged. The ship loitered on the calm sea while the oars came out and Tiphys consulted his charts. He set the course and they made for Lemnos, an island whose principle city, it was said, could be touched by the shadow of Athos' topmost peak at the summer solstice. All night the sailors pulled at the oars until, with their steady hacking lulling many to sleep, they raised the sail, and lashing the rudder, hove-to until Dawn first passed her rosy fingers through the fleecy clouds.

Refreshed, the men put their backs to it again. The prow cut the lightening sea, filled with stormy whitecaps. When Erginos complained that they were lost, the others grew excitable, piercing the calm air with cries of land at every appearance of deceitful cloud-forms in the distance. Jason urged calm. The murmurs did not end until Heracles angrily stomped his foot, nearly making a hole through the floorboards. In rueful silence, livened only by the strands of Orpheus' music, they flailed the oars until their broad ends began to come out of the water wrapped in fresh river-weeds.

This hopeful sign of proximate land was reinforced by the tunny-fish playing about the ship, as well as the flight of herons and pelicans bound in their same direction.

At last they came within sight of wind-ridden Lemnos, sacred to Hephaistos. Avoiding its northwest corner, which presented a rough and mountainous appearance, they swung down its western edge where the low-lying island spreads out, folding in the distance into barren, rocky, treeless hills.

Myrine, the principal city, lay under a jutting promontory behind a sandy shore. A long beach opened above the city, but as it seemed to have no natural or man-made harbor, Tiphys steered the ship around to the southern bay, where adequate anchorage presented itself along another broad beach, being the commercial harbor of the city. As Echion stood ready at the bows with the mooring-rope; and as the sailors rowed exultantly, ready for a long stop, dreaming of the delicious Lemnian wine, fat sheep and sleek pigs that awaited them, a strange sight greeted their eyes. From the city gates streamed a host of armed Lemnians, like bees clearing their hive for the flowery slopes. Assembling in silence up and down the beach, their ill-fitting armor clanged as they rushed to their positions. Jason, who had not been expecting a hostile welcome, as the original inhabitants of the island, the Thracian Sintes, had long been displaced by Pelasgians, and later by Greeks who arrived there for commerce, quickly had the crew ship the oars and gird themselves for battle. As the ship stalled at the shoals, Jason ordered all to be still so as not to provoke an incident. He then instructed their herald Aethalides, son of Hermes and brother of Echion and Eurytos, to go with his herald's staff and assure the Lemnians that they had nothing to fear.

After wading ashore, Aethalides was quickly surrounded by a knot of Lemnians and escorted into the city.

Atalanta, noticing how they walked, rhythmically swaying their buttocks, suddenly cried: "May Artemis ensnare me in my own nets if I lie: these are all women!"

Telamon, subject to the same suspicion said: "By the gods—it is true! Heracles, can they be Amazons who now prevent our landing?"

"If they be Amazons," said Heracles, "then by my ill-luck this day shall mark the third time I encounter these strange women in as many years."

&

Queen Hypsipyle, sitting on her father's throne, made from a single piece of the hard, vitrified rock that abounded on the island, polished so that it gleamed, and set with a filigree of green Egyptian peridot, received Aethalides in the palace's echoing council chamber. She wore a royal cape dyed purple from the saffron crocus, and pinned at the neck by a gold clasp in the form of a bee. As a good herald, Aethalides was sometimes compelled to resort to artifice to protect the interests of his employers; and so he told the queen nothing concerning the Fleece: only that they were Minyans from Boetia on their way to trade with the Athenian colonies of the Thracian Chersonese. A thing he immediately noticed, plain in its conspicousness, was the lack of any men anywhere he looked. He respectfully did not bring up the matter directly, but only praised king Thoas as a good and just ruler whom the Argonauts were keen to honor as they stopped briefly for food and water on blessed Lemnos. Hypsipyle offered no satisfactory explanations, only going in and out of the chamber throughout the day, so that the herald beseeched her late into the night to allow his companions to land and revictual their ship. She nervously agreed to provide him an answer in the morning and Aethalides returned to the *Argo*.

That night, all the women of the island assembled in the council room. Hypsipyle rose among them and said: "Dear friends, when we first spotted the ship entering our waters, the sunlight flashing on its flailing oars, we left our occupations, donned the armor of our husbands and fathers, and went out, in great fear and apprehension, to face what we thought was the arrival of vengeful Thracians. These men, however, appear not to present a threat to us. Let us furnish them with gifts: sweet wine and other supplies needed for their ship, so that they continue to remain outside the walls of our city; and when the winds are favorable, let them depart on their journey. If not, they will desire to come among us, and will no doubt soon learn what happened here; such evil news will be spread abroad, to our ruin. This then is what I propose. If any have other ideas, let her rise and speak."

At the conclusion of her speech, Hypsipyle sat back down.

Eyes now turned to her foster-nurse Polyxo, a priestess at one time loved by Apollo in the cool, dark, inner room of his shrine on the island of Chryse, where mice were allowed the free run of the storerooms and never killed. She rose in the midst of four unmarried maidens, with thick white hair, trembling with age, supporting herself with a staff, and greatly desiring to speak. From between hunched shoulders she raised her neck and head, hoary with age, and said: "As the queen suggests, let us by all means send these strangers gifts, since to be generous is always better. If these men leave us, however, and later the Thracians or some other enemy in time attack us, arriving unexpectedly like them, what do we do? Even if we remain unmolested, a greater danger threatens our future. When the older women pass on, and the younger ones attain old age without bearing children—fools, how will you survive? Will the bullocks yoke themselves to plough the fields? When harvest comes, will they gather the ripe wheat into the threshing-floor? Thankfully for me, I will be clothed in earth before that time comes, although the deathly spirits shudder to claim one as old and decrepit as myself. It is for you young ones I grieve. Seize the opportunity to save yourselves by admitting these men into your houses to enjoy your food and company. The god that favors Lemnos has brought them hither. Even Aphrodite, who cursed us toward our present misery, by her nature cannot hold us too long in reproach, and is bound to bless the act that will repopulate this island from your fertile wombs."

The assembly rejoiced in her words and filled the hall with sighs and gleeful noises. Hypsipyle, who had all along wished the same end in her heart, rose and said: "Very well; if this proposal is acceptable by all, I shall immediately send my herald Iphinoë to the ship to invite the strangers into our city."

The Argonauts watched the young Iphinoë run down to the beach, and it seemed she skipped along with the grace of a gazelle streaming across the tall grass in the first flush of morning. Standing on the shore, cupping her hands to her mouth, she cried: "I am sent by Hypsipyle, daughter of Thoas, to invite the captain of this ship, whoever of you he may be, to appear in her presence. She also permits his comrades, if they wish—and if their intentions are friendly—to enter our city." The Argonauts, consumed with curiosity about Aethalides' experience, but concluding nothing more from his report than that Thoas was dead, with the reign of Lemnos now passed to his daughter, scrambled excitedly to their seats to beach the ship until her keel sliced into the sand.

Jason pinned around his shoulders a sumptuous double cloak dyed red with madder root: a gift woven by the maidens serving at the temple of Athena at Thessalian Iton. One could more easily look upon the rising sun than at the brightness of its color. On a purple border all around were woven intricate designs in gold thread. In one place the Cylopes forged a thunderbolt for Zeus, hewing out one final, flashing ray with their red-hot mallets. On another edge Aphrodite held the shield of Ares, whereon a perfect reflection shone: from her shoulder, her unclasped tunic had fallen over her left arm. Heracles, had he cared to look, would have seen across the bottom of the cloak thick pastures, flowing with blood, where the sons of Electryon and the bandit Teleboans contested over cattle. And the top edge showed Phrixos listening to the warnings of the golden ram on his way to the mountain altar. All around in sequence the scenes appeared to dance upon the purple fringe, beguiling the eyes.

The crew disembarked lightly armed, including Jason, who took with him only the spear, tipped with broad steel, that Atalanta had given him. Heracles announced that he would remain, along with Hylas, to guard the ship. The fishy smell of the air made him suspicious of treachery. Old Iphiclos also stayed behind, grumbling warnings to Jason his nephew and those who cared to listen. When Heracles saw Polyphemos sneaking down the ladder, he clasped him by the shoulder and pulled him back up, saying: "Brother-in-law, where are you going? I don't want to tell my sister you've been off in the company of some silly Lemnian women. You shall keep company with me instead." And when he saw Orpheus lining up with the others he said: "I feel you go to have others pluck at your strings, you strange little fellow! Remember that love-making, however enjoyable, disturbs the rational mind." Orpheus, clasping his lyre under his arm, pretended to ignore him. King Augeias, before leaving the ship said to Heracles: "That Hylas is surely the handsomest lad I have ever seen! May I kiss him?" Heracles shook his fist at him and said: "You may not, sir. Although his bubbling cheeks invite such gestures, if you do act so importunely, I will cast you like a quoit far into the sea. Remember how I am not altogether pleased with you." Telamon called to him from the beach: "Comrade, as the very best among us, you deserve to feast and disport yourself on this fair island. Shall you leave Peleus and I without merry company?" Heracles replied: "As I can think of nothing but accomplishing the task before us, I have no stomach for revelry today. Your fair-haired captain already struts off toward the city like a preening peacock. Warn him not to tarry long. We should avoid unnecessary delays and leave at first light. Remember, however, your old friend and send down some roasted lamb-chops or swine crackling on the spit."

As Iphinoë led the Argonauts through the gates into the city, the Lemnian women thronged around them like Mainads who, having fallen upon young black bulls during their orgies on some desolate mountain-side, with greedy hands reach for hide and hair and tail, tearing at them in frenzy. So did the women, delighted by the strangers, appear to handle them; they could hardly disentangle themselves. Leaving the main body in the palace courtyard with the women, Jason followed Iphinoë, keeping his eyes modestly fixed on the ground. At the queen's chamber, the Thracian servants, awed by the sight of Jason, filled with grace and beauty, opened the paneled doors for him. Iphinoë led him through a porch shining on all sides with marble. Hypsipyle, observed his approach, turned away her eyes as a bloom suffused her cheeks. He had that brightness of the evening star whose red splendor charms the eyes of young brides, locked up in their chambers, waiting upon their marriage-beds.

Iphinoë offered Jason a seat on a golden couch opposite her mistress. Only then did he look up at the fair Hypsipyle, whose dark hair and eyes contrasted with his own. He offered her as a gift a delicate veil bordered with thistles, once his mother's; and a pair of bracelets inlaid with emeralds and agates.

Jason said: "It is beyond my power, O queen, to offer you sufficient gratitude for your kind compassion to us straggling men, who, far from our homes, are borne over the harsh sea to destinations still to come. You alone have offered hospitality; and for that may the gods, mine and those worshipped here, bless you and keep you safe and secure in your sovereign realm. Allow me, if I will, to inquire after the health of your father Thoas, a king of great renown and known by name in that part of Greece from which I come."

Hypsipyle turned to him, batting her long eyebrows and soot-painted eyelids over her dark, shining eyes. She told Jason: "It was not our intention or desire to leave you and your men so long without permission to land on our island. It is only that we have recently suffered a great misfortune, and this has prompted our wary behavior."

"Tell me, O queen," said Jason, "what great trouble has reached you?"

"I will be frank with you," said Hypsipyle, "and tell you the whole, unvarnished truth. While my father Thoas ruled, our men, fired by a desire for adventure, took to their ships to raid the Thracian mainland opposite. Their booty included young, nubile girls they brought back as slaves. At first our husbands bade us to welcome the slave-girls, a thing against our customs, telling us their only dutiful thought was to have them relieve us of our household chores. Ah!—but see how the path to Tartaros is often paved with good intentions. For her neglect the Goddess filled our men with lust, so that, shunning their lawful wives, they took these girls as concubines. We put up with this affront for a long time in the hope our husbands would change their minds and return to their marriage-beds, but the problem only worsened. The love of the men grew cold, obsessed as they were with the slave-girls wherever they were. Our children were supplanted by a bastard race. Virgins and mothers wandered about alone, without anyone to care for them. Fathers forgot about their daughters. At last us women could no longer bear the misery. Some god gave us strength to act. The next time the men returned from a pillaging raid, we closed the doors of our houses to them until they should come to their senses. They then took their slave-girls, and, by our permission, all the male children, and went back to Thrace, where they remain ploughing its snowy fields."

The eyes of Hypsipyle welled with tears. Jason, pained to witness such a lovely face so afflicted, would have fared worse had he learned the bitter truth obscured by Hypsipyle's dissimulation. The crime she hid from him had its foundations long ago when Zeus, unsuccessfully courting Hera, turned himself into a hapless cuckoo-bird, which Hera, taking pity, took to her fragrant breast. There Zeus resumed his awesome form to seize and couple with her before she could escape him.  Although they married, Hera always nursed bitterness over this embarrassing incident.  One day, as part of her revenge, she mixed a potent soporific with his nectar. Once Zeus fell fast asleep, she marshaled the other gods to chain him to his couch.  As she argued with Athena and Poseidon over what next to do, only Tethys, Lady of the Sea, hearing his groans, rose to Olympos to succor him.  She summoned the hundred-handed giant Briareos to free her lord; who, afterward grasping his bright thunderbolt, brought his enemies to their knees in fear and shame.  Taking Hera their ringleader by her hair, he depended her from heaven's edge, with a stone attached to each leg.  Her cries roused their feeble son, Hephaistos, who tried to aid her.  The offended Zeus took him by the foot and cast him off Olympos.  He fell for a whole day, and in the evening crashed down upon Lemnos like a meteor that, flashing through the sky, seems to drop behind some dark peaks.  There the Sintians found him, sprawled upon the rocks, and nursed him back to health; but he ever remained lame in one foot from the violent fall.  Hephaistos henceforth opened new forges in Lemno's deep caverns, where he beat out for Zeus thunderbolts, surrounded in black smoke and fire.  The island became as sacred to him as it had been to Aphrodite, whom, the Sintians called Cypris, or the great Mother Goddess, since her worship had spread there from Cyprus. But since that time that Hephaistos caught her, his new wife, in adulterous dalliance with grim Ares, she hated the people of Lemnos, who in turn, left her altars cold; while on her husband's they piled burnt offerings and left sweet wine and grains from the pregnant fields.  For when Hephaistos learned about his cuckoldry from Helios, who saw Aphrodite and Ares embracing in his dishonored bed on Olympos, he raced in grief to his fiery bellows on Lemnos to pour himself, stroke by stroke, into the greatest artifice to ever come from his workshop.  He hammered out a chain whose links could not be broken, not even by an immortal.  He wove these adamantine coils into a net at once so strong, yet so light, as is a spider's web that holds firm against the stirring wind and breaks not even with the capture of moths and beetles.  The net he fastened to the rafters over his bed and made to leave back to Lemnos.  The watchful Ares, seizing another chance to taste of the sweet, golden body of his mistress, took Aphrodite to bed, where their entwined forms were promptly ensnared. Not only Hephaistos saw them thus, but all the gods, who thereupon filled Olympos with immoderate laughter.

Aphrodite, bidding her time, still nursing a grudge long after the Sintians had passed from the island, struck the Lemnian women with an evil smell which repulsed their husbands, prompting them to seek wives abroad. She also inflicted them with the wild disorder of green jealousy over the imported slave-girls even as the men returned with their spoils. The Lemnian women. seeing these ill-bred Thracian girls, no match to them in honor or beauty, tattooed savages to whom the gentle arts of weaving and spinning were unknown, gathered together in secret in the desolate places under the stars to keen their laments to each other and to the gods who chose to hear. Aphrodite, adding fuel to the fire, taking the form of one of them, complete with suckling man-child, filled further their minds with hysteria and their breasts with fire, urging them to arm themselves with swords and torches, and to bring an utter end to the sex that had brought them to their present misery. To complete the theater, the once-gentle goddess flung to the ground the babe at her breast, inspiring all with greater madness.

Off the women go in a pretence, dancing, decking their temples with stringed flowers, preparing a feast to welcome back their men and their unwelcome guests. That night husbands and sons fill their bellies and drink wine without sense. At the appointed time, in the dead of night when foul deeds thrive, the most rabid of the women unsheathe their husbands' swords and stain their marriage-beds with blood. Aphrodite again descends on Lemnos, ushered in by lightning and shrill cries. Herself she leads a train of maddened women, breaking into houses, forcing her way into sleeping chambers, putting into the hands of reluctant wives, still moved by gentleness and pity, sharp blades and sickles. All through the night Lemnos shudders with groans and cries of pain and horror as the offenders, including their innocent male children, are hacked and cut and stabbed, overflowing Hell with mournful shades. Even those men who could awake before being struck down in treachery, girding themselves with odd pieces of armor, whatever they could grab, cower at the ghastly sight of wives lurking in doorways, for Aphrodite has made them seem large and looming, their shadows casting grotesque shapes in the firelight, so that it appeared that the denizens of Hell had been unleashed on them. Fire too mingled with blood, reducing once happy dwellings to ashes.

Amidst this scene of horror, of all the women, only Hypsipyle took no part in the awful crime. Instead, moved by filial piety, she roused her aged father Thoas, sword in hand, to help him flee the massacre. Supporting him, covering his head and face in a shroud, she led him from the palace to the shrine of Dionysos, hiding him at the foot of the god's painted statue, enveloped within his flowing robes. There she spent the night with him, ready to defend him against her terrifying subjects, who ranged all night over the island in the unwholesome enterprise of murder. When dawn arrived, the groans of the dying had faded with the night. Once more voices, human and composed, accompanied by tinkling cymbals, neared the temple doors, while its guardian lynxes roared in greeting to the new day. Quickly, Hypsipyle draws out her father, arranges his hair like that of a boy, decks his brow with a festive garland, and arrays him in the costume of Dionysos. She rips the ivy from the walls, curls them around her arms, and mounting a car with her father, drives him from the temple precincts, he holding up a ceremonial goblet spilling wine, while she holding aloft the sacred *thyrsos* and crying out: "Abandon these bloody streets, O you Giver of Wine Unmixed! Let the sea wash over the dastardly pollution and stink of death." She raced through the city on streets channeled with streams of blood, running roughshod over the corpses and dissected limbs of young and old, no one daring to oppose them, until she reached the woods, where in the deepest part she hid Thoas until nightfall; when, with the horror of her citizens still fresh in her mind, she conveyed him one last time to an abandoned beach, where she remembered lay an old rotting boat, left long ago as an offering to some marine deity, but now forgotten, its planks baked by the sun or worn away in the moist moonlight. With prayers for his safety, she pushed off the frail craft, watching it with tearful eyes float away into darkness.

Jason, loving Hypsipyle, opened his heart to reveal the truth of his expedition in search of the Golden Fleece. She said to him: "Stay and live with us, Jason, you and your men. You will find it pleasant to dwell on this island where milk and honey flow in abundance, and fat sheep bleat upon the hills, and no table is ever without bread piping hot and fresh. I offer you the throne of my father Thoas. You can reign over my people, I at your side, for as long as you wish, and as long the Goddess preserves us."

Jason touched her right hand and said: "That I cannot become your king, Hypsipyle, I do not do thinking it a mean position; but only because of the duty to which I am bound. But we will remain here for a day or so to take advantage of your kindness and the hospitality you most graciously offer. In that time, let us enjoy each other's company to the fullest, with the hope that my men can seed the furrows of fertile wombs and once more fill your land with needful sons."

Hypsipyle wisely did not press her heart with baseless longing. She sighed and leaned forward slightly, parting her lips, exuding the sweet fragrance of her breath. Jason pressed his lips to hers, but they drew apart quickly, blushing in the prime of their acquaintance.

The Argonauts meanwhile organized funeral games in honor of Thoas. When Erginos won the foot-race in armor, beating the sons of Boreas by dint of his perseverance, the Lemnian women laughed at him for his aged appearance. Taking the prize of a cloak from Hypsipyle, he said to her: "Such is my swiftness, with hands and heart to match. But it is a misfortune that even on young men gray hairs sometimes grow before their time."

Later the men went off where chance led them, invited by the eager women to their houses. As there were too few men to go around, they were compelled to keep their visits short, so as to please as many women as possible with their company. That night they returned to the palace, where Hypsipyle held for the Argonauts a rich feast, full of music and dancing, where each man's couch, covered in a blanket of Tyrian purple, was weighed down with numerous new companions, all vying for his attention, dropping almonds into his mouth, or figs, or dripping pieces of watermelon after he had filled his belly with roast beef and boiled mutton. Those who had never tasted Lemnian wine, pressed from black grapes after a late harvest, marveled at its treacly taste and floral aroma, so that they drank it unmixed as a dessert. When Butes announced he believed the wine had been fortified with fermented honey, the serving-girls assured him it had not, and brought him instead a jar of fresh honey for his opinion. Butes, sucking the golden syrup off of his finger, was left speechless, since it clearly had come from thyme-fed bees, and to an untrained palate would have been considered indistinguishable from the Hymettan variety.

Upon her couch before the long hearth, Hypsipyle rested on Jason's bosom, gazing up at him, hearing him describe his youth or talk of the building of the *Argo*, her heart afire, the marrow of her bones boiling like the bubbling pots of flesh-meat.

Atalanta entered the banquet-hall to no one's notice save Meleager's, who left with disinterest the women, entranced by his well-formed limbs, who surrounded him. She had been worshipping at the temple of the Great Goddess, who, though on the island was presently identified with Cypriot Aphrodite, was also no doubt originally the goddess Bendis whose worship the Sintians learned from the Thracians; she in turn was known to the Greeks as Artemis. Meleager brought her a trencher piled with meat, and the two sat together until the oil lamps dimmed and the dark corners sounded of merry love-making.

4

Back at the ship, Hylas watched the curdling smoke rising from the palace, and his ears delighted in the music and laughter that rolled through the town. "Nuncle!" he cried down to the beach, where Heracles prepared to broil some miserable sprats. "Cannot I go and partake of the feast? Father has given me leave to go, and wishes he can go himself." Heracles responded: "You had better stay here safe and sound. There's no telling what mischief you'll fall into. If that scoundrel Telamon had remembered us, we'd be feasting as well as they, without the headache of having to entertain women. I have nothing against them, surely. In themselves, they are as lovely as the lilies of the field and have a pleasing smell after bathing in rose-water; but when they rule a place it is best you flee as far from them as Colchis is from Iolcos. What? Is that a wagon I hear advancing? Throw me my bow, lad, lest this guest prove unwelcome."

But it was only Telamon, leading by the nose an ox pulling a cart of food and women. Despite Telamon's insistence to the contrary, Heracles made him send the women back, but not before they assisted to unload a side of beef, roasted to a crisp; three spatchcocked lamb rumps seasoned with pepper, garlic and rosemary; a basket of barley-loaves; and several tall stone jars of wine. Despite the welcome food, Heracles was cross with Telamon for delaying his supper for so long, and could only be appeased after Telamon agreed to sup with him.

The next day tall Palaimon roused Heracles from sleep. It was late afternoon, and raining. The agitated sea sent a heavy tide that reached the *Argo* where it had been hauled. Heracles awoke with a start, vigorously shaking the rainwater from his curly brown hair like a wet dog.

Palaimon told him: "Tiphys came down this morning to see

you, but your eyes were still too heavy from last night's wine. The rising moon for the fourth night in a row was misted, he said, which portends rough weather and storms. We will have to wait things out."

"How very convenient!" grunted Heracles, lifting up a wine vat to slurp the lees. He suddenly looked around. "Where is Hylas? And Telamon—was he not just here with me?"

"Hylas ran off into the city as soon as you fell asleep this morning. Polyphemos tried his best to catch him. And Telamon went back with Tiphys. Should I go find someone to relieve our watch?"

"Go relieve yourself and leave me be," said Heracles in a foul mood, since everyone had abandoned him. Palaimon hobbled off eagerly.

After two days of foul weather, by which Heracles had to sleep close under the shadow of the ship to stay dry, the shore-birds returned and the clouds drifted toward the north. Only Hylas visited him, bringing food and drink, explaining that he had been merely curious, and had only played at piggyback with some girls his age. At last Heracles' patience was exhausted. "Is this for what I joined?" he complained. "Is this what Heracles should be doing?— helping his shipmates to dally in bed day and night?" Leaving Hylas to guard the ship he marched angrily off into the city, trailing his club.

He came across the twin sons of Boreas first, wandering about the market-place, with a woman on each arm. His mere look terrified the women and they ran off. Heracles asked Zetes where the others could be found, but he honestly knew not. Heracles therefore went door by door, nearly knocking each off the hinges with taps from his club, and ordering all the Argonauts to return immediately to the ship. From doorways tumbled bleary-eyed, half-dressed shipmates, at first showing consternation at being so rudely disturbed; but when they saw who it was who summoned them, they thought it prudent to obey, leaving weeping women in their wake.

Heracles had to burst apart the palace doors, as no one, hearing him coming down the street bellowing, dared admit him. In the courtyard he found the rest of the men being fed their breakfast by their lovers. Polyphemos and Telamon looked at him sheepishly.

"Why do you vex us, Heracles, like the morning cock that crows at an inopportune time?" said Idas. "We are engaged here in work of a most serious military nature."

"How so, brother?" asked Lynceus

"Why—we levy an army for Lemnos!" roared Idas.

"Wretches!" cried Heracles. "Have you come so far merely seeking brides, scornfully leaving your own back home?  Does it please you to stay and plough the fields of Lemnos?  We will not win renown tarrying here with strange women.  No god will merely hand us the Fleece.  It will  come to us only by long travel and hard work.  Get back to business!  As for Jason, let him, for all I care, wallow all day long in the queen's embrace until he has filled Lemnos with sons—that will be his claim to fame."

The whole group stayed quiet, no one daring to look Heracles in the eye.  Jason rushed down from the queen's chamber in a night-gown.

"And there he is!" said Heracles with a derisive laugh. "Count me wretched too for having followed you, golden-locks. Nothing but the love of danger and the possibility of great deeds drew me to join this sorry lot.  I was looking forward to crossing the Cyaneian rocks again!  But if your goal is to live on this spit of land in the middle of the sea, then tell me now, and I will go off with Hylas and Telamon to finish what we started."

Hypsipyle appeared behind Jason, dressed in a long filmy gown dyed with dittany and trailing golden tassels.  She carried with her the odor of white lilacs.  Heracles grew silent and bowed his head in courtesy.

"You must be none other than the great Heracles," said Hypsipyle gently.  "Jason has not stopped speaking of you.  You honor me with your presence.  Set yourself down, please, and I will have my maidens prepare you a splendid breakfast.  Too long have you tarried outside our walls, while a warm hearth and a comfortable bed always here awaited you."

Heracles flashed an angry look at Jason, who straightened like a war-horse which, idling in its tether, suddenly pricks its ears at the clarion's call.  He ordered Argos and Tiphys to make ready for the departure.

Handmaids led Heracles to the banquet-hall, giggling as they caressed his slabs of muscle. He feasted merrily that morning, quite forgetting his anger at the postponement of the expedition.

Meanwhile Jason and Hypsipyle returned to her chamber, where they sat under a casement overlooking the sea. Seeing the men going to and fro along the beach, collecting the tackle, putting the gear in order and loading provisions on the ship, she groaned aloud with deep sadness, saying to Jason: "Dearest of all men, do you unfurl your sails so quickly at this first sign of clear sky? Why this eagerness? I think you were hindered here less by me than by the weather."

"If only the gods would release me from this toil!" cried Jason.

Hypsipyle seized his hands, wetting them with her tears.

"Go, if you must," said she, "and may Heaven bring you back, unharmed, bearing that Fleece for your king. This island and my father's ruling scepter will await you, should you choose to turn your prow our way on your return. Only remember me when you are far away, and on your sure return. Leave me with your bidding, which I will gladly do, if heaven blesses me with your issue."

Jason, filled with admiration, said: "May all things work for good, Hypsipyle, by the will of the gods. Hold me always in your favor, even though I bring you grief with my parting. If it is not in my destiny to return to Greece, and if you bear a man-child, when he is grown send him to Iolcos, where he can be a comfort to my father and mother, if living still."

Still weeping, she assented to his words by a gentle nod. Then from a clothes-chest she brought out a tunic rich with handiwork, a dark cloak, a sacral purple robe worn by her father, and his sword, bearing as its pommel the figure of a snake eating its own tail enchasing a lightning bolt. "Take it, a gift of the Smith god," she said, "that I may remain beside you wherever the battle is thickest. Go now, but forget not the land that in your need sheltered you in its bosom. And on the way back from Colchis' vanquished shore turn here again your sails."

She sank upon Jason's neck and said no more.

And so the city broke afresh with mourning at the departure of the Argonauts. That awful night a year before the women remembered with greater bitterness, now that once again they would be deserted; their hearts, opened briefly to wedlock, left to wither. They crowded the beach, restraining the men from their work by clinging to their necks, wailing as at a funeral. The men would have stayed, so great was their longing, had not Orpheus soothed their melancholy hearts with a song. Even the ship seemed reluctant to depart: the anchor-stones clung to the sand. When Jason and Heracles arrived, the men climbed aboard, raised the sail, and took their seats at the thwarts. They reversed the oars and pushed the ship slowly back into the sea-swell until she floated trimly once again. As a southerly breeze carried them off, they had leisure, with heavy hearts but happy memories, to wave and blow kisses at their sweethearts, who all plunged into the waves as far as they could go, with outstretched arms hoping to draw them back. Hypsipyle from her window watched the white sail diminish and blink out of sight.

❧

Day past day king Pelias wandered around his palace suffused with rage. Stopping at prince Acastos' room, he stretched himself on the floor to kiss where his son had walked. He had confirmed, after an extensive search, that Acastos had left on the *Argo* willingly, but no doubt tricked by Jason with empty promises of glory to join the foolhardy expedition. He imagined the myriad dangers along the way. No doubt he would be betrayed by the treacherous crew should it prove necessary. In frenzy he cried: "Jason, if you have my son, then I have your father!" With this he summoned the sergeant-at-arms for a ruthless errand.

That very hour, Aison, supported by Alcimede, led a young, nervous bull by the nose ring to a trench dug one cubit on each side in the middle of the open inner court of his house, where an ancient cypress grew, casting under its widespread branches a ghastly gloom. While his slaves held the skittish bullock, which panted and pawed the ground knowing its certain death, Aison, holding the white horns hung with dark blue ribbons and branches of yew, drew a sacrificial knife and slit the throbbing throat. Out poured the dark blood, splashing into the trench like a dry ravine swelled in a sudden rain. At his side Alcimede sprinkled herbs onto the blood, moaning and muttering orisons to the underworld deities. Aison, less prone to superstition, but in this instance following his wife in

303

the infernal rites, joined her in attempting to summon the shade of his father, longing for news about his son Jason. Soon a translucent mist seemed to form at the side of the trench, taking vaguely human shape, with an insubstantial face bent low and sipping the bull's blood. Once sated, the apparition looked up. By then the slaves had fled in terror. With black hollow eyes the ghost gazed on Aison and Alcimede, who turned pale with fear, recognizing the face of Cretheus.

"Be not afraid!" the shade whispered in a low, screeching voice that chilled the spines of his audience. "Jason, skimming the blue waters to Colchis, is well. He will return with a glorious spoil, and more. But you—why do you remain while a vengeful king plots murder in his heart, one brother against another? Why not escape your trembling limbs by your own hand? Come with me, my son. Already the Stygian mob calls you to our silent glades."

As quickly as it came to slake its thirst, the shade of Cretheus vanished. After chanting the spell backward to send the ghost back securely to its infernal home, Alcimede put her arms around her trembling husband and said through her tears: "In whatever you decide, I remain your partner. I, who endured his departure over the main, bearing it with sorrow, have neither the desire to prolong my days, nor see our son without you."

For long Aison remained still, unsure of what to do, and praying that Pelias might come to an evil end for committing his beloved son and his comrades to the sea. Then, taking a wine bowl, he bent down on aching joints to dip it into the trench. Suddenly they heard the tumult of soldiers bursting into the house. Together they quickly drank the rank, steaming blood until, clutching their closed throats in agony, they dropped to the ground. When the soldiers of Pelias, swords drawn, reached them, they could do little but look upon the aged corpses contorted in death, wept over by the terrified Promachos. In accord with their orders, the soldiers eschewed mercy and hacked the little boy to pieces.

5

No sooner had they left Lemnos behind than the wind abated. Out came the long oars. Orpheus instructed Jason to make due north to rugged Samothrace, where as many as wished could be initiated into the sacred mysteries of the unnameable Great Gods, permitting them to sail the unknown seas in greater safety and freeing them from fear of death. Any person, man or woman, slave or free, barbarian or Greek, could be admitted. The island's principal city, surrounded by ancient walls as massive as those at Tyrins, lay on the northern coast beside the sacred precincts. By evening, with difficulty they fought the fierce waves to beach the ship, since the island had no natural harbor. Lashing the mooring-ropes to the sea-beaten rocks, the crew members climbed down the ladders and were shortly met by Thyotes the priest, who came to the shore to greet them. Heracles was among those who did not involve himself in the observances. He questioned Thyotes at length about the nature of the underworld; and since Thyotes admitted that he knew only what he had been taught, Heracles considered his knowledge mere hearsay, and unworthy of consideration. As these mysterious rites cannot be divulged, nothing more will be said of the matter.

Tiphys waited two days for a good wind to drive them on. On the third day a northerly breeze began to build, for which Calais and Zetes took credit, basking in the after-glow of their holy initiation, and having spent a night in prayer to their father Boreas. They rowed to clear the battered coast of Samothrace, then under sail passed by well-wooded Imbros, until by evening they came within sight of the rocky tip of the Thracian Chersonese. As the wind continued blowing strongly from the north, they hove-to to discuss what action to take next.

Tiphys urged Jason to return for the night to Imbros, an

island inhabited by friendly Pelasgians; or else row the other way and moor the ship on the peninsula. With fog rolling in from the direction of Thrace, and lacking a tail wind, he believed it would not be possible to try to negotiate the Hellespont by night. Nestor added his concern that the Trojans, although thinking nothing of a Minyan ship passing by their territory, would, being no doubt trading partners of the Colchians, possibly become a hindrance on their return should they receive wind from Colchis of their despoiling of the Fleece. Most of the crew groaned at the thought of doubling back to Imbros, while others, fresh from a long rest at the oars, itched to continue onward. Jason, after pacing up and down the centerline, knelt at the prow before the Dodonian branch, hoping for divine wisdom. Soon Mopsos and Idmon joined him. Idas laughed to see the three of them contemplating the branch, saying: "We could have saved room by appointing that tree both captain and soothsayer!"

After some time the oracular branch, whose leaves, remarkably, still had not withered, shook with a change of wind. Nauplios raised a hand and announced that a south-westerly wind was brewing.

"Son of Aison," Heracles said, spitting in his hands to ready them for some rough work at the oars. "Telamon and I made this passage not long ago. In one night we sailed fairly up the strait."

"It is late," added Nauplios. "Let us reserve our concerns about the Trojans for our return journey. If Tiphys feels he cannot drive the ship, I shall do it. Besides him, there is no other sailor as experienced here as I."

Tiphys gave up the helmsman's seat to Nauplios, who asked Lynceus to climb on the prow and keep watch. In silence they turned the ship around, and with a good wind astern they made for the mouth of the strait. The sharp current at the lip slewed the *Argo*, so that she buckled like a war-horse yet to be broken in battle, fighting her rider's tight control on the reins. The crew heaved at the oars, helped by the wind dead aft, until the open sea closed up behind them. As they passed the delta of the river Scamander and its tributaries, they saw beyond the plains the twinkling lights of the Trojan citadel. Telamon remarked: "I have not quite forgotten that lovely maiden, Hesione, chained bare upon a rock rising from the sea, as Cytherea, at her birth, rose in the glory of her nakedness."

Heracles, setting the rowing pace, said: "I more remember the fine mares which Laomedon promised me." He called out to Jason: "On the way back, I task you to let me off here. I have some business to finish at Troy. Do not let me forget."

Nauplios, with the help of Lynceus, kept to a steady course closer to the Thracian side where the opposing current flowed weakest. Lynceus saw easily through the brume, since it was said he could see even underground and through trees. He would call out: "Starboard your helm!" which was passed abaft man by man to Nauplios, if the ship veered too close to the Thracian shore; or "Port your helm!" to bring it back to the middle of the strait. By the time the setting moon filled their backs with a wake of misty luminance, they had cleared the narrows where the crossing was scarcely nine stades. After hours of incessant rowing, their muscles trembled and dripping sweat ran down the bilge. The men, except for the indefatigable Heracles, begged to land for a rest. With the rising sun infusing the dark channel with rosy definition, Nauplios made them row a little farther past the region of Abydos, where ships crowded an excellent harbor, to a narrow, isolated beach backed by a long series of rugged, green hills. There the crew debarked to walk about until the blood returned to their legs and backs, and then settled down for breakfast. Jason congratulated Nauplios for his expert seamanship. When he thanked Lynceus for his vigilance, the latter remarked that, at one point looking deep down through the water, he saw that there seemed to be an undercurrent flowing up the strait in the opposite direction. Castor, hearing this, laughed him to scorn, remarking that, if true, it would have been faster for each man to hitch a ride on the back of seals. Lynceus, taking offense, and joined by his brother Idas, would have entered into conflict with Castor and Polydeuces had not Tiphys remarked that such rivers within rivers were known to seamen. Curious, Euphemos, an expert swimmer, crossed the channel to the Thracian shore, and returned two hours later, reporting that the water was cold, unruly and filled with jellyfish.

The wind shifted about through the night, but resumed blowing westerly in the late morning. They left Abydos astern and continued up the strait, staying closer to the Mysian bank, past the ridges of Percote and the town of Lampsacos, in which all had a merry row at the sight of a profusion of statues, large and small, on hill-shrines and rooftops, with erect phalluses, representing Priapos, who was said to have been born there of Aphrodite.

They broke out of the strait in the early evening. The dark sea and overcast sky opened up before them as they entered the Propontis, ploughing through eddies and riptides. They settled in for the night at the large harbor of Parium, but stayed with the ship, sleeping on the benches huddled in their blankets. Well before dawn Tiphys, back at the helm, roused the crew to their work. The wind had veered to the northeast, and so they left the sail folded up and rowed until, by midday, they came within sight of what appeared to be a very large island marked by a singular peak. Thereupon, Echion, after inspecting the storage jars and lockers, announced that they were in dire need of replenishing their supplies at the next port of call.

"That is not an island at all," said Acastos, son of Pelias; "but a peninsula, separated from the mainland by a narrow spit. I heard my father speak of it with his advisors as he plotted out the pitfalls of our course for his own satisfaction. Since it is peopled by Pelasgians who long ago were driven from Thessaly, called now Doliones, we will no doubt find ready hospitality. The principal city, Cyzicus, is situated near the isthmus."

A northerly Thracian wind bore the ship swiftly to the peninsula, where they found a little roadstead, open to the winds, on a prominent corner. On a plain beyond sprawled a suburb of mean dwellings, ending at city walls of considerable height, which extended in a wide and irregular circuit, broken in places by hexagonal watch-towers, all the way down and across the isthmus, where rose great buildings of granite and gleaming marble.

They lay at anchor while Aethalides went into the city to make enquiries. He returned at the head of a large body of citizens, who welcomed them in the name of their king Cyzicus, bringing choice flocks and jars of sweet wine. The Argonauts accepted these gifts, set up an altar to Apollo of the Disembarkations on the shore and made sacrifices. After sharing the meat with the Doliones, keeping little for themselves, they were urged to move further down the coast to moor the ship more securely in the city harbor, called Chytos. This they did, rowing down into a bay at whose eastern corner a waterway, extending into the city to form a spacious harbor, lay protected at its entrance by projecting moles and the seaward curve of the walls.  Another, smaller port, existed further south.  The city of Cyzicus lay partly on a hill called Bear Mountain, while its larger southern and western portions rested on the low ground of the isthmus, separated from the shore by a ridge of sand dunes built up by the wind and waves.

King Cyzicus himself came to the quay to greet the Argonauts, warmly clasping each of their hands in friendship.  He was a polite, spritely youth on whose face the first beard of manhood had lately appeared.

He told Jason, whom he admired for his own youth and princely bearing: "I would have you know that our father Poseidon, by an oracle, informed me not a fortnight ago to expect a shipload of heroes; and that I should welcome them—which I do.  Although we are strangers, soon we shall be fast friends.  You will see we enjoy here as high a level of civilization as your own;—unlike many of our neighbors in this rugged part of the world, circumscribed by a stormy sea."

They entered the city in high fashion, with all the Doliones marveling at the splendid band equipped in their armor, with their swords and stout shields.  Heracles did not volunteer this time to remain with the ship, having tired of this duty; and so Jason left Atalanta and Meleager, along with Echion and his brother Eurytos to keep watch.  The palace had already been well-furnished for a feast; for Cyzicus was in the midst of his wedding celebration to fair-haired Cleite, the daughter of king Merops of Percote.  After being bathed, preened and garlanded, the Argonauts were conducted to the banqueting-hall where they reclined on couches covered with jeweled brocade and pillows fringed with golden tassels.  The majordomo directed the activities of one hundred comely boys, who walked about with fleshpots and vats of a fruity white wine so that everyone's board never went lacking.  In time from behind a portiere appeared Cleite.  She was of a lithe figure, winsome, with a long, graceful neck and tiny hands and feet.  Heracles was so moved by the sight of her that he remarked to those shipmates around him: "Ah!—there is nothing in the world like a new bride, young and soft, untouched by the pangs of child-bearing.  Cyzicus must be the noblest of all men, that he would leave the sweetness of his bride's bed to come feast with us."  Cyzicus, hearing this, said heartily: "And if you consider, friend

Heracles, the priceless gifts I offered her father for her hand, you should now count me also as the poorest, yet the happiest, of men."

Cleite blushed deeply as she joined her husband's couch. Sitting together they seemed like a pair of doves cooing upon a tree branch.

Jason inquired from Cyzicus about the region and its various inhabitants. The king surrendered as much information as he knew about the neighboring cities along the remaining stretch of the Propontis, but beyond that he admitted his ignorance. He advised them to beware of the Bebrycians further up the gulf, who were ruled by a cruel tyrant. When he asked in turn the reason for the expedition, Jason answered vaguely, mingling mentions of trade and commerce along with encomiums for his host. When Jason noticed Cyzicus looking at him strangely, since to the latter the Argonauts seemed more like warriors than tradesmen, he changed the subject by presenting his drinking cup, curious to know about the engraved scenes of battle.

"These savages depicted here are Pelasgians who live up on Bear Mountain. When my people settled here, a portion did not wish to be subjected to Aeneus my father, and so they broke off and went into the wilderness, where they forgot their origins and came to believe they were born from the earth. In the early days there was always contention between us, with them coming down to harry us at night; but as you can see they were never a match for us, and we always sent them fleeing, having set their rafts aflame."

"But why are they here depicted as monsters with six arms?" asked Jason.

"Merely artistic convention," said Cyzicus. "They hunt, eat and wear the skins of the bears which are numerous on the mountain. Wearing the bear-skins, with their hanging paws, and painting their skin with woad, makes them appear from afar as monsters with six arms."

"Would that they should rush down tonight!" said Jason. "We would take care of them for good, your men and mine."

As they continued to talk, exchanging stories and bandying jests, Mopsos, who sat nearby, grew troubled at the sight of the head and golden mane of a lion affixed to a plaque on the wall. When he inquired as to this prize, Cyzicus responded proudly: "I bagged that one when on a raid on Mount Dindymon, where the natives run about the woods cutting their arms in honor of the Phrygian Mother Goddess. I saw it rise haughtily upon a crest, where it roared, thinking to scare us. But it ran as I gave chase, riding my hunting chariot, until I felled it with the throw of a well-aimed javelin." Mopsos said no more, afraid to offend the king, who, as a follower of Poseidon, had little regard for the ancient goddess who still ruled supreme in that part of the world. He obviously did not know—or care—that lions were sacred to the Mother Goddess; and given the size, beauty and nobility of the mounted lion's head, Mopsos entertained the possibility, to his dismay, that this could have been one of the lions that were known to draw her chariot.

Cyzicus detained them for two more days, unwilling to part company with such a gallant band; especially from Heracles, who astonished him with his tale of how he once travelled all that way to bed an Amazon. Of Jason his estimation waned somewhat, thinking his reticence about matters important, and endless gabbling on matters unimportant was intended to hide a diffident and saturnine disposition: qualities not admirable at all in a leader; and he wondered why it was he who led the enterprise, and not Heracles. Nevertheless, he walked arm in arm with Jason down to the harbor, weeping to see him go. Jason gave him as parting gifts a golden goblet and a fine bridle of Thessalian craftsmanship. Cyzicus gave Jason a helmet and spear his father had worn in battle; as well as a robe which Cleite had brought from Percote, heavy with golden thread. For the crew were brought fine wooly sheep, milled barley, mulberries and wine—not from Bithynia or Phrygia—but made from Lesbian grapes left late to ripen on the vine, so that the juice expressed thick and rich from their very weight. He also presented them with a new, heavier anchor-stone. The Doliones afterward preserved the original one in their town-hall, beside the sacred hearth.

While Heracles and the younger members of the crew remained on the ship making ready for their departure, the rest set off to climb Mount Dindymon to get a good view of the sea-routes. Although the wind blew favorably at the moment, Nauplios portended storms from the look of the leaden pallor of the northern sky. He urged Jason to cast off as soon as possible. As they came within sight of the look-out point, they heard the faint sound of a horn blown thrice in the distance. "Is that not the sound of the conch-shell that Argos keeps under the helmsman's seat, meant to sound an alarm?" cried Arcadian Ancaios.

It happened that Heracles had just settled between the thwarts for a short nap when a great splash flung a sheet of water over the port gunwale. He sat up to see a line of men, wearing bear-skins, start to make a great din on the cliffs above the walls that protected the harbor. While some scampered down to the cove, others hurled large rocks, trying to strike the *Argo*.

"We are under siege!" cried Telamon, seizing his javelin. "I had a queer feeling about these people. See how they now treacherously attack us."

"No—these are the Bear Men of which the king spoke," said Hylas. "See how that they have overcome the guards and now run wildly toward us."

Atalanta bent her bow, but her arrows fell short of the attackers throwing the rocks, one of which struck a piece off of the stern ornament.

"Allow me, lady, to rid us of these pests," said Heracles, fetching his bow and quiver. Pulling back the string so that his great bow groaned under the strain, he delivered death to the savages above the walls. They dropped one after the other. Meanwhile the other Argonauts scampered off the ship to head off the approaching contingent, except for Atalanta and Acastos, who, leaning over the gunwale, lent support against the nearer targets with their deadly arrows. Hylas then spotted a new force of savage Pelasgians rushing down the other side of the mountain armed with flaming pine-torches and fir spears; and, wishing to be of use, sought for a weapon. Instead he found Argos' conch-shell, and putting it to his lips, sounded the alarm.

Jason and the remaining Argonauts reached the cove in time to prevent their companions from being overwhelmed. Joined by the Doliones, they speedily put an end to the assault. At the conclusion of the slaughter, the Bear Men lay strewn along the shore, their bodies bathed by the waves, and fed upon by birds and crabs.

Later that day, Cyzicus had the *Argo* towed through a canal spanned by drawbridges to a small harbor on the eastern side of the isthmus. From there they gratefully sailed off, having saved the time it would have taken to circle around the mainland. Consulting charts provided him by the Doliones, Tiphys steered for the isle of Bebiscos near the outlet of the Rhyndacos River, which divided Mysia from Bithynia; and whose silty, yellow water stained the sea for a great distance from the shore. Steep and rocky, Bebiscos was inhabited only by goats.

With a fair, following wind they travelled a great distance into the night, until all sight of land was lost. Weary from the exertions of the morning's battle, most of them men slept, resting their heads on the shipped oars. Arcadian Ancaios, feeling pity for Tiphys, left his bench to sit by him awhile, urging the helmsman to retire and let him man the tiller, since the breeze had been steady all day and it seemed the sea graciously allowed them an easy passage. "How little you know about the sea," said Tiphys in response, "that you would for a moment put your trust in her, despite the calm demeanor she presents. And the winds, like women, are no less treacherous: they can change in an instant. No, dear comrade, while you rest I will remain here vigilant." Seeing that he could not move him, Ancaios shrugged his shoulders and returned to his bench, where he joined the others in their rest. Hour after hour, Tiphys leaned upon the helm, observing the stars and how the winds tilted the yard-arm. But he too was overtaken, though he fought it bravely, by that sweet release that droops the eyes and nods the head, sending one unawares into that pleasant vale of dreams. As the hours slid by, the ship became the plaything of the winds, turning the prow where it listed.

A cold blast of wind rocked the *Argo*, rousing the crew into a sudden state of confusion. Tiphys, looking about, could not get his bearing, since the night sky was overcast and the moon inveigled the starlight. Rain followed, and the sea grew raucous, thrusting high waves repeatedly against the sturdy hull. Argos unsteadily moved from one side of the vessel to the other, looking over the gunwale to see if the strakes still held firmly together. Tiphys at last announced that, by his reckoning, they were not far from Bebiscos, but closer still to the mainland, to which they should make a run with the change of wind, blowing from every quarter, but most powerfully from the north-east.

Lynceus presently spotted the dark outline of land. They beached the ship, tying her to a large rock, and wondered by how much, or how little, they had missed the Rhyndacos. As they gathered driftwood for a fire, they heard queer noises beyond the shore hills. There seemed to be a rushing, and a bustle, and whispers in the dark. Oileus, who was still aboard the *Argo*, alerted Jason that he had seen the glint of arms. A sudden fear seized the crew, as each man expected a sudden attack from an unknown enemy. "To arms!" cried Heracles, who was the first to climb aboard to fetch his weapons. The others followed in a desperate rush to gird on their armor. A trumpet then sounded, followed by a chilling cacophony of fierce screams as a great multitude swarmed the beach. With dull thuds spears struck the *Argo*'s topside as the men descended the ladder or jumped from the sides. Jason, slipping on his helmet, felt his heart beating through his leather cuirass from a potent mixture of anxiety and animation. About to experience his first battle, his mouth ran too dry to gainsay big Ancaios, who directed the men to form a tight group, locking shield against shield. Instead, he ran past them and into the thick of the attackers. The men, filled with admiration at their young captain's courage, followed in an unbreakable phalanx against an onslaught of flying stones and thrusting iron. Shields and spears clashed like a fierce flame that flares suddenly upon the kindling. Heracles, from the ship, at first picked off the enemies with his arrows; but growing tired of the ease with which he delivered death, he took up his brass-bound club and fell upon them like a woodsman in a virgin forest. Men dropped before him, their bones crushed, their brains spilling on the sand, like stalks of wheat bowing to the harvester.

When the attackers weakened and began to retreat, the Argonauts broke their tight arrangement and spread out in pursuit. Arcadian Ancaios, after lopping off one foeman's head, knelt to strip the body of an elegant corselet. "Leave the spoils!" barked Nestor at him. "That steel in your hand should be sufficient." Castor and Polydeuces, in the confusion, met and almost came to blows, had not each recognized the other from a strange radiance that illumined their faces. Hylas, too, did not shun danger. With Atalanta's bow in hand he slipped off the ship and sent more than one arrow to its mark.

Jason, steeped in others' blood, moved like a lion among prey, his locks flowing behind him as he ran hacking with the sword of Thoas in one hand, and thrusting with Atalanta's iron-tipped spear in the other. When he saw ahead of him a foe not retreating, but advancing, and that with great force and power, shouting taunts and urging his troops to stay and fight, Jason, filled with fury, ran and hurled his spear at him. The lance-haft hissed to its target, its point carving a path through the vaunted chest. The figure sighed deeply and then fell to the dust. Jason at that moment expected to feel exultation over his vanquished foe; yet he was filled with remorse and pity to witness such a champion so easily brought low. At his elbow he then heard a sob. From the gloom emerged Tiphys. He fell to his knees, casting dust upon his head. "O sea-gods!—what have you done?" he cried. "What ruin did a little rest bring? We have returned from whence we came, and wade now in the blood of our friends." Jason did not comprehend what Tiphys meant, until he heard Heracles calling for an end to the fighting. He ran to the man he had just speared, turned him over, unlaced his helm, and stared with disbelief at the pale cheeks of Cyzicus. Clasping the cold limbs, Jason wept. The others dragged themselves to the spot, heavy at heart and filled with dread at what they had done. Only Orpheus, who had not participated in the fighting, dared speak. Looking down at the body, but averting his eyes from the ashen face, he said to Mopsos: "You should have warned the king instead of gossiping to me the bitter end you saw in store for his insult against the Great Mother in hunting one of her sacred beasts."

At first light the Doliones left the city to gather their dead. Mothers wept over sons and wives prepared their husbands for burial. Wails, mingled with the groans and noises of the dying, rose from the desolate beach. The Argonauts remained by the ship, helplessly watching the mourners clinging to the piles of corpses. As for them, they suffered little injury; for their chirurg Eribotes, son of Teleon, had worked through the night tending to their wounds. When Cleite came out, her face veiled, walking slowly and gravely to where her husband lay, the Argonauts were cut to the heart.

Jason and Argos met with the king's chancellor and magistrates to work out terms of peace. After much discussion, the Doliones admitted that they were at greater fault. Spotting the *Argo* drawing swiftly to their shore, they thought it to be a ship-load of neighboring Macrians intent on a sneak attack. The Argonauts, not realizing they had landed back in Cyzicus, had no choice but to defend themselves when they saw troops swarming the beach.

Trees from the hills were stripped for pyres, upon which the dead, bestrewn with flowers, were laid. To the highest pyre, Jason helped convey the corpse of Cyzicus anointed with spring water and honeyed milk, and wrapped in a quilt of royal purple. He placed there in tribute the gold-threaded robe Hypsipyle had given him, as well as the helmet and sword-belt the king had worn in battle. In full armor, the Argonauts gravely marched around the bier to the doleful blasts of a trumpet. Then, racked with grief, they flung their pine torches to set the logs afire. The crowds watched in silence as the hungry flames leapt giddily until all was consumed and the red-hot ashes blew in the wind. Cyzicus' bones were transferred to the Leimonian plain, over which a large tumulus was heaped in his honor. Jason consulted with the priests Mopsos and Idmon as to how they could assuage their sorrow, ease their guilt, and purify themselves of the unintended murders. Mopsos instructed them to meet him quietly at dawn in a grove outside the city, through which a stream of the Aisepos river flowed on its way to the sea. There, Mopsos, in preparation, remained all night in vigil, offering up prayers and lamentations to Apollo. At the break of dawn, he bathed his body in the fresh waters of the stream, wreathed his head with olive leaves, dressed himself in a white robe he borrowed from Orpheus, and scribbled with the tip of his sword arcane markings on the ground.

Lights dancing in the gloom signaled that the Argonauts were wending their way from the beach, marching in a solemn procession, leading a pair of black sheep with gilded foreheads. Mopsos welcomed them with a wave of an olive branch. At the stream the men removed their shoes (Atalanta, having her bow taken by Hylas, and thus innocent of shedding any blood, excused herself), garlanded themselves with laurel, and lay prostrate to welcome the rising sun, as Mopsos instructed. The sheep, with heads bent downward, they slayed. As the men performed a triple march, Idmon walked among them bearing the bloody chine, touching with it their raiment and armor, until at the last turn he cast the pieces behind him into the sea. The rest of the sheep they allowed the altar fire to consume.

While the Argonauts waited, no one yet breaking their silence, Idmon set upright oaken pieces on the beach, all in a row, one for each Argonaut present. Each log he dressed with a piece of clothing or spare armor belonging to a crewmate, and assigned to each of them one of their names. Then in a hissing voice he chanted: "Leave us, you ghosts, and be content where you now rest. Follow us not on the sea, nor on land; haunt not our cities at home nor assemble at gloomy crossroads to bale about your unseemly murders. Send neither plague nor pestilence on our crops or beasts. Leave our children be." He performed this ceremony to confuse the ghosts, whom he knew to be capricious and persistent; they would stubbornly remain to haunt the oak logs instead, to which the blood-guilt was transferred, thinking them to be the Argonauts. In order to verify the effectiveness of the ritual, Idmon threw by a hollow bole the remaining portion of the meat and some wine and lees. Soon the ghosts, in the form of snakes, slithered out, with open mouths and licking tongues, to lap the sweet drops.

Afterwards the Argonauts competed with the Doliones in customary funeral games near the barrow of Cyzicus. Queen Cleite, her face still shrouded, watched some of the events from a dais, but she said nothing and made no gesture when any competitor won or lost. The Argonauts handedly won most of the events, except for the running contest, where Atalanta fell prey to unsportsmanlike trickery. She was on course to win the race, when one of her opponents dropped a shiny bauble in her way. She hesitated from natural curiosity in viewing the object, and lost by a hairsbreadth. When the Argonauts cried foul, another foot-race was held. This time Peleus competed instead, and won; he was given as prize a purple cloak. For wrestling, Samian Ancaios won a large, two-handled pitcher. No one could come close to Heracles in the weight-lifting contest, and so he was awarded a silver drinking-cup. Castor, winner in the chariot race, received a gold horse-collar. His brother, Polydeuces, boxed against the best pugilist among the Doliones and did not break a sweat. He received a woolen cloth woven with flowers. Jason entered the archery contest and lost, to the dismay of the Argonauts, any number of whom were better shots, not including Heracles. But he threw a javelin the farthest, and accepted for that only a crown of wild olive branches to seem modest. Finally, Orpheus won the musical contest with a song about the vicissitudes of life that filled all with both sweetness and melancholy, like the gourd, whose flesh, as it ripens grows bitter; but the pith remains sweet as honey.   Jason awarded him a pair of high boots to cover his bare feet.

For twelve days following contrary winds blew continuously, shaking the rigging and raising boisterous whitecaps over the swelling sea.  The crew slept fitfully on the beach, haunted by the faces of the dead and refusing any further comfort from the noble Doliones.  On the thirteenth night, exhaustion overcame them, weighing down their limbs and shadowing their eyes; and as they slept deeply and the third watch came, Mopsos and Acastos rose to keep guard.   Mopsos, sitting wrapped in his blanket, observed a small, bright-colored bird fly over the sleeping Jason, uttering shrill noises, before settling on the ship's stern-post. Mopsos trained his ears to listen to the bird's rattling call until Acastos threw a rock at it to shoo it away, saying: "Begone, you bothersome kingfisher!" Mopsos glared at him indignantly, but was much too excited to bother.  He shook Jason awake on his sheepskin bed and said: "Captain, I have just detected a message in the cry of the sacred halcyon, which breeds on a floating nest in the sea, and which prince Acastos wrongly assumed was a mere kingfisher.  This is what must be done.  You must climb to a holy place on Mount Dindymon and offer sacrifice to the Great Mother, who is above the whole company of the gods, in propitiation for the slaughter of the Bear Men, as well as of Cyzicus and twelve of his men.  If you do so, the winds will settle, allowing us to sail on."

Jason still half-asleep, mumbled: "But why should we Greeks have any regard for a Phrygian deity and her barbarous worship, full of noise and frenzy?"

"Hist!—hold your tongue, son of Aison," cautioned Mopsos.  "Upon the Great Mother Cybele, known to us as Rhea, depends the entire world: the winds, the seas, the earth; and even snowy Olympos rises by her will.  Do you not know that when she leaves her mountain abode to visit the heavenly realm, even Zeus himself steps aside, and all the blessed gods reverence her dread divinity?"

A new hope filled Jason's breast.  He jumped from his bedding to rouse his comrades, and told them of Mopsos' interpretation of the bird's call. Idas groaned with displeasure and would have gone back to sleep had not Orpheus taken up the augur's cause, imploring the group to perform the rites as soon as possible. They untied the mooring-ropes and rowed the ship to the harbor of their departure, from where they could more easily set upon the road to Dindymon; while Heracles, Atalanta and a few others remained aboard. Taking the choicest head of cattle, they followed Jason up the steep and wooded slope, taking the same route trod before when they had sought a look-out point, and which was called Jason's Way thereafter.

From the highest peak the whole seaboard to either side revealed itself as clearly as if they could touch it with their hands. Lynceus claimed to be able to see the misty entrance to the Bosporus, but others found that doubtful.

By a dried gully thick with trees not yet budding, Orpheus noticed a withered vinewood, unfit even for kindling, twisting wildly and stretching out its tendrils to the air. He called to Argos, who cut it down and skillfully carved of it a standing image of the Dindymene Mother flanked by two lions. This effigy they set upon a hill under the branches of lofty oak-trees. Beside it they built an altar of stones. Wearing oak-leaf chaplets, they killed the beasts in sacrifice, invoking the name of the Phrygian goddess, while Orpheus added mention of Titias and Cyllenos, two ranking Dactyls who attended to the infant Zeus in his Cretan birth-cave, and who danced noisily about him, along with the Curetes, clashing their weapons to drown his cries from the ears of Cronos.

Pouring libations upon the sizzling fat, Jason implored the Great Mother to forgo her anger and calm the winds. Orpheus then led the men in a war-dance about the holy image, beating swords on shields as if to drown out the lamentations of the Doliones over their king. After circling for hours until they could hardly drag their feet, they prepared a feast from the choice morsels, singing songs in praise of Cybele all night. At first light, the men awoke to great marvels. Down the gully trickled a stream; the trees were clothed in white blossoms; the ground was carpeted with new soft grass, amidst which grew patches of pale yellow primrose; and harts approached fawningly. Jason at once climbed to the look-out point and saw the storm-clouds pushed away toward Thrace, while the blue sea shimmered calmly under brightness of golden-sandaled Dawn.

Full of joy and promise, as if they were new men, they boarded the *Argo* and rowed away, helped by a slight wind from the direction of Dindymon.  Had they been less hasty to depart, they would have heard anon rising from the city a new round of keening: this time for Cleite, who, widowed and childless, wrapped around her fair neck a rough noose, and hung herself from the rafters of her chamber.  So subject to languishment did the Doliones become over this addition to their misery, that thereafter they subsisted for a long time on uncooked food, prevented by grief from grinding their meal at the mill.

6

As the crew appeared to be in good spirits and full of unused vigor, Jason proposed a rowing contest, with the victor receiving a jug of wine that had remained stored and sealed with pitch-pine for many years, and had no doubt acquired that delectable resinated flavor.  Once the sail slackened and the sea grew still, they all bent their backs and joyously pulled, propelling the ship forward like a racing swallow, while Orpheus chanted and strummed his lyre to keep the stroke.  Eurytos, at his brother Echion's taunting, was the first to strip to his breech-clout so as to not be encumbered.  When Idas saw this, he went further by becoming completely naked, to the embarrassment of Atalanta, who was forced by such effrontery to a seat next to Tiphys at the stern.  Soon the mens' chests gleamed with sweat and sea-spray as they groaned, but merrily, each trying to outvie the other.  The first to give up was Augeias, whose soft hands could no longer endure the rub of the oar.

"One down; forty-odd to go!" bellowed Heracles.  "Even my dear Hylas, young as he is, with his endurance puts many of you to shame.  See how he pulls without a word or grumble.  Come Jason—take Augeias' place.  Or do you not dare compete with me?  Show us how hard you can row."

Jason did not really wish to row, but he accepted the challenge earnestly, removing his shirt and settling down in Augeias' seat.  Heracles laughed at first as Jason missed some strokes, so that the oar butt kept striking him on the shoulder.  But the young prince soon fell into rhythm, keeping pace with Heracles, albeit without cutting the water as strongly as the latter.  Heracles rejoiced to see such honest effort.

By late afternoon, as they neared the mouth of the Rhyndacos, most of the Argonauts, exhausted, had shipped their oars and sat rubbing their calloused hands and strained muscles. Those left sitting across from Heracles, including Jason, now found it difficult to keep pace against the mighty man's tireless, wide stroke, causing the ship to pitch to port, leaving Tiphys in a constant struggle to keep her course straight. Only Jason, Heracles and Meleager still rowed as they passed the lofty cairn of Aegeon in the distance, a giant who fled Euboea and was drowned by Poseidon for besting him in a contest.

Suddenly recalling his next Labor, Heracles called for Orpheus to sit beside him. "Friend, I am certain you were brother to Linos, who was my music teacher. He was a decent fellow, but a bit punctilious. He pulled my ear for being clumsy with the lyre, and in a rage I mortally struck him. I ask your forgiveness in this matter." In response, Orpheus declared that he nursed no grudge over this. Happy to put the uncomfortable matter behind him, Heracles continued: "After I am done fetching the Fleece from Colchis, I must go off and find the Garden of the Hesperides. Might you know where it is and tell me?"

Orpheus gave him an astonished look and said: "Indeed, sir, no man living knows the location of that most sacred Garden, tended by the daughters of Evening, although some say it is somewhere in the land of the Hyperboreans; while others say in Libya, since it was from these very goddesses, keepers of the treasures of the gods, that Perseus acquired the helmet of Hades, the winged sandals of Hermes, and the wondrous satchel with golden tassels to hold the head of the Gorgon. If I may ask: for what purpose do you seek it?"

"I am to bring back from there some golden apples," said Heracles, at which Orpheus looked even more wide-eyed. "It is not my business: I am commanded to do it. Well, is there anything else you know about the matter? You are a queer-looking fellow, with a countenance bespoken of a grave intellect."

"I shall tell you what I know, in the hope that you achieve your end," said Orpheus. "Mother Earth brought forth branches heavy with golden apples to honor the nuptials of Zeus and Hera. From these a gilded glow like unto sunset canopied their marriage bed. Hera, delighted, entrusted the apples to the sister-nymphs called the Hesperides, daughters of Atlas and Hesperis, to plant in her favorite garden. From that branch grew a great tree, which the nymphs tended lovingly, singing as they pruned and watered it. The golden fruits hanging from the boughs were so delightful to behold that the Hesperides could not prevent themselves from picking them. Hera therefore appointed the earth-born serpent Ladon as guardian, who with sleepless eyes coils about the tree to prevent its despoilment."

"That is all well and good," said Heracles; "but if there is no more to tell, then off with you and let me row in peace."

Orpheus said, rising hastily: "It is said that certain nymphs, daughters of Zeus and Themis, about the river Eridanos know the location of this garden."

"Now you speak plainly!" said Heracles. "Sit here a while and play me a song to row by, since I shall soon be the only one left to drag this hull through the breaking waves."

As the day dimmed and they came in view of the headland of Posidion, the terminus of the Arganthonius mountain range, Meleager shipped his oar. Jason, his arms trembling from the exertion, toiled for a bit more, but then also dropped out. Although a furious stern wind whipped the whitecaps, Heracles alone remained at his oar, forbidding the raising of the sail, ploughing long furrows through the sea, sweeping the ship into the gulf of Cios, which narrowed as they went. Since Tiphys had announced landfall at the tip of the gulf, Heracles rowed for that objective as in a trance, without a moment's falter. As they came near the mouth of the Cios river, the channel through which the Ascanian lake discharges its murky water into the gulf, spreading out in streams and rivulets so that the district bloomed with marshes, the oar of Heracles with a loud crack suddenly shattered in the middle. With the loom still in his two hands, and the rest of the oar borne away on the tide, Heracles flew backwards into Menoitios' lap, who then, along with Eribotes beside him, fell atop Amphion and Iphitos. Heracles sat up, glowering about in silence to discover if any laughed at him. He then hollered: "Give me another oar! I am not used to such indolence." Augeias gladly thrust out for him his oar.

Impelled by hunger, the shipmates pitched in to row the ship to shore. They anchored in a marshy backwater overlooked by a sloping meadow. Heracles insisted Jason take the prize, since the latter hardly wavered in his stroke, and was the last to ship his oar.

Jason, in turn, insisted Heracles take the prize, since the latter so marvelously propelled the *Argo* so well and for so long and, in the end, singlehandedly, and could certainly not be blamed for possessing a rotten oar. Heracles finally proposed to award the wine pot to Hylas, who, though he was one of the first to surrender his oar, merited something for being the youngest participant among them. Augeias, seeing that many of the shipmates were displeased that the reward was wasted on a mere boy, remarked to Orpheus: "Ah! See how to the beautiful all things come so easily."

The Argonauts gathered firewood, stripped grass and rushes for bedding, and prepared their dinner. Heracles, sitting with Telamon, and eager to eat one of the roasting sheep purchased from the peaceable Mysians, who were a kind of Lydian, but spoke a unique and unknown language, clamored for Hylas to share his wine with him, with the admonition never to forget to mix in plenty of water, and to drink no more than three cups at a sitting, lest he transgress moderation. Hylas dutifully went about looking for fresh water; but the common store had been mostly depleted during the demanding rowing contest, and the rest went into a bubbling pot to cook oysters dug up from the shallows.

"Go fetch us more water from some cold spring, dear boy," said Heracles. "Meanwhile, while some light remains, and my supper still turns on the spit, I shall enter that wooded mountainside yonder to cut myself a new oar."

After finding a bronze pitcher, Hylas ran after Heracles, catching up with him as they entered the wood. Together they followed a well-worn path along the riverbank until the sound of rushing water compelled Hylas to go in another direction. While seeking a suitable pine-tree, Heracles chanced on a grove of ash-trees, which offer an even harder, but still pliant wood. When he found a tree, tall, straight and slender like a poplar, and free from burrs, he laid his lionskin aside and with the bronze tip of his club burrowed around the roots to loosen them. Then, wrapping his arms around the trunk, and pressing against it with his broad shoulders while keeping his feet wide apart for leverage, he jerked and thrust until the tree swayed. Summoning his prodigious store of strength, Heracles wrestled with the tree until the evening gloom set in, at last ripping it up, roots and all, spreading clods of earth, as when a sudden squall lashes a ship's mast, tearing it from the mast-crutch and snapping off the stays. He tied the tree in the lionskin and started back to camp, cursing his stomach for hunger, and dragging the load behind him.

Meanwhile, at the campsite, Telamon and Pelias were already slicing the sizzling sheep loins and heaping the meat onto waiting trenchers. As the night came on quickly, Polyphemos grew worried for his son, who had not yet returned. He kindled a torch and set off into the forest to search for Hylas.

Hylas, following the sound of the rushing water, arrived at a misty hollow deep in shade. He thought he heard also girlish chatter and laughter, but these noises ceased as soon as he came to the purling spring of Pegai, bubbling from a rock, around which grew dense bunch-grass, scarlet milkweed and green maidenhair ferns. As he knelt by the water's edge to dip his ewer, before him rose from the shimmering liquid surface a head of short, dark hair dappled with white water-lilies, and the slender face of a maiden as fresh as spring, and a long and graceful neck, and bare sloping shoulders, and tender breasts washed by the eddying spring. The naiad Dryope had been dancing with the other nymphs that haunted that lovely place, those guardians of the woods and mountain-peaks and the grassy dells, when the sound of the approaching Hylas startled them. They each fled away except Dryope, who hiding in the spring, was smitten by Hylas' sweet look in the waning light.

Dryope, driven by that desperation born of love, longing to kiss the boy's fair lips, and wishing utterly to possess him forever, reached out her dewy arms to clasp his neck. Only a brief cry was allowed to Hylas before he was pulled headlong into the black water, as when a falling star dips into the sea

Polyphemos, nearby, heard the cry. He drew his sword and ran around shouting for Hylas, thrusting forth his torch to dispel the gathering darkness at his feet. When at the fountain of Pegai he saw the bronze pitcher left crudely by the water's edge, he groaned with a heavy heart, fearing that Hylas had fallen victim to bandits or wild animals. Yet a father's hope could not be extinguished, and so he continued searching and calling out "Hylas!" until his voice grew hoarse. On the path along the riverbank he encountered Heracles dragging back the tree for his new oar. Distressed and out of breath, he fell upon the big man's arm, unable to muster his tongue for speech. "What is it, Polyphemos," Heracles asked him. "What terrible grief has gotten ahold of you?" In response, Polyphemos sobbed: "It is Hylas! Hylas has not returned. I found his pitcher by a spring, but no other sign of him. Alack-a-day! Wild beasts have borne him off to feast on him in their dens; or else roving bandits have seized him for sport or ransom. O! My boy—the son of my old age—to where have you gone?"

On hearing this, Heracles grew pale and sweat fell like rain drops from his brow. He grasped Polyphemos by both shoulders and lifted him from the ground, saying: "Gods beneath us! Are you certain of this?"

"I heard his cry—his final cry," lamented Polyphemos.

A sudden panic seized Heracles so that he felt the very air thicken in his nostrils. This feeling soon gave way to curdling rage as he imagined Hylas helplessly borne away.

"Hera!" he cried, raising his eyes to the tree tops. "Let your implacable enmity fall on me—only on me; and leave my friends be!"

Leaving Polyphemos and the felled tree, Heracles ran wildly into the deep shades of the forest, crying out "Hylas!" repeatedly. Only faint echoes responded. Blaming himself for the disastrous outcome of Hylas' foray for water, Heracles wandered in frenzy wherever his feet took him: raging and bellowing like a bull, stung by a gadfly, that rushes off from the herd, leaving behind the meadow where it grazed to plough blindly through the thickets. All night he searched the pathless woodland; as did Polyphemos, driven by despair.

When the morning star crowned the forbidding mountain-peaks, Tiphys awoke and hastened to the *Argo*. A good river breeze blew. Rousing Jason, he suggested that they take advantage of the wind. One by one the others woke. Telamon was the first to notice Heracles still gone.

"Hylas is also missing, as is Polyphemos," observed Philias of Araithyrea, binding his long hair into a braid.

"That lad is pleasant enough for sure," said Idas; "but we can do without him."

Pelias lit a fire, from which he, Telamon, Acastos, Meleager, Nestor and Atalanta fired torches. As a group they went inland, calling out for their missing shipmates. While they were gone,

Jason nervously paced around the camp, looking from the sea to the dark, wooded slopes. For a moment the comforting image of Heracles passing with his heavy stride, his quiver bouncing on his back, intruded into his clouded thoughts. He looked at the others huddled in their blankets breakfasting, and missed the big man's presence, feasting along with his comrades, tickling their ears with strange tales and their hearts with hope.

"The breeze sharpens, sir," called Tiphys from the foredeck. "I see clouds blowing from the south. If we leave now, we should have a fair wind at our backs after we leave the gulf. Further delay will cost us."

Jason said nothing, although Tiphys echoed his unfortunate thoughts. He waited until dawn and the return of the search party before he called the crew together.

"It could be that fate has taken the best man we have," he said. "Or it could be that in a moment we will presently hear a good word of him—of this I still hope. Give me your opinions. Do we set sail while the wind holds, or do we wait?"

The shipmates began to discuss the matter. This soon turned into a loud and bitter quarrel as they were split evenly in their support of each option.

Idas stepped forward and said: "Why shouldn't we put forth at once? Are not Polyphemos' best days behind him? He is good for nothing. That means we lack only one man of any value. But are we not all of noble blood? We are certainly stronger, when all acting in concert, than Heracles."

"But he is the best of all of us," said Admetos. "What other crew in all the world could boast of having a son of Zeus among them?"

"Bah!" said Meleager darkly. "Do not Castor and Polydeuces have the same divine sire?"

Lynceus laughed and said: "Sons of Zeus! A temple prostitute bore those two, and their father was some ill-kempt barkeep."

The raging speech of Telamon prevented a terrible fracas between the sons of Boreas and the sons of Aphareus.

"For shame!" he chided. "You are all scoundrels for dismissing Heracles so easily. You were not so flippant when he saved the ship from the Bear Men, were you? How then could you talk of leaving him behind?  Is not he one of us, a part of our noble band?  It is just not for his sake I complain: I wouldn't leave any of you behind either.  As the gods are my witness, we have not even begun our journey!  Savage lands and barbarous tribes still block our path, and we have no other Heracles among us, nor one with so valiant a heart."

Meleager stepped forward and said: "Heracles has gone missing all night.  What makes you think, Telamon, that he will now appear?  Do we wait another day, or until the moon conjoins its horns?  We could have been hard by the Bosporos by now had we left when Tiphys suggested.  Have you all forgotten your families back home that you have now all the time in the world to tarry here?  As for me, I'd rather wait for Heracles back in Calydon, in the comfort of my father's house.  Do not forget that Hera hounds him, and we took on the burden of her enmity when he joined our crew.  Why, she probably sent some new monster to occupy him.  I too have pledged myself to Jason, to fight and spill my blood against any foe.  So have Castor and Polydeuces—and we're all still here."

"What of it?" said Admetos.  "Heracles has not abandoned us willingly."

"Has he not?" retorted Meleager.  "He's a strange fellow, prone to dark moods and madness.  Perhaps his glory has gone to his head so that he no longer holds our common effort in any esteem, preferring instead to go at it alone.  Is that not the way we have seen him conduct himself?  What sane man would want to row an entire ship by himself?  I say here: have courage, and let us move on while we yet have the strength.  We'll have enough to worry about when we reach Colchis."

"Stop prattling," warned Cepheus.  "You are jealous of Heracles, as would be any man."

"What are you saying?" said Meleager.  "While you still lounged in your bed, I was out looking for him out of love and friendship, hoping against hope.  Even now I look continually yonder, hoping to see him descending the mountain-side.  Alas, friends, we have given overmuch to friendship, and have shed enough tears for one man.  Accept that some hazard or other has taken him from us and be done with it."

The shipmates fell silent as the moment of decision neared.

Jason sat on the ground, his head in his hands, his heart gnawed by irresolution.

"Meleager speaks the truth," said Calais finally. "Let us unmoor the hawsers and depart at once."

"By heaven—what a day this is for the Greeks!" exclaimed Telamon, ripping his shirt. "The savage Colchians would be proud to see us now. I do not remember, when we first embarked, hearing such mad boasts as I do now—that we are all somehow his equals!—when you all wanted Heracles as your leader. Where is your loyalty now? Yes, shed tears—and more tears! Will Meleager take his place now, or you, Calais? Lambs against a lion! I swear by the gods that the day will come when you, Jason, will face some danger, and will in vain call out for the strength of the very man you now despise and plan to abandon, and all this present boasting will count as nothing."

"Do not endanger us with such an ill-omened talk," said Tiphys. "Jason is our captain, and you must respect whatever he decides."

Telamon glared at Tiphys, and then looked down with gritted teeth at Jason, who was still seated on the ground. He said: "Sit there, will you. It is all plain to me now that it was your plan all along to abandon Heracles, that his glory may not overshadow yours should we ever make it home." Pointing a finger at Tiphys, he said: "Enough words! I shall go after him alone, without any of these friends who assisted you in this treachery."

Telamon, his eyes sparkling with fiery tears, charged at Tiphys. Zetes jumped in front of him and pushed him back into the arms of Calais, who in turn cast him to the ground.

"Stay here, then" said Zetes to Telamon. "Jason by his silence has spoken his decision. Come, Calais, let us take our seats on the ship."

One by one the Argonauts followed the mighty sons of Boreas. Peleus knelt by his brother, who remained where he lay weeping and fouling his head with dust. Jason, likewise filled with grief, rose, drying his eyes with his mantle. Just then Idmon, with Orpheus trailing, came running toward them, proclaiming between breaths: "The gods of the sea have spoken, noble comrades. Just now an old sea lion, encrusted with barnacles and sick unto death, washed up on shore. In its death throes it barked: 'Why do you seek to take Heracles to Aia against the will of Zeus?  His destiny is to complete at Argos all the labors of cruel Eurystheus, under strain of great suffering.  Think no more of him.  Polyphemos is destined to found a great city here at the mouth of the Cios, and his days to end among a savage people.  As for Hylas, a water-nymph has made him her husband.' Is that not so, Orpheus?  You too know the speech of beasts."

Orpheus nodded in agreement.  As he was the most trustworthy of all the Argonauts, Telamon could no longer contend against the general consensus and was forced to swallow his bitterness.  He took hold of Jason's hand and said: "Be not angry with me if in my foolishness I have sinned.  It was grief that prompted arrogant words that should never have been said.  Let the wind take away my fault and leave us friends again."

Jason lifted him up and said: "Your words, good friend, did indeed cut me when you accused me, in front of all the men, of having wronged that noble hero.  Since it was not for flocks of sheep or worldly goods, but for the cause of a comrade, that you raged, I shall not nurse a bitter wrath.  I hope you will do like for me, should a similar situation befall me."

With these words, the men embraced and returned to the *Argo* conciliated.  After the shipmates settled in their places, they were so moved by the sight of Heracles' empty seat, and their hearts so filled with melancholy, that one called "Heracles!" and another "Hylas!" as the ship pulled away from the Mysian shore.

7

Heracles searched the entire valley of the Cios, as far as the shore of the Ascanian lake and back, until the sun once more surrendered to the gloom, the breeze that stirred the tree-branches stilled, and the stars flickered like tinsel across the sky. He entered all the settlements and cities of the Mysians he came across, threatening to lay them waste, unless the people delivered Hylas, whom he assumed they had kidnapped, or else provided him news of his whereabouts. As no one had the slightest idea what he was talking about, they vehemently denied any wrongdoing and promised to look diligently for him so as to appease him; and as a pledge of faith they offered him their best sons as hostages. To this day, the inhabitants of this district conduct a ritual search for Hylas and offer sacrifices by the spring of Pegai, where the priest call aloud for him three times.

Like a lioness that has lost her cub, her wilting mane brushing the ground as she roams about in grief, Heracles knew not where else to look for the missing youth. He sank down at last, overwearied, pondering what type of report he would deliver to his sister Laonome, since even Polyphemos pledged, the last time they crossed paths that he would not return home without his son. In a troubled sleep he saw the form of Hylas bedecked with saffron weeds rise from a pool, telling him not to grieve, since he now lived happily with the sprites of the woodland. Heracles reached out his arms in vain to embrace the vision, but it vanished into mist. He awoke in renewed misery, since no hope at all remained to console him.

Remembering his shipmates, Heracles returned in haste to the shore. There he found only the Mysian hostages waiting for him; and of the campsite only charred firewood and animal bones. He was too troubled at first to say anything. When the young

Mysians reported seeing a ship the previous morning sailing far off to the westing, Heracles terrified them by stomping up and down the shore for an hour cursing Jason for his treachery.

After he had eaten, and his mind grew composed in proportion to the satiety of his stomach, he announced that he would set out for Colchis on foot to intercept the Argonauts. The Mysians groaned inwardly but dared say nothing, and so followed him for two days through mountainous country as far as the gulf of Astacos, where the Bithynians, remembering their defeat at his hands when he fought them on behalf of king Lycos of the Mariandynians, offered him whatever he wished as long as he left their district. Thinking at length on the matter, Heracles concluded it a fool's errand to attempt Colchis with a band of youths unaccustomed to hard marches in tow; he would do better to return to Iolcos and wait. He reckoned that it would still take many moons for the Argonauts to return, assuming they were not subject to unforeseen distractions or disasters along the way. Deciding that he could squeeze in his next Labor during the intermission, and still have enough time to catch up with them back at Iolcos, Heracles hired a ship to transport him and the Mysians back to Greece.

The *Argo* sailed on all day and night, propelled by a strong tail wind. None felt the pull of sleep, their minds still reeling from the loss of Heracles. Orpheus soothed them with the dulcet strains of his poesy until the Dawn chased away the stars, when a dead calm embayed them. Seeing a wide beach ahead, they pulled hard and made landfall against a lovely sunrise. After running the ship ashore, Jason sent a group to explore the land. In an embowered hollow, where a clear spring sated their thirst, Echion encountered a weeping youth, who looked up startled at his wide Arcadian hat. "Run for your lives!" cried the young man. As he was too shaken to divulge much more, they took him back to the camp; and after getting something to eat, the youth, named Dymas, informed them thus: "You have come to the Bebrycian shore: a terrible place where the sacred rights of guest-friendship are spat upon. Cruel king Amycos rules here, a self-styled son of Poseidon. He hates strangers—sailors most of all—so much that he challenges you to a boxing match, and then you invariably end up with your brains splattered. Hie to your good ship while there is still time! There's nothing here worth your lives."

Jason asked him: "And are you a Bebrycian, or a traitor to your lord that you tell us these things? Or a stranger, like us, looking for some hospitality? And how came you to escape this outrageous challenge you describe?"

Dymas quickly answered: "I stopped hither with Otreos, brother to king Lycos of the Mariandynians, on our way to Ilion, where my dear companion aimed to bring back a Phrygian bride, perhaps Hesione herself. We thought it safe, since the noble Heracles—you may have heard of him—had lately killed king Mygdon and subdued these savages. But his brother Amycos came forth and challenged Otreos, who, no sooner than I laced up his gloves, was clobbered so badly that his eyes nearly popped out of his head. Amycos dismissed me, unworthy of a hero's death, and left me here to die of grief. I could have returned home, but for what? To have my king come and avenge another brother's death? Gods forbid I endanger him or any more of my countrymen by luring them to this accursed place."

The crew listened listlessly, some doubting his words. Dymas therefore beckoned them to follow him to see for themselves the results of Amycos' deadly trials. He took them down the beach to a large cave under a beetling cliff, where no sunbeams danced on the sand, and the breakers sent up eerie echoes. Among the rocks thrashed limbs and other human detritus, solitary arms and hands still bound in sparring gloves, bones picked clean, and piles of skulls, some shattered beyond recognition. The Argonauts felt their hearts gripped by icy fear.

From the woods above, the ruthless Amycos saw them while herding his cattle, and in a huff raced down with his companions to the beach, where he encountered the crewmen as they returned to the ship. Without bothering to inquire who they were or why they had come, he blurted: "Listen up, you scallywags! I care not whether folly or madness dumped you on my shore; but here I have a law that foreigners must first contend with me before they're allowed to sail off. Who among your sorry lot will it be? Who will compete for entry into Hell—a prize all men win eventually? Choose now, or I'll choose for you. There's no escape from me."

The men now shook with anger at this wanton display of arrogance. The sons of Aiacos stepped forward, as did Meleager, his fists clenched, and Periclymenos and Idas. Courage stirred in Jason too, ready to take up the challenge. But Polydeuces burned the most, and removing his fine Lemnian mantle, replied: "Hold off your threats! We'll follow these rules of yours. I'll gladly take up your gauntlet." His brother Castor looked at him with misgiving, for though he knew his brother was a superlative pugilist, the present bout would be far from a gentlemanly Spartan competition. Amycos looked at Polydeuces with disdain, and laughed at his slight form, saying: "Step up, then, whoever you are. I'm ready to rearrange that handsome face until even your own mother won't recognize it. And these you call your friends, who'll let you die here at my hands?" Castor, taking affront, warned him to avoid mockery. But Amycos, leering at his opponent, paid him no one heed as he ripped off his thick cloak, not bothering to unpin it. They moved to a suitable spot, where the two groups sat down in the sand, leaving a space for the bout between them. While Polydeuces sparred against the air, testing whether rowing had made his hands less limber, Amycos stood still in silence, eyeing his prey. Compared to the son of Tyndareos, he was a beast, weighed down with scarred, knotty arms and flashing a breast as vaunted as a bull's. Hearts among the Argonauts sagged as they considered the worst.

A squire of Amycos threw down at their feet bull's-hide gloves, dry and toughened. Amycos said: "Pick the pair you like; you won't be able to blame me after losing. But tie your hands quickly: you'll find out soon enough with whom you're dealing." Castor bound his brother's hands in the stiff knuckle straps, while the friends of Amycos did the same for him. They then stepped into the ring, their weighted hands in front of their faces. Amycos betrayed his ponderous size with a swift attack, raining blows down on Polydeuces, who did his best to dodge and weave to avoid the deadly strokes. The Bebrycian king flailed like a sea-squall against a ship; and Polydeuces, like a master steersman, kept himself steady and unscathed against the relentless storm. Savage, wasteful swings were answered with feints and testing jabs, so that Polydeuces soon learned Amycos' artless style and uncovered his weaknesses. When he heard the heavy breathing and saw the sweat dropping from Amycos' brow, Polydeuces unleashed his prodigious skills, landing continuous blows on head and body. Amycos had to draw a little apart to catch his breath, astonished, as were his friends, that for the first time someone appeared to best him. Bellowing, Amycos renewed his attack, casting punches that hit nothing but air. Polydeuces, filled now with hope, danced like a butterfly, letting Amycos swing wildly with a left, only to sting him with a right cross; or ducking under a right hook, and then vaulting from underneath with an upper-cut. Blind rage, and the cheers of the Argonauts for their comrade, shattered Amycos' concentration. Exhausted, he could do nothing else but assail Polydeuces blindly, pressing with his heaving bulk, which the younger and lighter opponent turned to his advantage, feinting, retreating, but never failing to score a punch. In a desperate move, Amycos drew up on tiptoe, stretching like a man about to fell an ox, and dropped his heavy fist. Polydeuces nimbly stepped aside, receiving only a glancing blow down his shoulder, and finding Amycos open, closed in with blow after blow, each one snapping back his opponent's head. Amycos staggered off, his legs feeling numb, his eyes clouded with blood. Polydeuces followed him with a hard right, and then a hard left against the temple, which shattered the pompous ruler's skull and toppled him hard like a falling stone. Standing over him, Polydeuces cried: "Announce to the shades of Hell that it was Polydeuces of Amyclai, son of Zeus, who sent you there."

The Bebrycians sat stunned only a moment before rallying around the corpse of their dead king, readying their cudgels and light spears. Gnashing their teeth, they charged at Polydeuces, but his friends, armed and ready, encircled him. The two groups clashed in deadly battle; but the Argonauts, dominating the melee, sent the Bebrycians fleeing into the woods and mountains, carrying with them news of their king's demise, like shepherds who smoke out bees from their rocky hive. When Lycos heard it, he unleashed his Mariandynian troops to plunder the rich farmyards of Bebrycia.

The Argonauts, after rustling Amycos' sheep, bathed in the sea to remove the stains of death. Once they had satisfied heaven with sacrifices, they spread out leaves and rested on them as they dined, toasting Polydeuces and leaving for him the choicest morsels. But a few expressed still their disappointment at Heracles' absence, reasoning that the hero would have forewent the boxing match by putting a quick end to Amycos with his club.

All that night on the beach they camped, decked with laurel from a solitary tree to which the ship was lashed, tending to their wounds, continuing their thanksgiving offerings, and singing to Orpheus' sweet notes. When the sun crowned the dewy hills, and a following wind persisted, they loaded the ship with as much sheep as it could carry, untied the hawsers, and sailed out of the deep bay. With the wind on the beam, they brailed the sail tight to the yard-arm and by oars plunged into the narrow mouth of the Bosporos. They had not made it far against the onrushing current when sharp gales down blew from Thrace, whipping the already turbulent waters of the narrows, and raising towering rollers that would have wrecked the ship had not Tiphys skillfully maneuvered her from one shore to the next, bearing down and running her through counter-currents to speed her progress. All day they struggled up the strait, until, at the urging of the sons of Boreas, they moored the *Argo* at the Thynian shore, the last safe haven before the dreaded entrance to the Axine Sea. Their brother-in-law, king Phineus, ruled the savage Thynians from Salmydessos on the inner coast, a notorious wrecking place for ships on account of the wind-swept shoals; a thing which the Thynians took to their advantage, marking the shore with posts and claiming the right to plunder any vessel that floundered there. But they assured Jason he would experience no trouble.

Calais and Zetes, however, had not seen their relative for many years, and did not know that he had suffered not only exile, but a more terrible and miserable punishment from the gods. Living in a house close to the shore, Phineus rose from his bed when he heard the visitors approach, sensing by his prophetic powers that his deliverers had arrived. Blind, emaciated, his thread-bare skin caked with grime, he struggled from his bed and with his walking-stick tapped his way to the door. Reaching the courtyard, his knees gave way and he collapsed in a swoon. The Argonauts, entering, stood around marveling at the old wretch. Jason propped him against a wall, hoping to learn his identity, for not even the sons of Boreas recognized him. At length, Phineus, with labored breath, said: "Hail to you, Greeks, if that you are—and these vatic thoughts never deceive me. I once ruled this part of Thrace, from the shore to the mountains, but now live here in wretchedness and misery, an exile at the hands of my second wife, whom I brought from her father, a Scythian king, for half my flocks—a bride-price too steep to be rewarded with such callousness. I'll tell you what happened, that you may not consider your pity a waste. Happy was I once, married to the bride of my youth, who blessed me with two sons. But when she grew old and injurious to my sight, I put her away and remarried. Their step-dame, jealous of my sons, accused them of gross impropriety. Smitten by her youth and beauty, I believed her and allowed her to do as she wished. She pricked their eyes with a shuttle and imprisoned them. For this sin, I was laden with accursed gifts. Apollo burdened me with augury. Zeus offered me the choice between death and blindness. I chose the latter, and when I, in my distress, swore off the light of the sun, Hyperion sent those wretched Harpies to torment me. From some detestable abyss they rise whenever I sit to eat whatever morsels the peasants bring me in exchange for my oracles, swooping down and snatching the food from my lips, and befouling the rest with their excrement. Pity a poor, broken man: do not sail on and leave me, Phineus, the son of Agenor, once famed for riches, here a prisoner of awful Fortune."

The crewmen stood abashed at this report; but none more than Calais and Zetes, who were moved to tears. Zetes took the elder's hand and said: "Poor man! Is it truly you, Phineus, husband to our sister Cleopatra? Whereto your glory? We shall deliver you, if you swear such aid does not subvert Heaven's will."

Phineus raised his lightless eyes as if he could see Zetes' face, and said: "It is true that Heaven does not mete out more than man can bear, for with my punishment came the hope that the sons of the North Wind, and not some unknown foreigners, would someday return to deliver me. Fear not! May Hell consume me if I cause you to lose the gods' favor."

The brothers, emboldened by the oath, prepared a feast for the old man from the ship's victuals. While Jason and some others hid in the event greater assistance was needed, Zetes and Calais, with swords drawn, led Phineus to the table. As Phineus, with trembling hands, dipped his bread and put it to his lips, loud screeches rattled everyone's expectant nerves. The sky suddenly darkened, and in a black whirlwind down swooped dozens of gryphon-vultures.  In moments, harrying Phineus and beating him with their wings, they swiped away every bit of food.  The sons of Boreas swung their swords to scare them off, but the birds retorted by vomiting forth the putrid contents of their gizzards.  When they had, with mocking cries, flown off, Calais tried to disclose to Phineus the true identity of his tormentors, but he suffered such agitation that he failed to heed him.  Zetes, knowing the ways of birds, took with him some of the younger Argonauts to seek out the birds' nesting place, which they found in an abandoned turret of the house.  After scattering them and boarding the windows to prevent their return, Zetes joined his brother, and between them devised to put the mind of Phineus at ease.  They said to him: "These Harpies will be a nuisance no more.  They flew off fast, and we followed them closely—for we are equipped with wings on our shoulders—so that our finger-tips nearly touched their tail feathers.  We nearly overtook them by the Floating Isles had not Iris, the messenger of the gods, flown down and warned us to desist from harming the hounds of Zeus.  She then swore that inviolable oath only the gods can make that they would never again violate your house.  Iris returned to Olympos, the Harpies to their lair in Crete, and we outstripped the wind back here to Thrace."

Phineus, in gratitude for the happy outcome, raised his arms and prayed long while the Argonauts washed off his filth and prepared another feast, this time for all, sacrificing the sheep stolen from Amycos.  Calais and Zetes, after searching the rest of the house, found their nephews locked up in a vault, where a minion of Idaea, Phineus' second wife, would come at intervals to alternatively feed and beat them with a whip, so as to prolong their suffering.  The reunion of father and sons, who in their common blindness groped for one another, moved the assembly to tears.  When Phineus was set at the table before heaps of meat and redolent wine, he first quenched his thirst with pure, cold water, and then he dove into the banquet with relish, as a happy as a man caught in a delicious dream.  Jason, enjoying the sight of a man relieved of his suffering, and enjoying finally some peace, said to him: "August sir, now that your prayers have been answered, I ask that you answer mine.  With your far-sight inform us what perils we yet face in our voyage.  Thus far Heaven has smiled on our venture, but the sea is wide and there still remain long distances before us.  Although

Athena herself lent a hand in creating our vessel, and I feel Hera is on our side, I am as yet uneasy of mind. Tell us what lies ahead. Though I have among my crew two excellent seers, none may be so highly esteemed in prophetic gifts as you."

Phineus called for his mantle and asked for his head to be crowned with a laurel wreath. Conveyed to the hall, he sat among them. The pallor of old age left him, and his limbs were once again suffused with vigor. Within the circle of solemn hearth-light, he spoke: "Hear now what fate has in store for you. Such disclosures are the least I can offer for the inestimable service you have paid me. Though—gods forbid!—I cannot tell you everything that is to pass, I will reveal what I am able: Zeus himself wishes to keep men, when seeking oracles, partly in ignorance. From this place your path leads northward to the mouth of the sea and the two dark-blue rocks, towering cliffs that, displaced from the sea-bed, rush at intervals into one another with a violent crash heard and felt all along this coast, unleashing a sheer torrent down the strait. No ship, as far as I know has ever survived a passage between them. What you must do is to wait until the rocks stand farthest apart, and in that delay, let fly a dove. If she succeeds in flying between the rocks, then waste no further time and bend to your oars. The strength of your arms will be your salvation then, not your prayers. Prayer is by all means efficacious, but not at the moment when you must act. But if she turns back midway, do so likewise, or you will come to a miserable end."

At this point in Phineus' counsel, Telamon, shifting on his seat, sought to interject that he, with Heracles, had once passed that way on route to the land of the Amazons; and that they had found the idea of the clashing rocks a mere fable, since the only danger lay in a spur of rock between them, hidden at high tide, which could demolish a ship's keel if not avoided. But he kept silent after a hard look from Jason, who was loath to interrupt Phineus' revelations.

Phineus continued, detailing the lands and peoples the Argonauts would encounter thereafter, sprinkling his discourse with dire warnings that left the crew dismayed. "And when you have reached the river Phasis, which rises in the Amarantian mountains, drive your ship into the fens at its mouth. You will see the walls of Aia, king Aiëtes city, and the dark grove of Ares where he keeps the Fleece pendant from an oak-tree, guarded by a sleepless serpent."

After a long silence, Jason spoke: "You have in great detail carried us, through many hazards, to our destination. What I wish to learn now is whether we shall return safely to Greece? I have no great experience at sea, and even the most seasoned sailors among us have never reached the bounds of the world."

"Child," said Phineus, "once passed the clashing rocks, rid yourself of fear: some god will guide you back from Aia by a different route. Only know that you have no better friend than the goddess Aphrodite. On her depends the success of your journey. Now, question me no more."

## 8

After passing out of the Hellespont, they took a southerly route on account of the prevailing Thracian wind, stopping at the islands of Tenedos, Lesbos—where Heracles spent some time tasting the excellent wines—and then Chios, where beyond the rocky shore of Ariusia, vineyards produce undoubtedly the best wine of all Greece, blameless and painless. As with its wine, the beauty of the women of Chios is celebrated throughout the world. They sailed as far south as Leros, from where in a whole night and day they crossed the sea, arriving at fertile Naxos. There the natives introduced Heracles to laudanum, collected from the beards of goats where it clings during their foraging. The Naxians burned this as incense; but the clever Mysians mixed the substance with a little wine to produce a potent tincture that made Heracles sleep for days without any dreams. Though immensely pleasurable, upon awaking he vowed never to try it again.

From island to island they travelled until contrary winds wrecked the ship off the promontory of Caphareos in Euboea. From there Heracles led the Mysians to Chalcis, where by a wooden bridge they crossed into Boetia over a narrow strait of turbulent tides divided into two channels by a rock. They took then the road to Thebes where Heracles wished to see his mother and sister, and hoped to find Iolaos, whom he missed terribly, especially after the loss of Hylas. Laonome took the news with quiet composure, but then retired to her room to fill her pillow with laments. Iolaos, Alcmene told Heracles, had gone to pay a visit to king Ceyx of Trachis on the occasion of his wedding. There was evidently a related matter that upset her greatly, but she would not speak of it. Heracles set out the next day, returning to the harbor of Aulis to find a ship bound for Epicnemidian Locris in the Maliac gulf. With the Mysians he debarked and took the narrow pass of Pylai to the mouth of the Asopos, which he followed to the city of Trachis, situated on a plain at the foot of Mount Oeta near which the Asopos discharged from a mountain gorge.

The banquet was being prepared when Heracles pushed open the manor doors to stand insolently on the threshold surrounded by the Mysians, lightning flashing at his back. All the guests were abashed at the shadowy sight of the uninvited guest draped with a lion's skin, equipped with a ferocious club, great curved bow and rattling quiver. Even horse-driving Ceyx, reclining by his lovely-tressed wife Alcyone, did not know what to make of it. Heracles stepped out of the night into the light of the braziers, thumped his chest to salute Ceyx, and bellowed:

"The brave come uninvited to the banquets of the good!"

Ceyx, recognizing his relation, stood upright from his couch and welcomed Heracles, ordering his slaves to quickly arrange settings for the new arrivals. Heracles told him not to bother with the Mysians, and dismissed them to seek scraps from the larder mistress. Iolaos he embraced with great passion, squeezing his head between his broad hands and covering his nephew's face and neck with kisses.

Heracles admiringly heaped praise on Alcyone, who sat apart with her maids on a couch raised by ivory steps, beginning with her feet, which were as white and delicate as Parian marble. On her head she wore a new bride's towered crown, and her gaze was shielded by a yellow veil. As Heracles poured out a libation for their happiness, Ceyx remarked that he could not wait until the customary month, sacred to Hera, to marry Alcyone since she was so desirable. The allusion to Hera displeased Heracles, but he forgot about it when he was served a pot of honey sprinkled with sesame seeds. Ceyx's son Hippasos, holding Heracles in high esteem, wished to hear tales of his adventures; but his sister, Themistinoe, regarded him shrewdly, and did not care to be presented to him. Both were children from a previous marriage.

After listening to a discourse on his adventure with the Argonauts, Ceyx said to Heracles: "Did you say, Alcides, that Peleus son of Aiacos went with you? I would have you know that he arrived here last winter with his retainers and flocks of sheep and cattle, begging to lay roots in my domain. I did not press him as to why he had left his father's kingdom—and neither did he tell me.

As he is of noble birth and illustrious lineage I opened my doors to him and bade him settle where he wished. At that time I was still mourning the strange fate of my brother Daedalion; and when Peleus saw the gravity of my countenance I told him the whole story. My brother, a good man, but, unlike me, eager always for war and violence, had in his youth a daughter, Chione, unsurpassed in beauty. Not one, but two gods, among her thousand suitors vied for her hand. To Apollo she bore Philammon; and to Hermes, crafty Autolycos—was not he one of your teachers? You would think that, having found favor with the gods, Chione would have lived long and free from calamity; but when in words she esteemed her beauty greater than that of Artemis, in that she was wooed by the two gods, the Delian virgin transfixed her boastful tongue with an arrow. Never more did she speak; and died in my arms from her bloody gash. My brother four times dared to invade the funeral pyre, and thrust back, he fled in madness like a bullock under a hornet's sting. To a scaur of Parnassos he raced, as if on winged feet, and hurled himself off. But Apollo took pity on him, and as he fell gave lift to his flapping arms. His hair became feathers; his nose and mouth a curved beak; his fingers extended into claws. His boldness and courage alone the god left him. Now as a hawk, filled with rage, he chases the doves of Thisbe. Alas—how I grieve anew at the retelling! And as I recounted this to Peleus, his herdsman rushed in, breathless with dreadful news. As they watched the cattle resting on the yellow sand of the seashore, near a temple and ancient grove sacred to the Nereids, with sudden noise and violence a great, shaggy wolf sprang from the marsh willows, mad with rage and hunger. Pouncing on the herd it consumed some of the cattle, and tore apart the rest, until the seashore and marsh glowed red with blood. Peleus, strangely enough, did not appear agitated by the loss of his herds. I felt more concern than he, and called up my men-at-arms to join me in the defense. But Alcyone—my fair Alcyone!—with strewn hair, threw herself upon my neck, begging me to send aid, but not go myself. The sight of her tears at last stirred Peleus from his lassitude. 'Fear not, O queen; I wish no one to take up arms on my behalf,' he told her. I followed him to the top of the citadel, where from a tower a fire always blazed as beacon for storm-harried ships. From there we saw the beach, strewn along its length with blood and gore, and the wolf still at its dreadful business. Peleus, stretching out his arms, prayed to a sea-nymph he called Psamathe to lay aside her wrath. It seemed at first that his orisons fell lifeless into the sea, for the wild beast continued its awful carnage. But while the wolf held the torn neck of a heifer in its maw—lo! it suddenly, stance and all, transformed into marble. Except for the stone's grey hue, you would think the wolf still continues rampaging where it stood. The next day Peleus departed without further explanation. Have you, Heracles any further word from Peleus concerning these strange events, which, added to the circumstances surrounding my brother, have left me continually perturbed?"

Heracles, not wishing to dampen the festivities with ill gossip, failed to tell him of the murder of Peleus' brother Phocos, which ignited against Peleus the wrath of Psamathe his mother. He wondered, however, why the sea-nymph was so quick to forgive him, since the scorn of women cling to men like boiling pitch.

When the time came for Alcyone to unveil and be presented to Ceyx, Heracles, jolly with wine, announced: "Nay, the groom cannot take his bride until he has solved a riddle."

"What riddle is that, Alcides?" inquired Ceyx.

"I shall say presently," said Heracles. He emptied another cup of wine and eructed sonorously. "As you know," he continued, "the primitive Pelasgians of Arcadia are of a gluttonous and bibulous sort. After a feast, one of them once said to me, 'Heracles, we will go out now to gather, and then bring home their mother's mother together with her children.'"

The guests pondered this riddle while young men danced, twirling colorful silk handkerchiefs. At last, seeing in the winnowing-baskets the nuts and dried fruits used to shower the bride and groom in the procession to the bridal chamber, Hippasos asked to answer the riddle on behalf of his father. When Ceyx gave him permission, Hippasos said: "The Pelasgians went out to gather, roast and eat acorns. The acorn is the mother of the oak, and the oak its own mother. The children are bits of wood from the oak-trees, used as tinder to roast the acorns."

A slave came forward to inform Ceyx that two men were at the door seeking admittance. Ceyx asked him if the men wore wedding-garments, to which the slave replied that they appeared to be priests from their white vestments. Ceyx would have sent them off had he not been so felicitous. The two men approached him with bowed hairless heads and said: "Hail, lord of Trachis! We are priests of Apollo Farshooter. Kindly pardon our intrusion on this most festive of days. We wish you all happiness and invite you to Delphi to receive an oracle, which will no doubt prove propitious. We are here, however, to air a grievance and seek redress, for we count on your good will and sense of justice, known throughout all lands."

Ceyx answered: "What is it, then? Can you not see I am bound for the nuptial chamber?"

"We promise to take no more time than necessary," said the priests. "There is a certain Cycnos, styling himself a son of Ares and a prince, but in reality a bloodthirsty brigand, who ranges about eastern Thessaly and Phthiotis waylaying travelers and killing them. We are most distressed, in particular, that he preys upon innocent pilgrims on their way the Delphi, who traverse the byways laden with money and gifts for our sanctuary and holy work, and afterwards offers sacrifices to Ares from his illicit gain."

"There are many princes between Thessaly and Delphi," said Ceyx, nervously looking up at the ceiling. "Why do you come to me?"

"This outrageous behavior, you may imagine, has earned the enmity of Apollo, in whose name we speak, and by whose express command we have come seeking the Tirynthian Heracles for his assistance," said the priests. " For it was revealed to us not only that this hero could be found today in your house, but also that you are a relation of Cycnos, being his father-in-law."

"Yes; yes," said Ceyx impatiently. "He is the husband of my daughter Themistinoe. Alas, a man cannot always choose his relatives. Daughter can you not put some sense into that man? I certainly have little control over him."

Themistinoe said nothing.

"Allow me to parley with him," said Heracles. "Under usual circumstances I would dispatch such a knave, but for your sake, Ceyx, I shall do my best to convince him of the error of his ways. I have that business first with the golden apples, needing go up to the river Echidoros in Emathia to be advised by some nymphs—or was it the Eridanos? My head is swimming a bit and don't recall clearly."

"Please do so," said Ceyx. He dismissed the priests with promises to end Cycnos' crimes and to dedicate a treasury at Delphi. Themistinoe stole away to instruct a trusted servant to go to Cycnos and warn him, since she loved her husband despite his depravities, and had no doubt Heracles would attempt to harm him.

Ceyx and Alcyone, filled with exceptional joy, led the torch-lit procession to the bridal chamber amidst raucous clamor and hymn-singing. Before them went a child, whose parents still lived, crowned with mistletoe and bearing a pannier redolent with baked bread. Heracles, feeling too sodden to move, merely cheered the couple and poured libations, calling upon all the gods (except Hera) to bless their union. Seeing Iolaos in the reveling crowd, he called for him and compelled him to recline with him.

"It is certainly not proper to show up at someone's wedding-banquet without a gift," said Heracles. "Will you not go out tomorrow and buy one on my behalf, as I will probably sleep for half the day: perhaps a phial of rose-oil for Alcyone or a parasol? I have no money with me—ask Iphicles for a few obols. I shall pay him back. Speaking of my brother, where is he? And why did you not both join me at Iolcos? I have just been back from sailing on the *Argo*. The scoundrels marooned me in Mysia. Blast them! They will all wish Poseidon had sent a whirlpool to swallow them up when I get my hands on them, particularly that fop Jason who, I think, had it out for me from the start."

Iolaos, leaning on his breast, said: "He is not here, uncle. I have some news that will displease you."

"Speak, boy!" said Heracles. "And no riddles, if you please."

"My father detained me on some pretext or other so I could not join you at Iolcos," said Iolaos. "Then he went to Mycenae to serve king Eurystheus."

"What?" exclaimed Heracles, crushing the goblet he held in his hand. "Was this the matter that agitated mother? Iphicles has placed himself under that sniveling toad? Did he not think I would return? He will surely grieve afterwards for this mad folly. And you, hero Iolaos, whom do you follow?"

"Good friend, I follow you, of course," said Iolaos. "See there in a corner: I have brought your uncrushed shield all the way from Thebes."

Heracles saw it glimmering under the light of a cresset. His heart warmed at the sight. He wrapped Iolaos in the crook of his arm and squeezed with great affection, mussing his hair and planting a kiss on his neck.

On the second morning, when his body and mind had emptied of the sweet wine and rich foods of the banquet, Heracles set out. Ceyx equipped him with a lissome chariot drawn by two steeds born and bred on the Thessalian plains. With Iolaos handling the red-dyed reins they crossed the long and narrow valley of the river Sperchios around the Malaic gulf and made it deep into Achean Phthiotis by nightfall, hoping to cross the lofty Othrys range before retiring. Since the pass, at the edge of the sea, was narrow and declivitous, they did not attempt it that night, leaving it for the morning. When they came to the well-watered tableland of Thessaly, whose length and breadth is the greatest in all Greece, it opened below them up like a many-colored sea. In primeval times, the mountain-bound plain witnessed the Titans vie with the Olympians, when the ringing peaks quaked with the fury and thunder of their struggle. In the distance, under a leaden sky, the jagged Pindos mountains rose in interpenetrating layers of light and shadow.

While on the road to Pherai they passed through a rock-strewn river valley where an insolent robber called Termeros jumped in front of them demanding their purses. Heracles stepped off the chariot, and standing with crossed arms, asked Termeros what he would do if refused. Whereupon Termeros, kicking back dirt with his feet and bowing his head like a young bull incited by the flapping garment of a passing rustic, charged at Heracles, as he was accustomed to do against passers-by, so that he could strike and kill them with his bare head, which was as hard as rock. Heracles waited until he was within striking distance, and then pole-axed the robber with a heavy fist, crushing his skull so that his brains issued forth from his mouth and nostrils. In this way Heracles returned to aggressors the same treatment they intended for him.

At Pherai they paid a visit to Alcestis, who was at first so affrighted to see Heracles, thinking that he came to report some ill news concerning her husband Admetos, that she fell into a swoon for many hours. Heracles grew too impatient to wait any longer for her to revive and departed; but not without leaving word that the last time he saw Admetos he seemed well; unlike himself, whom the Argonauts ill-treated despite all the good works he had performed for them.

On the third day they reached lake Nessonis, which in the spring still swelled from the overflowing of the snow-fed Peneios. They went around it, crossing a shallow channel through which its superfluous waters pour into lake Boebeis an hundred stades to the south; and, reaching the swift Peneios beyond Mount Ossa, followed its foaming, turbid waters to the mountains into the chasm of Tempe, a narrow, rocky gorge through which the Peneios reaches the sea. They waited until morning to negotiate the pass, which offered the only way into Emathia. It was necessary to take the route on foot, pulling the horses and chariot behind them along the river bank through the narrow and overgrown defile, shadowed by the vertical walls of towering cliffs and edged with aromatic bay and mastic trees. In the eddying river did Apollo purify himself after killing the Python; and afterwards a temple was built on the right bank of the river, at which Heracles stopped to rest; and there he was reminded by the priests of the god's desire for vengeance against Cycnos. Heracles astonished the priests by stating that he was no god's lapdog, and that he would follow through on the assignment when he saw fit, and in the manner he saw fit, especially given the fact that he was already presently engaged in another's employment.

They forded the Peneios at the edge of the large morass where the stream runs into the sea and rode northward along the sandy coast, reaching the river Haliacmon by late evening, where they made camp and caught some rather large fish for dinner. In the morning they rode inland to avoid the fen, thick with tall sedge and swamp-grass, along the northern edge of the Thermaic gulf. After crossing the Axios it was not long before they reached the valley of the Echidoros and the lagoon at which the stream empties. Iolaos drove the chariot up the left bank as far as where the waters spilled from a ravine in the mountains, and then back, while Heracles listened for music, or sought to catch a glimpse of nymphs dancing or bathing in the midday heat. When he failed to spy any after a time, he grew indignant at their caprice and went down to the water's edge to holler for them. Just then he heard his name carried on a gentle breeze that stirred the tall grass: not in a maiden's call, but voiced hoarsely and bitterly. With clattering hooves a chariot-team appeared upon a hillock across the stream, rising from a cloud of dust. Its rider, in full armor, jumped off, and striking the boss of his shield with his lance-haft, cried out: "Wherefore do you seek me, Heracles? Mayhap for some debt you wish me to collect? Or do you merely wish to make the acquaintance of Cycnos, son of Ares, lord of the Phthian march?" Heracles hesitated, wondering how such an unexpected meeting came about. "Neither," he responded. "It is unfortunate we meet so prematurely, since at the moment I have greater things in mind. Be that as it may, I have been informed by the priests of Apollo of your brigandage and have no other design than to advise you against continuing your impiety, in the hope that you would turn from the evil path you have trodden to the righteous one. Such a choice every man must make at some point; and, while it is unexacting to choose the broad path of pleasure and filthy lucre, it is far better to take the narrow one of toil and sacrifice, which, though arduous, leads one to an impeachable reward." Cycnus filled the valley with his laughter. "Is that what you think?" he called. "Whether you permit me or not, Heracles, it is I who shall be your instructor this day. After all, you do not look to me like very much, unless the distance between us cheats my eyes. I too ventured to Iolcos to lend my strength and prowess to Jason's merry band; but he refused me, saying I was not worthy to join the other princes, despising me before all for my outlawry. I would have pierced that boy through the heart had he not had so many doughty men at his back, such as Meleager, and Nestor, or those twin sons of Boreas. Now prepare yourself; on you I shall avenge my outraged conceit." He rode off looking for a place to cross to other bank.

Iolaos, wrapping the reins around his forearm to hold the horses taught, said: "Look at that fellow, uncle! Strong though he looks, he does not frighten the son of Iphicles, and much less the son of Zeus! He will flee before us when I stir up these fleet-footed steeds and thunder down upon him."

Heracles walked back to the chariot and stood beside it, resting his arm on the rail. "Nay, Iolaos, not this day," he said. "If we engage, I will no doubt kill him, and thereby bring dishonor on

Ceyx, whom I love. It is better we depart at once."

Iolaos said, downcast: "If for my sake you refuse the fight, consider that I am nearly twenty; and though I have never killed a man, I am none the less courageous, and hope that my skill at other times has made me worthy in your eyes."

Heracles grasped his shoulder and said: "You need not prove anything to me, dear and best loved friend. I now recall, to my chagrin, that perhaps Orpheus rightly spoke of the river Eridanos, not the Echidoros, which sets before me a far longer and more arduous assignment than I anticipated. I urge you to turn back and wait for me at Iolcos. Should the *Argo* return before me, send word for me at Tyrins, or Mycenae, where I plan to complete my Labor by delivering to Eurystheus the treasure of the Hesperides. I shall take this horse, and leave you the car."

Despite Iolaos' protestations, Heracles untied one horse from the yoke and freed it from the pole. He mounted, and saluting Iolaos, rode off to the west. Iolaos, seeing Cycnos crossing the river, hastily turned around and hurried down the road he had taken there.

When Cycnos saw Heracles racing off, he tried to give chase, but gave up with fierce imprecations, as he could not close the distance.

9

Heracles rode hard to escape the wrathful Cycnos, as far that day as the town of Celestrum, situated on a peninsula extending into a lake, and which could only be accessed by a narrow isthmus as a safeguard from the surrounding savage tribes. He found there food and lodging for the night, and in the morning set out for Illyria, hoping to follow a similar course as when he returned with the cattle of Geryones. Not far from Celestrum he located the only break through the central range of the Pindos Mountains, a narrow defile through which flowed the river Eordaicos. He turned northward on reaching the rugged coast, ascending to the sea-facing heights at night to avoid the tattooed natives in the low valleys, where at dusk a foul haze descended and mingled with the stench of their human sacrifices. At the outset, Heracles could cover as much as five hundred stades per day over uneven ground; but of this pace his horse tired, needing more and more rest between the long rides. He reached Istria by the next new moon, where he considered taking passage on a ship across the gulf against the advice of the locals, who described the level tract at the head of the Cronian Sea as presently flooded by numerous streams swollen by the melting Rhipaian snows. Nevertheless, Heracles took that course, hindered at first only by a belt of shallow marshes as he left Istria. But as he proceeded westward he was confronted with violent streams and extensive lagoons. He rode slowly across the sandbars, taking circuitous routes, and then down the western coast of the Cronian Sea until he reached the vast delta covering the many mouths of the Eridanos, called Bodencus by the Ligurians, which signifies bottomless. Heracles crossed the wetland, stopping at villages of houses built on piles on the marshy banks to inquire about the nymphs of the place. Everyone he consulted had an opinion on them, pointing him this way and that.

The consensus seemed to settle on certain islets at the largest of the mouths, where amber in great quantities was said to exist, washed down the river from where the sisters of Phaëthon shed tears over his untimely death. Upon investigating, Heracles found only river-mouth lagoons where the islands were said to be located, and discovered them rich not with amber, but with guinea-fowl.

He rode inland long into the night, following the river-bank up the fertile valley. He grew dispirited. At a bend in the river where it meandered through low hills, Heracles led his horse to drink, thinking of halting for the night. After quenching his thirst, he lay on the spongy grass and drifted to sleep mouthing a prayer to Athena for assistance.

A sound, like leaves stirring in the wind, startled him. As he looked about dazedly, reaching for whatever weapon lay nearest, a childish tittering surrounded him. He looked up to see the moonlit mist, hovering over the black water, disturbed, as if a large damselfly had flitted across the stream. Three maidenly forms suddenly assembled on the far bank, dressed in white garments, with skin that shone like pearl in the moonlight. Though he could not see them distinctly in the gloom, Heracles spread his arms and prayed: "Daughters of Themis—if that you be—consider how I, Heracles, seek divine assistance, as did my forbearer Perseus, when he needed certain instruments to defeat Medusa. If you know the way to the sacred orchard of Hera, that garden kept by your sisters the Hesperides, where grows a golden apple tree, do reveal it to me. I shall sacrifice to you whatsoever you desire." With voices united in melodic polyphony, they responded: "We concern ourselves only with this river, Heracles, gamboling through this pleasant vale and playing innocent tricks on those who wander these solitary paths. Such we thought to do to you, until, observing you closely as you slept, your fearsome aspect made us apprehensive. Of other things we know but little. There is, however, an ancient river-god who often leaves behind the bustle of the sea to sleep in a cave by a lake beyond those hills. If you catch old Nereus unawares, he may tell you what you wish to know. But watch out! He is wily, and slippery, and will take many shapes to scare you off." With that they faded like mist at sunrise, leaving only a sprinkling of laughter behind them.

His heart burning with purpose, Heracles tied the horse to a bush and continued on foot through the hills. As the sun rose behind him, penetrating the retreating darkness like a rising bloom, Heracles reached a tributary of the Eridanos that widened into a sedgy lake ringed with osiers and poplars. Heracles walked around it to where the water lapped a rocky hill, and there, hidden behind a thicket, he sighted a small cave. He approached lightly so as to catch its inhabitant by surprise. Separating the flags to look into the den, he saw there in the dim light a supine form. As quick as he could, he reached in to grasp a foot. With shrieks of protest, the occupant kicked vigorously to free himself; but Heracles drew him out like an eel from the mud, and gripping a wrist with his other hand, pinned him to the ground.

Nereus seemed like nothing more than an old, spindly peasant, dressed in rags, with tufts of hoary hair and beard in disarray. "Why do you attack me?" he cried. "I am but an old man passing my last days in sleep, bereft of family and friends, with nary a coin in my purse. Free my limbs, and the gods shall reward your mercy."

Heracles regarded him a moment, wondering if he had mistaken a mere man for a marine divinity; yet he held him firmly, and said: "I would be remiss to free you until I have ascertained whether you are that one called the ancient of the sea, who always speaks truth; for I seek directions to the Garden of the Hesperides."

Nereus ceased his struggle and said: "It is certain that I am he; but I respond neither to extortion nor violence, and, though I strive to be always a gentleman, shall visit you on you the dire consequences of your rash act." Thereupon Nereus spit into Heracles eyes. Heracles blinked to clear his vision, loosening a grip to wipe off the spittle. Suddenly it seemed as if Nereus' legs merged together into a scaly and coiling fishtail, which flapped desperately. Heracles returned his hand to grip the fin, feeling his fingers sinking into the moist, slippery flesh. Nereus continued writhing, and with a groan his form narrowed and lengthened and became a thick Indian python. When Heracles would not free him, the snake bit his shoulder and then burst into flames. Heracles loosened his grip in surprise, but realizing the flames left him unharmed, redoubled his effort to hold Nereus fast. The fire flared and burst like a bubble into globs of water, which, coalescing, sought to trickle away. In response, Heracles drew in great armfuls of earth to contain the spreading pool. Thwarted by this means of escape, the water hardened, transmuting into a bundle of thew and pelt. A tail grew, a great maw formed, projecting limbs resolved into broad, clawed feet and a flowing mane flowered around the head. Heracles now held a lion as large as himself, but with bestial strength supplemented by the wiles of a god. Heracles did not know if all was illusion, or if Nereus did indeed assume such terrible shapes. Without waiting to discover the truth, Heracles wrestled the lion to the ground. Unable to get behind it, he thrust a forearm under its throat, keeping at bay the snapping jaws, but exposing his back to repeated swipes from a deadly paw. Despite the pain and the blood that sputtered from his lesions, Heracles would not release the river-god. After a short time, the lion's twisting subsided until it lay still, expelling hot and heavy breath, pinned under the massy body of Heracles. At last the beastly form contracted in size, shriveling back down to half-human shape; but no longer did the god resemble a rheumy old beggar. Instead of filthy rags, a resplendent tunic covered his body down to his fins; his hair and beard, growing full, changed color from grey to black tinged with sea-green; and his face, though ancient, shone with a supernal light. Heracles, exhausted and amazed, released him and fell on his back, drawing deep breaths.

Nereus, lying beside him, said: "I have not had to struggle this much since Poseidon led the sea-gods into battle against Dionysos and his allies, and with my trident I had to strike down the oliphants along the cliffs where Ganges is worshipped, the only river in the world that dares open its mouth to the rising sun. You are no doubt Heracles, the son of Zeus, since your strength surpasses all men on earth. Because you have bested me, I shall reveal what I know of the sacred Garden. No mortal has ever set foot in it, much less seen it; and Hera is so jealous of her orchard that she has ensured ignorance of its whereabouts even among the other gods, who fear her intemperate wrath. Only the Father of gods and men possesses the temerity to reveal its location."

"I have sought an audience with my divine father all of my life," said Heracles; "but he has ever remained hidden from me. Shall I go again to Delphi, or Dodona, to hear some cryptic phrases from the mouth of a priest?"

"No priest, even under direct inspiration, is able to describe the location of the Garden," said Nereus.

"How then shall I achieve this quest?" asked Heracles desperately, watching Nereus drag himself into the lake, pulling his curling fish tail behind him.  He disappeared into the water and then came up, only his head looming.

"You must dare to petition Zeus himself at a poor and lonely shrine deep in the wilderness of Libya," said Nereus. "Dionysos, wandering long ago in the desert, was led to a solitary spring where he took comfort. In gratitude he erected there a temple to Zeus, whom the misinformed Libyans call Ammon. Only there, in the cool and the quiet, it may be possible that he may answer you."  Nereus dove.  His tail rose and fell behind him, gushing water into the air.

## 10

The Argonauts continued in discussion deep into the night, until the embers died and they surrendered to pleasant sleep, some in knots throughout the house and others by the ship. At dawn, strong north-eastern gales prevented their departure, and detained them some days more. Finally Idmon had the crew build an altar to the Twelve Gods on the beach, and after laying offerings on it, had them sit down at the oars as if ready to depart. Some thought this a futile exercise until they saw the clouds begin drifting eastward. Without further delay, they unmoored the ship and sailed off toward the narrowest part of the strait, where, at the sight of shadowy cliffs all around them, fear struck every heart. A strange hissing now reached their ears, made worse by the ceaseless thunder of the pounding surf on the rocky shores. Rounding a bend, they came in sight of the mass of dark-blue rocks, which in the swirling mist and heavy waves seemed to be moving ever so slightly toward one another. Euphemos, punctilious in following Phineus' commands, released the dove he had carried aboard with him. All watched the bird to see if it successfully passed the rocks. But the *Argo* rocked terribly, sent into spins between the sharp current and the inshore eddies. Then Telamon urged Tiphys to guide the ship toward the eastern shore, for he saw the dark spurs of the rocks awash on the port side. Jason, seeing the dove make a clean passage, exhorted his friends to row with heart, and as an example took the place of the terrified Phaleros, seizing his oar. Orpheus struck up a song to battle the sea-borne sounds and the men, filled with shame, fell in behind their captain's stroke. Midway between the passage the northeast wind began again to blow, howling down from the headland. A monstrous, arching wave rushed at them, wheeling them toward the sunken ledge. Euphemos ran up and down shouting encouragement, and the men bent their oars like bows, answering him with their own desperate cries of exertion. With a horrendous crunch, the *Argo*'s struck a rock and part of the stern ornament broke off. Tiphys with both hands held the tiller firm as the backwash rolled under the keel, propelling the ship abeam. Feeling the ship caught in the overfall, the oarsmen expended all their remaining strength to clear the channel.

Once past the narrows where waves and winds contended so uproariously, the sky brightened and the vast sea opened up in every direction. The crewmen breathed easier, overjoyed that they had made it alive, so it seemed, through Hell. Tiphys was first to speak: "All is well and safe now, comrades. We owe our lives to Athena, who I saw standing in the roiling surge, her left hand bracing against the rock and her right pushing us forward in the nick of time. The *Argo* may not be caught, so it seems. Captain, now that we have surpassed such a point of peril, I pray you have no further fear of your king's assignment. Did not Phineus tell us that from henceforth we need entertain no further worries?"

Jason, weary from his unaccustomed work at the rowing bench, answered him gently: "Tiphys, why are you comforting me? Can you not see that I have terribly erred? I should have refused Pelias this task, even if in response he had torn me limb from limb. We have hardly begun our journey, and there are still such perils ahead that fill me with dread. It may be easy for you, Tiphys, to speak so cheerfully. You concern yourself only with your own life. But as leader of this expedition, I must worry for the lot of all. I do not even know how I shall bring us safely home."

Jason hung his head and sighed. At once the crew roared with acclamation and a renewed pledge of loyalty. Having received the response he had hoped, Jason announced with a bold heart: "Friends, your courage replenishes my own! I feel now that in company with such a stalwart band I can cross Hell and back. Let us keep to Phineus' course and hope for the best."

The crew returned to their work. Soon they passed the river Rhebas and the lookout peak of Colone; and not long after the Black Cape and then the outflow of the river Phyllis, where Dipsakos, son of a river-nymph, once welcomed Phrixos with the ram. His shrine in the spreading water-meadow, came and left their view; as did the deep stream of Calpe. A day and night without wind the oarsmen labored, like sweating oxen bound to the yoke, until—as the darkness receded, but as the day's light still lay hidden—they rowed into a cove of Thynias, a tiny, barren island. Stumbling ashore, each crewmember fought sleep to watch the brilliant sunrise speckle the water. Orpheus, long without blinking at the unfolding sun, reported that he saw Apollo streaming through the air, his golden blocks billowing, on his way from Lycia to the Hyperborean land. In his left hand he held that silver bow; and a quiver dangled from his back. No one else dared look directly at the god's splendorous eyes, but bowed their heads until Orpheus spoke. "Let us dedicate this island to Apollo of the Dawn," said he to the others; "and make offerings there on the beach. If he grants us a safe return home, let us remember to burn for him the thighs of horned goats. Lord, who wast revealed to us, be gracious!"

From shingle some built an altar by the lapping shore, while others searched the island for game. Catching wild goats, they killed them, wrapped their thighs in dripping fat, and burned them as they sang and danced hymns to the Healing God. Only Idmon refrained from the worship, since he knew, being a son of Apollo, that visions of the plague-dealing god could also prove portents of evil. Afterward, renewing the oath of loyalty to one another, the Argonauts heaped stones for a shrine to noble Concord.

On the third dawn, they sailed off in the wake of a westerly wind. They soon passed the mouth of the river Sangarios, the fertile lands of the Mariandynians, the outflow of the river Lycos and the Anthemoeisian mere. At night the wind dropped, and they coasted through the dawn into a harbor of the Acherusian headland, whose sheer beetling cliffs, topped with plane-trees, overlook sea-washed reefs on which the billows ceaselessly thunder. Inland lies a wooded hollow, home of a hell-mouth shaded by rocks and trees, from which an icy vapor each morning covers the ground with sparkling rime that thaws under the noonday sun. There too the river Acheron, through a deep ravine, pours from the promontory into the sea. Within that hollow chasm they moored.

King Lycos of the Mariandynians soon received word of their arrival from Dymas, who went ahead to break the sad news of his brother's death. Lycos welcomed the slayers of his enemy Amycos, particularly Polydeuces, in great style, feasting them in his palace. Lycos well remembered Peleus and Telamon, who had accompanied Heracles, and explained to all assembled: "Friends, what a man you have lost! I remember like it was yesterday how I entertained the bold Tyrinthian as he went to the fetch the girdle of the Amazon queen, as well as when he returned on foot, at which time he helped me take vengeance for the death of my brother against the Mysians. Not only that, he subdued the Bithynians as far as the river Rhebas and the rock of Colone; and the Paphlagonians as well. Since Heracles' departure, the Bebrycians have grown bold and suffer no compunction to seize my lands by force. To them I have lost another brother. But they have paid the penalty through you. I'll now return the favor by sending my son Dascylos with you as far as the Thermodon, as I did when Heracles needed a guide along this same coastland."

At dawn, after a long and joyful banquet, Jason roused the crew and led them to the ship. Lycos and Dascylos accompanied them, bringing many gifts. But as they were enjoying each other's company one last time, the seer Idmon, son of Abas, on a walk along the reedy stream-bed, roused from its lair a white-tusked boar that had been cooling its flanks and belly in the mud. The deadly beast, the sole denizen of those marshes, charged Idmon and gashed his thigh, severing bone and sinew. Idmon fell with a cry: not even his own mantic powers could save him. His friends answered in kind and ran to aid him. Peleus cast his hunting-spear as the boar retreated into the marsh, but as it darted out again, Idas ran it through. They left the monster where it lay and took up Idmon in their arms, but he died as they reached the ship.

For three days the Argonauts lamented their comrade, thoughts of their voyage forgotten. On the fourth, joined by Lycos and his people, they held the funeral rites and erected for Idmon a barrow, which they marked with a ship's spar of wild-olive wood dotted with sprouting leaves. But then, to add their misery, the helmsman Tiphys, having spent a long time sorrowing at the grave, was struck with a sudden fit of ague and also died. After interring him beside Idmon, they lay about the shore, overborne with grief, wrapped in their cloaks, without thought for food and drink. At length Ancaios the Lelegian approached Peleus and said to him: "It cannot serve us to remain here in this foreign land, neglecting our duty. Jason chose me not only for my fighting skills, but for my maritime experience. There are perhaps others here skilled enough to serve as steersmen.  Quickly now, spread this message: urge the men to remember our task."  Peleus, infected with his confidence, called out for volunteers willing to man the helm.  But Jason, despondent with sorrow, chided him, saying: "Son of Aiacos, where are these helmsmen you seek?  They're all crushed with grief.  If we're never to reach Aiëtes' city, nor make landfall again in Greece, I foresee us trapped here by a miserable fate, growing old for nothing."  Ancaios, however, renewed his pledge; as did Erginos, Nauplios and Euphemos, all as equally qualified:  but the crew unanimously chose Ancaios, whom Poseidon begot on Astypalaia by the river Imbrasos.

On the twelfth day, at dawn, they rowed out of the mouth of the Acheron.  Shaking out their sails to a westerly breeze, they came abreast of the hills of Paphlagonia and the river Callichoros, where, it is said, Dionysos, on his return from the fabled land of the rapid Indus, held revels before a cavern wherein he passed the solemn nights.  From there they came to a barrow on the beach, and were arrested by a curious sight: a wraith, like mist, rose up to the summit and quivered there to watch the ship.  Telamon, recognizing the phantasmal four-plumed helmet with scarlet crest, declared that it was the tomb of Sthenelos, grandson of Cretan Minos, who joined Heracles against the Amazons and died from an arrow-wound.  In awe, all hands witnessed the wraith sink slowly back into the gloom.  At the bidding of Mopsos, they furled the sail and anchored there for a time to observe the obsequies and raise an altar to Apollo, Protector of Ships.  Before sailing off with a strong wind, Orpheus dedicated his spare lyre.

They passed by the Maiden's Stream, where Leto's virgin daughter cools her limbs in its lovely ripples on her way heavenward after a chase.  After speeding through the night, they doubled Cape Carambis at day's break and for a full day and night, after a drop of wind, rowed along the vast strand of Paphlagonia. They squeezed in between a small island and the prominent headland of Sinope and disembarked to pass the remaining hours of darkness.  In the morning, some men, who had seen the landing from their small settlement in the hills, came down to see who they were. Recognizing Peleus, the three sons of Deïmachos, left behind by Heracles on his return from fighting the Amazons, rushed into their midst and begged Jason to take them with him, since they could not bear to remain stranded any longer in a foreign land. The sons of Aiacos put in a good word for them, and Jason readily admitted them to the crew, glad to replenish the rowing benches' empty seats.

As soon as the northwest wind cleared the sky of clouds, they made sail and sped further down the coast into areas unknown to all, leaving behind the rich water-meadows of the rivers Halys and Iris to round the lofty headland of Amazonia. Facing a rough surge and capricious winds, they anchored in the outfall of the Thermodon to wait out the weather. Autolycos urged them to leave as soon possible for fear of the Amazons. So as soon as a north-westerly wind spun up, the crewmen hastened aboard ship and sailed on past the territory of the Tibarenoi, a people with the following curious custom: when the women are ready to bring children into the world, it is the men who cast themselves on their couches as if in labor. Beside them, beyond the sacred headland of Genetaian Zeus, where the sand is black as soot, dwell the Chalybes. These neither sow nor reap, and do not busy themselves with livestock. Instead, they rive the earth to extract her ores and ever labor in their foundries filled with flames and black smoke.

The Holy Mountain appeared on their starboard next, where stood a temple to Zeus of the Fair Winds, beyond which on the hills dwell the fat Mossynoechians in tall wooden palisades resembling towers. Their customs and laws differ the most from other people's, for they are accustomed to do publicly what others do privately, and vice-versa: they do not, for example, blush to copulate in the open with whatever women they fancy, right on the ground like animals. Their king, however, dispenses honest judgment from his high wooden house: although, if he should err, the people shut him up all day without food.

After rowing for some time, since at night the breeze had dropped, they discerned the loom of a small island out of the mist. Remembering the words of Phineus to watch for a low-lying island beyond the Holy Mount, Tiphys turned the tiller to starboard. As they neared the lonely isle, a pointed feather fell from a swooping bird and struck the shoulder of Oileus. With a cry he released his oar, and all marveled at the bronzed, feathered shaft. Eribotes, the son of Teleon, sitting next to him, quickly pulled out the deadly pinion, loosed his sword-baldric, and with it bound the wound.

Another bird darted from the island toward them; but Clytios, son of Eurytus, bent his bow and with an arrow brought down the bird hard by the ship. Seeing all this, Amphidamas said: "Comrades, we are nigh to the isle of Ares, no doubt, as you can see from his unusual birds. If, following Phineus' injunctions, we are to beach there, arrows will avail us little. Let us devise another strategy for a safe landing. Consider that not even Heracles, when he came to Arcadia, was able to drive away the birds with his bow. I saw him climb to the top of a crag and shake a bronze rattle I lent him: in that way the birds scattered screeching in terror, only to migrate here, it appears. I have an idea for a similar trick." The crewmen listened and wasted no time in following his advice. After donning their lofty helms, half sat at the thwarts while the other half locked shields and spears to form a roof over the rowers. With a great shout they made for the island, but did not see any more birds until, reaching the shore, they thunderously clashed upon their shields. Suddenly, the deadly flock rose in a mass from the foliage. Fluttering about in a panic toward the mainland, the birds discharged a shower of bronze quills that fell like hail against their protective shields.

The Argonauts remained by the beached ship bewildered, for Phineus had advised them to wait there for a good turn. After some time four men, bedraggled and practically naked, emerged from the woods. One of them said: "Whosoever you are, we beseech you, by Zeus the god of strangers, to treat us kindly and help us in our need. A storm has destroyed our miserable boat and made us shipwreck. Give us rags to cover our bodies and take us with you. Have pity, I pray, on suppliants, for Zeus watches all."

Jason, sensing the prophecies of Phineus unfolding, questioned the men at length. They were the four sons of Phrixos—Argos, Cytissoros, Phrontis and Melas—who, after their father's death, and by his final command, had undertaken to travel to Orchomenos to claim the inheritance of their grandfather Athamas. On a vessel provided by king Aiëtes, they set out from Colchis not long before. But, caught in a northerly gale that grew in force and whipped the sea, their ship foundered; and grasping a spar, they were driven to the island in the dead of night.

On hearing their tale, Jason, much amazed, said: "We will certainly take care of you, since you are my kinsmen! I am the grandson of Cretheus, brother of Athamas. We are on our way to the city of king Aiëtes."

After providing clothes for the stragglers, in a group they went, as instructed by Phineus, to find the roofless temple of Ares, bringing with them sheep. Outside the marble shrine, built by the Amazon queens Antiope and Otere as they once went out to war, they sacrificed the sheep at a stone altar. The temple contained a sacred black rock affixed to the ground which the Amazons came from time to time to venerate and there make burnt-offerings of horse-flesh.

As they were feasting, Jason, eyeing the newcomers curiously, said to them: "Sooner or later Zeus cannot but smile on god-fearing men like us. Look at yourselves. First he rescued your father from his deadly step-dame and blessed him with wealth. Now he has preserved you through a savage storm. You now have a ship that can take you where you wish, whether east to Aia or west to Orchomenos. Therefore, be now our pilots and assist us to bring the Golden Fleece back to Greece; for I was sent to make atonement for Phrixos' attempted sacrifice that stirred Zeus' wrath against the Aiolids."

The sons of Phrixos listened in horror, knowing that king Aiëtes would give them a less than friendly welcome if their intent was to carry off the Fleece. Argos, speaking for his brothers, answered him: "Friends, whatever little strength we have will never fail to act in your service. But you don't know that cruel man! I dread even the thought of going back. He boasts himself the son of Hyperion and rules over countless tribes of Colchians. Apart from that, to reach the Fleece is no simple matter. It rests high up in a tree, protected by a monstrous, deathless and sleepless serpent, spawned by the earth on the heights of the Caucasus, where it is said Typhon was struck by Zeus' thunderbolt."

Hearing such grim notice, the others paled. But Peleus quickly said: "Friend, fear not! We're not wanting in bravery so as to cower before this Aiëtes. We are more than a match for him in arms, akin as some of us are to the blessed gods. I am certain that his Colchian vassals will prove of little help should he refuse us the Fleece."

Encouraged only slightly by his remarks, the others continued feasting and at last fell asleep. At dawn, feeling a gentle breeze, they hoisted the sail, which grew taut in the wind, and left the island of Ares astern.

As night came on, they passed the isle of Philyra, where Cronos, when he ruled over the Titans and Zeus was but a godling in his Cretan cave reared by the Idaian Couretes, lay with Philyra, daughter of Ocean. But his wife Rhea, catching them in the act, caused him to speed away in the form of a horse with flowing mane. In shame Philyra retired to Haimonia, where from the union she bore the Centaur Chiron.

Past many other tribes they sailed, borne by the light wind, until in the evening the end of the sea came in sight, and behind it the formidable scaurs of the Caucasus Mountains. Phrontis revealed that in one of those cliffs the Titan Prometheus lay bound to the rocks while a great eagle fed daily on his liver. The Argonauts made light of his words until they saw a bird traverse the darkening sky. Flying as high as the clouds, it still cast an immense shadow. As it swept over the ship, it shook the sail and stays with its loud, rushing wings, its pinions flapping like polished oars. Toward the mountains it darted and disappeared within its peaks. Soon afterward Prometheus' bitter cries of passion rolled over them. Gripped with fear, the crewmen fixed their eyes on the dark slopes until the eagle, having finished its repast, soared away with blood dripping like rain from its talons.

Since Argos wished the honor of bringing the ship to its destination, Ancaios passed him the helm. In the dead of night they came in view of the outfall of the Phasis They pulled down the sail and yard-arm, stored them in the mast-hold, unstepped the mast, and rested it along the deck. With oars extended they rowed into the estuary, plouging through the river's boiling current. On their left the Caucasus shadowed them; and on their right extended a vast meadow with the sacred grove of Ares and the Fleece. Jason blithely poured into the river libations of unmixed wine, as sweet as honey, praying for the assistance of the gods and the spirits of the heroes of the place. On Argos' advice, Jason ordered the ship steered into a shaded backwater, letting her ride at anchor among the high reeds. Each man stretched out in his place for the remaining span of night, with eager eyes longing for the dawn.

## 11

On the way back, Heracles stopped at sundry harbors along the Cronian Sea seeking, with little success, a ship bound for Libya. He descended into Istria, where at last, in the landlocked port at its extremity, he made the acquaintance of a young and ambitious Illyrian who, wishing to corner the market in silphium, had commissioned several galleys for that purpose, and was preparing them for their maiden voyage to the Libyan coast. As Heracles had no means to pay for his transport, he offered to safeguard the ships, which were carrying a great weight of gold and silver, against pirates. The shipmaster thought it prudent to agree.

The convoy travelled unmolested and with fair winds for seven days and nights as far the scythe-shaped island of Drepane, where they stopped for a day to rest and revictual. From there they passed between Leucas and fair Ithaca to various ports of call along the western coast of the Peloponnese. Before braving the open sea for the last leg of the journey they docked briefly at the deep harbor on the eastern side of the promontory of Tainaron, where stood the celebrated sanctuary of Poseidon, built of black marble. Near the shrine gaped a cavern that breathed dank mists, and was said to be one of the entrances to Tartaros. Heracles, learning of the cavern's existence too late, did not have the chance to explore it, and rued the moment the crew members called for all hands to sail.

Most ships taking the present route would have turned south-eastward and made for a penultimate stop at Crete, but since the death of Minos, rumors abounded of general political instability, making it best to avoid the island. They therefore plotted a beeline for Libya, rowing steadily windward for six days and nights. It was their intention to arrive at Phycus, the most northerly headland of the Libyan coast; instead, by a small error of calculation and a specific ignorance of those shores, they found themselves off course and within sight of the lofty promontory of Cephalai on the western side of Greater Syrtis. As they did not know the difference, they made for land; but a sudden gale from the south-east overtook them, lashing their sails with rain and spindrift, and enveloping the ships in dark clouds of sand blown from the coast. The ships retreated into the sea as the storm worsened, with everything around them turning to a blackness fractured by terrifying lightning flashes. As a result, the ships were scattered as far as the edges of Lesser Syrtis. When the skies brightened, the helmsman found his bearings, thankful that they had not been sucked into the perilous shoals of the deep bay, and as all the ships were accounted for, they anchored close to the sinuous mainland, prevented by the sunken reefs from reaching the beach, and wading ashore carrying their sails upon their shoulders, set about to mend them, find water, and rest from their ordeal. It was soon evident that no fresh water could be found, and so Heracles led a party inland where mountains loomed, with the hope of finding a stream. After searching long without success, the men began to despair under the stifling heat, crying to Heracles for assistance, since they believed that as a demigod he could accomplish all things. Heracles went off by himself until he came to the shore of a vast lagoon. Tasting the brine-laced water, he despaired. He was about to turn back and advise the men to board the ships and head to their intended landing, when, passing a jutting rock covered in moss, he heard a faint sough. Putting an ear to the rock, he rejoiced, hearing the rush of water from inside. With his club he struck the base of the rock three times in succession until a trickle escaped the fractured surface. He then kicked the ruined spot violently and a great stream of water erupted from a scissure and flowed down the dusty watercourse. All the men, like hornets massed about a bole oozing sap, rushed in to sate their thirst. Heracles let them drink first; and when his turn came he pressed himself to the ground to drink from the rock cleft until his belly ached and he lay prone and happy like a grazing beast.

They sailed off as soon as the repairs were finished. After four days, as they came within sight of cape Phycus, they were almost overtaken by Cyreneian pirates in little papyrus boats, who considered the few Greek merchants reaching their fairly unknown shores as easy targets. But Heracles, bellowing at them from the stern while gyrating his ponderous club above his head, scared them off. After that they came into a small harbor and a mean village on the western side of the mainland where the natives, at first refusing them entry, grew conciliated by the twinkle of their gold dust.

Heracles enjoined the ships' master to leave without him should he linger for more than a fortnight without returning. He found a toothless vagrant to guide him to the temple of Ammon and set out on a camel from the bold coast in the afternoon, when the air grew cooler, leading his escort upon horseback. The land rose gradually to a plateau through a succession of terraces marked by streams flowing through verdant ravines. Heracles, remembering the arid and inhospitable desert when he first traversed Libya on his way to Erytheia, could scarcely believe his eyes at the delightful environs. With cool breezes from the sea, and the hot breath of the desert kept out by a crop of encircling mountains, the district appeared so much a paradise that Heracles wondered if he had already stumbled into the Garden of the Hesperides. Progress slowed as Heracles had to stop each hour to feast on the abundance of dates and almonds and cucumbers that grew everywhere in great profusion, in the thick of great swaths of silphium and sweet-smelling flowers beds. In the evening they passed near a village of the naked Nasamonians, who ran out to invite Heracles to feast with them under the shady sycamore trees. It turned out that their headman was marrying a fourth wife, and as it was customary for the bride to have intercourse with all the guests, she offered herself first of all to Heracles. Although she was comely in her own way, with sunburnt skin and long black hair, Heracles declined, stating that he had not brought a gift for the bridegroom; and this explanation of his refusal sufficed. But he could hardly sleep that night from the noise of the riotous lovemaking.

The next day Heracles approached the mountains, where the sand began to encroach on the pleasing verdure of the table-land. At the edge of the desert there suddenly appeared a thick swarm of locusts that, enveloping them, blotted out the sun and sky. They took refuge behind the rocks that littered the place until the locusts passed. After another night within the shelter of the mountains, they began to descend by a steep ravine to the desert and encountered, at the base of the escarpment, a crude stone enclosure partially roofed with bleached skulls beside great piles of lion bones and bloodied pelts. As Heracles looked up, he was nearly struck by a jaw-bone sent flying from a den under a high bluff. Heracles' Libyan guide suddenly inserted two fingers in his mouth, blew a shrill whistle, and then ran off from whence they came. As Heracles, suspecting treachery, unlatched the great bow from his back, preparing to string it, he heard someone cry "Ho! Who dares trespass under the shadow of my alcove?" From the cave there then emerged a hairy, overgrown black brute clothed, as was Heracles, in a lion's pelt. The giant, blinking as if awoken from sleep, made his way calmly down the mountain-side until he stood level with Heracles, "I am Antaios, son of Poseidon, ruler of this waste." Heracles sized him as taller even than Geryones, but gaunt and bony, so that he seemed to be gifted less with strength than with stature. "Child of wretched men, if you wish to pass through this land," he continued, "you must agree to wrestle with me." Heracles had already been fingering the nocks in his quiver, and he could have facilely killed him with an arrow through the eye; however, as the giant came unarmed and without aggression, with a demand not wholly strange or unreasonable, Heracles agreed to his request. They moved to a clearing, where Heracles laid down his weapons and stripped off his lion's pelt. Antaios did the same, adding the curious ritual of rubbing his limbs with burning sand, as a contestant would rub himself with oil. Heracles thought nothing of this at that moment, thinking that Antaios considered it advantageous for his skin to be dry and mealy. They linked arms and hands in various clasps, which gave Heracles the chance to test the giant's strength. For long each man stood unmoved and equally amazed at encountering his match. Antaios was first to yield, emboldening Heracles with his gasps and trembling neck. Heracles thrust himself into his opponent, bending low to hook an arm around a reeling leg. Heaving upward with his shoulders, Heracles pitched Antaios over so that he fell flat on the ground. Heracles then pounced on Antaios to pin him, but as he did so, he felt the ground tremble. Before he could lock Antaios down, the latter heaved his body and cast off Heracles like a blanket, sending him sprawling several feet away. Antaios jumped to his feet with a scornful laugh, and it seemed his oddly palpitating limbs had thickened.

Heracles eyed the giant curiously, rising and shaking the sand from his back. They grappled late into the afternoon, with Heracles pressing hard, twisting limbs, and finally throwing Antaios by the hip. Just as before, the ground had scarcely drank the giant's sweat when up he bounded again, as fresh and ready as if he had not been wrestling at all. Heracles wiped the sweat from his eyes, squinting at the carrion-birds perching on the ledges. After falling again into a clinch, Heracles forced his opponent to a knee with a head-choke. Antaios, freeing himself, was ready to grasp Heracles in an underhook when the latter feigned a reach for his legs, upon which the giant seemed to fling himself to the ground. Immediately, he rose again, ready to continue the contest. Heracles now had some idea of the giant's secret. "You said your father was Poseidon," he said. "And who was your mother?" Antaios, anointing his limbs again with sand, responded: "If you must know, I was conceived by Mother Earth in that very cave." "I see," said Heracles demurely; "and that crude hut nearby, how came it to be?" The giant grew shifty-eyed. He said: "It is a temple I am building to honor my father. The roof is decorated with the bleached coxcombs of those who lose to me. But you are the most redoubtable fellow to ever come into these parts, and have nothing to worry about. Let us continue." Heracles agreed, but this time formulating a different strategy. As the two grappled, Heracles no longer made any attempt to throw Antaios, and neither did he allow the giant to throw himself of his own volition as before. Instead, Heracles twisted Antaios about, locking his arms or neck, but all the while keeping him on his feet. As suspected, Antaios merely tried to break free, without any hint of trying to throw Heracles. Thereupon Heracles positioned himself behind Antaios, wrapping his arms around the giant's arms and chest as if he planned to flip him over. Instead, Heracles, arching backward, lifted the giant until his feet dangled, and holding him aloft squeezed mightily until the ribs began to crack. Antaios howled in pain, writhing and kicking to break free; but growing weaker the longer he was out of contact with the ground, from which Heracles rightly guessed he renewed his strength, he failed to loosen the grip that enveloped him. In this way Heracles bore the giant until the chill of death stole over him, and then cast him down in a heap, trusting that the earth could never more revive him.

Despite his opponent's imposture, Heracles could not deny the pleasure he derived from such a prodigious struggle. Therefore, wishing to avoid any offense to Antaios' shade, as well as to Poseidon or Mother Earth, Heracles heaped a barrow of great stones and earth over the corpse, resulting in a mound of such size that it took the form of man stretched out at full length, and by which he also despoiled the carrion-birds of their fulsome feast. In time the natives pointed out the hillock to passerby, claiming that the removal from it of a clod of earth would cause unceasing rain until the hole was refilled.

As he worked, Iphinoë, Antaios' wife, emerged from the cave, bringing him bread and water, evidently not at all troubled by her husband's decease. She invited Heracles to her hovel and there, by means of certain allurements, convinced Heracles to have union with her. In time she bore a son, whom she called Palaimon in honor of her husband the wrestler.

Leaving that place, Heracles wandered deeper into the desert, hoping to find some village or passing caravan that could point him in the direction of the shrine of Ammon. Night came, and with it a chill air, and the cries of jackals that seemed to circle him just out of sight. Heracles slept between a line of hills, keeping a fire burning all night to scare away the wild beasts which eyed him from the cliffs, and the snakes and scorpions that seemed to breed around him from the very sand. The next day, his march plunged him in a sea of orange sand, where even the stunted vegetation of the stony plain dared no longer grow. The sand sucked at his feet, slowing his gait, until it seemed another fruitless day would never end. For days he continued on, traversing the barren landscape that shifted from sandy plain to endless, undulating dunes broken by low hills and rocky ridges from which the hot sand blew in a crystalline mist. Through this his lionskin proved both a curse and a blessing. On the one hand, oppressed by the heat, he wished to strip it off; but on the other, it served as the only barrier against the sun's relentless, scorching oppression. By the fourth day, as he wrung the last drops from his waterskin onto his swollen tongue, Heracles entertained the thought of turning about and heading back to Cyrene where the sweet spring water beckoned, and the date-palms bowed with heavy fruit, and the sweet breath of the north wind blew continually. Tormented by hunger as much as thirst, he had tried to hunt the swift gazelles in the early morning when they sprung from behind the sand dunes to feed, but they outraced his arrows.  At last he fell on the sweltering sand, lonely and without strength.  He dragged himself to a rocky place to wait for the sun to pass its highest point.  From his lodgment he could see far into the shimmering desert waste.  Under the strain of the monotonous visage he thought he saw winged gazelles skimming over the plain like swallows, dissipating the broiling heat under their flapping wings.  When he had confirmed the illusions that tricked his eyes, he then believed he saw scampering nearby an extraordinary creature with the body of a lioness, the head of a hawk, and a long upright tail ending in the shape of a lotus-flower.  Rubbing his eyes did nothing to improve or remove the sight of the fantastic animal. He reached for his bow, settled an arrow against the cord, and with certainty transfixed the monster, for it roared and ran off.  Heracles, although consumed with curiosity, felt encumbered by a languor that after over time grew increasingly pleasant.  He stopped begging Zeus for rain.  He considered that to die in such a state of enervation would not be difficult.  As the sun dipped behind the western mountains, strange, new constellations adorned the sky, and the evening air blew through his lion's pelt, he had a great desire to close his eyes and drift into sleep.  But suddenly ashamed at his debility, he struggled against himself to move deeper into the shelter of the rocks, knowing that if he failed to start a fire soon the lions, jackals and spotted leopards would come out to make a feast of him.  As he settled in a different corner of the rocky formation he disturbed a nest of ichneumons, in which, to his great delight, he discovered several cracked eggs, some still dripping with yolk. These he consumed and his strength renewed; and hope also, since the little animals were known to live close to water.  On the following day, Heracles ventured out again, compelled by the fair prospect of finding, if not an end to the desert, at the very least an oasis.  By midmorning, with the sun poised at the zenith, he grew heartened to see lamb-vultures appearing from the south, flying toward the outcroppings where he had spent the night, and back again.  It meant, he hoped, that animals congregated nearby, most likely at a water-source, since the lamb-vulture disdained rotting flesh and waited patiently near the living for death to prematurely strike.  After a laborious march through gravely desert he came to a line of crags at the edge of the table-land. He climbed up a furrow to the top and found below him a vast depression holding in its midst a verdant oasis of coarse grass and palm-trees spreading out beyond the horizon. To the south extended a still lake perfectly reflecting the cloudless blue sky, and from its edge spread an overgrowth of mud-brick buildings surrounding a flat-topped rock supporting a prominent stone structure. His heart palpitating with excitement, Heracles plunged down the steep edge of the scarp, losing his foothold and tumbling to the bottom of the basin. Recovering himself, he ventured into the field of trees, where he shook the bowed date-palms until the fruit clusters rained down on his head. Villagers approached to watch Heracles eat his fill with gluttinous abandon. When finished he accosted several in the crowd, demanding with exaggerated gesticulations where water could be found. When no one could answer him, since nothing could be made of his foreign speech, he tore through the town to the edge of the lake, where, after plunging in his arms, he pulled them out covered in bloody striations from the work of sharp salt crystals that coated the surface. Exasperated, he stormed back into the midst of the mud-brick houses, cursing its inhabitants, until a child came forward. She seemed not at all afraid of Heracles, but rather bemused. Taking his finger, which she could barely encircle in her small hand, she led Heracles to a wide and deep well shaded within a palm grove. Heracles immediately tore off his covering, and bounding toward the spring-fed pool, sprung off the edge and dove into the water, which was said to run coldest in the noontide heat. Heracles swam this way and that, taking in mouthfuls of the cool, life-giving water at every turn, ducking under the surface and bounding up like a cormorant after having caught a fish, to the evident delight of the Libyan child. He floated on his back for a long while looking up at the blue expanse through the encircling palm-fronds, no longer minding the penetrating rays of the sun against his damp flesh. Feeling refreshed and renewed after his immersion, he climbed out of the pool and like a shaggy dog shook off the water from his head and beard. The little girl now brought him dates, olives and spelt-bread in a basket, which she left at his feet before being pulled away by an apprehensive relative after being alerted about her activities. After his repast Heracles turned his eyes to the stone edifice upon the flat rock rising from a sea of trees to the north of the village. As he neared, he saw that that it was neither large, nor ornate—out of character indeed for an oracle of Zeus—but certainly imposing from its position on the height. A line of priests with sun-burnt hairless pates, dressed in white linen, streamed down the single path that wound up the side of the hill to greet him with an inordinate amount of familiarity. Heracles, remembering the words of Nereus, mentioned the name of the Egyptian god Ammon, at which the priests excitedly and obsequiously bowed and pointed up at the hill. They led him solemnly up the path to the summit, where a crenellated wall enclosed the sacred precinct. A gate of palm logs opened to an avenue that passed between storehouses and priests' quarters to a narrow open court in the northwest corner, accessed by some steps, whose walls abutted the edge of the cliff on two sides. A multitude of exotic visitors from the east, awaiting access to the augural shrine, made way for Heracles as he followed the priests through the court and into a large, empty, windowless hall lighted only by oil lamps resting in wall niches near the rafters. Through the gloom, impregnated with the thick smoke of frankincense, Heracles could make out another door in the north wall. The dim light bathing the side walls revealed them covered with colorful drawings of men and creatures sharing human and animal forms, surrounded by strange inscriptions and glyphs in orderly columns completely indecipherable to Heracles. A long panel depicted scenes of men presenting, to what seemed to be a group of deities, drawn larger than their subjects, jars of wine and baskets of bread. One deity possessed the head of an ibis; another that of a jackal; and the third, a female by her slender shape, wore a crown in the form of a vulture with outspread wings, from whose belly coiled out a red viper ready to strike. On the opposite wall the drawings seemed fainter, weathered with age, losing their coloration as they spread down the surface. Beneath images of rivers and well-watered groves, sitting sphinxes and gryphons like he had seen in the desert, he discerned faded wedge-shaped signs, different and more primitive than the rest, carved within an ellipse. Beside it was pictured a homunculus wearing a sidelock and grasping two coiling snakes. Heracles followed the illustrations with his eyes, through light and shadow, to the adjacent panels. Their principal subject seemed to be a figure of a man with the head of a sparrow-hawk, surmounted by a disk within a golden crescent.  In one place he wrestled a lion; in another a bull.  Here he stood before a king bearing an ibex across his shoulders.  There he fought with a falchion a three-headed serpent rising from an ocean.  Heracles looked on in wonder at how the images appeared to depict with intriguing similitude a number of his own Labors.  The remaining panels were effaced by cracks in the wall; but one last illustration seemed clear in depicting the figure in some cavernous, subterrene place sitting above a population of indistinct, spectral forms.  Heracles called for one of the priests to come and explain the meaning of the drawings. After a great deal of murmuring among them, one appeared in the inner doorway to beckon him.  With a trembling hand he stopped Heracles at the threshold of another room that seemed the same size as the first, but darker still, illuminated only through two small apertures atop the left wall.  "*Hotep, Neb-I,*" said the priest (that is, "Peace, my lord"), and stood in the doorway as if to guard it.  Heracles, trying to peer into the room above the head of the priest, could discern the glimmer of gold thread embossed on a curtain of heavy fabric draped across the door to another chamber directly opposite.  A pale, flickering glow escaped beneath the edge of the curtain.

"*Em Heset Net Amun!*" a female voice called suddenly from within the next space (that is, "Be in favor of Amun!").  Then, in a manner, though labored, that Heracles could understand, she continued by crying: "Life! Strength! Health!" Gripping the doorjambs, Heracles pushed in deeper into the second hall against the guardian priest and said, thinking there was someone hiding behind the curtain in the inner room, "Who is it that speaks?"  The voice responded: "It is the Oracle of Amun that speaks.  Ask and you shall know."  Heracles called out: "I seek the Garden of the Hesperides."  The voice at once answered: "Only forethought can show you the way.  Heracles waited for further explanation of the cryptic message; but when none came his ire rose.  With one hand, Heracles dislodged and jerked the priest behind him and boldly entered the second hall.  As Heracles stepped toward the curtain, the voice grew strained and agitated.  "Come not closer to the sanctuary!  Suppliants are permitted only in the forecourt!"  A throng of priests crowded at the doorway weeping and begging him to desist. Heracles roared at them to become silent; and they did.

"If this be indeed a dwelling of Zeus, I wish to see and hear from him," demanded Heracles. "If not, I will put a quick end to this mummery."

A wail, like the cry of a hyena that fiendishly disturbs the night, sounded through the room, stopping Heracles as he reached for the curtain. From a narrow corridor beside the sanctuary emerged the Oracle: an exceedingly tall woman, for the Ammonians were an admixture of Ethiopian and Egyptian, attired in a simple white garment without folds, so slight that the form of her body was visible through the sheer membrane of the fine linen. She held a crucible before her, and her eyes shone through the thick smoke of the bubbling incense.

"Very well!" said the Oracle, her voice suddenly deep and troubling. Her eyes stared forth vacuously, as if oblivious to the presence of another. She wailed again, her mind gripped by the madness of the god; so that Heracles felt a few hairs stand erect on the back of his neck. "Amun will show himself to you," she said; "for you are Chonsu, son of Amun and Mut, who slays the king's enemies and devours their hearts. You must wait outside in the forecourt until all is ready." She uttered then a series of instructions to the priests.

Heracles suddenly lost the will to argue the matter. He slowly stepped backward, watching the form of the priestess become indistinct behind the glow of the incense burning on smoldering coals. He passed quickly through the first hall and out into the courtyard, longing to fill his lungs with the fresh air. Sitting on a stone bench until his lightheadedness passed, he watched the priests draw in a young ram with horns beginning to curve. After slaying and flaying it with a flint knife, they cut off the head and carried it and the fleece into the temple. Shortly thereafter a priest beckoned at Heracles from the door. Heracles returned to the second hall, where he found no sign of the priestess, and the light beneath the curtain extinguished. Heracles slowly drew aside the heavy curtain. The gaping entrance to the sanctuary appeared like it revealed oblivion. No light at all could penetrate inside; iciness reached out to touch him. Heracles bowed his shoulders to enter the small room, letting the curtain drop behind him. He could smell the sanguine and gamy odor of slaughter.

"Father?" whispered Heracles, afraid to adversely disturb

with any impropriety the delicate balance of a ritual he did not fully comprehend. He desired to reach out into the darkness for palpable proof of either a great mystery or a great deception. After what seemed like a long while, he heard a small, still voice call his name. Heracles peered about him blindly. "Here I am!" said he, feeling overwrought. His breaths grew short, choking on the overbearing odor of incense. He tried to speak again, but was struck dumb. Slowly he stretched a hand until he felt the soft down of a fleece at his fingertips. Abruptly, the thing before him toppled with a loud noise. In surprise, Heracles lurched backward through the entrance, pulling down the curtain and revealing now in the dimness, lying on the ground behind a pedestal, a painted statuette two cubits high, with the ram's fleece and horned head piled up beside it. Confused, Heracles looked about him; it appeared that all the priests had fled the temple. He stiffly shambled out to the courtyard, past the flayed carcass of the ram lying in its own smattered blood, and descended back down the great rock. Only when he reached the bottom could he speak again. His anger now burned hot, and he had half a mind to storm up to the sanctuary and tear it down stone by stone. He recalled then the voice that called to him, and could not deny the air of dread and mystery he felt in the darkness. Perhaps Zeus did appear near to him, covered with the fleece and holding the ram's head before him. Did not Semele, daughter of Cadmos, seen by Zeus washing off the blood of sacrifice in the Boetian Asopos, afterward in their affair ask to see him in all his glory? Bound by oath, he did so; and she was immolated in his glorious majesty. This cruel end, it seems, he was spared; yet, how strange, Heracles countered, that the god who clothes himself in thunder and lightning should become but a whisper in the dark.

There was no point in returning to the temple. He had his answer, as inscrutable as any an oracle can deliver. Perhaps more would be revealed in a dream; or, given time, some important clue would appear by sustained mental exercise. After filling his haversack with olives, dates, and pieces of dried mutton, Heracles took the road out of the depression. Standing at the edge of the vast cavity, he contrasted the bleak and endless landscape before him with the cool and moist sea of trees below. It was difficult to leave the pleasant oasis to plunge back into the desert, knowing only to head northward until he reached the sea. He had gone half a day when he realized that his waterskin was nearly empty, having drunk the remainder immoderately after forgetting to fill it. He cursed himself for not having the forethought to collect an ample supply, while he could, of the most important necessity of all. Knowing he could scarcely survive if he continued his journey so poorly equipped, he turned back to Ammonium. As the day waned and night crept out of the edge of the desert, a certain insight struck him so smartly that he dashed his palm against his brow for his dullness. In telling him the he needed *forethought* to find the Garden of the Hesperides, the Oracle cleverly concealed the name of the one who would surely know its location: Prometheus, for his name signified that very quality. Prometheus was brother to Atlas, father of the Hesperides; and of all the gods, he was perhaps the only one possibly accessible to mortals on earth, since, the poets said, he lay chained somewhere in the Caucasus mountains as punishment for stealing fire from Zeus.

## 12

Jason deliberated on the best way to attain the Fleece, in his mind creating and discarding plans until the rise of day. The clear air now revealed Aiëtes' mighty city upstream framed by the loftiest mountains he had ever seen; and, across it, the gloomy groves where the Fleece was kept. Aia covered the shoulders of a hill, rising steeply to the white palace at its summit, rose-colored from the touch of dawn. Layers of curtain walls, high pennants waving from every drum tower, wrapped the city's many levels, pierced by a wide, paved road leading down to the royal harbor crowded with galleys.

The crewmen waited patiently until their chief, hunched over in the bow, stirred from his ruminations.

"Comrades," Jason began, "I will explain what course seems best to me; but I will leave it to you to approve it; and let no one remain silent if he has better counsel, lest the burden of our failure fall on him. I will go and see Aiëtes and ask him to yield the Fleece. The king will straightway reveal himself as friend or foe. I feel it is better to speak to him first than try to rob him of his possession. Many a time a good word succeeds where force fails."

All agreed to this proposition. Augeias at once volunteered to go with him, since he had a great desire to meet Aiëtes, whom he considered a kinsman. Jason, taking Hermes' herald's wand from Aethalides, added also Telamon and the sons of Phrixos to his embassy. They descended from the boat, crossed the reed-bed to dry land beyond, and set out across a plain where grew in rows willows and tamarisk-trees from which dangled strange bundles. Argos explained that the Colchians' chief divinities being Heaven and Earth, they consider it a terrible sacrilege to bury or burn their dead, and instead, wrapping them in untanned ox-hides, hang them from the highest boughs of the trees far from the city;   although they consign the women to the ground as to not leave the Earth deprived.  Jason, curious about this custom, inquired whether Phrixos after his murder had been so entombed.  Argos replied that the royal family was not subject to those strictures and showed him a mound within a ring of poplars by the river-bank which he described as Phrixos' tomb.  Beside it stood a marble cenotaph for Helle, depicting her clutching the ram, caught between her wicked stepmother and the unforgiving sea.  "And our father died a victim of old age rather than Aiëtes' hand," added Phrontis with certainty. Jason wondered whether king Pelias had lied to him about Phrixos' demise and his unburied bones, or whether he had been misinformed.

As they made their way through the countryside to the high walls of Aia, Jason remarked how all seemed deserted.  Argos explained that Aiëtes brother', Perses, fomenting rebellion against him, made allies with the Scythian tribes to attack the city.  But, unable to breach the strong walls, the attackers arranged a truce with Aiëtes and retreated to their encampments.  Thus matters stood at the Argonauts' arrival.

They found the city tightly guarded and in a state of turmoil, for the threat of war made everyone skittish.  As they neared the single open gate, a fog rolled in from the coast and clothed them in mist so that they passed through unnoticed.  The sons of Phrixos led them straight up to the palace, where the Greeks stood amazed at the monumental gates, shadowed by tall fluted columns upholding a stone cornice decorated with brazen triglyphs.  Seeing the sons of Phrixos, the royal guards made no move to challenge them as they entered the courtyard.  Vines there sent their green shoots high along the walls, and below gushed four eternal fountains built by Hephaistos in gratitude to Helios who aided him in his weariness during the Gigantes' revolt  From one flowed milk, from another red wine; the third produced fragrant oil; and in the last ran water warm at the setting of the Pleiades, or cold at their rising.

When Aiëtes' daughter Medeia, going from room to room in search of her sister Chalciope, saw the group passing into the colonnade of the inner court, she gave a cry of alarm. Chalciope and her maid-servants dropped their yarns and spindles and ran outside the doors.  Seeing her sons with the two strangers, she threw up her arms in joy; her sons did likewise and they tearfully embraced. Between sobs she said to them: "Well now! Although you left me anguished, you were not meant to go very far. Fate has brought you back! Woe is me! What a passion for Greece your father's dying words bred in you! Why would you go off to that Orchomenos—whoever he is—and leave your mother here in bitter sorrow?"

As she was speaking Medeia came out, and remaining in the shadow of the colonnade, stared at Jason. Growing up surrounded by the kinky-haired, dark-skinned Colchians, she had never seen, except among her own family, another man of such stature, with such long golden-hued hair and such sky-blue eyes. He seemed like a god in the glow of his youth and peerless beauty, dimming everyone beside him. She felt the sudden pain of infatuation ravage her wildly-beating heart. Thinking of nothing but him, she became aware of a new and unknown agony flooding her soul with a sweet sorrow.

Queen Eidyia appeared, followed by Aiëtes, a towering monarch with an austere, imperious countenance made prominent by his steady, shining eyes, almost golden in sheen, a mark of the sons of Hyperion. Without a word to the newcomers, he ordered the household to busy itself with their care and prepare for the night's banquet.

After being bathed and dressed in new clothes, fragrant with myrrh, Jason and his companions were brought to the banquet-hall noisy with the chatter of the king's numerous courtiers, allied princes, nobles and other men of mark. As they gorged themselves on rich foods and flowing wine, Argos pointed out prince Apsyrtos seated next to the queen, whom Asterodia, a nymph of the mountain-range, bore to Aiëtes before he married Eidyia. He was tall and broad-shouldered like his sire, and in so many respects so outshone all other young men that the Colchians called him Phaëthon. Next he showed him Albanian Styrus, prince of that mettlesome tribe living around the eastern reaches of the Caucasus, who by his animal-skin tunic advertised the wildness of his nature. He was newly-arrived to the court and betrothed to Medeia, but the marriage had been postponed by the civil war. Argos began to speak of the winsome bride, sitting behind the queen with her maid-servants and nurse-maid when king Aiëtes made his entrance, brightening the room by the shimmer of his gold-spangled robes. On his snow-white locks rested a crown fringed with polished yellow jasper reflecting the lamps with glowing rays; and his broad hands wielded like lightning a crystal scepter. He sat, and looking around the room, fixed his eyes on his sons-in-law. As a crooked smile violated his habitual scowl, he addressed them: "Sons of my daughter and of Phrixos, whom I honored above all other strangers, what brings you back to Aia? Did some disaster strike you on the way? Well I warned you about the long voyage, which I once travelled in my father's chariot when escorting my sister Circe to the lands of the west, and we arrived at a headland on Tyrrhenia's coast where she now dwells still. Tell me now plainly what befell you. And who are these men with you? And where did they land their ship?"

Argos, fearful for Jason's purpose, answered hastily but gently: "Sire, that vessel you gave us broke up in a storm and we were lucky to cling to driftwood until we washed up on Enyalios' isle. Some god saved us surely, for even his fearsome birds were gone, driven off by these men who had landed there the day before. By Zeus' pity for us they delayed, and they gave us food and clothing after hearing me mention the famous name of Phrixos and your own, since to this city were they sailing. If you must know their business, I will not hide it. A certain king, fearing for this throne and possessions, banished this scion of the Aiolids, sending him off on a perilous quest: for it is fated that that the house of Aiolos would never escape Zeus' wrath, or the pollution over Phrixos' attempted sacrifice, until the Fleece is returned to Greece. Pallas Athena built their ship; and not along Colchian lines, of which we chanced on the worst one, torn apart by winds and waves. But their ship's bolts held fast all this way through every sort of wind and tide. In her he gathered the best of Achaia's heroes. And after wandering over land and sea, he's come here in hope of the Fleece. His name is Jason, son of Aison, grandson of Cretheus; and if truly of Cretheus' stock, then he is our kinsman. With him come Augeias, whom you may also know as another of Hyperion's sons; and Telamon, son of Aiacos, begotten by Zeus. So too the rest of his crew calls some immortal father or grandfather."

Aiëtes boiled hotter with every word he heard. Rage

swelled his breast, especially against Chalciope's sons, since he thought they were the cause of Jason's coming. Sundry dreams, oracles and portents revolving around the Fleece whirled in his mind. After the death of Phrixos, not only did a new constellation in the form of a ram adorn the night's sky, but Phrixos' ghost appeared to him in a dream to warn him of the dire consequences of losing possession of the Fleece. From Hyperion's oracle he further learned to expect treason from within his own family. Of his daughters he had no worry in this regard; or of his son Apsyrtos. He had welcomed Phrixos to his country—and this was how his sons repaid him, by returning with a band of evildoers to strip him of his throne? With eyes beneath his brow spurting flames, he berated them: "Wretches! Depart at once with your trickery! No Fleece brought you and your Greek henchmen here: but a craven desire to seize my crown. Had you not eaten from my table first, I would now rip out your tongues and chop off your hands, sending you back with nothing but your feet to deter you from further machinations."

Telamon's temper choked him over the king's opprobrious accusations. He was about to answer him with a bitter retort when Jason restrained him, speaking first with gentle words: "Your majesty: we have not come here with evil designs. We threaten no violence. Who would brave the vast depths to rob his host? No, blame this venture on Fortune and the orders of a tyrant. I do as I am ordered. The gift we ask is ours by right: and yet we make no demands, but trust in you to be as kind to us as you were toward Phrixos. We are more than ready to repay you for the Fleece by aiding you in war against your brother Perses and his Scythian allies, or whatever other tribe you wish to subdue. Let us then join hands as friend and allies. Accept these gifts, all adornments of my father's, which we have carried for you over the seas: an opulent cloak woven by my mother and died blood-red from a Tainarian caldron; a Lapithian bridle; and a sword inset with gemstones along the hilt and pommel."

Aiëtes struggled with two choices: whether to leap up and slaughter the strangers, or to destroy them by less direct means. Deciding on the latter course after a period of sullen pondering, he said: "Stranger, why continue? If your race indeed comes from the gods, or, having come to a foreign shore after another's goods, consider yourself not the least inferior to me, I will give you the Fleece—once I put you to the test. I bear no grudge, you see, against good men, as does this Greek king of yours. The trial I set before you is one I myself can perform with my bare hands.

"Out on the field of Ares I have two marvelous bulls, the like of which you have never seen, for they walk on brazen feet and from their mouths gush flames. I yoke this team to a heavy plough, with the pole and yoke and shares all of one solid piece, and drive through the rough field to plough two hectares, from ridge to ridge. Next, I sow in the furrows not the barley-seed, but the teeth of an ancient serpent, and out rises an armed host that I cut down with my spear. I start at dawn, and end with my harvest at dusk. If you can do as I do, I will give you the Fleece; but not before, since it is unseemly for a brave man to yield to a coward."

Medeia marveled at her father's cruelty. Her face, rose-tinged, turned pale. She trembled to think of Jason actually taking up the challenge. Jason, with eyes affixed to the ground as Aiëtes spoke, sat speechless, completely at a loss. At long last, after every turn of mind, he made his desperate response:

"Aiëtes, you have every right to challenge me. This trial, though outrageous, I shall undertake,  even if death be my lot: for there is nothing worse imposed on men than harsh necessity—the very thing that drove me to come here at a king's command."

"Go join your company, since you're eager for the toil," said Aiëtes grimly. "But if you're afraid to yoke the bulls or shrink from the deadly harvest, know that I will end this business by making sure others think twice before coming here before their betters."

Shaken by the king's blunt words, Jason rose from his seat. Augeias and Telamon followed him out, as did Argos, who by a sign warned his brothers to remain behind. Even in his distress, Jason's beauty and charm held him in distinction. Medeia, holding her silver-colored veil aside, gazed at him filled with wonder. Her heart blistered with pain as he passed from her sight, and her thoughts stole after him as in a dream, following in his steps.

In the deathly quiet of the banquet-hall—for none dared to gainsay the king—Chalciope hastily departed, withdrawing with her sons to her rooms. Medeia also excused herself, harried by love's assaults and unable to drive the thought of Jason from her mind: his bearing, his clothing, his manner of speaking, how he sat and how he left. His voice continued to whisper in her ear. She wept over his fate, sealed on Ares' plain, and invoked Hecate for his deliverance.

## 13

From his days as Cheiron's pupil, Heracles learned a vague notion of the geography of the world, which in its entirety was not yet known, since no Greeks had ever travelled as extensively as he, whether into the blistering sands of Libya, westward to the shores of the Axine, eastward to the edge of Ocean or northward to frigid Scythia. The Caucasus mountains, he knew, lay at the extreme of the Axine, near the land of Aia whither he was headed on the *Argo*. Had not the impious Argonauts abandoned him, he would have no doubt arrived in the vicinity within a fortnight. If he hurried now, eschewing any delay, he could perhaps catch Jason at Colchis, whom he planned to soundly and justly trounce after achieving the Fleece in his stead, for such a lout could not be allowed to bask in any glory. Pleased with this plan, he considered how to best punish each Argonaut in turn as he marched back to Ammonium. Arrived there, he climbed to the sacred precincts and dashed in the doors to the priests' quarters, pulled one from his bed, and demanded from him a camel and some more waterskins. The priests, affrighted out of his wits, conducted him to the home of the local governor, who, on the insistence of the priests, took no measures against the unruly intruder by calling to his aid the members of his small garrison, but instead equipped Heracles with two sturdy camels and two casks of water, indicating by stretching out his arm how, as the way to the coast was represented by the distance from his shoulder to his elbow, the way to Egypt encompassed the length of the whole arm.

Heracles took the road eastward to Egypt, riding one camel and pulling the other in tow into the face of the new moon, large but dim, and embroidered by an endless sprinkling of stars. Beyond Egypt lay Arabia, and then perhaps Ocean, although that was disputed. His geographical knowledge then grew hazy, but he considered that by continuing northward through Phoenicia he would eventually reach the Axine, and from there it was a simple matter to follow it around to the land of the Colchians and the Caucasus mountains.

By hard riding, covering twice the distance each day he would otherwise have achieved on foot through the deep, shifting sand, sleeping sparsely in rocky places during the hottest parts of the day, and eating nothing but hares, Heracles came to where a wall of mountains everywhere decorated the horizon. Within three days he reached these limestone hills, crossed through them by means of narrow paths, and came to the steep edge of the table-land.

Below him spread a long and narrow valley, bounded everywhere by the same pale limestone hills, and with the tortuous gray-blue ribbon of the Nile river coursing through a green sward. Everywhere the land was dissected by watercourses and covered by flat green fields and clumps of palm and sycamore-trees. A splendid-looking city straddled the river, of which the western half was the strangest and most astonishing. As Heracles on foot wound his way carefully down the escarpment, leading the camels behind him, he could see more clearly how from the very sides of the mountains were hollowed out, as if by the hands of giants, what seemed like immense temples and galleries, so that the whole stony expanse, from one direction to another, appeared pockmarked like a vast unnatural honeycomb. These colossal structures expanded to greater breadth at the edge of the mountains, all in a line, with roads descending from them; and surrounded on all sides by gardens and storehouses. And in the valley, as far as the river, lay scattered, like cracked eggshells, monuments and tiny pyramids, gleaming in the sun.

Heracles reached one of the rock-hewn, colonnaded terraces and, leaving the camels outside, walked into sudden coolness and shadow between the massive carved columns. Within a wide hall, decorated with colorful reliefs, he looked up at a row of colossal statues over whose heads birds flapped about the cavernous interior. The quiet and sterile grandeur of the place, the lack of industry of the town below, the pyramids and monuments soon led Heracles to realize that, in contrast to the town opposite, this precinct seemed to be nothing less than a vast necropolis.

A shuffling sound disturbed the quietude. Having left his

club and bow with the camels, he hurried quickly outside, and for a moment was blinded by the intense sunlight breaking on him. Against shielded eyes he saw a line of soldiers, small men as black as smoke dressed in nothing but linen skirts, armed with light lances and clubs, at the edge of the terrace. More soldiers streamed up a ramp, pushing against their comrades until in a close-ranked bristly throng they surrounded Heracles. Their lighter-skinned captain, wearing a leather apron over his skirt, and carrying a threshing flail, commanded Heracles in words he did not understand; and when Heracles failed to do as he instructed, raised the flail against him. Heracles plucked it away with one hand, and hurling back the haft, cracked the skull of his attacker so that he fell dead. Seeing this, the soldiers pressed in, ready to pierce him with their lances, but Heracles, twirling the flail menacingly about him, kept them at a distance. One managed to sneak up and prick his calf below his inviolable lion's skin; while another, darting in as Heracles turned, struck his head with a cudgel. They now pressed in thickly on his right hand and on his left, striking and kicking him, and using the butts of their lances to trip him. Heracles viciously lacerated them with the flail until it snapped; and afterward, spattered with blood and bursting into a maddened laughter by the orgy of violence, he continued his defense by pummeling them with closed fists, thrashing them about, or ripping off gobs of flesh with his teeth. Yet not even his great strength could save him from being enveloped by the hostile forces. A mass of gnarled, spindly black bodies soon covered him completely, as weaver ants, rushing out from a hollow tree, overspread the unwelcome wasp. Buried under a mound of writhing men, their bodies dripping blood and sweat, he could scarcely move or breath. From repeated blows to the head and lack of air, and despite his frantic effort, darkness covered his eyes.

⁊

Heracles awoke abruptly, blinking repeatedly against the painful, stabbing light. He struggled to lift his head to look about him, finding himself bound from neck to ankle in coils of rough palm-fiber rope to a pallet resting on a wagon and hauled by a pair of bristly-backed oxen. A cadre of soldiers marched grimly around the vehicle, while before it the prince of the necropolis was borne aloft on a sedan-chair. The procession reached the river's edge, and passing through the flowering rush, which aroused the marsh-birds into a frenzy of flight, stopped at a little jetty. There a dozen of the soldiery came near, and lifting the pallet, carried it to a waiting barge. Men by long sticks pushed off the bank and guided the barge across the river through the waving tufts of papyrus reeds, past leering crocodiles and peering hippopotamuses, to the other side, where the prince of the town proper waited upon his own sedan-chair. The bound Heracles was deposited on another wagon and conveyed first past fields of barley and spelt and clover pastures, and then through the broad paved street running the length of the town crowded with courts and richly colored houses constructed of Nile mud. The wagon came to a stop before an imposing complex of quarried stone near the edge of the town, surrounded by a lush garden whose foliage could be seen overspreading the garden walls. Heracles' pallet was now hoisted on numerous shoulders and conveyed into the forecourt of the palace on the heels of the prince. At the other end of the forecourt stood three small buildings shielded by a row of columns. A balcony decorated with hanging carpets and malachite extended from the central building. The prince of the town waited with bowed head before the balcony, fanned by his attendant with a palm frond. Presently two men appeared on the balcony. The taller man was clothed in a narrow dress reaching from his breast to his ankles; and the skin of a young leopard, fastened around his neck, mantled his shoulders. The shorter man held a tall wooden crook and wore a circlet about his head adorned with ostrich feathers. The prince knelt to kiss the ground and addressed the taller man in his own speech: "Busiris—Hail! Beloved of Ma'at, the goddess of truth, prince and high priest of Amon-Re at Thebes, I bring to you this tribute: a stranger—behold! he has come within our borders and entered our sacred precincts. May Amon defend us, and Horus cover us by the plumage of his outstretched wings!" Busiris straightened his braided, black sheep's wool coiffure and rested a hand on the pommel of a small decorative dagger sheathed in his waist-sash. (It was he who drove Proteus, father of Polygonos and Telegonos, from Egypt.) He looked inquisitively down at Heracles, who raged futilely against his bonds, and turned to impart some words to his companion, the herald Chalbes. The latter stepped forward, knocked the crook thrice against the floor, and made a solemn pronouncement. At once more soldiers arrived to surround Heracles, armed with lances and tall square wicker shields that nearly covered their bodies. One of them withdrew a falchion from his belt and approached Heracles, who was lowered to the ground. Unafraid to die, Heracles suspended his struggling. He was touched only by a sudden sadness over things left undone. He did not wince as in one sweep the soldier cleanly rived the ropes. When Heracles realized he was left unscathed, he pressed against the weakened cords and burst them all asunder. Bounding to his feet he cried, pointing an accusatory finger at the occupants of the balcony: "Is it the practice of this realm to treat strangers so poorly?" Busiris brushed past Chalbes and said: "Pardon us, noble stranger. Hostile forces from without, as well as deserters and traitors from within have in recent times beset us. And so, my princes mistook you for a tomb-robber. Tell me, are you a Cyprian, or perhaps a Phoenician? and what is your purpose here in Thebes?" Heracles glared at the wall of shields surrounding him, spear-points pressed between them. "Neither," said he. "I am Heracles of Tyrins, a Greek merely passing through Egypt on my way across the world. I must tell you that lesser men have paid dearly for affronting me. If you allow me to continue unmolested on my business, I shall not take any revenge upon you and your city." Busiris exchanged a knowing look with Chalbes, and turning back to Heracles said: "You must by all means allow me to make amends for the ill-treatment you have suffered. Enter my palace, noble guest, and at once I shall call the leeches to treat your wounds, handmaids to wash your body, the chief fuller to mend your clothes, and singers from my harem to bring you merriment. Then tonight and tomorrow you shall dine with me on the finest goose-flesh and black wine from the Delta. On the third day you will assist me in sacrificing to Amon for the good of the land and the health of the good god, his majesty, my Lord Pharaoh, Ramesses, the King of Upper Egypt and the King of Lower Egypt (who is strong in truth, the chosen of Ra, the beloved of Amon, and the giver of eternal life like his father Ra!); it is by his beneficence that I reign in Thebes in his stead, since he has moved his throne to the east of the Delta, called it the house of Ramesses, and is now engaged in war with the Chittim and the Canaanites." Busiris clapped his hands and the wall of shields parted so that Heracles could pass through. Heracles hesitated; the thought, however, of relishing a fine meal and resting in a comfortable bed, given his recent long sojourn in the harsh desert, overpowered any sense of duty or urgency. Heracles agreed to be Busiris' guest and followed a pair of black slaves to a guest chamber where he was bathed and rubbed with oil fragrant with myrrh and broom. While the lionskin that ever covered him was away being washed, he was attired in a short skirt and belt held by a metal clasp in the shape of a cockchafer; and around his shoulder was draped a panther's skin with ribands tied to the hind paws. He declined to have this head and beard shaved off in the manner of the Egyptians, who prize cleanliness above all, but assented to the thorough removal of lice followed by a light trim with shears.

Busiris declared a public festival in honor of Heracles and held a lavish dinner-party that evening in the great dining-hall. The room, supported by fluted pillars, quickly filled with guests, curious to see the stranger and his magnificent bare chest and back. After attendants poured water over Heracles' hands and decorated him with flowers and necklets, he was free to peruse the large dining table and the smaller tables around it, covered with dishes of roast meat, bowls of fruit and baskets of flat, round bread, to partake of whatever his heart desired. Heracles consumed nearly half the contents of the main table, clamoring for more as he threw down the empty bowls, keeping the servants busy running to and from the kitchen. He enjoyed the goose immensely, roasted slowly on a spit over live embers on a low slab of limestone that served as a hearth. When he was satisfied with goose-meat, he turned to the boiled mutton seasoned with juniper, dishes of antelope and ibex sprinkled with crushed fennel, and blood sausage. These delicacies he washed down with a curious black-colored beer made from ground barley, which he supplemented with pomegranate wine, spiced with honey and date juice, poured from large jars wreathed with flowers.

His belly near to bursting, Heracles dropped at last into a thickly-cushioned arm-chair of ebony near Busiris, his consort, who wore a head-dress in the form of a vulture, and their son Amphidamas, who still wore a youthful side-lock on the right side of his head despite being a grown man.  As fan-bearers cooled his body, warm from wine and food, the grandees and ladies, wearing lotus buds on their elaborate coiffures, came to admire him and, if possible, touch his limbs in seeming veneration.  He allowed the women to indulge in this habit, but forbade the men, thinking it unnatural to be caressed by them.  One woman dressed in a simple garment narrowly covering the form of her body, after kneeling and kissing his feet, placed a ball of aromatic ointment on his head. Heracles, his senses dissipated by the wine, took in the scene while the oil-cake melted in the heat and drizzled down his face.  Since his grudge had lapsed with the merriment brought on by the festivities, he did not allow himself to ruminate on the strange circumstances of being nearly murdered one moment, and celebrated the next. Neither did he wonder why Busiris passed the night in hushed conversation with Chalbes and a circle of priest and scribes, all of who at intervals looked conspiratorially in his direction.  Instead he called for more white wine and beer, and drank until his eyes swam. Only the thunder of kettledrums revived him long enough to witness a troupe of girls dressed in transparent dresses twirling about with castanets and tambourines in their hands, and bending their bodies in unimaginable ways.  Dancing, they sang:

> *Breath the sweet odors;*
> *Anoint thyself with oil;*
> *Wreath the lotus 'round thy limbs;*
> *Let song and dance be merry toil!*
>
> *Place myrrh on thy head;*
> *Adorn thyself with beauty.*
> *Wrap thyself in fine linen;*
> *And cast thy cares from thee.*
>
> *Until cometh the day we draw*
> *Toward the land of silence.*
> *For no one take with him his goods;*
> *And no one returns from thence.*

Presently a small effigy of a corpse, wrapped in strips of linen, was brought forth and carried about by the servants to remind the revelers of the shortness of life and the inevitability of death. The guests wept or grew silent at this reminder; but as soon as the effigy was removed, they fell again into laugher and loud discourse.

Heracles, eager to question Busiris, called out to him: "Tell me: do the gods of Egypt consort with the gods of Greek Olympos? I have come lately from a sanctuary in the desert where Zeus was said to dwell, and yet the natives of the place call him Amon there, and not Zeus. Kindly explain such a thing to me, if you please."

"My priest tell me," said Busiris, "that the Egyptians were the first to recognize and name the twelve great gods, from which all nations then derived their own epithets. Amon signifies *the unseen*, or *the unknown* god, and is reckoned as no less than the king of the gods. You see, then, how it is that we call Zeus by the name of Amon. I myself am a son of a Libyan god you call the Earthshaker, although he is not known in Egypt; and the daughter of Hapi, god of the Nile."

"Poseidon is your father?" exclaimed Heracles "We are cousins-germain, then, since I am a son of Zeus! Furthermore, I came across a giant in the desert who also claimed the sea-god as his parent. Antaios he called himself."

"That is my brother!" said Busiris in surprise, and then his countenance grew dark. "How came you to meet him? He is quite jealous of his little kingdom and does not suffer strangers to pass through it."

"I must confess that I killed him in a wrestling-match," said Heracles contritely.

Busiris withheld any word or action that would betray his alarm at the news. He merely waved his hand dismissively, saying: "Let us avoid any more unpleasant talk, for tomorrow we together shall honor with all happiness the great god Zeus Amon with a worthy sacrifice."

"That is all well," said Heracles, "since I too can be considered an Egyptian."

"How so?" asked Busiris.

"I hail from the line of Perseus," said Heracles, "who was himself a descendant of Aigyptos, who ruled this country and lent his name to it."

Busiris looked to the priests for their opinion, thinking this statement to be controvertible. One of them replied: "Barbarians, O prince, possess an imperfect knowledge of our sacred history, although his words contain some truth. Ten generations ago there ruled a nomarch of the Thebaid nome, when it encompassed Chemmis, named Belos, whose wife Anchinoë bore the twin sons Aigyptos and Danaös. Aigyptos went to war against the Arabians, and returned triumphantly on Belos' death. To him were born fifty sons by several wives. Danaös, instead, conquered a part of Libya and sired fifty daughters by several wives. The two brothers had no light row over who was to succeed their father until Aigyptos proposed a wedding between their offspring. Danaös, suspecting treachery, fled with his daughters across the sea to Greece; thither followed the sons of Aigyptos, seeking an alliance in exchange for them. When Danaös refused, they laid siege to his city until he capitulated, and distributed his daughters among them. After the wedding celebration, Danaös gave each daughter a dagger with which to dispatch her husband on the bridal night. In this way all the sons of Aigyptos were cruelly murdered, except one, Lynceus, who became the great-grandfather of Perseus, who told us this story when he passed through Egypt with the head of the Libyan Gorgon. At Chemmis, there stands a sanctuary dedicated to Perseus, whose bloodline clearly began there. The people there say Perseus sometimes appears. They also say they one of his sandals turns up there from time to time. It is two cubits long and causes the land to flourish when it appears. As you know, O prince, we Egyptians despise the customs of other nations. But at Chemmis the people hold athletic contests in Perseus' honor, much like the barbarians. So you see that this stranger speaks some truth, but he is ill-informed in thinking that Egypt derived its name from Aigyptos, since it has been known as such for millions of years and is the oldest of all nations, except perhaps that of the Phrygians."

Heracles had fallen asleep during this discourse. Busiris had him conveyed by five stout slaves through a court adjacent to the dining-hall to a secluded apartment, where he was deposited on an immense bedstead piled high with pillows. His snoring could be heard in all parts of the house and drove the guests to depart the banquet prematurely.

## 14

As they retraced their steps across the plain, Argos said to Jason: "Son of Aison, you may think little of what I am about to suggest, but in dire straits one ought never to discount any counsel. That girl I pointed out, the younger daughter of Aiëtes, is a priestess of Hecate, and greatly skilled in sorcery. If we can win her to our cause, you'll have no trouble with the contest. I only fear that my mother will not support us in this matter. In any case, I'll return and make entreaties on your behalf, since we'll all certainly hang together if you fail."

Jason heartily agreed, but the thought that their fate lay in women's hands increased his distress.

Back at the ship, the crewmen greeted them cheerfully. But when Jason broke the terrible news of the coming ordeal, each looked at the other in despair. Finally Peleus broke the silence: "The time has come to take action. There is more profit in the strength of our arms than in words. Jason, make yourself ready if you plan to go through with this. If not, no need to look around; I'll do it! The worst we can suffer is death."

Telamon, stirred in heart, jumped up; as did Idas, mouthing prideful words. Castor and Polydeuces would not be left behind, and neither would Meleager. But the rest kept still and silent.

Said Argos to the six brave volunteers: "Friends, we're at the end of our rope, although I think my mother will aid us. Stay by your ship a little while yet instead of recklessly rushing into doom. I mentioned to Jason the daughter of Aiëtes, an adept in herbs she finds on land and running water. With her charms and spells she can quench a fire, halt rivers, bind the stars in their courses and arrest the holy moon. It is possible that my mother— her sister—will come to our aid as a go-between. If you approve, I will return to the palace to entreat her."

As he spoke, a terrified dove, fleeing a hawk, settled in Jason's lap; but the hawk, diving at high speed, smashed against the sternpost. At once Mopsos said: "The gods give a sign! They bid us to speak to the maiden and seek her aid, which she will not refuse if the words of Phineus are true. The dove is sacred to Aphrodite, on whom all our hopes he said depend. Call on Cypris to assist us. Listen to the son of Phrixos."

The Argonauts assented, with the exception of Idas. Leaping to his feet, he cried: "Well now, are there more women here beside Atalanta that we've resorted to beg from the goddess of love rather than the god of war? And now you look to doves and hawks keep you safe! Hang you all! Forget that you are fighting-men and spend your time courting silly girls."

Although many of his companions murmured behind his back, none dared to gainsay him. As Idas, fuming, sat back down, Jason cheered them with words of encouragement, sending off Argos on his mission. They then, at Jason's command, trundled up the anchor-stones and rowed the ship out of the backwater closer to dry land and in view of all.

❧

While Aiëtes met with his Colchian councilors to announce his intention of burning the *Argo* with its crew once Jason lost his life on the field of Ares, Argos arrived at the palace. He pleaded with his mother to convince Medeia to come to Jason's assistance. She herself had been of such a mind, but fear of her father had dampened her resolve. Meanwhile, a deep slumber brought relief to Medeia's troubled mind. In her dreams she sees Jason accept her father's challenge, not for the Fleece, but for her sake: to free her from a forced marriage to Styrus, who offends her with his uncouth ways. Jason is the first man she ever loved; and he, loving her, promises to make her his wife. In the dream, she strives with the fire-breathing bulls, making light work of it. Her father discounts her efforts, since the task was Jason's to perform. A serious row ensues between her father and the strangers, leaving Medeia as the arbiter between them. She takes the side of the Greeks. The screams of her enraged parents pull her out of her dream.

Medeia awoke trembling and peering around her. Her agitated mind prevented her from returning to sleep. "Madness!" she whispered to herself in the dark. "What possesses my mind to think of nothing but this stranger, come from so far off? What have you done, Medeia? Let him take the Fleece and leave—that's all he wants. Or is it? Let him be gone forever, for he shall never return and we shall never visit Haimonia's cities, wherever that is." She forces her eyes shut, willing back the slumber that ever attended her wearied body. Unable to find comfort, she sits up on her bed, saying: "O! how my heart flutters for this stranger. It would be better if he goes back to woo some Greek girl and leaves me here bound to a wretched marriage. No! What am I saying? I must do something. Though I have no shame left, I will first seek my sister, who must be anxious for her sons."

She rose. Barefoot, wearing only her night-gown, she opened the door of her chamber and crossed the threshold on the way to her sister's rooms. But there she stood a long time, arrested by shame. She went back inside and then out again, unable to commit to coming or going in her tergiversations. She gave up at the fourth attempt, and threw herself face downward on her bed to weep.

One of her maid-servants, hearing her sobs, saw Medeia lying there in tears and ran off to inform Chalciope, who at that moment sat in converse with her sons on how to win over her sister. Alarmed, she rushed to Medeia's apartment. Finding her in anguish, her cheeks reddened with scratches, and her eyes swimming, she cried: "My darling, why such tears? What has happened? Are you ill? Or has our father told you what he has planned for me and my sons? How I wish I could be far, far from this place!"

Medeia, sitting up, grew flush. She was eager to give her an answer, but shame checked her. But as love had her heart and tongue bridled, she addressed the matter indirectly, hoping to make Chalciope entreat her: "Sister, my heart is wrenched for your sons, lest our father destroy them along with the strangers. Just now, as I dozed, I saw an awful vision—may some god circumvent it and keep you from grief!"

Chalciope, pained with terror at her words, said: "It is for that very reason I have come, Medeia: to enlist your aid. But swear by heaven and earth to keep secret what I tell you. By the blessed gods, by your own parents, do not let evil befall my sons, or else I will die and return with them from Hell to haunt you."

Chalciope could no longer hold back her tears. Clasping her sister's knees, she buried her head in her lap. Throughout house one could hear the faint sound of their weeping.

"You scare me with such talk!" said Medeia. "Would that I had the power to save your sons! Behold the Colchian's awful oath you make me swear, by great heaven above and beneath the Earth, mother of the gods! As I have the power, I will not fail you."
Chalciope readily answered: "Can you not then devise some ruse to help the stranger, for my sons' sake? Argos approached me on his behalf. He waits back in my chamber for your response."
Medeia's heart leapt for joy and a deep blush mantled her white skin. With misty eyes she said: "Chalciope, I will do your pleasure. May my eyes never again see the shining dawn; may you no longer see me among the living, if I do not look to your life and that of your sons, to me almost like brothers. And you—I am your sister and daughter, for you held me to your breast when I was a babe, or so mother has declared. Go now; but keep our business hidden from our parents. At dawn I shall visit Hecate's temple to prepare a potent charm against the bulls."

Chalciope joyfully departed to inform her sons of her sister's promise. But once alone again, Medeia was seized with shame and terror. To think that she plotted against her father's will for a stranger's benefit! As stillness enveloped the deepening gloom, sleep fled further from her. She could think of nothing but Jason meeting a horrible end before the awful bulls. Her heart beat wildly within her: like sunbeams, reflecting off an urn's tremulous water, dances upon the walls. As she wept uncontrollably a wasting pain shot through her, searing her body, starting at the nape of her neck. She did not know whether to carry out her promise and fetch the charms; or to die herself; or to do neither and with patience await her fate. She long debated with herself the reason for such unfilial devotion to a stranger. "O! How I wish that Artemis had put an end to me with her swift arrows ere I saw that man!" she wept. "How I can help him, and not be discovered? Alas, whether he lives or dies, misery is my lot. Away then with shame! Let him go where he pleases, saved by my help. Then I'll kill myself. But how the Colchian women will despise my name—a girl who betrayed her father for a stranger's love! How I now regret my weakness before this consuming passion!"

With wild eyes she looked about. The thought came to her to end her life that night and avoid disgrace rather than carry through her scheme. On impulse she rose to fetch the casket in which she kept her many drugs. One bitter drink, she thought, would loosen the grip of fatal love. Placing the casket on her knees, she wept, dropping great tears upon her lap. She fumbled with the lid's latch. But, suddenly struck with the horror of death, she stayed her trembling hand. The sweetness of life, even with all its cares, could not escape her. She thought of its many pleasures; of her happy playmates; of the sun's delectable light. She could neither take her life, nor take control of it. Resigning to her fate, she put away the chest and waited for the dawn.

## 15

Awaking with a considerable headache, Heracles found his arms and legs weighed down by chains and manacles. Instead of a comfortable bed, he lay once again on a wagon pulled by a team of oxen down a paved avenue shadowed by immense red granite sphinxes. To one side, beyond the thick bulrushes, flowed the rushing Nile. Ahead, a pair of red granite obelisks, and behind them two seated statues of white alabaster, guarded the monumental entrance to the great temple of Amon. The light of the rising sun broke through the flanking towers of the pylon, richly carved with colored figures, and topped by flag-staves.

Priests in immaculate white linen marched gravely and quietly in front, while behind trailed what seemed the entire populace of the city, cheering loudly and led by dancing women gaily twirling ribands and snapping castanets. The festive atmosphere ceased as they passed through gold-plated doors under the gateway, where all but Heracles and the priests were prevented from entering. The golden doors were closed and the people piled before it offerings of wine, incense, honey and oil; bouquets of flowers; loaves of bread and platters of fruits and meats; jugs of beer and sacks of finely milled durra and barley.

Beyond the door spread an open court surrounded by a colonnade of massive stone pillars. In the middle of the court temple-servants fed a deep fire-pit with coal and timber, fanning the flames so that they crackled high into the air. Heracles turned his face from the intense heat as he was rolled past.

The wagon halted before the porch to the dark interior of the hypostyle hall. Temple-guards, ten on each side, pulled Heracles from the wagon and led him, bowed with chains, to stand before the porch. He did not resist, as he was curious what mischief the Egyptians wished to work on him now. He called to the herald Chalbes, who stood among the priests nearby, and asked him what was to be done with him. Chalbes explained that, years before, after a series of bad harvests, Egypt was struck with want. Busiris, unable to receive an answer from the gods as to how to remedy the situation, called for a famed seer from Cyprus named Phrasius, who advised him to sacrifice a stranger to Zeus Amon each year in order to restore prosperity. Busiris, ever cruel, zealously followed the command by first sacrificing Phrasius, after which the god seemed pleased by sending a plentiful harvest. Since then, Busiris scarified a stranger each year; preferably one of red hair or complexion, since such men were rare in Egypt, and, when found, were no doubt strangers. In addition, the priests added, red was the color of the god Set, the enemy of mankind, and his symbolic representation in the human offering augmented the efficacy of the sacrifice.

Busiris, wrapped in a black mantle, emerged from the hall, carried on an ebony stool inlaid with ivory, and holding out an arm, enjoined silence. A priest approached with a bowl, from which he took out a some strands of hair to show Busiris. He said: "O High Priest and First Prophet of Amon and chief of the secrets of heaven: the stranger's hair possesses a ruddy luster in the sunlight; by this alone we know Amon-Ra is pleased to send this offering." Busiris nodded in acknowledgment. At this, Heracles lifted his head and said: "I charge you, Busiris, with a double crime. Not only does your cruelty and treachery offend the laws of hospitality; but even worse, your plan to sacrifice a man and not an animal is abhorrent and an unspeakable evil, especially to Zeus, whom you pretend to worship." Busiris beckoned Heracles forward. He was compelled up the steps and chained to the two central columns that held up the porch so that his arms were outstretched. In the dimness of the hypostyle hall, supported by massive pillars and lighted only by small square windows under the roof, he could make out a multitude of priests.

Busiris said: "Far from being cruel, Heracles, I carry out the wishes of the great god to save my people. Would you allow one to live and many to die? It is meet that one man should die for the good of all."

A reciter-priest came forth to read from a scroll the sacred prayers while the hypostyle hall was incensed. Then, as the priests withdrew beyond the hall into the holy place to prepare the image of the god for a public procession, Heracles was sprinkled with lustral water infused with hyssop and, as he raged against the chains that held him, crowned with lotus flowers. He spat at so ignoble an end, strung up like a beast for an unholy sacrifice.

Mingled with sweet incense wafting from the hall came the noise of a sistrum. A tight brood of priests, chanting discordantly, walked forth between the columns holding up on their shoulders by poles a small barque manned by a crew of small bronze figures, with a little deck cabin in the center covered with canopy of fine linen dyed blue. Heracles bowed his shoulders and pulled with might and main until the manacles cut into his flesh. Giving up, he let out an anguished cry that echoed through the pillared hall. At the bruit, the priests apprehensively halted their procession.

"There is no need to hide the god from me," said Heracles wryly.

"The image of the god cannot be exposed to profane eyes," said Busiris

"I say there is no need," Heracles countered, "since we have already become acquainted, when he appeared to me not long ago wearing a ram's head and fleece."

Busiris sprang from his seat and struck Heracles with the back of his hand, commanding him to be silent and cease his blasphemy. As Heracles glowered from the affront, his eyes fell upon a badge hanging from Busiris' neck. The amulet, shaped from hollow gold and inlaid with glass, depicted the face of a goddess with cow's horns, heavy braided plaits and twinkling eyes of lapis lazuli. Busiris, noting Heracles' curiosity, said: "I bear the image of Hathor, the celestial mother, consort of Amon-Ra and protectress of the Theban necropolis."

Now Heracles burned with fury. He growled through gritted teeth and rattled his chains. "I see by her cow-eyes," he said ruefully, "that she is none other than Hera, here present to ensure my murder. It shall not be this day! No one takes my life from me." Busiris, taking alarm, stepped back into the company of Chalbes and Amphidamas. Craning his neck to glimpse the sun beyond the edge of the cornice, Heracles cried: "Father! If it be your will, show these impious Egyptians that you have sent me forth into the world to cast out the insolent and bring lawfulness to men. If not, then let me die with them!" Silence descended on the sacred precinct, as the superstitious priests, filled with perturbation, expected some heavenly response to the somber entreaty. Suddenly an eagle, holding in its claws a writhing serpent, and so large that some called it a phoenix, flew over the walls and circled twice overhead. On the third go-around the serpent slipped from it grasp and fell into the court, from where it slithered away into the shadows of the colonnade. The priests, though struck with awe, did not know what to make of the sight. Heracles, taking heart from the omen, drew in so great a breath that his stature seemed to increase and the muscles of his arms and back thickened like limestone. Turning about his hands within the fetters to grasp the chains, with deep groans he relentlessly pulled until blood dripped from his fingers. Busiris at first watched this deranged exertion with trepidation, unable to comprehend what it was Heracles attempted. Looking then for reassurance at the massive pillars and the high roof of the porch, he laughed nervously and cried to Amphidamas, thrusting a sacrificial flint knife into his hand, "It is time! Slay him!" Amphidamas looked from his father to Heracles and back. Afraid to disobey, he took a few faltering steps toward the struggling hero, who convulsed with the ferocity of a boar caught in a hunting-net, but froze at a loud noise from above, like the clack of lightning in a field. Dust and flecks of stone fell upon him. One temple-guard, seeing a crack rising through the entablature, exclaimed: "Surely, he is the son of Amon!" Heracles uttered one final cry. The pillars to which he was chained shifted slightly from their plinths, and then a moment later toppled with an unavoidable and horrendous rapidity, bringing down the porch roof in a deadly rain of masonry upon Busiris, Amphidamas and Chalbes, who had stood there stupefied.

Heracles flew backward off the porch as the pillars crumpled, narrowly missed by a chunk of the cornice that crashed down beside him. As he, considering his good fortune, unpinned his shackles, the remaining priests and temple attendants ran off through the dust in a panic, leaving the sacred barque of Amon overturned on the floor of the hypostyle hall. Heracles found his lionskin and weapons in a pile by the fiery pit, which would have been, had all gone as planned, committed with his dead body to the flames. In the few moments it took to gird and equip himself, the city's garrison was already at the gates. Heracles climbed atop the ruined temple porch and picked off with his arrows the first intrepid soldiers to venture inside. Bruised and spent beyond all human endurance, he thought it wise to avoid a fight. He retreated into the hypostyle hall, through a small open court, and into the chapel area. He investigated the dark, empty chambers, and the adjacent storerooms, until he located and struck open a door, long fallen into disuse, which opened to a path leading down to the river. There he found a number of boats. He climbed aboard the smallest one, spread the square sail into the breeze and pushed off, guiding the vessel to midstream by a single large oar extending toward the back, while sitting, hidden from his enemies eyes, under the rush canopy of the pilot's cabin.

The north wind, blowing continuously, in little time propelled him up the meandering river, past Egyptian Thebes and the necropolis to a verdant island at a widening of the Nile, called Elephantine because it was shaped like an oliphant's tusk. The island appeared heavily fortified, with castles all around its eastern side. Heracles steered clear of it, and from smaller inhabited islands nearby, and sailed boldly upstream through the shallow rapids, where hard rocks and islets obstructed the river's flow. The river churned through the cataract; and as roiling white froth descended from a gorge framed by sandstone cliffs. As Heracles sought for a convenient place to debark, he felt what seemed like hail striking the cabin. Suddenly an arrow lodged by his feet. Heracles crawled forth to face a smattering of falling arrows and spears. Tall, half-naked sun-burnt Ethiopians crowded the cliffs to each side, running across the ridges to keep pace with his boat while they attacked. Heracles nocked an arrow, pulled his bow into a circle, and held the arrow to his cheek as he surveyed who best to first dispatch. He picked out one Ethiopian poised on a crag ready to cast a spear, exceedingly tall, his face smeared with white chalk, draped in a leopard's skin and wearing an elaborate head-dress of ostrich and goose feathers. Guessing him their leader, Heracles discharged the arrow straight into his breast. He fell headlong still grasping the spear-haft and tumbled down the rocks. Unbeknownst to Heracles, he was Emathion, brother of Memnon, a son of Tithonos and the Dawn, and king of the Ethiopians. Witnessing the death of their king only emboldened his subjects, who renewed their attack with wild cries.  Straightway Heracles, under the danger of whizzing arrows, wheeled the boat around, tore down the sail, and released it to the current.  The Ethiopians followed in tandem as far as the rapids, which marked the border with Egypt, where they dispersed, afraid to arouse the ire of the Elephantine garrison.  Heracles felt like he was riding a feather in the wind as he struggled to avoid being thrust upon the boulders jutting from the riverbed.  Once past the cataract, the river became navigable again, and carried him past Thebes with no incident, since he stayed hidden in the cabin, with only his legs and club, of necessity, sticking out.  For a long way thence Heracles saw only ploughmen preparing their fields or tending to their dykes and sluices for the coming summer inundation, when the Nile spread its gift of black mud.  The next day he passed Memphis, a city on the western bank of the river that rivaled Thebes in the grandeur of its temples and structures.  Above Memphis towered the three great Pyramids of ancient renown, each larger in succession, gleaming through the desert haze like fiery beacons.  Beyond these wonders the river bifurcated.  Heracles steered into the eastern branch, lower and narrower, to better view an army of slaves on a great plain baking mud bricks under the watchful eyes of their taskmasters, until it drained into the vast swamp of the Delta, lined with marshes and the flowering rush, stocked with crocodiles, hippopotamuses and wading oxen, and swarming with a cloud of marsh-birds.  Heracles, plagued by hunger, used an Ethiopian spear to catch a few silvery fish.  He drew the little boat onto a sandbank, and there passed the balmy night watching the sun drop below the Libyan hills.

16

At first light, Medeia bound her golden tresses hanging over her shoulders in disarray, rubbed clean her tear-stained cheeks, and anointed her skin with sweet-smelling ointment. She dressed in a splendid robe decorated with fine brooches and wrapped around her lovely head a shining veil. Pacing around the room, feeling nothing for past or future, she called upon her twelve unmarried handmaids, who slept outside her fragrant apartment, to yoke the mules and harness them to a wagon for a trip to Hecate's shrine. While they rushed to obey their mistress, Medeia took from her casket its most potent potion, distilled from a special flower engendered in the life-blood of Prometheus, having dripped from the ravening eagle's beak upon the mountain-slopes where chill winds and hoarfrost tempered its stem and leaves. In a Hyrcanian seashell she had gathered the black sap from this flower, which in color and appearance much resembled the saffron-crocus, a cubit tall, growing upon a double stalk, and whose bulbous roots had the look of severed flesh, on a moonless night, naked, crying and howling, after having bathed in seven perennial streams, and seven times called on night-wandering Hecate, queen of the dead. And as she cut the root with a bronze sickle, covering with a hand her eyes, the earth shook and it seemed as if the groans of the Titan himself rolled over the land.

She concealed the simple in the fragrant girdle girding her bosom and, hurrying out, mounted her wagon. With a handmaiden on either side she herself took the reins and goad and raced through the town, while the others ran along behind with skirts hiked up to their white thighs. The citizens shunned the princess' gaze. She drove out of the city and across the plain, straight to Hecate's shrine. Dismounting, she told her playmates: "I've made a grievous error, my dears, in coming out here while these foreigners wander about. Our city is gripped with terror, and it is no wonder that this shrine lies empty of women. But since we are here, let us enjoy ourselves somewhat in gathering blossoms as we're wont, and then later return to our house at the usual time. But friends—one thing more. You'll go home laden with gifts if you follow a little plan of mine. Argos and Chalciope are trying to mislead me. Keep all of this quiet now! They said I ought to help the stranger, the one that took up the challenge with the bulls, in return for some gifts. I've agreed to their words, and asked him to meet me here alone. He will bring the gifts, which I will divide with you, while I will give him a charm more deadly than he thinks. You must leave me when he arrives."

⸙

Argos had returned to the ship during the night, leaving his brothers at the palace in order to find out what Medeia had a mind to do. When they turned up and told Argos that Medeia planned to go to Hecate's temple at dawn, Argos drew Jason apart to inform him. They set out for the temple, taking Mopsos, since he was skilled in interpreting omens.

On the road near the shrine they passed a black poplar-tree, thick with leaves, where chattering crows came to roost. One of them, eyeing Mopsos, said: "There's a dim prophet, who knows not what even children do: that no maiden will speak sweet words of love to a young man if there are others present. Go away, sorry seer! It is not you that Cypris favors." Mopsos understood the crow's speech, and smiling at the portent, told Jason to continue alone to the shrine, while he and Argos waited.

At the infernal goddess' shady precinct Medeia found no amusement in her disport. Her eyes continually wandered from her playmates to the far-off paths. More than once her heart skipped a beat at the sound of a footfall or of wind rustling the leaves.

Then she saw him, as if for the first time.

He appeared like the Dog Star's sudden rising from the sea in the grip of summer, fair and bright, but bringing dire woe upon the fields. Her heart grew still; her eyes dim. Fire overspread her face. Rooted to the ground, she could not move. Her love, languishing in indecisive torment, ignited like a spark buried under ashes rekindled by a breath of wind.

The handmaids, as bidden, melted away. The two stood face to face without a word, like oaks or lofty pines stand silently upon a mountain side by side in the still air: but when a breeze rustles them they murmur to no end. Medeia, moving back her veil, longed for Jason to say her name. He saw the flush of her cheeks mingling with the pallor of her distress, and felt wonder at the golden sheen of her eyes.

"My lady, why so fretful that I come alone?" said Jason with a kind smile. "I am not now, and never have been, like those vainglorious fellows. You may ask or tell me anything you wish. As friends we come together in this holy place, and far be any offense from it! Only do not beguile me with honeyed words, since you promised your sister to give me some helpful gift. I implore you, by all that is sacred, to help me, since without you I cannot surmount your father's trial. In exchange I promise to exalt your name throughout all Greece. Remember Ariadne, virgin daughter of Pasiphaë and king Minos, who saved Theseus from certain death, and stole away with him on a ship. She was much beloved by the gods for this. So too shall you the gods love you should you rescue me and my crew. You certainly look like one not unused to acts of kindness."

His comforting words melted her heart like rose-dew dissolving under the morning sun. She turned aside to lose a smile and then thought to speak, but the words fled her lips. She could not bring order to the tumult of thoughts and expressions that weltered within her, roiled by an admixture of fear, love and shame. At length, raising her eyes to him, she reached into her sweet-scented bosom to clutch the phial of Promethean unguent. But she checked herself, and with mild defiance said: "If you put any hope in your gods, or if your strength alone suffices to save you from doom, I pray, allow me to go guiltless back to my father." And as the stars faded from the sky, with tears she withdrew the potion and held it out. Overjoyed, Jason immediately laid hands on it. She luxuriated in his need of her.

In quiet suspense they stole glances and sweet smiles. Forcing herself to speak, she explained to him the ritual he had to perform to effectuate the potion that would make him withstand the savage bulls.

"Yet it will make you mighty for one day only; still, do not flinch from the encounter," she concluded. "I will tell you something else. After you have yoked the deadly oxen, and by your strength have ploughed the stubborn ground and seeded it with the teeth, when you see the living crop commence to rise, cast a great stone into their midst. They will fall on it like devouring dogs and slay each other. Seize that moment to reap the bloody harvest."

Medeia hesitated a moment and then said distractedly: "Yes: your task done, you will carry off the Fleece far, far from Aia. Leaving here, you shall go where you wish."

Medeia dropped her eyes in silence as warm tears wet her fair cheeks from the thought of his departure across the seas. Then, feeling a sharp pang in her heart, she grasped his right hand and said: "Forget me not. I swear I shall remember you always." Holding him in her eyes, she continued rapidly: "Tell me, then, about your home. What sea-route will you take there? Will you come near rich Orchomenos or pass by the isle of Aiaia, home of my aunt Circe? And tell me more of that maiden you mentioned before, the famed daughter of my father's sister Pasiphaë."

Moved by her tears, Jason too felt the pull of love for the sheltered girl. He said: "Of one thing only am I sure, Medeia: if I escape and live to reach Haimonian Iolcos, never by night or day shall I forget you."

Jason, thinking that he could sooth her by gentle speech, remarked her sudden agitation. Once more wracked by grief, she sputtered earnestly: "May some whisper reach me from a far-off land, or some bird bring me news, when you forget me. Then let a swift wind snatch me up and bear me across the sea to Iolcos, that I may reproach you to your face with reminders of who it was who saved you! It shall be then that I sit openly in your halls!"

The sluice of her piteous tears opened anew. Jason, cutting her words short, said: "Dear lady, let the winds and birds blow where they list. You speak in a silly manner. Do you think that I can accept your help and then desert you? Far better that you should abandon me, take back this charm, and release me to my death. How could I return home unless all Greece welcome and honor you? And who but you will tend to the bed of our nuptial chamber, where nothing will come between our love unless death enfolds us? By the powers that sway alike the gods above and below, by the stars whose course you turn, by this very hour of trial: I swear that if I forget this night, this kind deed for my sake—the flight from your father and home—then let my triumph be short-lived; let your cunning art find and destroy me; let no one be near to help such an ingrate; and if you can think of penalties worse than that then include them as you turn away amid my terror."

Jason said the words she had waited all night to hear. But her joy could not surmount the fear that gripped her heart. Scarcely able to speak, Medeia said: "There is yet a greater peril once you vanquish the bulls and defeat the sown men. The Fleece you seek has a dangerous warden. May you have faith in Hecate and me, and in our powers! See what is to pass!"

Medeia waved a hand before Jason's face. Suddenly he saw before him the dim phantom of a monstrous snake, coiled around a tree, rearing its head. In dismay, he bared his sword, but just as fast the vision melted against the darkness of the grove.

"This yet remains," said Medeia; "but I too shall be there with you."

The maid-servants, at a distance, began to hitch the mules for the ride home, for the hour required Medeia's return to her mother. Medeia was loath to be separated from Jason. But he, mindful of the risk of their discovery, bid his farewell, promising to meet her again soon at the same place. Medeia returned to her handmaids, who flocked around her: but she, her soul enraptured to the clouds, paid them no heed. Absently climbing her wagon, she took reins and lash in hand, and set off for the palace. Chalciope, in agony over sons, sought her as soon as she arrived. Oblivious to her questions, Medeia settled on a stool at the foot of her bed, leaning to rest her cheek on her left hand, and with tearful eyes pondered the evil about to be born from her schemes.

Jason joyfully returned to Argos and Mopsos, who waited by the poplar-tree, and, after recounting what Medeia had told him, returned with them to the ship. Jason showed his companions the princess' potent charm and all rejoiced save Idas, a man of action, who sat apart to nurse his rage at their credulity and misplaced trust in women. After breakfasting, Jason sent his herald Aethalides, and Telamon as a bodyguard, to the city to secure from the king the dragon's teeth. These Athena had divided between Aiëtes, as a gift when he governed Corinth, and Cadmos, who slew the monster.

For after Zeus, in bull's form, carried off Europa, her father Agenor commanded his son to either find her or suffer exile from their Phoenician land. With his companions he roamed far in vain, until, wearied of the search, he sought Delphi's shrine for guidance on a settling-place. He was told to follow a heifer, whose neck was never burdened with a yoke, to where it lay to rest, and there to found a city. He soon met one passing by, unguided by any herdsman, and followed carefully her trail to the Boetian land, which he called Aonia. After fording the river Cesiphos, and crossing the fields of Panope, the heifer raised her horned head and lowed before kneeling to rest on the grass. Cadmos, filled with gratitude, kissed the foreign soil and, to prepare for the thanksgiving sacrifice, sent his servants to seek fresh water from a spring. They came to an ancient forest, whose gnarled boles never suffered an axe, and found a stream gushing from a shaded grotto. No sooner had they dipped their urns into the flowing waters than the cave's guardian, a monstrous sky-dyed serpent, thrust out its head. As the men stood unmoving, trembling, their blood running cold, the dragon slithered out the rest of its scaly body, and rearing upward, with a hiss puffed open the frilled skin around its head. The men vainly fought or tried to run. Twisting and darting from above, the snake attacked them, killing some with its fangs, crushing others with its sweeping tail, and poisoning the rest by its pestilential breath. As the shadows of day's end crept into the wood, Cadmos went in search of his companions. Seeing their bloated bodies, and in their midst the coursing serpent lapping at their bloody wounds, Cadmos lifted a rock and heaved it on the monster, which repelled against the viper's plated back. Next he let fly his javelin, which entered betwixt the scales, driving the iron point deep into the serpent's belly. Hissing with fury, the serpent coiled itself and sprung. Cadmos resisted the thrust with his lion's hide shield, and drove his lance into the horrid maw. The snake, biting furiously with its triple-banked teeth, forced the spear-point to greater damage, and poisonous blood dripped from its palate. Unable to withstand the son of Agenor, the serpent tried to flee, slithering away on undulating coils. But Cadmos ran forward and cast his hard lance, pinning the creature by the neck to a stout oak-tree. There the slimy bulk writhed until it perished. Athena, then, flew in from the sky and dashed out the serpent's teeth. Giving him his share, Athena ordered Cadmos to plough the ground and scatter the teeth like seed. He did so; and as he dug the furrows, behold! from the ground sprang lance-heads and plumed helmets: a crop of armed men in battle-array. Alarmed, having not other arms at his disposal, Cadmos cast rocks among them. Rather than fight him, they turned on one another and fought in bloody frenzy until only five remained standing. These made peace among themselves and pledged their fealty to Cadmos, who on the spot founded the city of Thebes.

Aiëtes, surprised to see the messengers, handed them the yellowed teeth in a shiny bronze helmet. In the unlikely event Jason succeeded in yoking the bulls, he knew that what awaited thereafter would prove his undoing.

When grim night overspread the Colchian land, at that witching hour between dusk and dawn with the bleary moon yet three nights short of filling out its horns, Jason stole out like a thief, leaving his friends asleep under the hawsers, and made his way across the plain with what he needed for the rites Medeia prescribed. At a lonely spot by the river's side, open to the sky, he first bathed his body in the cold, running water, and wrapped himself in the black robe Hypsipyle had given him at their parting. He next dug a pit a cubit deep, piled it with kindling, and over it cut the throat of an ewe Argos had procured for him from a farm. As he burned the carcase whole, pouring out on it libations of milk mixed with bitter honey from Butes, who had searched out for him a hive, Jason invoked the mysterious Hecate for aid. He withdrew from the pyre, as Medeia had told him, and not once looked behind as he fled, though the terrible sounds that followed behind him nearly crippled with him terror. Had he turned, he would have witnessed the awful sight of dread goddess, having heard him from the nethermost abyss, rising from the mists, surrounded by the howling of her hellish hounds and crowned with an oak-leaf coronal entwined with gruesome serpents. The river-meadow trembled at her feet and glowed as with countless torches; while the nymphs haunting the marshes cried out in fear.

Jason rejoined his crewmen as daylight broke over the snowy peaks of the Caucasus. He wasted no time in melting Medeia's unguent, and sprinkled with it his shield, spear and sword. As a test, his friends assailed him on all sides with all their might, but not one could make a mark in his shield or arms. Seeing this, Idas furiously hacked the butt of Jason's spear with his mighty sword, but the blade leapt from it like a hammer from an anvil. Jason then anointed his body. Straightway a new potency coursed through him. His hands and arms grew plump with strength. Filled with manly vigor, Jason leapt about in a frenzy, flashing his shield and thrusting his ashen spear, brimming with confidence and valor.

At Jason's word, the oarsmen took to the benches and rowed the *Argo* swiftly upstream to the plain of Ares where a large crowd of Colchians crowded the mountain spurs to watch the spectacle. Aiëtes, in full armor, his head weighed down by his golden, four-plated helmet shining like the sun, wheeled around the river-side grounds on his mighty chariot. As soon as the hawsers were made fast, Jason vaulted from the ship with his shield and arms, and the casque full of teeth; and strode with his bare, glistening chest, like that of glorious Apollo, onto the field to where the enormous brazen yoke and the plough of adamantine-strength rested together. He fixed the end of his heavy spear into the ground, rested the casque against it, and set off to examine the deep tracks of the bulls. Meanwhile Aiëtes took his seat on the dais beside his wife, with Medeia and Apsyrtos on either side, and behind them the nobles and allied chieftains. Draped in a golden robe reaching to her bare feet, Medeia held a gilded mask to her face, through which, nipping her lips, she watched Jason with her glittering eyes.

At a signal from Aiëtes trumpets sounded. From a grotto within the rocky outcroppings framing the river came a great noise, and from a belching of black smoke emerged two enormous bulls as black as jet, their thumping feet and curved horns shod in bronze. The Argonauts gasped; and even Idas, shuddering, looked in Medeia's direction hoping to see from her some immediate aid.

Seeing Jason, one of the bulls, pawing the ground in anger, snorted and charged at him, thundering against the earth as it ran. Jason planted his feet apart and resolutely held his shield, confident that Medeia's magic would protect him. But as the bull came nigh, his heart misgave, and shifting his stance, received a glancing blow from the stout horns. Jason staggered sideways from the brunt, but remained on his feet, to the exultation of the spectators, who had witnessed none but Aiëtes in his youth do the like. Jason set off after the trotting bull, and as it turned toward him, shaking its broad back, he reached out to grasp the tip of its brazen horn. The bull bellowed, trying to shake free, but Jason hinged his shield-arm over its high shoulder-crest, and held fast as it raged about leaping and thrusting to cast him off. When the beast for a moment ceased its struggle to catch a breath, Jason dropped his shield and grabbed ahold of the other horn. The bull once more rampaged, dragging him in circles around the field. But Jason pressed down on the muscular neck, and by a several kicks to its legs brought the bull, weary from the constant struggle, down to its knees. As Jason held it's snout against the ground, feeling the heat of its arduous blasts of breath, he called out to the Dioscuri, who raced onto the field as they had rehearsed, picked up the yoke and carried it to Jason. Meanwhile the second beast, charmed by Medeia's quietly muttered spell, tractably approached and sunk down beside its companion. Jason, unable to believe his good fortune, forced the yoke onto their necks, bound it tightly, and fastened the bronze pole in between. After hitching them to the plough, Jason took up his shield from the ground and slung it on his back. Holding the heavy teeth-filled casque in the crook of his arm, he pricked the bulls' flanks with his spear, and with a firm hand on the handle began to drive the plough and scatter the unnatural seed far behind him into the cloven sod.

Jason toiled until the wheeling sun fell deep into its westward course. When he had left long furrows from one end of the plain to the other, he freed the oxen and scared them off. The crowds grew silent. Seeing the fallows devoid of the expected crop, Jason returned to the ship where his comrades pressed around him with heartening words. He dipped the casque into the river to slake his thirst, and then, still nourished by divine mettle, bent his knees to keep them supple, foaming at the mouth for the next ordeal.

Aiëtes, meanwhile, marveled at the young man's strength. He had fully expected to see Jason already dead and the destruction of the *Argo*'s crew begun. He glanced with suspicion at Medeia, who sat still and erect, her face hidden behind the mask. With a tap of his scepter, he inaugurated another flourish of trumpet-blasts.

Clods of earth stirred throughout the plain. The upturned sod glittered here and there. As Jason looked, the furrows began to sprout crested helmets. Men rose as if from the grave, pulling up with them stout shields and double-tipped spears. At once Jason sprang among the nearest and with whirring blade sliced through necks and shoulders, pruning the rising warriors like bushes, leaving them lying on their faces, or on their sides, half-emerged. But the field grew abristle with threatening spears as armed men by the dozens, freed from the ground, converged on him. Jason, maddened by the effect of Medeia's decoction, still believed he could overcome them until he spotted a huge round boulder; remembering Medeia's instructions, he heaved it on his shoulders and cast it at the advancing horde. Medeia, by her dark arts, inflamed the Scythian mercenaries, who had waited in tunnels beneath the plain for Aiëtes' signal to emerge, to attack one another at the sight of the boulder falling in their midst. As Jason crouched behind his shield, they turned their spears and with angry shouts leapt on each other in savage frenzy until the furrows ran with their blood. Jason, with fevered brow and pounding heart, rushed into the fray when there were only a few left standing, and completed the slaughter. In the end they lay like saplings flattened by the heavy rain.

While Aiëtes, appalled and amazed, surveyed the unexpected scene, Jason, blood-soaked, bathed in the river and returned to his company on the ship. A new mood lay hold on the Argonauts: the Golden Fleece was now theirs by right, and they would not shrink from seizing it by force if necessary.

17

The dawn glowed beautifully, reflecting like blood in the flowing canals. Heracles considered continuing on foot from the Delta, but then thought it more expedient to sail across the sea to Phrygia, since the wind had changed to the south. As soon as he washed out of the mouth of the Nile he regretted his decision. The tide pushed his little boat back three times into the bulrushes. After detangling himself from the mud, he caught a good wind gust, and made it a bowshot from the shore before the waves contested with the winds to buffet the little vessel. Heracles, discontented to be bested by the elements, strove mightily with the steering-oar to keep the boat on as steady a course as he knew, which, as he was not by natural ability or training a navigator, was marked by a broad margin of error. For two days he rode the main, and on the morning of the third spotted mountains rising to the west. A head sea pushed him back, so he sculled with the steering-oar until he came to a rocky beach down from a broad harbor busy with ships. A well-appointed town rose above it on the side of a hill, looking south. Heracles, his belly rumbling and his throat parched with thirst, wandered into a field where he saw a cowherd driving his cart. He grabbed the bullocks by the horns to stop them. "Off with you!" said the drover. "I need hire no help; as you can see I manage quite well by myself." Heracles, despite his poor state, laughed and said, "I am not here to deprive you of your work; only of one your bullocks. Give one to me that I may sacrifice it to Zeus for saving me from the Egyptians and bringing me safely to—where, pray tell, am I?" The drover laughed also, but in mocking way, and responded, "Did you not arrive at Thermydrai yonder, the harbor of Rhodian Lindos?" Heracles, pleased with himself, said: "By his beard! I am not far from Phrygia, then." He proceeded then, despite the protestations of the cowherd, to unyoke one of the bullocks. As he led it away, the cowherd stormed off to the top of a nearby hill, and there flung at Heracles a continuous stream of censure, laden with the most execrable and injurious words imaginable. Heracles took this in good humor, since by leaving the other bullock untouched he had not deprived the man too badly of his livelihood, and took apart a stone wall to build an altar. After slaying the bullock and sacrificing it to Zeus, he sat and filled his belly with the sizzling meat under the continuous carping, leaving at the end only a pile of bones and offal. The Lindians ever remember this incident, and for this reason utter curses whenever they sacrifice to Heracles, thinking it of especial efficacy for the fertility of their fields and animals, since the drover whose bullock was taken never encountered any barrenness in livestock thereafter.

Heracles took passage, at no expense, on a vessel of burden bound for Ephesus, since the supercargo considered him a ward against the Samians, who were notorious for their piracy. Heracles disembarked in the territory of Miletos, where he went to visit the temple and oracle of Apollo, said to be as ancient and venerable as that of Delphi. He did not enter there as an adorant, content only to observe the sacred buildings and the laurel grove where a small temple housed the image of the god. From Ephesus Heracles struck out on foot, following along the Meander river to the outskirts of Maionia.

Medeia reached her chamber atremble and terrified, certain that her father would not fail to detect her hand in Jason's triumph. There existed no country distant enough, she knew, where she could flee his wrath. Even if she could dissuade him of her complicity, she feared too the loose tongues of her handmaids, who had been privy to her secret meeting with Jason. Medeia paced her room with burning eyes and haunted by a fearful roaring in her ears. For want of air in the depths of her misery she clutched at her throat. Gnawed by grief, she tore her hair and groaned in anguish. Once more her poisons came to mind. She poured her phials in her lap, ready to consume them all, when a hopeful thought pierced the dark cloud of her despair: to flee with Jason and the sons of Phrixos was her only option. She put away her potions. With trembling lips she kissed her bed. She kissed her door-posts. She fondly stroked the walls which contained her happy childhood. She cut off a long golden tress and left it on her pillow for her mother, saying: "O mother! I go, leaving here this in memory of me. Farewell Chalciope! Farewell father, for whom I weep: if only I might leave warmed by your tender embrace. Farewell my home! Had you never come to Colchis, Jason! Had the sea dashed you to pieces on your way."

Weeping silently, Medeia stole from the palace, the doors opening of their own accord in response to her hurried incantations. In bare feet she ran down narrow alleyways, lifting up the hem of her robe and hiding her face with a fold of her mantle. By a secret way she was able to leave the city undetected by the night's watches: one she well knew from her nocturnal excursions in search of corpses or noxious roots as witches use. In fear, nevertheless, she hurried from the city's walls down to the river's high bank, from where, looking across, she remarked the gleam of the campfire the Argonauts kept blazing through the night as they reveled in Jason's victory. Through the gloom her voice was recognized by Phrontis. At Jason's urging he replied, until thrice they exchanged words. The men extended their oars and rowed eagerly across the river, where, with hawsers hardly secured, Jason vaulted from the foredeck to the ground to meet her. With him followed Phrontis and Argos. Seeing them, Medeia dropped to her knees and with outstretched hands cried: "Save me, friends, and yourselves from king Aiëtes! All is discovered. Let us escape in your swift ship before he harnesses his swift horses!"

Jason, full of pity, said: "Medeia, in you alone I have found my reward, even without the Fleece. In your goodness, and through your great power, grant that I may accomplish that for which I came and bring home that great relic."

"I will give you the Golden Fleece," said Medeia, "after dealing with its guardian. But now you, in sight of your companions, take heaven to witness the solemn vows you made to me; and, once far from here, to not bring shame on me when there are no more kinsmen to protect me. For your sake, Jason, I leave my father's house. A princess no longer, I shall henceforth live as an exile, abandoning all I have to follow my heart."

Jason gently raised the sobbing girl and comforted her in his arms. "Dear lady," he said; "I swear by Olympian Zeus, and his consort Hera, patron of wedlock, that on our return, I will bring you to my house as my wedded wife."

Jason clasped his right hand in hers as confirmation of his pledge.

Medeia urged them to row speedily to the sacred grove in order to make off with the Fleece while it was yet night. They took her on board and pushed off from the bank to row upstream with alacrity. As the glittering city receded, Medeia, stung by sudden regret, stretched her arms over the gunwale, wishing to be taken back. But Jason, going to her, soothed her grief with comforting words.

At seventy stades from the city a thick wood overspread the riverbank. There Argos, son of Phrixos, directed them to moor, hard by a meadow called the Ram's Resting-place, for there the golden beast first bent its weary knees carrying the children of Athamas. Jason, with a small contingent of the crew, followed Medeia ashore. Nearby stood the smoke-daubed base of the altar Phrixos established to sacrifice the ram to Zeus, savior of fugitives. They followed a path into the dark and trackless wood until their eyes detected a fiery gleam punctuating the gloom. Medeia said nothing until they reached the edge of a clearing, where before them stood a massive inclosure of seven walls of polished stone five rods high, arranged in a circle, and defended by towers and gilded battlements. Three bronze gates pierced the walls; and on atop one of the gateposts perched a fearsome statue of triple-bodied Hecate cast in black Corinthian bronze, holding in her many hands serpents, daggers and torches burning with real flames. The image revolved slowly around its base, scattering the shadows with its radiance.

Jason drew back at the sight, the memory of his nocturnal rite still fresh. Only Atalanta stared in wonder untainted by dread of the goddess, for she was known also as Artemis of the Gate. She was about to step boldly out of the shadows of the boughs when Medeia checked her, explaining that the towers were filled with savage Taurian guards ready to strike down any who came near. After instructing Jason and the others on what to do, Medeia went forth alone, her bare feet stepping lightly on the grass, until, caught in the menacing illumination of the fortress' whirling guardian, she became visible to the guards. They rushed out, spears and swords ready, to accost her. But when she drew back the mantle from her face and addressed them in their own Tauric speech, the guards, abashed, obsequiously rushed to open the principal gate before her, keeping their faces averted from her royal visage. As soon as the gateway was opened, an arrow from Atalanta's bow whizzed forth from the forest edge and struck dead one of the guards. With great shouts Jason and his companions rushed out and slew them, catching them by surprise; except for one who, pursued by Calais and Zetes, fled into the wood. Fearing that her father would be alerted, Medeia hastened Jason over the threshold. In the sacred grove within grew laurel and cornel-trees, and thick grass bedighted with tall asphodel, bright maidenhair, aromatic galingale, pink verbena, golden sage, fragrant honeysuckle, creeping goldilocks, sweet-smelling basil, healing nightshade and cat-thyme, bursting dittany, flowering saffron, pepperwort, thorny greenbrier, soothing chamomile, black poppy, and heal-all; and also white hellebore, and deadly, tight-rooted wolf's-bane. In the midst, a tall oak overspread the grove with its branches. On a long branch, high above their heads, impended the Golden Fleece, rufous like a cloud bedewed by the fiery sunbeams of morning. Jason, rapt in wonder, hardly noticed the stir from the tall shrubs at the foot of the tree. The guardian serpent, seeing them from afar with unsleeping eyes, roused its terrible form, covered in horned scales, to twine huge coils around the trunk, rising like black smoke spiraling endlessly into the sky. Lifting its crested head, and extending the terrible jaws, it's ferocious hiss set the air a-crackle. Reeling with fright, Jason could barely draw his sword. Medeia placed a reassuring hand upon his arm and said: "I am its mistress, whom it knows and fears. Do wish to approach it now, when it is awake and will devour you? Or will you let me come again to your aid?" Jason drew back, astounded at the serpent's girth and enormous length, like that of the *Argo* from prow to stern.

Medeia stepped boldly toward the writhing creature, locking its crimson, flashing eyes with her own. Sweetly she called on Sleep to descend on the serpent, and supplicated night-wandering Hecate for the success of her essay. "Your duty is at an end," Medeia told the serpent, whose sinuous coils had begun to relax. "Turn away from the treasure you have loyally guarded, and rest. I am here to guard it now. After your long vigil, sleep." Yet the serpent struggled to hold aloft its head and keep astir its eyes. Quickly,

Medeia severed a branch from a juniper-shrub, and with a potion from her casket, soaked the leaves. While chanting spells, Medeia sprinkled the drug into the serpent's eyes. Overcome by the enchantment, the eyelids fluttered, and then the scaly head dropped lower, jolting and nodding in drowsy struggle, until it touched the ground, sending one last convulsion coursing along its enormous frame.

Medeia ran to the stricken head, shedding tears in shame at her cruelty. Stroking it gently, she said: "Not so were you when in darkest night I brought the holy offerings; and not so was I when I dropped honey-cakes into your mouth. And now here you lie! At least I spared your life. On awakening, no longer will you see the Fleece dappling the shadows of your wold. Forget me, I pray. Flee to some other grove to pass your old age. Let not your fearsome hissing hound me!" Then she urged Jason to quickly fetch his prize; but as he did not know how to reach the Fleece, Medeia bid him to stiffen his courage and climb the serpent's dormant coils still wrapped loosely around the tree. Jason set his shoulders, took a deep breath, and commenced the ascent up the serpent's tail to the heights of the tree. He plucked the sheepskin, overspreading the foliage like a golden cloud, and brought it down to where Medeia still smeared salves on the monster's head. For a moment Jason forgot the world. He joyfully held aloft the Fleece, in size like a yearling's hide, and its splendor settled on his cheeks and brow in a ruddy blush. He was like a girl who catches on her garment the waxing moonlight shimmering into her attic room. Jason bestirred Medeia to hurry with him from Ares' grove. As he hastened back to the ship, Jason draped the Fleece like a mantle over his left shoulder; or he clutched it tightly, rolled up in his arms; and all the while it made the ground at his feet luminant.

Hardly had they cleared the wood at dawn's break that they heard the clash of arms. Perses, brother of Aiëtes, hearing of the Greeks' arrival, had thought to make common cause with them, and with some troops marched down to the ship, hoping for a parley: for he had always counseled Aiëtes to restore the Fleece, or else suffer the curse of its possession. But Acastos, seeing them afar off, and thinking them the vanguard of Aiëtes' army, raised the alarm. The Argonauts armed themselves and rushed out to meet them.

Jason, shunning the battle, hastened to the safety of the ship. As he passed by, those Argonauts who caught sight of the shining Fleece marveled, and dropping their weapons, reached out their hands to touch it. But Jason kept them back, hurried Medeia aboard, and spreading the Fleece over the stern-bench, covered it with a newly-woven mantle. He quickly donned his armor, and rushing to the prow, called for the men to break the fight and return to the ship. They streamed back and took to their seats, half of them locking their shields along the length of the ship to guard against the attackers' assaults. Drawing his sword from its sheath, Jason slashed the hawsers at the stern and the *Argo* leapt under the strain of the oars. "Hoist the sails for home!" he cried. "At last our mission is fulfilled, thanks to this maiden, whom I shall take home and make my wife. Hasten now: I am certain Aiëtes will also attack by sea and try to bar our passage. We hold the fate of our children, our dear country, our aged parents, in our hands. We can bring them back either grief—or glory!" In moments they swept off in the strong current. Leaving Medeia sitting on the Fleece beside the helmsman Ancaios, Jason took stock of the crew. Argos, Atalanta and Meleager had suffered slight wounds, which Medeia treated with her vulneraries. Only Iphitos, son of Naubolos, did not make it back.

Aiëtes, learning what was afoot from the escaped Taurian guard, assembled his forces. With a rounded shield in his left hand, a pine-torch in the other, and his spear couched beside him, he rode high on his chariot, driven by Apsyrtos, down to the riverbank across from Perses' confounded troops. But he had no time to think of his traitorous brother. With thunderous cries he drove hard along the river, his countless Colchians streaming behind him, but the *Argo* by then had cleared the estuary. Apsyrtos reined in the horses and Aiëtes leapt out, shaking with bitter fury. He raised his hands to the rising sun and threatened his people to find Medeia and bring her to him, or else suffer the most terrible retribution. Apsyrtos and the Colchian commanders at once prepared to launch their fleet.

18

Heracles crossed the mountains into the uplands of Phrygia, marching as far as the western curve of the great Halys river in ten day's time. He was careful not to kill any oxen, having been warned by the people that doing so was punishable by death, and so contented himself with hunting wild boars and goats. He could find nowhere to cross the Halys: the melting snow at its sources in the mountains engorged its great breath with a continuous torrent. He therefore followed its long course eastward as far as the territory of the Macronians, where Heracles tried to get his bearings. As he was crossing a river, the Macronians, armed with wicker shields and lances, lined up on the opposite bank to sling stones at him. Considering them too numerous to engage in battle, Heracles thought it wise to disarm himself and sit cross-legged as an advertisement of his peaceful intention. The gambit paid off; after some time, a delegation of Macronians crossed over. Heracles gave them an Ethiopian lance he still carried with him as a pledge of amity; they offered him one of their handsome hair tunics in exchange and allowed him to continue on his way. Since Heracles had found it difficult to communicate with the Macronians, he could not ascertain whether he had reached the extremes of Phrygia. He therefore headed due north, hoping to fix his location on reaching the Axine Sea. After spending a day crossing the mountains, his heart gladdened when the endless, misty sea opened up before him.

He followed the broad bend of the seaboard, crossing numerous mountain torrents and passing through humid forests, until he arrived at the river Phasis and the villages of the Colchians. For a moment, Heracles believed himself back in Egypt, for the Colchians looked identical to the Egyptians. They were of slight build, dusky-colored, possessed kinky hair and wore the same type of linen clothing. By their twittering he came to confirm that they were descendants of a great Egyptian army that had in antiquity ventured into that region.

Heracles continued on upstream. In the distance towered the Caucasus range, with its many offshoots, and its hoary ridges lost in the clouds. Unlike the Rhipaian mountains, with their sharp peaks, the summits of the Caucasus were flat or rounded; even so they appeared to be some of the loftiest mountains in all the world. Heracles was moved to tear off into those desolate heights to search for Prometheus, but he had to first inquire about the Argonauts. Coming at last after two days in sight of the stout walls and battlements of Aia on the opposite side of the Phasis, from where Aiëtes ruled, he thought it strange that the river quay was entirely devoid of ships. As he searched further up the riverbank for a way to cross, he arrived at a scene of battle. Crows, disturbed by his presence, flew shrieking into the sky, leaving lances set in the earth and bloody heaps of cloaks and armor covering the dead. As Heracles upturned some faces, hoping to recognize some of his comrades, he heard a sough. In a nearby thicket he found lying Iphitos, son of Naubolos, sore wounded unto death. He raised the stricken man, laid him gently aside, and from his water-skin moistened his lips. "Without you, Heracles, I never thought it could be done," gasped Iphitos; "but he did it, by Zeus! Jason, by the aid of the witch Medeia, achieved the Fleece. King Aiëtes surprised us as we, waiting for Jason's return from the sacred grove, made haste to launch the *Argo*. A few of us were wounded, including Argos and Meleager, and all save I managed to make it aboard. I did not cry after them for my own sake, Heracles, as lesser men would have done, but rejoiced instead that the object of our long journey had been secured. Do not begrudge our chieftain, Heracles, since only after long deliberation over your absence did he decide to sail from the Mysian shore. Blame rather the sons of Boreas, who with strong will and vehemence discounted you; and also perhaps Meleager, who stood with them."

Iphitos coughed up blood and lay still. Heracles held him until he died, and then buried him in a shallow trench.

Before Aia, on neighboring ridges, stood encamped two great armies, that of Aiëtes and that of Perses, swelling with massing hordes of Scythian allies. With the wronged brother, who in the confusion of the Argonauts' departure, with the Colchian forces weakened, chose to make his stand, stood the Alani and the fierce Heniochi, led by Anausis, who felt slighted that Medeia had been betrothed to Albanian Styrus; Bisaltan warriors, whose shields bear the image of a thunderbolt with twinned golden serpents; the Thracian Coilaletoi, who fight from their wagons, draped with sewn hide; and men from wooded Hylai. The wily Sindi, born from slaves of Scythian masters who in their absence took their wives to bed, flocked in the wings along with the Corralians, whose barbaric standards are a field littered with broken wheels, porcupines and battered herms. The Batarnai too had their companies, who fight with unordered ranks of intermingled. horsemen and footmen. Troops from the glens of Hyrcania brought their ferid hounds, which enchased in black armor dash into battle at the trumpet's call. The Hiberians sent contingents, as did the Iazyges, who never grow old, since at life's ebb the fathers give their sons a sword and demand from them release from miserable life. The Mycaei, of the fragrant locks, had their cohorts; as did the Thyrsagetai, who in times of eld marched with Dionysos into the eastern wastes.

After crossing the Phasis by one of its many bridges, Heracles made a wide circle around the Aiaian countryside and climbed a hill to observe the battle, uncertain of who it was fought against the innumerable Colchians. When trumpets shattered the placid air, armed hosts poured into the plain, stamping through the morning rime with rapid march, closing the narrow space of land between them. Lances and arrows produced a temporary night, and at its breaking blood overspread the field like blooming anemones. The Colchian defenders, in a tight array, locked their shields as the whirling Scythians, in a headlong rush, freed their swords and pikes for more intimate work. As the center held against the enemy, king Aiëtes rode into the battle, with his resplendent panoply flooding his dusky troops with light. At orders from his awesome voice, commanders charged with their cavalry, first on the left wing, and then on the right, and began to cut through Perses' troops, driving them toward the river.

After the Scythian forces sounded the retreat before Aiëtes' blazing chariot, Heracles from a distance gazed at the morass of blood and gore, the piles of mangled corpses and dead horses, the ruined standards, broken weapons and the shattered chariots, left revealed on the battlefield. It became clear to him, from his vantage, how little the gods cared for human affairs. Fortune ruled all; and only death was free of it.

There was nothing else for Heracles to do in Colchis. He headed into the well-wooded valleys of the mountain foothills. The closer he came to the Caucasus, the more diminutive he felt. The mountain range filled the eyes to either side, with its central portion loftier than the rest, and as the sun waned the black crags grew darker still, and filled the heart with foreboding. Where in this vast formation could Prometheus be? Heracles thought to himself; and what madness possessed him to think that he could search such an impenetrable stronghold, filled with cold and death, which not even the natives dared far venture into? All the tribes that lived about the Caucasus recognized it as place lost in time, haunted by an ancient divinity, known to them by different names. It was a place of nightmares, of woe, of dreadful suffering; a howling wilderness resonating with bitter disaffection.

Heracles first came upon the Soanes, a people always filthy, dwelling at the foot of the mountains; they in the summer followed the springing ibex up into the lower summits. These explained that Prometheus was said to be fettered somewhere near the sea, as mentioned by the mariners, who, sailing to the emporium at Dioscurias, not only hear his groans, but from their ships witness the flight of a monstrous golden vulture: one that, against nature, is able to fly toward the sun without being troubled by its bright rays. Remembering his experience in the Rhipaian mountains, Heracles took from the Soanes a pair of snow shoes constructed from broad disks of wood wrapped in raw hide and covered with spikes. Unable to accept them at their word on account of their slovenliness, Heracles commenced to thread his way up the mountain, ready to commit himself to a long search if necessary, when by good fortune he came across some Troglodytes in their caves, who, without hesitation, confirmed what the Soanes had reported. Heracles therefore descended to the other side of the mountain branch, and headed westward across the thickly-wooded valleys. When the mountains once more hemmed him all about, he ascended as far as the first summits above the tree-line, where the cold air blew down and whipped his lionskin.

19

Propelled by a propitious following breeze, the *Argo* for three days sped through the sea, landing, at Medeia's direction, on the Paphlagonian coast by the river Halys, where she offered sacrifices to Hecate. Overcome with exhaustion after the long haul the crewmen slept part of the day, until Ancaios roused them, fearing the pursuit of the Colchians. Jason, remembering how Phineus had told them they would return by a different route, was at a loss as to what bearing they should take next. Phrixos' son, Argos, addressed them: "We are told that long ago, before the stars were set on their courses, before even the Greeks ruled the Pelasgian land, that from Egypt, known then as the Misty Land, the mother of mankind, a certain king went forth with his hosts throughout the world, founding cities as he went. Though many have crumbled in mists of time, one of these, Aia, still survives, and its people are descendants of those men the king settled there. In our sacred temples we have stone tablets, preserved from those bygone days, on which their ancestors engraved maps showing the boundaries of the land and sea. They describe a broad river, called the Istros, the farthest branch of Ocean, on the far side of the Axine Sea. Its headwater rush down from the Rhipaian Mountains, beyond the home of the North Wind. For long it flows through endless plains until, reaching the borderlands of Thrace and Scythia, it divides: one branch discharges into the eastern sea; and the other flows into a deep sound of the Cronian Sea—the same that washes your own land, if I am correct in thinking that the mighty river Acheloös flows into it."

Erginos, on watch from the prow, caught sight of the white sails of the Colchian fleet through the mists, like an endless flight of birds. "Son of Aison!" he cried. "The enemy nears! We have the

Fleece, but our troubles have only begun. We cannot risk passing again through the Cyaneian Rocks. Let us follow this fellow's advice and head upstream, where perhaps we may find another sea-route home." Jason still appeared indecisive until a portent appeared suddenly in the sky: a falling star left a bright trail to the north. This sign of heavenly favor aroused Jason as if from a stupor and he asked Ancaios to plot a new course. They left there the son of Lycos and sailed off. They did not round Cape Carambis, but plunged northward into the unknown waters under a coastal breeze.

The Colchian fleet, unable to close on the *Argo*'s lead, split into two search parties. Half the squadrons continued on a false trail toward the Bosporos, while the other, commanded by Apsyrtos, made for the river Istros. Near the island of piney Peuce, which divides the Istros' outfall into two streams, Styrus, who with his Albanian fighters had joined Apsyrtos on one of the ships, spotted the top of the *Argo*'s mast and with great shouts compelled the rowers to outstrip the rest of the flotilla to reach its target. But a coastal squall, whipped into strength by the cold northerly winds, swept against the Colchian vessels. Apsyrtos, seeing the rest of his ships swaying and bobbing on the billows, gave the signal to lay ahull. But Stryrus, mad with jealousy over Medeia, thought he could ride out the squall and forced his ship into the wind's teeth, thinking he could defy the gods. The ship broke up as it reached the beach; and although Styrus escaped the wreckage and almost made it ashore, the waves drew him back into the cold depths.

Apsyrtos wisely waited out the storm, and then turned his fleet into that channel called the Fair Mouth at the lower end of Peuce. But the Argonauts, to escape the foul weather, had rowed hard to the upper end of the island, and gained the Istros not long afterward by way of the other stream called the Narex.

And so the Argonauts, thinking they had outstripped the Colchians, sped up the mighty river, but remaining always several leagues behind the Colchian warships. All the way Medeia sat wrapped in her mantle silently weeping, feeling ignored by the crew and troubled with doubts about Jason's sincerity. No Scythian lakes or streams could help but mourn the lost princess as she passed, and even the Hyperborean snows melted at the sight of her. Not even Jason, speaking kind words or bringing her things to eat, could lift her grief.

The Colchians left Mount Angouron and the plains of the Thracians astern, and in time came abreast of the Cauliac spur, where the Istros divides in a narrow, smoke-filled gorge. Fighting against a fearsome current, they pushed into that branch of the river that washed over the Laurion Plain and in time debouched into the Cronian Sea. Apsyrtos came ashore among the Histrians, and learning from them that no other ships had been spotted leaving the gulf, became convinced that the *Argo* still followed them. He therefore scattered his ships to guard every cove and block every route to the open sea as far as the river Salangon and the Nestaian frontier, making allies of the local inhabitants with bribes of Colchian gold.

When the Argonauts emerged into the gulf behind the Colchians, they found every landfall and every island barred against them, except the two Brygean islets near the coast, sacred to Artemis. These the Colchians had left alone, in deference to Hecate, whom they identified with the daughter of Leto. One island contained a temple to the goddess; and in the other the Argonauts took refuge. Leaving Medeia on the ship, Jason drew apart with his crew and sat with them in council to decide what next to do. Augeias of Elis, clearing his throat to command attention spoke first: "It is clear by now that we have no hope of escape; and that any attempt to fight our way past this blockade will end in disaster. Surely prince Apsyrtos commands the Colchian fleet, and being of the Sun's kindred like myself, he is no doubt touched by that practical enlightenment common in our race. Let us arrange a parley with him. He cannot in good conscience deny us the keeping of the Fleece, since king Aiëtes promised Jason he could have it on the accomplishments of his allotted tasks."

"You are too accustomed to having your way, king," said Peleus. "What makes you think the Colchians will not kill us at the first opportunity?"

"If that was their wish," said Augeias, "they would have done so already, would they not?"

"They dare not shed blood on an isle sacred to Relentless Artemis," said Atalanta.

"There is but one thing the Colchians want back," said Nestor; "and that is Medeia. Though her plight touches me, it is the Fleece we are bound to bring back, not her."

"Not so," said Orpheus. "We were all witnesses of the solemn pledge that Jason made concerning her."

"What a fine predicament you have put us in, prince of Iolcos!" said Idas with distaste. "Let whatever gods there are know that I, from the start, knew the danger of getting entangled with this foreign woman!"

"Though Idas is oftimes a fool, he this time speaks rightly," said Meleager, stroking the wound he had received in the escape. "Why should we expose ourselves to further dangers on her account?"

Atalanta, who had grown attached to the princess, gave Meleager a black look.

Augeias, feeling vindicated, said: "Let us leave her in the goddess' temple where some local king can act as arbiter: whether she is to go home to her father or stay with us. Apsyrtos will surely respect that judgment, and release us should the decision fall in our favor."

"And if it does not?" said Jason, but no one returned an answer. He glanced at Medeia, and lolling his head in defeat, agreed to send envoys to arrange the terms of a peaceful settlement. Peleus and Aethalides, with a white cloth tied to his herald's wand, boarded a dinghy and paddled off to the nearest Colchian vessel. In the evening they returned with the happy news that Apsyrtos, concerned with the veiled threats against his sister if he did not comply, but confident that she would ultimately be entrusted to him, had agreed to their terms. This Aethalides, proud of his diplomatic accomplishment, proclaimed loudly in Medeia's hearing. Appalled and shaking with distress, she climbed down from the ship and drew Jason away from his companions. Then, well apart from the others, she looked at him squarely and, before he could say a word, burst out: "Jason, did you really think you'd keep this a secret—this plot concerning me? Has your success blighted your memory? And what of those promises you made me in your hour or need?—those oaths, delivered with honeyed words, by Zeus, the suppliant's god? For them I abandoned all modesty, and have left parents and country and all that to me is dear. Alone I'm carried now over the sea with the mournful halcyons for your sake; when I preserved you through your trials on Ares' plain; and then foolishly helped you attain the Fleece. What ruin I have brought upon my sex! As your wife I thought to come to Greece—and so stand by me now, instead of abandoning me! Do I not deserve your protection? Stand by your pledge and take me away; or else draw your sword right now, slit my throat, and recompense my insane passion. Think for a moment on my misery if these judges deliver me to my stepbrother. How shall I face my father? While you enjoy your homecoming, there is no revenge, no torture, so cruel he will not mete out to me. No: may the Queen of Heaven on whom you rely turn her back! May you remember me one day in the midst of suffering. May the Fleece, like a nightmare, vanish into darkness. And may the Furies haunt you and drive you from your home. Mark my words! you have broken a mighty oath. No longer will I be mocked when this treaty you and your crew have conjured comes to naught. It is because of me that they're bound for home at all, and now they're ready to abandon their only hope!"

Medeia stormed off in a boiling rage, crying aloud and tearing at her tender cheeks like a frenzied Mainad, of a mind to set the ship ablaze, to destroy it all, and then cast herself into the flames. Jason raced after her in alarm.

"There now, my lady," he said soothingly, thinking quickly. "I like this business least of all! But all we seek is some way to avoid a fight, seeing that we are outnumbered and overpowered for your sake. See you these campfires encircling us? The people of this country are eager to help Apsyrtos carry you back to your father, like a captive maid; while we should suffer a bitter end should they all coordinate an attack and take you by force. This truce will buy us time to do something about Apsyrtos, after which these people will think twice about assisting the Colchians, whom I will not hesitate to then engage in the open if they deny us passage."

Medeia by degrees grew strangely calm. Jason's hackles rose at the vacuous look of her once-bright eyes. She delivered her sudden, deadly response couched in a heavy aspiration: "Listen now. Ill times move us to ill designs, as from the first when I erred by some god's will. Save me and I will lure him into your hands. Then, if you can do it, kill him—it would be nothing to me—and make war on the Colchians."

Jason backed off, in full agreement with her, but pricked by her coldness. When heralds for Apsyrtos arrived the next morning to confirm their truce, Jason left for him a pile of exquisite gifts, among them the Lemnian queen's sacred purple robe, passed to her father Thoas by Dionysos, and still redolent with a wondrously sweet scent from when he lay on sea-girt Dia, drunk with wine and nectar, embracing Ariadne, whom Theseus carried away from Crete. And as the heralds collected and loaded the tribute into their vessel, Medeia approached them with a message for her brother, telling them lyingly that she had been abducted against her will. She wanted to meet him secretly at the goddess's temple to hatch out a plan to steal the Fleece and return with him to Aia. The heralds departed fully persuaded by her words and spellbinding, for she had scattered into the air some magic dust to follow them.

That night, witnessed by both parties, Medeia was left on the lonely isle, where a single old priestess made her abode. The *Argo* returned to the other island, while the Colchian flagship anchored on the mainland. Apsyrtos, to mask his whereabouts, transferred later to another vessel and had himself conveyed to the island in the dead of night. In the portico of the temple he met Medeia. For long they talked, planning every detail of her apparent treachery against Jason. But as Apsyrtos turned to leave, confident that the Greek kidnapper and thief would soon be delivered into his hands, Jason, who had been waiting in ambush, sprang on him with upraised sword. Medeia quickly averted her eyes, covering them with her veil as Jason struck Apsyrtos like a butcher fells an ox. Apsyrtos fell on his knees, vainly trying to stanch with both hands the black blood spurting from the mortal wound, and in his violent throes tinct with crimson Medeia's silvery veil and garment, though she drew away from the horrid scene.

The priestess, who the Colchian maiden had taken into her confidence, reverencing her as a devotee of Hecate, made as if she saw and heard nothing as Jason thrice licked up Apsyrtos' blood, and spat it back into the dead man's mouth. Then, to prevent his ghost from taking vengeance, Jason pricked the eyes and sliced off some of the extremities, stringing the severed parts together and tying them under the armpits. While he buried the corpse, Medeia stood at the shore with a firebrand. Spotting the prearranged signal, the Argonauts rowed quietly across the channel, their lanterns doused, and laid up their ship sidelong to the Colchians'. Arrows from Atalanta and other archers struck the surprised sailors as boat-hooks bit into their deck to keep the vessels close. Scarcely able to properly arm themselves, the Colchians took up whatever was at hand to defend their ship, even their oars, hanging off the gunwale to exchange blows with the Argonauts. As blood foamed the water and corpses piled up between the hulls, the Argonauts stormed the ship and swept through it like a woodland fire, killing every last man. Jason eagerly came to join them at the end, but they no longer needed his assistance.

The crew then sat together to debate what to do next. When Medeia came among them, some shuddered at the blood upon on her raiment, and moved their seats to avoid being near her pollution. Others, however, held her in greater respect for her unshakeable resolve to sever all the natural ties of kinship and come wholly under their captain's protection.

Peleus offered the most sensible plan, saying: "We must embark now while it is dark, and row opposite to where the enemy is massed. Though by dawn they'll discover what we've done here, I am convinced that they, now leaderless, will give up the chase and disperse. It will be easier then to return this way and resume our original course."

At once they embarked and headed into open water to avoid any Colchian vessels, coming to rest within a lagoon at the mouth of the river Eridanos. The Colchians, meanwhile, failing to fall for the Argonaut's diversion, were hot to scour the sea for them over Apsyrtos' murder. But as they began their reconnaissance, the skies lit up with fearful lightning. The Colchians, thinking the portents directed at them, lost heart, and afraid to return to Colchis and face Aiëtes empty-handed, drifted apart and sought out new settlements.

After two days, Jason, thinking Peleus' plan had worked, gave the order to embark. They passed first by the Brygean islands, and, seeing no Colchian sails in any direction, continued sailing southward, plunging into a thick cluster of innumerable islets. As they found it difficult to continue the passage through the narrow channels, they veered toward the coast of the Hylleans and anchored there. These people, under the influence of Apsyrtos, had beforehand planned hostilities against the Argonauts. But when they learned that Jason had been a friend of Heracles, they helped them on their way. In gratitude, Jason rewarded them with one of a pair of tripods he had received at Delphi when he went there to seek guidance concerning the voyage. The oracle declared that whatever country possessed them would be free of enemy attacks. Their king, killed shortly before the Argonauts' arrival while defending his cattle against raiders, had been Hyllos, who claimed Heracles conceived him on the water-nymph Melite when he had gone to Drepane seeking purification from king Nausithoös after murdering his children. On reaching manhood, Hyllos, chaffing under the watchful eye of Nausithoös, who was concerned about the young upstart, collected a party of his countryman, and with happy assistance from the king himself, migrated northward to the present district. The Hylleans buried the tripod deep in the earth near their principal city so that no one would find it.

## 20

For weeks Heracles searched, subsisting on small game and wild berries, his face burnt by sunshine and frost, climbing higher into the snow and ice, or else descending into shadowed gorges; at times glimpsing the glint of the sea, at others the mysterious, dancing red fires of the northern horizon.  At night he took refuge in caves, where he watched the shadows flicker on the walls until he was overcome by soft sleep.  Although he never completely yielded to despair, with each fruitless day hope receded like the ebbing tide, so that the morning came when his spirit failed to move him from the shelter of his eyrie, and he remained huddled there with hoarfrost covering his beard.  Among all the ways of death, the only one man fears is the way he has begun to die.  For the first time, as the cold slowed his heart, he felt this fear: to die in such loneliness, too feeble even to rage against death.  But one morning, when a passing shadow darkened the grotto's mouth, Heracles struggled to climb out and saw in the distance an enormous bird, whose wingspan could easily cover the *Argo* oar to oar.  He hastily assembled his gear and dashed off across the frozen crags, trying to keep the bird in sight; until, he saw it, after circling several times, swoop down behind the cliffs overhanging the sea.  Thereafter, more than once did the summits shake from inhuman howls, filled with equal parts wrath and sufferance.  Frenzied, pitiable groans followed, erupting with such palpable force that great rocks and chunks of ice dislodged and thundered down the mountainside. Heracles covered his ears against the violence.

Heracles hurried across the mountain ridges where no man had yet trod, risking life and limb after the god's place of durance vile.  As evenfall approached, and the scarred moon revealed itself behind dark clouds, the Tyrinthian managed to reach the edge of a deep crevasse, not far from where the cliffs impended the sea.

What he saw both astonished and petrified him. Against a mountain column stood chained by every limb a being of such imposing size and fearsome aspect that an awe-inspired dread caused Heracles' heart to thunder against his ribs. As tall as a mountain-ash, his face and shoulders lay hidden under an inordinate tangle of hair and beard seared in frost; his nails had grown long and curled like tree branches; his skin, exposed to the injurious elements, had thickened like hard bark; and billowing rags barely covered his immense, gaunt frame. Not only that, but a monstrous golden Caucasian eagle, with glimmering eyes and a beak as large and curved as a ship's prow, perched beside the helpless giant, furiously gnashing and clawing at his side, tearing off gobs of his liver, while blood and bright ichor gushed from the wound and dripped like rainwater off the stony ledges.

Prometheus, seeing Heracles, rooted still in place by amazement, cried out in anguish: "Come you, whoever you are, to see this spectacle of woe?" The words came forth like the sound of thunder that rolls long after the lightning stroke, filling the heart with apprehension. Heracles, snapped back into the moment, raised a hue and cry until the eagle, disturbed at his gruesome repast, like a thousand screech-owls screamed, and, raising a great wind under its wings, took flight. Heracles straightway took up his curved bow, nocked an arrow to the cord, and with one eye following his target prayed: "May Hunter Apollo speed my arrow straight!" The fearful arrow freed from the cord, it sliced the limpid air and transfixed the third of the ghoulish spawns of Echidne in the breast, so that the monstrous bird spiraled down to death flapping in vain its long-pinioned wings.

Heracles climbed down the rocks until he stood in the shadow of the Titan. Prometheus, tears of joy filling his eyes, said: "For one thousand—or is it thirty thousand?—years have I been fettered to these rocks by the will of Zeus and the cruel hand of Hephaistos, who fashioned these thick chains of bronze and clamped unbreakable adamant around my limbs. I know not how many centuries I have stood here in dreadful agony, waiting miserably each day for the winged hound of Zeus to gnaw at my liver, which each night grows back again to ensure my continual suffering; while I powerless, vainly long for a death that does not befit my station, for I come from that ancient race, born of Earth and Heaven, cousins to the Olympians, and thus also shackled with unendurable immortality. But, you may ask, how came I to this bitter torment? It pains me to tell; but also to keep silent, since for long ages not a soul has ventured here to give me company or succor. And what a woeful tale it is, full of cruelty and injustice against a friend! When Zeus plotted to overthrow his sire Cronos, as the latter had done to his father before him, I advised my fellow Titans that not by brute force are great ends achieved, but by cunning—this my mother oft taught me. They failed to heed my advice, and seeing their ruin close at hand, I went to fight on the side of Zeus, who, by use of my counsel, proved the victor. Forthwith he took charge of earth and the empyreal realm, while to his brothers he apportioned the sea and gloomy Tartaros, where his enemies were cast to dwell in darkness. Looking down, Zeus grew disdainful of mankind, for at that time they crawled like vermin upon the earth and lived in caves, and set his mind to destroy them and start a new race. I championed the side of mortals; by that I began to earn Zeus' enmity, sharpened when he saw how I taught them to make houses of wood and bricks; how to discern the heavens to know when to plant or sow; how to bend the fearsome beasts to the yoke; how to divine from dreams and omens; how to extract the treasures of the earth. I taught them also the arts of medicine, of writing and numbering, and all those sciences useful for man, for he is composed of two natures: a lower one like the beasts, for which he fills his belly; and a higher one like unto the gods, for which he fills his mind. I taught them also to fear the gods, but not at their own expense. When the gods quarreled over which portion of the sacrifice was theirs, I killed an ox and prepared two offerings: for one I wrapped the unwanted bones in gleaming fat; while for the other, consisting of the roasted flesh and offal, I placed inside the stomach. Zeus did not deem the latter very appetizing, and reached for the former; and though, condescendingly, he claimed to see through my deception, his wrath waxed so great that he withheld from men the gift of fire. Again I fell into my man-loving ways, and stole fire from the bellows of Hephaistos, hiding the lively spark in the pith of a fennel-stalk. For that affront Zeus, forgetting my original benefaction, repaid me foully, riveting me for eternity to this forgotten rock. Such is the disease of tyrants—to have no faith in friends! He did not hold men guiltless, either.  At his bidding Hephaistos fashioned from earth and water a new thing called woman, modeled after the goddesses.  She was called Pandora, for all the gods not only imbued her with their best qualities, but altogether offered her as a dangerous gift to man.  Aphrodite bestowed on her grace and bewitching beauty.  Athena dressed her, adorning her with a veil and crown of spring flowers, and instructed her in  the domestic arts. Hermes taught her how to spin words, dripping with honey, to bend the wills of men.  She was presented in marriage to my foolish brother Epimetheus, who accepted her into his house despite my warning never to accept gifts from Zeus.  As her dowry Pandora brought with her a great jar which the crafty messenger of the gods instructed her never to open.  Unbearable curiosity naturally possessed her, which she could only cure by lifting the lid.  Out flew all manners of evils and diseases that have become the bane of men.  Pandora stoppered the jar too late; yet a drop of Hope remained securely just under the lip: the only antidote men have against suffering and the terrors of death.

"Hope too has preserved me these long ages, entombed in these jagged cliffs, tormented by the hail and storm, and the ravening bird.  Despite all this, I held over the head of Zeus the certain knowledge of his defeat and overthrow, and often he sent Hermes to pry from me this awful secret; but I planned to keep it hidden until he should deign to unbind me. But in helping me, you have committed a grave offense in killing the minion of Zeus. Who are you, brave and rash mortal?  Don't tell me!  I think—I hope!—I know, for all things future are in my purview.  My mother Themis taught me that after thirteen generations, there would come one, a descendant of wandering and kind-hearted Io, to free me from my punishment.  A priestess of Argive Hera, Io was so lovely that Zeus loved her; and, to hide her from jealous Hera, he transformed her into a white cow. Hera, undeceived, demanded the cow, and placed her under the guard of many-eyed Argos, who never slept.  But Hermes, at Zeus command, slew Argos by first lulling him to sleep with the sound of his reed-pipes, and then hewed his head with a sickle.  Thereon Hera tormented Io with a gadfly, and caused her to wander the earth.

"Though your name I know not, by your actions I feel that you are he.  There is yet more you must do for me, my son; I feel no offense in calling you so, for I myself fashioned humankind from clods of earth when once these hands were free and dexterous. Believe not those tales that men sprang ready-made from the earth, lying under the ash-trees like fallen fruit: for, how can something ever come of nothing? Come up here and see if you can break apart these fetters. Though of unbreakable adamant, they will surely yield their strength to my deliverer."

"First, it is meet to repay one good turn with another," said Heracles. "I have wandered through many lands, crossed mountains and seas, suffered hardships, thirst and hunger in search of the garden of the Hesperides, from which I am bidden to bring back golden apples. Pray tell where it is, for I am told you know."

Prometheus shot him a look of alarm. "It is one thing to find the garden, and quite another to steal its precious fruit; since the tree from which it hangs is guarded night and day by hundred-headed Ladon, a sleepless dragon. And if you touch the fruit, or eat of it, you shall surely die. The orchard itself lies in a shady vale in the land of the Hyperboreans, high above a narrow gorge where a river, the northernmost branch of the Ocean Stream, voluminous in both summer and winter, divides. It is hidden in mist from human eyes—but if your father is indeed divine, your eyes will see it— and enwalled by my brother Atlas in fear of our mother's prophecy that someday a son of Zeus would come to despoil the tree. Be not rash and attempt to find the garden and seize the all-golden fruit. Rather, seek out Atlas, who at the tallest mountain edging the earth stands guarding the pillar that keeps heaven and earth asunder, bearing on his shoulders, as it were, the celestial sphere, inset with gleaming stars. Such was his punishment as foe of Zeus, as this was mine. Offer to lighten his burden for a time by relieving him of his watch  if he should go and fetch the apples for you. But be wary! He will not want to take his burden back."

At these words, Heracles grew downcast. "Alas!" he cried; "you have been entombed too long, without news or knowledge of the doings of the world. My ancestor Perseus, returning from Libya with the head of Medusa, asked to be his guest, weary as he was from his battles with the soaring winds. Atlas, however, refused him on hearing he was a son of Zeus, calling his claim a fable, but no doubt thinking of that prophecy of which you spoke; and with insolent words rebuffed him. Perseus, a small thing compared to him and no match at all, requited such inhospitality with a deadly gift. Turning his back, he held aloft the Gorgon's head and made Atlas into stone. It is said that he is now indistinguishable from the mountain mass. From his hair and beard grew woods; his shoulders and arms became ridges; and his head is now a mountaintop. He continues to bear the heavens indeed—whether he wants to or not!"

"Distressed as I was of my brother's fate," said Prometheus, "I am doubly bitter now to hear the news. I am consoled only in that he will no longer grow weary at his post."

Heracles climbed to a narrow ledge. Doubtfully inspecting the adamantine ring through which the harsh chains bound the Titan to the column, he said: "Tell me also, most ancient one, the secret of life and death: why do the gods enjoy immortality, while men suffer dissolution?"

Prometheus with a grave expression answered: "Does not the ox at times collapse while harnessed to the plough? What if vines never withered, or dreams never ceased? Even the love of friends fades. Nothing truly endures. Of necessity all things in this universe must end; even the universe itself, when it ends in fire. But each has its own time, whose relentless passing nothing can escape. In the face of eternity, is a moment any different from a day, or a million million years?"

"And shall I, who have seen the ends of the earth, too die, never to rise again?" asked Heracles.

"Why, mortal, do you exhaust yourself with toil unceasing? What is the end of your wanderings, scion of the horned virgin?" said Prometheus. "You also will not escape the doom of men. Live, then, and be merry. Fill your belly. Enjoy the wife of your youth: for death will come all too soon."

"If an endless night beckons me with eternal repose," said Heracles, "then I must continue my work while light endures."

Heracles raised his brass-bound club, and by a single blow, erupting flaming shards, shattered the Titan's bonds. With the tension of his arms suddenly loosed, Prometheus, sapped of vitality, his limbs atrophied from ages of disuse, rumpled to the hard ground with the reboant noise of a crashing oak-tree. Raising then his hands he cried: "O Zeus, sovereign monarch of heaven, only by your will could I have been freed this day. I finally divulge, then, the hidden thing of your distress:

*Thetis is she who'll bear a son,*
*By which his father'll be undone."*

Then turning his ancient face toward Heracles, he said: "You seem too brave and mighty to call both parents mortal. For a moment, I almost thought you were that offspring of Zeus destined to rival Zeus." Heracles responded: "I am Heracles, begotten of Zeus on Alcmene of Thebes." Prometheus sighed deeply and said thus: "Then, Heracles, you have brought glory to your father this day." The Titan's body now convulsed with sorrow and great tears fell from his frost-seared eyes like clumps of melting snow. "I well remember now," said he, "the taunt of Maia's son, who called my punishment eternal until some god should come and take upon himself my woes, and of his own will agree to descend in my place into the sunless realm of Tartaros. Such is the inoperable will of Zeus! Leave me now, Heracles, for though you have freed my body, my soul remains fettered forever to these lonely haunts." The soft moon now lengthened the shadows of the cliffs. Heracles thought for a moment and then said: "Perhaps in this also, great benefactor of mankind, I too can be of assistance. Give me but a little space and I shall find you an heir for your torments." Prometheus, his breast enlarged once more with hope, painfully reclined his broken body against the jagged slope. He reached up, tore a branch from an olive tree growing on a beetling crag, and twinned it into a wreath for Heracles. "By this," said he, "you take my fetters upon yourself until you fulfill your promise." He then, from a piece of adamant reaved by the club of Heracles, formed a ring, saying: "And by this, I will ever carry on me a remembrance of my durance."

And as Prometheus slipped the ring on his finger, he vanished from sight. Into Tartaros he went until Hermes' prophecy should come to fulfillment

Heracles, overcome with weariness, slept until the morning star first rose above the summits and the Bear receded toward the north. He departed and crossed the remaining ridges of the Caucasus, descending finally where the mountains ended abruptly at the seashore. Before him extended a vast, uncharted plain which no Greek had ever reached, nor any geographer ever mapped. Keeping close to the sweep of the coast as he marched on, he saw neither houses nor villages, nor any trees. It was a long time before he saw any persons, until he encountered long-haired nomads living in wagon-houses. He avoided intercourse with them and continued on; soon afterward, however, he heard the thunder of hooves behind him. Sauromatian warriors, their armor formed from mare's hooves, stitched together so that they looked like lizard scales, rode up and surrounded him on tall vigorous horses. Each man carried a bow in one hand a bone-tipped spear in the other. One of them drew a noose and expertly ligatured Heracles' neck, attempting to draw him like a beast. But Heracles grabbed hold of the cord and by a strong pull extracted the warrior clean off his mount. The others were so astonished at this feat of strength that they invited him to take the defeated man's horse. This Heracles did and followed them to their encampment, where they slaughtered and ate a mare and drank fermented mare's milk. But when Heracles, finding that some of their furtive wives looked somewhat familiar, realized they were Amazons, they took up arms and wanted to kill him. Their husbands with great struggle held them in check and then related to Heracles how they acquired them. It so happened that on one of Heracles' ships, sailing away after the battle at the Thermodon, the captured Amazons turned on their abductors and massacred them. Having no knowledge of boats, they drifted on the sea until they came to the northern shore and the land of the Royal Scythians. The Amazons, wandering about, seized a herd of horses and commenced to plunder the land. The Scythians, unable to recognize the invaders, whom they took for young men, fought against them; and it was only afterward, examining the corpses left on the battlefield, did they discover they were women. Considering the Amazons the very image of health, vitality and prowess, they wished to have children by them, and so sent away some of their men to reside near the Amazon camp and do there everything the Amazons did. As they appeared to pose no threat, the Amazons left them alone.

The Scythians observed all of the Amazons' habits, and when one of them went off to relieve herself, as they did singly or in pairs, a young Scythian did likewise; and drawing near to her, he proved so charming that she agreed to company with him. Unable to converse, since their languages were foreign to one another, by hand gestures they agreed to meet again the next day, except that the Scythian was to bring one of his companions, while the Amazon one of her sisters. This happened, and by degrees each of the young men was able to find a wife.

After some time, a disagreement arose amongst the couples, for the Amazons did not wish to return with the men to their city, since they looked down on Scythian women, and could not bear to displace their vigorous pastimes with domestic chores. And so they urged their husbands to go home, secure their inheritances, and return to them. This they did; but then the Amazons further objected that they did not feel safe in the region, since they had on their arrival caused such mayhem and misery, they convinced their husbands to follow them beyond the Tanais river, through a land known to their forebears, and settle there.

Heracles left the camp forthwith, unable to bear the presence of the Amazons and leery of the Scythians' slanted, shifty eyes. He rode the gifted horse until he reached the coast of that body of water called the Mother of the Axine, which sits above the latter and pours its water into it through a strait similar to that connecting the Axine with the Propontis, but shorter and narrower. In ten days' time since leaving the mountains he came riding through feathery snowfall to the Tanais river, which divides the land of the Sauromatai from that of the Royal Scythians. He was not certain at all about the geography, but felt it safe to continue his journey following the coastline, hoping at some point to reach the river on the other side of the sea, as Prometheus instructed. The weather was very cold for spring-time, but the grass still grew thick and tough under the feet.

From the Royal Scythians, who are the most noble of the Scythians, dwell in villages, and consider all other of their kinsmen as their slaves, Heracles received a rope girdle, a golden libation cup and a bent Scythian bow. The Sauromatian horse he exchanged for two mares and a chariot, finding them more suitable for long travel. They advised him not to wander too far to the north to avoid arriving among the Man-eaters, who were not Scythian and were the most barbaric of all the races of men. Passing then through the land of the Scythian nomads, and then, across the Borysthenes River into the farmlands of the Scythian ploughmen, he saw trees for the first time since quitting the Caucasus, arriving in a well-wooded district between the mouths of the Hypanis and the Borysthenes rivers, which empty together into a great marsh. A strange adventure befell him there. Tired after hard riding, and chilled to the bone, he fell asleep, drawing his lion's pelt around him. Awakening to the frigid dawn, he found his missing chariot-mares, which he had unyoked and left to graze. After a long search in the woods he came to a grotto aglow with firelight. Inside, on a nest of sorts, sat a prepossessing and buxom woman. When she arose he saw, to his utter amazement, that while from the buttocks upward she seemed no different than an ordinary woman, her lower extremity consisted of a long, scaly snake's tail, gleaming by the firelight, on whose coils she supported herself upright, swaying to and fro. In order not to appear impolite, Heracles went straight to the matter at hand and inquired if she had seen his mares. "I have seen them," said the double-formed woman, making room in her nest. "They are safely in my keeping. You may have them back if you come hither and company with me." Heracles agreed to her proposition, thinking he would make short work of it. However, she delayed his departure many days afterward with various excuses until he could wait no longer. Returning the mares, she told him: "When your mares strayed in this wild and inhospitable land, it was I who saved them. You have more than paid for their salvage; for I bear in my womb your three sons. When they grow up, what shall I do with them? Do you wish they remain here in my land, or do I send them to you?" Heracles answered: "When my sons reach manhood, watch them, and when you see one of them bend this bow as I bend it, and tie about him this girdle, choose him to remain; while those who fail, send away."

Heracles strung the Scythian bow and entrusted both it and the girdle, on which dangled the golden cup, to the woman. He then yoked the mares to the chariot and continued on his way. The she-viper bore three stout sons whom she called Agathyrsos, Gelonus, and the youngest, Scythes. Remembering the instructions from Heracles, she offered the trial to each son. Only Scythes passed the test and remained to rule the land, while his brothers were banished. From Scythes, it is said, descend the kings of Scythia. It is also worthy to note that to this day Scythians carry a goblet suspended from their belts.

In any case, this is the tale told by the Greeks living about the Axine, who thought the she-viper was none other than the monster Echidne. The Scythians no doubt originated this legend, since they worship Heracles as a god and consider him their progenitor.

## 21

Running before the wind, the Argonauts headed south, past the Liburnian islands abandoned now by the Colchians, and Black Corcyra, somber-looking from its shadowy forest. They coasted by Melite, steep Cerossos, and saw, on the horizon, the island of Nymphaia, which powerful Calypso, daughter of Atlas, once made her home. But as they spotted the coastal mountains of Ceraunia through the far mist, a strong gale struck them hard abeam, and turning to a head wind, swept them all the way back to the Amber Islands. It was then that all heard an awful soughing coming from the prow; and Mopsos, putting his ear to the Dodonian branch fitted to the ornament, turned pale at what he heard. Raising his voice against the howling wind, he informed the rest of Zeus' anger at the murder of Apsyrtos. They would suffer endless wanderings across the sea's tempests, he explained, unless Jason and Medeia where purified by the great witch Circe. Then Mopsos turned to Castor and Polydeuces, and begged them to invoke the gods for permission to enter Ausonian waters. This the twin brothers did at once, raising their hands in supplication, while the rest sagged in their seats from terror. As the wind died, to the wonder of all, violet sparks of fire danced shrilly on the twin horns of the yard-arm before running down the fore-stays behind the sons of Tyndareos.

Jason turned to Medeia for guidance on finding her aunt Circe, who lived, she explained on an island in the Tyrrhenian sea, off the western coast of Ausonia. Completely at a loss as to what other route to take there, Ancaios steered the *Argo* up the river Eridanos, hoping to find some outlet to the opposite sea. They sailed to the very source of the river, the deep lake where Phaëthon, half-consumed, plummeted in his sire's chariot, and where his smoldering body still discharged noxious fumes so that even birds failed to cross the watery expanse without fluttering down helpless into the roiling steam. As the Argonauts searched the backwaters and tributaries for a channel leading south, by day they were vexed, unable to eat or drink, by the stench of the moldering corpse; while at night they were assailed by the Heliads' lamentable keening, whose tears like oil-drops were borne past them on the stream.

They would have mistakenly rowed up another river flowing through the Hercynian fastnesses had terrifying cries from the dark forests around them, thick with fir and pine-trees, which Mopsos interpreted as a warning from Hera, not dissuaded them. They turned around, and by trial and error located a great seething confluence where branches of the rivers Eridanos and Rhodanos met, and passing down the latter wrapped in mist through uncharted regions of the Celts, at last came to the sea. Castor and Polydeuces were the first to notice two small islands, the Lesser Echelons, across from the river's central mouth, where they put in for several days to rest and gather provisions.

From there they sailed for two days, hugging the coast, and settled in at the isle of Aithalia, where the beach is strewn with variegated pebbles. Medeia, bidding them to depart, took a position at the prow to observe the Tyrrhenian coastline as they rowed. At her signal, they turned toward what seemed an offshore island, buzzing with spiraling sea-hawks, but really a rocky promontory connected by a flat, sandy neck to the mainland. They ran ashore on the western side of the cape of Aiaia, anchoring inside a coastal lagoon surrounded on all sides by woodland and sandy hills.

On the pleasant beach Circe was bathing her head in seawater in ablution after an ill-omened dream in which she saw the walls of her houses streaming with blood, and fire devouring her magical potions, which she managed to douse with sacrificial blood gathered in her hands. Rising and ringing out her long golden tresses, she caught sight of the Argonauts, and they of her. She approached them, dragging through the sand the tail of her purple dress stiffened with embroidered gold-work. The Argonauts, looking at her intently, immediately considered her, from her regal form and gleaming eyes, the sister of Aiëtes. Circe spoke sweetly to them all, inviting them to accompany her back to her home. She strode off, turning once to give them a beguiling look, which was enough to compel the Argonauts to follow the enchantress like panting hounds. When Medeia, however, held back Jason by the arm, he ordered the company to halt, and taking only Medeia with him, followed her into the forest of elm, cork and scrub-oak, seeing, midway, puffs of blue chimney-smoke ascending. The path ended at an open glade and a house of polished stone. In the garden sprawled wolves and mountain-lions, as mild as could be, licking their paws or twirling happily on the soft grass. On seeing Circe, they came near with twitching tails and tried to fawn on Jason, but he drew behind Medeia in fear. Circe, prodding the beasts aside with a staff, led her guests down the long hall of her house and invited them to sit down while she set out golden cups in which she planned to mix her evil drugs with wine to work some mischief. Instead, Medeia prodded Jason toward the hearthstone, and they both crouched there silently in the posture of suppliants: Medeia hiding her face and Jason planting the silver-hilted sword that killed Apsyrtos point-first into the ground

At once Circe knew that they were fugitives suffering blood-guilt, and without a word, following the inescapable laws of Zeus, commenced the rites of purification. First she took a suckling pig, whose sow still lay with swollen dugs, and holding it over them, cut the throat so that the stream of blood splashed on their hands. Next with libations she propitiated Zeus to listen to the murderers' supplications while her handmaids carried outside the polluted refuse. Finally, staying by the hearth, burning cakes of meal, oil and honey, Circe prayed that the Furies relent from their wrath and that Zeus would once more smile on those who committed such irreparable sin.

With the prescribed ablution completed, Circe raised them up and had them sit on polished chairs, carved and silver-gilt, while she sat nearby to question them. As soon as Medeia looked up from the ground, her dewy eyes gleaming golden in the hearth-light, and spoke to her in the Colchian tongue, Circe recognized her kinswoman. After sharing a long embrace, Medeia, still speaking her native language, recounted all that had passed since leaving Colchis, but out of shame left out her brother's murder. Circe, nevertheless, learned all by her power; and though she felt some pity at her weeping niece, said to her: "Miserable wretch! By your intolerable deeds you've wrought for yourself a most shameful homecoming and will not escape Aiëtes wrath for long, for he will soon show up on your doorstep to avenge his murdered son. But, since you are my suppliant and kinswoman, I will devise no further ill against you. But begone!—you and this stranger, whoever he may be, that you have taken against your father's will. Kneel no more at my hearth; I can never condone your grave misconduct."

An immeasurable grief overbore Medeia. Hiding her eyes in a fold of her robe, she wailed until Jason, quivering with fear, took her hand and led her out of Circe's house. Jason found his crew engaged in diversions by the ship, playing at quoits or out hunting wild boars in the marshes. As the cove was very pleasant, the winds light, and game abundant, few heeded Jason's order to make sail. Jason, emptied of resolve, went off by himself; while Medeia remained huddled and sobbing in the shadow of the dark hull. Peleus, however, who had observed the footsteps of Thetis forming across the water's surface in the calm, called Nauplios over to him to confirm his conjecture. By looking up at the clouds, Nauplios presaged an imminent shifting of the wind. Peleus therefore roused the men to end their games, prepare their supper, and make ready to depart in the morning, making them feel shame for their heedless attitude toward their captain.

As Nauplios predicted, a westerly wind came with the dawn. They sprang aboard, unfurled the sail, and were carried off in the fresh morning breeze. At midday they entered into a windless calm. They were rowing past limestone cliffs topped with scrub until Jason, hearing a strange singing, as natural and variable as the wind and waves, ordered the oarsmen to clear the oars. The ship drifted along on waves of seaweed while the crew gossiped in their inactivity. Before long, through the mist appeared three little rocky islets, close together, treeless, but covered in scrub and yellow daffodil. A sweet melody rose from there, wafting across to them on the heavy, still, scented air. All now heard the bewitching sound, and filled with an exquisite longing for the rocky shore, took to rowing, following Ancaios' unrestrained turns of the steering-oar.

Orpheus alone resisted the tempting pull. "Avast, friends!" he called. "Turn away from the Sirens' isle! I see them there, perched like birds upon the rocks, while around them are piled the moldering bones of sailors trapped, their minds dulled by their bewitching song, never again to see their wives or homes. Steer clear, or such a doom will befall us all!" Raising then his Thracian lyre, Orpheus spun a lively tune to compete in their ears. As the lyre chords began to defeat the Sirens' ethereal refrains, the west wind rose to his aid, carrying the ship to seaward. Although the singing faded as the waves drove them onward, Butes, maddened by the sound, vaulted overboard before anyone could stop him and made for the flowery islets. His friends watched him in despair until both he and the lonely rocks dropped below the rim of the sea.

In gloomy silence they sailed on. Finding the coastline devoid of any good anchorage, they spent the nights sleeping aboard the ship. One morning, they awoke to find that they had drifted a long way into the open. Rowing hard to near the mainland, they came in sight of a great mountain rising solitary from the sea, its summit wreathed in clouds of smoke. Already they could hear the roaring surf when suddenly, as they drew nearer, the mountain-top burst horrendously, spewing fire and rocks and a rain of thick ash into the air. In terror not a few dropped their oars or clung steadfastly to their bench-mates. Jason raced to the stern to exhort Ancaios to steer away, in the direction of another leeward island, a steep-to rock rising skyward in sheer cliffs; and then, as rollers began to choke the sea-lane with chunks of pumice, the oarsmen set their backs to give a wide birth to the drifting rocks. They considered it a sign of heaven's favor, as they left the frightful islands astern, to see dolphins gamboling about the ship.

They furled the sail and kept at the oars for lack of wind. Nauplios, though unfamiliar with those waters, recognized the landmarks from sailors' tales, and seeing in the distance the mountains of Trincaria rising in a blue haze, warned Jason of the approaching danger, the greatest since they had escaped the Colchians.

"We come now to a strait the likes of which a man should be spared the sight," he said. "One one side is a great crag of sheer cliff, and in its midst a cavern where lurks the monstrous Scylla. She has six heads, they say, borne aloft on serpent-necks; and for limbs twelve great tentacles that she uses to snatch passing dolphins or dog-fish, and bigger game besides. No ship has ever crossed her without suffering loss, for men she finds a rare delicacy. Opposite her lair is a whirling maelstrom called Charybdis that three times a day, they say, swallows the sea and anything in it, and then eructs it forth, seething the waters as in a bubbling caldron."

"And so by which side should we pass?" asked Jason.

"That I cannot say," said Nauplios. "You are in charge. But I would rather lose a few men, than the entire ship."

Nauplios' response was heard by those sitting nearest, who then passed it on down the line. Although the older men laughed at his superstitious concerns, the younger members of the crew protested in fear, urging Jason to find another route. Ancaios, leaning on the tiller, countered that to do so would unnecessarily add many more weeks to their voyage, since they would have to skirt the mainland before turning east again. As the discussion grew heated, Medeia, who had hardly spoken a word since leaving Circe, rose from her seat beside Ancaios. Jason called for quiet.

"What Nauplios speaks is true," she said. "Scylla is a daughter of Hecate, whom I have served since my youth. If you place your trust in me once again, I pledge to get us through."

Idas snorted and spat, but the others urged Medeia to act in their best interest. Following her instructions, they rowed to within sight of the narrows, and then hove-to for two nights until the veil of cloud lifted from the moon's face. At the third watch, the men, girt in full armor, had to bind their eyes and row slowly and quietly, while Medeia took charge of the tiller, with Atalanta's assistance, since she had not the strength to handle it by herself.

Unable to see, the Argonauts trembled to hear the horrible clamor of the wind and waves contending at the mouth of the strait, which they took for the bark of Scylla, who was said to have dog heads jutting from her belly. On the right side loomed Scylla's yawning cavern, exhaling a phosphorescent mist. Medeia cried out her incantations in frenzied Colchian couplets and scattered her mixed potions into the water and air. Only Periclymenos the wizard, dared to draw down his blindfold, more curious about Medeia's magical artistry than the channel's threats. What he saw in that instant froze his blood. As they hugged the brooding cliff, enormous black tentacles, dripping ooze, danced for a moment in the shadow of the hollow. And dead across, under a shaggy wild fig-tree growing high on a spit of land, a whirling vortex formed in the wake of a bore that tossed the *Argo*. And when she crashed down into the swell, Charybdis, swallowing the tide, tore at her keel. But their distance from the whirlpool saved them; and as the men in panic rowed for their lives, the monstrous eddy disgorged its hidden depths into the air with a violent roar, seething the *Argo* in a storm of spindrift.

Carried on the swift current, they left behind the terrors lurking in the narrows. As Dawn brightened the world, pushing back the mantle of waning night with her rosy fingertips, they came within sight of Mount Etna's lofty peak wreathed in clouds, with ribbons of fire quietly coursing down her dark ravines. A sheltered, curving cove, with two bright streams coming out to the sea close by, beckoned the frightened and exhausted sailors along the otherwise barren coast. Though a westerly wind began to blow, the men begged to be let ashore to eat, rest and refill their water stores. As Ancaios, wishing to ride the homebound breeze, reluctantly turned the *Argo* toward the shore, the lowing of cattle and the bleating of sheet mingled in their ears. Augeias jumped from his bench.

"Keep a wide berth, Ancaios!" he cried. "We near, no doubt, the country called Trinacria and the pasturage of the Sun. These fine herds and flocks, immortal, are tended by his gentle daughters, the nymphs Phaëthousa, the younger; and Lampetië, with her staff of shining oricalc. Sure will be our destruction should we molest these sacred beasts."

As they came close inshore, through the clinging mist they saw milk-white heifers grazing along the river-meadow, shaking their golden horns at the brazen sky. Astonished, the men said no more, and let Ancaios take them out into the open sea.

❦

Guided by the sun by day, and keeping the Plough on his left hand at night, Ancaios aided by a quartering wind, steered the *Argo* across the Ceraunian Sea. Within a fortnight of leaving Trinacria's coastland, the unmistakable contour of the island of Drepane, like that of a hide-bound shield, dark with mountain-forests of cypress and ilex, came into view. Nestor, who knew the coast well, had the ship avoid the iron-bound western coast, circle the island, and pull in on the leeward side, opposite Thresprotian Epirus.

The Argonauts marveled at the fair harbors of the Phaiacians, their tall ships, their great walls and spacious public squares. Likewise the people streamed down to the wharves, and shipwrights left the dockyards, to gaze at the *Argo*; for though the Phaiacians excelled in building ships to cross the sea, they had never seen another vessel as sleek and handsome riding high into their port of Hyllos.

The arrival of the *Argo*, a ship which had been on all men's lips, was soon known to all. Emissaries of king Alcinoös invited the Argonauts to the royal palace. He was the son of Nausithoös, who had led a migration of his people to the island from Trinacria to escape the plundering Cyclopes. Leaving a few of the crew to guard the ship, Jason, Medeia and the rest of the Argonauts went up into the city by a narrow causeway leading from the harbors. They came to the king's estate, enclosed in a palisade, planted with blooming trees whose fruit never failed through all the seasons of the year: moist pears, sweet pomegranates and figs, dark olives bursting from ripeness. There too stretched a flowering vineyard, and the vintners' vats overflowing with fragrant purple juice. One clear spring watered the orchard, and another coursed through the courtyard for the use of the household.

The Argonauts, awed by the luxuriance, entered through the courtyard gate and crossed a threshold of bronzed tiles. The mansion entryway, flanked by gold and silver statues of seated hounds, opened into a tall vestibule ringed by high and airy rooms, wide corridors and spiraling staircases. They filed into the great hall through golden doors framed by silver sill and lintel. The walls were empanelled in bronze and ringed with molding and friezes of lapis lazuli. Tall golden sculptures of boys on plinths, holding aloft burning brands, encircled the room with bright light. King Alcinoös, sitting on his chair before the hearthstone, rose to greet them. Not quite middle-aged, he wore a tip-tilted beard like all Phaiacians and moved with a young man's agile grace. His young queen Arete, whose grandfather was Alcinoös' father Nausithoös, sat nearby in the shadow of a colonnade with her fifty handmaids busy at the loom.

Said Alcinoös: "Welcome sailors of the far-famed *Argo!*" Then, after calling on Pontonoös, his chief squire, to rally the servants for the supper preparation, he had the Argonauts sit on high-back chairs placed along the walls and covered with embroidered rugs, with Jason and Medeia beside his own throne. As they feasted on dripping chines of beef and lamb and seared Rhodian dog-fish, chased down with honeyed wine pressed from his own vineyard and served in golden goblets, Alcinoös interviewed Jason, who described his expedition in the best possible light: stating that Aiëtes, wishing to do honor to his ally Pelias, had not only willingly surrendered the Golden Fleece in obedience to the will of the gods, but had also sent his daughter to become the wife of Jason or any other Iolcan prince she fancied as a sign of his unbreakable amity.

As the Argonauts were enjoying the evening's festivities, feeling as joyous among the friendly Phaiacians as they would among their own people, Pontonoös entered hurriedly to whisper in the king's ear that a squadron of war-ships, the party that had pursued the *Argo* out through the Cyanaian rocks, had entered the harbor and the armed crews were on their way to the palace. Jason, who had overheard somewhat, hardly had inquired, fearing the worst, when the golden doors opened and in walked a troop of dusky Colchians. Their leader, seeing Medeia, doffed his helm in her direction, and then addressed the king.

"Mighty lord!" he said. "I am vice-admiral of the Colchian fleet. I am here to return the lady Medeia, without any argument, back to her father's house."

Alcinoös glanced with concern at Jason, and replied: "The princess, I am told, has accompanied these sailors of her own free will."

"Whoever has told you this must be a scoundrel and a despiser of the gods," said the vice-admiral. "Since summertime, our fleet has been pursing these pirates, who absconded not only with the king's daughter, but also with one of our national treasures. I am afraid that if we face any resistance in fulfillment of our mission, we will unleash on these people a terrible reprisal; and a greater one you will suffer later by the hand of our king Aiëtes at his coming."

Alcinoös called for Echeneos, his most trusted councilor, and after discussing the matter with him turned back the Colchian vice-admiral and said: "It is clear that we have here a quarrel between two parties that, as is often the case, are convinced of the sincerity and rightness of their respective cause. The hour is later, and prudence forbids any hasty decision. Let us assemble again in the morning, when cooler heads prevail, and I shall listen carefully to each side before making any judgements. In the meanwhile, return to your ships in peace. We shall all be the poorer if thoughtful negotiation cedes place to unnecessary strife."

The Colchians, weary from their excursion over so many seas, agreed among themselves to honor the Phaiacian king's request and wait until morning. They returned to their ship surrounded by an armed escort, the sight of which dampened their resolve to engage in armed struggle against their hosts.

Jason sent the Argonauts back to the ships telling them to arm themselves, maintain a watch, and be ready to depart at a moment's notice. Alcinoös would not hear of Jason or Medeia sleeping outside the palace that night, and so installed Medeia in a painted bedchamber he had ready should Arete bless him with a daughter; while Jason made his bed on thick rugs and coverlets the handmaids stretched out for him in the cool of the colonnade.

As night sprinkled the world with sleep, the king and queen retired as usual to their bed. Lying there in the dark, Arete, embracing her husband, divulged the preoccupation of her heart.

"Dearest," she whispered lovingly, "do something to save this harried girl from the Colchians, whose king, whom we don't even know, is from far away; while the men who brought her are from lands close by. Poor Medeia broke my heart with her entreaties just now. Unable to sleep, she came to me in tears as I dressed for bed, and touching my knees, said, 'Majesty, show mercy! Do not give me up to the Colchians to be returned to my father. See how a little sin can lead to ruin! Yes, I was thoughtless, but not wanton. I swear by the sun's holy light and by the rites of Perses' night-wandering daughter that it was never my intention to sail off with these foreigners. Rather, only after helping Jason out of love to gain the Fleece did fear move me to take flight. But my virginity remains unspoiled. Have pity, gracious lady! Entreat your husband on my behalf. And may the gods grant you peace and honor, and beautiful children, in this city ever free from war.'

"My lord, as you can see, witless from love, Medeia tried to cover one wrong with another by running away from her overbearing father's wrath. But Jason, she revealed to me, has bound himself by solemn oaths to wed her. If this is the case, my dear, let no decision of yours help to break his covenant; nor be the cause of Medeia having to suffer her father's unremitting outrage, since fathers are much too jealous over their daughters, as you will no doubt discover some day. Consider what Danaë suffered, set adrift by her father's cruelty; or, not far from us, Metope, the daughter of Echetos, who drove bronze spikes through her eyes."

Thus Arete moved her husband's heart, and he replied: "I could by all means drive out the Colchians by force, taking the side of these heroes for Medeia's sake. While I dare not defy Zeus' judgment I also find it unwise to ignore Aiëtes, as you demand. There lives no mightier monarch than this man; and though he is far, he could bring war upon us if he wished. No; I must render a judgment that the whole world will view as just. This is what I propose. If Medeia possesses her maidenhead still, I will send her back to her father. But if she shares a man's bed, I will not separate her from her husband, nor will I hand over any child she bears to her enemies."

Saying this, sleep conquered him. Arete, taking his words to heart, at once rose from her bed, and going through the house followed by her bustling handmaids, sought her herald, whom she entrusted with shrewd counsel. The herald first awoke Jason from his slumber, and hurried with him to the harbor to inform his shipmates. Delighted, they straightway began to carry out the marriage rites. In a bowl they mixed wine for the blessed gods, dragged sheep to the altar, and that very night prepared for Medeia a bridal bed in the sacred cave of Macris, daughter of bee-keeping Aristaios who too discovered the olive's bountiful yield. It was Macris who in Euboia nursed the infant Dionysos, and smeared his parched lips with honey as soon as Hermes pulled him from the fire. Driven off by Hera in her jealousy, Macris settled in the sacred cave among the Phaiacians, prospering them. In that selfsame grotto did they prepare the marriage-bed, spreading out the Golden Fleece on a matting of rushes under a covering of bull's-hide suspended from upright spears. Palace maidens, like nymphs of hill and wood, gathered many-colored wild-flowers; and as they brought in the blossoms, the bright splendor of the Fleece, like firelight, danced on their white arms and touched their eyes with sweet longing: but not one dared to touch it.

When Medeia came down from the palace, dressed in the finest of Arete's gowns, Jason took her by the hand and together proceeded into the cave, passing behind a curtain of scented veils. Outside, the Argonauts, gripping their spears and garlanded with leafy withes, sang the marriage song to the tune of Orpheus' lyre. Though suffering regret over their makeshift arrangements and apprehension over the power of Alcinoös' judgment, Jason and Medeia delighted in one another, their mingled bodies bathed in the effulgence of their golden bed, knowing full well that the gods do not grant joy without weeping.

When dawn's lustral beams banished black night, and island beaches and dewy paths crossing the fields laughed in the sun, the whole city rose and filled the streets, longing to see the princely Argonauts. Alcinoös, holding his golden staff of justice, came down to the assembly ground by the shipyards. Behind him came the nobles and ranks of armed Phaiacians ready to keep the peace.

When the Colchians arrived from the far harbor, the people grew quiet. Alcinoös arose from his seat on a smooth stone bench, and with lordly mien declared: "Friends, guests and countrymen! Zeus of the black cloud has shown me his will in this matter. I declare that if princess Medeia has been duly married, she shall remain with her husband; but if she is found a virgin still, and thus under the authority of her parents, she is to return to her own country."

The Colchian vice-admiral, looking suspiciously at Jason and the Argonauts, who could hardly contain their laughter, said: "We accept your judgment, O king. As far as we know, the princess is not, and has never, married, although she is betrothed to prince Styrus of the Albanians. Bring her to us, therefore, and we shall make preparations to depart."

Arete, tugging at her husband's arm, had him invite Jason to speak. Jason faced the Colchian and said: "You shall indeed depart, but without Medeia, who is my lawful wife."

The Colchians, outraged, demanded proof of his assertion. The sons of Phrixos came forward as witnesses, as did Atalanta, who pretended to have handled Medeia's virginal girdle, when the Colchians refused to accept the testimony of blood-relations. Finally ivory-skinned Arete laid the matter to rest by declaring that the marriage had been arranged under her auspices, and consummated in the island's sacred cave.  At this the palace women broke into the second-day's hymeneal song and danced in circles around the bride and groom, giving thanks to Hera for the king's wise decision.

Alcinoös would hear no more of the Colchians' protestations and threatened that he would close his harbors to them if they did not accept his ruling and depart forthwith.  But after discussing the matter among themselves, the Colchians, afraid to face the wrath of Aiëtes after having failed in every aspect of their mission, besought Alcinoös to accept them as allies.  And so they remained on the island.

On the seventh day the Argonauts sped off at dawn with a fresh tailwind.  Alcinoös plied them with many gifts, as did Arete, presenting Medeia with twelve Phaiacian bridesmaids to attend her, replacing the ones she had left behind in Colchis.

The oarsmen, eager for home, cut through the sea with a full sail, passing inshore from the green humps of Paxos and Propaxos.  They left behind the Ambracian Gulf, threaded the narrow channel between Ithaca and the Acarnanian coast, coasted through the scattered Echinades, and were in sight of Pelops' land when a howling northerly gale swept them off.  The sail they lowered when it began to tatter, unstepped the mast, and rowed incessantly for the lee of some island or the shelter of a cove.  But hard as they pulled, the swell, the current and the steady wind conspired to push them far out into an endless void of sea and sky.  The Argonauts watched in utter despair as familiar shores faded from view.

22

Ten days after crossing the Tanais, Heracles arrived at the mouth of the river Tyras in the land of the gold-loving Agathyrsoi. Trying to cross it at a shallow point, a chariot wheel shivered on some hidden rocks. Abandoning the chariot, Heracles unyoked the mares and drew them the remainder of the way through the stream, leaving a large footprint on a mud-covered rock on the opposite bank, which is still shown to this day. From there he rode one mare down the western coast of the Axine, which is heavily indented with bays, pulling the other beside him as a pack animal, and came to the land of the Thracian Getai. Knowing some words of Thracian from his old nurse, Heracles learned from them that the river he sought was called the Istros, the remotest branch of Ocean, and conducted him to its many mouths encompassing a delta as great as that of Egypt: a vast, reed-covered marsh, relieved at intervals by singular hills covered with beech-trees, oak and willows. But, eager to hear of his travels, they detained him for some time. When he told them that he hoped to one day achieve immortality, the Getai laughed at him and said, "Do you not know, sir, that you go through much trouble for nothing? It is certain that by nature we already possess immortality." (They said this because they thought that at death they went to be in the company of their chief divinity, called Gebeleizis). As proof they carried out before Heracles a strange ceremony. Quinquenially the Getai dispatch one of their own with certain requests for Gebeleizis. As Heracles watched, they selected one person by lot, grabbed him by the hands and feet, and vaulted him through the air over three men holding javelins upright. The unfortunate victim impaled himself and died quickly, which meant that he went to their god with evident success, who would, based on his instructions, grant them whatever they wished.

Heracles now set his face westward, following the

serpentine course of the wide Istros through a flat, featureless plain, until a low range of hills appeared to accompany him, broken at intervals by vistas of green valleys and silvery streams. The next day the leaden sky brightened, the clouds grew thin, and in the distance a stretch of mountains materialized: a long, glittering row of snow-tipped peaks shimmering in the bursting sun of morning, so artfully transparent in their beauty, so concert in their coloring, so grand and perfect in their sweeping lines, that the sight filled his mind with wonder. The river now widened to nearly twenty stades, its rushing waters obstructed by numerous islets of all sizes, some simply rocks jutting from the water, others covered in trees from which innumerable wild-fowl fluttered to darken the sky. Immense flocks of ducks ruled the air; while pelicans and white herons littered the riverbank, their eyes keen for soaring hawks. And on the bare rocks midstream perched vultures with red eyes and lolling heads, caricatures of noble patience.

Heracles left the riverside to hunt the shaggy, short-horned bisons in the meadows, easy targets as they lazily cropped the thick grass, providing him ready and delicious meat. Beyond the ranging herds the plains narrowed and the land grew hills, reaching to the water's edge, covered in low, sparse woods. The sprinkling of willow-trees gave way to a forest of noble birches on either side of the river, fringed by golden sunflowers; while travel along the banks, moist and spongy, covered in a green morass, grew exceedingly difficult. Heracles, forced to higher ground, saw now the extent of the beech woods clothing the deep undulating valley. The haunted wilderness seemed impenetrable, a place frozen in antiquity before men filled the earth, unspoiled and untouched, breathing a cold, forlorn loneliness.

The valley narrowed on reaching a spur of the densely-wooded mountains, from whose recesses flowed numerous streams and tributaries breaking over scattered boulders until they washed into the Istros. The river-bed now coursed through a deep rift, inclosed by high, precipitous rocks honeycombed by murky caverns. So high and close were the cliffs piled that the formation induced an early sunset, filling the valley with deep shadows, after which a cool twilight lingered.

It grew difficult again to traverse the riverbank, bracketed by rocks and woods, rising at once steeply, and then sloping gradually away. Heracles therefore, nine days after leaving the shores of the Axine, dismissed the mares and journeyed onward on foot. The mighty mass of the river flowed calmly past him until the valley narrowed once more, squeezed between the cliffs. As the river bent sharply this way and that, mountain peaks appeared above the treetops to the south. The river tumbled down in a succession of falls, rushing with white spume over obtruding rock ledges, and roiling in dark eddies livened with leaping silvery trout. Beyond these cataracts the river widened for a space, and then once more the gorge constricted to its narrowest point thus far, of less than ten fathoms wide, nearly impossible to traverse for lack of level ground. The rushing river, dividing into two branches within a smoky abyss, roared through hemmed in by vast, precipitous white wooded cliffs between which hawks flew like distant wisps of grey mist. The spectacular defile filled Heracles with awe, as if he had found himself before the grandeur of another Titan; but even more so. The serpentine trails of the river through the formidable rampart of the mountains and endless mantle of shrouding forest primeval—in all its desolate, gloomy, mysterious wildness— impressed the rude and boisterous sensibilities of Heracles more than the cypress-haunted valleys of Arcadia, the vast well-watered plains of Thessaly, or the spreading haymeadows of Boetia. The savage land was all beauty.

Was this not the fearsome gorge at the river's divide discussed by the Titan? His heart, agitated by nervous excitement, filled for a longing to plunge into the dense wood. Up the declivitous cliff-face he climbed, borne at each step by jutting rocks or roots, pulling his weight forward by grasping the boles and branches, until he reached the summit and a steep ravine, washed by a mountain torrent and shrouded by gnarled oak-trees. He followed the crystal stream for hours through the beech wood carpeted with ferns and velvet mosses, passing here and there a grassy stretch or glade livened with scented violets and rosy cyclamen, until the beech-trees, in the gathering twilight, welcomed here and there a lonely fir-tree. Heracles collected timber in plenty, started a fire, and settled within a close-set grove. The night he passed in restless sleep, imagining that the shadowy outlines of the trees turned to monstrous shapes. The shrill cry of wild-cats raked his ears, as well as the baying of wolves, which scoured the cliffs in packs after the springing ibex. The ground seemed sullied with dark, creeping things; and the wispy shades of the dead appeared to flit about. The nightmarish sights and sounds of the haunted wood ceased not until the arrival of the misty dawn, when the shadows fled and Heracles awoke to see a gigantic black bear digging nearby for roots. Heracles reached for his club; but the bear, no less fearful of the human invader, scurried off. For breakfast, Heracles shot a roe-deer, and roasting the flesh until it crackled in the cool morning, he ate it with dewy strawberries hanging thickly from sun-dappled rocks. Thus fortified, he marched on through the thick forest maze, populated now exclusively by the fragrant pine, through bogs and briers, following the sound of gurgling water to a gully strewn with boulders and vertical wall of rock swashed by a vaporous cascade. A steep climb conveyed him to the top of the waterfall, overlooking a larger valley, deep and lonely, shut in by pointed crags on all side, artfully set as if by a giant hand. Looking behind from his high perch, Heracles could see the silver ribbon of the Istros undulating through the mass of billowing green trees, mottled randomly by fading autumn with yellow tints; the cold, bare mountains, the highest peaks rarely free of snow, stretching like a fishhook to the north and west, their bases draped with alternating folds of oak, beech and fir; and to the south, below the listless clouds, more restless white crags shadowing rich, emerald plains.

Searching the valley with his eyes, Heracles noticed a silvery stretch of forest, at its center strangely touched by a golden tinge, as by the impertinent hand of autumn. Heracles waited, lest the sunshine played a trick on his eyes. Even when the sky grew overspread, and that bright cast by which the forenoon sky blushed crimson faded, the patch of forest glimmered still.

The valley floor was free from undergrowth, carpeted with short, coarse grass and showered in wind-strewn rose-petals. The forest consisted of silver-fir, stunted and misshapen by the harsh winds. In little time Heracles reached an open glade, beyond which a grove of sundry trees encircled in a lively garden a stout apple-tree bowed with bright, golden apples. Here the virgin laurel-tree stood beside the pointed cypress; there the overspreading elm shadowed the soft linden-tree. The tall mountain ash was not loath to share a space with the green boxwood; and the lithe tamarisk, draped with vines, mixed her foliage with many-hued maples. Wild thyme, scenting the air, grew among violet hyacinth, yellow crocus and delicate damask-rose. It seemed that all of nature, in a perpetual springtide, had adorned herself in an exuberant plenty of fringes and curls.

But lo! the scaly coils of a great tawny serpent infolded the trunk of the apple-tree; and against the still serpentine bulk comfortably rested three maidens clothed in long garments of varying hues, with harps and shepherds' pipes embraced in their long white arms  Though gales blew to and fro across the valley, not a leaf within the grove stirred, and all seemed as still and quiet as a bucolic painting. It was only when Heracles stepped within the ring of outer trees and beyond a silver trellis demarking the garden that his footfalls made a noise, causing the maidens to stir. At once they drew apart, looking at Heracles with fear and dismay.

"Beautiful and kindly divinities," said Heracles reassuringly, "be gracious to me, whether you be heavenly goddesses, or of the lower world, or nymphs of the wood. Allow me please to take but a few those golden apples hanging abundantly from every weighted bough. Surely you can spare some! I wish to do no harm to the tree's custodian, appointed by the gods; therefore, feed it dainties that it may be appeased; or sprinkle it with dewy honey and drowsy poppies, that it may remain quiescent while I pick a fruit or two."

Then the nymph Aigle, daughter of Atlas, said: "Man most foul, grim and violent!  Wherefore molest our solitude? I see those eyes flashing beneath your scowling brow.  No man may touch these treasures and live: as you will soon discover."

The Hesperides dispersed, their fleeting forms dissolving into dust and earth. As Heracles took a step toward the tree, from its leafy aureate canopy shot out a dozen tawny snouts on long, sinuous necks, animated with darting, forked tongues, and eyes glittering red like shards of chalcedony. More serpentine heads followed, darting in and out of the gilded leaves, so that the tree, trembling, seemed alive with a myriad of moving tentacles. Heracles tightened both hands on his club as the heads hovered above him. All at once the mouths of Ladon spoke, each in a different tongue, yet in harmonious polyphony, so that the garden seemed filled with a sacral song. From the torrent of sounds Heracles heard words he understood, and they ran gently thus: "We know who you are, offspring of the most high. That you have both found and entered this grove is reward enough. Do not essay any mischief, lest you bring down heavenly anger upon your head. Turn back now to whence you came and all will be well with you."

"Nay," said Heracles. "I have travelled, at the command of an unjust king, long and far to find this tree. Blame him with impiety if you must, but not I."

The serpent-heads bent and coiled, and from the highest bough plucked a gleaming apple in its maw. Arching down from above, it presented the holy fruit to Heracles while other mouths said: "Were you warned not to touch the fruit of the tree, lest touching it you shall die? You shall not die. Take, eat, and become a god." Heracles saw that the apple was fair and delightful, perfectly round and lambent in the rays of the midday sun. With abandon he reached for it, but Ladon pulled it back ever so slightly, so that Heracles, dropping his bow and club, was drawn closer to the encinctured tree. With ear-piercing hisses, Ladon's hundred ghastly heads, with snapping jaws, suddenly darted forth, seeking to bite or entwine him. Heracles grasped one neck in a stony grip, struck at another with a fist, and a third he crushed under his foot. Twisting free, he leapt beyond the serpent's reach, which, to extend it striking length, by continuous undulations of its long body uncoiled itself from the bole. Quickly Heracles reached for his bow, and from his quiver drew one of the two remaining arrows stained with Lernean poison. He sped an arrow into that section from where the heads branched forth, pining the horrid scales to the wood of the tree. The writhing heads dropped one after another and the surging bulk sagged listless in loosened coils. Only the tip of the tail still twitched. A darkness settled on the grove as clouds hid the sun; and a sudden wind tore the blossoms from the trees. Flies collected around the guardian's festering wound.

Heracles with some hesitation plucked an apple from the lowest bough. He turned it about in his hand, admiring its delicious loveliness. Crystal dew-drops ran down the golden skin, wherein his countenance numinously reflected. With one bite he could die, as said one god—or become one, as said another. The temptation, savored with indecision, gripped him only for a moment. As no ill came to him from handling the fruit, he tore off two more, depositing all three into his satchel. One more thing he carried away with him from the grove—an olive spray: a sweet desire for the enchanted garden's shadiest tree possessed him.

Heracles climbed out of the valley and then descended the trackless mountain-side back to the narrowest part of the Istros, where through the strong current he swam across to the opposite steep bank. He climbed again the soaring rampart of the gorge, and then set out across the southern mountain-ridges until they melted into wooded hills, passing after many days into a realm of sandy hillocks and finally the wide, barren lowlands north of Thrace, hemmed in by rugged mountains and coursing with rivers.

## 23

For nine days and nights the *Argo*, shipping water, ran southwestward before the raging blasts, which finally drove her deep into the gulf of Syrtis on Libya's coast, a vast waste of shoals and tangled seaweed, where a flood tide swept her high onto a beach, with her keel, at the ebb, left hardly touching the water. The crew leapt down from the ship and in grew numb at the desolate landscape of marsh and sand, like an endless haze, stretching as far as they could see, without paths or pleasing groves, and muffled in a dreary silence.

They were all at first bewildered, for nobody understood how they ended up where they were. Ancaios and Nauplios joined the Boreads to scout the area, and came back to inform the others that a colossal wave must have carried them over barren rocks and reefs, where the ship would have surely perished, and stuck them on the backshore of a vast coastal lagoon. The simpler-minded rejoiced that they had been saved from destruction. Ancaios, however, could not hide his grief.

"Comrades, we're doomed," he said. "With the tide retreating, we are left high and dry in a strange land, mired in seaweed, and with surf barely deep enough to wade in. There are shoals everywhere. Even if we could cut a channel through the sandbar to the sea, the coast is bound by leagues of black reefs and sharp rocks which we would not be able to overcome. There's little hope of getting home now, I tell you. Let someone else, then, fill the helmsman's seat and take us out of his bind if he can. It is obvious to me that Zeus bars our return."

"But surely, the great Zeus will not let the Golden Fleece rot here with us?" said Augeias.

"A lot of good the Fleece has done us," muttered Menoitos, the son of Actor.

Ancaios wept, as did all the skilled shipmen among them, for they knew he spoke the truth. Periclymenos pointed a bony finger at Medeia, who sat near the ship in a stupor surrounded by her sobbing bridesmaids.

"And what of her?" he said. "I saw how with dark magic she saved us from the perils of the strait. She certainly could have calmed the winds if she had wanted. Perhaps she meant all along to entrap us. Women are vindictive in that way."

"Be silent, brother," said Nestor. "Your words do little to relieve our present distress."

"Indeed!" said Castor to Periclymenos. "Do you not call yourself a sorcerer and conjuror? We have seen precious little of your powers, while from Medeia we have witnessed mighty works. Why didn't *you* save us from the storm?"

"It is no use. The gods have turned their backs," said Palaimon, from the ship, remaining there due to his lame feet. "Even knowledge of the sacred mysteries of Samothrace could not preserve us."

Everyone recognized that there was little point in arguing. Though on leaving Drepane they were well-provisioned, they had discarded most of their chests and jars to lighten the ship when they were scudding across the sea. There was only enough food and drink to last a day; and when these had been consumed, the sailors, turning pale with fear, strayed from their landing place and wandered like phantoms over the endless beach, each one ascertaining for himself the extent of their doom.

The gloom of night only deepened their despair. With tears they embraced one another, said their farewells, and went their separate ways to lie in the sand, wrap their heads in their mantles, and wait for death. Medeia had not moved from where she sat listlessly since the morning, huddled with her handmaids who spent all night piteously wailing, their tawny tresses fouled with dust, like unfledged birds chirping for their mother after falling from their nest upon the rocks.

Jason too lay despondently near his beloved, tossing in troubled sleep deep into the next day, when at high noon, under the scorching sun, someone lifted the cloak from his head. He looked up and saw three maidens wearing goatskin capes reaching to their waists. Recognizing immediately that he was in the presence of some divinity, he averted his eyes. But they spoke to him in a friendly tone, sharing one voice.

"Poor wretch, why despair?" they said. "We know of your quest for the Golden Fleece and all the hardships you endured in your wanderings through the world. We are wardens of the Libyan shore: the nymphs who found Athena after she sprang fully armored from Zeus' head and bathed her in the waters of the Tritonian lake. Up with you now! Rouse your men! When Amphitrite unyokes the steeds from Poseidon's swift chariot, then you must repay your mother for her sufferings bearing you in her womb. Whereupon you shall see once again your hallowed land of Greece."

They vanished into mist. Jason could not tell if he had dreamed the vision, or seen it with his waking eyes. He leapt to his feet and shouted for his crew, bursting to hear their opinions, since many heads are better than one. But they at first paid him no mind, thinking him mad from heat-stroke. Only slowly did they shuffle back, dejected. Jason made them sit with the women by the ship and explained the matter. They listened in amazement, and as they pondered the meaning of the riddles, a booming noise drew their attention toward the sea. Over the reefs bounded a massive, white-crested wave, like a herd of outsized horses galloping toward them, their snowy manes waving in the rushing air, and inundated the shoals with a terrifying hiss. The Argonauts fled to escape the breaker, which lifted the *Argo* from the clogging sea-weed and floated her over a league down the lake, where her stern grounded in the sand and her prow was left dancing on the bubbling spume.

The Argonauts did not know what to make of this in light of Jason's vision. Finally Peleus, filled with joy declared: "It is clear that Poseidon's wife has just unyoked her husband's team! Our mother, I am sure, is none other than the *Argo* herself, since she has carried us within her as in a womb, groaning all along. Let us follow where she leads, and mayhap we'll find an outlet to the sea."

Blasted by the torrid sun, they trudged wearily through the sucking sand. While Ancaios and Nauplios took soundings around the ship, the others, parched with thirst, went off to find fresh water. Orpheus, climbing a ridge of sand, found on the other side a small oasis of grass and tender shoots, and in the midst of three tall saplings in full leaf, a small pool fed by a thin rill of water. And as

Orpheus reached the fortunate spot, hardly believing his eyes, he was struck with a sudden awe. Perceiving he was on holy ground, he cast off his sandals and dropped to his knees. Addressing the poplar, elm and willow trees that shaded his head, he prayed on behalf of his friends: "Kind spirits, be gracious to us, whether you are goddesses of Olympos, or the underworld, or are the guardians of this place. Make yourselves known and show us where we can slake our burning thirst. If ever our ship sees home port again, you will, above all, receive our most grateful offerings."

And it seemed to him as if the trees assumed the forms of maidens. She who had been the willow, her golden head cradled in her white arms, said to him: "A great brute was he! Wearing the untanned hide of a great lion and carrying a club of olive-wood, he invaded our garden, killed the guarding serpent with his bow, and stole our golden apples. With our sacred grove despoiled, we fled to this desolate place at no great distance from our father's mountains. Consider yourselves fortunate, however. Though he brought to us unspeakable grief, he did you a good turn. Like you he wandered through these parts, parched with thirst. In vain he searched for water until, whether on his own device, or at some god's prompting, he smote a rock by the lakeshore with his foot, and out gushed a refreshing spring."

As Orpheus next winked his eyes, the nymphs vanished and all was as before. Orpheus followed the rill to an outcrop, where he found sweet water bubbling from the cleft in a rock. His cries of exultation alerted the others, who rushed thereto from all directions. Delighted, the ravening crowd swarmed around the spring like burrowing ants, or flies upon a drop of honey. Learning from Orpheus that it had been Heracles, while searching for the Garden of the Hesperides, who by a stroke of chance had saved them, they resolved to send out a search party for him, thinking that he still trudged through the area. As they could not locate his tracks, effaced by the shifting sands, five of those best fitted for the task volunteered to fan out in different directions. The two sons of Boreas went off first, and then fleet-footed Euphemos, followed by Lynceus, who could rely on his farsightedness, and finally Canthos, a good friend of Polyphemos, who was anxious to learn from Heracles of his fate.

As the night winds began to howl, Lynceus returned to the

camp, saying that he thought he saw the lonely figure of Heracles tramping off in the distance, as when a man first sees a sliver of the new moon through the clouds, and that it would prove impossible to overtake him. Euphemos and the sons of Boreas, without success, also returned. As for Canthos, the son of Abas, after venturing along the seaboard, he found a grazing flock and was driving them back to his hungry crewmates when the shepherd, to defend his property, threw a stone at him and killed him. His name was Caphauros, great-grandson of king Minos, who had banished his daughter to Libya when she was found carrying a child by Apollo. When the Argonauts heard Canthos' dying cry, they seized their weapons and chased Cephauros until they caught up to him in the morning, killed him, and took his sheep. They recovered the body of Canthos, already moldering under the hot sun, and buried him on the spot.

While this was happening, Mopsos too could not avoid a bitter death, though he was a prophet. With his left foot he stepped on the tail of viper as it lay burrowed in the sand to avoid the midday sun. Though by nature sluggish, this time the serpent, writing in pain, coiled itself around his leg and sank its fangs into his calf. Mopsos, who felt little pain, bravely stanched the wound. But as he went, he was struck with palsy, a dark mist veiled his eyes, and his hair dropped from his head. His limbs grew heavy and he slumped to the ground, seized by a deadly cold. When his companions found him dead, they were astounded at the swift rate of decay, although he had been lying in the sun only a short time. Starting from the wound, black rot had spread, baring his bones, bursting open his belly, and melting his entrails all out on the sand. Quickly they dug a deep grave with their mattocks and gave him a solemn burial, thrice marching around him in full armor. Over him they raised a barrow and set up a broken oar-blade as a memorial.

Though stricken with grief, the Argonauts set to work on freeing the *Argo* and finding an outlet to the sea. Reversing the oars, they pushed her along, tortuously probing various channels between the shoals. When it seemed they were getting nowhere, Orpheus suggested that Jason offer the great tripod, inscribed with ancient glyphs, he had received at Delphi to the local gods in the hope that they would lend further assistance. Going ashore, they set up the tripod. And as they prayed, a horseman appeared from behind a dune. He was dressed in white robes and a long clump of hair extended from the front of his head. When he began speaking to them, Euphemos, who understood a little Egyptian, was able to translate from the similarity of words.

"He says," explained Euphemos, "that his name is Eurypylos, king of this land, and that his father is Poseidon. He understands that we have lost our way and wishes to help us reach the sea."

Euphemos offered him the tripod, and in return Eurypylos gave the Argonaut a clod of earth as a welcoming gift. He then pointed to the sea and spoke at length. After listening, Euphemos continued: "He says that over there, where the water is darkest and deepest, lies a narrow channel running through the foreshore frothing with surf. Beyond it stretches the misty sea. Once in the open, hug the coast until you see the headland running northward in the distance. Make for that point, avoiding the dangerous gulf, and as soon as the shoreline slopes again to the east, you may safely sail straight out to sea."

Embarking at once, the Argonauts shoved the ship through the shallows indicated by Eurypylos, who followed along on horseback where he could, uttering a prophecy that one hundred Greek cities would be built around lake Tritonis should a descendant of a certain Argonaut ever take back the tripod. (When the Libyan natives heard of this, they buried the tripod in the sand).

After three days, having finally reached clear water, with the wide blue sea before them, they rejoiced; and some, thinking they had seen Eurypylos ride into the lagoon at some point and disappear holding aloft the heavy tripod, considered him a beneficent marine divinity. They therefore urged Jason to kill for the god the finest of the sheep they had aboard. Jason did so, raising the sheep over the stern and uttering: "Sea-god who appeared to us—whether the daughters of the brine call you the wondrous Triton, or Phorcys, or Nereus—be gracious and grant us a safe return." As he prayed, he slit the victim's throat and cast the offering overboard.

Exhausted and windbound, they dropped anchor a short way down the coast and came ashore to rest. There Medeia, inspired by a dream, took Euphemos aside and told him to guard well the clod of earth, saying the he had received it from Triton disguised as a man. On returning to Tainaron, he was to cast it into one of the chasms there, and thereby win for his descendants, starting in the fourth generation, the right to colonize Libya. Thereafter Euphemos was very careful with the clod, keeping it near his bosom when he slept and entrusting it only to the most responsible hands whenever it was his turn to row.

At dawn they spread the sail and rode the west wind, keeping the barren shoreline to starboard for a day and a night. Early the next morning, the deep gulf came into sight: a frightening morass laced with shoals and flotsam, and beyond it the long jutting cape. From there they struck out, borne by a southwesterly wind that rattled the cordage. But by nightfall, the wind dropped and the crew had to furl the sail, lower the mast, and extend the oars. For two days and nights they rowed hard over empty sea, landing at last on rugged Carpathos, where Nauplius knew of good anchorage on the eastern side of the otherwise inaccessible island. At first light they embarked, intent on crossing over to Crete to resupply the ship. But as they drew near the harbor on the eastern side, the island's chief judge, who travelled around Crete thrice a year to enforce the laws and maintain political stability after the death of Minos, ran out to a high rock, dressed in his bronze armor, and began to pelt the *Argo* with large stones to prevent it from docking, since he was wary of strange ships. At once, though thirsty and weary from a day of rowing, they backed the ship from the shore, consigning themselves to an arduous voyage to the next port of call after Periclymenos convinced them that their attacker was none other than Talos, who in Cretan legend was the sole survivor of the ancient Age of Bronze.

As they bore down to turn about, Medeia cried out: "Listen! I believe that only I can defeat this man, whoever he is, unless there is some immortal part of him in that bronze body. I only ask that you keep the ship nearby, but out of his range, while I work out his downfall."

They took the ship a little out where the stones could no longer reach them and then rested on their oars to see what Medeia would do. Covering her cheeks with a fold of her purple mantle, she took Jason's hand and walked up to the foredeck. There she fixed on Talos her baleful stare and three times wove her incantations, calling upon the death spirits, the swift minions of

Hell that haunt living men, feeding on their souls. Grinding her teeth in a ravishment of wrath, she assailed him from afar with undiluted malevolence, projecting from her eyes deadly phantasms into his mind.

Ensorcelled, Talos lost his footing as he tried to heave another rock and fell from the spur where he perched, scraping his ankle as he went, severing an artery, and dying quickly in a pool of blood.

They put into port and spent the night at anchor in case the townspeople proved hostile. They were afraid of Medeia, however, and did not venture from their houses. At dawn the Argonauts filled their water-jars and raised a shrine to Minoan Athena before settling at the oars and casting off.

After rounding Cape Salmonis, they ventured again into open sea. But as night deepened, they grew terribly frightened to a man, for low clouds blotted out any sign of moon or stars, and surrounded by the wide sea on all sides, without a landmark or coastal lights to guide them, they were under, as it were, a shroud of darkness. It was as if they were adrift in deepest Hell. Jason, despairing, raised his hands and with tears beseeched Apollo to guide them, promising to leave the god gifts innumerable at each of his principal shrines. Soon the horizon seemed aflame, the waves whitened and newborn sunbeams breaking through the dispersing clouds revealed the humps of two rocky islets behind them, and before them, reflecting brightly on its bare peaks, appeared the little island called Membliaros; but they did not know this, and thinking they had discovered it by the grace of the god, called it Anaphe. They found a beach on the eastern side, and after running the *Argo* up into the shingle, set up an altar for Radiant Apollo in the shade of a cluster of trees. As the island was uncultivated and devoid of any animals fitting for sacrifice, the Argonauts could do nothing more than pour libations of water upon the burning brands, since they had also run out of wine since leaving Phaiacia. Medeia's handmaids, accustomed to the rich sacrifices of oxen at Alcinoös' palace, could not contain their laughter. The men, seeing likewise the humor of the situation, shot back at them with some coarse jests. Thus began an exchange of ribald raillery, which did not end until Atalanta threatened to unleash her bow on the next person to continue the scurrilous badinage, since the indecorous language hurt her virgin ears.

In the morning a fair wind saw them off. They had not gone far when Euphemos screamed in anguish, for he had placed the clod of Libyan soil beside him on the rim of the gunwale when he first sat at his bench, and forgetting it, noticed that it had washed out from a sudden bow wave in the direction of the island of Calliste, which they were passing at the moment. Thinking his future renown voided, Euphemos left his seat and ran abaft to prostrate himself in silence before Medeia, who, pointing to the island, prophesied that his descendants would still rule Libya, but starting from there in the seventeenth generation.

After Anaphe they landed next at Oinoe, where fishermen had pulled a skiff from the sea containing an old man who in his delirium claimed to be Thoas, the king of Lemnos. The Argonauts, discounting his pretension, made fun of him and departed. They skirted the scattered islands, keeping always at least one of them in sight, and took a slight detour toward Aigina, since Peleus expressed a great desire to see his father. But after having some trouble putting in there, since the island was surrounded by reefs and shallows, Ancaios grew fretful that the southerly wind which had accompanied them since leaving Anaphe would break, and urged his shipmates to waste no time. They therefore did nothing more than draw water, turning the process into a game to hasten it. And so they raced one another carrying the heavy water-jars to and from the spring called Asopos.

Jason would entertain no further stops after leaving Aigina. They hailed the coast of Attica, sailed inside Euboia, passed Aulis and the cities of Opuntial Locris. And nearly seven months after their departure, they joyfully reached Pagasai.

24

The coastal town of Pagasai lay quietly under the thrall of night.  Only the doleful baying of some distant hound welcomed them.  Jason was the first to step ashore, followed by Acastos, who was eager to report to his father, whom he still loved although the old king was irascible, violent and overbearing.  But Jason wished first to make a sacrifice to Apollo of Disembarkations.  As they were building up a fire, a townsman, who kept a sloop tied up nearby, approached from curiosity.  On seeing the great ram's head jutting from the *Argo*'s prow, he turned white with fright and ran off screaming.  Calais and Zetes, quick on their feet, apprehended him and brought him back to Jason.

"My lords," the man said, wildly agitated, "either the rumors are false, or you are ghosts let loose into the world by the mercy of the Other Zeus."

Jason pressed him to explain, convincing him with a slap to the face that he was no less than flesh and blood.  Regaining his composure, the man revealed how everyone believed that the Argonauts had perished on their voyage; thereupon, Pelias, desiring to remove all remaining threats to his rule, killed Jason's father by forcing him to drink bull's blood, compelled his mother to strike her breast with the sword, and cut short the life of his infant brother.  On hearing this Jason, speechless, rent his garment and bobbed his head in anguish, wringing from his eyes great tears.  The others, noticing his distress, gathered around him and likewise received the news with horror.

"I say, and I hope I speak for all of us, that we must assist Jason to revenge himself on this impious king," said Meleager.

Most agreed and cried out for Pelias' blood.  Acastos, naturally, shrank back, unable to believe that his father would stoop to murder Jason's kinsmen.  "I am certain there has been a misunderstanding," he said. "Let us go into the city and inquire for ourselves, rather than believe the word of this prattling commoner."

Admetos then spoke: "A son, when it comes to his sire, sometimes confuses fear for love. I am married to Alcestis and well recognize my father-in-law's temperament and savage nature. You know as well as I, Admetos, that he murdered his own stepmother, although the case can be made that she had it coming to her. There is no end to Pelias' ruthlessness. See how he kept his own brother under heel. I see no reason to disbelieve this citizen."

Nestor nodded his head in agreement, since Pelias, in seeking dominion over Phitiotis, had banished his father Neleus.

"I, for one, am ready to fight at your side, Jason," said Polydeuces. "Let us put away words and take up our swords. We can take the city while it is yet night."

"Hear, hear!" cried many of the men.

"Don't be foolish," said Asterion of Peiresia. "What can a few dozen men do against Pelias' royal garrison? Did we not scurry from Colchis with an army at our heels? We should rather wage a general war, each man first returning to his city and raising a body troops."

While they argued over the best way to make the attack, Medeia, who had been quietly observing the discussion, left the company of her handmaids, and entering into their midst, said: "I alone shall punish Pelias and deliver the palace to you."

Astonished by her bold statement, the Argonauts besought her to expose the scheme she had in mind. She told them only that she had many drugs in her possession; and though beforetime she had never used them to destroy human beings, she would not now shrink back from wreaking vengeance on those who were deserving of punishment.

While Jason stood numbly off to one side, Medeia worked out her plan. She first had the shipwright Argos construct a hollow image of Artemis, as he similarly had done on Mount Dindymon, made to look as frightful as possible, and in which she secreted various potent concoctions and charms. While this was being done, she sent Orpheus to fetch for her certain native roots and flowers, borrowed from Thessalian Autolycos his knife and from Palaimon his walking staff of olive wood.

Taking her handmaids with her, she went off into a little

coppice nearby. The Argonauts stood around the campfire in silence waiting, unable to see her, but hearing little cries and noises coming from the shadows of the trees. In time emerged an old wizened crone, her garments in tatters and her white hair disheveled. Jason had to peer closely at her before he realized that underneath the wrinkles and mottled skin she was still Medeia in an ingenious disguise. Likewise, like bacchants, her Phaiacian handmaids followed her, barefoot and white-faced, wearing twig wreaths around their heads and carrying sticks topped with pine cones.

When it became clear to Acastos that the threat to his father was real, he tried to sneak off unnoticed. But Telamon tripped him with his foot. When Jason ordered Acastos detained until the conclusion of their plot, lest he alert the king, Telamon looked to Peleus for his assistance. But Peleus, a vassal of Pelias, adamantly refused to lift a finger to assist in his demise, although he promised not to interfere with others intent on so doing. Acastos was carried up into the *Argo*, gagged, and tied down between the thwarts.

Following Medeia's instructions, the Argonauts, except for Atalanta, who remained on the beach with her, embarked and quietly rowed the *Argo* out to a roadstead, keeping the sail under wraps. They were to look out for a signal from the palace: smoke if by day; fire if by night. Then they were to row to Iolcos and attack the city with full confidence.

Medeia sent Atalanta ahead of her into Iolcos to seek the temple of Artemis and inform the priestess there that the goddess was coming that night from the distant land of the Hyperboreans to bless the city and the king with good fortune. Atalanta quietly slipped into the city, found the old priestess Iphis, and made the pronouncement, handing her a cluster of amaranth-flowers. Since Atalanta was a well-known devotee of Artemis, Iphis had no reason to doubt her, and working herself into a frenzy from the thought of seeing the goddess, went forth to prepare for her arrival.

Meanwhile Medeia led her handmaids in a procession toward the city, carrying in their midst the image of Artemis, ruddled and wrapped in a golden shawl. They arrived before the gates at daybreak, and already the populace, aroused by Iphis, filled the streets in anticipation. On seeing the image of Artemis, they all bowed in reverence, making a wide path for Medeia and her followers to walk through.  But in a loud voice, Medeia chided them for their ill manners, and reminded them that the Lady of the Wildwood was not a prissy deity, but a lover of action.  Encouraged by the Phaiacian girls, who, intoxicated from chewing ivy leaves Medeia had given them along the way, began to wildly dance, the womenfolk did likewise, twirling their skirts immodestly.  The men too sprang into the celebration, bringing out their yearling lambs for sacrifice and joining their wives and daughters in the merrymaking.

With the whole city distracted, Medeia shuffled toward the palace.  With a wave of her hand the doors unbolted and opened before her.  In the hall she found Pelias and his nine daughters, roused from sleep by the religious fervor gripping the city.  When Pelias saw the image of Artemis seemingly floating above the heads of Medeia's manic handmaids, he pushed through the cordon of his royal bodyguard and in superstitious fear demanded from Medeia an explanation.

"Artemis has come for you, Pelias!" screeched Medeia. "From distant Hyperborea, in a chariot drawn by yoked winged dragons, she has flown over land and sea searching for the most pious king of all to establish her worship forevermore.  She soared over the vale of Tempe, scanned the heights of Ossa, of Pelion, of Orthrys and of snow-clad Olympos, and finally steered her chariot over fair Haimonia, where goddesses get short shrift."

Medeia drew from her satchel a handful of magic dust, and casting it into the air, caused visions of winged yellow serpents with fiery eyes to circle around the image of the goddess.

"And what does the dread goddess want of me?" asked Pelias in alarm.  His daughters, terrified, crowded around his throne.

Medeia answered with a cackle: "She has commanded me, her chief priestess, not only to lengthen your life, but to renew your youth, so that you may live again the years that you once knew."

Pelias, growing suspicious, since his court magicians often entertained him with similar tricks, said shrewdly: "Whoever heard of a man growing young?  Show me some proof of what you speak, old woman.  Show me how you bring to bloom again your shriveled teats."

Medeia, anticipating this reaction, turned her attention to Pelias' daughters.  Squinting at them and extended a gnarled hand in their direction, she asked the eldest, Alcestis, for a bowl of pure water, identifying her as the wife of Acastos, whom she confirmed had perished with the rest of the adventurers on a distant shore. On hearing this, Alcestis cried out in anguish, her heart broken anew; but in obedience, with a trembling hand, she brought Medeia the water in a goblet.

Medeia hobbled into an alcove in the shadows of the colonnade. There she washed her body clean of the potent simples that had altered her appearance. When she reappeared, Pelias, amazed, fixed his gaze on her; for where a decrepit crone had been, now stood a maiden suffused with health and beauty.

Pelias, unable to discount the evidence before his eyes, believed all that Medeia had told him. He beckoned for her to approach him, eager to get on with the ritual that would restore his youth. In his ear Medeia urged Pelias to order his daughters to do whatever she commanded them, since it would be through them that she would, in due time, effect the miracle she had promised him. He did so, and invited Medeia to lodge in the palace as long as she wished.

That night, after Pelias had retired to bed, Medeia called his daughters forth from their apartments and said to them: "Do you really wish me to lift your father's weight of years?" The daughters, whose names, besides Alcestis, were Pelopia, Hippothoë, Evadne, Peisidice, Antinoë, Amphinome, Medousa and Asteropeia, were unanimous in their agreement. Again Medeia asked: "Do you really wish to see your father's head and beard turn black again?" Again, they consented. A third time Medeia asked: "Do you really wish to expel loathsome old age from your father's limbs?" Tiring of her questions, they urged her to tell them what they should do.

Medeia said nothing for a little while, as if in doubt. The daughters waited anxiously for her to break her silence. At last, with feigned solemnity, she said: "Hearken to what the goddess orders! To return Pelias to his youth, he must be born anew by being cut into little pieces and boiled in a caldron seething with magical herbs and potions. Find yourselves knives and hatchets, therefore, and perform your filial duty!"

Seeing how the daughters stiffened with horror, Medeia said: "There must always be pain and blood at every birth. But is not all forgotten with the child's first cry on coming into the world?

I shall inspire a greater confidence. Bring me that old ram I see you keep as a pet and I will do to it as I plan to do to Pelias."

Eager for an incontrovertible proof to lay to rest their doubts, the daughters of Pelias brought a shaggy ram which they had fed with milk since it was a lamb, pulling it by its curved horns, to the kitchen where Medeia attended to a brazen caldron seething and foaming with her potions. She cast in it the Thessalian roots and petals Orpheus had found, precious Colchian stones, grains of sand from Ocean's shore, hoarfrost gathered under a full moon, a screech-owl's desiccated wings, the tripes of a werewolf, the liver of a long-lived stag, the head of an ancient crow and scales from a Libyan serpent. With Palaimon's staff she stirred the boiling mixture, which displayed it potency by making the dried wood sprout leaves and tender olives. As soon as she saw this, Medeia drew Autolycos' knife and cut the ram's throat; but by its great age, hardly any blood dripped out to wet the blade. When the beast fell dead, she severed apart its limbs and plunged the pieces into the vat. After uttering incantations in the Colchian language, which the daughters mistook for Hyperborean, a thin bleating sounded from the caldron. While the daughters of Pelias still wondered, out jumped a lamb, shook the broth from its back, and skipped off in search of a plump udder.

The daughters, feeling that they could then explicitly trust Medeia, insisted on completing their gruesome assignment. She swore them to an oath of secrecy and told them the time was not yet ripe. And so on the fourth night Medeia by a sorcerous melody put the entire household, except for Pelias' daughters, into a deep sleep. She followed them to Pelias' chamber, where they stood in a ring around his bed, tightly gripping their freshly whetted tools.

"Why hesitate?" Medeia said. "Now is the time to act. Lift your knives and swords and axes; drain his blood and I shall fill his veins anew. In your hands rests his life and youth. Perform your duty if your filial love is true. Let your blades rid him of hateful old age."

Spurred by Medeia's words, and thinking that they were truly doing right by their father, the king's daughters commenced the fatal strokes; unable, however, to watch, they closed their eyes or turned their backs as they hacked with their blades. Only Alcestis dared not lay hands on her father, and fled the room before the first blow fell. Pelias, suddenly awaking into a nightmare, his flesh in shreds and spouting blood, could do little more than raise his arms toward his daughters before death took him, crying: "What are you doing? Who has driven you to take your father's life?" At this his daughters lost their courage and drew back in horror at what they had done. But too late. As soon as Pelias expired, Medeia said: "Quickly, take your lamps and accompany me to the roof, where I must pray to the moon for the efficacy of this ritual, since it is more difficult to restore youth to a man than to a beast." They ascended to the highest roof of the palace. Medeia went apart to engage in long repetitious prayers in the Colchian tongue to afford time for the Argonauts to make the attack.

Lynceus, seeing the distant gleams of light upon the palace roof, roused the men from sleep. They rowed the *Argo* hastily to the beach of Iolcos, leapt ashore in their armor, and headed for the city, which they found undefended, for the people were still recovering from three days of feasting and reverie. When they burst into the palace, easily overcoming the drowsy sentinels who opposed them, the daughters of Pelias were in the process of boiling their father's remains in the kitchen caldron; but this time Medeia had merely sprinkled the water with harmless and impotent herbs.

25

When Heracles arrived at Iolcos, he found the city nigh empty, for the populace had all gone outside the walls to a stony field to witness the funeral Games of king Pelias. Iolaos, who had been waiting at Iolcos as Heracles had instructed him, was the first to spot him bounding over a hill and with cries incited the Argonauts, who were busy helping with their mattocks to clear out running lanes and the like. At once they ran to him, their throats hoarse from shouts of joy, recounting with great enthusiasm how he had saved them from certain death in the desert of Libya. Heracles had quite forgotten how from kicking a rock he uncovered a spring in the rocky heights beyond the Syrtis, and so looked with puzzlement at those who crowded him. Only Calais and Zetes remained aloof, pretending not to notice him.

Heracles, seeing Jason, pushed all others aside, and stomped toward him as if indignant. As the shadow of Heracles came over him, Jason felt numb in his knees. Heracles, however, considering it his good fortune to have caught up with the Argonauts not long after their arrival, and forgetting past grievances by his generous spirit, grasped his shoulder and said with a hearty chuckle: "Well done, prince of Iolcos. You must show me the Fleece when you have the chance, although in my haversack I have some small things of no less import." He thereupon allowed everyone a quick peek at the golden apples, which sparkled like captured sunbeams. All marveled at the sight.

King Acastos invited Heracles back to the palace, where after a bath, he feasted until early afternoon. Medeia once passed the door to the banquet-hall, and Heracles remarked the glint of her bewitching eyes; but they did not speak to each other then. Since Heracles had not been an accessory in Pelias' murder, Acastos bore him no ill will. He had been freed from his bonds by Peleus and

Admetos, who altogether made it to the palace to see the sobbing Peliades wish to make an end of themselves. Jason, taking pity on the young women, restrained them from taking any rash actions and exhorted them to have courage, since it was not by any evil design on their part, but by the deception of Medeia, that they had committed the terrible crime.

"Foul parricides!" Acastos jeered at them; and then turning to Jason said: "What now, pauper prince? It will be a toothless king who next sits on Cretheus' throne."

"How so?" asked Jason innocently.

"Did you not say to my father," said Acastos, "that all you wanted was the scepter and throne, while he could keep all the wealth of the kingdom?"

Jason, who could not contradict him, agreed.

"Then all the wealth devolves on me," said Acastos. "And I shall use every bit of it to harass you, with the assistance of my allies."

Jason, seeing how Acastios pointed at Peleus and Admetos, said to them: "Friends, do you withdraw your support from me and give it to prince?"
Peleus, answering also for Admetos, said: "While we will always with fondness remember our adventure, Jason, it is now time to return to our daily affairs. As Pelias was our liege-lord, and it was not for his downfall that we enlisted, we must in this case continue our allegiance to his line."

Medeia entered the hall. The Argonauts drew back, avoiding even her glance, for they felt her dark power. Jason went to her and they talked quietly for a time. She urged him, in light of the night's events, to resign the throne to Acastos. They could then go to Corinth, where, as daughter of Aiëtes, she had a legitimate claim to the throne.

Though it proved a bitter pill for Jason to swallow, he said to Acastos: "Though it is right that a man should take vengeance on one who wronged him first, and I feel I have inflicted a less severe punishment than the evils I myself suffered, let it be as you wish. I release all claims to my ancestral kingdom."

"You conduct yourself honorably," said Acastos. "But what of these murderesses, my sisters?"

"It is only right that I should assume responsibility for

them, except Alcestis, whom Medeia tells me had no part in this." said Jason.

Acastos, touched by Jason's magnanimity, allowed him to remain at Iolcos until the conclusion of Pelias' funeral games, which he, as the new ruler of Phthiotis, inaugurated the next day. Heracles, still a bit wearied from his recent long wanderings, consented to be the President of the Games and planted himself in the officiating seat. As it was late in the day, only one event, the two-horse chariot race, was held. Of the Argonauts, Polydeuces, Admetos, Euphemos, son of Poseidon, and Asterion, son of Cometes, participated; they were joined by one Pison, son of Perieres, and long-lived Bellerophon, son of Glaucos, who in his youth slew the Chimaira. The story of Bellerophon was well known. After accidentally killing his brother Deliades, he fled to Proitos at Tyrins, who purified him. As the gods had given him beauty, and filled him with bravery and charm, Stheneboia, wife of Proitos, fell in love with him, seeing him every day performing manly exercises in the courtyard. When she made known to him her secret lust, he honorably refused her. Mad with scorn, the queen then accused the youth of trying to seduce her, and demanded his death. Though filled with rage, Proitos shrank from slaying Bellerophon with his own hands, and sent him instead with a letter to his father-in-law Iobates in far-away Lycia. There he was well-received, and after ten days of feasting Iobates asked to see the letter, which, under a secret cipher, instructed Iobates to put the bearer to death. This also the Lycian lord was unwilling to do himself. Thinking of a roundabout way ensure his destruction, Iobates ordered Bellerophon to slay the awful Chimaira: a monster as terrible as it was hideous, whose body consisted of the foreparts of a lion, the hindparts of a dragon, and, protruding from the middle, the head of a she-goat breathing blasts of fire. Bellerophon at once set out after the swift-footed monster. Unable to capture it, he slept one night in a temple of Athena, who in a dream left beside him a golden bridle for Pegasos, a wondrous winged horse foaled from the blood of Medusa. He surprised Pegasos drinking at the sacred fountain of Pirene in Corinth, and mounting him, flew off to the Chimaira's lair. Dodging and weaving on his winged steed the blasts of projected flame, Bellerophon at last slew the triformed monster by showering down arrows from above. Iobates then sent

Bellerophon on other hazardous missions, against local savages and even the Amazons: but over all he proved invincible.  For one final trap, Iobates organized an ambush on his return, employing the most stalwart men of Lycia.  Bellerophon too escaped unscathed, killing all his attackers.  Filled with wonder at the youth's strength and courage, Iobates gave up as hopeless any further schemes, and urged Bellerophon to remain at his court, showing him the letter encoded for his demise.  He gave him Philonoe his daughter in marriage, and after he died left him the kingdom.  But Bellerophon, filled with pride, tried later to ride Pegasos to Olympos.  Just off the ground, Pegasos, stung by a gadfly sent by Zeus, bucked and cast Bellerophon from his back.  He fell into a thorn bush and was left crippled and blind in one eye.

Though he was invalid and past his prime, all bets were still on the great hero's victory.  Cheered on by his father Glaucos, Bellerophon maintained a firm lead until Euphemos, inspired by his own divine parent, maneuvered his team like Poseidon riding his foamy steeds.  Rounding the last post he tore ahead and won handedly.  Acastos presented him with the winner's wreath and an inscribed tripod plated with orichalc.

The Games continued for two more days, which gave time for additional contestants to arrive.  Admetos and Polydeuces competed in the boxing contest.  Admetos excelled; but Polydeuces the more so, making a quick end of all his opponents by knocking out their teeth. When the time came for them to fight each other in the final round, Alcestis gave him some water mixed with wormwood (procured from Medeia, who thought it was the least she could do), causing him to see double, and thus induced him to drop out of the contest.  Polydeuces, to the chagrin of those who expected a good, bloody time, was the declared winner by default.  Because he had not won by skill, but by luck, he dedicated his victory to Mopsos, son of Ampyx, who had died in Libya from a snake bite.

With flute-players in the background spinning lovely refrains, Eurybotas, son of Teleon distinguished himself at quoits; but Telamon upset him by six paces. Meleager made the longest cast with the javelin.  In archery, Eurytos, son of Hermes, proved unsurpassed, only because he did not have to go up against Heracles.  Cephalos, son of Deion, and grandfather of Laertes, a youth who was coming up in the world, and who had assisted Amphytrion in the war against the Taphians and Teleboans, won at the sling. In wrestling, Jason contended against Peleus. Castor could have easily defeated both, but he was keen for the foot race and wished to avoid injury. Jason, however, seeing vigorous Atalanta standing by chomping at the bit, since women, to preserve their modesty, were not allowed to participate in athletic contents, appointed her to wrestle in his place. Peleus, feeling the sting of insult, stormed off, but was soon compelled to return to the wrestling-pit by the tumult of the commonalty, who were not about to miss a contest of prurient interest; as well as by the direct order of Heracles, who, as President of the Games, had the power to bend the rules. Peleus fell in in a desultory manner, thinking that without much effort he could pin down Atalanta. She proved more difficult to restrain than the wind, stronger than pliant willow, and quicker than a frightened ostrich. By sheer ferocity of effort she wore down Peleus and defeated him.

The contestants for the foot race were two strangers: Neitheus and Argeios; Melanion, the son of Amphidamas; and three Argonauts: Phaleros of Athens, Iphiclos, son of Thestios, and Castor, who, supremely confident in himself, haughtily looked down at the others. Melanion, also known as Hippomenes, grew so flummoxed over Atalanta that he stumbled at the fourth stake. Iphiclos, naturally swift, sped past Castor and received the wreath[6]. The long race was won by swift Zetes; and the double course by his brother Calais, who flew through it as if he had wings on his shoulders. Heracles, overcome by his grudge against them, jumped off his seat, threw off his lion's pelt, and demanded opponents for all-in wrestling. As no one was man enough to volunteer, Heracles returned to his seat broodingly, wreathed the Hyperborean olive spray around his head and set his mind to found his own Games.

The final day of the contests proved the most exciting. Iolaos, with a team of four fine Thessalian horses, gifts of king Ceyx, surpassed all others in the chariot-race, even against the favorite Glaucos. Glaucos, a son of Sisyphos, and thus the oldest of all the competitors, once ruled Corinthian Asopia. How he fell

---

[6] According to Hyginus (*Fabulae* 273) it was Castor who won.

from power came in this way. When, long ago, Poseidon and Helios contended for the land of Corinth, the hundred-handed Briareos, serving as arbiter, awarded the Isthmus and the great bare rock above the plain, afterwards called Ephyra, to Helios. Helios gave Ephyra to his son Aiëtes; while to his son Aloeus he gave the territory of Asopia, which lay separated from Ephyra by a small river. Aiëtes, however, going to Colchis, left the government in the hands of Bounos, a son of Hermes. On the death of Bounos, Epopeus, son of Aloeus and then ruler of Asopia, annexed Ephyra to form a unified kingdom. When Epopeus died, crafty Sisyphos arrived from Thessaly to make a play for the throne; since Marathon, son of Epopeus, unable to bear the violence and lawlessness of his father, had left for Attica. Sisyphos ruled a short time before he died, and after returning from the underworld abdicated the throne to live as a private citizen until he died a second time in his old age. Meanwhile his son Glaucos, who lived at Potniai near Thebes, reluctantly assumed the throne of Ephyra, since he liked nothing more than to care for his horses, which he fed on human flesh to make them formidable in a race. In order to abridge his political duties, Glaucos invited his cousin Lycaithos to take control of Asopia. But Marathon, unwilling to lose his inheritance, returned for a short while to ensure that his sons, Corinthus and Sicyon, regained control of the realm. Since it was unlikely that Bellerophon, abroad on his adventures, would ever return to succeed him, Glaucus ceded the government of Ephyra to Corinthus without protest; he changed the name of the city to Corinth after himself. Likewise his brother took over Asopia, naming it Sicyon after himself. When Sicyon died, a son of Hermes, Polybos, succeeded him, having married his daughter Chthonophyle. It was he who raised the foundling Oidipos. When Corinthus died childless, Creon, son of Lycaithos, became king of Corinth. But the people were not happy with Creon, since they considered the Sisyphids usurpers.

Rounding the last post, Glaucos' horses suddenly grew skittish and uncontrollable. Glaucos fell from the chariot entangled in the reins and was dragged to his death. The horses then turned about and began to devour his mangled flesh. Some thought it was the ghost of Pelias, lurking about, who affrighted them; or that they were induced into a frenzy after feeding on hippomanes at Potniai.

Others thought the judgment of Aphrodite fell on him, offended that he prevented his horses from breeding to contain their animal vitality. But the truth was that Glaucos had no alternative but to restrict his horses' diet to vegetables while attending the Games; and craving raw meat, they turned on him. Ever after the ghost of Glaucos was said to haunt the Isthmus, scaring horse and the like.

Cycnos, son of Ares, backed by a rabble of ruffians, made an appearance. Admetos, wishing to appear diplomatic despite Jason's protestations concerning his fulsome character, said nothing against him. Seeing Heracles, who failed to recognize him, Cycnos sheepishly skulked around the field, at last joining the sword-fighting contest. All the Argonauts competing there withdrew, leaving only a handful of Iolcans and strangers. Cycnos proved the better fighter in all matches, growing bolder and more dangerous at each turn. In the final bout he fought one Pilos son of Diodotus, whom he reprehensively ran through the gut with his sword. As no one knew the victim, the outcry was muted.

Finally Eumolpos, Heracles' old music teacher, surpassed all in the song contest by the sweetness of his voice. He wished to be crowned with laurel by no other save Heracles, to whom he whispered a prophecy about his next Labor. He was accompanied on the flute by Olympos, a pupil of the satyr Marsyas, who was bound to a tree and flayed alive by Apollo for presuming to be a better musician. Olympos, in turn, took the prize in his category. Orpheus brought the games to a close with sweet refrains from his lyre, narrating a long and mystical poem about the expedition to Colchis, but one in which he magnified his role. The Argonauts, though perplexed by his radical recollections, still found the performance quite moving, and to a man joined in the adulation.

At the conclusion of the Games, Acastos proposed that the Fleece be dedicated to Laphystian Zeus. No small dissension then arose, between Jason and the Minyans who though it fitting to deposit the Fleece at the original sanctuary near the summit of Mount Laphystios in Boetia, where Athamas planned to sacrifice his children; and those on the side of Acastos, who pointed out that there existed a similar shrine to Laphystian Zeus outside of Alos, the city founded by Athamas after being banished from Boetia for the murder of his son Learchos. After some time wandering, Athamas inquired at Delphi where he should settle. The oracle told him to stop at a place where wild beasts would feed him. Reaching Thessaly, he came across a pack of wolves devouring a sheep's carcass. Seeing him, they fled, leaving him the bloody remains. Thinking the prophecy fulfilled, Athamas settled there. Acastos had more than piety to account for his insistence. After ruling in the region for some time, Athamas by a prophecy was called to die as a sin-offering for the people. Just as he was about to sacrificed, it was said someone saved him, an act that greatly angered the gods. Thenceforth the oldest member of the royal house of the Aeolids would be duly wreathed and sacrificed if he ever entered the town-hall of Alos, where offerings to Laphystian Zeus were deposited, and then went out from thence. Acastos found this practice impious, and wished to end the vicious circle by the ultimate offering of the ram's Fleece. They cast lots, and the lot fell to Acastos, who duly carried the Fleece down to the *Argo* and draped it over the prow ornament. The Argonauts assembled for their last voyage together, rowing the *Argo* across the bay of Pagasai. They debarked and solemnly crossed the Crocian plain toward Alos, situated within a short distance on the eastern extremity of Mount Orthrys. Acastos, followed by the Argonauts, boldly marched into the town-hall bearing the Golden Fleece; and to the shock of the sentinels there, just as boldly walked out in defiance of the ban. As a scowling Heracles went with them, none dared dispute the act. To the sacred grove above the city they then repaired, where Jason and Medeia at the shrine reverently hung the Fleece.

In the shadow of the ship that had carried them through so many perils, the Argonauts tearfully embraced over the breaking of their fellowship. As they prepared to depart to their native lands, Heracles said: "Comrades, though I count myself as the least of you, allow me to propose that, in view of the unexpected turns of fortune, we should exchange oaths amongst ourselves to fight at the side of whosoever shall need aid." To this, all of them heartily assented. "Furthermore," continued Heracles, "we can do no less than honor Zeus, greatest of the gods, for preserving us in our distresses. To that end let us choose a most excellent place in Greece, and there to his glory institute Games and celebrate a festival open to all men." After swearing by solemn oaths to aid the other in his time of need, they asked Heracles to organize the Games as he seemed fit. Augeias said: "As to the site of the

Games, Heracles, there is none better suited or more beautiful than a plain in my own land of Elis, between the Alpheios and Cladeos rivers, surrounded by green hills of pine and ilex. There is a grove of plane-trees there suitable for a shrine." The proposed location pleased all except the Thessalians, who were prejudiced about their own land. Heracles, having seen the country when he had cleaned Augeias' stables, agreed that it was most suitable and settled the matter by resolving to hold the Games in two years' time.

From there those Argonauts who lived north set off on foot. Jason, Argos, Heracles and the remainder sailed the *Argo* down the Euboean strait and around Attica, dropping off crew members at Opos, Aulis and Athens, and came to the Isthmus, where at the narrowest part they beached her in an inlet. After performing a sacrifice, Jason dedicated the *Argo* to Poseidon for being kind enough to bear her on his broad back. Heracles and Iolaos bid farewell to Jason and proud Argos, who with heavy sighs contemplated his handiwork, and set off for Mycenae feeling bittersweet.

# BOOK III

## THE HARROWING

### 1

When Heracles arrived at Mycenae, the golden apples weighed heavily in his haversack. Heracles walked unopposed into the great hall, where Eurystheus, sitting on his high throne, and surrounded by his men-at-arms, received him, having known ahead of time through spies of Heracles' imminent arrival. He had hoped for the end of Heracles, perishing either in long wandering in search of the elusive treasure; or else, having against all odds obtained the prize, at Hera's hands for his profane pilfery. When he heard that Heracles had apparently succeeded in his quest, his mind turned through many moods, from incredulity to disconsolation. In desperation he consulted seers and soothsayers to discover the most arduous task imaginable for a mortal: one so utterly impossible so as to make a man wish he had never been born rather than be compelled to attempt it. His hackles rose when he heard the answer. Believing now that the end of his despised cousin could be assured, he determined to receive Heracles one final time so that, with cruel jubilation, he could seal his doom.

The chattering of the court grew silent. Only Eurystheus' immodest plaudit resounded hollowly. "Do not merely stand there, cousin," said the king. "If you have achieved the quest, show us."

As Heracles unloosed his satchel he saw Iphicles sitting among the king's retainers. The latter gravely held his gaze for a moment, and then looked away. Heracles in one hand withdrew the golden apples, holding them forth for all to see. They sparkled in the light of the cressets. Priestesses of Argive Hera from her sanctuary near Tyrins came forth with a basket, into which Heracles dropped the apples. Without touching them they examined the sacred fruit, and after some discourse, presented them to Eurystheus with words of approbation. Eurystheus stared breathlessly at them, his countenance bathed in a golden glow, until his curiosity was satisfied. He ordered that apples returned to Heracles as his reward, to the dismay of the priestesses, who tried in vain to persuade the king of such continuing impiety regarding Hera's property. The king dismissed them, wishing to compound Heracles' crime.

Eurystheus then had his courtiers drape him with the kingly robe and scepter, and placed the double crown of Tyrins and Mycenae upon his head. He sat up stiffly, and with a grim smile across his lips called forth the herald Copreus to deliver the following pronouncement: "As your final Labor, Heracles, the king orders you to journey to the lower world and from there bring back that creature said to guard its gates—the watch-dog Cerberos. Accomplish this task and you shall freed from your bond."

The hall filled with gasps. Even Heracles felt as if he had been subjected to sudden blast of desert wind, though he remained indifferent in expression. Iphicles, whose outrage rekindled a sudden solicitude for his brother, protested: "My lord, far be it from me to ever question your august judgment—but what you ask of my brother is beyond even his reach! No living man has ever dared enter the realm of the dead, much less return to tell about it. Do you mean to send Heracles to certain destruction?"

Eurystheus grew pale, his forced pomp suddenly withering under the unexpected outburst. He lifted the oversized crown, which had slid nearly over his eyes, and in a flush of anger answered: "Iphicles, your words ring hollow, at least to my ears. Did you not long ago arrive at my court, gloating that Heracles would never return? I remember with what satisfaction you maligned your brother, cursing him to the winds, for making you twice removed from this royal seat. You dog! I would as sooner make Heracles my chief attendant than you! Be silent, or hang with him if you'd like. It makes no difference to me. What say you, Heracles? I know a quick way to Hell. Shall I tell you? There's one by rope and bench." Met by laughter from the court, the emboldened king continued: "There is also another way, but you must beat your own path—with pestle and mortar." The court grew silent, since no one understood his reference.

Heracles broke the tension with a grim laugh. He crossed his arms and said: "You speak of hemlock, I think. No, that's too deathly cold a way to go. Your shins grow numb before you start!"

Eurystheus trembled with rage at the raucous laughter.

"We all shall be guests someday in the gloomy house of Hades; some sooner than others," said Heracles. "While I do not know the way, nor if such a realm verily exists, I do not fear to essay it, whatever the cost. With my own hands I shall bring the hell-hound to you, Eurystheus. May you be here then, as you are now, to so kindly receive us."

The king in silence endured the ensuing fevered chatter of the court, for never before had anyone there witnessed such a contest of wills. Taking the golden apples with him Heracles departed, going directly to the sanctuary of Athena, where he left the gleaming fruit as an offering, since he was loath to have any further dealing with something that belonged to Hera. While driving him to Tyrins, Iolaos pressed him for the details of his final Labor. Heracles remained reticent until he had eaten and then plainly divulged the hopeless errand. Iolaos misunderstood him, thinking that he had first to die to make the descent. Heracles consoled him with the example of Dionysos, fathered, as he was, by Zeus on a mortal woman, who descended into the underworld to rescue his mother from death. The world contained numerous chasms leading to the infernal realm, one of which, at Phlegrai, he had seen with his own eyes. Another, it was held by all, existed at Tainaron, a promontory at the extremity of the Peloponnese. "I shame myself, Heracles," Iolaos lamented; "since, in feeling this to be your last Labor indeed, from which you will never return, I cannot bring myself, as at all other times, to pledge my assistance. Such a great fear overtakes me when I consider the Stygian horrors that would await us! For who truly knows what is in death? At that evil hour all our joys, sorrows and struggle for life cease, yielding to maggots and the conquerer worm. Who would desire to march into the grave ahead of his time? To enter seems simple; to get out impossible."

Heracles responded: "Fear not, great-hearted Iolaos. I neither ask nor require assistance, not even from the gods. In this flesh, as out of it, I shall reach the Stygian shore alone, relying only on this mind and these mighty arms. There is one thing, however, needful to do. I recall what Eumolpos, my old music teacher, told me at Pelias' Games. He said I should go up to Athens and inquire into the Mysteries of Eleusis. By this he prophesied my final Labor, for those initiated into the Mysteries are said to safeguard themselves from the torments of Hell."

Iolaos quickly replied: "But Heracles, did you not already observe the Mysteries of the Great Gods at Samothrace while sailing on the *Argo?*"

"The Great Gods—whoever they are—promise only safety while at sea. I see you have another objection. What is it?"

"It is that only Athenians have ever been allowed to partake of the Mysteries," said Iolaos.

Heracles considered and said: "Indeed! Now I have no rebuttal. Let us go up to Athens tomorrow and inquire."

❧

They did not set out for Athens until midday. The ride across the Isthmus was long, but pleasant, and they took in a sunset, which was always beautiful and breathtaking as the ember-red rays dissolved through blue sky. As they passed the proud city of Eleusis, rising on a rocky height not far from the sea, Iolaos remembered the song of the Trinacrian bard about Persephone and Demeter, who had established her Mysteries there. None who partook of the Mysteries could divulge their secrets, on pain of death. What they contained or enjoined Iolaos could only guess, although in the time he spent at Athens after escaping from Crete with Theseus he had come across more than a few initiates. Slave or free, they seemed different, changed, filled with something almost divine.

Through a narrow pass in the mountains they entered the Attic plain and soon came in sight of the great rock that was Athens. At the city walls they were stopped until the guard-house could receive word from the palace to allow them entry. Security seemed heightened. A forest of javelins crowned the battlements. They were escorted up the steep road on foot to the Acropolis, where at the inner gate Theseus met them, having seen them from the palace terrace. Theseus begged pardon for turning Athens, once so open and welcoming, into an impenetrable camp. His desire was to unite all of Attica into a great commonwealth, but he was meeting resistance from certain quarters that wished to preserve their independence, and hostilities were liable to break out at any time. Only the Eleusinians stood with him, since in the reign of Erectheus, after declaring war on Athens, they were soundly defeated, and agreed to submit to the king as long as they could retain management of the Mysteries. Heracles contested Theseus' desire to impose a federal government, esteeming the freedom and independence of each city as preferable for the general happiness of mankind. Theseus argued that it was natural for those cities of the Greeks within a circumscribed region to wish to form a compact for mutual trade and defense; and once united it was equally as natural that all should look to a king to lead them.

After a splendid supper, they settled down to the matter at hand. Theseus at once declared his intention to accompany Heracles into the underworld; and although Heracles forbade him, the thought ever afterwards stuck in his mind. Concerning the Mysteries, Theseus had no power to grant or deny anyone access to them, that being a prerogative of those that controlled the sanctuary of Demeter at Eleusis. And so in the morning they travelled in retinue to Eleusis, where Heracles appeared before the city magistrates and the priestly college to plead his case, but without disclosing the content of his next Labor. The Eleusinians for the most part desired Heracles to wear the myrtle wreath on account of the great esteem he would bring to the city, but those older and wiser remonstrated, appealing to their ancient laws that not only restricted the privilege to Athenians only, but forbade attendance of the Mysteries to those under a sentence of capital punishment, or who were guilty of murder. They sought to exclude Heracles for many rash acts, but chiefly for his slaughter of the Centaurs upon Mount Pholoë, for which crime he had never thought to be purified, since the twiformed Centaurs seemed to him to lack the excellency of humankind. To resolve both objections, Theseus advised that Pylios, a leading Athenian citizen, could adopt and purify him; after which he himself would sponsor him for the initiation. Uncertain whether an adoption would qualify Heracles as an Athenian, the Eleusinians demurred, until Eumolpos came forward and declared that Demeter, in a vision, charged him with establishing certain preparatory rites, which were to be called the Lesser Mysteries, by which any virtuous Greek could subsequently partake of the Greater. As the latter were held in honor of Demeter and Core, the former were to be for the glory of Core alone, in celebration of her ascent; as well as a reminder of the sufferings of Dionysos, who also descended to the lower world and returned. After long discussion the particulars of the new rite were agreed upon. It was to be held near Athens each year in the springtime. Those initiated into the Lesser Mysteries then qualified after at least one year to observe the Greater Mysteries, which took place every five years in the late summer, when the leaves first leaf. When Heracles, to make clear the exigency of observing the Mysteries, revealed how he planned shortly to travel bodily into the lower world, the Eleusinians were left speechless and urged Eumolpos to make for him an exception so that he could be duly fortified by all the advantages afforded an initiate.

Heracles returned with Theseus to Athens, where Pylios purified him of the slaughter of the Centaurs and formally adopted him. For this, Heracles had to crawl forth between the legs of Pylios' wife, as if he were a new-born babe exiting her womb. He then wintered at Tyrins, eating moderately and living chastely, reading books and preserving his stamina by running from one end of the palace to the other bearing furniture. When the buds began to bloom, he called for Iolaos, who resided with his father at Mycenae, to fetch him in the chariot and take him to Athens.

Among the great multitude assembled there from all quarters of Greece, for word of the establishment of the Lesser Mysteries could not help but spread, causing great excitement among those of alien birth who wished not only to live happily, but to die with a fairer hope, Heracles saw his old shipmates Castor and Polydeuces. He learned from them what they knew of what became of the other Argonauts. Jason was received by King Creon at Corinth. Peleus, who had been purified by Eurytion of the murder of his brother, settled for good in Phthia, where Eurytion gave him his daughter Antigone as wife, along with a third of his domain. Meleager had married Cleopatra, the daughter of Idas, brother of keen-eyed Lynceus, and was living comfortably at Calydon. Idas had married Marpessa, daughter of Evenos, king of

Aitolia, who liked to challenge her suitors to a chariot race, killing those who lost. When Idas carried her off, Evenos pursued him as far as the river Lycormas, where, realizing that he could never catch up, slaughtered his horses and hurled himself into the river. Heracles inquired particularly after Zetes and Calais, whose treachery he had not yet forgotten, and learned that they were last seen on Tenos.

For nine days the catechumens fasted until evening, avoiding especially mullet, beans and pomegranates, and lived chastely, waiting for the Eleusinian clerics to arrive. In a solemn procession they swept into Athens at night by the light of torches, carrying with them holy things in lidded baskets. Their official herald, assembling all on the Pnyx, enjoined a holy silence before the rites could begin. Quietly the throng left the city carrying with them a sow, and marched down to the harbor, where they washed it in that part called the Cantharos, so called because the natural enclosure, protected by two arms of land, resembled the contours of a drinking-vessel. From there they returned to the city, and then left by the South Gate, circling about its great walls to the southeast, to where the river Illissos bounded it, into the district of Agrai. By the lovely bank of the Illisos, shaded by plane-trees, near where the fair-flowing spring Callirrhoë issues from the foot of a ledge of rock and from whence expectant brides gather bathing-water, stood a sanctuary to Demeter covered with vines. Under the direction of the hierophant, whose flowing locks, wreathed in myrtle, fell over his long purple garment, the priests of the altar sacrificed the sow to Demeter. A portion of the sacrifice was reserved for them, but none for the neophytes. Heracles, who in his piety had scrupulously observed the long fast, could hardly contain himself against the delicious smell of the crackling flesh. The hierophant was a relation of Eumolpos, both of whom belonged to that sacred family descended from Thracian Eumolpos, son of Poseidon, the first priest of Demeter, who was killed in the war between Athens and Eleusis. The hierophant was a citizen of Athens who inherited the office and held it for life. He was known by his title only, discarding his former name, which was written on a leaden tablet and cast into the Saronic Gulf. While celebrating the Mysteries he remained celibate, anointing himself with the juice of hemlock, which, on account of its coldness, was said to be a remedy against the fiery passions. The same is true of heracleon, which resembles the white water-lily, and is named after a nymph who was said to have died of jealousy over Heracles. The finest specimens grow in Boetia, where it is called madon. Those who take it in drink become impotent for twelve days and are no longer troubled by lascivious dreams.

On pain of arrest by the civil authorities, none could pass beyond the vestibule of the sanctuary of Demeter. After taking an oath of secrecy, the candidates were instructed for the next two days either singly or in small groups. Eumolpos took charge of Heracles' instruction, meant to prepare him with the knowledge of certain terms and symbols, but yet veiled in mystic language and difficult to understand, which were to be revealed with greater clarity during the Greater Mysteries. On the second night each candidate went naked into the Illisos, where they were purified by a priest termed Hydranus. The next morning, reminded of their oath, all, now called initiates, were released.

As Iolaos, manning the chariot-reins, conveyed Heracles back to Tyrins, he burned with a desire to know something of what Heracles had learned or experienced. While Heracles intended by all means to honor his oath of secrecy, he felt no harm in revealing some of the more basic precepts to his friend. "Did you know, Iolaos," he said, "that we owe unbounded gratitude to Demeter, who taught men not only husbandry, that they could rise above the level of brutes; but also entrusted to us these Mysteries, which fills our souls with sweet hope in a future world?"

"How so, Heracles?" said Iolaos. "What hope have we of happiness beyond this life?"

"As I have learned, Iolaos, much in every way!" said Heracles. "Consider chief of all the operations of a lowly seed. It must first be planted in the fertile earth, where it dies under the hoarfrost, only to live again in springtide when the green shoot breaks through the clod."

"Is our only hope against the shadow of death, then, based on such flimsy thing, well-known to even the meanest peasant?" asked Iolaos disconsolately.

"Nay, there is more than this," countered Heracles. "Did you know there is no need to wait for death, for even in the midst of life we are in death?"

"How so?" said Iolaos. "Now you speak harder things."

Heracles took the reins for a while and said: "Our soul, like the seed, imprisoned in a terrestrial body, ever yearns for felicity. Is it not true that even in the midst of plenty, after you have filled your belly and gotten all things you have desired, that you look upon the world with certain sadness, feeling empty of mind? It is the soul which languishes so, striving, as it must by its nature, for truth and beauty; yet, hindered by this body, which can so often pollute it, it is bound and disconsolate, like Core when she must leave the blissful company of the gods to dwell with her gloomy consort below the earth. She yearns for that season when she returns to the higher world, where all is clear and bright. The Mysteries are meant to purify the soul, so that, both in this life and in the next, it can live freely, unpolluted by material nature. This, as far as I know, is what I have learned."

"Would it not be better then, Heracles," said Iolaos, "that once purified, one should end his life to prevent the soul from being further tainted?"

"When once set out on a journey, what good is it if half-way through, a man leaves the road out of fear or sloth?" said Heracles. "Should he not finish what he started? I deem there to be greater glory, against all struggles and pains, in finishing the race. The industrious contestant, however, prepares himself by eating and sleeping well, stretching and oiling his limbs, and keeping his eyes fixed on the goal. In the same way, before embarking on my next Labor, I do everything possible to insure myself against failure by fortifying not only my body, but also my soul through these mystic rites."

When Heracles emerged from his lustration in the Illisos, he felt filled with good-will and unburdened by any care. But back in Tyrins dark thoughts and moods once more invaded his mind. He set out for Nauplia looking for a ship bound for the islands of Minos. After debarking on Tenos, a mountainous island brimming with serpents, he ranged about the chief cities until he found the Boreads by a famous spring, whose water was said to be unmixable with wine. From a covert nook he dispatched Calais with an arrow in the back, and as Zetes took flight, not knowing from whence death was coming, felled him also. Afterward Heracles, seeing the corpses of such stout youths lying haphazardly in the dust, was struck with great remorse and beat his breast, lamenting the difficulty, despite the aid of a hallowed cult, of conquering evil impulses. He heaped earth about them and informed the villagers of the identity of the stalwart men that lay beneath the barrow. As this was not enough to placate his guilt, Heracles also erected two sepulchral columns, one standing upright, and the other laid upon it like a crossbeam. The columns were balanced so cunningly that the top one rocked slightly whenever the north wind blew, a marvel to behold. Heracles returned to Tyrins and practiced no further mischief while he waited for the start of the autumnal Mysteries.

## 2

Since Castor and Polydeuces were not granted the same indulgence as Heracles, and had to wait at least a year to continue on to the Greater Mysteries, Heracles found himself without an acquaintance among the initiates who gathered at the market-place of Athens in the ides of September. Theseus also was absent from the city, having left for Calydon at the behest of Meleager, who promised a great adventure to those who answered his call. In his absence he appointed three magistrates from among the wealthiest citizens, one to handle civic issues, another to handle military issues, and a third to oversee the religious arrangements. Pylios was awarded the latter office, and so on the first night of the ceremonies, after performing sacrifices for the well-being of Athens, he proclaimed before the assembled initiates: "Come, you who are pure and uncontaminated! Come, you who have live uprightly and seek justice! Come, you who speak without guile! But begone you with tainted hands, double tongue or impure soul; for such cannot observe the Mysteries." He then added: "Each celebrant must pay one obol a day, or begone also!" The hierophant—the same who had presided over the Lesser Mysteries—assisted now by a female hierophant, both clad in purple robes, then commanded the people to wash their hands, for which jugs of consecrated water were provided, admonishing the impious with terrible punishments and the anger of the gods. After this, a herald reminded all to remember their sacred oath of secrecy and to observe silence for the remainder of the ceremonies, which were to last ten days. Jewelry or costly garments were forbidden while in the sacred precinct of Demeter, for such were an affront to the goddess, who fared through the earth in humble attire while she suffered her loss.

The initiates assembled again on the second day by the

grassy banks of the Illisos, where the gentle breezes fluttered the leaves of the plane-trees, and waited until eventide. Presently a swineherd appeared prodding numerous suckling pigs. The herald in a strong voice cried: "To the sea, initiates!" and ordered each one to secure a piglet for himself and carry it down to the nearest inlet of the sea. When the piglets saw themselves pursued, they scattered into the night, betraying their positions only by their incessant squealing. Heracles was one of the last to find one for himself, since he was so big, and the creatures so small, that, running between his legs, they continually eluded him. After scooping up the heaviest of the litter, he fell in last in the procession, which marched solemnly toward the harbor. At the water's edge each confessed his sins to the priests, and then purified himself through immersion in the sea water. Those with the most egregious trespasses were directed to plunge into the water more than once. Heracles had to immerse himself and his suckling pig nearly a dozen times to cover all of his killings. After rising from the water each person disrobed and was provided a fawn-skin to wear to symbolize that he was a new creature, having left the old in the briny water, which was considered a laver of regeneration. After careful consideration, Eumolpos, who was astonished to hear of all the violence Heracles had committed during his life, directed him as an additional precaution to further purify himself by sacrificing an ox to the infernal Zeus; afterward he had to lay out the skin of the animal and squat upon it on his left foot until the torchbearers, who thought very highly of themselves at being additionally responsible for directing the purifying rites, permitted him to end his penance.

The foregoing purifications were not completed until the third and fourth days, when, after a general sacrifice by Pylios for the well being of Athens before the temple of Demeter at the foot of the Acropolis, each initiate had to slaughter his little pig upon the altar, allowing it to become wholly consumed in the fire. After being sprinkled with the animals' blood, the initiates began a strict period of abstinence from both foods and sensual pleasures, lasting until nightfall, in remembrance of the sorrow of Demeter, when they were allowed to eat only parched wheat sprinkled with sea-salt, seed-cakes baked with tiny horns, pomegranates and wine mixed with milk and honey.

On the fifth day the sacred objects, brought to Athens from

Eleusis on the day preceding the start of the Mysteries, were gathered secretly from the temple of Demeter and hid in covered baskets. These, along with a statue of a godling called Iacchos, thought to be son of Demeter, or of Core, were conveyed on a cart drawn by black bulls with great pomp ahead of the initiates as they proceeded along the Sacred Way to Eleusis. The votaries of Dionysos, who identified their god with Iacchos, accompanied them bearing winnowing fans and the *thyrsos*, stalks of giant fennels stuffed with ivy leaves and topped with pine cones. They, along with the spectators lining the road, whipped the entire company into such a frenzy by their dancing and jubilation that all cried out "Iacchos! O Iacchos!" at regular intervals, sang paens and sacred hymns, and made a great din by beating on kettle drums. Along the way they stopped to offer sacrifice and pour libations at various places deemed holy for their connection with Demeter. There was the house of Phylatus, who received the goddess in her wandering, along with a fig-tree deemed to have been her gift for his kindness. At a bridge over the river Cephissos waited masked men, who commenced to hurl vulgar insults and railleries at the initiates. Heracles, taken aback at the jeers and abuse, made ready to hurl stones at them when a bystander explained that it was the custom of the people of the district to act in such a crude manner during the procession, following the example of Iambe, who consoled Demeter by her jests and buffoonery.

Beyond the bridge the road wound past olive groves and into a deep and shady gorge where the barren mountains divided the plains. Twilight filled the dark Pass of Daphne, stilling by its somber mystery the shouts and excitement of the throng, which, having attracted from all around men and women, youth and maidens, had grown in size to many thousands. All around the narrow pass, candles and lamps twinkled in niches cut into the bare rock. But as the gloom deepened into blackest shade, the initiates lit torches to illumine the way, and led by the torchbearers, continued toward Eleusis bedaubed in pitch-smoke. As the pilgrims crossed the river Rheitoi, the descendants of one Crocos, who once ruled the Eleusinian Plain, arrived to tie saffron-colored ribands around their right hands and left legs. After a period of rest the torchlit procession continued well into the night, coming in sight of the Rarian Plain and Eleusis near the midnight hour.

Entering the city by a special gate meant only to admit those observing the Mysteries, they stopped first at the well where Demeter, on her arrival overcome with grief and fatigue, stopped to rest, and then wound their way up a hill above the Bay of Eleusis to the shining sanctuary of Demeter. Once there the initiates alone followed the torchbearers two by two around the temple porch, passing the torches from one to another so that the flames appeared ever in movement and the smoke fanned out through the columns.

The next day the initiates devoted themselves to fasting and various lustrations with consecrated water. After sunset they assembled again in the outer court, dressed in fawn-skins, where the herald, after ordering the profane to withdraw and by means of secret questions precluded any interlopers, for the third time administered the holy oath to preserve in inviolate secrecy the sacred rites. The doors to the sanctuary were opened and the aspirants filed inside the Hall of Initiation, observing a holy silence.

Under a ceiling high and lost in shadow, the whitewashed walls around the cavernous hall depicted in fading tableaus Demeter's trials. The hierophant, assisted by priestesses and acolytes, carried in the baskets containing the holy things and deposited them before a free-standing marble tabernacle in the shape of a small barn at the other end of the room—built on the foundations of the original shrine to Demeter. From coffers in the door of the inner room he removed chalices filled with barley grains harvested from the Rarian plain and gave them to the priestesses, who, balancing these and oil-lamps upon their hands, danced around the hall, forming circles and spirals by their movement while the initiates, filled with anticipation, watched from their tiered seats lining the walls.

In an epicene voice, and in a speech unknown to the initiates, the hierophant pronounced collects and chanted invocations, accompanied by unseen flutes and cymbals. The priestesses returned the chalices of meal to him, which he poured into a large bronze mixing-bowl along with spring water and crushed pennyroyal. After blessing the holy potion, which commemorated that which Demeter preferred instead of wine, he distribute it to the initiates, who, after drinking it from small cups, returned to their seats, declaring: "I fasted; I drank the mixture."

When all had partaken of the sacred draught, the officials doused the lamps and cressets, and closed the doors, leaving all assembled in silence and darkness.

In little time a strange feeling came over Heracles. Cold sweat dripped from his brow and his heart throbbed. He heard first a pair of striking cymbals near his ear, then a multitude, filling the hall with monotonous crashing. Shadows, darker than the darkness, moved before his eyes. His belly heaved unwholesomely and his head swam as if he was standing looking down from a great height.

Brilliant light, like a flash of lightning, tore apart the darkness. In that brief moment of visibility monstrous shapes appeared to surround them, as if the bowels of Tartaros had burst and all the horrors therein irrupted to torment them, replete with unearthly howls and bellows resounding from every side and underfoot. The lurking madness of the world, and all evil and death seemed revealed without pretense in one unending terrifying tempest. Heracles wished to fight, to flee, to weep but his body felt both paralyzed and scattered, so that he was everywhere and nowhere at once. And just as the horror, the sound and fury escalated to an almost unbearable degree, just as the world seemed fractured and contaminated beyond redemption, a noise like a thunderclap shattered the dire cacophony, ushering divine voices, pleasant odors and sweet harmonies. The doors of the tabernacle flew open and a blinding light burst from the threshing-floor within, flooding the hall with a warm glow, chasing away the foul visions that had for a moment seemed triumphant. The hierophant's diaphanous form emerged holding forth the sacred objects hereunto hidden from their eyes, and in a stentorian voice announced the culminating formula of the rite, the words that elucidated the Sacred and Profound, proclaiming all in attendance no longer initiates, but witnesses of the ineffable. Heracles basked in the beauty of what filled his eyes and ears, carried off to fair sunlit meadows as in a long and pleasant dream, knowing all secrets, thinking all thoughts, at one with the twin Goddesses in whom life and death lost their distinction.

Upon exiting the great hall, the initiates, startled, quivering, enraptured, and still suffused with inescapable wonder and joy overflowing, were rewarded with the myrtle crown. In the morning, the seventh day, the image of Iacchos was returned to

Athens in a solemn procession, during which the worshippers once more paid their devotions at the shrines of Demeter along the Sacred Way. Heracles spoke to no one along the way, for there were no words. On the eighth day a spotless victim was offered at Athens to the Two Goddesses to secure their continued blessing on the health and wealth of the land. The final day was marked by a curious ceremony involving two flat-bottomed earthen vessels, which were filled with wine and then each overturned, one toward the rising the other toward the setting sun, so that the wine ran in two directions while the initiates turned their eyes first to heaven, saying "Rain!", and then to earth, saying "Be fruitful!" Afterwards the hierophant dismissed the fortunate celebrants to their homes with the cryptic words, said to be Egyptian: "*Cogx Ompax!*"—that is, "Be watchful—and do no evil!" And thus the holy and most venerable Eleusinian Mysteries ended.

While waiting for Theseus to return to Athens, Heracles contentedly spent the days walking in the pleasant groves by the Illisos in company with Iolaos, who, knowing better than to question an initiate, held out until curiosity overcame him. As they came to a fair place, settling under a lofty and spreading plane-tree, Iolaos said: "Uncle, be not angry with me. I do not wish to know all you have learned at Eleusis; but if you let fall but a crumb, I shall be content." Heracles, filled with love for the youth reclining on his breast replied lyingly, since he believed all men had to learn their own the way to death: "I have learned nothing beyond what I explained before, Iolaos. I have seen and I have felt—that is all. Look here at this resting-place, filled with the sounds and odors of pregnant springtide. Or this stream flowing at our feet, so bright and cold. I saw them truly, as I never saw them before, Iolaos. And I long now to see them again no longer with my bodily eyes, from which so much detail escapes, but with my soul, when it is freed from this body, and goes off to know the divine. I have joined my trials to the sufferings of Demeter and been redeemed by the sweetness of that communion; and look forward to joining in her company, and that of the other noble gods, in the same manner as Core, who ever conquers the grave by her return with her divine—I have said enough. Therefore with all confidence I shall soon descend bodily into Tartaros, and by all means return: for I am Heracles, the son of God."

3

Heracles and Iolaos departed Athens shortly after the conclusion of the Mysteries, figuring Theseus was long delayed, bound for the southern extremity of Laconia and a famed cave said to be an entrance to Tartaros, which Heracles had missed examining during his outward journey to the lands of the west in quest of Geryones' cattle. To reach the grotto it was necessary to cross the rocky promontory and on foot descend into a deep and gloomy ravine where the dark and misproportioned trees wreathed themselves into fiendish shapes. There gaped a bleak wide-mouthed chasm, from which unwholesome exhalations clambered over the withered grass. Iolaos, in mortal fear, hung back as Heracles, wearing a cuirass under his lion's pelt, strode to the cavern's mouth, where he peered into the interminable darkness. Iolaos crept forward and said: "While I cannot come with you, Heracles, I shall certainly keep watch in this forbidding thicket until your return." Heracles returned to his friend, and resting a hand on the youth's shoulder said, "I know not how long I shall remain in the sunless world; nor how or to where I shall return. Go, therefore and see to Megara at Thebes, whom I have not visited since that awful day when I deprived her of posterity. Tell her my Labors will soon be at an end." Iolaos departed weeping, thinking that never again would he behold the cheerful visage of his friend.

As Heracles prepared to light a torch, he thought he saw a glimmer through the trees. Calling out, in response came a maiden's voice, who cried: "Sir—have you seen a young hart, whose horns have barely grown beyond its ears, skirt this hill? I have chased him from noontide to now, and no closer have my arrows come to piercing his lovely red hide." A huntress stepped out, accoutered with a bow and quiver, her hair streaming in the breeze. Her form seemed no less bright beyond the slanted sunlight that feebly speckled the wood. "I have seen no living thing stir through this unhallowed valley, maiden, besides you and me," said Heracles. "Come not near this foul cave, which is a portal only for the dead, and not for one so ruddy and full of life as you. But tell me plainly if in some disguise you are a goddess, or nymph? If so, have you come to proffer me some aid before I proceed into undergloom?" The maiden laughed with delight as her grey eyes sparkled. "I am as you see me, sir—nothing more. Yet, in long hunting this desolate valley, my ears have picked up stories here and there. If you desire to enter yonder cave, I shall then call you impious—even a madman! for all in this district know whither that black maw goes; and none who have ever ventured forth, whether from curiosity or love of ill-gotten gain, have ever returned. But I recall one man—a seer perhaps, for he carried about a curious staff carved with entwined serpents,—who wove ghostly stories for his friends as they nearby passed the night. He said that anyone still breathing the upper air and desiring to descend into Tartaros should first, in the dead of night, offer up the blood of a black bullock to the infernal king as an atonement. Then, at the first gleam of dawn he will feel the earth move and hear the howling of the shades as the portals of the dead open to welcome him. But he must not yet attempt to pass inside without having in hand a special offering for Persephone: a golden bough that grows without fail in the darkest part of this savage forest. Should the gods favor you, the bough will yield to your hand, and in its place will grow another, golden in stem and leaves."

Heracles considered her advice and said: "I have heard such a thing before, in another land, from that prophetess called the Sybil. Sacrifice a black bullock for my sake if you like; after having endured the Great Mysteries, I feel I have no need. As for the golden stem necessary for admission, I'll leave the latest nursling for another to come after me." The maiden sighed deeply and said: "Ah Heracles, I have watched over you since plucking you as a helpless babe from that stony field. You will ever hew your own way in this world. Do, then as my must, for in your own way you are already exalted above men. Rely on your cunning and awesome strength—I cannot accompany you further. Nock an arrow and have it ready. Here you must leave behind all hesitation. Here every form of cowardice must meet its death." She spoke, and as she turned her form grew exalted and shone with rosy, sweet-scented loveliness.  Heracles cried: "What goddess is this?—my heart tells me that you are Athena!"—but she had vanished from sight.

Heracles lit his firebrand and boldly plunged into the cavern, looking back only once to see the dying embers of the day halted at the mouth by the hopeless darkness.  The descent was steep and rough underfoot, narrowing as it went, until Heracles could no longer proceed upright, but had to hunch his shoulders and bow his shaggy head.  The passage, sometimes straight, sometimes winding, appeared interminable; and as what seemed like hours passed, the air grew stifling and torrid.  By the time Heracles reached the bottom, his lungs aching with unbearable oppression, his billet had burned down to a glowing stub: only a ruddy luminance from what purported to be the end of the long tunnel guided him through the remaining distance.

Heracles emerged from the other end of the chasm into a twilit wilderness.  It seemed to be night-time; but no moon showed her horns and no stars twinkled from the apparent firmament.  The only illumination, feeble as it was, came from a fiery incandescence that ringed the distant horizon.  This murky simulacrum of the upper world seemed devoid of life.  No cicadas played their shrill nocturnal song; no owls screeched from the leafless trees; no acorns littered the bare ground; and no bough was burdened by a single fruit or blossom.  Low and narrow hillocks, like grave-mounds, interspersed the melancholy grove of black poplars and listless willows.  Heracles proceeded along an up-sloping path until he arrived at the brink of a deep valley clothed in mist.  In the distance he could discern the outline of a vast marsh, and from its edge came the roaring hiss of an unnatural confluence where a river of bristling flame debouched.  Heracles descended, and as he neared the eddying morass he saw a multitude of evanescent forms swarming about the sedge-choked shore, flickering like passing shadows, and rushing about like leaves swirled by the wind.  Young men and old, crones and maidens, as thick as birds crowding the strand before a restless sea, held out their arms pleadingly toward the marsh, twittering like bats. And as Heracles watched, a dusky skiff glode forth through the sulfurous haze, punted by a hideous, squalid old man with unkempt white hair, draped with a filthy mantle tied by a knot at his shoulder. Staring with unblinking, fiery eyes Charon pushed back the shades with his punting-pole, barking orders through a misshapen, toothless mouth, allowing only certain ones to enter his bark-sewn coracle. The abhorrent ferryman saw Heracles as he approached and cried: "You there!—whither in such haste?—and armed too! Halt where you stand and tell me why you've come. Come now, speak!" The shades fled as Heracles plied through them, dissipating like the cold mists mantling the meadows when dawn breaks.

"I seek entry into the realm of the dead," said Heracles. "Convey me, if you please, to the far shore, if that is the way."

Charon shook his pole at Heracles and said: "That is the way: a land of shadows and never-ending night; but not for you, since you seem of firmer build than these and an ancient law forbids me to carry living bodies across these Stygian waters."

"I am not accustomed to be faced with disagreement," said Heracles. "Therefore allow me entry to your spacious boat."

When Charon again refused and tried to poke him with his pole, Heracles snatched it from his hands and brought it down upon the boatman's naked shoulder. Charon winced for a moment under the blow, and then, to Heracles' surprise, sprung back like a tough, green twig. Heracles struck him twice more before Charon relented, noticing the Eleusinian myrtle wreath upon Heracles' brow. He cleared the gangway of the cowering shades and admitted Heracles to his boat, which immediately sunk, groaning under the unaccustomed weight, into the mire, its stitches bursting.

Heracles asked Charon: "What is the meaning of the swarming mass upon the shore? Why do you ferry some across and not others?" Charon replied: "We cross the mere of Acheron, the great bourn between our worlds, into which the four infernal rivers sink. Here drains the Styx, by which even the holy gods fear to swear falsely; the frigid Cocytus that passes by the Vale of Mourning; the Acheron, from which the marsh takes its name, and the fiery Pyriphlegethon. Only those dead who have been duly buried are allowed passage into the dark kingdom, and that for a fee of one small coin. While their bones wait still for rest, they must wander these banks for one hundred years, until I can allow them to cross with the others." As Heracles pondered the fates of the dead, the boatman continued: "It is evident by your myrtle wreath that you are privy to the mysteries of our Terrible Queen. What business brings you hither before your time, bold man? Do you not know that your days are numbered; and whatever you may do, it is but wind?" Heracles spoke no more, flipping Charon an obol for his trouble, which he had brought with him cognizant of the passage fee required of the dead, as he disembarked on the opposite bank As Charon's coracle disappeared back into the mists, Heracles set out through the lonely and shagged valley of the Styx, compelled by an echoing clamor ahead. Clambering through a ravine, he came to a hollow with a cave at one end. A pall of silence fell as he drew near. In the darkness of the cave he sensed a movement, like a shadow within a shadow. Suddenly three sets of flaming orbs blinked at him, accompanied by long, truculent snarls. As Heracles hesitated, he could hardly believe his eyes when a black, bloated three-headed beast padded forth stealthily. It resembled in most respects a dog, but bore a mane of bristling serpents; and its long tail, capped with a snapping maw, whipped furiously against its haunches. Neither the Hydra, nor Troy's sea monster had induced in him more trepidation. Steeling his nerves, Heracles crept near with his club, and then burst before the monster ready to pummel it into the submission. Surprised by the sudden hostility from one entering its realm, the hellish watch-dog barked furiously from its triple mouths, snarling and flashing its rows of sharp teeth dripping slaver. When Heracles did not wince, but instead stepped forward boldly swinging his club, Cerberos fled its hovel. Heracles pursued it out of the valley, but soon lost track of the monster, which by its great bounding stride easily outchased him.

Heracles wandered about the region until he came among another vast multitude of phantoms inhabiting a meadow full of tall-sprouting asphodel whose pallid blossoms waved like a grey veil over the cheerless waste. On seeing Heracles they drifted toward him, like a shoreward rollers gaining strength. When Heracles saw himself surrounded by such a vast, rustling assemblage of shades, twittering like bats, grasping at him with their ghostly arms, he was overcome with deep horror and revulsion, and whirled about, ready to flee the place. But he suddenly faced an even more dreadful apparition. A disembodied head, unnaturally large and looming, rushed toward him. It bore the hideous visage of the Gorgon Medusa, frozen in a final scream of agony. At once Heracles dropped his club, unsheathed his sword, and sliced through the snake-haired fiend—but the blade passed through nothing but a dissipating vapor.

A haunting laughter drew Heracles' attention back to the ghostly meadow. A glint of shining armor drew his eyes. Against the retreating mass of shades, fleeing now the hero's presence, advanced a ghostly paragon, in life a stout and comely youth cut down in his bloom. Heracles sheathed his sword, opened his quiver, and from it drew a bronze-tipped arrow. He was ready to draw back his clear-sounding bowstring when the shade cried out: "Son of Great Zeus!—stand where you are! Stay your deadly arrows. You have little need to fear us; for we are empty ghosts, like that Gorgon, whom your ancestor Perseus bravely slew, spreading her blood on the Libyan sand." Heracles astonished, replied, "What god or mortal raised you? And who dared slay such a lordly youth?" The phantom, in a blink, traversed the distance and stood before Heracles. At once Heracles recognized his spear-wielding comrade Meleager, whose wispy form managed to retain something of his princely mien.

Meleager spoke, his pallid eyes wet with a mist of tears: "I am gratified that you, at least, are not yet one of us, and are no doubt here to fulfill one of your many Labors, for there is nothing in earth or under the earth too difficult for Alcmene's son. I see you afflicted with many doubts and questions; and so I shall explain first how I came to this bitter end.

"On my return from Colchis, my father Oeneus greeted me with news of a bounteous harvest. He had offered the first-fruits to the gods: barley-grains to Demeter; wine to Dionysos; oil to Athena; to each divinity his own special gift. But—from negligence or carelessness, I do not know—he failed to honor Artemis, goddess of wild things, with her due, leaving her altars devoid of fragrant incense. We learned too late that the gods too are swayed by wrath. Although my father tried to entreat the virgin goddess with sacrifices of goats and red-backed cattle, her anger remained unquenched: before the grain could reach the threshing floor, she sent to our lands a boar so immense that it could prove a match for any bullock of green Epirus. Why—when Theseus saw it, he declared it could be none other than a spawn of the Crommyonian sow he slew on his journey to Athens! His eyes pulsed with blood and fire; his stiff, high neck, seemed impenetrable; his bristles stood rigid and sharp like rows of spears; as he grunted hot foam dashed his broad flanks; his long sharp tusks could match that of the fantastic oliphant; and his breath scorched as he passed the unreaped shoots. In his rampage, like a raging flood, he tore through vine-rows heavy with grapes; cut down the young trees bearing fruit; and slaughtered with his tusks whatever beasts or men that crossed his path.

"When it became clear that nothing, neither hounds nor herdsmen, could protect our livelihood from the boar's destruction, my father, counting on the fame and honor wrought by our expedition to Colchis, called for a band of brave young men to come and stand with him in defense of the fields of Calydon, promising to give the boar's pelt as a prize to whoever succeeded in killing it. As he was to too old to take to the field, he placed me in command. In short order there streamed into Calydon the noblest of men. I am surprised, Heracles that you did not come seeking glory—did you not get the call? Your brother Iphicles was there, as was Iolaos. Jason arrived from Iolcos, as did Samian Ancaios, Idas and Lynceus, the twin sons of Leda, and many others comrades who shared the thwarts with us aboard the *Argo*. Inseparable from Theseus came Peirithoös, not wishing for a second time to miss a glorious adventure. The sons of Thestios, my uncles, came from Pleuron representing the Couretes, ready to join the chase. You may remember Echion and Eurytion—they too came; and Nestor from Pylos; and brave Laertes, son of Acrisius, from Ithaca; and Hippomenes, son of Amphidamas, who competed in Pelias' funeral games. Hippocoön from ancient Amyclai sent his sons; as did Actor, with the blessing of Augeias, to bring glory to brilliant Elis. Peleus, Telamon—so many others also answered the summons; including one woman, hot for the chase: Atalanta, from wild Arcadia, who made us forget the inadequacies of her sex when she sailed with us.

"For nine days we feasted in my father's hall. On the tenth, as we gathered our equipment, ready to set out, Ancaios, Cepheus and some others remonstrated against Atalanta, for they chafed at having a woman compete with them in the hunt. That Ancaios joined the protest surprised me greatly, since, being her relation, he had defended her when she wished to join the *Argo*'s crew. With great effort and choice words I soothed their wounded pride, and finally compelled them to accept the fair Tegean; all except Peleus, who still smarted from his defeat by her at Pelias' funeral Games.

"A thick forest there was, which for long centuries no axe had touched, rising from the plain, and overlooking the fields. We received notice the boar had taken refuge there. For six days we hunted the beast, ever ready with our nets and hounds. Atalanta, to her credit, often found his spoor; she tried to organize the hunt, but none would listen to her save I. At last we encircled the boar in a deep dell where the rain-water drained. At its lowest point lay a reedy marsh of supple willows, osiers, and sedge-grass. Some of the hunters, overeager, rushed in and roused the boar, who charged out like a flash of lightning from massed clouds, laying low the tall bulrushes and crashing against the trees. The dogs piled on, trying to stop the mad charge, but they were scattered or killed by the force of his sidelong strokes. This was what the hunters waited for! Echion was the first to cast his lance, which, missing, struck a maple-tree. Jason, then, launched his: it would have surely hit the boar's broad back, but overshot from two much force. The beast felt now the mortal threat and grew incensed. You could see fire sparking from his eyes! Like a rock flung from a catapult, he rushed against the nearest group of hunters, laying low Eupalamus and Pelagon on the right. Eanesimus, in fear turning to run, drew the beast's attention. He charged and hamstrung the son of Hippocoön. In rage my dear brother Agelaus rushed forward with his pike; but the boar darted clear, and then returned, raving, in a frontal assault, goring Agelaus and Hyleus beside him. Nestor narrowly escaped by vaulting with his lance-haft into the branches of an oak-tree; from where, after whetting his tusks against the bole, the boar dashed against Hippasus, ripping open his thigh in one sweep. Castor and his brother now rode up upon their milky steeds, chasing the boar with their hunting-spears into dense woods. Brave Telamon tried to follow, but tripped on a projecting root. While Peleus came to his aid, Atalanta, running behind, her hair streaming in the wind notched an arrow and let it fly. The arrow grazed his back and lodged beneath the ear, staining the bristles with a spray of blood. When the others saw the lucky shot, they flushed red with shame; and spurring one another on in reckless courage, the hunt turned into a wild affair of flying missiles, all missing their mark. Then it was that blustery Ancaios, wielding his two-headed axe, cried out: "Comrades, make way! Learn how far a man's weapon surpasses a girl's! Even with Artemis no doubt guarding this beast, my right hand will still destroy it." Lifting the axe overhead, standing on tip-toe, he prepared to strike; but the boar, foreseeing his rash act, wasted no time in closing the distance. Through his groin struck the sharp tusks; and down fell mighty Ancaios, unmanned, his entrails pouring out and soaking the ground with blood and gore. An augur had told him that he would not live to taste the wine from his own vineyard. Indeed, hearing of the hunt, he ran off leaving his cup untouched on the table. Thus he fulfilled the proverb: 'There's many a slip betwixt the cup and the lip.'

"Peleus, seeing his comrade brought low, without thinking or precision cast his spear, missing the mark and striking Eurytion his father-in-law instead. I too, in the confusion, slew Iphiclos and noble Aphares, my mother's swift brothers. Alas—how terrible to see such slaughter!

"Amphiaros was next to draw blood, transfixing an eye. Afterward Peirithoös rushed in, pike in hand; but Theseus admonished him, saying: "Keep away!—O dearer to me than my own soul: my soul's counterpart! No shame exists in battling from a far; see how Ancaios paid for his rashness." Then, after carefully balancing a heavy lance, Theseus let it loose. A leafy branch waylaid the careful aim. Jason again tried to pierce the bristly hide: a hound, and not the boar, felt the sting. Seeing an opening, and impelled by rage and grief for my uncles, I cast a spears from each hand. One landed upright in the earth; the other struck deep the beast's arching back. The boar raged round and round, gushing fresh blood and foam. Retrieving my brother's gleaming pike I goaded him into frenzy, and then plunged the point deep under his shoulder-blade, piercing the heart, and bringing an end to the cause of all our misery.

"Our soaring spirits soon tumbled to earth when we saw about us the heavy toll of our success. As I set about to skin my hard-won prize, the sons of Thestios assembled, protesting that Iphiclos had first struck the boar and deserved the spoils. No small dissension ensured over that boar's head, continuing all the way back to Calydon, where we bore the corpses of two uncles I had unintentionally slain. Thestios, enraged more by missed honor than the death of his sons, from Pleuron settled on war. The Couretes marched out against us. While I fought, we resisted them bitterly, holding them at the city walls. But then I learned what my mother Althea had done, and, swollen with rage, I departed the ranks of the Aitolians for my own house. She had been in the sanctuary bringing the gods gifts for my success when she saw her brothers borne in on catafalques. Beating her breast, and filling the city with her laments, she changed her golden dress to black; but on learning the author of her demise she wept no more and went forth to bring about my destruction. Home she rushed and from a secret place brought out that charred billet that held my fate. You see, while my mother carried me yet in her womb, the Fates who spin the thread of life appeared to her. One, seeing a log burning on the hearth, declared: 'To your son and that billet we assign the same span of life.' At once my dear mother snatched the wood out of the fire, doused it in water, and locked it away, thinking that as long it was safe my life would never end. But now, with the fateful brand in hand, she called for pine-knots and kindling for a cruel flame. I was told that four times she made to toss the log into the flames; and four times she resisted. No doubt the mother in her warred with the sister: like a ship, driven on one side by the wind and on the other by tide, contests with both forces. A servant who was with her reported her to say: 'Will he someday become king, while my brothers lie beneath? Let him die!—and drag down with him his father's house. O, but I am a mother, who bore your pains for nine long months! How can I choose? If only I had left the billet in the flames, your end would have spared me this present sorrow. What misery! But you win, my brothers: I can only see your ghastly wounds. Turn your eyes, avenging Furies! Now death must be paid for by death.' Having spoken, with trembling hand she flung the brand into the flames, turning her back to spare her eyes from the sacrilege. I tell you, Heracles, that at the very moment the fire consumed the wood, I felt the heat of that same flame. My body burned. When word came of my mother's curse, nothing could contain my agony.

"The battle continued to rage. When it seemed the Couretes would breach the city walls, the magistrates sent the high priests to implore me to resume my command, promising a great reward of fertile land. My father too came often to plead with me, as did my friends and dear sisters. I merely languished beside Cleopatra, my wife, and would not listen. It was not until I felt the very walls of my house rattle from the siege that my heart was moved to action. My lady in her soft gown sealed my resolve when she, weeping, recounted the horrors awaiting a fallen city. At once I donned my shining armor and marched out to join the fray, leading my countrymen in a rout of the enemy. Back to their native city we pushed them, where I slew the rest of the sons of Thestios. Before their towers, as I was about to slay Clymenus, Daipylos' valiant son, I fell—whether from some lance's steel point or arrow, or from my mother's curse, I do not know—and, feeling my soul and strength diminishing, my last breath went forth in tears, and forever the light was shut from eyes."

Heracles wept, for the first time in his life, over such a ruin of youth and beauty. In commiserating with his comrade, he forgot completely Meleager's assent to his abandonment in Mysia.

Sorrowfully, he said: "It is best indeed never to be born; never to look on the light of the sun. Tell me now: what is this place you haunt?"

"This meadow, covered in ghostly asphodel, is the place of those whose work is done," said Meleager. "Here assemble the vast horde of the dead, awaiting judgment. Those who have committed grave evil in life are cast into the Tartarean pit from which there is no escape. But the good and just, the noble warriors and the poets who made rich our lives with art, are rewarded with passage to the Elysian Fields. I am not yet permitted to leave this place, but accompany me and I shall show you the neighboring regions."

Heracles followed Meleager to the edge of the meadow, near to the rocky haunt of Cerberos, where could be heard a loud wailing: cries of sorrow without torment. "In this lonesome dell," said Meleager, "dwell infant souls. Never did they taste their share of life's sweetness, torn in that dark day from their mothers' breasts. Here they remain, neither rewarded nor punished. Next to them are those condemned to die on a false accusation, awaiting their turn to plead their case before Minos the judge." From there they passed into a dense and pathless wood where the fruitless trees bore leaves of black and branches gnarled and knotted. Amid the tangled briers they heard a melancholy soughing. Heracles stopped, bewildered, not knowing from whence the moanings came. "Tear but a little twig from any of these branches, and you shall know who wails so," said Meleager. Heracles reached out to snap a stem from a great thornbush before them. At once the plant shuddered and cried out: "Why do you tear me?" Dark blood dripped from the broken branch. Meleager said: "Here dwell in sorrow those who flung their lives away by their own hand, loathing the light. The soul, savagely torn from the body, lands where fortune wills within this wood; like a grain of barley it sprouts and grows into a tree, yielding no fruit, but only bitter thorns. How any of them would now endure poverty and travail in the world above! But they are forever bound beyond the seething marsh, trapped within the nine-fold coils of Styx."

Under the shade of eternal night they passed beyond the dreary wood to another meadow spread on every side and surrounded with myrtle-groves. "And what is this place?" inquired Heracles, seeing dim forms with downcast faces traversing secluded paths. Consumed in deep sorrow, not one of them paid heed to the visitors. "The Vale of Mourning it is called," said Meleager. "Here the woodland conceals those who wasted away, pining for love. Not even death releases them from their torment." After they had walked a little way, Meleager with a great sigh said: "Upon my death my sisters filled Calydon with their lamentations. My corpse upon the bier they kissed and wet with tears. At last, it is said, Artemis took pity, clothed them with feathers, and changed them into guinea-hens. Only two sisters were spared, of which Deianeira, with her neck golden-hued like a fresh olive, is left at home, as yet unsubdued by love. You would forever honor me, most worthy Heracles, to take her someday as your bride." Heracles recalled his love for Megara, which, though undiminished, seemed forever lost under burden of his enormous crime. He always knew, though he was loath to admit it, that he could never return to a life with her. He gave no answer to Meleager's shade, keeping all things in his heart.

They continued through rising ground to a rocky eminence overlooking a panorama so inconceivably desolate that Heracles from consternation clung to the brushwood girding the brink. At last the source of the flaming horizon he had seen at the underworld's entrance became clear. Stretching for an immeasurable length between ramparts of beetling cliff ignited to the highest reaches by many-colored flame, stood a fortress ringed by triple walls and encircled by a swirling current of white-hot flame choked with crashing boulders. Columns of black, rolling smoke, pregnant with floating embers, swirled to the heights of a massive gate supported by adamantine pillars which no great troop of man or gods could overthrow. Above rose an iron tower, its summit glowing, upon which three infernal creatures most ghastly and foul had their seats. In shape they seemed like women, wearing bloody robes pulled up about them; but for hairs horned vipers quivered and with taloned hands they beat and tore their breasts, uttering chilling wails. Meleager cried: "Hide from the unsleeping eyes of the Furies, who ever keep watch over the gate of Tartaros!" Heracles did so, crouching in a thicket. "That is Megeara on the left," said Meleager. "Allecto, weeping, sits on the right. And between them, ready with her whip is hollow-eyed Tisiphone, whose blackened lips expend corruption. How long do men in the world above put off atonement! At death they assemble in that great plain of judgment you see there stretching out from Tartarean Pyriphlegeton. When sentence is pronounced on those without redemption, Tisiphone leaps down to lash them and drive them through the prison gates. Behold! The avenging spirits flee their posts. Another horde of wicked shades are consigned to their punishment! The horrid gates rattle, opening to admit them." The interior now released groans and lamentations, the sounds of clanging chains and bestial tortures. Heracles, astonished, asked, "What is that noise rising from within? What evils deserve such dire punishments?" Meleager answered: "The dead dwell in sundry regions, and each are punished according to the measure of their wickedness. There go the foul parricides, the fraudulent, the hoarders of wealth, panders and adulterers, murderers, the tyrants and the traitors. In the center of that dungeon lies the darkest and deepest place, an abyss twice as profound as cloud-girt Olympos is high, where the ancient race of the Titans is forever consigned. It is their ceaseless clangor we hear most of all."

Heracles commenced to descend toward the plain by a narrow path. Looking back, he saw Meleager still on the cliff. The shade called out: "I can go no farther, Heracles. The boundary of my own prison has been reached. Here I must remain in temporal punishment for my sins. Ho! I see the fire of eternal curiosity, that thirst for adventure and things unknown, in your eyes. But I beg you not to go near the opened gates. It is impossible for any pure soul to cross the fiery river, much less pass beyond those battlements. Take instead the road to the right, which will lead you to the palace of Pluton, and beyond that, they say, to the Fields of the Blessed, where I hope to someday dwell once my purification is complete—if that is the object of your journey here." Having spoken, the shade of Meleager grew dim and faded like a passing mist.

The path wound down to another crag, a bowshot away from the hissing current of the flaming stream. From that vantage, the clamor from Tartaros washed over Heracles like a foul wind. Looking for any sign of Cerberos, Heracles shuddered at what he saw beyond the massive gates, opened and admitting an endless line of naked, newly dead harassed by the swirling Furies.

He first beheld, in the threshold, sitting on a vulture's hide atop a pile of filth and bones, the bloated daimon Eurynomos, his flesh a color between blue and black, like that of flies that breed on rotten meat, snatching certain ones from the harried throng to strip off the flesh with his teeth.

Behind him, Heracles could not miss a gigantic form stretched and pinned by fetters over numerous square rods of plain. He was none other than the giant earth-born Tityos, who in some forgotten time tried to take Leto, favored of Zeus, by force. Since then his agony is prolonged by twin vultures that feast on his vitals, fluttering within the sundered cavity of his breast. Beyond him, a forlorn figure rolled an enormous rock up a hill. This was Sysiphos. Heracles watched him reach the summit of the hill, after which the tottering rock rolled back down the hill again, prompting Sisyphos to begin the arduous labor anew. How he came to his eternal punishment was said to have happened in this way. Sisyphos, king of Ephyra, one day saw Zeus, who had abducted Aegina, daughter of the river-god Asopos, passing nearby. When Asopos arrived asking if anyone had seen his young daughter, Sisyphos promised to reveal the ravisher's identity if Asopos caused a spring to gush below the citadel. Asopus did so, and the truth was revealed to him. Zeus at once wished to kill him for his impiety, but crafty Sisyphos, sensing death near at hand, ordered his wife not to pay him the required funeral honors: to keep bare the altars of offerings of oil, grain and honey. On reaching the underworld, Sisyphos decried before Hades his wife's sacrilege, and begged to make amends for daring to enter the realm of the dead without due rites by being allowed reentry into the living world to punish and harass her. His request granted, Sisyphos returned to life and lived long in infamy, until for a second time his thread of life was cut. Now, hemmed in by a futile exercise, nevermore shall he find release from the infernal realm.

Another criminal Heracles recognized from bedside tales: Ixion, king of the Lapiths, hoisted spatchcocked upon a turning, flaming wheel. When once he married Dia, daughter of king Deioneus, he repudiated the bride-price he had promised and treacherously threw the king into a trench filled with burning coals. The crime elicited such horror that Ixion could find no one to purify him; except for Zeus, who took pity and removed his madness. Ixion repaid him by trying to take Hera by force. Zeus gave him another chance to make amends, and to test him fashioned from a cloud a form like Hera's. Ixion at once, without compunction, lay with the phantom, and from the unnatural union came the Centaurs. For his recalcitrant impiety, Zeus condemned him to his present punishment, making him immortal so that he should suffer bodily in flames for eternity.

The vista now obscured through distance and torrid fumes, Heracles could barely make out an emaciated figure standing neck-deep in a pool and overspread by boughs pendant with pears and pomegranates, shiny apples, juicy figs and ripe, dark olives. As he dropped his lips to drink, the water drained down to his feet, where the black mud boiled in a sultry wind. And if he raised a hand to pluck a fruit, the branch retreated from his reach. What crime led to such a punishment for Tantalos, a son of Zeus who reigned in Phrygia, was no longer certain. It is said he betrayed his privilege of feasting with the gods by stealing nectar and ambrosia, divine foods, to share with mortals. Or else he once, to test the wisdom of the gods, slew his own son and served him up to them. From that same pool in which Tantalos stood a bevy of maidens came to fill broken water jugs, from which the water ran as fast as they filled it. These were, Heracles recognized, the forty and nine daughters of Danaös, who, scarcely married for a day, murdered their husbands that same night.

The mighty gates of Tartaros began to close as the Furies, after circling about for one final pass, like shrieking eagles patrolling the mountain hollows for prey, returned to their perch atop the iron tower. Heracles laid low, hidden from their searching eyes that seemed like pairs of red, pulsating flame, retreated back along the narrow pathway, and descended to the plain by another way. In the great distance he saw a vast welter of phantoms, mere shadows against the night, crowded around three great thrones on which sat shining forms, each bearing a golden staff. At every judgment delivered the dark realm shuddered, and the formless assembly appeared to wilt like a rill in summer, fissioning into three great trains, only to swell anew, bolstered by the fecund sepulcher. He followed quickly alongside the opposite road from Tartaros until all was again quiet and empty, and all fleeting apparitions were left behind. For long he crossed an indistinct waste, without moon or stars to guide him. He thought he caught the trail of Cerberos, and followed the taloned imprints through rocky uplands. Ahead it seemed that morning had broken through a fissure in the earth, for the edge of heaven exhibited a growing flush. He came to a bluff and stood aghast as a vast edifice rose from the valley in dark majesty. It had the form of a temple, bright as molten brass, set with obsidian columns about its Cyclopian walls, and spanned by a golden entablature embossed with precious stones and monumental sculptures more like life than art. A dozen arching gates looked into spacious halls and porches fulgent from endless rows of lamps and cressets.

Heracles approached the majestic palace in awe. As he entered past the brazen doors, a violent barking assailed him. Cerberos stood before him with arched back, each canine maw growling and baring its teeth in violent protestation. When Heracles unsheathed his gleaming sword, the infernal watch-dog fled again. Heracles pursued him through immense galleries surrounded by marble colonnades. The chase ended inside a great hall whose lofty, vaulted ceiling was lost in gloom: sparingly did gleams of fretted gold or rich paintings reach the eyes. Opposite the entrance stood two lofty thrones of black marble under which Cerberos cowered, half-heartedly growling.

From a deep alcove suddenly sounded impassioned pleas

for assistance. Looking there, with an eye still trained on Cerberos, Heracles found two naked men sitting on stone couches, their feet dipped in a pool of writhing serpents. He was struck at first sight by a sense of familiarity, which only grew stronger as he approached them and saw their countenances with greater clarity. The men, their eyes turgid with tears, stretched their arms toward him, imploring him by his great strength to release them. Heracles, in astonishment, thought he recognized Theseus; but the man before him seemed past middle-age; his hair graying, thinned and scraggly; his face mazed and haggard. "Is it you, Theseus?" Heracles cried; "but how so? Did I not see you in Athens but a month past? Have you perished since and your shade grown old?" Looking closely at his companion, who seemed spent alike, Heracles declared: "And you!—Peirithoös, are you as inseparable from noble Theseus in death as you were in life? Explain, if you please, how you find yourselves here in such a dismal state."

Both men looked befuddled, and only increased their piteous lamentation. Heracles reached down to grasp Theseus by the arms, but could not dislodge him without agony from his seat, for it seemed the very rock entwined around his flesh. Heracles tried again, the second time with less force but greater care, like a man pulling a thorn from his foot, needling Theseus until he wrenched free, leaving behind a bloody swatch of fundament where the two disparate surfaces were spliced. Heracles now set to free Peirithoös but could not budge him a finger without mutilation. As Heracles persisted, the ground commenced to tremble. A fulminating roar, like unexpected thunder, rolled through the antechambers, halls and galleries. The mighty columns appeared to sway as spandrels snapped and crashed down around them. Heracles looked for Cerberos, but found that the monster had quitted his refuge beneath the thrones. Lifting Theseus on his back, Heracles rushed back the way he came.

Outside it seemed all of Hell had broken into turmoil. The hard ground fissured to belch flames and torrid smoke. Blowzy flakes of fire drifted down like slow mountain snow. Rocks cracked and rolled down the hillsides. Heracles carried Theseus across the blighted landscape into a mountain cleft, far from the palace, which reflected on its marble complexion the rage of the funereal deities, fulgurating from the blue of burning brimstone to the gloss of the blood-red moon.

"I know you, sir!" said Theseus at last, cowering in Heracles' borrowed lionskin, after they had overcome their fright and distress. Occasionally a sound like thunder still rolled through the valley. "Heracles!—why yes, how could I not remember? You've come down to fetch up Cerberos, have you not? I beg your pardon: I feel like I have been suddenly awakened from a long sleep. I am not a phantom, as you can see. A heart still beats beneath this breast. Are you the same, or is this another trick of Hades?"

"I am as you see me," said Heracles. "But how was your youth lost?"

"And how was yours preserved?" asked Theseus, equally puzzled, as memories rushed back to him. "Four long years I sat on that siege perilous—or at least years they seemed to me, although there was no moon to count the months. How Pluton mocked us for our rash daring once we were pinioned to our seats! I recall now a thing I overheard in my confinement: that in this realm the stream of time flows differently than in the world of living men, slower and more leisurely. A generation may pass here for every day consumed above. O, Peirithoös, noble companion, are you lost, trapped forever in the house of Hades?"

"He is beyond hope," said Heracles. "The road back seethes with molten rock and plumes of fire."

"How shameful it is to betray a man and friend hostilely seized! But well was the god's ire reserved for him, preventing any escape; he it was who dreamed up this hopeless and scandalous enterprise," said Theseus sorrowfully. As he comforted his friend with a light hand upon the back, Heracles spied something stirring in the burning plain. Stone sepulchers, some lidless and empty, riddled a region inclosed by a low crumbling wall. From one half-opened tomb a wizened hand desperately clawed the air. Heracles ran to the grave-yard and heaved off the heavy lid. Out jumped a pitiful creature clothed in rags. He groveled at Heracles' feet and, kissing his knees, said: "Bless you, sir, for releasing poor Ascalaphos! At one time I tended Hades' orchards. But I tattled on the Dark Queen when she tasted the pomegranate seeds, for which trespass her mother buried me beneath the rock."

"He is a daimon—a denizen of this infernal realm," said

Theseus, arriving at the side of Heracles.  Then to the prone figure he said: "Which way lies passage out of Erebos?"

Ascalaphos, suppressing laughter, responded: "Who dares to flee the underworld without permit of its lord?  Cerberos shall catch you and grind you between his teeth like wheat!  Only for your kindness to me will I reveal the way.  Across these mountains lie the blessed lands, beside which flow the waters of Lethe as far as the bounds of Ocean.  There, on cliffs along the broad shore, you will find twin gates and an escape into the upper air.  Through one door, the Gate of Horn, only true shades are permitted to pass when it is so commanded by the gods.  The other gate, of ivory, you will now by its radiance.  Through it the dead send false dreams to vex the living.  If you are quick, you also may pass out from it."  The daimon suddenly turned in fright, darting his eyes about.  "Who calls me?" he screeched.  "Is it you, Mistress?  Woe upon woe!"  The daimon scurried off toward the palace.  It is said that Persephone threw into his face a handful of water from the burning Pyriphlegeton, and he grew a beak and feathers and became a screech-owl.

As they wended their way out of the stewing valley, Theseus began his tale.

Spoke he: "After Peirithoös lost fair Hippodameia, he came to me, filled with grief and longing, to persuade me that we should attempt to find for ourselves new wives of quality, who therefore could be no less than daughters of the highest gods, since we ourselves were sons of the same: he of Zeus and I of Poseidon.  We discussed the possibility of marching against the Lacedaimonians in order to abduct the famed Helen, sister of the Dioscuri.  It was said that Zeus, taking the form of a swan lay with her mother, Leda; that her mother bore an egg; and that Helen sprang from it.  A widower myself after Phaidra's death, and having reached my fiftieth year, the plan seemed agreeable at the time, for there is no lonelier man than he who outlives a wife.  Helen, though but a child, was rumored to possess a beauty above all the women on earth."

"Phaidra, you say?" asked Heracles.  "The daughter of Cretan Minos?  You must start there, or I shall be wholly lost."

"Pardon me, brother Heracles!' said Theseus; "but I must keep this prologue brief, since these events will be well known to you when the time comes.  I never quite forgot red-haired Antiope from our expedition to the land of the Amazons. As we pressed together in the fray, our bucklers grinding, the flush of her cheeks colored mine; and I felt against me the heat of her sweet breath. With Peirithoös I sailed again to the valley of the Thermodon, waged war against the Amazons, and brought Antiope back with me to Athens. Though she loved me as I did her, she was loath to demean herself with marriage, but agreed to remain my consort. Orithya, angered by the abduction, rallied her Amazons. Allying herself with the Scythians, she marched her army overland, through Thrace, into Greece. But the Amazons, deserted by their auxiliaries after some disagreement, alone reached Athens and camped on the Areopagus, there sacrificing to Ares for hope of victory. I marshaled my forces and hard fighting waged for four months. The left wing of the Amazons moved to the place now called the Amazonium, while the right occupied the Pnyx next to the temple of the Muses, where we sallied forth to meet them. The Athenian right wing moved down from the hill called Museum to attack the Amazon left wing, but was routed and forced to draw back to the temple of the Furies. With fresh fighters arriving from the Palladium, Mount Ardettus and the Lyceum, we streamed out and, in a decisive move, drove the Amazons back to their tents, inflicting heavy casualties. In all this Antiope fought heroically at my side against her sisters. The war continued in this way until, with Antiope's help, a treaty was concluded.

"Afterward Minos' son, Deucalion, who ruled Crete after his father, offered me the hand of his sister Phaidra in an effort to normalize relations between our two kingdoms, which had been in upset since the murder of Androgeos. Antiope objected severely to the new arrangement, and gathering up some remaining of her sisters, who had settled in at Megara, she tried to intrude upon our wedding-feast with the intent of murdering Phaidra and the guests. I was able to bolt the doors to prevent their entry; and it was with your help, Heracles, that we subdued them outside."

Dark, brooding cliffs surrounded them. By way of narrow passes choked with brakes they crossed the mountains and reached a river-valley. On the left wound a sluggish stream, clear and dark, unlit by sun or moon, and in which nothing could hide. A white cypress tree shaded its sharpest bight, where the water overflowed the banks. To the right, separated by sloping hills, a small lake, fed by the surrounding mountains, poured its waters into a rocky pool under a spreading white poplar. This tree Hades planted as a memorial to the nymph Leuce, once his mistress. Shades drifted down the hills, most to drink of the stream, and some others of the lake. Theseus at once ran to the pool, affrighting and dispersing the ghosts, to lap greedily its cool water. "The pool of Memory," announced Theseus, after he slaked his thirst. "Those initiated before death know to drink from here, and to avoid the waters of the river Lethe, which but a single drop will plunge their memories into oblivion. My own wits are now restored with the help of this healing draught. Come Heracles; let us continue on our way. Elysion must be near, and not far from there a doorway out from this gloomy world." They hastened from the place to avoid the ghosts, which like pigeons after a sudden fright flocking back to their feeding, converged again upon the plain. But Heracles first took a branch of the white poplar with him, and wore it as a wreath.

Theseus continued his story. Antiope had borne him a son, Hippolytos, who, after his marriage he sent to Troizen, to be reared there by the brothers of his father's mother. Hippolytos grew to be a chaste and handsome youth whose principal occupation was venery, spending days in the greenwood hunting wild beasts, some say in the company of Artemis herself, to whom he was as devoted as his mother had been. This, and his general scorn of women— for outside the divine company of the virgin huntress he saw no other need—angered Aphrodite; she soon took revenge.

Coming from Eleusis, where he had participated in the mysteries, Hippolytos passed through Athens to see his father. When Phaidra saw him, dressed in white linen, his white skin bathed in sun, his hair garlanded, she imagined it was Theseus in his youth and, due to the influence of cruel Aphrodite, fell immediately in love with him. Phaidra followed him to Troizen while Theseus was away. There she built the Temple of Peeping Aphrodite overlooking the gymnasium, where she could watch the naked Hippolytos at his manly sports. Adjacent to the temple grew a myrtle-tree, under which the hapless Phaidra would sit, nursing her passion, and pricking the leaves with her bodkin.

After returning to Athens, Phaidra hoped that in the absence of Hippolytos her lust would subside. But she received no relief. She could neither sleep nor eat, and walked about daily in an irritable mood. When Hippolytos returned to Athens to compete in the Panathenaic festival, Phaidra rose before dawn to secure a place beside the temple of Aphrodite on the Acropolis, by which the procession would pass and from where she could see the young man among the victors. When she did, all the passions she kept locked in her heart bubbled forth and she fled, weeping, to her old nurse, who had guessed at the cause of her debility, but was not certain of the object until Phaidra finally confided in her. That night Hippolytos would lodge in the royal place. The old nurse, foolish and blind with devotion, urged her mistress to compose a letter, which she herself promised to deliver to Hippolytos.

Returning to his chambers that night, Hippolytos found the letter, fragrant with sweet honeysuckle, on his bed. He opened it immediately and read the disclosure in horror. He had only spoken to her two or three times in his life, following his usual custom of not countenancing women; but now he sought her chamber and burst in, casting all manner of aspersions on her. Phaidra threw herself at his feet and cried: "You have read my letter, beloved Hippolytos. Even foes read each others' letters, and yet do not enter into such a frightful display. Hear me; allow me to profess what I could barely put into words. I've tried to speak to you, but the sound died on my lips, my love mixed with shame. You have filled my marrow with a greedy fire! But don't look at me like that. I have never sought to dishonor my marriage in this way—inquire on my reputation if you wish! This love has come late, and how it burns. Imagine a young ox chafed by the yoke, or a wild horse bearing for the first time a harness—so, with rawness, my heart suffers a new love. This love, this guilt, becomes an art if learned in early years. Later it is insufferable. So accept me, free of sin, and let us both be guilty. If Hera herself were to offer me Zeus, her brother and husband, I would take you instead! Look how I have changed. You'll find it hard to believe, but I love now the greenwood, and follow Artemis like you. Let me go with you to Troizen, to be your companion on the hunt. I revel in nature as in a Bacchic frenzy—frenzy for your love. I think it is the curse of my race: remember my grandmother Europa, ravished by the bull; and my mother Pasiphaë, inhered with the same lust; and my sister Ariadne, cruelly abandoned by your father. And where is Theseus now? How could you love him—the man who put your own mother to the sword; who would not consent to marry her to prevent a bastard from attaining kingdom. Oh, how could I have any shame—it is fled. If my mother could a bull seduce, why can't I man?"

Hippolytos, filled with repugnance, cast her off and ran from the chamber. Phaidra, losing all sense, her love turning to loathing, ripped her clothes, and alarmed the household with her cries. That morning Theseus returned to Athens. He found all of the servants in mourning. Rushing to his chamber, he saw Phaidra hanging from the lintel. She had found it impossible to endure rejection from the one for whom she burned. In wounded pride, she hastily scribbled a note, which she still held in her cold fingers. Theseus read it and tore his vestment, for it accused Hippolytos of trying to ravish Phaidra, who decided, so she claimed, to take her own life rather than dishonor her husband. Theseus would not countenance his son, and ordered him banished from Athens forever. Hippolytos mounted his chariot, lashed his four swift horses, and sped away to Troizen, thinking himself fortunate to have escaped a worse fate.

Theseus, full of anger and melancholy, closed the casement curtains and sat brooding in the darkness. The crime he thought committed merited no less than death, but how could he put his own son to the sword? Then he remembered the promise Poseidon had made him. The god once pledged to fulfill three of his wishes. "Then let my only wish be this: destroy Hippolytos for bringing shame and dishonor upon me," cried Theseus.

Hippolytos at that moment raced his chariot at the foot of the rugged mountains overlooking the landlocked bay of Troizen, where groves of fruit-trees, topped by soaring cypresses, clothed the strip of fertile shore. A massive wave suddenly rose from the sea, so high it could surpass the Molurian Rock, and roared toward shore. From its awful foamy crest it seemed a great white bull bellowed, ready to spring. The horses, mad with terror, veered toward the cliff-edge; but Hippolytos held them in check, since he was an expert charioteer. When the wall of water thundered down upon him as he rounded a bend, the horses once again lost their course. In a mad lashing to keep them steady, the reins caught in the branch of a sprawling olive tree. The chariot swerved sideways and crashed into the rocks jutting from the hill-side, breaking into pieces. Hippolytos, entangled in the reins, was first dashed against the tree, then the rocks, and finally dragged to death behind his horses.

Theseus sighed heavily as he recounted the death of his wife and favored son. "And so," said he, "Peirithoös and I led a small force into Laconia. We surprised Helen dancing in the temple of Unbending Artemis at Limnai, where slaves are scourged to stain the altar with blood, and carried her off. We were pursued as far as Tegea, where we drew lots for the girl, agreeing that the winner would help the loser secure any wife he so chose. I won her, and as she was not yet nubile, sent her in secret to Attic Aphidai to be cared for by my trusted friend Aphidnos and my mother Aithra. There was yet great confusion in Laconia over what happened, and no one knew where Helen was taken, or who had taken her. I was at Athens for some time when Peirithoös arrived to remind me of our agreement. He claimed that Zeus appeared to him in a dream to suggest he claim Persephone, wife of Pluton, as a bride! At first I laughed at the outrageous proposal; but he held me to our oath, and I had no choice but to follow him in the mad escapade. We were emboldened that you had once already penetrated into Hell and returned. And so we descended by the same way you did, through the cave at Tainaron. We encountered the infernal ferryman, who violently denied us transport, although we offered him money, and even gold, crying that he had once already been put in fetters by Hades for a year for giving you passage. Peirithoös tried to reason with him, stating that he, as a son of Zeus, had greater claim to Persephone than her uncle. He would not budge. As we could see no other way into Erebos, we lay in wait until Charon's boat returned to its moorings. Then, stripping off our clothes, and carrying an obol in our mouths, we braved the company of the chilling ghosts and were able to secure a seat on his barque. All the way to the other side, Charon wondered why the craft rode so low in the water. He discovered us, however, too late, for we sped off as soon as the prow touched the far bank. We wandered about naked for some time until we came upon the palace of Hades. Drunk with foolish madness we were seeking out Persephone to abduct her when we heard the voice of Hades kindly bidding us welcome. Not knowing what to make of his hospitality, we obeyed his instructions to sit on that stone couch. It straightway held us fast as we heard the god's grim laughter. Snakes coursed beneath us and Cerberos came to maul our thighs. From our position we could hear and oftimes see the somewhat horrid business of the infernal court. Only once did we see the gloom pierced by a great light, when Persephone—or so we thought—passed by the alcove, whispering words of encouragement in a dulcet voice. She told us the mighty Tyrinthian would come one day to take us back to the upper air. 'We give him leave,' she also said, 'to take Cerberos; but only if he can master him with hands alone, without the use of arms, and returns him without delay.' Our spirits lifted; but we soon forgot that grain of hope, since our memories were continually purged by the wilting power of our confining seats."

They followed the river Lethe through misty woodland. The water coursed by their feet with a gentle whisper that made them long for a soft bed. Midway on their journey, the night sky, visible in patches through the creeping foliage, grew copper-colored. Soon, the bleary wood brightened as with the first flush of morning. The leaden mists dispelled; shafts of light, melting through the branches, dappled the path. One bird answered another with gay chirps. With new vigor they dashed to the edge of the forest where, lifting their eyes, they saw the rising sun dousing with rathe brightness the shoulder of a hill. Overcome by the unexpected sight, they ran up the slope to embrace the fledgling light. From the mount's crest they saw endless fields, fresh and bright, moist with glistening dew. The vista of a new world opened, clothed in radiance, with its own sun and dimming stars, as breathtaking as sight of the Tartarean frontier was harrowing. Heracles thought he had escaped already into the upper air, and for a moment forgot his cares. Theseus brought his right mind back by urging him not to tarry any longer. "Though I yearn to flee this netherworld, let us put our heads together to find Hades' watch-dog," he said. Heracles shook his head and said: "Friend, I refuse your offer of assistance, as it will diminish my glory and make Eurystheus discount my Labor. It is here that we must part: you to freedom and I to continue my quest, even if it leads me down into the Titans' deepest dwelling-place."

Theseus, alarmed said: "Are you mad? See how time has been to us unkind and full of artifice. Who knows how many turns the world has made while we linger down below?  Perhaps we too have become but shadows ourselves, insubstantial, existing in a dream where yesterday enjoys the permanence of tomorrow." Then full of consternation, he bitterly lamented: "And what of me? With my taper burning low in its socket, what shall I find when I reach the land of the living?  Will Athens still stand?  Will the whole of Attica still make common cause with her king?  I rue the day I took Helen away.  She will be the woe of nations."

With tears running down his cheeks, Theseus left him. Heracles followed him part of the way into the valley, but then turned along another path where he thought he saw again the spoor of Cerberos in the pliant earth.  It led him to a meadow scented with laurel where shades, brighter and more substantial than those encountered before, lounged at ease or occupied themselves in merry sports.  Some raced or grappled in sand-strewn pits.  Some tended to their shining arms and chariots, or gazed at their sleek horses freely grazing.  Others feasted at long tables laden with delightful things, or danced, or joined their voices in a chorus of song.  Heracles recognized the poet who held them spell-bound with his lyre's nine strings.  He addressed long-robed Orpheus, whose brow was dressed with a snow-white riband: "What? Another Argonaut fallen from the world?  I see some great misfortune haunts the steps of those who joined to steal the Fleece. Tell me, blissful soul, what sort of death laid your body in the dust." Orpheus stilled his lyre's humming strings and said:  "No greater thing is there but Love, which overcomes all things.  Its searing flame consumed me for Eurydice, most beautiful of all the naiads, whom I married in the dark vale of Tempe not long after our return from Aian Colchis.  That very day, with my happiness complete, as she strolled with her sisters not far from the river Peneios, god-fed Aristaios, accosted her.   She trod on a serpent as she fled his embrace and fell dead.  After I wore myself with mourning, I set my course to search for her among the shades.  Emboldened by your example, Heracles, I descended to the gates of Acheron through a cave at Thresprotian Aornum.  Charon, charmed with my song, gave me passage.  I crossed this vast and silent realm until I stood before the lords of the dead.  I played for them the loveliest of melodies, expressing my purpose by this song:

*Gods who rule the world subterrene,*
*To where all of mortal birth descend,*
*I speak without pretense of a scheme,*
*Wanting such ruse on which liars depend.*

*To see dark Tartaros I have not come;*
*Neither to enchain the horror of three necks.*
*Only to seek my wife, by viper overcome:*
*She fell envenomed by a single peck.*

*Though I tried to bear it all alone,*
*I had not the power to contend.*
*Love has won, and in me sown*
*The selfsame Love you comprehend.*

*I beg you now, repair the threads*
*Of her subtile, short-spun fate.*
*From this great abyss, filled with dread,*
*Return my wife to her former state.*

*For though we tarry above a little time,*
*All things return to you.*
*At the ebbing of the springtime,*
*All men come to pay their due.*

*To your lorsdships shall she submit,*
*When ripe of years she breathes her last.*
*To me this once Eurydice remit:*
*'Till one day Acheron grips her fast.*

*And if the Fates deny me once,*
*Then shall I here remain.*
*All of Erebos will rejoice:*
*Death can claim not one, but twain.*

"O how the shades shed tears at my refrains!  Tantalos lost his hunger and his thirst.  Ixion hung frozen from his wheel.  The vultures for once gave Tityos respite.  The Danaïds felt no need to fill their urns.  Sisyphos' stone sat still.  Even the Furies for the first time wept. Persephone graciously inclined her head in agreement to my plea; and dread Hades followed her advice. They called Eurydice from among the newly dead. She came, faltering in her steps, her wound still causing her distress. I took her hand and led her off, bearing only one command: should I turn to see her with my eyes before the upper air, she would be lost to me again.

"The upward slope was steep and dark, full of silence and clouded with mist. At the threshold of the day, seized by some mad desire, I turned to gaze behind. At once she slipped back into the depths girt by ruinous night. In vain I stretched my arms. I cried, "Eurydice! Come back!" But in response came only one faint "Farewell"—and she was gone. Stunned and filled with fright, like those who saw the hell-hound you brought up through the margin of the earth, I raced back to where Charon moored his boat—and already away she floated on the Stygian barque. I begged and pled, but he chased me off; no further pity did he have. For seven days I sat on the bank clothed in filth, feeding my grief with tears. Then, inveighing against the gods of Erebos, I took refuge back in the heights of wind-swept Haimos, pledging to scorn the company of women evermore, for none could replace Eurydice.

"I poured my heart into composition, and sat day and night upon a hill making lays of my laments, drawing birds and trees and even stones, enthralled. I taught too what I had learned from my visit to the darkling realm, revealing secrets even you withheld. I learned to worship the sun, and nothing else. By these acts I angered Dionysos, for I soon had more disciples among the Thracians than he. He roused the Mainads against me, who hated me also for my scorn of womankind. Waving their vine-wrapped wands, and with hair streaming in the breeze, they came against me in a swarm. One cast a spear that fell short of the mark, deflected by my song. Another flung a stone, which too succumbed to my lyre-strings. But soon their howls, breast-beatings and discordant sounds, from drums and Berecythian flutes, drowned the power of my lute. They attacked first the savage beasts that still stood tame, attentive to my song. After these the wild women encircled me and commence the awful assault. They struck with hands and wands, branches and rocks; even with implements found in a field, left behind by horror-struck husbandmen. My voice no longer availed me.

"They say that when, with bloody hands, the Mainads went away, leaving my torn limbs bestrewn, the birds wept, as did the beasts and even the trees, shedding their leaves. The streams swelled, and the rivers, with their tears. They say my head and lyre, thrown in the Hebros, floated out to sea and washed up on Lesbos. But my tender mother and the other Muses collected my limbs and buried me at the foot of Mount Olympos, where nesting nightingales sing more loudly and sweetly than others. Only then could my soul descend beneath the earth. Going through the places I visited before, I once more sought for my Eurydice. Finding her in these blessed fields, I took her in my eager arms; and here we walk, side by side, or one leading the other. No longer do I fear to lose her from my sight."

Heracles lifted his eyes to where Orpheus stretched a hand. There, on a plain clothed with dazzling light, danced Eurydice, her tresses streaming in the gentle breeze and her long gossamer gown twirling behind. He had glimpsed these very meadows at Eleusis.

Heracles said: "Thracian, your minstrelsy almost overbears my eyes with tears. I should have paid you greater mind when together we sailed. Have you knowledge of my father Amphytrion, or of my children, felled by my own hand, if mayhap they dwell in this fortunate land?"

"None in this countless throng has a fixed home," said Orpheus. "We live in shady groves and meadows laved with streams. We bed beside the Eridanos, which, rising here, flows through secret channels to the world above. If you wish, you may search them out from among the countless shades, but only a gift of warm blood will restore the wits and speech of these who have imbibed the water of the winding Lethe. For after making satisfaction for their sins, they drink from the Lethe and then are welcomed here among the blessed."

Heracles left him; and climbing a little hill, sat for long observing the blessed spirits hovering over the bright fields. By and by, some long-horned kine, as ruddy as the Erytheian kind, came wandering. Heracles sought out the largest and most perfect of the cattle and slaughtered it, allowing the blood to pool in a shallow ditch. At once the ghosts drifted near, impelled by the warm and fragrant blood. Heracles allowed some shades to drink, and then with drawn sword kept the rest away, hoping to spot among them the bright faces of his children or his father by his stately amble.

One then came running over the hill crying, "Hang you! What do you think you're doing?" Heracles turned to face him. The man shook his crook at him and said, "I know you! Heracles, is it? Defrauder of Geryones! I saw you once pilfer his herd. And now you dare touch the cattle of Hades?" The herdsman commenced stripping his garments. "No need to report you to the master—not after I, Menoitios, finish giving you a thrashing. T'will be the last cow you ever take!" Menoitios sprang upon Heracles, hooking his leg and with a heave toppling him to the ground. Heracles, surprised by the strength and speed of the daimon, wasted no time in getting on his feet. He allowed Menoitios to rush again; and then, grasping an arm and sliding under him, threw the herdsman over his shoulder. In a flash Menoitios, unfazed, was on him again, trying to lock arms around Heracles' neck. Heracles slipped from his grasp, and, coming around, seized him by the middle. Menoitios thrashed to free himself, but he could not prevail against Heracles' grip. As rib bones cracked, and Menoitios cried for mercy, Heracles heard a three-fold barking. From the hilltop above them Cerberos filled the valley with his mad howls. Heracles released the herdsman and climbed the slope, determined not to let Cerberos escape his sight. He pursued the beastly hound across fields, through groves and thickets, into a rustling forest along the riverbank of Lethe. They emerged at last where mountains overlooked the broad, black Ocean. Starless night arose from the horizon, threatening like a ruinous storm to overtake them. Heracles kept close in breathless pursuit as Cerberos climbed the high ridges, until man and beast stood upon a crag where the mountain-side gaped open in two places. Two great gates, embedded together in the rock, framed dark grottos. The lintels, jambs and pediment of one were of polished horn; and of the other shining white ivory. Cerberos stood guard between them, throbbing with rage and snarls, unwilling to allow an unauthorized escape. At his feet Heracles found the lionskin, discarded by Theseus at the threshold of escape. Girt once again with Nemean armor, Heracles let drop his bow and sword, and untied his quiver. Seeing him disarmed, Cerberos charged, pouncing in feral might. With head bowed low to avoid the snapping maws and snaky manes, Heracles threw his arms around the hell-hound's throat, where the three heads branched, and instigated a firm grip. Back and forth they swayed, and fell rolling to the ground, until they almost toppled from the cliff. With double-edged talons Cerberos tried to tear at Heracles' side; and with barbed tail his back impale; but though the lion's pelt deflected the assault, Heracles felt the shock of every blow. Though in agony, Heracles would not relent, and slowly chocked the air from the heaving bulk. At last the three necks limped. Cerberos dropped wheezing to his side, the three red tongues spilling from the jaws, all his vigor gone. With his last remaining strength, Heracles struggled upright and planted a foot on the monster's flank. Cerberos whimpered like a child, and getting feebly to his feet, with bowed heads licked his conqueror's hands.

From between the twin gates Heracles uncoiled an adamantine chain used to secure Cerberos when he made the rounds guarding each Tartarean portal. After securing his weapons, he bound the offspring of Echidne about the neck and dragged him through the Gate of Ivory. Cerberos trembled as he went, baying and digging in his paws, for he feared to leave the underworld as much as men feared to enter it.

The way out was long and dark and winding, made more arduous by the intractable guard-dog, who resisted every pull of Heracles' mighty arms. When Heracles at last felt an ampler air as he neared the upper boundary, his strength renewed. Cerberos, struck by sunlight for the first time, went mad with terror. He barked furiously the rest of the way out of the chasm, the same through which Dionysos once brought up his mother Semele. Heracles at first did not know where in the world he emerged; but he soon recognized the city of Troizen nearby. He remembered nothing of his harrowing adventure beneath the earth, save that he went thither to fetch Cerberos; and here he was.

Heracles shunned the road to Mycenae, preferring to cross the fields to avoid encountering anyone. Along the way, wherever Cerberos flicked his slaver, there suddenly grew the deadly aconite. Those few unlucky to witness the terrible sight of Heracles, whose visage seemed grimly altered, and of big, black Cerberos, fled in utter fright. As they neared Mycenae, Cerberos slipped loose and ran off as Heracles tried to take a drink from the spring of Cynadra, which flowed between the city and the sanctuary of Hera. Heracles surprised him in a barley field, trying to dig a hole back under the earth, and kept him on a short leash thereafter.

Standing before the Lion's Gate holding back the inflamed Cerberos, Heracles called for Eurystheus. The hound of Hades, forgetting his subjugation, jumped at the guards massing atop the citadel walls provoked by their arms and shining armor. The Cyclopean stones rattled with the ferocity of his raging barks. Eurystheus had been offering a sacrifice in the courtyard of the palace when he heard the boisterous baying and Heracles' booming summons. Cowering behind the altar, he had Copreus go out and confirm what he most feared. As soon as Copreus returned bearing with marked perturbation an unvarnished description of the infernal hound, Eurystheus, blanching with terror and struck with incredulity, jumped into his bronze jar and did not emerge for three days.

After Copreus, on instructions from Eurystheus, announced Heracles free from his period of servitude, having accomplished all of his Labors, Heracles took Cerberos, padding quietly beside him, his muzzle low, beating his flanks with his snaky tail, back to the chasm near Troizen. Cerberos eagerly jumped down into the darkness, looking back only once with his fiery-red eyes.

## BOOK IV

---

## THE ANGER OF HERACLES

### 1

Autumn had passed into spring while Heracles traversed the netherworld, where his sojourn appeared to occupy but days in comparison. The valleys were clothed in green, and one could already see the golden barley breaking through the furrowed glebe, watered with rivers swollen by the melting snows. He returned to Tyrins to rest and refresh himself. Walking along the citadel's high walls, where he could see the world bursting with new life, he thought about his own. For the period of a Great Year and more, he had been singularly occupied in his Labors. At the conclusion of one, another waited. But he was now free of his servitude to an inferior man, which relieved him; but his new freedom revived that abiding restlessness gnawing him since his youth.

When he arrived at Thebes his mother Alcmene embraced him, her eyes brimming with tears. Her face, though blushing still with a hint of her former beauty, had grown careworn from anxiety over her son's long absence. Although he honored her, he had nothing else to give her, not even an obol acquired as a spoil from his Labors. Seeing his destitution, she begged him to reconcile with Megara and settle again with them at Thebes, where he was known and loved. He fell silent at the mention of Megara. His mother, seeing the burden on his heart, knew not to press the issue, and allowed him to go on his way.

Heracles returned to the home he had not seen in over ten years. He leaned his club and bow against a porch column and placed his quiver, filled with rattling arrows, beside it. As he crossed the door some maidservants saw him first, and with tears ran to him, falling on their knees, gabbling about food, drink and a warm bath. Surrendering his lionskin, he asked them only for the whereabouts of Megara. They led him to the courtyard, where, under the cool shade of a tamarisk tree he had planted after their marriage, Megara sat, still, after all the years, in her black mourning clothes. She looked up in surprise, hearing the footfalls against the flagstones, and held Heracles long in her veiled eyes. Heracles approached, and, gripping a tree branch, said, "Wife, has Iolaos treated you well?" She nodded faintly as tears flooded her eyes. Heracles turned away, for he felt his own heart breaking. He said: "Our marriage turned out most inauspicious. Had the gods any pity, it would have never been. Forgive me the anguish I have caused you." Heracles waited for an answer. Megara said finally: "How can I? You took away everything dear to a woman's tender heart. First, our children; and then you yourself, off pursuing monsters and dreadful beasts, while here I have sat, a widow before my time. In this team we were miserably yoked, you and I. Whatever you have suffered, I have twice over; and in a greater way, since I have no glory or fame to comfort me. You will emerge from your plights against serpents and boars and ravening lions none the worse. I will ever remain wretched."

Heracles knew all along that the road back to Megara was forever closed. There was no question of his return to his former life. "You speak the truth, wife," said Heracles, sighing deeply; "wherefore, I release you from our bond of matrimony. I shall offer you to Iolaos, if it pleases you. He has been my faithful companion throughout my Labors and no greater reward can I give him than that jewel once mine. He will love and honor you throughout your days. You will bear new children: boys as stout as I; and girls more beautiful than the Olympian goddesses; and their laughter will once more fill these empty halls."

Heracles lightly touched her face. She briefly pressed her cheek against his rough and calloused hand and then ran into the house, wracked with sobs. Heracles remained alone in the courtyard until the shadows of eventide deepened, thinking back on happier times.

Heracles remained at Thebes for the wedding-banquet, where he broke the sad news of Hylas' loss to his sister Laonome, telling her that the beautiful boy had captivated the heart of some woodland sprite, who claimed him for her own. By this tale, which, unbeknownst to him, contained some truth, he hoped to soften the blow of a mother's greatest anguish. As for her husband Polyphemos, Heracles could only relate that they had parted while searching for Hylas; and, though his whereabouts were presently unknown, he was confident the Argonaut would find his way back again to Thebes. But the truth was that Polyphemos, after founding the city of Cios, set out overland in hope of rejoining the *Argo* and died among the Chalybes, who buried him on the seashore under a tall white poplar-tree.

Iphicles appeared on the final day of the festivities, having been expelled by Eurystheus, who now hated not only Heracles, but all of his relations. Iphicles, however, told Heracles that he left on his own account over his brother's ill-treatment; and, calling him the better man, pledged his eternal loyalty and service. Heracles, his heart enlarged with much wine, embraced him, and they were fully reconciled. As the shades of the evening drew on, Heracles found refuge on a couch, from where, through half-lidded eyes he looked with contentment at his gathered family.

Heracles installed Iolaos in his own house at Thebes. Anxious to begin a new life, he departed for Tyrins, preferring there to keep his residence. Iolaos, loath to be separated from his greatest friend, offered to continue as his charioteer, but Heracles instructed him to make the rounds of his marriage-bed instead.

Passing through the market-place, Heracles heard news that piqued his interest. He took the road to Aulis and crossed a bridge over the turbulent narrows into Euboea. A short walk from Calchis brought him into Oechalia, the city of Eurytos, who had in his youth instructed him in archery. Eurytos was said to have been a son of Apollo the Archer and as expert a marksman as his divine father. He had four sons and one daughter, fair-haired Iole, who, turning nubile, had bloomed bright and fragrant like a violet. Eurytos was offering her to any man who could outshoot him or his sons. In truth, he had no intention of marrying off his daughter, since he could not bear to part with her. Given his consummate skill with the bow, he was confident no man could defeat him, and made the announcement merely to keep up appearances. He first pretended not to know his former pupil, having heard of the

Tyrinthian's fearsome skill. But his youngest son, Iphitos, greatly admiring his comrade from the *Argo*, endeavored to stoke his memory until he could affect ignorance no longer. Heracles then feasted with the king and other suitors until the appointed day for the contest arrived.

For the first event, the participants were to shoot successively at three targets, each farther than the other. Eurytos' son Clytios, another of the Argonauts, bested all the other suitors until he faced off against Heracles, who struck each target closest to the bull's-eye. For the second event, a fluttering dove was tied by a cord to the top of a tall post. Each man bent his bow and waited for his name, shaken from a helmet, to be called. In trying to wing the bird, the first dozen or so either missed the slender pole entirely, or transfixed the wood with arrows. Deion then let his arrow fly, and, through skill or luck, cut through the cord that bound the dove, freeing it. Deion cried out in triumph and looked to his father for recognition of victory. As he did so, Heracles shot his arrow high into the air. Seeing the bird as barely a speck against the clouds, everyone thought he had shot as a conceit, and sniggered. But all ridicule ceased when the dove, still pierced by the arrow, dropped lifeless at Eurytos' feet.

Eurytos called now for a third and final event between himself and Heracles. Taking the place of his sons, he dropped his purple mantle from his shoulders and called for his favorite bow[7]. His great, backsprung bow was brought to him, along with a quiver full of arrows. Attendants, meanwhile, set up six pairs of double-headed axes firmly in a line. Eurytos said: "All that is left, Alcides, is to shoot an arrow straight through the crossing axe-head flukes. If you manage as clean a shot as I, my daughter's hand will be yours."

Eurytos examined his bow, balancing it on his hands. Thrusting one golden tip into the ground, he braced the bow frame against his leg and with great strength bent it so that he could fasten the bull's sinew over the ends. The bow snapped back into place.

---

[7] This same bow passed on to Odysseus, who, leaving it safely in his storerooms while at Troy, used it to dispatch the importunate suitors on his return to Ithaca.

He took his position, fitted an arrow to the cord, called upon Apollo for assistance, pulled and let it fly. The arrow cleanly traversed each narrow ring and struck a bull's-eye on the other side. Eurytos returned to his seat amidst great acclamation.

Heracles bent his knees to peer through the line of axes. He had certainly never encountered such an event before. Success involved not only accuracy, but lightness and dexterity, since the rings barely fitted an arrow-head. Looking at his large hands, for a moment his confidence faltered. He stepped back to the shooting line, twanged the bow-string to test the tautness, and nocked a brand-new arrow. Taking careful aim, he drew back the cord to his chest with less tension than was his custom, and released. Straight through the iron sped his shaft and came out cleanly on the other side, splitting Eurytos' arrow down the middle.

The sons of Eurytos were astonished and dismayed to witness an archer who could outshoot his father. Two of them raced back to the palace in a huff. Only Iphitos stepped forward to congratulate Heracles. Eurytion, plunged into a dark mood, glared with rheumy eyes. Then, affecting a more hospitable disposition, he called Heracles to him and led him into the city.

Heracles, inflamed with the thought of meeting Iole, had to wait until the evening to see her, when she came out at the start of the banquet to sit beside her father's couch. She was as young and lovely as Heracles had imagined her. She rose to serve honeyed wine: first to her father, then her brothers and next to Heracles, who breathed in deeply as the folds of her fragrant garments wafted by him. Although he won Iole without question, Heracles strove to act in a gentlemanly manner, decorously refraining from grabbing or even making eyes at her until she had been formally introduced to him by her father. In the meantime he drank wine and ate roasted meat to his heart's content, oblivious to the degree the sons of Eurytos were discomposed because of him.

As the night wore on, Heracles did not think it importune to finally say: "Lord Eurytos, you truly have a daughter who has no equal, not among the Argives or Achaians, or in any other place of the world that I have seen. Since I am at your disposal, having lately been released from other responsibilities, I would most gladly plight her my troth this very night, if it please you."

Deion, bursting to his feet, exclaimed on behalf of his

brothers: "Father, does his brutish lout take you for a fool?  I would do well to remind you of his miserable history.  How he murdered his own children is well known; and then, for all we know, later cruelly discarded his wife.  What glory is there in that, even if he is a renowned slayer of monsters?  How can you entrust our dear sister into his hands?"

While Eurytos sat silently, brooding over the admonishment, Iphitos, who reclined next to Heracles, said: "Have you had too much wine, Deion?—or have you, Toxeus and Clytios, for I see how you both sit flustered at the edge of your couches, ready to join your brother in protest?  Is this how you treat a guest—one who in all sincerity came to our city to compete against all the other gallants, and, having fairly won the prize, sent them all home to nurse their broken hearts?  Heracles needs no word, good or ill, from any of you.  He is a hero known throughout the world; and we should be honored that he desires our sister for his wife."

Toxeus said: "Be silent, little brother!  Do you take the side of a stranger over us?  May the gods show you the worth of putting your faith in a madman!"

"Most true, brother," said Clytios.  "He will surely go mad again and kill any offspring begotten on Iole.  He is like a careless gardener who fumbles about his garden treading the flowers underfoot.  That, remember, is his nature.  If he cared not a whit for his first family, how can we entrust him with ours?  Send him home, I say!"

At that the three brothers drew swords and cudgels. Eurytos, emboldened by the resolution of his sons, said: "Alcides, though I have known you from your youth, and your father commanded all my loyalty and respect, I shall not give you Iole. She is of too much worth to me to risk entrusting her to such a dangerous man as you.  Go and seek a wife from the fighting Lapiths, or perhaps the Amazons!  You will find among either a helpmeet of better parity, I think."

Iphitos countered: "Father, you cannot, in your good honor, break a pledge once made!"

"There he goes again," said Deion.  "Why don't you marry him, Iphitos, since you come so often to his defense?  Let us ask Iole her say in this matter.  There is your husband, sister.  Is he the one you desire in your marriage-bed?"

Iole, trembling, fell grasping her father's knees.

Heracles, assailed by the numerous protestations, sat dumbfounded and a bit drowsy from his full belly. Toxeus came up and struck him on the shoulder with his cudgel, calling him Eurystheus' slave still. Heracles raised himself unsteadily, looking for his club. He had left his weapons by the door. The sons of Eurytos pressed in closer. Heracles, taking one last look at Iole, said to Eurytos: "I shall refrain from dishonoring you today in the maiden's presence, lord of Oechalia. But rest assured that pledges cannot be so easily broken nor guests so vilely treated without the Father of all taking notice."

Heracles, draping on his lionskin, strode out with such fierceness that Eurytos suppressed a shudder.

2

When Glaucos, a young son of Minos, while pursuing a mouse, fell into a vat of honey and drowned, Minos consulted the Delphic oracle to resolve his disappearance. Since among his herds he possessed a bullock born with a dappled hide, he was told that the person who could suggest the best analogy for the prodigy would find success in restoring the child to him. Minos dutifully assembled the augurs, and a certain Polyidos provided the best answer: he said the bullock was like a mulberry tree, whose fruit is first white, then red and, when ripe, black. Polyidos, however, had no idea where to find Glaucos until, watching for omens, he saw an owl chasing bees over the wine-cellar. But after locating the boy's body, Minos, who adhered to a literal interpretation of the prophecy, demanded that Polyidos restore him to life. Polyidos, considering such a feat impossible, beseeched Minos to employ the services of Asclepios, a son of Apollo, who was then gaining fame from his extraordinary healing skills. Minos fetched Asclepios, and as the latter could do little for his dead son, shut both him and Polyidos in the wine-cellar with the corpse. There, while Asclepios pondered what to do, a snake crawled forth and entwined itself around his staff. Distractedly, he struck and killed it. A short time later, another snake appeared, bringing with it an herb sprig in its mouth, which it applied to the head of its mate. Instantly, the dead snake revived. Securing the herb, Asclepios revived Glaucos in the same manner.

Zeus, fearing that men would continue to cheat death, threatened to strike Asclepios with a thunderbolt should he persist in attempts of revification. Apollo, who loved his son above all others, went mad with rage. He sought out Zeus' smiths, the Cyclopes, and killed several of their sons. For this crime Zeus, who stands supreme, would have hurled Apollo down to Tartaros; but as his mother Leto interceded before him, Zeus commuted the sentence to a period of purification on earth: he was to serve a mortal for one year.

Prince Admetos of Pherai in Thessaly was the man Apollo approached in the guise of a rustic, willing to work without wages for the allotted time. Ignorant of the stranger's identity, Admetos nevertheless treated him kindly and appointed him his herdsman. During that fortunate period Admetos enjoyed a stupendous harvest: his livestock multiplied three-fold, and all the cows, producing cream instead of milk, bore twin calves. After succeeding his father Pheres as king, he sought to marry the beautiful Alcestis, daughter of king Pelias of Iolcos. Before that, however, Pelias imposed a condition on all suitors: he would only give his daughter to the man who could yoke a wild boar and a lion to his chariot and successfully drive the team around the race-course.

One day, Admetos came upon a strange sight: in a shady vale his herdsman sat playing the pipes so sweetly that even the animals crowded around him to listen. At once Admetos guessed him to be a god, and threw himself at Apollo's mercy. But the son of Leto had nothing but praise for the honorable Admetos. Promising that Alcestis would be his, he taught Admetos how to yoke the two wild, disparate beasts. Admetos fulfilled the condition imposed on him, and brought Alcestis to Pherai as his wife. He had neglected, however, to honor Artemis on his wedding-day. That evening, on entering the bridal chamber, he found snakes rolled together in a heap as a sign of her displeasure.

Apollo not only reconciled Artemis to him, but did a thing that went beyond any boon given a mortal by a god. He plied the Fates with unmixed, sweet Cretan wine and convinced them that, should the time come for Admetos to die, he could be spared by finding someone to die voluntarily in his place. Apollo kept the knowledge of this final gift from Admetos until the thread of his life was about to be untimely severed. In his prime, with a wife still beautiful, with lovely children surrounding him, he foreswore to die. At the same time, he loathed how little he thought of asking another to bear his cruel fate. But he was a ruler, after all—and would not there be one among his many subjects willing to trade places with him? He believed that his life, in the great scheme of things, had greater worth. He sent out soldiers into the streets to find this person. At the end of the day, they came back empty-handed, reporting that while the populace, young and old, rich and poor, were shocked and dismayed at the news of their king's impending death, no one took up the offer. Next he asked those of his household. But they all politely refused, clinging dearly to this life, just as he. While he considered facing his end with manly courage, he thought of his aged parents. Surely they, in the twilight of life, would trade places with him. In response, his father Pheres said: "Though our days are perhaps short, I find no use in haste. Vainly do old men pray for death, for when death comes nigh, no one wants to die, and old age is no longer a burden. This is one favor I cannot grant you, my son. It is not a law of our ancestors that parents should die for their children! Too sweet is the sun's light. You were born to live your own life, whether miserable or fortunate." As for Alcestis—he tried his best to keep her ignorant of his dilemma; but when she discovered it, her resolve was firm and immediate. She approached Admetos and solemnly swore— and how he tried to prevent her!—that she would take his place. When the words left her lips, however, the Fates heard, and the course was set. Alcestis, his dear companion, the mother of his children, in the full bloom of life, full of pity and unselfish love, would die for him. "My beautiful Alcestis, I cannot allow this!" cried Admetos. "You were never part of this bargain." Alcestis responded: "It is done, dear husband, because your life is dearer to me than my own. Already, I feel the darkness surround me. Call my children, that I may embrace them one last time. All I ask of you is that when time passes, and memory of me grows dim, that you do not give our little ones a cruel stepmother." She went then to purify herself in lustral water in preparation for the end. Admetos, his heart sundered, went off to weep alone, cursing himself for the evil lot fallen on him, and swearing that he would never re-marry, for there could not be another such noble, kind and selfless woman in all the world.

The next night Alcestis died, surrounded by her husband and children. Her body was washed, anointed with oil, dressed in her finest garment, and placed on a high bed. All of Pherai was plunged into grief. For three days processions of veiled keening women roamed the streets. Shops closed. All bartering ceased.

Forges grew silent. Into this scene walked Heracles. After leaving Oechalia, he felt such bitterness that his only desire was to get drunk with some old comrades. He first went looking for Peleus in Phtiotis, concerned how he had fared after accidentally slaying Eurytion during the Calydonian boar hunt. Being told he had fled to Acastos for purification, Heracles continued on toward Iolcos, but stopped at Pherai along the way. The servants had no choice but to admit the intimidating stranger to the palace, where in due time Admetos, dressed in a mourning robe and with his hair shorn close, met him. Although happy to receive a visit from his old friend, Admetos greeted him with a forced enthusiasm, so difficult was it to mask his true disposition. Despite his friend's dissembling, Heracles could not help commenting on the many faces marked with grief: "I must be arriving at a bad time, comrade, for it is clear that someone has died. Tell me: was it a servant, or perhaps your father or mother?"

Admetos said: "No Heracles, son of Zeus! It is never a bad time for a guest. Someone indeed has died—a foreigner—a woman—no need to be too concerned about it! My home is yours for as long as you wish. Come, wash the dust off those feet! You there," he called to a servant, "take Heracles to the guest-chamber. Bring him meat and bread and wine that he may dine. You will be at the far end of the palace, Heracles, so you're not disturbed by all this commotion."

The servants led Heracles to the guest-chamber, far from the sounds of grief. After being bathed and oiled, Heracles banqueted until the night grew deep, lying on his lionskin and crowned with garlands. Afterward he entertained himself singing and plucking a lyre. He thought about lovely-tressed Iole and nursed revenge against her father for his ill-treatment.

In time the house steward entered with another flagon of fragrant Lesbian wine. Heracles noticed the old man's downcast face, and how he avoided looking him in the eye. "You look like you need a drink, my good man," said Heracles jovially, patting him on the shoulder. "Here, fill yourself a cup, and drink with me!" The servant, afraid to refuse, meekly poured some wine for himself. "Now tell me what this is all about. I heard someone's died. A distant relation of the king's perhaps?—but that is no reason for such gloom."

"A distant relative, you say, sir?" said the steward in distress. "She was not as distant as you think!  My lord must be very hospitable to admit such a light-hearted guest at such a time as this."

"And why shouldn't I be?" said Heracles, growing angry. "Admetos made no great fuss over this unknown woman—why should I?"

"Unknown!" ejaculated the exasperated steward.  He had been strictly warned by Admetos not to reveal the truth.  He turned to leave and said: "She was not unknown to us, sir."

Heracles sprang in front of him and shut the door.  "I think perhaps Admetos is keeping something from me.  You're not going anywhere until you tell me the truth," said Heracles, and would not release the old man until he revealed that Alcestis had died, and why.

At the news, the Heracles' heart was cut to the quick.  He put down his cup, and threw off the festive wreath of myrtle sprays that crowned his head, ashamed of his frivolity.  He paced about the room deep in thought.  "Has such a thing ever occurred in all the world?" roared Heracles.  "Is it even possible that Admetos could lose his wife, and yet show his friend such unsullied hospitality?  Hark!  The house is silent.  Where went the procession?"

"To the burial grounds, on the road to Larissa," said the steward.

Slipping on his lionskin, Heracles left the palace in haste and stumbled down the road.  When he reached the graveyard just before dawn, he found it empty and resounding with a mournful stillness.  Alcestis had already been interred.  Heracles did not have to search long for Alcestis' grave, newly dug, marked by a brightly painted marble monument depicting the noble woman in relief, seated, surrounded by her children.  On the base was inscribed:

NO GREATER GIFT DO GODS MEN SEND,
THAN SHE WHO IS BOTH WIFE AND FRIEND.

"Must death always be the victor?" said Heracles to himself. He considered once again descending into the underworld to bring back Alcestis as he cast his eyes about the mournful mounds and monuments overshadowed by still cypress trees. Presently he saw—or thought he saw—a shadow skulking behind the monuments. Heracles, crouching behind Alcestis' gravestone, witnessed the floating wisps of darkness swirl and coalesce and take the shape of a man hidden inside a black cloak and cowl. The gloomy figure knelt against the freshly-dug mound to lap up the sacrificial blood poured out during the funeral rites. Heracles' soul, initiated at Eleusis and aneled by his journey through the underworld, could now penetrate to things dark and divine.

Heracles flung off his lionskin, and in his booming voice cried: "Begone, foul Death, hateful to men and horror to the gods! You will not take her this night." He remembered from the Mysteries that, though a shade on sundering from the body can haunt the earth for three days, pitiless Thanatos—Death himself— never fails to claim his due.

Thanatos rose, a gruesome figure a cubit taller than Heracles. From his sleeves protruded gnarled, bony hands; and from within the cowl two baleful eyes on a wan, skeletal face peered at him.

"I have come for what belongs to me," said the daimon in a voice cold and harsh.

"I said begone!" repeated Heracles. "There is nothing here for you. It was not yet time for Alcestis, who is in the flower of her youth."

Thanatos laughed and said: "I win great honor when the victims are young."

"Even so," responded Heracles, "she died to save her husband; it would be a great injustice if you took her."

"One of this household has already escaped me. Shall another? Death is a debt which all must pay," said Thanatos.

"Very well," said Heracles, spitting in his hands. "If you want Alcestis, come and take."

With this Heracles leapt upon Thanatos and grappled with him, as he had done with Menoitios. The burial grounds shook and the monuments toppled by the fury of their engagement. Bony Thanatos was as hard as iron, and as strong as a lion. Every move that Heracles tried, Thanatos turned right around. It seemed Heracles had finally met his match. Cold arms locked around his neck and his breath drained way. But Heracles broke the icy grip in time and, jumping behind him, wrapped his arms around Thanatos' waist, picked him up, and dashed him to the ground. Three times, he did this; and then sitting upon his back, he applied an unbreakable strangulation hold that ended the contest. Since Thanatos could not die, Heracles maintained his hold until concession was unequivocal. Death, bitterly moaning, slunk away among the other graves and disappeared.

Heracles, although exhausted from the ordeal, pushed over Alcestis' monument, dug out the earth with his bare hands, stripped away the lid of the sarcophagus, and looked down at Alcestis' face, still lovely even in death. Observing no change in her after a long while, he thought the night had been a dream. He was about to replace the lid on the sarcophagus when suddenly, taking a greedy gulp of air, Alcestis opened her eyes just as first light began to chase away the gloom.

Heracles helped Alcestis out of the grave, and pulling her veil across her face, led her back to the palace. There he found Admetos, crouched upon the steps in abject misery, his head covered by a fold of his robe.

"Friend, you did wrong in not informing me of the death of your wife," said Heracles in a serious manner. "And here, like some common lout, I entered your house and feasted while it was filled with lamentations. I blame you for my impiety, Admetos. But since you are in such deep sorrow, I will not prolong my stay. I ask you only this: take this woman into your house and guard her for me for a little while, until I am back from Iolcos. I lately won her in a contest."

Admetos uncovered himself and looked up in surprise, wiping away his tears.

"You misunderstood me, Heracles," said he. "I meant you no offense. It would have grieved me doubly to have you turn to another man's hearth last night. You know the customs of the Thessalians! We honor our guests above all. (But this woman— how strange!—I almost see the form of Alcestis!) There are surely other households in Pherai to welcome her. She can't stay here. Looking at her, I feel the tears almost ready to gush from my eyes. Where would I keep her, in a house full of young men? Neither can I install her in my wife's chambers. The citizens would reproach me, thinking I had betrayed my wife, and on the day of her funeral!

By the gods—just take her away, if you please!  I am already a broken man.  Do not insult me further."

Heracles shook his head sorrowfully and answered: "O if only I could bring back your wife from the underworld as I did Cerberos!"

"I know you would do it if it was possible," said Admetos. "But how so?  The dead are nothing—are they not?—and cannot return to the light of day."

"How true," Heracles lamented.  "Why then sorrow over what cannot be changed?  You are still young.  Another wife will bring you cheer."

"Never!" said Admetos in horror.  "No woman shall ever lie again on my marriage-bed.  I lack even strength to enter my own house.  I cannot bear to hear the children calling for their mother."

"Your devotion is praiseworthy," said Heracles; "but refuse my request no longer.  Pray, take this woman into your house."

"How I wish you had not won this woman!" cried Admetos, but after being pressed, and unwilling to offend his friend, he called for a housemaid to conduct her to an apartment.

"Nay, I cannot leave her in the hands of slaves," said Heracles, a twinkle in his eye.  "Lead her in yourself!"

"I cannot touch this woman, Heracles!" said Admetos, rising up.  "I have accepted her—is that not enough?  Let her go in, or take her yourself."

Heracles would not hear of it.  After further argument, Admetos relented.  He reached out to take her hand, but with head askance.

"You hold her like she's made of fire," roared Heracles with delight.  "Are you sure you've gripped her hand?"

"Yes, can you not see?" replied Admetos, growing impatient.

"Then keep her," said Heracles, parting the veil to reveal Alcestis.  "You can never say I was an ungrateful guest!  Yes, look at her closely.  She does resemble your wife somewhat."

Admetos slowly turned his face—and behold, he saw his wife!  Incredulous and almost fainting from emotion, he said: "Are you really my wife Alcestis?—or a phantom?"

"This is indeed your wife," said Heracles.  "I fought Death last night for her, and I have the bruises to prove it.  She will not be able speak, however, until the dawn of the third day, when the bonds of death are finally loosed.  Take her now.  She is yours again."

Admetos clasped Alcestis in his arms and both wept for joy. Heracles went on his way, thinking that he had actually wrestled Death.  The truth, however, was that the infernal gods were so admiring of Alcestis' bravery, and so shocked at her untimely appearance before them, that they considered it no great improbity to send her back.

3

Heracles tarried a short time at Iolcos, where he found Peleus, once more in exile, at the court of Acastos. Acastos would have turned him away, smarting still from the murder of his father Pelias, had it not been for his wife Astydamia, who, secretly in love with the son of Aiacos, used all her womanly wiles to convince her husband to purify him of the death of Eurytion. In any event, Peleus was now, by his marriage to Antigone, the king of all Phthia and Acastos considered it prudent to maintain friendly relations with all the chieftains of Thessaly. When Heracles recounted a dim recollection of what the shade of Meleager had told him about the death of the sons of Thestios at the Calydonian hunt, Peleus said: "And you believed that lying spirit? What really happened was this. Meleager, lovesick over Atalanta since our days sailing on the *Argo*, presented her with the spoils: the head of the white-tusked boar and its bristly hide. This certainly angered us all, and set us murmuring. Two sons of Thestios, outraged, went so far as to snatch the prizes from her hands, saying that Meleager had no right to give them. Meleager, gnashing his teeth in uncontrolled fury, cried: 'Watch me teach you the difference between deeds and threats, you who dare claim another's rights!' and drove his spear-blade through Plexippos' heart. Toxeus, hesitating nearby, wishing to avenge his brother but not at the expense of his life, shared the same fate when Meleager likewise warmed his spear in his blood."

Around this time it was reported to king Eurytos of Oechalia that twelve of his prized brood-mares, along with twelve mule-colts, still at their udders, disappeared from his herds on the hills outside Oechalia. Eurytos at once accused Heracles of the theft, considering he had done it out of revenge for being slighted over Iole. Iphitos once more came to the Tyrinthian's defense, claiming that though Heracles could be accused of being headstrong and violent, there never was an instant where he was said to have indulged in thievery.  His brothers rebutted him by pointing out how it was told that Heracles despoiled Geryones of his famous cattle, to which Iphitos replied that Heracles had done so under authority, and so acted out of duty rather than license.  Iphitos, intent on absolving Heracles, took on himself the responsibility of finding the missing horses.  After searching around much of Euboea, he learned that the team was seen being driven into the mainland.  He made the circuit of the Peloponnese, inquiring at major towns in Argolis, southern Arcadia and even venturing into Lacedaimonia.  At Pherai, while staying at the home of Orsilochos, he made the acquaintance of a youth named Odysseus, the son of Laertes of Ithaca.  Odysseus had been sent by his father to obtain reparations from the Messenians, who had raided flocks and even herdsmen from his island.  Finding they shared a common purpose over the loss of property, the two became fast friends.  On parting, Iphitos gave Odysseus his father's backsprung bow, which he had wielded since his youth.  In return Odysseus gave Iphitos a sharp sword and stout lance.  Iphitos resumed his search for his father's mares, doubling back through Arcadia to take the road to Argos and Tyrins across mount Parthenion.

Heracles, on his way back from Iolcos, by chance met Iphitos at a crossroads.  Bidding him surmount his chariot, he brought him to the gates of Tyrins.  When Heracles inquired what brought Iphitos to the area, the latter rather tactfully explained the issue of the missing mares, without intimating the possibility of Heracles' involvement, since, though increasingly suspicious, he could not bring himself to subscribe to it.  He merely asked Heracles for his assistance in locating them.  Heracles listened quietly to this discourse.  He had regarded the son of Eurytos with fondness over his support of his case for Iole; but something about the man's overly cautious demeanor discomfited him.  When Iphitos, over supper, talked of nothing other than the mares, Heracles grew sullen since Iphitos, through veiled and florid words, let slip hints of his hidden suspicions.

Afterwards, flush with wine, Heracles led Iphitos up the Cyclopean walls of Tyrins to the highest tower of the palace.

Heracles, waving a hand to show him the surrounding grasslands, said: "I shall be delighted to assist you in finding the mares. Tell me, do you see them grazing anywhere?"

Iphitos, bracing against the battlements, looked down from the dizzying height and said: "I do not see them."

"But you believe they are somewhere here?" said Heracles.

"Indeed," said Iphitos. "I have carefully followed their trail."

Heracles, his mood darkening said: "Tell me, then, and do not refuse me a plain answer. Do you think I had a hand in this?"

"Gods forbid!" cried Iphitos quickly. "My father was quick to blame you, but not I! It was perhaps that famed thief Autolycos who did it!"

"Yet I have good cause to take them, do I not, over the issue of Iole?" asked Heracles.

"You certainly would!" stammered Iphitos, feeling hemmed in on the narrow parapet.

"Then you betray yourself!" Heracles stormed. "Why else would you come to Tyrins if you did not believe I was the culprit? Dog-faced liar! you will pay for your false accusation!"

With that, Heracles, by a shove, caused Iphitos to tumble from the wall. His head cracked like an egg on the flagstones below and his brains gushed out. Heracles peered down at the sprawled corpse. Unable to comprehend what had just occurred, he remained standing there, whipped by the winds, until his anger, fueled by the present slight as well as Iole's loss, subsided. He looked down a second time at the body of Iphitos and shook his head at the young man's demise, absent a full realization that he had caused it.

Heracles retired to his apartment to sleep. Only in the morning, upon first waking, was he afflicted with remorse. He went out and buried Iphitos, building a barrow for him besides the great walls. His purification at Eleusis had been undone by one rash act. When word got out of the murder, the people of Tyrins begged him to leave at once and seek expiation from the High King lest his presence bring calamity upon the city. But Heracles would countenance no such thing, wishing never again to become beholden to Eurystheus. He therefore packed his satchel and set out, and on the road met with his young cousin Oinos, son of Licymnios, one of his playmates as a child, who had come from Thebes for a visit after hearing from Alcmene that Heracles had accomplished his Labors.    Licymnios was a half-brother of Alcmene, who had gone into exile with Amphytrion to Thebes after the death of Electryon and married Amphytrion's sister Perimede. Oinos was duly aggrieved on hearing of Heracles' plight. Believing Heracles' contention that Hera had maddened him once again, as on the day he killed his children, Oinos pledged his unqualified assistance.  Heracles first asked him to accompany him to Thebes where he could submit to Creon.  Oinos dissuaded him from this idea, arguing that Creon was old, distempered, and could hardly be counted on to forgive the murderer of his grandchildren another violent episode.  Was he not pitiless in keeping the blind Oidipos still a prisoner?  Heracles knew well the circumstances.  After coming to the throne of Thebes, Laios, son of Abdacos, plagued by childlessness, sought counsel from the Delphic Oracle.  He received the grim answer that any child born to his wife Iocaste would become his murderer.  This curse, it is said, came from his abduction of Chrysippos, Pelops' son, from Pisa.  Thereafter, Laios kept distance from his wife; but one night, drunk with wine, he had union with her, which resulted in the birth of a man-child. Unwilling to tempt fate, Laios took the child from his nurse, pierced his feet with a brooch-pin, and binding them together so he could not crawl away had exposed him on Mount Cithairon.

There the herdsmen of king Polybos of Corinth came across the foundling and entrusted him to the king's wife Periboea, childless herself, who nursed him to health and passed him off as her own son, calling him Oidipos because of his swollen feet.

Coming to manhood, Oidipos surpassed all other youths in strength and courage.  But when they jealously taunted him, questioning his birth, he set out for Delphi to discover the truth. The oracle warned him not to return to his country, since he was destined to murder his father and have union with his mother. Believing that he had really been born to Periboea, he decided to avert the prophesied disaster by not returning to Corinth.

After leaving Delphi, as he was riding through Phocis toward Daulis, it happened that at the Cleft Way, where three roads met, he encountered king Laios, on his way again to Delphi after prodigies pointed to his imminent death at his son's hands.  As the midmost road was very narrow, Laios' charioteer Polyphontes rudely ordered Oidipos to move aside.  When he refused,

Polyphontes killed one of his horses. As Oidipos jumped off his chariot, Laios ordered Polyphontes to drive on, bruising Oidipos' foot with a chariot-wheel. Enraged, Oidipos slew Polyphontes with his spear, dragged down Laios, and—not knowing he was his father—killed him. After Oidipos fled the scene, Damesistratos, king of Plataia, found the bodies and buried them under a mound of uncut stones, which can be seen to this day.

With Laios' killer still unknown and at large, Creon, brother of Iocaste, succeeded to the throne of Thebes. Not long afterward the Sphinx, offspring of Typhon and Echidne, flew into Thebes, perched upon nearby Mount Phicium, and terrorized the region. The monster, hideously composed of a woman's face and breast, a lion's feet and tail, and a bird's wings, made a bargain with Creon: she would depart only if someone correctly answered a certain riddle she had learned from the Muses. Creon therefore made a proclamation that any who could answer the Sphinx would be rewarded with the kingdom and the hand of the late king's widow Iocaste. Many came to try their luck, including Creon's own son, Haimon, but none could solve the riddle, and were devoured.

When Oidipos, who had been wandering around Phocis and Boetia, heard the call, he straightway went to Thebes and confronted the Sphinx, who posed to him the following:

> *What thing of one voice be*
> *That has four feet, then two, then three?*

After pondering for a moment, Oidipos confidently said: "The answer is plainly Man: for as a babe he crawls on all fours, walks upright as an adult, and resorts to a walking-stick in old age." The Sphinx became so distraught that she leapt to her death into the rocky valley below.

The Thebans, in gratitude, proclaimed Oidipos king. He unwittingly married his mother Iocaste, who bore him two sons, Eteocles and Polyneices; and two daughters, Antigone and Ismene.

A plague of barrenness, affecting man and beast, fell on Thebes for this pollution. Oidipos sent Creon to consult the Delphic Oracle, which replied that the murderer of Laios had to be expelled from Thebes. Oidipos pronounced a curse on the unknown criminal, ordering him banished when found. The blind seer Teiresias then appeared at the court to reveal Oidipos' guilt in killing his father and becoming heir to his bed. No one believed him until news came from Corinth of Polybos' death. Subsequently, Periboea visited Oidipos and confirmed the truth of his adoption. A final proof was provided by the man who had exposed him, Menoetes, who identified Oidipos as son of Laios by the scars on his ankles.

Oidipos, realizing that he had participated in such atrocious crimes, tore a brooch from his mother's garment and pricked his eyes. Meanwhile Iocaste, unable to bear the shame and grief, hanged herself.

As Oidipos' children were not yet of age, the throne devolved once again on Creon, who kept Oidipos a prisoner in the palace lest news spread of the disgrace. But his sons hated him; and he cursed them for placing the silver table and golden goblet of Cadmos before him, thus reminding him of his birth; and for serving him meat from the haunch rather than the shoulder.

And so Heracles instead pinned his hope on king Neleus, who would not refuse him, seeing that two of his sons, Nestor and Periclymenos, were his comrades aboard the *Argo*.

They crossed Arcadia in Oinos' swift chariot. Along the way Heracles killed a Centaur he had driven from mount Pholoë, Homados, who, it was reported, had once attempted to ravish Eurystheus' sister Alcyone. Those who later heard of this marveled at Heracles' virtue, since he performed a good deed even for an enemy. Arriving at Sandy Pylos, Nestor received Heracles warmly, Periclymenos less so, and brought him before the aged Neleus. The king did not remember how he had once sacrificed with Heracles when the latter was on his way to Erytheia; but after having his mind refreshed by the eloquent discourse of his youngest son, Neleus did not forget the compulsion of hospitableness and entertained the guests in his well-appointed manor. When Heracles at last stated the object of his visit, Neleus listened gravely. In response, the king said gruffly: "I must by all means refuse to purify you. While I have no reason to dispute your honor, seeing in what high regard my son Nestor holds you, you have nevertheless killed the son of Eurytos, my close ally. As we must always endeavor, according to ancient dictum, to succor our friends and bring harm to our enemies, I must, as friend of Eurytos, henceforth consider you also my enemy." Nestor impassionedly tried to persuade Neleus to reconsider; but the king, in retiring from the hall, made it clear that Heracles was to be gone by the morning. Heracles, though outraged, maintained his composure for the sake of Nestor, and departed with Oinos that very night.

Oinos now urged Heracles to seek an audience with Hippocoön, the king of Sparta. Heracles at first refused, since he held Hippocoön in low esteem. On the death of his father Oibalos, Hippocoön, on pretense of being the oldest, seized the throne and banished his brothers and half-brothers: among them, Tyndareos, father of the Dioscuri, who fled to Aetolia to the court of Thestios and subsequently married the princess Leda. Oinos countered that since Hippocoön and his twelve sons were all men of violence, Heracles would find among them a sympathetic ear. Given that Heracles, weighed with guilt, was running out of options, he agreed to venture to Sparta.

The chief city of the Lacedaimonians was situatd in the upper valley of the river Eurotas. As they looked down into the valley and saw the city, Heracles, underwhelmed, remarked: "Is this the greatest city of Laconia? Though the land is exceeding beautiful and fertile, with the slopes covered in vineyards, wheat fields and olive-groves, I see nothing but some villages and edifices spread out on low hills, with no great walls to defend it." Though his travels had taken him throughout the world, he had never before been to the celebrated city, built on a number of contiguous hills and an adjoining plain that stretched to the right bank of the river. Oinos responded: "The Spartans have no need to hem themselves behind walls. As you can see, the lofty ramparts of these two mountain ranges, the Taygetos and the Parnon, rising on either side, gird this valley." They continued on along the left bank of the tranquil river, teeming with white swans. A bridge spanned the Eurotas, passing over a small island overgrown with oleander. The road led into a shrouded hollow through the opposite bank of hills. Under a temple to Athena, built on a lofty hill rising from thick woods, the way passed directly into the spacious market-place, surrounded by marble colonnades and public buildings. Here the two friends parted while Oinos sought to have mended the splintered felloe of one of his chariot-wheels. Heracles proceeded down the principal street toward the southern and more level part of the city, and there found the palace of Hippocoön, as unimpressive as the rest of the city, since the Spartans were unconcerned with personal luxuries and lived frugally. Hippocoön, who was disdainful of all strangers, received Heracles grudgingly, and then evinced a marked discourtesy when he realized Heracles had kept company with the Dioscuri. He at once accused Heracles of being an agent for Tyndareos, seeking his overthrow. As the argument grew heated, a commotion outside distracted them. Heracles ran out and saw Oinos lying bloodied and near death. When he angrily demanded to know what had transpired, one of the sons of Hippocoön came forward and said: "When we saw this knave loitering outside the manor, gazing at it like a plotting housebreaker, my bothers sent out our great Molossian hound against him. He threw a stone at the bitch; thereupon the twelve of us ran out in force, armed with cudgels, and gave him his just desserts." At this the sons of Hippocoön made merry with crude jests. Heracles was so enraged that with his club aloft he charged against them. Lycon managed to wound his hand with a lucky arrow; while another, Hippothoös, clipped his hip-joint with a spear-thrust. Soundly outnumbered and dripping blood, Heracles fled from their midst. Mounting his friend's chariot, with cries and frenzied lashes of goad and reins, he wheeled about, leaving the sons of Hipoccoön in his wake, white with stirred-up dust. But they scrambled to their own chariots to pursue him.

Heracles rode hard out of the valley, losing himself in the wilderness of the Taygetos, the haunt of wild animals. In the shadow of the mountain peak called Taletum, where sacrifices of horses are made to the Sun, Heracles found a sanctuary of Demeter. There he took refuge, and was hidden by the healer Asclepios while treating his wounds with the salutary juice of the mistletoe-berry. Asclepios, so he told Heracles during his convalescence, was the son of Apollo and Coronis, daughter of Phlegyas, the king of the Lapiths. Apollo, who loved her, left a raven to superintend her while he was away. Although with child, the madness of love made Coronis share her bed with an Arcadian prince. The raven at once flew to Delphi to tattle to Apollo the notice of her treachery. The raging god slew the maiden on the high bank of Lake Boebis, filling her bosom with his deadly arrows. "Your punishment is meet!" cried Coronis as her life-blood slipped away; "but why did you not wait until my labor?—alas an innocent dies with me!" Too late Apollo regretted his jealous act. He cursed the meddling raven, turning its plumage, white as that of doves hitherto, black. And when he saw Coronis lying on the high funeral pyre, her body wrapped in flames, his tearless sorrow broke anew: for no tears may ever a god's cheeks bedew. He anointed her breast with fragrant myrrh; and after completing the appropriate rites, watched in despair as ashes swirled with the smoke. Unable to bear, however, the destruction of his offspring, he at the final moment reached into the fire to pluck the unborn from the womb, naming him Asclepios. To windy Pelion Apollo sent him to be tutored by Cheiron in the healing arts.

On hearing this, Heracles declared: "Why—I remember you now! You were that quiet boy who sat at the back of Cheiron's cave crushing herbs or mixing potions while the rest of us sharpened our lances and learned to hunt the wild things of the wood. I am grateful now that you serve mankind in a different way than I." In gratitude for his kind words, Asclepios gave Heracles a brazen reliquary containing what he called a lock of the Gorgon's hair. He carried also with him two phials of Gorgon blood, given to him by Athena. One contained blood that flowed from the veins on the left side, which could put people to death; and the other held blood from the right side, which could save their lives. Asclepios, however, would not part with either of these relics.

Heracles healed completely in short order, although he still retained a small scar in the hollow of his right hand. Asclepios, sensing Heracles' distress of soul over the death of Iphitos, recommended that he seek purification from Deiphobos of Amyclai, who was a well-known and pious priest of Apollo.

(Long afterward, when Artemis, chasing game in the wooded slopes of Troizen, heard the crash, she feared the worst and sped down to cradle Hippolytos' broken body in her arms. She remembered then how Asclepios had revivified a son of Minos who had fallen in a vat full of honey. She begged him to repeat the miracle. Although he was afraid to offend the gods again by breaking the bonds of death for another person, he felt pity for the virgin goddess. Opening his phial of Gorgon blood, taken from the veins of Medusa's right side, he applied the blood as an unguent, and incanting certain charms, raised Hippolytos from the dead.

Artemis, overjoyed, enveloped her mortal companion in a thick cloud and whisked him to her sacred grove in Hesperian Aricia. Hades thereon registered a complaint with Zeus that he was being unjustly robbed of his subjects. The Fates—Clotho the Spinner, Lachesis the lot-giver and Atropos the Cutter—sided with Hades, for if the gods were not allowed to change the destiny they wove, how could mortals? Zeus understood the gravity of the situation. With a thunderbolt he killed Asclepios, making good on his original threat.)

The town of Amyclai was situated upon a hill only twenty stades south of Sparta. Although horrified that Heracles had murdered his own guest, Deiphobos nevertheless agreed to expiate and purify Heracles of his blood-guilt at the command of Apollo, who envisioned a greater penance for him in the days to come. Deiphobos had Heracles first wade into the reeds that grew thickly along the river-bank and immerse his blood-stained hands in mud, after which he had to rinse himself in the river-water. Then, to complete the ceremony for such a heinous crime, he sacrificed a piglet and had Heracles laver his hands again in the animal's blood.

At the conclusion of the purificatory rites, Heracles felt no better. Guilt still fettered him. He wished once more to experience the peace of mind he had found at Eleusis. He returned to Tyrins and for subsequent nights was plagued by evil dreams. Then, one morning, he awoke to find his body afflicted with sores. Heracles was certain the ghost of Iphitos was haunting him and ordered his servants to fumigate the palace with brimstone. The sores afterward turned into oozing boils. In desperation Heracles set out for Delphi to inquire from the Oracle an end to his troubles.

Heracles auspiciously arrived at Delphi when the Oracle was in session, since only certain days in the month were set apart for this purpose. As there was a large throng of suppliants waiting, lots were drawn to determine the order of admittance. Since the magistrates easily recognized in the crowd the towering figure of Heracles, they gave him the honor of bypassing all others. After paying the customary fee, Heracles had to purchase a goat, which he turned over to the priests for scrutiny. Pouring water on the goat and seeing it tremble, the priests pronounced it healthy and a good victim. Heracles sacrificed it, wholly burning the remains on an altar stacked high with fir-wood. Then, wearing a laurel-garland decorated with wool ribands, Heracles approached the priests in the porch of the sanctuary and in confidence requested how to rid himself of his affliction. The priests then entered the sanctuary.

Heracles did not have to wait long before the priests returned with harried looks. One of them said: "The Pythia refuses to answer your question, saying that she has no oracles for one who murders his friends!"

Heracles, whose itching sores and lack of sleep had plunged him into a severe distemper, wagged a finger at them and cried: "No oracles for me you say? Then I shall institute an oracle of my own!" Thrusting the priests aside he stormed into the temple. In the center, over a small chasm in the living rock sat the Pythia Xenoclea upon a high tripod. When she saw the sacred precinct invaded by one with such dogged determination, she leapt from the tripod in alarm. Heracles accosted her: "No oracles for me? You were not so reticent when you sent me off to labor for Eurystheus! Give me an answer, or I shall plunder this place for good!" The enclosure was fragrant with laurel burnt as incense. Xenoclea raised her arms and pleaded: "Hurt me not! I am only an agent of the god!" The chasm suddenly belched that noxious smoke by which the Pythia, inhaling it deeply, delivered her revelations. The reeking vapor wafted through Heracles, who was standing over the opening, and for a moment he grew delirious and saw strange visions. The Pythia, meanwhile, fled into the innermost sanctuary to take refuge before the golden statue of Apollo and the altar upon which burned an eternal flame. Intoxicated by the exhalation, Heracles teetered like a tree shaken by the wind. He shook his head vigorously to clear his addled brains, and grasping a leg of the tripod, carried it off with him, making good on his threat to found his own oracle. The priests, the Delphian magistrates, and the temple guard, however, barred his way at the door. When Heracles threatened to smash the tripod over their heads, the high priest of Apollo, moved by religious fervor, jumped into the fray and grasped the tripod by another leg. There then ensued a struggle as Heracles pulled the tripod one way and the high priest, no small man himself, pulled in another. When the tripod was on the point of shivering, the tussle was interrupted by a sudden thunderbolt, which, striking in midst of the sanctuary porch, left eyes blinded and ears ringing. As it was a clear day, even Heracles recognized the omen of Zeus the Thunderer and desisted, releasing the tripod to the custody of the high priest. Then a voice, augmented by divine authority, resounded from the midst of the sanctuary. The Pythia, kneeling over the chasm, her hair streaming in a new blast of augural effluvium, sang:

*Father Zeus is filled with wrath*
*That you have chosen this ill path.*
*For by sempiternal dictate,*
*He holds a guest inviolate.*
*To end the reign of foul disease,*
*Ill dreams and blains that so displease,*
*You must again descend to be*
*A bondsman for time triennially*
*And the price your slavery'll fetch*
*T'will be for the sons of that poor wretch*
*You impiously cast from th'looming wall*
*And came to perish from the fall.*
*Be off far across land and sea!*
*Slave now of mighty queen Omphale!*

Heracles said not another word. Accepting his fate, with his head lowered, he left the temple muttering an oath of revenge upon Eurytos as the author of his present misfortune. The Pythia then two more verses sang:

*Tyrinthian Heracles, a different sort,*
*From th'Egyptian one, of kindlier port.*

(By which she meant that when in ancient times the Egyptian Heracles visited Delphi, he conducted himself with more decorum.)

4

King Eurystheus was more than pleased to convey Heracles across the sea at his own expense, sending his trusted herald Copreus to arrange the transaction with the Maionians. Copreus, wearing a golden ambassadorial robe and holding aloft his herald's wand wrapped with yellow wool, was first to step out on the quay at Smyrna, leading Heracles in fetters. At the market-place he sought out the agents of the Maionian queen, and, informing them of the pronouncements of the Delphic Oracle, artfully commanded a princely sum of three talents for Heracles, without informing them of his identity. They first balked at the price, until Copreus ordered Heracles to lift up the side of a loaded wagon with one hand; they were then confident that the queen would reward them for their astute purchase of such a strong-armed slave. Heracles said not a word during the exchange, wracked with apprehension that, as he could eat whatever he wished while serving Eurystheus; now, in a much different circumstance, he had to content himself with a slave's meager barley-cake rations. On returning to Greece, Copreus promptly remitted the three talents to Eurytos, who as promptly refused it, saying that only blood could pay for blood. Copreus did not press the point, and returning home, happily paid it into his master's treasury.

Queen Omphale, daughter of Iardanos, had lately inherited the throne from her husband Tmolos. While hunting on Mount Carmarorium, he grew enamored of the huntress Arrhippe, a disciple of Artemis. She fled to her patron's sanctuary, where Tmolos impiously ravished her upon the goddess' very couch. In shame, Arrhippe hung herself from a beam. Thereon, the outraged goddess sent a mad bull after Tmolos. Taken by surprise and tossed in the air by the bull, he fell on sharp scree and broke his neck. His son by a previous marriage, Theoclymenos, buried him on the great mountain in the center of Maionia, renaming it Mount Tmolos.

Sharing a wagon with other newly purchased slaves and wares that had been traded for gold, saffron and sweet, black Maionian wine, Heracles was conveyed to the capital city of Sipylos, situated on the eastern slope of a mountain of the same name, between Smyrna and the river Hermos. Once at the royal palace, the slaves were herded into an enclosure beside a sty while they awaited their new assignments. Heracles, being the strongest of the lot, was tasked to plough the queen's extensive farmlands. Commanding a team of enormous oxen, which he yoked himself to an oaken stock, he laid straight furrows from dawn to dusk each day; and each night he retired to the slaves' hovel to eat his scanty meal and sleep. Through hard toil he was gradually relieved of his afflictions. During this time he learned much about the Maionians, finding them very much like the Greeks in custom and temperament, except that the common people prostituted their unwed daughters, by which means they had an opportunity to accumulate their dowries.

The taskmasters, realizing the value of Heracles' indefatigable labor, soon set him to dig dikes and design waterworks to better irrigate the fields during the hot summer months after the first appearance of Orion's Dog. Discarding his lionskin, Heracles worked bare-chested in the fields. One day, Queen Omphale wished to see the extent and quality of her demesne and was conveyed on a palanquin to a hill from which she could view the laborers. At once she spotted Heracles as the sunlight gleamed on his dripping sweat, employed in breaking through rooted boles and tough roots, his enormous musculature rippling with every swing of his Amazonian double-axe. At her word she was brought near Heracles. Omphale, parting the curtains of her litter, called: "You there—what is your name?" Heracles, catching sight first of her golden sandals and delicate feet, dared not look any further. With head bowed, he responded: "I am just a slave, O queen: a living slave." Omphale, admiring the perfection of his physique, said with a laugh: "You're as strong as an ox, and as big as a bear—and as hairy as one too!" The jest pleased Heracles. Growing bolder, he cast a surreptitious eye at the queen and felt stung by her beauty. Her jeweled coronet barely contained her golden locks, flowing down past her shoulders like an Arcadian spring, twined with roses and while lilies. Her long neck, encircled with gemstones set in mother-of-pearl, graced bare shoulders wrapped in a fragrant, silken gown. Her eyes, the color of cinnamon, fluttered like startled butterflies; and she spoke thus to the overseers through lips as red and glistening as pierced pomegranates: "Let others work the fields; I wish him for a man-servant." Settling back into her fragrant bolsters, she was carried back to the city.

Omphale delighted in observing Heracles perform the house-chores. Merrily and without complaint, he butchered meat, scrubbed the kitchens, carried water and emptied the cooking-pots. "Alcides," Omphale said to him, using the only name she knew him by, "what reward do you expect for your faithful service?" To this, Heracles, smiling graciously, responded, "The pleasure of being near you, O queen, is reward enough for me." Omphale, blushing like a maiden on her marriage-night, said: "I see, Alcides, how you look with longing at the blue sky and the greensward each time you pass a window with a heavy pot in your arms. You were not made for house-work, but for heady undertakings. If I give you a bit of freedom, do you promise to return to me? Since my husband's passing, lawlessness has festered throughout the land. Malefactors have been emboldened, perhaps, by the fact that I am a woman and have not as firm a grip on authority and justice as had Tmolos. I wish you, therefore, to go forth and rid Maionia of all manner of bandits and ruffians."

The new assignment delighted Heracles. Donning his lion-skin, he first cut for himself a new cudgel out of a yew sapling, light but strong. Then, requesting a bow and quiver from the royal armory, he set out as Omphale had commanded looking for adventure. He had not gone far when he came across a force of Itones plundering Omphale's lands. Rousing the local populace, who armed themselves with clubs, mattocks and whatever other utensils were available, he drove the Itones off as far as their own city, which he razed for good measure. Recovering the spoils, he distributed it among the citizens until all were made whole.

On his way back to Sipylos, flush with success, Heracles grew tired and fell asleep under a tree near Ephesus. Feeling a slight tug at his arm, under which his weapons rested for security, he awoke to find a pair of unbearably ugly, pot-bellied gnomish figures trying to rob him. Had it been darker, he would have taken them—covered everywhere in yellow hair, with long arms, upturned noses, and brows furrowed like a crones' wrinkles—for clever and dexterous Libyan apes. These were two of the Cercopes, thievish vagabonds who went about the world stirring trouble. Heracles reached out a long arm and caught the one called Olos by the throat. The other, Eurybatos, he tripped with a leg as he tried to flee and pinned him under his foot. Heracles thought to kill them, but as they had done him no harm, and had such a droll appearance, he decided to allow Omphale to decide their fate. He trussed them screeching and screaming, hung each one head-downward from the ends of his club, and carried them off on his shoulders swinging like milk-pails. After a little distance, the Cercopes' frantic cries of protest turned to uproarious laughter. Heracles, who thought the amusement came at his expense, demanded to know the cause of the sudden diversion. After Olos, suspended behind Heracles, caught his breath, he said: "Our good mother always told us: 'Ware the great Blackbuttock!'" "And who is that?" asked Heracles. "Why, sirrah, since your buttocks are so hairy, and as sun-blackened as an old piece of leather—it must be you!" cried Eurybatos, at which the Cercopes erupted in a fresh round of laughter. On hearing this absurdity, Heracles too was overcome with so much merriment that he had to sit upon a rock to steady himself. The Cercopes, taking advantage of his good humor, persuaded Heracles to release them, promising never again to rob or commit any evil acts in Maionia. It was said they kept true to their promise, but going to another place they tried to defraud Zeus himself, who turned them into stones, or else, as some say, monkeys.

Omphale, hearing of a cruel vine-dresser named Syleus, a son of Poseidon, who seized passing strangers and forced them to dig in his vineyard, sent Heracles to look into the matter. Heracles, pretending to be lost, wandered into Syleus' farmstead, where he saw numerous poor wretches, malnourished and unrecompensed, laboring among the vines. Syleus, seeing Heracles, thought that he had found a hireling worth his weight, and, since compelling the hero was out of the question, falsely promised him a tidy gold sum to till his orchard. Given a mattock, Heracles set to work. When

Syleus went away that afternoon to conduct business, Heracles dismissed the other workers from their bondage and then tore up all the vines by the roots.  Packing most of the vine-wood into a stout wheel-barrow, he brought it to the manor-house, where, feeling hungry after a hard day's work, he set the pile on fire to roast bread and meat.  Selecting Syleus' finest bull, he sacrificed it to Zeus the Hospitable.  Slicing and spitting the meat, he cooked it in the fire until the fat fairly crackled.  Missing drink, he wandered about the house trying to locate the cellar door, which he broke open to bring up a fine two-handled wine-jar.  Xenodike, Syleus' unmarried daughter, hearing the noise, ran off to find her father.

Heracles happily feasted when Syleus appeared at the door, indignantly demanding an explanation.

"To your health!" said Heracles, raising his cup.  "Come and sit!"

Syleus, filled with rage, shut his ears, gnashed his teeth and hurled curses at Heracles for the space of an hour.  Heracles continued eating in the face of such incivility.  When he was done, he sprung from his chair, mattock in hand, and in one downward stroke crushed Syleus' head.  When he looked about for his club and lionskin, he found them missing from where he had laid them aside before starting his supper.  Through an open window he happened to see Xenodike running away with them.  Heracles dashed out of the door and bawled for her stop her pilfery; but as she refused to heed him, Heracles drew his bow, and taking aim, grazed her thigh with an arrow.  He had meant only to arrest her flight by a slight flesh-wound, but when he went to recover his belongings, she had bled to death.  As the homicide, by the nature of its precipitation, was entirely justified, Heracles felt no concern at all about her ghost, especially since the victim had been merely a woman.

Heracles roamed far and wide in the service of Omphale.  It is said that he ventured into the uncharted lands at the world's eastern reach.  The people there are similar to the Ethiopians in appearance, being dark-complected, but possess straight hair.  These Ethiopians who live toward the rising sun are very numerous and wealthy.  While there, Heracles wedded many wives, but had only one daughter, whom he called Pandaia.  He gave her five hundred oliphants and a necklace of sea-pearl, which he discovered while trolling the seashore. These people record that Heracles, whom they called Dirsanes, thrice assaulted a certain rock called Aornos, washed by a river called the Indus, but was repulsed. A certain tribe, called the Sibai, claims it is descended from those that accompanied Heracles on his expeditions, and, like Heracles, wear animal skins, carry clubs, and use the brand of a cudgel to mark their beasts of burden. Others relate how Heracles subdued the land in the company of Dionysos. But it is evident, given the circumstances, that these accounts are mere fables, unless it was the Egyptian Heracles, and not the Theban one, who accomplished these things.

Heracles did, however, venture into neighboring Phrygia. On the road beside the river Meander he saw a figure familiar by his fox-skin cloak and syrinx hanging from his belt. "Friend Heracles!" cried the herdsman Daphnis son of Hermes, who had sung with the sweetest notes the story of Demeter and Core when Heracles and Iolaos found themselves on the island of Trinacria during his tenth Labor. Looking closely at Heracles, he said: "I see by the glow upon your brow that you are no longer a stranger to the Mysteries." Bounding up to him, Heracles declared: "I drank the drink! And you—what brings you here so far from your own land? And why the forlorn look?"

Daphnis answered: "I come here seeking my beloved Pimplea, who was abducted by pirates and, I have discovered, sold as a slave to a Phrygian landowner named Lityerses."

Lityerses, another brazen abuser of hospitality, was a bastard son of king Midas. Midas once possessed an astounding gift: he was able to turn anything he touched into pure, soft, yellow gold. The old fat Satyr Silenos, having strayed away from the retinue of his foster-son Dionysos as the latter passed through Asia, fell fast asleep in the mountains of Phrygia after consuming large amounts of wine. Found by some rustics, who feared his half-goat appearance, they bound him and took him to Midas at the city of Pessinus, by the upper course of the river Sangarios, from where he ruled. Having once participated in the Mysteries, Midas recognized his esteemed prisoner, set him free, and afforded him all honors. For ten continuous days they celebrated a festival, and on the eleventh Midas assisted Silenos in rejoining Dionysos. The wine-god, rejoicing to have his foster-father back safe and sound, offered

Midas any gift he desired. Midas, not long in thinking said: "Grant that whatsoever I touch should be turned to gold!" The god reluctantly fulfilled his request, concerned that Midas, prey to his avarice, had not asked for something nobler. Off went Midas rejoicing in his new power, testing it by touching whatever he came across. The green twig of an oak-branch became gold. An apple, falling into his hand, would have fooled a Hesperide by its sublimation. Even a clod of earth, touched by his fingers, hardened into the precious metal. But when he sat at his table, the bread and the meat he hungrily grasped became gold; and the wine he tried to drink dribbled down his chin molten. No longer did he find pleasure in his magical gift, but cursed it, for now he was rich but perennially hungry and parched with thirst. After pleading to the god, Dionysos appeared to tell him that, to rid himself of the gift, he should seek the source of the river Pactolus, high in the Lydian hills, and in that tumbling fountain immerse his head and body. Midas obeyed, and from his lustration the river assumed the golden touch, ever afterward awashing the banks in shiny electrum.

After this, still encumbered with a loathing of wealth, Midas stravaged through fields and woods, worshipping the god Pan. One day, during a musical contest between Pan and Apollo, where one god pitted his fitted reeds against the other's lyre, Midas sided with the horned son of Hermes. Apollo, thinking that ears so dull should scarcely keep their human form, punished Midas by changing their form and function. His ears lengthened and grew shaggy, and from that moment wore those of the plodding ass. Shocked and embarrassed, Midas sought to hide his deformity under the folds of a purple turban. His slave-barber, privy to the secret shame, dared tell no one, but at same time burst for the telling. He dug a hole in the ground and buried in it words of the appalling, yet risible sight. In time reeds grew thickly there that, when stirred by the breeze, betrayed their sower by soughing his buried whispers.

Now, Lityerses was a big eater who daily consumed three ass-loads of bread, and was fond of calling his wine-cup, which held the quantity of three full wine-jars, but a trifling measure. He would offer hospitality to wayfarers, and when they had been comfortably set in their new lodgment, forced them to compete against him in a harvesting-contest. He waited for their strength to flag, and beat them with a whip. In the evening, having handily won the contest, he beheaded them and disposed of their bodies in sheaves.

Although Heracles proffered the assistance of his strong arm, Daphnis, who eschewed all forms of violence, wished to strictly adhere to gentlemanly negotiation and so continued on his way. Nevertheless, Heracles followed him closely, reluctant to leave an acquaintance in a lurch.

When Daphnis arrived at Celainai, situated on a high cliff at the sources of the Meander, Lityerses received him at his estate, lavished on him every conviviality, and allowed him to see Pimplea. He promised, however, to release her to his custody only if Daphnis competed against him in reaping the harvest. As Daphnis was a shepherd, and unused to manual labor of that sort, he feared to lose the contest, and thus Pimplea. But he could not refuse. As he was about join Lityerses in the field, Heracles appeared and offered to take his place. Taking a reaping-hook, Heracles indefatigably mowed the fertile banks of the Meander, where the wheat-stalks grew as tall as a man, easily surpassing the work of Lityerses. When Lityerses late in the day caught up to him, Heracles, who had beforehand seen evidence of Lityerses' crimes among the wheat-shocks, clove his neck with a sickle and cast the trunk in the river. To Pimplea he gave Lityerses' manor-house as a dowry, and leaving the happy couple, proceeded on his way.

The Phrygians begged Heracles not to depart from their land until he had done something about a gigantic serpent that slithered about the muddy banks of the river Sangaros, destroying crops and eating any men who came near. From a hill, Heracles saw the serpent and shot it dead with an arrow, piercing its scales. In this river there is a found a stone, which after the setting of the Pleiades is said to shine at midnight like fire.

Before returning to Omphale, Heracles climbed Mount Sipylos to see for himself the figure of weeping Niobe turned to stone in grief over the destruction of her children, when she boasted they were of greater worth than the divine twins of Leto. The rock was much worn with wind and time, but possessed the unmistakable posture of a grieving woman when viewed from a certain direction. Niobe was the first among mortal women with whom Zeus consorted, as her descendant, Alcmene, in the sixteenth generation, was the last.

Learning from foreign emissaries the true identity of her new slave, Omphale accosted Heracles on his return, chiding him for keeping secrets from her. Yet her awe of his person and noble lineage was magnified; and, pleased with his good works, allowed Heracles to feast with her at her own table and served him vittles with her own hand. Delighting in each other's company, they played games long into the night, including dice and knucklebones, which the Lydians invented during a severe famine, to take their minds off their hunger.

Heracles continued to rid Lydia of brigands and highwaymen. Then, taking command of the Lydian fleet, he sought to rid the coast of the depredations of pirates. He chased the Samian corsairs far out to sea, where he sunk their vessels on the reefs of the island of Doliche. Disembarking there for water before heading back to the mainland, Heracles noticed a rather large collection of feathers bobbing in the waves. He thought at first it was an unusually large bird, but as it washed ashore with the tide, it turned out to be the incorrupt body of Icaros son of Daidalos, his arms still clad in what remained of the wings his father had made for him. Heracles stripped off the plumage, wrapped the body in a blanket, and dutifully buried it on the beach. To the winds he said: "The gods are often cruel to men, but at times they dispense some kindness to them, as crumbs from a table fall to the little dogs. Rest assured, Daidalos, that dirt has covered your son's bones." Heracles renamed the island Icaria in the youth's honor. When Daidalos heard afterward what Heracles had done, he held him in higher esteem than any man who walked the earth; and everywhere he subsequently went, he built the Tyrinthian great monuments.

Omphale could no longer bear to have Heracles gone long from her. She kept him continually beside her. Enthralled by her, Heracles forgot the glory begotten of daring exploits, and proceeded to grow soft in the luxuries of oriental life, feasting on fat mutton, chines of beef and sweet Maionian wine. He followed behind Omphale wherever she went, holding a golden parasol over her to shade her white neck from the withering sun. On the eve of a feast-day to Dionysos, as they passed through the vineyard of Tmolos, they came to rest in a retired grotto by a purling brook. After her servants prepared two sumptuous couches in the cool shade of the cave opening, draped with swags of vine, Omphale, wishing to amuse herself, ordered Heracles to discard his clothing and assume her own wardrobe. As he could not disobey, he first snaked himself into her girdle, which promptly tore asunder. Then he assumed her gauzy purple gown, which reached down only to his waist. Her golden, jeweled bracelets broke on his burly arms. His oafish feet split her dainty shoes. Omphale, after a good laugh, then put on his lionskin, resting the forepaws on her breasts and using the rear-paws to conceal her pudenda; and, unable to lift his club to her shoulders, dragged it about, thumping her chest in mock imitation of the hero. Heracles could not help but be both aroused and amused by her antics and delighted her all the more by performing crude curtsies and pirouettes.

At dinner, Omphale, chewing meat off the bone, as Heracles would have done, observed:

"You have ever been a slave of women, Heracles. Throughout your long bondage to the Mycenaean king you were, in reality, doing the bidding of the immortal Hera—who, as you said, tore you as a babe from her own breast. Whatever it is you seek, whatever compulsion drives you, be at ease! You are mine now. Rest at last from your labors in the comfort of my fragrant bosom."

As the glow of sunset left a sweet farewell in the dark foliage, they lay for slumber, still cross-dressed, on beds apart, yet side by side; for they could, at dawn, honor the discoverer of wine only in a state of purity. But at midnight a shadowy form passed through the gloom, and with outstretched arms searched out the couches, stepping lightly with his cloven feet. He was none other than Pan, who beforehand seeing them from a hill ambling through the vineyard, became instantly enamored of the Maionian queen, whose scented locks streamed down her shoulders. He came first to one couch where, reaching under the duvet, felt the bristly lionskin, and recoiled in terror, as a wayfarer jumps back when a snake slithers across the path. He parted next the drapes of the adjacent couch, confident he had found the object of his love, and quietly mounted beside the sleeper. Lifting the bottom edge of the garment before him, the old lecher prepared to take his pleasure, when all he felt were scabrous, hairy thighs. Heracles, stirred from his slumber, drew a foot and kicked him off the bed. The sudden crash awoke Omphale, who, calling to her attendants for lights, soon discovered the bruised divinity groaning on the hard floor.

They had a good laugh at Pan's expense as he scampered away back to his mountain-cave. Since then, Pan has eschewed clothing, which deceives the eye, and commands his followers to practice his rites in the nude.

Omphale, taking Heracles as her consort, bore him three sons: Lamos, Agelaos and Laomedon. Heracles, who grew fond of carousing in bed until noontime while the sun's beams warmed his face, once pulled in one of the maidservants who came to wash him, and by her begot two additional sons, Cleodaios and Alcaios. Omphale scolded him for this license, beating him with her golden sandal.

Heracles, continuing to dress in womens' silken clothes, which felt wonderfully comfortable against his skin after wearing the lion's pelt for so long, took up the art of weaving, daily working his weight of wool. He would sit at the loom in a yellow petticoat among the slave-girls, stretching the fine warp upon the beam and making passes with the shuttle to thread the woof. Or, as he teased strands from the wool-basket, spinning with distaff and spindle, he spun stories for Omphale of serpents throttled in his infant hands; of the Tegean boar with its lair on cypress-covered Erymanthos; of Thracian mares made fat with man-flesh; of the triformed herdsman of Eytheia; and of the hellish watch-dog who barred his escape from the netherworld. At first his creations were ugly and ill-threaded; but by time and practice his large, clumsy fingers acquired the discipline to prepare splendid wools shawls, inwoven with threads dyed in Tyrian purple, and embroidered along the edges in gold thread.

Perhaps Heracles would have served Omphale for the remainder of his days, playing her husband, forgetting who he was or what he had accomplished in the world, had a group of new domestics not been brought to the court; who, ignorant of the state of things, laughed at Heracles when they saw him so gaily dressed. An onrush of anger, so long unfelt in the midst of his voluptuous new life, restored Heracles to his senses. He at once broke his distaff, threw his spindle across the room, and tore off his shawl and petticoat. Charging into Omphale's apartment, he demanded his lionskin and weapons, which she had long hidden from him in the fear that he ever wished to return to his bold adventuring.

"O heartless!" cried Omphale, the fear she long tried to

delay finally realized. "Can our love not hold you? Or our sons, already walking with tottering steps? If I ever did you a good turn, or showed you a bit of kindness, remember the sweetness of our life here away from all the noise of the world. The three years are past—yes I know! I have dreaded every turn of the gnomon that tracks the luminous god across heaven. Have pity on me, bereft of my first husband and now about to lose another."

Heracles, his passion drained, looked at Omphale tenderly and said: "I deny none of what you say, O queen. Never, to the end of my life, will your memory be forgotten. Men like me, you surely know, are not born for ease and indolence, but for toil and danger. I leave not because I want to; but because I must."

"At least you do not slip away, like a thief in the night, which perhaps would have been less cruel," said Omphale with downcast eyes bubbling with tears. "You are like that proud lion, caught in the nets, too beautiful to slay. The hunter brings him home, chains him to a post, and hopes to tame his wild ways. But ever the lion chafes at his fetters, wishing to return to his woodland haunts, or else turn upon his captor with ravening hatred. I truly believe that of all things, it is a hero's death you seek. Go then, Heracles, before you consume me utterly. I shall never forget you, greatest of men."

Heracles, gently taking the slight Omphale in his powerful arms, said: "I am much less than you, O queen, for you have vanquished me; and never shall I feel shame in that. In wearing my armor, you have become heir of my exploits. Farewell."

Omphale, carrying herself bravely despite her broken heart, released him and showered him with gifts, of which he accepted only a gleaming baldric. In return, he gave her Hippolyte's whetted double-headed axe. She accompanied him to the coast, where a ship lay ready to carry him home. From the quay at Smyrna she watched the flapping white canvas grow small against the brilliant blue sea.

5

Heracles had no sooner settled in Tyrins after his exile over the death of Iphitos than restlessness again possessed him. To mind came all those who had slighted him or had been inconsiderate during or after the commission of his Labors; since it always seemed fitting to him to repay with interest both those who had helped him and those who had done him harm. Foremost was the impudence of king Laomedon of Troy, who, promising the snow-white mares, gifts of Zeus in recompense for ravished Ganymede, contemptuously reneged on his offer after Heracles had risked his life to save princess Hesione from the sea-serpent. He therefore called upon all of his brothers-in-arms for their assistance. First to answer the call was Iolaos, who, leaving the sweet marriage-bed of Megara, came thirsting for adventure, since men are content to lie in idle love only for a short spell. Heracles told him: "The time has come to recompense my enemies a hundredfold."

With Iolaos Heracles first recruited soldiers in Tyrins for the expedition against Troy, afterward collecting men from as far as the Isthmus while declaring Laomedon's doom. Iphicles from Thebes joined them, bringing with him Heracles' magnificent Trojan shield, which had been stored at their mother's house. Peleus too answered the call. He had returned to Phthia, where he took the throne formerly held by Eurytion. Under his command came a small contingent of Myrmidon vassals, fierce Thessalian fighters, who, dressed in black armor, looked like ants when they scurried about in a battle. They were descended from Myrmidon, whom Eurymedusa bore to Zeus when he came to her in the form of an ant. The Argive Oicles, son of Antiphates, grandson of Melampos and father of Amphiaros, who later met an astounding end in the war of the Seven against Thebes, arrived next at Tyrins, not wishing to miss in the spoils and glory of a foreign war; as did Boetian

Deïmachos, who claimed to be a Minyan.

Heracles, in need of one more captain, with his companions paid a visit to Telamon at Salamis, whom he found feasting in celebration of his wife's Periboea's imminent parturition. Heracles, asked to pour out the first libation, received the gold-trimmed cup from Telamon and, raising his hands, said: "Father Zeus, if ever you have, with willing heart, listened to my prayers, I ask you now to grant Telamon a brave son, as invulnerable as this Nemean lion's pelt I have around me, and with spirit to match." While sitting at meat, they saw through the casement a great black-winged eagle soaring through the clear sky. Heracles, thrilled within by a sweet joy, turned to his host and said: "Telamon, the son you wished shall be given to you. Name him Aias after the king of birds. He will become the bulwark of our people." When, near the end of the banquet, Periboea gave birth, the stout babe was brought in to Telamon. Seeing him, Heracles wrapped him in his lionskin; yet, the lion's pelt covered not the babe's neck or armpit, where the strap of Heracles' quiver crossed.

Telamon assembled eight small ships of twenty oars each, putting them at Heracles' disposal. With each comrade commanding a ship, and Heracles two, they set sail across the sea. Making their way through the islands of Minos, they stopped at Paros, where Alcaios, on a visit from Thasos, not knowing what to expect from Heracles, refused to leave his palace to greet him. Heracles, however, had no other designs there than to raise altars to Zeus as well as Apollo, hoping to avoid the latter god's displeasure for attacking one of his favored cities.

Fair weather carried them swiftly across the sea. Rounding Tenedos, the flotilla widely dispersed so as to avoid drawing attention from the look-out posts there, and, arriving in staggered fashion, beached the ships on the narrow arm of an inlet across the bay from the Trojan plain, at the entrance of Hellespont, from where they could make out, over the hills, the pennants atop the Trojan citadel. Heracles was the first to leap to the sand, throwing down his arms before him. As Iolaos strapped on his corslet, Telamon said: "Never since that day you marched into the Mysian wood have I seen such grim resolution on your face, Heracles. With you we are eager to storm the city, but as we have rowed continuously since leaving Lemnos, where we expected to find hospitality from queen Hypsipyle (who, we discovered, had been sold abroad as a slave to Lycourgos, king of Nemea, when the Lemnian women discovered that she had spared her father Thoas[8]), it behooves us to renew our strength with meat. Let us hunt some goats there in the hills and prepare a feast while it is yet light, remembering to pour libations to Zeus and Poseidon for our safe passage."

Oicles agreed, saying: "We are well-sheltered by the rocks and out of sight of the city or its outposts. Since we are small in number, stealth is our greatest ally. Let us wait until nightfall, send a few men to scout out the area, and then determine the best course of action."

Taking a deep breath of the briny air, Heracles was reminded of his own hunger. Peleus and Iphicles ran off to find their supper. They returned with the carcases of several goats and some live sheep, which they had purchased from a roaming herder. After flaying each animal and stripping off the meat, they threw some pieces in the fire to honor the gods and roasted the rest. They ate and drank on the beach, watching until the fading sun lit as with fire the arching headlands of the Troad and the nearby coast of Thrace.

When the stars pendant from the celestial sphere appeared to begin their nightly turn, Heracles led his captains into the hills where they could get a good view of the city. The walls were as high and impregnable as he remembered them. With such a small force, and without siege-works, he could not expect to be successful

---

[8] She was forced to care for his Lycourgos' son Opheltes or Archemoros. When the Seven marched against Thebes, they met her. Showing them a fountain where they could get water, she put down the boy on a bed of parsley, and he was bitten by a snake and died. Lycourgos, who had been warned in an oracle not to allow his son to touch the ground until he had learned to walk, wanted to revenge himself on Hypsipyle, but Adrastos, leader of the Argives, protected her. Hyginus relates (*Fabulae* xv.) that she was instead sold in slavery to king Lycos of Thebes. It was this Lycos who, in the absence of Heracles, tried to destroy Megara and killed Creon, king of Thebes. On his return from his last Labor, Heracles killed him. (Hyg., *Fabulae* xxxii.; Euripides, *Heracles*). But as Lycos would have ruled Thebes prior to Creon's second regency, and for other reasons, this particular legend does not fit into our chronology.

in a direct assault, since Troy could simply close and bar the gates against them.

Heracles postponed any offensive that night, expecting a night's sleep to impress on him new ideas. They bivouacked on the beach, and in the morning, Heracles led most of the men across the Scamandrian plain to the ford of the river Xanthos. They quickly overcame the soldiery manning an outpost, securing two chariots and horses. Leaving the men hidden behind the high banks of the river, Heracles and Iolaos mounted a chariot and approached the city along the main highway. The sentries atop the walls quickly spotted the pair, girt for war, and alerted the garrison. Heracles reigned in the horses as troops sallied forth with heavy spears held in defensive posture.

Heracles lowered the cowl of his lion's pelt and cried: "Laomedon! It is I, Heracles! As promised, I have returned for my hard-won mares." Heracles waited while his demand was communicated to the palace. After some time, Idaios, Laomedon's herald, hurried through the gates, and, bowing deeply, said: "King Laomedon remembers you, Heracles. He states, however, that he owes you nothing beyond his gratitude. It would be impious, he says, having once received a gift from God, to give it up to another. The king bids you to go in peace, since there is little you can do here."

Heracles, fully expecting such an answer, said calmly: "Since your king stubbornly persists in defrauding me, I must proceed to defraud him of his city." He nodded at Iolaos, who took up Heracles' great round shield by the straps and braced it against the front rail. Ensconced behind, Heracles drew his bow and with an arrow pierced the greave of the garrison leader. In reaction, the spearmen flung their spears. Most fell short of the chariot; but one struck Heracles' shield and poised there quivering. "Quickly, Iolaos, back to the river!" ordered Heracles. Iolaos exchanged the shield-straps for the reins and whip, wheeled the chariot about, and rattled away in a cloud of dust.

The spearmen, pursuing them on foot, were quickly overtaken by whatever horsemen or charioteers could hastily arrange their equipage with such short notice. Iolaos deliberately slowed their car after the initial rush in order to give the Trojans time to catch up. As they neared the river, up sprang Heracles' men-at-arms from their coverts and felled the horsemen with spears and arrows. Dcïmachos was the first to draw blood, impaling a rider through the chest, so that the bronze spear-point passed through his corslet and came out of the back. The charioteers, seeing the ambush, stopped short to await the spearmen, who, as soon as they arrived, spread out along the riverbank in an attempt to overwhelm and push back the attackers. All along the banks the fighting raged, and the dusky waters of the Xanthos grew crimson with blood. Iphicles, lunging with his spear, transfixed one Pergasos through the mouth, blowing off his casque, out of which spilled his brains behind him. Unable to dislodge his lance, Iphicles drew his sword and plunged into a knot of Trojans, hacking and slashing. One named Polyaimon, he freed of his sword-hand, and then, to remove him from the earth pierced his lung right through his breast-plate. Telamon used his bow until he ran out of arrows, and then, grabbing a spear, proceeded to gut several Trojans. Peleus, seeing the bodies piling up before his brother, doubled his efforts so as to avoid being surpassed. He too sent a fair number of Teucrians to sleep in the dust.

Heracles rode up and down the riverbank, picking off Trojans with his arrows where the fights were fiercest, urging his men to take possession of as many horses and chariots as possible. Seeing Iphicles suddenly surrounded and pinned against the stream, Heracles jumped off the chariot and, like a dislodged boulder rolling down a mountain-side, gaining speed and force at each turn and bounce, he hurled himself irresistibly through the massed enemy, sweeping away bodies with his stout shield and battering heads with his club. This way and that swung his cudgel, and no piece of armor could resist it. Treading crumpled bodies underfoot he reached Iphicles by a willow thicket, who said to him: "Brother, we did not expect to be met straightway by such a force. I see already more Trojans racing across the plain. Soon we will all be overwhelmed against the river and killed or drowned. Let us retreat, defend our end of the ford, and take a respite for now on the other side." Heracles, seeing the men hard-pressed, concurred. He made his way to the ford, killing whatever Trojans crossed his path, and once there called on his captains to lead the retreat.

Meanwhile Laomedon, who from a high tower on the citadel held a commanding view of the plain, witnessed the struggle by the river. Surrounded by his councilors, Panthoös and Ucagelon, he said: "Heracles must be a fool to incite to war against me. Since my father Ilos left Dardania to found this city, sanctuary of the sacred Palladion, no enemy has every succeeded in taking it. Besides, see what greater security we have now, shielded by our walls divinely-wrought? Nevertheless, we must take all intimations of danger seriously, especially when the instigator is one as deranged as this Heracles, who calls himself a son of the divine Father. Do you not see the patent absurdity? Can Zeus favor two of his offspring, bitter enemies, at once? Either Zeus is with me, for I too can claim divine descent through Dardanos, who begot Erichthonios, who in turn begot my grand-sire Tros—or with him." Laomedon then called his sons Podarces and Bucolion, born to him by the nymph Calybe; and his eldest son Tithonos, who arrived in a burnished bronze corslet. To Tithonos he said: "Take three hundred of our best men and, after finding the camp of these invaders, push them back into the sea." And to Podarces and Bucolion he said: "Lead the remaining garrisons into the field against this ill-fated advance of theirs. Crush them utterly. Bring Heracles to me, dead or alive."

Tithonos, who played the lyre and composed hymns to the Dawn, at once mounted his chestnut steed, whose speed was matched only by Laomedon's divine mares, and led his cavalry upriver, fording the Xanthos near the foothills of Mount Ida. He led his troop across the plain and followed the coast up the narrow headland that formed the eastern arm of the bay, guessing correctly the location of Heracles' desolate landing place. Runners, posted on the rocky ridges by Oicles, who had been left to safeguard the ships, saw the Trojans riding hard and sped to inform the camp. Oicles, who with his men had been digging a trench around the beached flotilla, armed hastily and prepared for battle. The cavalry first met resistance from archers in the hills, who with their arrows cut down a fair number, sending men and horses tumbling into one another. But the Trojan horsemen thundered on up the narrow strand and fell against the scanty defenders. Oicles threw his long lance at the vanguard. The speeding shaft flew over Tithonos' shoulder and pierced the gorget of another Trojan, slicing through the neckbone so that he recoiled off his horse, as if by a violent gust of wind, and landed sprawled on his back. Tithonos, loving his life too much, at once drew back. Witnessing this, Oicles unsheathed his broadsword and pursued him. The Myrmidons, seeing Oicles about to be trampled among the charging horses, rushed in and by expert sword-cuts brought down the Trojans from their mounts.

The Trojans now prepared torches, and having crossed the ditch, came near to the ships. Those defenders on board resisted them with pikes or by hurling down spears. When the ranks of these Trojans dwindled, another wave supplanted them; and one was able to cast a flaming brand onto a ship's deck, setting afire the furled sail. Oicles, having lost sight of Tithonos in the melee, mounted a wayward horse and rode back swiftly to the ships, crying: "To sea, comrades, to sea!" Heeding his command, the defenders streamed back to dislodge the chocks and push the ships into the water while the Myrmidons defended their backs. As the remaining men were too few in number to row all the ships away, they commenced to hoist sails to take advantage of the seaward breeze. Two ships, aflame, were abandoned. Another two managed to slip away untouched. Trojans boarded the remainder and a desperate fight ensued, sword against sword and shield-boss against shield-boss, until the bilges ran slick with blood. Oicles valiantly ran from ship to ship, repulsing the swarming Trojans with a spear in each hand, thrusting at their bellies or backs, piercing shields and plated corslets. By his actions, the Greeks freed the other ships from the sand, throwing the dead Trojans by the boards as soon as they were at a safe distance. Oicles alone remained on the beach, encircled by the Trojans. From the ships his comrades watched with parched throats as Oicles, despite the odds, continued jabbing at the rabid Trojans, keeping them at bay like wild dogs. But they overwhelmed him like bees against an intruder of the hive, swarming over him so that there was not a man who did not get his spear or sword-tip in him. Tithonos arrived last of all to deliver the final stroke, by which he cleaved Oicles' head from his shoulders. Seeing that the ships now floated safely offshore, the Trojans collected their dead and trampled off. The Greeks wept to see their fallen comrades bestrewn in blood across the strand, like the leaves of purple crocuses shaken by the wind.

❧

Heracles was the last to cross the river, keeping the Trojans at a distance with his armor-piercing arrows. When the two princes arrived leading the chariotery, Podarces drew back the men, assembling them in ranks by the tomb of Ilos in the center of the plain. Standing on the far river-bank, he called to Heracles: "Unlike my father, I bare you no ill-will, Tyrinthian. You know well how I spoke up for your interests when you rescued my sister. I must, however, defend Troy at all costs. Why not break off his engagement? Send some men back to this side to collect your dead, and then leave our shores."

Heracles' determination to exact revenge against Laomedon moderated when he looked at his weary companions, spattered in blood and grime. He replied: "Of all the Dardanian brood, you are the most wise and righteous, young prince. Such qualities may preserve your head some day. Let us observe a truce while we collect and burn our dead."

"A truce, then, between foes," said Podarces sadly, since he had hoped not to fight against Heracles.

When Bucolion saw the Greeks collecting their dead compatriots, he confronted his brother, saying "I see you first having a parlay with Heracles, and now this! Our father will be most displeased by this dishonor, Podarces. You know our orders."

"Brother, haste in war is no better than quiescence during peace-time," said Podarces. "While you may be older than I, you are also a bastard, while I am legitimately born, and thus possess the greater authority."

"Fie on you, callow youth!" spat Bucolion; then, marshalling his companies, he led them across the deep river. Heracles with his arrows killed three teams of horses, causing their bodies and stalled chariots to temporarily choke the ford and prevent further passage. Joining Iolaos on the chariot, he led his men to the high rampart, still extant between the beach and plain, built for him when he fought the sea-monster. There battle was joined. The Greeks had managed to secure a number of horses and chariots in the first skirmish, so they were not entirely at a disadvantage against Bucolion's squadron, although a number of Trojan bowmen now took part, raining down death upon them. Iphicles took an arrow to the thigh, and had to retire to the shadows of the rampart, where Iolaos tended his wound. Heracles raged, spreading panic with the gleam of his shield. After disabling a chariot by smashing its pole, Heracles killed both occupants of the car simultaneously with a single downward strike of his long club. Peleus, nearby, ordered his driver to stop and leapt from his chariot to confront three Thracian mercenaries, whom he chased as far as a small knoll known as Bramble Hill, but also as the Tomb of Bounding Myrine after the great Amazon queen. There Peleus fought them all at once, killing one with a sword-thrust through the baldric upward into the belly; another by a slash to the neck; and the third by striking his face with a rock, which shattered the nose and eyesockets, causing blood and brains to ooze out of the cavity. Deïmachos confronted Bucolion from a distance, casting a spear at him with all his might; but it lost force, flew low, pierced the chariot wall and killed his squire when the sharp point reached his groin. As Bucolion drew back for a return spear-cast, Heracles already had him in his sights, and sent an arrow burrowing through his neck. He stood erect for a moment still gripping his spear-haft, and then toppled over the chariot-rim.

When Podarces saw his brother fall, he was wracked by anguish and rued that he had held back his companies from pursuing Heracles. Mounting a charger, he rode along the lines calling the troops to order, making ready to cross the Xanthos with them; when suddenly, the imperial clarion sounded across the plain, signaling the closure of the gates, and calling all the Trojans back to city.

"What means this trumpet-call?" asked Telamon as their foes disengaged and streamed back across the plain in a dark wave. "Shall we pursue them, Heracles?"

"Had the two princes been in accord," said Heracles, "I fear they would be now pursuing us. Back to the ships! I meant to only to test the hornets' strength by our little ambuscade; but it seems we have aroused the entire nest. Once the Trojans have barred the gates, lacking our full complement, we stand no chance; unless Laomedon deems to take the battle out to us here."

After despoiling the Trojan dead to secure additional arms, they hurried back to the camp, taking a Trojan prisoner with them, where they found only the two smoldering ships laid up on the beach. Peleus climbed up into the rocks to scan the sea and reported he could detect no sign of the remaining ships. Iolaos found the corpse of Deïmachos, which Heracles burned first before all others. They then marched inland and took refuge in the cliffs along the coast, hiding out for the night in caves.

Although heartened by Tithonos' report that Heracles' reserve forces were scanty, Laomedon was concerned that six ships had escaped. Bewailing the death of Bucolion, whom he loved the best of all his sons, he vowed to girt himself in armor and lead his army like had done in his youth. Panthoös, urging restraint, said: "My lord, while our forces clearly outnumber those of Heracles, we are in no position to involve ourselves in further engagements at the moment. Do you not see how many fires now consume our brave dead? Little did those men know that by nightfall they would be wandering in the cheerless halls of Hades. Had we burned all of the ships, we would now be in a better position. But the reality is that they will return, perhaps in greater number. We must assemble our army, dispersed now as the men tend to their fields. Only at full strength should we attempt offensive action. Heracles is ruthless and crafty beyond description: a man never at a loss; and if his reputation holds true, filled constantly with melancholy and madness—and we all know how he will not stop until he ensures our destruction. Our best course is to wait and see what Heracles tries next. As long as our gates are shut, we are safe. He will not dare attempt a siege, knowing full well that our impregnable walls will outlast him."

Laomedon agreed to this counsel, but also ordered the navy to scour the coasts for Heracles' flotilla.

6

Heracles' companions watched disconsolately as Trojan vessels patrolled the waters from Tenedos to deep within the Hellespont. They were trapped, lacking provisions, except for what they carried, and without hope of rescue. The remaining ships, wherever they were, could not risk returning for them. Only Heracles felt unconcerned. Sitting apart, he only brooded on how to perform the impossible task of ravaging Troy. Observing Peleus roasting a little hare for breakfast, Heracles remarked, "Tell me, son of Aiacos, was not your father employed in building Ilion's walls?" Peleus nodded vigorously and said: "Indeed! Poseidon and the son of Leto summoned him as a fellow-worker, not only for his piety and justice, but because of the skill he displayed in fortifying the coasts of Aegina against pirates." At the mention of Aiacos, the Trojan prisoner, whose name was Antimachos, trembled violently, and falling at Heracles feet, begged for mercy. Heracles assured him that he would not be harmed if he explained the reason for his sudden incitement.

"If this indeed is the son of Aiacos the Aeginetan, then I and my people are doomed, so it will not be to my further detriment to tell what I know," said Antimachos.

"Out with it, then," said Heracles impatiently; "or I shall kick you off this cliff."

Antimachos, grasping Heracles' knees, said: "My father once told me that, as soon as the wall was completed, three gray-green serpents thrust themselves against it. The two that had struck those parts of the wall wrought by the gods fell down dead. The third, however, forced its way into the city through chinks in that part built by Aiacos. Thereupon Apollo prophesied that the city would fall at the hands of the sons of Aiacos: in the first generation, as well as the third."

Heracles, filled with wonder, raised his hands and prayed: "I thank you, Father Zeus, that you have led me to bring with me not only one son of Aiacos, but two!"

Antimachos, to whom Heracles promised safety for himself and his family in return for his assistance, agreed to lead them to that stretch of wall he believed to have been the work of Aiacos. It enclosed the lower city on the western side at the farthest extent from the citadel and its palaces, where lived the merchants and craftsmen. While most of the city rose up from the very edge of a steep, rocky hill, the western portion rested on extended tableland, buttressing a desolate elevation, thickly wooded and overgrown with brambles. Leaving Iolaos as look-out on the sea-facing cliffs, Heracles and his companions crossed the plain and made the arduous climb under cover of darkness.

While some men set about hewing young trees and constructing siege ladders, Peleus and Telamon scouted the fortifications. They returned to report the appearance of a double-circuit wall, with the inner one higher than the outer, which was slightly inclined and protected in front by a wide but shallow ditch that seemed to wrap all along the western and southern sides. The outer wall, though battered by time and weather, still presented a smooth finish to withstand escalading. Its foundation was built of large stone blocks, a rod thick, set without mortar; and upon this rested mud-brick battlements strengthened with timber. Only one guard-tower, at the turn of the southern wall, was visible in their vicinity.

As the gloom deepened at the third hour, Heracles put his stratagem into play. He dispatched some men to the region alongside the tower, where they set the brush and brambles afire. Stirred by the winds sweeping the plain, the flames, leaping high, soon engulfed that part of the hill, drawing hither out of curiosity or concern all the soldiery in the vicinity. Heracles then led his forces down to the edge of the ditch, where with arrows they swiftly dispatched the remaining sentries that still patrolled behind the parapet wall. Hoisting their long siege ladders, they climbed to the battlements, Heracles leading the way. To speed the assault, they tied hempen lines around the merlons and dropped the ends for the most agile to climb. They soon met resistance as they fought their way to a flanking tower, from where they could cross to the inner wall. A general alarm was now raised, and trumpet-calls resounded through the city, stirring soldiery and citizens alike. Pinpricks of light appeared throughout the sprawling lower city as the commotion roused men from their beds.

Once on the ground inside, Heracles divided his forces, wishing not to directly engage the more numerable Trojan defenders, but to fan out through the dark streets in small cohorts committing acts of sabotage. They had strict orders, however, to spare women, children and old men who could no longer raise a sword. Under the command of Telamon, one group, who had outfitted themselves completely in Trojan armor and vestments, he tasked to secure the armories and garrisons. Another went forth with burning brands to set houses on fire. Trojan defenders now streamed in from all quarters.

Panic filled the commons as the flames spread from house to house. Men and animals, laden with belongings and towing wives and children, clogged the streets, impeding in the pell-mell an orderly response from Troy's defenders. Though the Trojans knew their city better than their enemies, Heracles, with Peleus and Deïmachos, managed to draw them into alleys and narrow streets, where under darkness they killed them in scores. In this way, street by street, the Greeks fought their way to the city's heart, causing havoc as they infiltrated, like a river, swollen by thawing snow, overflows its banks and lays waste to the tender, green shoots.

In the morning, Troy still burned with a din and roar. Heracles and his men concealed themselves in abandoned houses, from which they went forth at intervals to harass the Trojans. In one house Deïmachos found an aged woman and her daughter, who, on account of their penury, had refused to leave their habitation despite the threat of war. Falling madly in love with the daughter, named Glaucia, Deïmachos had union with her, afterward learning from the mother that she had bore her to Scamander the river-god. Deïmachos, his brains addled with passion, quite forgot why he was there and for a time lost contact with Heracles, who over the next night and day continued his struggle to reach the citadel.

Laomedon, confused about the scope of the attack, and thinking that Heracles had returned with a larger army, ordered all of his troops to abandon the lower city in defense of the upper.

They therefore quit their posts and fortified positions, and retreated haphazardly behind the great ashlar walls of the redoubt, higher and thicker than the outer fortifications, reinforced by bastions and flanking towers at regular intervals. Heracles, wrapping himself in a cloak of Trojan purple, celebrated the victory by feasting with his men and offering sacrifices.

Having now the leisure to better prepare for another attack, the Greeks set about constructing siege works, including ladders, moveable towers, catapults, mantlets and battering rams housed inside siege-sheds covered with uncured bull-hides. Their army's ranks swelled with slaves and disaffected peasants, for after Heracles threw open the Scaean gate, many joined him out of hatred for the oppressions of Laomedon and the Trojan nobility.

At the appointed time, the besiegers marched up the principal street to the main gate of the upper city, flanked by two watch-towers. Heracles strode forth in view of the Trojans soldiers, who made the walls abristle with upright spears and shields.

"Hear me, brave men!" Heracles cried. "My suit is not with you, but with your king. Open the gates to be spared further suffering and bloodshed."

The Trojans, to a man, defied him. Heracles, filled with wrath at their intractability, since he had no patience for a long siege, ordered an immediate assault with everything at his disposal, offering the captain who would first breach the walls the pick of the royal spoils. Up to the walls swarmed his forces, pulling the siege engines. The Trojan showered them with arrows, spears and rocks, killing so many in the first wave of the assault that bodies were piled as high as the waist. Ladders were hoisted, but repulsed. The towers were no more brought near the walls that they were set on fire. Only the catapults proved their worth, lobbying great stones and bursting through the mud-brick and wooden outworks, toppling Trojans off the walls like leaves shaken from the tall trees. The battering rams, in their coverts, were then rolled to the walls, one at the gate and another at the flanks of a bastion, by a fig-tree, where the mortar-work would be weakest. Heracles was the first to work the battery against the gates, singlehandedly swinging the iron-tipped beam into the stout doors with a mighty crash, rattling the jambs and lintels—but they held.

The siege continued for three days, with mounting losses on

each side. Laomedon's councilors begged him to release the divine mares to Heracles; but he refused vehemently all the more, stating that they had food and water enough to survive a long investment. He also had faith that Troy's allies—Dardans, Lycians, Mysians and the cities along the coast—to whom he secretly sent word of his distress, would soon arrive to relieve him. His wife, Leucippe, and his daughters—Astyoche, Cilla, Proclia, Aethilla, Medesicaste, Clytodora, and lovely Hesione—he confined to the highest rooms of the citadel. From the balcony there Hesione watched the furious struggle beside Podarces, whom his father had relieved of duty for his spiritless actions at the ford.

"Tell me, brother," she said to Podarces; "who is that handsome, gallant Greek who follows in the shadow of Heracles?"

"That is Laomedon," said Podarces. "Don't tell me your fickle heart has turned with the wind. I remember your fondness for your savior Heracles; now your eyes flutter at another—at an enemy no less! In all my days I shall never come to understand a woman's heart."

Heracles ranged up and down the line, organizing each attack. He promised ten ingots of gold from Laomedon's treasury for the first man to scale the walls. Some intrepid fighters did, but perished as soon as they reached the parapet, and could not claim their prize.

At last large cracks began to appear at the corner of the bastion. Seeing them, Telamon took command. He had the other battery wheeled to the bastion's adjacent face, relieved the current crews and replaced them with the stoutest men in the ranks. The stone faces were battered in turn to the sound of clashing cymbals. By nightfall, the masonry began to crumble. The foundation stones dislodged and split apart, pushed inward by the relentless force of the swinging beam. When a fissure began to appear, Heracles set bowmen to provide cover for a contingent of spearmen, who with siege hooks attempted to enlarge it. As soon as the hole was big enough to pass a body, the Trojans massed about it on the other side, filling the breach with a hedge of spears. But brave Telamon, taking up a stout bronze-plated shield, was the first to push his way inside, crying: "Unto the breach, dear friends!"

Fighters streamed in after Telamon, fiercely engaging the Trojans. When the defenders abandoned the wall to aid their compatriots on the ground, the Greeks once more raised their ladders. Seeing now their enemies entering from every side, the Trojans panicked. Deïmachos, leading a charge, broke through their defensive line, forcing the Trojans into the plazas and broad avenues. But as Deïmachos reached the treasury, a lance thrown by Clytios, son of Laomedon, pierced his breast and jutted out of his back. Deïmachos fell with a groan in a clattering of armor and his last thought before darkness stole over his eyes was of Glaucia.

Raging Heracles pushed his huge form through the breach, too late to claim the glory. He charged into the Trojan ranks with shield and club, his mouth dripping slaver, his eyes glowing beneath his lowering brows. The Trojans fell beneath him like meadow-flowers crushed under the thundering herd. When he saw Telamon in grim struggle against prince Lampos, madness overtook him. Dropping his shield and club and drawing a sword, Heracles advanced like a howling lion, anxious that his friend would be remembered for the victory and not he. Lampos fled on catching sight of the pouncing Heracles. Telamon, considering that he was the object of Heracles' fury, and struck suddenly by his presumption in being the first to breach the wall, fell to his knees and began to heap stones upon another. Heracles stopped in his tracks at the odd sight; and brought back to his senses, he asked Telamon what was his intention. Telamon looked up at the grim visage and said: "I am building an altar to you, Heracles the Noble Victor!" Heracles, greatly affected by Telamon's humility and cautious ingenuity, praised him. Then, tasting victory was at hand, Heracles parted from him and continued his rampage.

While fighting raged throughout the upper city, Heracles thought only of reaching the palace at the highest point of the citadel. Heedless, through Trojan spears and spinning arrows, he reached the double doors, which his companions were already trying to wrench open under threat of stones and tiles thrown by defenders on the roof. Heracles first bent his bow to topple many of these down, and then thrusting aside his own men, he bashed in the doors with his club, gaining entrance to the vestibule. There waited a Trojan troop, guardians of the palace, who in a mass smashed against the invaders like a billow against a scudding ship. After killing a fair number of Trojans, Heracles broke from the melee. When Tithonos saw Heracles running through the halls and courtyards yelling for his father, he was drained of hope, and fled the palace by a secret door, which led him out of the city by the postern gate.

Heracles found Laomedon in an open courtyard huddling beside an altar shaded by an old laurel tree. Girt in his armor, and grasping a spear, he sat wearily, his spirit broken.

"Take them!" cried Laomedon. "Do as you wish with the blasted mares. They are yours!"

Heracles, shaking his head in disapproval, said: "We have arrived too late at this agreement. Let the world ever remember that you let Troy fall over a gift once given."

Laomedon rose, reared back, and desperately cast his spear. It missed and caught on the door-post. Heracles strung an arrow, bent his bow, and let fly the deadly missile. Though Laomedon raised his buckler in time, the pronged arrow-head pierced raw-hide and wood, and struck him under the collar-bone. Laomedon staggered back and fell against the tree trunk, his shield pinned to his useless arm. Heracles, his bow armed anew, approached Laomedon deliberately until he loomed over him, blotting out the stars. Against the commotion, the wails, the din of battle, Laomedon heard only the strain of the bow as Heracles drew back the arrow that ended his earthly life.

7

On hearing of their king's death, the demoralized Trojans, instructed by Panthoös and Ucagelon, laid down their arms and sued for peace. The remaining sons of Laomedon, except Podarces, who with his sisters were captured, managed to escape the city in the same manner as Tithonos, unwilling to share the same fate as Bucolion. Heracles rewarded the Trojans with clemency, and desisted from razing the palace or looting the temples.

The captives, members of the royal house, were herded before the temple of Athena. The daughters of Laomedon, hair loosed, huddled together like doves under the shadow of the circling hawk, wept inconsolably as Heracles consulted with his captains. After killing Laomedon, Heracles had sought the royal stables and found them empty. Now he angrily demanded to know the whereabouts of the divine mares, casting fiery glances at the frightened group. Finally a hostler stepped forward, green with fear, to explain that he had seen the Dardan Anchises, grand-nephew of the king, remove the horses as the siege of the upper city began. Heracles sent out a search party after the mares, but it never returned.

Hesione, wiping her tears, confronted Heracles, striking his chest with her small hands and heaping on him curses as would make a sailor blush. Enjoining silence, since her wails hurt his ears, Heracles entrusted her to Telamon as a reward for his exemplary service, along with a gold-rimmed goblet. Though he was married, and had already claimed one Theianeira as part of his spoils, he could not pass on taking a concubine of such noble lineage. He did his best to comfort her, but her resentment could not be assuaged. She followed on Heracles' heels expressing her disgust. Finally, Heracles gave her permission to ransom any of her fellow captives.

Thinking that Heracles planned to kill the sole remaining royal prince, she selected Podarces, offering her golden veil in payment. Heracles agreed, and to everyone's astonishment, declared him king, renaming him Priam since he had been redeemed. After announcing that, other than acquiring the mares, he had no further designs on the city or its polity, he released all of the captives and enjoined them to go about their business.

Just then Iolaos came running, frantic and breathless. He had spotted the remaining ships of their flotilla sneak away from the far side of Tenedos, where they were hiding, and take refuge a long way down the coast behind a headland where mountains sloped into the sea. Furthermore, he reported the alarming news that a large army of Mysians was said to be crossing the river Simois at the very moment on their way to the aid of the besieged city. Considering forfeiture of his prize a small thing in relation to the satisfaction of his revenge, Heracles lost no time in assembling his companions, and any local volunteers who wished to accompany him, for a hasty march to the ships. As he neared the Scaean gate, a woman broke through the crowds, threw herself at his feet, and begged him to take her. She was Glaucia, who by a dream discovered that she carried Deïmachos' son. On this evidence, and in honor of his fallen comrade, Heracles agreed to take her with him. On his return home, he put her in the care of Cleon, father of Deïmachos. In his house she bore a son, named Scamander, who afterwards obtained a parcel of land in Boetia demarcated by two streams: one he called Scamander and the other Glaucia.

As Iolaos reported, they found the ships anchored in narrow cove sheltered by tall crags off the coastal plain of Larissa, within hearing of the discharge of the river Satnioeis. Blessed with a land breeze, they made sail and took to the sea.

Now Zeus had left bright Olympos for the reaches of Mount Ida, where he could sit and observe the affair in Troy at his pleasure. Feeling no greater satisfaction than in the triumphs of his son Heracles, he turned to Hera, who had accompanied him to keep watch on his passions, and said: "There is surely no man on earth like Heracles, is there? Did you see how he, with only a few men, plundered mighty Ilion? You must be pleased, wife, since a soft spot for Troy has never existed in your heart." But Hera hated Heracles more than she hated Troy, and forcing a smile to hide her rage, she went a little apart to where Zeus could no longer see her. There she summoned Sleep and ordered him to lighten Zeus' eyelids. Poor Sleep, gift to men, heedless of the consequences of such an act, cast his spell on Zeus' heart and wrapped him in sweet repose. Having now the freedom to act without interference, Hera blew upon the sea, whipping it into frenzy. Heracles' six ships had scarcely lost sight of land when the violent storm overtook them. The sky grew dark with seething thunderheads; and all else was eclipsed by the scouring spray. Raging billows scattered the ships and the north wind ripped the sails from the yardarms. Everything not battened down, including provisions, spoils, and even men, went by the boards from the constant deluge that overwashed the decks. For three days the tempest roared without relief, roiling the ships in a welter and endless night, until more than one foundered and was lost in the pitiless deep.

The storm subsided with the same rapidity as its arrival. Clear sky burst through the dark clouds. Heracles awoke from a water-logged stupor. He pushed himself to look over the gunwale. He could see no other ships. His own vessel drifted idly, leaning on its counter, within sight of a mountainous headland. Heracles took stock of his shipmates. Iolaos and Iphicles, who took passage on Heracles' ship on account of his wounds, had survived along with Glaucia and fifty others. As for Peleus and Telamon, Heracles feared the worst and gave them up for dead.

They took to the oars and with alacrity rowed the battered ship for land, feeling that it would founder at any moment. But as they neared the coast, the local inhabitants crowded the cliffs and, taking them for pirates, commenced to pelt the ship with rocks. As no one could guess where they were, making further exploration— in the ship's present poor condition—unwise, Heracles grew determined to make landfall at that place. And so they rowed the ship back out to a safe distance and waited until nightfall.

Under the lustrous full moon they rowed the ship to the lee side of the cape and disembarked, thankful for feeling earth again beneath their feet. With some weapons, saved from the wreck, they headed inland. As they neared a large town amongst the mountains, they saw a shepherd watching from a hill his resting flocks. From him Heracles learned he had arrived at Meropian Cos. Since he and his companions were famished, Heracles asked the shepherd to give up one of his rams to them. The latter, a stalwart youth of solid build and full of mettle, laughed at Heracles and said: "If I were to extend charity to every shipwreck spit upon my land, I would soon be destitute. But as you could possibly relieve my tedium, let us wrestle. If I am worsted, a ram shall be yours."

Heracles, though weary, agreed to wrestle with him. The two stripped off their clothes and fell into a clinch. The shepherd, though quick and strong, was no match for Heracles, and so resorted to dirty tricks, such as casting handfuls of dirt in Heracles' face. This angered Heracles greatly and moved him to try to pummel the youth. His friends, who had assembled to watch the match, deplored the abuse, crying, "Does the stranger not know with whom he deals? Does he not know that this is Antagoras, the son of king Eurypylos of Astypalaia?" before joining together to attack Heracles. Iolaos, standing by, rallied the other companions to resist the Meropians. A fierce brawl ensued, growing larger as Antagoras' fellow citizens joined the conflict. Antagoras' brother Chalcodon managed to wound Heracles with a sword-cut to the back of the thigh. Heracles and his band, sorely outnumbered, were forced to break off the fight and flee for their lives.

On his way, Heracles came across the home of a stout Thracian woman. On learning that he had antagonized the citizens of Astypalaia, against whom she had an old grievance, she admitted him into her cottage and offered refuge. In little time, soldiers sent out by king Eurypylos, to whom Antagoras had reported the arrival of the armed cohort, were at her door. As Heracles was too big to hide under the bed or in a closet, she disguised him by dressing him in her own brightly-colored clothes, which fit him snugly. Having escaped detection through the woman's contrivance, Heracles ate and slept to regain his strength. The next day, his wound healed from the woman's unguents and poultices, he set out looking for his companions. He found that they had been welcomed in a nearby town called Ptelea, which happened to be populated by Pelasgians from Thessaly. To his joy, he was reunited with Peleus and Telamon. While Heracles had reached cape Laceter on the island's southern extremity, the sons of Aiacos managed to reach Stromalimne, the town's harbor, on the northern seacoast, after their ship foundered. Hesione too had survived, along with a good number of Myrmidons. Theianeira, however, pregnant by

Telamon, swam to Miletos, where she hid in a forest. King Arion rescued her and raised her infant son, Trambelos, as his own.

Ptelea, famous for producing a wine flavored with elm-catkins, had long been embroiled in a feud with Astypalaia, instigated by Eurypylos, who wished to subjugate all of the island's towns; the Meropes being a haughty people, and addicted to violence. Seeing in Heracles a kinsman and natural leader who could free them from their oppressor, the Pteleans gladly joined him when he declared his intention to fight against the Meropes. Heracles once again organized his remaining forces, devised a battle plan, and marched forth, strengthened by additional volunteers from the towns of Haleis and Lycope. Eurypylos, seeing them afar off, stirred up his troops, appointing his son Chalcodon as his lieutenant. The two sides engaged in a valley midway between the two towns and fought a bloody battle until dusk, when they separated until the next day. Eurypylos, though incurring heavy casualties on his side, refused to surrender and fought until Heracles with an arrow took his life. Heracles did not allow himself to be waylaid again by Chalcodon, and pursued him vigorously across the fertile fields back to Astypalaia. He caught him on the steps of a temple to Demeter, amidst baskets filled with pears and apples and the first-fruits of the summer-harvest, and was about to kill him, when a sweet voice cried for mercy. Chalciope, Eurypylos' daughter, running to the scene, covered her brother's body with hers, willing to share with him the fatal stroke from Heracles' sword. But the sight of the beautiful girl, dressed in purple linen and fragrant with perfumed ointment, stopped Heracles cold. He freed Chalcodon and allowed him to rule Astypalaia on the condition that he ceased all of his father's depredations. When the fighting ended later that day, it was found that the Meropes had been nearly decimated.

Heracles remained at Cos for some time while his remaining ship was under repair. On a whim, unable to keep her out of his thoughts, he married Chalciope. But when the women of Astypalaia heard from the Thracian matron—who possessed the shortcoming of being a notorious gossip—that Heracles at her house had dressed in women's clothes, they thought this most unseemly, and, highly offended, abused him daily as he worked on his ship. But the Coan men, to this day, welcome home their brides in similar attire.

Chalciope was not at all happy to be married to the man who killed her father, and showed her displeasure by being quarrelsome and peevish. So when Heracles departed for Greece, he left her behind without any regret. She later became the mother of Thessalos, who came to rule the island.

Now Zeus, awaking from induced stupor, quickly surmised what Hera had done, and flew back on a storm-cloud to Olympos. In bubbling fury over the outrage done to Heracles, he accosted all the gods about the great hall, looking chiefly for Sleep, who escaped by taking refuge with Night, conqueror of gods and men. Turning then to Hera, whose wily charms failed to deliver her, he lashed her arms with golden thread, weighed her feet with anvils, and dangled her from Olympos' highest peak amidst white clouds. Those gods who sought to aid her, great Zeus caught and hurled from the heavenly citadel.

8

King Augeias of Elis, after his return from the expedition with Jason, fretted all the more over the threat of Heracles, whom he had defrauded of any recompense for the cleansing of his byres. Preparing, therefore, for a fight in case Heracles at some time decided to march on Elis, Augeias made allies of Amarynkeus and the sons of Actor, called the Moliones after their mother, who possessed a willful and forthright personality. Amarynkeus was a valiant soldier whose father had come to Elis from Thessaly. Actor's father was Phorbas, son of Lapithos, and so was descended on the maternal side from Epeios. This Epeios was the son of Endymion, who held a race for the throne at Olympia between his sons. Epeios won it and became king; and thus his people were called Epeians thereafter. Since Epeios sired no heirs, the throne passed to his brother Aitolos; but he was exiled for manslaughter when at the first funeral games ever celebrated in Greece, he ran over with his chariot a certain Apis of neighboring Arcadia. Thereupon, the throne passed to Eleios, son of Poseidon and Endymion's sole daughter Eurykyda. The people then gave up the name of Epeians, and took the more suitable name of Eleans instead. Augeias was the son of this Eleios, and not, as was supposed, of the sun-god Helios, which misunderstanding Augeias often used to his advantage. To secure the loyalty of his allies, he assigned a third of his realm to Amarynkeus and another third to Actor and his nephews, Eurytos and Cteatos, who were said to have been born from a silver egg and possessed such a profound concomitance in their thoughts and deeds that it appeared they shared but one mind and body.

Those companions of Heracles who had fought with him at Troy urged him to consider another enterprise for the purpose of recouping the spoils they had lost at sea. In consequence, Heracles, recalling how king Neleus of Pylos had refused to purify him for the death of Iphitos, prepared in indignation to march to the coast. Telamon, though eager to continue fighting at his side, he dismissed to give him an opportunity to return to Salamis and enjoy the embraces of his new Trojan concubine. And Peleus, hearing rumors of dissensions in Pthia over his absence, raced home with his surviving Myrmidons.

After recruiting additional fighters from Tyrins, he set out for Lacedaimonia, crossed the river Eurotas near Sparta, and traversed the lofty Taygetos range through the narrow winding gorges that lead to Pherai and the gulf. He reached sandy Pylos after only four days of hard marching, taking the Pylians by surprise by the haste of his arrival. Despite assistance from neighboring allies, including the sons of Hippocoön, who raced from Sparta eager for battle, the city fell. Heracles sacked and burned it, in the process killing all of the sons of Neleus save Nestor, who was away visiting Gerenia. Nestor hastened to Pylos when he heard of the attack, arriving only to smoke and ruins. Old Neleus, who had survived by hiding in a cellar, wept for joy on embracing his sole remaining heir.

"I should have listened to you, son," he said, "when you urged me to accommodate Heracles during his previous visit—he who has now come upon us with his army, overwhelming our beloved city like a plague of locusts that darkens the midday air. I watched from the tower as he came near with fire and sword until I could no longer stomach it. Why, my rheumy eyes saw the very gods try to withstand him in our defense—and they could not! Athena came with him, you see, standing high beside his chariot, shaking her awful ægis. She engaged Ares foremost, that lover of bloodshed; while Heracles bandied with Poseidon, trident against club, until the sea-god withered—if you can believe it—under his divine strength. Seeing Athena in a bind, he ripped a spear from the ground and thrust the point through Ares' shield; though he could not penetrate the buckler, thick with hard-wood, bronze and gold, the stupendous impact dashed Ares to the ground. Before Ares could recover, Heracles drove his sword into the god's thigh, slicing open the divine flesh and releasing the crystal ichor. Heracles, after wounding Hera in her right breast with a three-barbed arrow, next turned his relentless bow on Hades, who had appeared merely to collect his battlefield spoils, and inflicted on him a terrible wound as he stood amidst the corpses.[9]"

Nestor, who feared his father's brains addled from the terrible ordeal, gently urged him on to a more prosaic reporting concerning his brothers.

Neleus continued: "A plague on the Tyrinthian!  One by one your valiant brothers fell, no match against the wielder of that tree-shattering club.  The last to face him was Periclymenos, who, as you know, Poseidon granted not only prodigious strength, but the power to assume whatever shape he desired, whether that of an ant, bee, snake or some other thing.  To show you there is no love lost among friends, Heracles though nothing of assaulting a fellow Argonaut.  Good thing my boy changed himself into a lion, and so held his foeman off for a time.  When he could withstand Heracles no longer, I saw Periclymenos take the form of a serpent, and then, to escape a detection, that of a blow-fly.  Heracles noticed him resting on the chariot-yoke and reached for his club; but Periclymenos transformed himself into an eagle and flapped about Heracles' head attempting to tear at his eyes with hooked bill and sharp talons.  After batting Periclymenos away, Heracles pierced him with an arrow beneath a wing.  He tried to fly to safety, but from his wound his pinions could no longer support him, and he plunged to earth.  On impact the unlucky arrow was driven upward into his neck, killing him.  O that these old bones had perished rather than he!"

While Nestor assisted his father to rebuild the shattered kingdom, the Eleans wasted no time harassing them in their weakened state, since they resented that Pylian outposts encroached on the territory of Elis as far as the river Alpheios.  The greatest outrage occurred when king Augeias confiscated the four horses that Neleus sent to compete for a tripod in the chariot-race at Olympia, sending the driver home vexed and embarrassed.  Nestor, bristling at the continued setbacks, led a raid into Elean territory, where he killed Itomeneos, son of Hyperichos, who came to the

---

[9] The only people in the world who worshipped Hades were the Eleans since they mistakenly considered this event to have occurred during Heracles' later attack on Elean Pylos.

defense of his herd, and drove the spoils from the plain: fifty herds of oxen and as many flocks of sheep and goats; fifty droves of pigs; and an hundred and fifty mares with their foals. By night he took them to Pylos, where Neleus' heart grew glad that so much booty had been captured by his son, though unskilled in war. At daybreak Neleus' heralds announced reparations for those Pylians to whom the Eleans were indebted, and the former assembled to claim their share of the spoils, with Neleus keeping for himself a herd of cattle and flock of sheep, along with their shepherds, to recompense him for the loss of the prize-winning horses.

After three days the Eleans came in great numbers, fully panoplied, on their chariots, along with the Moliones, who as of yet were inexperienced in fighting. They surrounded the Pylian frontier-town of Thryoessa, perched upon a rock by the river Alpheios, but sent their main force down the coast toward Pylos. The Pylians, fully expecting battle, set themselves in array and went out to confront their enemies. Neleus, to keep Nestor from risking his life in the fight, hid his horses. Undeterred, Nestor ran along with the horsemen, who waited until morning at Arene, where the river Minyeus falls into the sea, to join up with the foot-soldiers. By noon they reached the Alpheios, where they offered splendid sacrifices to Zeus, Poseidon and Athena. Passing that night fully armored, at sunrise they attacked the Eleans who had yet failed to storm Thryoessa. Nestor was the first to register a kill, spearing Mulius, married to Augeias' eldest daughter, golden-haired Agamede, who knew the virtue of the herbs nourished by the earth. Taking possession of the warrior's chariot, Nestor swept down on the Eleans like a dark tempest, seizing fifty chariots. He would have assailed the Moliones, but in plain sight they were suddenly shrouded in mist and caught away by Poseidon, who was said to be their true sire. The Pylians, enjoying the upper hand, chased the Eleans over the hollow plain as far as Bouprasion, abounding in wheat, and the Olenian rock, where a hill called Alesion rises. There the Pylians, having completely routed the men of Elis, turned back, giving glory to Zeus among the gods; and to Nestor among men.

When word of the victory reached Tyrins, Heracles, reminded of the great debt owed by Augeias, sought to take advantage of his discomfiture. Assembling again his countrymen, along with Iphicles and Iolaos, and a large contingent of Cleonians, who hurried to join him, Heracles crossed the breadth of Arcadia. Along the way numerous Arcadians swelled his army, so that he reached the territory of Elis with a formidable force. The people of Elis for the most part lived in unwalled villages, and offered little resistance. Heracles began first by raiding towns along the river Alpheios to replenish provisions, punishing those loyal to Augeias, but not molesting those of the native Epeians of Triphylia, who were originally Pelasgians of Arcadian stock, and chafed at being ruled by the Eleans, who had come from Calydon. The Pylians, however, fighting for Elis, put up a struggle, as did the Pisaians, who could not believe Heracles' audacity in marching an army across their sacred grounds. Heracles for the time being left them alone, preferring to concentrate his energies on taking Ephyra. Situated on the river Ladon, near where it flowed into the river Peneios, the walled citadel crowned a sharp hill, giving it a commanding view of both the plain and the river-valley. The lower city straddled the river and for the most part lay indefensible. The twin Moliones, who had learned much from their engagements against the Pylians, deftly led the chariotry while Amrynkeus commanded the infantry. Coordinating their defense, they checked Heracles' army and would not allow him to besiege the city, sweeping clean the plain and pushing him back into the hills. While encamped there Heracles fell ill with the dropsy. His captains would not attack further without him, some murmuring that not even Heracles could overcome two; and even Iphicles urged him to cease hostilities until someone could fetch some bathing-water from the river Minyeus, which, though sluggish and marshy, and affected with a foul odor, was said to be a sure cure for numerous diseases. Heracles, unable to walk, reluctantly agreed, and sent heralds to Ephyra to arrange a truce with the Moliones: without, however, making any intimation of his illness. But days later they got wind of Heracles' condition, and confidently marched out to attack his forward positions, manned by Cleonians. A fearful slaughter ensued in which Menedemus the Elean, who fought alongside Heracles fell; as did Dameon, son of Phlious, who was killed by Cteatos with the horse his rode on (and was buried with it in the same grave); and three hundred and sixty brave Cleonians. Heracles, cursing the sons of Actor for their dishonor in breaking a solemn truce, dragged his swollen limbs into his chariot, and leaning on his driver Iolaos, led a reckless charge, ready to take with his unerring bow two Elean lives for that of every Cleonian killed.  His first victim was Amarynkeus, whom he shot through the eye.  The Eleans lost heart seeing their champion fall and despoiled of his armor, and for a time were rebuffed.  At one point, Heracles had the Moliones in his sights, for they always rode in the same chariot and were so marvelously coordinated that they looked from afar like a single person with two heads, four arms and four legs.  Being at the peak of their youth and daring, they eluded him and went after Iphicles.  While Eurytos handled the reins, Cteatos cast his spear.  Iphicles, fighting the Epeians on foot, was struck beneath his left shoulder-blade; the spear passed through his body and the bloody point came out of his right breast, near the nipple.  With a groan he fell in a clattering of armor, and with his remaining strength scratched at the earth.  At once the Epeians began to drag away his body in order to despoil him of his armor, since he carried not only Heracles' embossed shield, but wore a golden sword-baldric that had belonged to his father Amphytrion.  Iolaos, at the woeful sight, leapt from his chariot and singlehandedly fought off the Epeians until friends managed to convey Iphicles to a place of safety behind the lines.  Heracles quit the battle to attend to his brother.  Filled with grief, Heracles laid beside him, fiercely glowering at any, save Iolaos or the chirurgeons, who came near.  Already darkness impinged on Iphicles' vision; yet he fought for every breath.

"Brother," said Iphicles; "we lay again together, like in younger days when we slept upon our father's great shield, which he covered with soft lambs'-down for our comfort.  I must tell you now something I remember, though I wonder if it will displease you."

"Pray tell, brother," said Heracles.

"Recall that most celebrated incident, when as a babe you strangled the serpents that had slithered into our crib.  Mother told you Hera had sent them, out of her enmity toward you."

"Yes I remember," said Heracles.

"Well, the truth is—as I lay there, drifting in and out of childish dreams, a footfall stirred me.  I half-opened my eyes and saw our father treading lightly into our chamber, carrying a basket.

He lifted the lid and poured two serpents upon the cold floor. As he left, shutting the door behind him, I, frozen in terror, saw the two snakes slither about looking for a warm place to nestle. They crawled up to the table that held our makeshift crib and menaced us. It was then that I let out a cry that awoke the household. Father did such a thing to discover which of us was sired by Zeus, a fact the blind prophet of Thebes had revealed. He loved you best after that, and I least, who have since endured living under the shadow of your greatness."

Heracles, caressing his brother's head, said: "While, I lacking hearth and home, wandered the world as another's slave, you cared for mother and maintained our patrimony; you raised a fine son who has lightened the heavy burden of my Labors; a champion of Thebes—you garnered fortune in your own way, as each man must. You see, brother, how no man on earth is born to be fortunate in everything. Whatever I have accomplished, I would give up to have you whole and fighting again beside me. I pledge we will both be immortal, brother. Your name will not be far from mine when poets, in times to come, recount the great exploits of this age."

Iphicles, fainting from loss of blood, said nothing else. Heracles had him conveyed to Pheneos in northern Arcadia, where their paternal grandmother, Laonome, lived.

The battles in hollow Elis continued for many days, with no side gaining the advantage. The bodies of men and horses, overturned chariots and discarded arms filled the wide plain, with rills of blood running between. As the brightening dawn brought out the tired armies again for more fruitless struggle, Corinthian heralds on swift horses arrived to announce the Peace of the third Isthmian Games. The Isthmia was founded by Sisyphos of Corinth in honor of Melicertes, who perished with his mother Ino when she cast herself into the sea between Megara and Corinth. The body of the boy was retrieved by a dolphin, and hung upon a pine tree. Sisyphos found the body and, under the instructions of a Nereid, instituted his worship under the name Palaimon and established the Games. Theseus compelled the Corinthians to open the games to all Greeks—hitherto merely a series of local nightly rituals—after which it was rededicated to Poseidon, who was much better known by all men. He also bargained for the best seats for Athenian visitors, in as large a place as could be covered by the sail, fully spread, of the galleys that conveyed them thither across the Saronic Gulf. The victor of the Isthmia was awarded a garland of pine-leaves, and his feats were extolled in lofty odes.

All warring cities were compelled to suspend hostilities during the period of the Isthmia to allow athletes and pilgrims to travel safely to the games. Heracles, with his army continuously routed by the Moliones, had no choice but to retreat from Elis, bitterly ruminating on his lack of success in taking Ephyra, as he had Troy. Thinking he could wait out the truce, and then resume his objective, he brought his army north to Olenos to the home of Dexamenos, who ruled also over Dyme. He was the father of Eurypylos, who served with Heracles in the Trojan campaign; and also father-in-law of the Moliones. Given his strained relations with Augeias, Dexamenos thought it not improper to receive Heracles, who arrived in time to attend the wedding of his daughter Mnesamiche to an Arcadian prince. Throughout the banquet, Heracles wryly observed a Centaur called Eurytion, who, as the evening progressed, grew more agitated while downing ewers of wine. He always expected trouble whenever Centaurs, wine and women came into close proximity. True to form, Eurytion commenced by interrupting the speeches of the nobler guests with horse laughs and caustic japes. When Dexamenos commanded him to desist, Eurytion turned over the tables, galloped toward Mnesamiche and tried to violently extract her from the protective arms of her betrothed. Heracles, who had been fingering his bow, nimbly strung an arrow and shot the Centaur under the arm-pit. His heart and lung pierced through by the barbed arrow, he trot off spitting blood, but collapsed in the vestibule.

In the meanwhile, the Epeians forwent any celebrations for their victory over Heracles in place of holding funeral games for their champion Amarynkeus, who was the first to relinquish his life in the struggle, and who was buried by his sons at Bouprasion. The games were open to all comers, even to the Pylians, who had lately worsted them. Nestor, in the prime of his strength, arrived to compete. All the Epeians now had an opportunity to see on display the prowess of the heir of Neleus. He handily beat Klytomedes, son of Enops, in the boxing-match; and followed this victory by mastering Ancaios of Pleuron at wrestling. He outraced Iphiclos;

and threw the quoit and spear further than Pyleus and Polydoros, respectively. Only in the horse race was Nestor beaten, when the Moliones crowded him at the turns, one twin tightly holding the reins while the other lashed with the goad, and at the end raced past him to claim the greatest prizes.

9

Dexamenos urged Heracles to forego his enmity with Augeias and the Moliones, for the peace of the realm and the sake of his own twin daughters, who, being married to the Moliones, he did not relish the possibility of seeing widowed. Heracles, not wishing to displease such a kind and hospitable friend, grudgingly agreed to abandon the inauspicious enterprise, and prepared to march his army back to Tyrins. But when a local lad called Polystratos, whom Heracles loved, fell ill and died, he built for him a memorial at Dyme, leaving on it a tribute of his own hair. On the way back, Heracles' Arcadians allies returned to their homes with nothing to show for their bitter efforts.

At Tyrins he found the palace door barred and guarded by Eurystheus' men-at-arms. Heracles, with Iolaos and a band of loyal Tyrinthians still at his side, would have entered into a struggle with them had the herald Copreus not waddled down the street at that precise moment. Bowing to Heracles, he delivered the announcement that king Eurystheus, worried about Heracles' recent foreign intrigues, raising of armies, waging of wars and other suspect activities, had come to believe that all such things were meant as a springboard for one invidious proposition,—namely, that Heracles no doubt had designs on the high kingship of Argolis; which honor, against any and all claims to the contrary, Zeus devolved upon none other the current occupant of the throne.

Heracles, stunned to hear this admission, wavered between incredulous hilarity and fulminating rage. Settling for the former after so much bloodshed on the plain of Elis, he placed a hand on Copreus' shoulder and genially asked to see Eurystheus to discuss the matter and dispel any notion of treachery on his part. Copreus, who trembled like a leaf under his heavy hand, extricated himself and moved within the safety of the armed guard before declaring, with fitting sonorous finality, that Heracles was thereby banished from the Argolid until such a time as the High King allowed him to return. Heracles forgot his civility, and hoisting his club, stood ready to force himself into the house. Iolaos fell before him, and with impassioned pleas directed his eyes to the walls and roofs, where bowmen stood perched like watchful ravens.

Heracles could not dream of fighting Eurystheus. Not only did he command a formidable army, but the fortresses of Mycenae and Argos, not to mention Tyrins, were unassailable. Heracles paced around under the fretful watch of Eurystheus' soldiers, debating inwardly as to the best course of action. Finally he turned to Iolaos and asked him what he would do. Iolaos answered soberly: "No man can do all things. Let us go to Pheneos where we can look in on my father, to see if he is well or ill."

Heracles first went to Thebes to fetch Alcmene, who up to then had received no news of Iphicles' injuries. She travelled with him and Iolaos to Pheneos, where they found Iphicles carefully nursed by Bouphagos, son of Iapetus and Thornaxe, and his wife Promne. Iphicles appeared in a much more salutary state, but possessed of an inconsonant exhilaration, which worried Heracles, since he had often seen such overjoyed rapture in men on the threshold of death.

While residing at Pheneos, Heracles did much for the benefit of the citizens. The road to Pheneos leads through a ravine, at the middle of which rises a spring. Under heavy rains, the spring once poured forth and flooded the Phenean plain. Heracles therefore excavated chasms below mounts Oryxis and Skiathis to draw off the water. He also, to bring a consistent supply of fresh water to the city, dug a channel through the middle of the plain, fifty stades long and thirty feet deep, to provide a new course for the river Aroanios.

One day, an Arcadian ally came to report that the Eleans had sent a procession to offer sacrifices to Poseidon at the Isthmia in Corinth, and that at the moment it passed through Arcadia, the Moliones included. Heracles allowed the idea of vengeance to sprout seed in his mind until, fully flowering, his head throbbed with the pressure to act. Without telling anyone his intentions, he slipped out of Pheneos one night. He caught up with the procession as it crossed the river Asopos and out of sight tracked the Moliones until they arrived at the frontier of Argolis, where he ambushed them from a roadside thicket below Cleonai outside the narrow mountain pass from Argos.  He sped arrows into the backs of Eurytos and Cteatos, killing them instantly, but attacked no one else in the party.

Uproar ensued, since the procession had been under the protection of the Isthmian truce.  Molione, made doubly zealous by her agony, could find no rest until she arrived at the truth of the matter, and made inquiries far and wide to discover the identity of her sons' murderer.  Coming to the resolution that it was Heracles who had slain her children, she compelled Augeias to demand satisfaction from Eurystheus, since Heracles was still believed to live at Tyrins.  But Eurystheus washed his hands of the matter, referring him to his recent public pronouncement of Heracles' exile.  Next, Molione appealed directly to the Corinthians to immediately place the entire Argolid outside the peace of the Isthmia.  The Corinthain magistrates, though deploring the impious fracture of the religious truce, attributed the murders to the depraved actions of one individual, and thus saw no need to exact punishment against cities or territories on behalf of a public spectacle that was supposed to enhance the ties of peace and friendship.  Frustrated by all of her failed attempts to gain satisfaction, Molione laid a solemn curse on every Elean who took part in the games.  The Eleans ever afterward boycotted them.

While these events brewed, Heracles bid his time at Pheneos, losing his concern over Augeias now that he had revenged himself on the sons of Actor.  But when Iphicles took a turn for the worst and died suddenly, Heracles once more became enwrapped in a gloomy and dangerous humor.  Iphicles was buried in a tomb on a hill at the foot of the acropolis, by where a stadium was later built.  As for his caretaker Bouphagos, he was afterwards slain by Artemis for entertaining a disordered affection for the virgin goddess.

Heracles, disinclined to postpone any longer his war against Augeias, raised a new army in Arcadia, adding to it Thebans, and, in disobedience to the command of Eurystheus, recruiting also countrymen from Argos.  He was about to set out from Pheneos when he took a fancy to the horse of his ally Oncus, who ruled Telepousan Onceium in southern Arcadia, and asked to borrow it.  This horse, named Arion, with a coat as blue as lapis lazuli, had a fabulous origin. When Demeter wandered the world in search of her daughter, she came to the sandy river Ladon where she deigned to escape Poseidon, who lusted after her, by turning herself into a mare. Poseidon, seeing through her ruse as she grazed with other mares, adapted the form of a stallion and covered her. Demeter subsequently bore a daughter, whose name it is impious to divulge, and the stallion Arion. At first Arion acted so wild and reckless, insatiable in his eagerness to gallop, that even his sire had trouble handling him. But after taming him somewhat with a golden bit, Poseidon set him as trace horse for his ocean-skimming chariot. When Oncus built a shrine to Furious Demeter at Onceium, since she had been filled with wrath at her violation, Poseidon entrusted Arion to him.

Arion, still spirited and capricious, proved a handful for Heracles; but he managed to tame him in due course. On blue-maned Arion's back he led his army back into Elis. Deprived now of their most important champions, the Eleans fought dispiritedly, despite being led into battle by Augeias himself. Heracles forced Augeias back into Ephyra and besieged the city until he surrendered. Allowing his men to loot the city to their hearts' content, Heracles settled in the palace, keeping Augeias in custody while he summoned prince Phyleus from Doulichion. Now that he had mastered Elis, Heracles felt no enmity toward his crewmate from the *Argo*, and left him unpunished. When Phyleus arrived, Heracles handed him the throne of Elis; and out of respect, since Phyleus had defended his suit against Augeias, Heracles released to him his father as well as all other prisoners. Phyleus, having no desire to rule, intended to return to Doulichium, where he had established himself in society, and gave the kingship back to Augeias. But out of gratitude to Heracles for his faithfulness, Phyleus urged him to marry his daughter Astyocheia. Heracles, disinclined to be burdened with such a young wife, merely had union with her. Nine months later she bore him a son, Tlepolemos. He also had relations with a daughter of Augeias, Epicaste, who bore to him a son, Thesalos.

After noticing how he had despoiled Ephyra of her young men, Heracles encouraged the widows to marry his soldiers. For the most part, the Elean women were pleased at this, and prayed to Athena to fructify their wombs. Since their prayers were fulfilled, the widows founded a sanctuary to Athena the Mother and called that place Sweet where they first met their husbands and experienced such delightful pleasures at their unions; and the stream passing by it they called a word which in the local dialect means *sweetwater*.

Heracles now wanted to take vengeance on Elean Pylos and Pisa for prolonging the war through their support of Augeias and constant harassment of his army. He destroyed Pylos, and was about to march on Pisatis when a solemn procession from Pisa brought him the following Delphic oracle: *"Pisa, my father attend; I, the Pythian mountain glen;"* that is: as Delphi belongs to Apollo, so does Pisatis belong to Zeus. The warning saved the Pisaians.

After returning from Pheneos, near where Heracles built a sanctuary for Phenean Apollo in honor of those who failed to come home from the Elean campaign, Heracles remained with his army encamped outside Pisa through the summer in anticipation of upcoming Games that were held at Olympia at irregular intervals. But since Elis, which oversaw the Games, had been crushed by Heracles, no preparations had been made that year. These Games were of great antiquity. Some say that a conical hill in Olympia was the site of a wrestling match between Zeus and his father Cronos for supremacy; and that thereafter, Zeus, to celebrate his triumph, instituted the Games, wherein Apollo proved a formidable contestant, besting Hermes in a race and Ares at boxing.

Heracles took a tour of the plain at Olympia, a beautiful hollow couched within low, pine-covered hills between the rivers Alpheios and Cladeos, with the intent of re-founding the Games with the spoils of his warfare. The grounds were overgrown with weeds and purple wild-flowers and in use for pasture by local herdsmen. Heracles set his men to clean up the place and grub up all the thorns while he marked out a sacred precinct, shaded by spreading plane-trees, in honor of Zeus, planting there the sprig of wild olive he had carried since returning from the land of the Hyperboreans. After raising six altars to the Olympians, one for every two, he offered sacrifices to Zeus, burning the victims on a fire fed with only white poplar, calling on him as the Averter of Flies in the hope he would dispel the buzzing swarms that vexed the valley. Iolaos, who had been learning the history of the place from the locals, asked Heracles, "Is this not the place where your great-grandfather Pelops achieved notoriety?" Heracles knew the story well. Pelops was a son of Tantalos, the wealthiest king of Phrygia. Such was his prestige that he was allowed to consort with the gods at their feasts. Puffed with pride by his divine associations, Tantalos thought to test the omniscience of the gods by killing young Pelops and serving him in a dish. The gods immediately discovered the impious ruse and patched Pelops back together. Only Demeter, distracted by her grief over the loss of Persephone, consumed a shoulder; but Hermes, at the order of Zeus, installed in him a new shoulder of ivory. Pelops emerged more handsome than ever; and beloved of Poseidon, was carried off to Olympos for a time.

Pelops, after coming back to earth, sought the hand of Hippodameia, daughter of Oinomaos, the king of Pisa, an act fraught with peril. Cruel Oinoamos forced all suitors to compete with him in a chariot race. He allowed them to set off ahead of him, with Hippodameia on board, while he tarried sacrificing a lamb to Zeus. On his chariot pulled by immortal horses, gifts of Poseidon, Oinomaos afterward speedily overtook them and killed them with a spear-thrust. When Pelops learned that twelve suitors before him had expired in his manner, he persuaded Myrtilos, the king's charioteer, to sabotage, in exchange for a night with Hippodameia, his lord's chariot by replacing the linchpins of the wheel-axles with waxen substitutes. When Oinomaos sped off in pursuit of Pelops, the wheels detached and he was thrown from his chariot and killed. Pelops repaid Myrtilos with death, they say because he tried to kiss his betrothed. As he died, Myrtilos laid a curse on the House of Pelops.

Pelops not only married Hippodameia, but also took control of Pisa and Olympia, and by his skill at diplomacy and the carefully arranged marriages of his numerous children, gained great influence throughout the Peloponnese, which was called after him.

Heracles discovered the purported grave of his ancestor Pelops, long neglected by the Pisans, near the sacred grove, and constructed around it a low, pentagonal stone fence. He dug a sacrificial pit, uncovering in the process a gigantic shoulder-blade, which he entrusted for safe-keeping to the Pisaians[10], and sacrificed to Pelops as hero a black ram as the moon rose and the golden light of day retreated behind the hills.

Heracles the next day stepped out a new arena, for foot and chariot-races, making it one stade long according to the distance of his stride. And when all was ready, he sent out heralds with the pronouncement that the Games would begin on the second full moon after the summer solstice. Contestants soon began to arrive from all quarters, many of them fresh from the Isthmian Games.

For five days, under the hot sun, men competed, completely naked and dripping aromatic oil. Unlike other sacred Games, Heracles allowed at Olympia only athletic events, and no married women were permitted within the precinct. They had to remain on the far bank of the river Alpheios.

Iolaos won the four-horse chariot race driving Heracles' chariots and his mares, establishing the precedent that competitors need not drive their own horses. In the horse-race, the Arcadian Iasios outstripped all others. Once more Polydeuces could not be equaled in the boxing match; and his brother Castor proved the fleetest in the foot-race. Two soldiers of Heracles' army, Phrastor and Niceus, won at the javelin-throw and quoits, respectively. Although Heracles declined to enter the wrestling contest, allowing Echemus of Tegea to win glory, he agreed to compete in the all-in fighting contest, held on the final day. But, since no one dared challenge him, he won by default.

In the evenings, under the beautiful light of the fair-faced moon, all the people in attendance feted the victors in grand banquets brimming with meats and myrrh-laced wines. With each win, they received pine branches and colored ribands to tie around their arms. On the final day, each champion was given as a prize an olive-branch wreath: this was to be the only reward, Heracles declared, since he had performed all of his Labors without payment.

––––––––––––––––––––

[10] When the Greeks found the war against Troy prolonged, soothsayers augured that they would not take the city unless they were in possession of the bow and arrows of Heracles and a bone of Pelops. The latter they secured from the Pisaians. Returning after the fall of Troy, the ship carrying back the bone succumbed to a storm off Euboea and the relic was lost for a time.

Since then, the olive branches are lopped with a golden sickle by a high-born boy, whose parents still lived, from the sacred tree planted by Heracles.

Daidalos, who had come as a spectator, when he heard from Heracles how he had found and buried Icaros, was so overwhelmed with gratitude that he made a statue at Pisa in the hero's likeness. Heracles, failing to recognize it as he passed by one night, threw a stone at it, taking it for a living person: so exquisitely life-like was the statue's construction.

All departed the Games in high spirits and filled with goodwill. Heracles took the success of the endeavor as proof of his own maxim never to be the cause of evil to anyone. But the Eleans say that the Games were actually founded by a gnome called Heracles the Dactyl, who, with four younger brothers, served as protectors of Zeus in Crete after his birth. They established a precedent by holding a foot-race amongst themselves, with the winner receiving an olive chaplet. It is clear that the Eleans contrived this story to spite Heracles the son of Alcmene, who had laid them low.

Having finished the business of the Games, leaving it in the care of the Pisainians, Heracles was passing through Triphylia when to his remembrance came the mocking advice of Lepreos, who, when he had pleaded with Augeias for his rightful recompense, had advised the king of Elis to fetter him. Heracles made a detour for Lepreum, where he first buried the bones of Menedemus close to a pine-tree, and entered the city with a small contingent at his back, in case of trouble. Thinking that Heracles, on a rampage, came to harm her son, Astydameia persuaded Lepreos to receive Heracles hospitably and plea for forgiveness. Arriving at the house, Heracles, thinking the youth's effrontery a minor offense, asked his father Caucon to punish him. When Caucon demurred, Astydameia, through sweet entreaties, at last moved Heracles to suspend his dislike for Lepreos, who was, after all, a good-looking and well-built young man. Coming to admire Heracles' resolve in conquering Elis, which had often treated subject Lepreum with a heavy hand, Lepreos apologized for his previous boorish behavior, and, in a spirit of youthful competitiveness, challenged Heracles to a series of contests. Heracles, who could not find it in himself to turn down a challenge, committed himself to whatever Lepreos proposed. Lepreos first competed against Heracles in throwing the quoit and in bailing out water from a caldron. In both events Heracles prevailed. Lepreos, considering himself a superlative trencherman, then challenged Heracles to an eating contest. Each man killed an ox, flayed it, cut it, cooked it and prepared his meal. Heracles was first to clear his trencher. Finally Lepreos, unable to keep up with Heracles in a drinking match, ended up so vexed that he rashly seized his weapons and challenged Heracles to single combat. Moved by a mother's tears, Heracles tried to calmly dissuade the hot-headed youth; but Lepreos refused to retract his impetuous words. Before Heracles could attempt further diplomacy, Lepreos, with drawn sword, rushed at him. Heracles parried and pushed him away, shield-boss against shield-boss. Lepreos tried again, this time employing a sword-thrust against Heracles side. The backward stroke drew blood from Heracles' wrist, raising his ire. He commenced to ferociously batter Lepreos until the latter cowered below his shield, hardly able to bear the blows. Heracles cast away his shield, and with sword-hilt grasped in both hands, plunged the sword downward with so much force that it penetrated Lepreos' hide-bound buckler and smote him through the belly, bathing the blade in hot blood and viscera. Lepreos, mourned by his parents, was buried at Phigalia. Because Heracles had eaten a whole ox in record time, he won the title of Ox-Eater during this incident.

10

After disbanding most of his army, Heracles proceeded down the coast to Pylos, where he extracted from Nestor an acknowledgement of his supremacy over western Messenia. As a result, he returned the Pylian realm to Nestor, but had him keep it in trust for his descendants. Because he had spared his aged father, Nestor maintained a begrudging respect for Heracles, and was the first to swear by him. Heracles grew to love the young man as much as he did Iolaos or Hylas.

As he left Pylos, Heracles swore that Hippocoön and his sons would not go unpunished: principally for the murder of his cousin Oinos; and also for arraying against him when he tried to take Pylos. Though the size of his army was now greatly reduced, compared to the numbers at his command when he marched on Elis, Heracles still felt confident that he could take on the unwalled Spartans with a little assistance from some powerful chieftain. So he swung north, passed through Arcadia, and came to call on Cepheus, son of Aleus, ruler of Tegea. Cepheus, who, as may be recalled, had been his comrade on the Argonautic expedition, was not unsympathetic to Heracles' cause, since Hippocoön had often signaled his intent to extend his dominion into Arcadia. He was concerned, however, that if he and his twenty sons left Tegea unattended, the neighboring Argives would take the opportunity to raid his territory. In response, Heracles gave him the lock of the Gorgon's hair which he received from Asclepios. Should Tegea's enemies try to attack while Cepheus was away, his daughter Sterope had but to wave the lock of hair three times from the city's walls. Provided she kept her gaze averted, enemies would be put to flight. The charm proved sufficient for Cepheus, who agreed to go with Heracles to war.

Cepheus and his twenty sons joined his army to Heracles'

on the Tegeatic plain, and, as soon as Castor and Polydeuces arrived from Aetolia ready to fight for their father, the combined force set off southward through the valley of the river Alpheios. On reaching the junction of the rivers Oeneus and Eurotas, they split ranks. Cepheus' army continued onward to cross the river Eurotas by Amyclai, and thus attacked Sparta from the south. Heracles and the Dioscuri took the more direct route to the bridge, where Hippocoön and his sons resisted them. But Heracles broke through, and a fearful slaughter ensued in the hollow way saddling the Spartan heights. A great din of clashing arms rattled the fruitful valley. The fighting continued past sunset and almost to the dawn, when, as light overspread the hills, the grim results of desperate combat became evident. The Spartiates bore the brunt of the casualties. Hippocoön and all his sons stewed in their own blood. Cepheus too perished, as did seventeen of his sons. But without further resistance, Heracles marched triumphantly into the city center. He restored Tyndareos, who had been abiding at Pleuron with Thestios, to the throne with the provision that he hold the kingdom in trust for his descendants, should they ever claim it.

While Heracles stayed in Sparta, he found the bones of his cousin Oinos and buried him with fitting honors in a new tomb close by the city wall. He built also a sanctuary to Athena of the Tit for Tat, since he felt she was always complicit in his victories. On the road to Therapne, across the river, he raised a sanctuary in honor of Asclepios of the Hip-joint, since he was artfully cured of the wound he had received there when he first encountered the sons of Hippocoön. By this he anticipated that Asclepios would someday become a god. And, animated by an inordinate zeal over his conquest, he even founded a sanctuary for Hera, since she had not, for once, opposed him in his latest adventure. Having no other victims at hand, he was compelled to sacrifice to her goats; and this is why, to this day, the Lacedaimonians are the only Greeks who surname the goddess *Goat-eater*.

Heracles took the bodies of Cepheus and his sons back to Tegea. Aleus, a devout believer in superstitions, hoped that Heracles would not ask for the lock of the Gorgon's hair to be returned. Having quite forgotten about it, Heracles was content to merely enjoy Aleus' hospitality for a few days before returning to Pheneos. From his guest-chamber Heracles enjoyed a view of the temple of Athena, where a white-mantled priestess caught his eye each time she came forth to perform her rituals in the upper courtyard.  One night, flushed with wine, he crept into the sanctuary to watch the virgin-priestess, a slip of a girl with long auburn hair bound with a golden fillet in a coiling mass, dance beside a marble fountain.  Moonbeams limned her lithe body through her filmy gown as she quivered in graceful curvets and caracoles in honor of the goddess.  When she had accomplished her devotions, and knelt to gather up the leaves that the wind had blown into the enclosure, Heracles emerged from the shadow of the colonnade praising her beauty with honeyed blandishments. She, taking fright, tried to flee; but Heracles swept her up in his arms and pressed her lips together with a finger until he was certain she would not raise a scandal.  He released her, offered her wine to drink, and adorned her wrists with golden bracelets and other jewelry from the spoils of Sparta.  Heracles carried out the same seduction each night until the naive girl, forgetting her chaste vocation, led Heracles to the sacred couch of Athena, above which hung the tusks and hide of the Calydonian boar.  She relented of her incitation at the last moment; but Heracles, drunk and unstoppable in his ardor, deflowered her.

Heracles departed without ever learning that the girl was Auge, daughter of Aleus.  While on a visit to Delphi, Aleus learned that his wife Neara's two brothers would die by the hand of her daughter's son.  Since his only daughter, Auge, had not yet married, he tried to prevent the fruition of the prophecy by installing her as priestess to Athena under the threat of death for unchastity.

When Auge could no longer hide the swelling of her belly, Aleus angrily demanded to know from her who had committed the outrage, thinking she had been violated.  When Auge revealed it had been Heracles, he could not believe it.  Beside himself, Aleus dragged her to the market-place, where she fell on her knees pleading for mercy, thinking he planned to kill her in public.  But he sought his man of business, Nauplios, and entrusting his daughter to her, relayed to him in confidence that she should be drowned in the sea.  Nauplios set out with Auge across Mount Parthenion, taking the pass leading to *Argo*.  Along the way Auge was afflicted with birth-pains, and under the excuse of needing to micturate, withdrew into a thicket.  There she quietly gave birth to a male child. Wracked with grief, she left him hidden in the bushes, hoping that some god would take pity and spare him, and returned to Nauplios who waited by the road, preferring the uncertain outcome of exposing her son to the certain outcome of his death alongside her own. Nauplios, taking no notice that she had been delivered of her child, arrived with her at the seashore, but had not the heart to carry out Aleus' instructions. He took her instead a little further to Nauplia, where at the harbor he sold Auge as a slave to some Carian merchants about to set out to sea.

In the meanwhile, herdsmen belonging to king Corythus found the son of Auge being suckled by a hind. Incredibly, not far off, they also came across Atalanta's infant son, whom she had borne to Meleager, but exposed so as to continue the illusion that she was still a virgin. For this reason, he was named Parthenopeus. Corythus took in both boys, but only raised Auge's son as his own, giving him the name Telephos since he had been sustained from a doe's teat.

Reaching manhood, Telephos set out one day and inadvertently killed his maternal uncles Hippothoös and Nereus on the road to Tegea. In their last moments, remembering the prophecy, they cryptically acknowledged their killer, mumbling something about the king's daughter and Heracles—although Telephos had no inkling what they meant. Greatly troubled, and wishing to know more about his mother, Telephos sought answers at Delphi, where he was told to seek king Teuthras in Mysia. Taking his friend Parthenopeus with him as his spokesman, since he had been left speechless from the ordeal, he came to Mysia and found Teuthras under siege by the Argonaut Idas. Teuthras promised Telephos not only his kingdom, but also his daughter in marriage for his assistance. Aided by his friend, Telephos overcame Idas in a single battle and forced him back to his ships. Teuthras, honoring his commitment, handed both the throne and his daughter to Telephos.

Telephos, however, did not know that Teuthras' daughter was his own mother, Auge (who had been sold to Teuthras by the Carians, and whom he then adopted, lacking children of his own); and Auge did not know that Telephos was the son she had exposed on the mountain. On the wedding night, while Telephos lay on the marriage-bed awaiting his new bride to complete her toilet, Auge quietly approached, sword in hand, ready to slay him, since she had vowed ever to be faithful to Heracles her first love. Suddenly a large serpent crawled out from the under the bed and slithered between then. Auge, in fright at the omen, dropped the sword, prompting Telephos to rise in alarm. When Telephos learned what Auge had planned to do, and was about to kill her, Auge, in desperation, cried out for Heracles her ravisher to save her. On hearing this, Telephos recognized his mother; and, with disaster averted, Auge recognized her son. The next day, Telephos took his leave of Teuthras and brought Auge back to his homeland.

# BOOK V

---

## THE PASSION OF HERACLES

### 1

After spending four years at Pheneos living with his mother, who had thought nothing of giving up her patrician comforts at Thebes to be with her son in exile, Heracles decided to leave the Peloponnese. During his sojourn in Arcadia he had not been idle in enjoying the company of several women. One was Phialo, the daughter of Alkimedon, who lived in cave on mount Ostracina, on the road between Mantinea and Methydrium. When Alkimedon noticed she was pregnant, he waited until she gave birth, and then expelled both her and her child to die on the mountain, binding Phialo to a tree to ensure her demise. The newborn babe, named Aichmogras, lying on the rough ground beside her, cried piteously. A jay-bird heard his wails and imitated them. Heracles, who happened to be walking along the road for a visit, heard the bird's cries; and thinking it was that of a child in distress, followed the sound. Finding Phialo, he untied her and rescued his son. A neighboring spring has been called after the jay-bird ever since. There was also another woman, from nearby Stymphalos, Parthenope, who bore him a son, Eures; but, now leaning on middle age, and with grey flecking his curly hair and beard, Heracles longed for a suitable wife again, legitimate children, and, in his current fancy, the simple pleasures of home life.

Iolaos took the news badly. Although he had remained at Thebes, he travelled often to visit Heracles and hunt with him on the slopes of mount Cyllene. Sitting on a rocky spur overlooking the plain of Pheneos, their bows, lances and nets set aside, they shared fond reminisces of the years gone by. Iolaos tried to dissuade him from abandoning his homeland and even, with stubborn resolution, vowed to go away with him. Heracles, sighing deeply, said: "Noble Iolaos, more of a son to me than all those bastards I've left scattered through the world, you are now a man, and with all a man's responsibilities. Your place is in your own house, with Megara your wife, and your daughter Leipephile, who, even from her cradle, shines with a beauty that surpasses that of Aphrodite or Athena. I, on the other hand, have finished my Labors. I have settled my scores. I grieve still over the deaths of my kinsmen, Oinos and Iphicles. I do not know what death the Fates have in store for me, whether falling yet in some future battle, or—gods forbid—dying on my couch from hateful old age. It seems no matter what dangers beset me, death avoids me! Nevertheless, I will not wait here to find out. I long now to regain a bit of what I once had, that happiness I felt in the good old days, when the sun seemed to shine a bit brighter, and the winds blew with unsurpassing gentleness."

"But where will you go?" asked Iolaos.

"To Calydon," said Heracles. "I heard somewhere that Meleager left a sister, Deianeira. I think about her from time to time: whether her hair is golden or brown like roasted chestnuts; whether her eyes possess the hue of the beryl or that of lapis; whether her voice sounds like a freshet gently flowing—things of that sort, which occupy the thoughts of idle men. If she is yet unwed, I will most happily make her acquaintance. Do you think, Iolaos, that such a fresh young thing will countenance an old goat like me?"

"Why Heracles," exclaimed Iolaos, "it is well known how Old Age fears you. Just yesterday I could swear I saw you squeezing him by the throat, while ready to strike his balding head with your club!"

Arrived at Thebes to return Alcmene to her house, Heracles found a woman, surrounded by a murmuring crowd, waiting for him at the door; who throwing herself down, and clasping his knees, fixed on him her golden-sheened eyes.

"Mercy!" she cried. "I am Medeia, Jason's wife."

Hearing the crowd calling her a witch and murderer, Heracles ushered Medeia inside and demanded to know the reason for her visit. Trembling and fretting greatly, she told how, after being expelled from Iolcos, she had lived contentedly with Jason at Corinth for nearly ten years, bearing him many sons and one daughter. But as time dimmed her beauty, Jason grew enamored of Glauce, king Creon's daughter, and wished to marry her in order to ensure a political advantage for himself and for his children since he felt no confidence in Medeia's own dynastic pretensions. Medeia at first pleaded with Jason, offering to poison Creon so that he could seize the throne. And when, unwilling to change his mind, he threatened to put her away, she reproached him, reminding him of the solemn oaths he had made in Aia before all the gods.

After Jason married Glauce, Creon, fearing the people, who clamored for Medeia as their rightful queen, banished her from Corinth. Given only one day to prepare for her exile, the scorned woman thought of using her magic to change her appearance, steal into the palace at night and set it afire: for she had a little root, discovered by Circe, which when kindled was difficult to extinguish. But in her torment, she devised an even more sinister plot. Rubbing a fine robe and crown with a pernicious poison and garlic, she sent them to Glauce as wedding gifts. The innocent bride, thinking nothing of it, put them on, and straightway burst into flames. In her anguish she threw herself into a fountain, still extant and now called Glauce's Spring, but to no avail. In her final throes Creon tried to rescue her, and coming near, was too engulfed in the fire so that both were consumed.

Since they were too young to take with her, Medeia left her children as suppliants on the altar of Hera upon the heights of the mountain overlooking the ancient city, below the temple of Heavenly Aphrodite, knowing that Jason would attend to them. But Creon's supporters found them, and driving them forth, stoned them to death. Thereafter, as they spread the rumor that Medeia had done the deed, a terrible plague descended on Corinth, causing all the children to perish. An oracle ordered the Corinthians to offer sacrifices in honor of Medeia's children each year and to raise an altar to Fear; and only in this way was the plague lifted.

And as Medeia fled the city, she prophesied that Jason would suffer a baleful death; which he did, when, broken and sick at heart, he wandered penniless through many countries, lastly returning back to the place where he had left *Argo*. But while sleeping under the rotting hulk, dreaming of his past glories, a beam fell down and crushed him.

Medeia reminded Heracles that the Argonauts had vowed to defend her rights when Jason pledged to marry her and keep her as his life-long companion, and begged for asylum at Thebes. Heracles, stating he had not been there, and could not be beholden to her claims, nevertheless promised to do the best he could for her. In gratitude, she administered to him certain simples to cure his occasional fits of madness. But the Thebans, claiming she had flown in on a chariot pulled by winged serpents, would not suffer a regicide among them, and expelled her.[11]

When the day for Heracles' departure arrived, Alcmene, still standing tall and supple like the slender alder, saw him off with a tender kiss, her cheeks wet with a mother's tears. "You must find a noble husband, mother," he urged her. When she remonstrated, he observed: "You must surely despise mankind to still withhold your charms." For this, she pinched his jutting chin. At the head of a loyal band of Arcadians, who had served him throughout his recent campaigns, Heracles set off for Aegea, from where he sailed across the gulf to Calydon.

When Heracles arrived at the court of king Oeneus, he found it crowded with kings, princes, noblemen, wealthy yeomen and distant high-born relations, all suitors for the hand of Deianeira. They caroused and ate meat from the king's board, played games and discoursed loudly and officiously over which of them the king's daughter would choose to marry. To look his best, Heracles had bathed and oiled himself, trimmed his hair and beard, and put aside his lionskin for a tunic and cloak.

With the feasting under way, all heads suddenly turned at a bellows from the door. "None of your lot!" cried a frightening figure as he strode in with thundering steps. Acheloös towered over all the men present, save Heracles, possessed a build as hard and massive as a Tyrian keystone to match, and wore over his body a bull's hide, with the head for a helmet, from which jutted two

---

[11] There are severe anachronisms with the various traditions of Medeia's activities during this period. Most accounts have her fleeing to Athens, where she marries Aigeus and clashes with the young Theseus. In another she consorts with Sisyphos. Both views are incompatible with our chronology.

massive, white, polished horns with gilded ends. Standing in the middle of the hall, giving everyone a black look, he said: "Only one present is meet for that lovely virgin, as the good king well knows; for, choosing to consort only with great men, he once entertained Bellerophon the Chimera-slayer for twenty days, after which they exchanged gifts: he received a belt of Tyrian purple, while the king a two-handled goblet. There sits that very cup, at the head of the table, before the king's seat. Who dares put his lips to it?" When no one rose to take the challenge, Acheloös lifted a flagon of wine, so heavy that it needed two men to carry it, filled the goblet, and grasping it by the two handles, sucked down the unmixed wine with such abandon that streams of the sweet juice flowed down his shaggy beard. Heracles, watching this display of bombast with amusement, said nothing since he was new to the court. Instead, he turned to a suitor, who hailed from Ozalian Locris, to discover the identity of the insolent newcomer. The suitor replied: "He is warden of the river Acheloös around these parts, renowned for building embankments to keep the mighty stream within its course. For arresting the ravages of the river, he is worshipped as a river-god by the commons, who think he can assume the form of a bull or a speckled serpent. More likely those ideas come from the roaring sound of the rushing waters, and the meandering course the river takes, turning this way and that. He has let all that nonsense go to his head, I think, and struts around with those bull horns like he is a god after all. Indeed, since they say Deianeira is really the daughter of Dionysos, he considers himself the only one among us worthy of her."

Someone jubilantly roused the assembly, which, like a herd of oxen released suddenly into the flowering meadow, rushed to crowd around the windows. "She rides in from the field!" cried one. "If Athena had a twin, it would be she!" called another. Heracles pushed his way through the throng to get a look. His heart leapt at the sight of her. Rather than the fragile, spoiled princess he had imagined, wrapped in fragrant linen folds, and walking mincingly on gold-laced sandals, the girl dismounting her chariot and caressing the foam-flecked neck of her hard-charging team seemed practiced in the art of war. Her long legs were covered in greaves of gold; her waist girt with a glittering belt; her ample bosom bedighted by a shining corslet of mail. Around her broad shoulders draped a crimson cloak, clasped at her neck by a jeweled brooch. As she walked, exuding a majesty that filled her suitors with awe, arrows clinked in her quiver. And when she removed her helm, decorated with golden plumes, her russet locks, like soft vine-tendrils, cascaded onto her shoulders. Many a man longed to caress those cheeks, blooming rosy from exertion and drizzled with delicious sweat; or to kiss those full, puckering lips, curving like a Scythian bow.

The appearance of the king broke the suitors' lovestruck reverie. The men all stood reverentially in line until Oeneus was seated. They then returned to their couches to await the night's festivities. Oeneus was rather tired of the whole circumstance. The suitors had been enjoying his largesse for year; his daughter had long resisted taking a husband, though he pleaded, threatened and cajoled her. She rarely came to court anymore, convinced that, since none had theretofore pleased her, it was unlikely any would do so thereafter. And so night after night, the king had to listen to the new applicants plead their suits, while continuing to act hospitably to the older ones, since he hoped to retain valuable alliances upon her marriage. Too, he was burdened with a young and querulous wife, Periboea, daughter of Hipponoös, a grandson of Sisyphos. Her father, angered that she claimed she was with child by Ares, sent her away to Oeneus with a request that he do away with her at the earliest. Oeneus, having lost his son and wife, was not willing to slay the girl, but married her instead and begat by her a son, Tydeus.

Since the arrival of Acheloös, less new wooers appeared at court, and the existing ones increasingly gave up and departed for their homes, for he spent his time boasting and making threats. Heracles still attended, however, keeping quiet and sitting apart from the rest so as not to draw attention. The Locrian urged him to make his case before the king, curious as to his identity, since Heracles by equivocations concealed it, thinking it impractical to speak without Deianeira in audience.

One night, after supper and the usual entertainments, a silence overtook the high-beamed hall. Deianeira, by her sudden appearance, dispelled the gloom under the waning cressets. She swept in like rosy Dawn, who, rising in the orient, dissolves the lingering clouds of night, bringing new hope to forlorn men. An eternal springtime clothed her with all the supple charms of youth and loveliness. Surrounded by her ladies-in-waiting, who ensured the trail of her gown did not befoul itself across the dusty floor, she first greeted her father with a kiss, plucked a date from a dish, and went to sit upon her couch. With marked indifference she cast an eye about the room, and then settled back upon her bolsters to weave colored flowers into a garland. The suitors, one by one, approached to praise her excellence or leave gifts by her delicate feet. She afforded each man a single glance, and perhaps a smile, but otherwise not a word mingled with her honeyed breath. Heracles marveled at her turning shades of character: she was one who neither feared life in the woods and fields, nor disdained the comforts of domesticity.

Now Heracles unwrapped his cloak and strode forward down the middle of the hall, tall and erect, borne on powerful thighs that pulsed like a racing horse's flanks. His tunic barely contained his massy chest, and the sinews of his enormous arms stood out like frapped cordage. Even Acheloös took notice of the newcomer, and straightway considered him his only true rival. Heracles bowed before Oeneus, and opening his generous mouth, began: "Most illustrious ruler of Calydon and Pleuron, I am Heracles, formerly of Tyrins. I was acquainted with your noble son, prince Meleager, with whom I sailed aboard the famed *Argo* with Jason son of Aison, our captain. It was Meleager who first described your fair daughter to me; and, with all due respect, I must declare him rather miserly in his introduction, for he failed to adequately prepare me for the sight of her unsurpassed loveliness."

Oeneus, caught by surprise, declared: "Heracles! Who does not know Heracles! You honor us by your presence, and may the gods smile upon you as you throw your lot into this game, which, I believe, has gone on far too long." He arched an eyebrow at Deianeira, and was about to follow with a look of urgency, when he caught her staring at Heracles in rapt attention. Never before had he witnessed in her such a reaction to a suitor's blandishments. Thinking that, after all, she was fated to marry Acheloös, Deianeira saw at last her savior in Heracles

"Moreover," continued Heracles, stealing a glance at Deianeira, "should I marry your daughter, not only would she bask in the glory of my Labors, feats unmatched to this day, but she would have Almighty Zeus as her father-in-law."

Heracles would have continued his disquisition had not a hoarse laugh interrupted him. Acheloös, standing beside him shoulder to shoulder, scoffed: "This man is an outlander. He can say anything he pleases, and are we supposed to take him at his word? I too have heard of these legends. Some lion he subdued, or some boar caught, or some mares he wrangled. What proof is there? I, on the other hand, am well known through all the lands that bear my namesake river's unruly flow—the greatest and most ancient in all of Greece. Ask the Dolopians or the Agraians who I am. Inquire from the Acarnians, and they will tell you that I, by my power, have turned their marshes into fruitful fields. Indeed everywhere sweet water flows, I am known. I am your countryman; but this man is plainly a nobody, a smooth talker, and by the looks of him, not very bright at all. Theseus—now that is a man to contend with. Were he here, I would forthwith give place. I recall, after the hunt for that wild boar, when you, your majesty, assembled together the most illustrious men of Greece—(if Heracles is so noteworthy, why was he excluded?)—that Theseus[12] and some companions in the chase found himself blocked at my river's edge by water swollen with the spring rains and melting snow. I tell him, 'Take shelter in my house, famed son of Athens. The river is now impassable; see how the current roars past, bearing with it trees and rocks! I've witnessed men and beasts swept up in its relentless eddies. Rest while the waters run their course, and settle back within their bed.' And so they came into my home upon a high bank, with walls of pumice and coarse tufa, a floor of damp moss, and ceiling paneled with conchs and purple shells. My barefoot nymphs at once laid out a feast. Lelex, the hero of Troizen, with a bit of gray at his temples, enjoyed my hospitality; as did brave Peirithoös and others. After we had our fill, and reclined drinking savory wine in jeweled cups, Theseus, looking toward the sea beyond the river's mouth, asked me: 'That island—what is it called?

---

[12] Ovid in book viii. of the *Metamorphosis* presents the Calydonian hunt as occurring after Heracles had fought Acheloös and lost his horn in the process, since Acheloös entertained Theseus while hiding his head-wound beneath a garland.

Is it only one? Being far off, it is hard to tell.' I responded: 'What you see is not one island, but five; the distance deceives the eyes. They were once five naiads who, after sacrificing ten bullocks, invited the other rural divinities to their sacred feast—all except me. In my rage I stirred the waters until they swelled and rampaged against nature, sweeping away woods and fields. The naiads and all things around them were washed away into the sea. Whole pieces of land, torn off by the violent discharge, became the islands beyond the river's mouth, called the Echinades. But there is yet another isle—look carefully, it lies apart from the rest—that is dear to me. Sailors call it Perimele. Once a girl bore that name, and I loved her. Her father, Hippodamas, bitterly opposed our marriage, and he cast her off a cliff to drown in the deep. I caught her, but in the welter she was torn from my arms. I prayed to the trident-bearing god to shelter her—and as I watched her floating on the waves, land embraced her body, and an island grew around her.' Peirithoös alone doubted my tale, disbelieving, and mocked the gods. Lelex, older and wiser, rightly reminded him that the powers of heaven have no limit, and gods do as they wish."

Heracles tried to register a rebuttal, but Acheloös continued over him: "And as for this business that Alcmene's son sprung from Zeus—either he is not your father, or he is—to your shame. If your claim to Zeus is true, does it not mean you were conceived in adultery? What is it, then? Is Zeus your father or not? Admit your lie, or confess that your mother was made a strumpet!"

Heracles, who had been glaring at Acheloös during his peroration, though stewing in white hot anger, suppressed the impetus for violence before such high company. He said only: "My hand is superior to my tongue. I am better suited for fighting than debating."

Oeneus interrupted them with nervous laughter, saying: "Ah, see how late it is! Let us end this discussion for the night. Tomorrow is another day. Come back then with cooler heads, dear friends. Perhaps Deianeira will have made her decision by then."

The next morning, Gorge sensed Deianeira's distracted mind, and said: "What spell possesses you, sister? Is there a man, at last, found worthy of winning your heart?" Deianeira, who had been stroking the lovely, colored plumes of the guinea-hens that strutted about their apartments, responded: "How like our brother

Meleager is this stranger!  Of noble bearing, manly, possessed of that same dark and brooding countenance.  I could hardly sleep; he found his way into every dream."  Gorge, delighted said: "At last!  One to strike your fancy!  But do you lay down, bruised by Eros' painful shaft, so easily?  Be certain that your time will be consumed with children and wifely duties.  No longer will you race your chariot across the fragrant meadows or hunt alone the fleet-footed roebuck.  Is this truly what you wish?  And what will happen when he goes off to battle, as men like him do, and perchance dies in some foreign land?  Or, once tired of you, his roaming eye delights in some neat-ankled hussy?  Be married, dear sister, by all means; but let time and prudence conduct you to a sound decision."  Deianeira, her thoughts in a jumble, her heart suffering from an unaccustomed ache, was not listening.  She put a hand to her moist brow, fevered by inward flames.

A house maid interrupted their breakfast to announce, with great alarm, that two of the suitors had entered into a heated argument in the hall and were now on their way to settle the score by the riverbank.  Deianeira, having no doubt as to the identity of the battling wooers, kicked off her sandals and ran faster than anyone else to the crest of the high river, where she saw Heracles and Acheloös already contending by the water's edge.  Acheloös, with strong arms, fended off each of Heracles' assaults, who repeatedly rushed at him, trying to entangle him in the tall sedge.  Heracles, in disgust, stooped to gather a handful of dust, which he flung at Acheloös; but the wind blowing through the reeds pushed it back into Heracles' eyes.  Heracles rued that he had been enticed to fight Acheloös on his own turf.  Heracles then went for Acheloös' mud-splattered neck, his finger slipping in the grip, while at the same time trying to hook one of his legs for a throw.  But Acheloös, Heracles found, was laden with greater bulk than it seemed, and stood immobile, like a rock fixed against the wind-swept surge.  They drew apart, as fighters do to catch their breath, and then clashed again.  Each held firm, determined not to yield.  Brow against brow, hands clasped, they pressed their weights, just as strong bullocks strive to impress the fairest heifer of the pasture, while the terrified herds awaits a winner.  Heracles tried three times to disengage, and at the fourth succeeded in breaking from Acheloös iron grip.  Without pause, Heracles swung his hammy fist and stunned Acheloös with an upper cut, sending him spinning. Jumping on his back, Heracles caught Acheloös in a crushing embrace. The river guardian managed to thrust his arms, dripping with sweat, into the hold to loosen it. Heracles, without giving Acheloös pause, moved to a stranglehold. Acheloös, unable to break free, fell to his knees in the muck, and then his face hit the ground. With flailing arms Acheloös drove their struggling bulks into the river, where he hoped to gain some advantage, contorting his body, trying to wriggle from out of Heracles' deadly squeeze. "Personating a snake now?" mocked Heracles. "Fighting snakes was cradle work for me!" But Acheloös had managed to turn partly about, and had both hands now working to break apart the mighty choke. Before he could succeed, Heracles moved to wrap his fingers around Acheloös' neck. Acheloös summoned all his strength to pry off the vice-like grip, pushed Heracles back with a kick, and regained his footing. Then, bowing his head, he charged with his helmet's deadly horns. Heracles vaulted aside, threw an arm around his opponent's neck, and pulled him down so that his horns thrust securely into the ground. Exhausted, Acheloös, his mouth filled with dirt, finally yielded. Heracles obliged him, but not before wrenching off one of the horns as a sign of victory. Acheloös, looking up to see Deianeira, to hide his shame covered the mutilated stump in a clump of weeds, and departed.

Heracles climbed the riverbank to where Deianeira stood watching the battle in wonder. He took a knee before her and said: "My lady, between the two of us we have scared away all your other wooers, and now only I am left. I hope I have not made too unseemly an impression on you; but in insulting my mother, he raised my ire."

From that moment, Deianeira knew her love was sure.

Heracles presented Oeneus with the horn, which the king put to good use as a fruit-bowl, in imitation of the horn of Amaltheia, the nurse of the infant Zeus after his birth on Crete, which never ceases to overflow with fresh herbs and autumn fruit.

Oeneus, delighted to gain the formidable Heracles as his son-in-law, celebrated the marriage in high style. The smoke of a hecatomb rose for ten days as the feasting continued; and Oeneus, who possessed extensive vineyards, did not spare the choicest wines from his cellars. Alcmene never before saw Heracles, surrounded by friends and relatives, in such high spirits. Heracles was given a residence beside the royal palace, and there he settled with Deianeira.

Heracles did not long remain idle, but after his honeymoon stirred from his marriage-bed to perform deeds of benefit to his new countrymen. As one example, he diverted the river Acheloös by digging canals, through which he regained for the Calydonians large tracts of land for fruitful husbandry.

At Oeneus' command, Heracles marched with the Calydonians against Thresprotian Ephyra, in the district of Elaetis, captured the city, and killed its king, Phyleus. It was curious how Elean Ephyra had also a king by that name, the son of Aigeus.

After his victory in Thresprotia, Heracles stopped off at Dodona to inquire of the oracle, curious as to what things were still in store for him. He received a prophecy that disturbed him; namely that if he did not die in fifteen months' time, he would instead live the rest of his life in quietude. In addition, he was given the following command. He was to call on king Thespios, whose daughters each had bore him a son, to send two or three sons to Thebes, forty to colonize the island of Sardinia, and to keep the rest at Thespiai. Since the boys were still young, Heracles asked Iolaos to take general command of the colonization effort. Iolaos, inclined to another adventure, agreed. He sailed to Sardinia with the Thespians and an Athenian contingent, provided by Theseus, and subdued the native inhabitants, composed of Libyan emigrants. Iolaos divided the most desirable inland tracts into provinces, leaving deserted the coastal strips which, filled with marshes and lagoons, yielded a most insalubrious climate; and planted fruit-bearing trees. Daidalos he summoned from Sicania to build great monuments, such as gymnasia and court-buildings, to ensure the success of the fledgling state. The Thespian sons of Heracles held Iolaos in such affection that they considered him a second father, and consented to be called Iolaosians after himself. When all was settled, Iolaos returned to Greece by way of Sicania, where many of his followers remained, attracted by the beauty and fertility of the island. Iolaos was welcomed throughout Sicania, since the inhabitants remembered him from his time there with Heracles.

Heracles, in the meanwhile, continued to live happily at Calydon with Deianeira, who was admirably suited for him in every way. She continued to hunt and practice the arts of war, sometimes along with Heracles, and there was nothing she was wanting from her former life; instead she enjoyed now much more. Within three years she bore him Hyllos, Ctessipos, Glenos, Hodites, and a single daughter, Macaria. Heracles spent his days playing with his children, and was known to warn visitors who tried to distract him, saying: "I'm at play!—a welcome change from my toils."

But what mortal happiness can last without attracting the attention of the jealous gods, who then bring men down to misery? One evening, a little boy, the son of Architeles, a kinsman of Oeneus, eager to befriend Heracles, approached him at the commencement of the feast to pour water over his hands. Noticing that the boy, not knowing any better, used a foot-bath for the purpose, Heracles became enraged and flicked him on the head with a finger. When Heracles witnessed the boy crumple to the floor, killed instantly, he cried out in anguish, took up the limp body and pressed it long against his breast.

Despite the forgiveness of Architeles and the king, Heracles refused to make his case an exception to the law, and chose voluntary exile over the accidental killing. Despite the entreaties of Oeneus, Heracles packed his belongings, and taking Deianeira and his children with him, set off for Trachis, where he hoped to take refuge with his friend king Ceyx.

They came to the river Euenos, swollen and overflowing its banks. Heracles, fearless for himself, but anxious how to get Deianeira across the flood, choked with debris and teeming with whirlpools, stood mutely on the riverbank, blocked by the impassable stream. Just then, a Centaur galloped down from the hills to offer his assistance. While Heracles did not recognize him, since all Centaurs to him had the same appearance, the Centaur did recognize Heracles. He was Nessos, who had escaped the slaughter upon Mount Pholoë as Heracles passed by in search of the Erymanthian boar, after which very few Centaurs remained there. Pursued by Heracles, they had fled in various directions. Some, such as Nessos, went to dwell by the river Euenos; others fled to Malia, where they thought to dwell with Cheiron; a few made it to Trinacria, where the Sirens destroyed them. The remainder fled to Eleusis, where the god Poseidon hid them.

"Hullo!" cried he; "because of my impeccable honor, the

gods have seen fit to appoint me ferryman. I am strong and know all the fords well."

Heracles said: "Very well, carry my wife across."

"Delighted," said Nessos. "With my help, for a small fee, she'll stand safe on the other side; while you, using your mighty strength, can swim."

Heracles set Deianeira, pale and trembling, dreading both the surging river and the burly Centaur, upon Nessos' high back, and then commenced to organize with his Arcadian allies for an orderly crossing. Heracles piled his chariot high with his belongings, tied them down, and after setting his son Hyllos at the top of the heap, waded into the river leading his horse Arion by the bit. Although the water soon reached his breast, Heracles cried: "I'll beat one more river yet, now that I've begun!"

The current, strong as it was, seemed trifling against Nessos strong legs and broad back. He confidently passed through the flood with Deianeira, for dear life, clutching his breast. Almost at the opposite bank, Nessos looked back to see Heracles barely begun, and evil designs entered his mind. Once across, Nessos crouched to allow Deianeira to dismount. In watching her wring out the hem of her dress, with the fabric wet against her bosom and her fragrant hair dripping water, Nessos grew mad with unlawful desire. He trotted slowly toward her, excitedly swishing his tail. Deianeira, seeing his wanton eyes, desperately dashed toward the river, screaming for Heracles.

Heracles, midway across the stream, heard her cry above the roar. Wiping the water from his eyes, he saw how Nessos attempted on the far bank to haul Deianeira into his arms.

"You ravisher!" he yelled. "Where are you taking my wife? I should have known better than to trust a Centaur!" And as he saw his struggling wife borne away, he raged, his eyes red with fury: "Stop there! Trust your horse-strength, if you will, you foul, two-formed monster! You'll not escape me!" Heracles drew an arrow from his quiver, the remaining arrow tainted with the Lernean Hydra's blood. He prepared his shot, and holding his bow in his outstretched left hand, he carefully measured off the distance to the mark. It was as if Nessos heard the bowstring sing, for he made a leap before the shaft, cutting a wide arc through the air, pierced his back. Down went Nessos, tripping on his hooves; but he was careful to keep Deianeira cradled in his arms to prevent her injury in the fall. She crawled out of his grasp, sobbing inconsolably, too weak to stand or do anything else but sit there trembling.

Nessos, seeing the barbed arrow-point protruding from his breast, agonizingly broke it off, and reaching painfully behind him, extracted the shaft. Blood spurted from the double wound, searing his skin and smoldering the sunlit grass on which it dripped. Seeing this, he knew the arrow had been dipped in a powerful poison, which employing his blood as a reagent, had been transformed into a caustic substance. "I will not die unavenged," he thought.

"Woman, allow me to make amends!" he pleaded, stretching his arms toward Deianeira. "My baser nature took advantage of my good sense. Come here; I have something to give you before this wound does me in."

As Deianeira watched, Nessos broke off a hoof, damaged already from his convulsions, which he filled with his streaming, tainted blood. "For you; take it!" he said desperately, trying to mask his agony with altruistic resolve. "It is a love-philter, which you may need some day. Your husband is Heracles, after all, who in the wildness and rashness of his nature has much in common with my sort. Come near, I say. You have nothing to fear from me now."

Deianeira, confused, scared, afflicted even still with a new bride's jealous love, reached out just enough to lift the mixture from the Centaur's fingers. Nessos, seeing Heracles climbing the river-bank, said hurriedly: "Keep the talisman from light or heat, lest you ruin its power. In that day when your husband's love begins to wane, anoint one of his garments with the blood. He will be forever yours; and nothing but death will separate you."

Stanching the bloody flow with his fist and mustering his remaining strength, Nessos rose from his haunches and galloped off. He made it as far as Ozolian Locris, where he perished of his wound. His corpse remained unburied, putrefied, and filled the area with a fetid odor. Similarly, the Centaur Pylenor, whom Heracles shot before Pholos' cave, infected the waters of the river Anigros in Elis with a horrible stench after he washed his wound there.

Deianeira kept Nessos' gift secret when Heracles arrived at her side.

As they passed through the country of the Dryopians,

Heracles came across their ruler, Theoidamas, son of Dryops, ploughing his fields with a yoke of oxen. Since Hyllos was hungry, and numerous provisions had been lost crossing the river Euenos, Heracles interrupted Theoidamas' labor to ask for a bite to eat. When the latter insolently waved him off, telling Heracles he did not suffer beggars, Heracles in anger slew him, unloosed one of the bullocks from the plough, slaughtered it, and feasted with his family on the spot. When the Dryopians, who lived in the fastness of Mount Parnassos, learned of this, they were enraged and organized for war under Phylas, Theoidamas' successor. No sooner had Heracles settled in at Trachis than the Dryopians threatened to enter the Malian plain looking for him. Heracles, assisted by the Malians, marched out and subdued the Dryopians in a single day. He then expelled the Dryopian tribes to the frontiers of Phocis, and awarded their land to the Malians for their assistance. The leading Dryopians he took as slaves to Delphi. Since the shrine had no use for them, they were sent off to the Peloponnese, where they threw themselves at the mercy of Eurystheus, who used them to build several cities in the Argolid. In the fighting, Heracles killed Phylas and carried off his daughter Meda, on whom he begot a son, Antiochus. But he did not bring Meda to Trachis for fear of offending Deianeira. She learned, however, of his indiscretion, which served only to augment her jealousy. While at Calydon, Heracles had been an attentive husband and father, ever at her side and in the company of his children. Since arriving at Trachis, however, he had spent less time in the house, and more time feasting with his Arcadian companions, allowing his restless mind to dwell on further adventures.

Heracles one day was sought by Aigimos, king of the Dorians of Histiaeotis, who offered him a third part of the kingdom for his assistance in a border dispute with the Lapiths of Mount Olympos. Seeing that the Dorians were outnumbered, Heracles, reunited with Iolaos, who had recently returned from his assignment in Sardinia, as his charioteer, joined his Arcadian army with them and defeated the Lapiths. On the battlefield he met with his shipmate Coronos, son of Caineus, who ruled over the Lapiths, and was forced to kill him when he refused all offers of diplomacy. Aigimos faithfully held a third part of his kingdom in trust for Heracles' descendants. Since that time, an enduring bond existed between the Dorians and the descendants of Heracles.  On his way back to Trachis, Heracles heard that the Dryopian Laogoras, a man of violence and ally of the Lapiths, was abusing his visit to Delphi by feasting in the temple of Apollo.  Heracles burst in and slew him, along with his sons.

While at Delphi, Heracles remembered his vow to Prometheus, who told him that there would no end to the Titan's sufferings unless a god was found willing to die and descend to the underworld in his place.  Heracles thought long on the matter while walking the sacred paths of the sanctuary; until, with the exultation of sudden discovery, he ordered Iolaos to hitch the chariot and take him to Mount Pelion.

When they came to Ormenium, a small city on the foot of Mount Pelion, king Amyntor would not let Heracles pass through his territory since he was a known associate of Peleus.  Peleus had once defeated him in battle and had taken his son Crantor to be his armor-bearer.  Amyntor was also the father of Euaemon, Astydameia and Phoenix.  The latter he blinded for having an affair, at the instigation of his wife Cleobule, with his concubine.  Cheiron, however, restored his sight.  He later sought protection under Peleus, who made him king of the Dolopians when Peleus gained possession of Pthiotis.  Heracles, pricked by Amyntor's nerve, attacked the city and slew him.  Seeing that his daughter, Astydameia, was lovely to behold, Heracles spent a night with her.  In time, she bore him a son, called also Ctesippos.

Heracles left Iolaos at Ormenium while he alone climbed the slopes of Pelion.  He remembered well the location of Cheiron's cave of ancient rock, where the Centaur's loyal wife Chariclo received him and conducted him to the room from which Cheiron never stirred, incurably sick but unable to die.  Heracles, who did not know how he would be received by his old teacher, stood quietly until Cheiron noticed him with his rheumy eyes.  He had been tutoring a plump fair-haired infant in music, plucking for him different harmonies from the cords of a lyre.

Cheiron wept on seeing Heracles, who knelt by his side when the Centaur tried achingly to rise on his haunches.  As they shared news of the years that passed between them, the tiny boy, affected by the grief and melancholy he detected in their words, stroked Cheiron's frail hands, kissed them, and whimpered: "Live, I pray! Don't leave, dear father!" Heracles asked to know the boy's identity, and Cheiron, handing the boy a piece of dripping honeycomb, began thus: "I gave him the name Achilles. My condition prevents me any more from filling these deep tunnels and shady groves with pupils; but this lad I could not refuse to adopt and attempt to shape his tender years. He reminded me so much of you as a lad, and Jason, and tragic Actaeon, who in the bloom of youth had the ill-luck of seeing Artemis naked, bathing in a pool, while he hunted on the slopes of Cithaeron. She turned him into a stag and his own dogs in a frenzy consumed him. When not a morsel of him was left, the dogs looked for their master with great howls, coming at last to my cave, where I carved an effigy in Actaeon's likeness to console them.

"This child, nourished on milk, marrow and honey, will grow to become the last of the great heroes of our age. After him, these times will pass into legend and song. He will turn crimson the vine-covered plain of Mysia, but will perish in his prime. He is immortal, you see, in every part but one, which will doom him to share the lot of every man."

"Immortal, you say?" Heracles exclaimed in disbelief, as the boy could not resist touching the shaggy pelt of his lionskin.

Cheiron said: "I will explain how that came to be. You may know that Peleus, my grandson, sought the protection of Acastos after killing his father-in-law in the boar hunt. While staying at Iolcos, Acastos' wife Astydameia fell madly in love with him. Peleus, the chastest of men, rejected all of her indecent proposals. She, contriving to take vengeance, sent a message to Peleus' wife in Phthia that he was about to marry Sterope, Acastos' daughter. Believing the false tale true, she hung herself. Moreover, Astydameia then accused Peleus before her husband of attempting to seduce her in his own bed. Acastos, believing his wife, but unwilling to stain his hands with the blood of the man he had hospitably received and even purified from a crime, took him up this mountain under the pretense of a hunt. After a long day at the chase, Peleus, greatly fatigued, fell asleep under a tree. Acastos, grasping the opportunity to let Peleus be killed by wild beasts, concealed his sword—a fine one, wrought by Daidalos—and left him alone in the wilderness. Some wayward Centaurs found him, and thinking him one of the Lapiths, our mortal enemies, they tried to kill the defenseless man. Thankfully I had yet some strength in me in those days, and was out for a walk in the shade, when, after finding the sword in a thicket, I managed to find Peleus after casting a bit about.

"I tell you: nothing can raise the spirits like a visit from a good friend or relative! Peleus abided with me for some time; and he would go hunting as he used to, bringing back hares and fragrant apples for Chariclo. He was so aggrieved over his wife, however, that I pressed him to try his hand at gaining the sea-nymph Thetis, who came often into a Thessalian cove swimming with the dolphins. Like all marine divinities, Tethis is crafty, and has the power to assume any form she wishes. I instructed Peleus to seize and hold her fast, despite what shape she evinced. A myrtle wood grows close to this bay, where naked Tethis in a grotto slept. There Peleus, laying in wait, snatched her. Though to escape she took the form of a bird, and then a tree, and finally a spotted tigress, Peleus would not relinquish his grasp until she yielded to him, saying: 'For you to conquer me, a god must be your ally.' Having won the reluctant goddess, he wed her on this mountain—and what a wedding it was, honored with the presence of the high gods, who arrived in mortal guise! I gave Peleus a heavy spear of Pelian ash, polished by Athena and capped in bronze by Hephaistos. The other gods presented him with splendid arms and armor: a corslet shinning with embossed stars, a pair of bronze greaves fitted with silver ankle-straps, a silver-studded broadsword, a vast, bright-rimmed shield, wrought beyond the telling; a bright casque brushed by a horsehair plume; and two immortal horses, Balius and Xanthus, foaled by a Harpy and sired by the West Wind, were Poseidon's gifts. Delighted, Peleus washed their manes in spring water and anointed their tawny hides with olive oil.

"In this very cave, on a bed of leaves, was this illustrious child conceived. Tethis bore Peleus six other children, but these she burned in a secret place to test their immortality. Ligyron, as the babe was first called, alone survived the flames, which Tethis applied to burn away the mortal parts inherited from Peleus; while during the day she anointed him with ambrosia. When Peleus one night discovered Tethis in the midst of her ritual, he cried out in terror and snatched his son from the fire, where only his foot had been burnt. Tethis fled back to her sisters. Thereafter Peleus entrusted the boy to me while he went off to assemble an army to besiege Iolcos.  He slew Acastos and Astydameia, tore her asunder, and passing between her strewn limbs, marched his men into the city."

Cheiron called for his wife to take little Achilles, for he wished to be alone with Heracles.  She came in with another babe in her arms, Patroclos, whose father the Argonaut Menoitios wished to be educated alongside the son of Peleus.  As soon as she carried the boys off, with a heavy sigh, Cheiron said: "How well my daughter—Ocyrhoe, for she was delivered beside a swift river—prophesied my fate!  When Apollo brought the child Asclepios to me, fresh from his mother's fiery bier, in she came—I remember how her auburn hair fell upon her shoulders—and turning frantic at the sight of the child, declared he was to be the healer of the world; but he would overstep his bounds in bringing life to the dead, and pay for it with his own life.  And about me, she said: 'And you, dear father, though meant from birth to enjoy life eternal, shall one day long to die, vexed by the serpent's venom; and so shall you suffer, until death takes you and you are freed from your immortality.'  Saying this, her voice turned into a whinny; her hanging locks became a flowing mane; her hands and feet hardened into hooves: she lost all semblance of humanity, becoming a mare before my very eyes, silenced forever by the Fates.

"Here I now lie, cursed by a wound that no poultice of blended herbs can cure; my blood, corrupted by Lernean poison, has reached every extremity.  I take pleasure no longer in endless life.  No longer do I enjoy the light of day or the sweet draught of the vine.  I desire, Heracles, to die."

With a hand on his mentor's shoulder, Heracles with a heavy heart said: "Dearest friend, how I can I repay your patient instruction in my youth, or ever make amends for the grievous hurt I inflicted on you?  Perhaps there is some remedy in this.  On one of my Labors I came across the great god Prometheus enchained on a high mountain.  Zeus would never pardon him—he told me—until some god could be found ready to take on his sufferings and descend willingly to Hell."

Cheiron bestirred himself in a sudden alarm.  Looking intently at Heracles, he asked: "Did you manage to unfetter him?"

"I did," said Heracles.

Cheiron, with tears in his eyes, after a moment cried: "How clear it all becomes to me now!  O, my good son, can you not see with what providence the great Zeus handles the affairs of gods and men alike?  Prometheus knew a secret, told to him by his mother, that if Zeus married Thetis, she would bare a son more powerful than he.  Since you freed him, Prometheus must have finally divulged the secret, prompting Zeus to forestall the danger by arranging for a mortal, Peleus, to marry Tethis instead.  Now all that is left is to complete the ancient bargain.  Prometheus is immortal—he will never die.  If I am to die for Prometheus, I must exchange my immortality with mortality."  And then, grasping his oaken staff, he urged Heracles to assist him out of the cave.

They went forth a little ways, and in a glade Cheiron knelt to pile some stones for an altar; while Heracles he dispatched to fetch a ram from his herd.  They sacrificed it; and as the savory smoke swirled above the flames, Cheiron, raising his arms, prayed: "Almighty Zeus, I take the mantle of mortality from Heracles. Grant that when the Fates cut short the thread of his life, he take on the mantle of my immortality."

Heracles, stunned, said: "Cheiron, as dear a father as my own, do you know what you say?  Do you so willingly discard everlasting life for me?"

"There is no greater good than to lay down one's life for a friend," said Cheiron.  "Did you think, son of Zeus, that there would be no reward for your Labors?  As great as you have been among men, greater shall you be in the company of the blessed gods."

The sound of a distant thunderclap affirmed his pronouncement.

Sadly leaving Mount Pelion, knowing the he would never again see Cheiron alive, Heracles reunited with Iolaos and set out with him back to Trachis.  Along the way Heracles, as a means to relieve his downcast spirit, concocted a fable for Iolaos about his penultimate Labor.

"Now  Prometheus advised me not to go after the apples myself," said Heracles, "but to pay a visit to his brother Atlas in the northern waste, where on the summit of the highest mountain he stands holding up the sky, and ask him to fetch the apples instead while I for a while minded his burden. This I attempted, climbing for weeks through the howling snow and blistering frost, until I reached the mighty Titan.  He was relieved to see me, and happily, with a heave and a snort, hoisted the heavens on my shoulders.  I nearly crumbled under the weight!  Imagine the whole of the celestial bodies circling in their wondrous epicycles at once placed on the back of a puny man!  But after shifting the burden a bit, by which some dislodged stars fell in flames to earth, I set myself in a position where I could subsume, at least for a little while, the god's magnificent labor.  At length Atlas returned from the holy garden, and holding out three golden apples in his hand so I could see them, offered to take them to Eurystheus himself while I continued bearing the sky.  Prometheus had warned me about this, and so I hastily replied: 'Very well.  But here, take back the sky for a moment while I find a pad for my head.'  Atlas considered my request not unreasonable, put down the apples and bent down to take the sphery load from me.  As soon as I was freed, I picked up the apples, bade him farewell, and departed."

Passing near Itone in Phthiotis, a chariot came to stand before them on the road.  Recognizing Cycnos, son of Ares, standing tall in his car, his polished armor gleaming under the torrid sun, Heracles called out: "Cycnos!  We meet again!  But why set your swift horses against us, men tried in pain and labor?  Step aside from our path.  We have no time for you now.  To Trachis we drive, to honorable king Ceyx, whom you know well, for you have his daughter Themistonoe as wife."

Cycnos responded with a snarl: "I have long sought for a new match with you, Tyrinthian, since you ran away at our last one.  Gird yourself, and let the son of Ares give you sound instruction in combat."

"Fool!" exclaimed Heracles.  "Ares will not deliver you once we meet in battle.  They say that I cast him to the ground when he came to defend sandy Pylos, transfixing both his shield and thigh with my spear-thrust."

Cycnos slipped on his plumed helm, and readying his menacing spears and shield, had his driver move a small distance away, squaring for the fight.  Heracles said to Iolaos: "Come, friend, quickly take the reins of our swift horses.  This time we will not save face.  Have courage in your heart and drive straight onward.  Fear not this talk of Ares.  It is against men that we contend."

Iolaos, burning with excitement, said: "The Father of gods and men must greatly honor you to deliver such a strong fellow into your hands! He fails to frighten the son of Zeus; and the son of Iphicles even less! Quickly put on your armor before our chariots join. At your age, you must take every precaution."

Heracles, glad at heart and smiling at his words, returned: "Hero Iolaos, rough battle is at hand. As you have borne me oftentimes with your skilled maneuverings, do so again, wheeling black-maned Arion this way and that, and assist me as you are able. Although I am not accustomed to it, I will do as you ask and don my armor."

Heracles clasped on his legs greaves of bronze, fastened a golden corslet around his breast, laid on bronze spaulders and set a close-fitting casque on his head—all valued arms from the first Trojan expedition. He covered his back with a bristling quiver, gripped two spears in his left hand and held aloft in his right the glorious shield glittering with white ivory and electrum. Arion neighed loudly as Iolaos snapped the goad, and, with a leap, led the charge against Cycnos' onrushing chariot. Spears struck shields with the noise of thunder as horses and chariots collided in a whirl of dust. Both combatants, still standing, leapt from their cars and fell on one another with great shouts like two lions vying for a deer's carcase. Cycnos, eager to kill Heracles, struck with his brazen spear, but could not penetrate the thick targe of Heracles emblazoned with chilling Fear and frightful Strife. Heracles, in turn, drove his long spear between Cycnos' helm and shield, piercing his foeman's neck below the chin. Cycnos fell like an oak or pine-tree smashed asunder by Zeus' thunderbolt, dropping to the dust in a clattering of armor. Iolaos helped Heracles strip Cycnos of his armor and took it with them back to Trachis. Ceyx recovered his son-in-law's corpse and buried him in the valley of the river Anauros; but, at Apollo's command, the swollen river washed away his gravesite as punishment for despoiling the pilgrims heading to Delphi.

2

Deianeira found, as some years passed, that Heracles grew increasingly short with her, chiding her for every trifling thing. He stopped going to her bed or appearing publicly beside her, except at official functions at the behest of king Ceyx. That burning passion in him, surpassing even the very necessities of eating and sleeping, had cooled to warm embers. When she questioned him about his disinterest, he grew reticent, and then fell into a long distemper. Deianeira could only vent her sorrows to her nurse, or to the handmaidens she had brought with her retinue from Calydon. She was convinced that some mistress pleased him more than her, now past that beguiling bloom of maidenhood so quickly plucked, like a fruit at the peak of freshness; but when once overripe, it is cast from the branch.

Deianeira could not know that the visage of fair Iole of Oechalia never departed entirely from her husband's thoughts. As time advanced, she loomed ever more prominently in his desires, and it gnawed at him that he did not possess her. He tried to forget her, to be content in his present station, but how could he be refused a mere girl—he who had ridden Nemea of its pest, who had ended the Hydra's reign, who had torn open the Tartarean gates, who had despoiled mighty cities on the Thermodon and the Scamandrian plain? Passion once more animated him. Anxiety breathed new life into his powerful limbs, so long listless. Before the end, he had yet one final score to settle, and one final prize, rightly won, to claim.

Heracles assembled a formidable army composed of Malians from Trachis, Arcadians and Epicnemidian Locrians to attack Oechalia. With him went his herald Lichas; Hippasos, the son of Ceyx; Menoitios, the son of Actor; Adrastos, king of Argos; Iolaos, and the sons of his uncle Licymnios, Argeios and Melas.

Only to these captains was the true object of his expedition revealed; the common soldiers were recruited to fight on the idea that Eurytos had been exacting an unjust tribute from the Euboeans.

Heracles marched into Euboea and made a surprise attack on Eurytos, routing his forces, killing him along with his son Toxeus, and capturing his other sons, Molion and Clytios. On his side, Hippasos fell, as well as the sons of Licymnios. The latter had been unwilling to allow his youngest son Argeios to join the expedition, but agreed when Heracles swore to bring him home again; this he did, by returning home his ashes. After burying the dead, Heracles took the city and sought Iole in the palace. Despite treating her with gentleness and courtesy, she spat at him and ferally resisted every overture. Overcome with anger, Heracles brought her remaining brothers before her, threatening to kill them if she did not at least acknowledge that he was now her master. She forced Heracles' hand by refusing to do so; and so he killed her brothers before her very eyes. Her resolution melted by anguish, Iole tore away from him, dashed outside onto the balcony, and madly jumped off the walls. Appalled, Heracles ran to the balustrade. To his relief, he found that Iole had been saved by her flounced petticoat, which, swelled out by the wind, broke her fall.

Confident that Iole would, in time, grow to love him, Heracles entrusted Lichas to take Iole, and other captive women, to Deianeira at Trachis, along with a vast train of booty. To celebrate his victory and offer thanksgiving, Heracles decided to visit the sea-girt Euboean promontory of Cenaion, whipped by eastern gales, where stood an ancient temple of Zeus. He intended to sacrifice from the Oechalian spoils nine bellowing bullocks for Cenaionian Zeus, two for Poseidon, and a long-horned, unyoked ox for his guardian Athena, who always ensured his victories. He also awarded the horse Arion to Adrastos, who became the third master to tame him.

Back in Trachis, anxiety consumed Deianeira. She had been without news of Heracles for at least a year, perhaps more. Before departing on his next campaign, which he described as only for the purposes of righting a wrong done to him by a Euboean chieftain, he had been unusually kind and affectionate with her, confirming to her mind that he still loved her as he once did. Despite this, certain

"And why does not Lichas bring me the news himself?" asked Deianeira.

"You should see how he is mobbed by the people, my lady," said the old man. "I am sure you shall see him presently."

Deianeira could no longer contain her joy. She leapt from her couch to share the news with all of her ladies-in-waiting. Lichas' arrival soon interrupted their dancing and merry-making. With him came a throng of Oechalian women, Iole among them.

Deianeira ran to him, saying breathlessly: "All hail to the herald so long delayed—as long as he brings a joyful message! Tell me, dear friend Lichas, is it true I shall see my husband alive and well?"

"That is how I left him—hale and hearty!" said Lichas, ordering the captives to sit on the ground before their mistress.

"But is he here, or still abroad?" said Deianeira, looking with eagerness past his shoulder.

Lichas said: "In Euboea still, offering holy sacrifices to Zeus."

"And these," said Deianeira, looking at the captives, and lingering on Iole most of all; "who are they? They elicit my pity."

"Captives, my lady, from the sack of Oechalia," said Lichas.

The captive women, huddling together on the ground as if wracked by some bitter cold, followed Deianeira with their eyes. Their clothes were torn and dirty; their hair defiled by dust; no glint of jewelry adorned their bare skin.

"I have every right to rejoice at my lord's good fortune, do I not?" she asked, as if in a soliloquy. "A strange pity, however, has taken hold me at the sight of these poor women, exiles like me, homeless and fatherless in a foreign land. O Zeus, withhold from any child of mine a fate like this, at least while I live." Then, standing over Iole, she said: "Hapless girl, who are you? You seem noble-born. Lichas, whose daughter is she? For the anguish marring her lovely face, I pity her most of all."

Lichas, marked by sudden disquietude, shrugged his shoulders and said: "How should I know? Why ask such a question?"

Deianeira, despite being taken aback by his familiar manner, pressed calmly: "Is she of the royal line there, perhaps?"

Lichas, realizing his discourtesy, replied more reservedly: "I do not know. I do as I am told without asking many questions."

"Perhaps you know her name, having heard it from one of her companions?" asked Deianeira.

Not receiving an answer from Lichas, Deianeira asked Iole directly, distressed by her ignorance; but the girl maintained a firm silence.

"That one has not opened her lips since we left the conquered city," said Lichas. "Not a word I've heard, only tears. Grow not, I pray, impatient with her; they all come as gifts from Heracles to serve in your house."

"Very well," said Deianeira. "Let her be at peace; I must not cause her more grief than she has already." Calling her nurse, she ordered her to conduct the women to the servants' quarters. Lichas went along to ensure the installation happened without incident. As Deianeira followed them, the old messenger, who had been waiting patiently, detained her, saying: "Tarry here a bit, my lady, to learn who it is you bring under your roof. If my former tale was worth an ear, so will this one, I think. Stay, I pray. I must communicate with you alone."

Deianeira, looking back at the last of the captives as they went into the house, said: "Well, sir, they are gone; kindly proceed."

"That man has given you a dishonest report," said the messenger. As Deianeira pressed him for an explanation, he continued: "I heard that man say, before many witnesses, that for this maiden's sake Heracles toppled the walls of Oechalia. For love, I say, and not for other reasons; and now the herald has pushed out love and prattles something else. Since Eurytos, years ago, would not surrender the maiden to him, Heracles, on some pretext or other, returned to make war, slew him, and sacked the town. As you see, he sends her to your house, but not as a slave for long. Knowing these things, which many have already heard in public, I resolved to tell you, O queen. Forgive me if my words, though truthful, bring you grief."

Deianeira stood speechless. Wringing her hands she said: "What bane have I admitted into my house? So who is she? Has she a name?"

The old man replied: "A name as illustrious as her birth. She is Iole, the daughter of Eurytos."

Deianeira staggered back, darkening the door-sill with her

faltering form. With a trembling hand to her fevered brow she called for a housemaid to bring the old man food and drink, bidding him to tarry a while longer. Through her apartments the wife of Heracles wandered, rushing about or standing still as her frenzied heart moved her; while pallor displaced the angry flush of her cheeks. Her old nurse heard her groans across the house and hurried to find her.

Deianeira, beating her breast, lifted her eyes and cried: "Heavenly Queen, why do you search the far reaches of the earth, and even the dark realms beneath, for horrid beasts to send against Heracles, monsters from which even he would turn his eyes? Why not change my heart into some evil thing? In this breast, boiling with rage, you will find monsters enough to terrify him. And more than you, Cypris has been his bane. You have crushed him; but she has trod upon his neck."

"My child, control your grief! Show yourself the wife of Heracles," begged the nurse.

Deianeira lowered at her like a god-possessed Mainad. "Shall this captive Iole give my sons brothers?" she wept. "Although the world owes its peace to you, false husband, a worst pest than the Hydra is here—a wife's wrath. What good have my prayers over his perils done? He returns in safety for *her*! Grief, with what revenge will you be assuaged—a punishment unthinkable and unspeakable? So I please you no longer, and a slave is preferred to me? Nay—that day that ends our marriage will end your life."

Alarmed, the nurse said: "Of what crime do you speak? To slay him who is kindred to the gods? All of Greece will rise to overthrow your father's house and the whole Aetolian race. Grieving one, you will surely die."

"Then die I shall, the wife of glorious Heracles!" cried Deianeira. "Day will rise from the western ocean and the Scythians will grow black under the Sun's burning car before the women of Thessaly see me abandoned. With my own blood will I quench that girl's marriage torches. Let him add me to his bevy of conquered beasts; let him add me to his toils. To his couch will I, with body dying, cling. But if that harlot has conceived, I will tear the child from her out of time. What have you gained, Alcides, if by this final vileness you blot out all your glorious deeds?"

The nurse pleaded: "Poor soul, why do you feed the flames of your anger and grief? He did perhaps love this Iole while yet her father reigned, when it was a king's daughter he sought. Love has lost its power; look at her now—a slave, her charm stolen by her hapless lot. We love what is forbidden; which, once granted, we desire no more."

"It is pity that stirs his love!" exclaimed Deianeira. "He dotes on captive women—I know of them all."

"True, he loved the Trojan princess," recalled the nurse; "but he gave her to another, did he not? The Arcadian maid, Auge, whom he lusted after in her sacred dance—what love does he still have for her? Should I mention others? The daughters of Thespios are forgotten. Picture him sitting there at the distaff beside the Maionian queen, mad with love, having laid aside his lionskin, a turban wrapping his head, his locks fragrant with myrrh. Yes, everywhere he wandered, he burned with love; but burned with a feeble flame. How can he possibly love a slave and foeman's daughter to you?"

"I'll tell you," said Deianeira. "Beautiful are the groves when the first blush of spring clothes the naked wood; but when the winter gales strip off the leaves, nothing is left but a mass of trunks. Such is my beauty, diminishing with time. Whatever he saw in me has vanished. Old age and motherhood have robbed me of my charms. But see how this slave has not lost hers? Her beauty shines through her every misfortune; for nothing save her realm has she really lost."

Deianeira fell weeping into her nurse's lap, as she did in tender years. Between sobs, she said:

"That man you see puffed with fame, going from city to city, girt with a tawny pelt and carrying a massive club—glory really means nothing to him. He wanders seeking love and womens' chambers. He whom a thousand feral beasts could not overcome, love overcomes. Given this, why do I wait for his madness to return, when he'll strike my sons and I dead? Thus does he put away his wives and makes the world thinks his stepmother is the cause of his crimes! Come, Deianeira, do not weaken in your resolve. Do what you must!"

"Slay your husband?" uttered the nurse.

"You mean my rival's husband."

"The son of Zeus?"

"Of Alcmene also."

"With a sword?"

"Yes; a sword."

The nurse, patting her head, said consolingly: "My child, think on it. It is a light offense that he commits."

Deianeira sat up with a start. "Do you think a mistress is a small evil for a wife?"

"Come now! Has your love for Heracles gone?"

Deianeira laid down her head again. Having cried out her passion, she felt terribly weary. After a long while she said quietly: "Yes, dear nurse, my love for him remains, deep and fixed in my heart. It is true that to be angry with one's love brings on a great madness."

The nurse, filled with relief, said: "By magic spells and prayers do wives retain their husbands. We will bend him by my charms; you'll see."

"What herb is there from the far-off Axine, or growing on the slopes of the Pindos, that I can use to conquer him? Even if the moon leaves her starry bed to come to earth at your bidding; even if grain ripens amidst winter frost; even if the thunder-bolt be made to stand still—nothing will bend him."

"But love has conquered even the gods."

Moved by her nurse's words, Deianeira's countenance brightened with a new thought. She sent her nurse to a fetch the fine white linen shirt she had woven in Heracles' absence; while she retrieved from a secret place a casket where she had stored for all that time the tainted blood of Nessos. Lifting her eyes, she prayed: "Winged Eros, aim unerringly a shaft at Heracles, and not one of your lighter ones, for only by great force can he feel love's power. Let him learn again to love his wife; to turn his rough heart to me again. Extinguish every flame kindled in his breast by Iole's beauty; and rekindle it with mine. Often have you conquered the Thunderer Zeus; often the Stygian lord who rules the darkling realm; now gain yourself another triumph: conquer Heracles."

3

Heracles on the wind-swept headland consecrated several marble altars in a grove sacred to Cenaionian Zeus. Wreathing his head first with hoary poplar, he put on the embroidered shirt brought by Lichas, carefully packaged by his wife, sealed with her ring, and entrusted to the herald with the warning to keep the shirt from light and fire until delivered into Heracles' hands.

While twelve bullocks waited in line for sacrifice, Heracles kindled the altar-flames. Soon the roar of the crackling tinder overbore the din of the bulls' bellowing and sound of the poundings surf. While Heracles cast frankincense into the sacred fires, poured wine on the altars, and commenced to offer thanksgiving for all of his accomplishments, his attendants killed the victims, flayed and cut them up, and committed select portions to be burnt. But as he stood near the flames, praying serenely, the heat from the smoking offerings and resinous pine activated the bane besmearing his shirt. He began to sweat. Stepping back from the flaming altars, he found the oppressing heat undiminished. Confusion turned to distress as he felt his new shirt melting on his body, blending with him, smoking, filling his nostrils with the reek of his own burning skin. As Heracles tried to rip off the shirt, pieces of his flesh came off with it. In frenzy he tore at the poisoned fabric on his arms, hoping for relief; but his hands extracted gore and he exposed to his horror his own bloody, throbbing sinews and even bones where his great muscles dissolved within his limbs. As long as he could, Heracles stood rooted to the spot, trembling, burning, and casting woeful looks at his terrified companions. But when the extremity of pain at last overcame his endurance and manly fortitude, Heracles, possessed with wild and involuntary motility, ran amuck, filling the wooded grove with his anguished cries. Like a wild bull, who flies pierced with spears, of his words and actions had disturbed her. First, he discussed how his estate was to be divided on his death, and in the presence of notaries apportioned his inheritance among her and his sons. When she persisted in knowing the reason for such a sudden contingency, he revealed the vatic utterances he had heard beneath the Chaonian oaks, that after a year and three months on leaving his final home, he was either fated to die in battle, or, having achieved his task, be released from his toils and find rest.

That time, by her reckoning, was at hand. To her nurse, she lamented: "They say of old that, until death, one cannot judge a mortal's lot in life, whether it is good or evil. But even before death, I know that my life is nothing but sorrowful and bitter. Even in the house of my father Oeneus I suffered like no other maiden before me. As a suitor I had that bestial Acheloös, whom my father from impatience would have had me marry; meanwhile I prayed for death rather than be forced to go near such a bed as his.

"At last Heracles came to deliver me. Whatever joy I gained did not long last. Since the slaying of that little page-boy we have been exiles here in Trachis. Fear after fear has haunted me every time Heracles has taken to the field. I am almost certain, after so long a time that some evil has befallen him."

Her nurse replied: "Mistress, I have often been a witness of your tears over Heracles' wanderings and indiscretions. If I may be so bold to presume you'll accept the counsel of a slave, let me say this: send one of your sons, perhaps Hyllos, to seek news of your lord."

Just then, the nurse saw through a window someone hurrying to the house. She alerted Deianeira, saying: "Hush, mistress—no more words of ill-omen. I see a man approaching. He wears a wreath, as if ready to deliver glad tidings"

An old man, widowed and penurious, entered. Bowing low, he said: "My queen, know that the son of Alcmene lives and brings hither the first-fruits of battle!"

Although Deianeira's heart jumped at the news, her long anxiety made her cautious. She said calmly: "How do you know this?"

"Lichas the herald proclaims it in the meadow. I flew hither to be the first to deliver the news and thus gain some favor from you, and perhaps a little reward.

while the hunter hides in fear, Heracles overturned the altars, uprooted trees, and scattered the mountain rocks. His companions, even faithful Iolaos, thinking his old madness had returned, fled from him. With his boiling blood hissing in his ears, with his desiccated flesh dropping from him like the brittle bark of an old tree, he raised his hands and cried, still ravening:

"Come Hera, feast on my death! Look down from your high seat and feast on me, cruel step-dame. Witness my end and gorge your savage heart with my anguish. If I deserve any pity, then take my life, one never lacking in suffering and toil. Was it for this, that I slew the Egyptian, who with the blood of strangers defiled his temples? For this I deprived Antaios of his strength, or showed no fear before Erytheia's monstrous shepherd or the triple-headed guardian of the Styx? Could it be these hands once yoked the Cretan bull? Elis certainly knows my labor there; and the Stymphalian marsh; and the Parthenian woods. Was it for this that my hands secured the golden prize of the Amazons; or my strong arms snatched the sacred fruit from under the dragon's watchful care? No Centaur could stop me, or the boar that laid waste to Arcadia's fruitful fields. Was it for this end that the Hydra failed to renew her strength under my fiery attack? It was I who took possession of those Thracian steeds engorged with human blood and tamed them with their own master's flesh. With these arms I conquered the Nemean lion in his cave. Even you, cruel Hera, have wearied of imposing on me toils, while I never tired in performing them. But now a new and strange catastrophe overwhelms me: one not valor, not strength, not the use of arms can withstand. Devouring flames prey on my limbs—but still Eurystheus is alive and well! Ha! And yet some still believe in the gods!"

Heracles found Lichas hiding in a cleft. He accosted him furiously, accusing him of treachery in giving him the fatal shirt. Lichas, trembling and begging for mercy, explained in what manner Deianeira had entrusted to him the gift, accompanying with it instructions that no one but Heracles should wear it, and that it should be kept free from light of fire until the end. While he yet spoke, trying to embrace the hero's knees, Heracles seized him by the ankle, and with mighty strength whirled him four times around before catapulting him off the cliff into the Euboean Sea. It is said Lichas was transformed into a crag washed by the waves, still frightening sailors, who see in it the semblance to a human form.

❧

Back in Trachis, Deianeira left her chamber, pale and trembling, and crying for her nurse. Finding her, she gripped the old woman's hands and with a stammer spoke: "After sending the shirt away with Lichas, I retired to my chamber fretful and agitated. I began to think: did the Centaur all along plan some evil thing, some treachery against my lord? After all, he forbade me to expose his blood to sunlight and fire. His words should have forewarned me! It happened that I threw outside the blood-stained rag I used to daub the shirt. Exposed to the sun's strong light, undimmed by clouds, the shred of wool in the heat writhed and burst aflame before my eyes. It melted first like incense sprinkled on an altar-fire, and the remainder shriveled into dust; while bubbling froth seethed up beneath from between the flagstones."

"Flee, mother, far away—to some foreign land, or sea, or to the world beneath!" came the anguished voice of barefaced Hyllos, a youth already growing in the mold of his great father. "The guardian of the world is no more. He who vanquished monsters was himself vanquished by some wasting plague. How I wish that you had died, or were my mother no more—you who have slain the noblest man in all the world." Deianeira, shocked into silence by horrid presentiment, listened as her son, who had gone to seek news of his father, detail the tragedy on the sea-washed cape as he had heard it from Iolaos, who had just arrived alongside suffering Heracles by ship. Deianeira could hardly contain herself. She fled from the presence of her incensed son, fainting as she reached the refuge of her chamber. Fresh tears wet her pillow as her nurse tried everything to sooth the deep wound she on heart inflicted. To Hyllos the nurse went next as he busied himself constructing a litter, declaring how his mother had sinned without intent, inveigled by the Centaur's murderous craft.

While the nurse thus reasoned with Hyllos, Deianeira crept down to hear them; and seeing the litter destined to bring home her dying husband, she suppressed a moan and fled back into the recesses of the house, falling before the shrines, roaming haltingly until she reached Heracles' chamber. She took a double edged sword with her into the large bed.

"Alas," she groaned, looking fearfully at her reflection on the shining blade, "what have you done, Deianeira?  Why now hesitate to die?  Shall your lord perish, and you, the cause of so monstrous a deed, remain with life?  Alas for my own house!  Agrius has unseated my poor father from Calydon's throne.  My brother Tydeus roams exiled on some foreign shore.  Meleager has perished.  Our mother too has left this world.  Wicked thing!—still you hesitate?"

She unclasped the gold-wrought brooch that held her gown.  With trembling lips she cried: "Meleager, now you will see a sister worthy of you!  Farewell, aged father, sister Gorge, my beloved homeland!  Farewell, sweet light, last to strike my eyes."  And after a final farewell to her bridal couch, she plunged the blade through her bare left side and into her fractured heart.

Her final scream summoned Hyllos in a panic.  He was the first to see her tragic end.  Convinced now of his mother's unwitting sin, he threw himself on her cold body, wetting with her blood his clothes.  Planting kisses on her lips and eyes, he lamented, no longer knowing which misery to bewail: "Alas, I live now bereaved of both father and mother!"

Heracles, though unconscious when he was carried into the house, awoke from the wailing surrounding him.  Hyllos wept loudest of all, seeing his father's huge frame shriveled, the worst hidden under a coarse blanket.  Heracles weakly raised his head from the litter, ignorant at first of where he was or of the plaintive faces that crowded him.  He gave a loud cry as he felt the poisoned heat seeping into his lungs and the marrow of his bones.  His breaths grew stertorous.  "How is it that my great limbs satisfy not yet this noxious pest?" he lamented.  "Cruel curse!  Behold, all of you, what remains of once-great Heracles.  What!—how came this dew upon my cheeks?  My face, harder than the clashing rocks, has learned finally to weep."  Recognizing Hyllos, he stretched out a trembling arm, nothing now but protruding bone and ragged strips of charred flesh.  He said to him: "Shield my visage from the world, my son, that none may see these tears forced from unwilling eyes.  No man should ever say he saw me thus."

He then raged against his companions: "Most ungrateful of all the Greeks!  I wore out my days ridding the world of monsters and evildoers—and now that I suffer, will no one relieve me with his sword. What? Will nobody with one stroke sever my head from this ruined body?"

Heracles once more fell from pain into a swoon, and as quickly recovered, but more delirious. With his son cradling his head, he cried: "Athena! Where are you now? O! I am tortured anew! My son, pity me! Find a sword. Smite your sire here, beneath my collar-bone, and end the pain with which your godless mother has imprisoned me." Lifting then the blanket covering him, he elicited a round of gasps at the sight of his wasted form, a great and awful ruin of strength. "O end most foul! Heracles is undone by a woman's hand. Know this, though I can hardly move a step: she who did this deed will feel my heavy hand. She shall learn to declare before all that I, in my death, as in my life, am bane to the wicked."

Hyllos pleaded: "Hear me, father; though afflicted, accept my counsels and learn how your resentment is unwarranted."

"Speak then, though in my wretchedness your words come forth as riddles."

"I must tell you of mother."

Heracles shook in fury. "Dare you breathe that foul woman's name?"

"I must; silence now would be unjust."

"What is it, then?—but careful what you say lest I find you complicit with her."

"O father! Dead she is by her own hand."

"Alas, would she have died by mine!"

"Hearing it all will allay your wrath. She sinned, but with good intent."

"Was it good intent to slay your father, wretch?"

"She only thought to bind you with love-philter when she saw your new bride arrive," said Hyllos, spent with sorrow. "The Centaur Nessos begot this snare when your own arrow poured out his life, and convinced her that his gore—tainted with the Hydra's poison—had power over wayward hearts."

Heracles in agony covered with both scarred hands his face. After a deep groan, he said: "At last I recognize my awful plight. All is lost. Go, my son, and assemble your brethren and Alcmene my mother, for there are things I must reveal before my end."

"Your mother is not here; she is at Thebes with the other children. But say what you will and we here will do your bidding."

Heracles said no more, his senses overborne with the gnawing anguish. In such a languor did he lie that his companions thought he had breathed his last. When they saw that his ruined breast still slightly heaved, they all drew back; none daring to fulfill his wishes and end his misery. Iolaos and Licymnios at once sped off on horseback to seek a cure from Delphi, determined to save their friend. Hyllos sent others to bring back Alcmene from Thebes.

Heracles awoke after several days in response to his mother's tender caresses. "Do I still see Trachis amidst her rugged hills?" he rambled, deranged. "Or am I set among the stars? Who opens heaven for me? I see you, father! And what sound is that? Hera calls me son!" Coming slowly out of his delirium, he began to weep: "And what is this? Heaven's gates are shut against me; I am dragged down from the starry field. But a moment before I loomed over Oeta and the earth lay beneath my feet."

Noticing Alcmene, he said to her: "Why turn your eyes away, mother? It is Heracles you see, but only now a shadow. Are you ashamed to call me son?"

Alcmene, nearly speechless with grief, beating her aged breast, responded: "What son like you has mortal woman ever borne? What Heracles can I again Zeus bare? What son so great will ever again call me mother, his Alcmene? Too happy were you, my Theban husband, who descended beneath with your son still living, where all the shades were filled with fear that you were called his father, although not in truth. Where shall I flee? To what corner of the world shall I go where I will not be known in you, hated by sons lamenting their murdered sires?"

Iolaos and Licymnios at that moment returned from their errand. Choked with tears they reported that the oracle offered no cure, but only the unkind command to take Heracles, with all his arms and armor, to the summit of mount Oeta, where his final fate would unfold.

Hearing this, Heracles became lucid, and with sudden vigor said: "This the prophetic oaks once declared: that by the hand of one slain, I should be slain. Thus Nessos did to me—the dead outdid the living. As well, the meaning of another oracle is clear:

that after a certain time I should either die, or end my toils. No retiring life was mine. My toils must cease in death."

Hyllos he had swear an oath to carry him to mount Oeta and lay his body on a burning pyre. But the tortured youth could not promise to kindle the flames. "Consent, then, to take Iole as your bride," said Heracles, recognizing his son's great love. Turning to his mother, Heracles said: "Hail mother! Cease your sorrows. Your Alcides lives. My heroic deeds have made Hera seem a concubine. Dry your tears now, greatest of all Greek mothers. What son like yours has Hera borne, though she rules the sky? She envies a mortal woman, though she is queen of heaven."

At Heracles' command, his friends carried him, girt in his Trojan armor, to mount Oeta. In a long procession they climbed to a lofty mountain-meadow where white hellebore sprinkled the tall grass. Iolaos and Hyllos with their axes felled trees of every type and size. Upward they piled a heap of logs: beech and fast-burning pine, tough oak and ilex, wild-olive and poplar.

When the pyre was finished, and the sun, hidden behind clouds, stood suspended directly overhead, the sorrowful company drew back: none was willing to assist Heracles to the final act. Heracles without assistance raised himself, gathered his lionskin and arms, and like a huge, suffering lion roaring in pain in a Libyan forest, staggered in his clanging armor to the pyre. Slowly, wracked with immeasurable pain, he climbed the groaning beams.

Heracles spread out the lionskin and lay on it, with his knotted club as a pillow. For a long while he searchingly gazed at every part of heaven. Stretching out his hands, he prayed quietly: "Heavenly father, from whatever quarter you witness my passion, if the bounds of the trackless sun, the Scythian wastes and every burning strand sing my praise; if crimes and sins have ceased; if peace now fills the earth, reserve a place for my spirit among the stars. I have no fear of the gloomy realms, but to return to those gods I overcame as nothing but a shade ashames me. If that be your will, then pass me again through the Stygian abyss— but prove me first your son. All else I count worthless. Scatter the clouds that you may gaze on me consumed."

Then he sat upright and called for someone to light the pyre; but none came forth, not even Iolaos, who hung his head in shame.    As he railed at them, upbraiding their cowardice for deserting him in his last hour, a shepherd, Poeas, appeared, attracted from another valley, where he had been tending his flocks, by all the commotion.   With him came his young son Philoctetes. Spotting them, Heracles cried: "Make haste and seize a torch, good man.   Show my step-dame how well I can bear the flames."

Poeas, intimidated by the curious spectacle, ordered his son to fetch a burning pine and do as Heracles commanded.   As the boy circled the pyre, daubing it with flames, Heracles in gratitude cast down for him his bow and quiver, destined one day to again see Troy.

As smoke swirled around Heracles, he heard through the crackling flames the distinct grief of his mother.   Though he could no longer see her standing near the pyre, he said: "Dear mother, by your tears you disgrace my death.   Why give Hera further joy by your weeping?   Strengthen your heart; it is a sin to strike the paps that nourished me."   All marveled at how calmly he faced his end. Alcmene dried her tears, striving to share in her son's resolve.

As    the    flames    roared    higher,    Heracles,    undaunted, unshaken, counseled and encouraged his friends, urging them to follow his example in choosing not the pleasantest and easiest of lives, but rather the noblest and most ambitious.   He told them to observe moderation, to follow nature and to devote their lives to serving their fellow men.   So great was his fortitude in the face of death that he even shifted some logs about to speed the flames. Finally, circumscribed by heat and death within and on every side, he lay down still, as if reclining on a banquet-couch.   Helpless and alone, all things seemed like a dream he had made for himself.   He remembered then the loveliness of the Western sun melting into Ocean; the snow falling as feathers in the Northern wastes; the wild solitude   of   the   blue   Istros   couched   within   lofty   steeps;   the mouldered ruins awash in the endless shimmer of Egypt's sands; the splendor of the silent stars mirrored upon the desolate sea.   And as the greedy fire licked his limbs and seared his eyes with the final darkness of absolute night, he prepared to discard his life in the purposelessness of death.   But as the clouds scattered and the midsummer sun in full vigor embosomed his blighted form in golden light, he surrendered, not to death, but to that infinite longing after Beauty.   "The heavens open!   Father—I come!" he cried as his melting flesh doused the flames; and in a whisper followed his final words: "It is finished!"

All mourned the end of that great-souled bulwark of gods and men, the dissolution of that noble bearing, the silencing of that sounding voice.

And at the moment of his final breath, on the wooded slopes of Pelion, an old Centaur placed two children gently aside, and lay on his bed of grass for the last time.

The pyre crashed down and burned for hours, even to the setting of the sun. When his companions searched the rubble for his bones, they found nothing but his empty armor lying in its place.

4

Hyllos, in accordance with his father's command, married Iole when he came of age, although he resented her all of his days as being the principal agent in the death of his parents. He remained at Trachis with Iolaos and Ceyx. Other sons of Heracles lived under the care of Alcmene in Thebes or were found in other parts of Greece. They were known as the Heraclids.

High King Eurystheus grew increasingly paranoid over the sons of Heracles, fearing, after seeing their great numbers at Heracles' funeral games, that they would someday band together to depose him and lay claim to illustrious Mycenae by virtue of their Perseid descent. He therefore, for the rest of his life, undertook the audacious task of expelling them all from Greece; first by diplomacy, and then by threat of force against any kings who harbored them.

Eurystheus sent word to Ceyx to expel from Trachis the Heraclids, Iolaos, the house of Licymnios and all of Heracles' Arcadian allies. Ceyx could not hope to resist him and implored them to go forth and seek a stronger ally. Along with Hyllos, the persecuted band left Trachis and stopped at many cities as suppliants. Only the Athenians under Theseus sheltered and settled them at Tricorythus on the plain of Marathon.

As for Ceyx, the peace-loving king took a ship, despite Alcyone's pleas, to Delphi to inquire about his brother, and to investigate the evil doings of the lawless Phorbas and followers of Phlegyas, who were making travel to the oracle unsafe. Caught in a terrible storm, his ship foundered and he perished. Alcyone one night in a dream was visited by what seemed to be the shade of Ceyx, pale and naked, his hair and body dripping with brine. When morning came, rushing to the seashore, she saw her husband's body borne on the waves. From a mole which held back the crashing waves she leapt into the surge, but the gods, taking pity on her, gave her wings, so that as a halcyon she skimmed the waves. To the floating cadaver she flew and with her cold beak kissed his face. Ceyx too took avian form and even now men see that pair of birds, mated forever, fly over the broad sea; and for seven days in winter's midst peace calms the flood as Alcyone broods over her nest.

When Eurystheus learned that Theseus refused to surrender Heracles' sons and followers, he assembled a great army and personally led it, along with his sons, against Athens. Theseus joined with Hyllos and Iolaos in an alliance. By then Iolaos was an old man. Taking up his weapons and armor, he prayed that his youth be restored for a single day. The petition was granted. As he set out, two heavenly lights came to rest on his chariot-yoke and a dark mist enveloped him. From the haze Iolaos emerged, young and strong; once more gripping the reins with a firm hand.

Before the battle was joined, an oracle declared that victory could only be achieved after the sacrifice of a high-born maiden. Macaria, the sole daughter of Heracles, willingly slew herself at Marathon, giving her name to the Macarian spring.

The Athenians defeated Eurystheus and killed his sons, Alexander, Iphimedon, Eurybius, Mentor and Perimedes. Eurystheus fled in his chariot back to Mycenae, but Iolaos captured him by the Scironian Rocks as he tried to cross the Isthmus. Although the Athenians pleaded for his life, considering it dastardly to execute a sovereign, Alcmene, on account of all the suffering Eurystheus had inflicted on her beloved son, ordered his execution. Hyllos beheaded him; and, on presenting the head to his mother, she gouged out the eyes with weaving-pins. The Athenians gave him an honorable burial, interring the head at Tricorythus and the trunk at Gargettus, since before his death the king had foretold that, as long as his body lay in Attic soil, it would protect them from the Heraclids in the future.

An oracle informed the Mycenaeans to choose a son of Pelops as their next king. The Pelopids were related to the Perseids in many ways since several of the sons of Perseus had married the daughters of Pelops and Hippodamia. Two sons of Pelops, Atreus and Thyestes, contended for the throne. They had been installed at Midea as vassals of Sthenelos after he seized Mycenae. Atreus felt he had the greater entitlement, since Eurystheus had entrusted

Mycenae to him during the war against the Heraclids. To prove further that his claim had divine sanction, Atreus pointed to a golden lamb born among his flocks. But Thyeses, after seducing Atreus' wife Aerope, stole it; and at a meeting of the leading citizens to settle the matter, proposed that the throne should go to him who possessed the golden lamb. Atreus, of course, agreed. Thyestes then produced the golden lamb and claimed the throne of Mycenae.

Thyestes' artifice with a holy portent angered the gods. Zeus sent Hermes to inform Atreus that his claim to the throne would be confirmed by the even more startling omen of the sun reversing for a day its course. Feeling the weight of divine displeasure, and fearing that the portent would indeed occur, Atreus abdicated and went into exile.

When Atreus discovered his wife's infidelity with his brother, he drowned her and then recalled Thyestes, promising an end to their disagreements. On the day Thyestes arrived in Mycenae, Atreus killed, boiled and served up his sons as a meal, omitting the head, hands and feet to conceal the gruesome nature of the feast. When Thyestes finished his repast, Atreus set before him the severed extremities and exiled him a second time.

Alcmene, at the age of ninety, died before the second expedition against Thebes by the sons of the Seven Champions, who ten years before had perished in the struggle to restore Polynieces, son of Oidipos, to the throne after he was exiled by his brother Eteocles. As her sons were about to bury her, they found the coffin heavier than warranted. Removing the lid, they were astonished to see a stone in a place of their mother's body. Hermes, on Zeus command, had taken her to Isles of the Blessed, where it was said she wed Rhadamanthys. The Thebans set up the stone in a sacred grove. When Iolaos died, the Thebans established for him a hero's shrine, where lovers to this day make solemn pledges.

After their mother's death, Hyllos and his brothers remained at Thebes where, assembling at the Electrian Gate, they discussed amongst themselves the propriety of subduing the Peloponnese, since as Perseids they had a legitimate claim to Argos, and even Laconia and Messenia, where Heracles had left land in trust for them. Mustering an army, they entered the Peloponnese and, after conquering several small cities on the frontier, maintained a presence there for one year.

When a plague spread over the whole Peloponnese because the Heraclids had returned before their appointed time, they withdrew to Attica for a period, and then went to dwell with the Dorians, who had settled in the Dryopians' former territory in a valley of the river Peneios between Mounts Oeta and Parnassos, claiming the rights left in trust with them by Heracles; where their king, Aigimios, adopted Hyllos as his son. Hyllos inquired of the oracle at Delphi when next to attempt an invasion of the peninsula, and received the following answer:

> *Through a narrow passage by the sea,*
> *At the third harvest find your victory.*

Taking this utterance literally, Hyllos and his brothers waited for three years. During that period the citizens of Argos, at the urging of their king Adrastos, who wished to continue relations with the house of Heracles, invited Tlepolemos and his great-uncle Licymnios to their city. Tlepolemos, while angrily beating a slave, accidentally killed the aged Licymnios when he interposed himself between them. At the order of the Delphic oracle, he sailed with some Dorian followers to Rhodes, where he founded numerous cities. Having grown wealthy, he led the Rhodians in nine ships to fight at Troy, and was killed there by a descendant of Bellerophon, Sarpedon, king of Lycia.

When Aigimios died, his two sons, Pamphylos and Dymas, submitted to Hyllos. Firmly allied now with the Dorians, the Heraclids confidently marched back into the Peloponnese through the Isthmus, which they took to be the narrow passage meant in the prophecy. There they were confronted by the great mass of defenders. To avoid a long and arduous struggle, Hyllos cast a challenge between himself and a champion on the opposing side, with the outcome being that, if won, the Heraclids would be allowed to reclaim their ancestral lands; and if lost, the Heraclids would withdraw and refrain from any antagonism for a period of no less than fifty years. Echemos, king of Tegea, an ally of Mycenae, volunteered to fight and killed Hyllos in single combat. Honoring their pledge, the Heraclids returned for a time to Doris. Thirty years after the Trojan War, Cleodaios, son of Hyllos, thinking he could disobey the oracle, led an unsuccessful invasion; as did his son Aristomachos at the conclusion of the truce, when, remembering the oracular response about taking a narrow passage into the Peloponnese, assumed it naturally referred to the route over the Isthmus of Corinth. His attempt too ended in disaster.

A generation later, the Heraclids prepared for their last and greatest campaign under the sons of Aristomachos: Temenos, Cresphontes and Aristodemos. First, however, they travelled to Delphi for guidance, and hearing the same pronouncements as before, registered a complaint that all of the oracle's instructions had proved consistently fatal to those who followed them. The oracle chided them for their lack of comprehension and revealed the true meaning of its riddles. By the third harvest the oracle meant the third generation of men; and by the narrow passage, the oracle meant, not the long land route across the Isthmus, but the short route across the Gulf of Corinth at its narrowest point.

They began to construct a fleet at Naupactos in the territory of Ozolian Locris. But before they could sail, calamities beset them. An Arcananian soothsayer, Carnos, came among their troops reciting frenzied oracles. Although he meant no harm, Hippotes, son of Phylas, killed him with a javelin, thinking he was a sorcerer sent to ruin the army by king Teisamenos, who had inherited the thrones of Argos, Mycenae and Sparta from his father Orestes. Because of the murder, divine retribution destroyed the ships by storm and the land forces by famine, forcing the abandonment of the campaign. Moreover, Aristodemos was murdered while on a subsequent pilgrimage to Delphi by Medon and Strophios, cousins of Teisamenos.

At wit's end, the Heraclids sent Temenos to Delphi for additional guidance. The oracle informed him to banish Hippotes for ten years; and if he wished to be successful in his expedition, to take as his guide the Three-Eyed One. Some Heraclids, out on the futile search, came across a certain Oxylos, a descendant of the Calydonian king Thoas, sitting on a one-eyed horse. On questioning him, they learned that he had been in exile at Elis on account of a murder, and after a year was returning to Aetolia. Taking him with his horse together to represent the thing with three eyes spoken of in the oracle, since the horse had been partly blinded by an arrow, they made him their guide.

After reassembling the army and repairing their ships, the Heraclids sailed across the strait of Rhium to the coast of Elis and then advanced confidently into the Peloponnese, where they, with the aid of Dorians, Thebans, Trachinians and many others, defeated Teisamenos and all other hostile chieftains, making themselves finally masters of the peninsula, as Zeus had willed.  Among their allies fell Pamphylos and Dymas, the sons of Aigimios.  As a reward for his service, Oxylos requested the fertile region of Elis; which was fitting, since the royal Aetolian family hailed originally from that region.

Temenos, Cresphontes and the twin sons of Aristodemos, Proeles and Eurysthenes, established altars for Paternal Zeus, offered sacrifices, and cast lots for each principality.  Cresophontes secured Messenia for himself in the following way.  After agreeing that the first lot drawn be for Argos, the second for Lacedaimonia and the third for Messenia, Temenos and the sons of Aristodemos threw stones into a water-jug; however, Cresophontes cast in a clod of earth, which naturally dissolved in the water, and allowed the other two lots to come up first.  In this way Argos went to Temenos and Lacedaimon to the sons of Aristodemos, although it was agreed that Theras, brother of Aristodemos' wife, would rule as regent until they came of age.  As confirmation of their allotments, Temenos found on the sacrificial altar a frog; Theras saw there a serpent; and Cresophontes a fox.  The soothsayers explained these omens as signifying that those meant for Argos best remain there, since the frog had no strength when it walked; that those meant for Lacedaimon would be formidable in the attack, as is a serpent; and that those meant for Messene would be cunning, as is the fox.  Arcadia was left undisturbed after king Kypselos arrived at an agreement with the Heraclids, forming an alliance with them through marriage.

Temenos, ruling at Argos, favored Deiphontes, the husband of his daughter Hyrnetho, above his own three sons.  The eldest son, Ceisos, drove Temenos from the throne, forcing Deiphontes to flee to Epidauros with his Argive followers.  Medon, son and successor of Ceisos, saw his authority much reduced, and ruled as king in name only.

At Messene, Cresphontes married Merope, daughter of Kypselos, who bore him three sons.  Another descendant of

Heracles, Polyphontes, in a rebellion killed him and two of his sons. The youngest son, Aipytos, survived, having been staying with Kypselos at that time. Polyphontes, learning Aipytos was alive, offered a talent of gold to any who would kill him. When Aipytos came of age, he returned to Messenia under a false name, claiming to have killed the wanted person. Merope, in a forced marriage to Polyphontes, tried to kill Aipytos with an axe as he slept, thinking he had murdered her son. But when from a servant she learned his identity, she plotted with her son to kill Polyphontes. The next day, at her insistence, Polyphontes invited his guest to assist at a sacrifice. Given a sword for that purpose, Aipytos turned on the usurper and slew him. The son of Cresophontes, taking the throne, ruled justly, and proved popular among rich and poor alike.

Procles and Eurysthenes ruled jointly at Sparta because no one could distinguish among them as to who was the eldest, but lived in constant quarrel. Fittingly, they married twin sisters, Lathria and Anaxandra, who were daughters of the Heraclid Thersandros. Thereafter two monarchs always reigned at Sparta.

Hippotes, in his exile, fathered a son, whom he called Aletes to commemorate his wanderings. Aletes, with a force of Dorians, seized Corinth from the descendants of Sisyphos. He also tried to conquer Attica, but was thwarted by the valor of Codros, Athen's last king. When an oracle announced that his death would safeguard Athens, Codros, disguised as a peasant, entered the Dorians' camp, provoked them, and was killed. When Aletes heard of this, he withdrew his army. The neighboring city of Sicyon was conquered by Phalkes, son of Temenos; but since the king of Sicyon was also a Heraclid, Phalkes agreed to share the throne with him.

## EPILOGUE

*Now on the subject of Heracles if we have dwelt over-long, we have at least omitted nothing from the myths which are related concerning him.*

Diodorus Siculus, *Library of History*

The followers of Heracles built a barrow over the remains of the pyre and sacrificed to Heracles as a hero. The Thebans adopted the same practice. The Athenians, however, became the first to honor Heracles as a hero and god.

Some on Mount Oeta reported that by divine action lighting fell and consumed entirely the pyre. Others thought they saw a cloud carry Heracles to heaven as thunder rolled; or that a swarm of locusts flew out to ravage the countryside. But that Heracles as his final Labor conquered death and achieved that which he most sought, immortality, is well established; for when Odysseus, returning from the Trojan War, on the advice of Circe visited the underworld seeking guidance from the shade of the Theban prophet Teiresias, he saw Heracles; who, girt in a curiously wrought baldric, by his terrible glance and nocked arrow, set the dead aflutter. But Odysseus confirms that what he saw was merely a phantom, and that the real Heracles—that immortal part inherited from Zeus—was happily feasting with the gods, having made their acquaintance at last. Heracles, abashed at meeting Zeus, had Athena accompany him to make the introduction, and at last father and son were able to converse face to face. The poets add that Hera, at the urging of Zeus, reconciled with Heracles, a bastard among the gods, and adopted him as her own son. To accomplish this, Hera lay on a bed and allowed Heracles to emerge from between her legs, as if she had given birth. Or else she gave him her breast again to suck. Afterward, he was given neat-ankled Hebe, the goddess of youth, as his wife; and she bore him two sons, Alexiares and Anicetos.

Zeus wished to include Heracles as a god among the Twelve Olympians. Heracles could not accept this singular honor, the first and last ever extended to a mortal, thinking it preposterous that at his enrollment another god would be deprived of membership.

No; he is content merely to mind the Olympian gates, where he waits each night for Artemis to return from the hunt. After he removes from her chariot the day's haul, the gods laugh to see him carrying by the hind foot a struggling bull or wild boar; but if he finds any other lesser prey he chides her playfully: "Men will call you helper, as they did me, if you confine yourself to shooting at wild boars and oxen, which trample the ripening wheat. Leave hares and deers to feed upon the hills; what harm have they done?" Heracles still eats and drinks the fragrant nectar contentedly at every celestial banquet, and then with a full stomach departs to the ambrosial chamber of his ever-youthful wife.

And there were many other things which Heracles did; which, if every one were written down, not the world itself could contain all of the books written.

# AUTHOR'S NOTE

*Of the stories told concerning this god, some are largely legend and some are nearer the truth.*

Dionysos of Halicarnassus, *Roman Antiquities*

*While it is very easy to tell stories about Heracles, it is extremely difficult to compose a history.*

Petrarch, *On Illustrious Men*

"Nothing without Heracles!" was a popular saying among the ancient Greeks.  It is difficult to imagine today the widespread influence Heracles enjoyed in antiquity.   He had temples throughout the Greco-Roman world and beyond.  Kings claimed him as forebear.  He was the subject of more epic poetry, lyric poetry, lyric odes, tragedies, comedies, prose, historiography, oratory, philosophy, sculpture and art than any other god or hero. Even after Christianity became the official religion of the Roman Empire, the cult of Heracles was still pervasive.  The "hero god" was worshipped well into the 5th century.  It light of this, it is astounding that, apart from summaries in late mythological handbooks like those of Diodorus Siculus and Apollodorus, not a single complete epic work or dedicated biography about Heracles from antiquity survives, although we know a number of them were composed. Panyassis, a relative of the Greek historian Herodotus, wrote an epic poem in fourteen books about Heracles, as did several other more obscure writers like Peisander, Phaedimos, Cinaithon and Herodoros.  Sadly, we also lack Plutarch's *Life of*

*Heracles.* The problem these writers probably faced is still with us today. There is simply so much material about Heracles that Aristotle, for example, recorded his dissatisfaction with what he had available, finding them farragoes of confused and disparate legends.

In this novel—or more aptly, prose narrative—I have attempted something not done since the Renaissance: a reconstruction, from all available primary sources, of the complete mythic history of Heracles. But was Heracles "real"—a historical person who flourished about a generation before the Trojan War of the early 12$^{th}$ century B.C? Today most would classify him as "mythical" as Beowulf's Grendel or unicorns. But here we must pause to consider the distinctions between myth, legend and fable. Myth we get from the Greek *muthos*, which meant simply a report or story, without the modern connotation of untruth. The myths were tales meant to convey facts, not fictions, albeit under a dramatic guise for didactic purposes. On the surface myths are entertaining; beneath they communicate secret or sacred truths, explanations of natural processes or rituals whose causes have been lost in time. Legends enjoy a firmer foundation. They are embellished traditions based on real people and real places. Even fables, ostensibly the product of pure imagination, sometimes develop from kernels of truth. When scholars say that a poet or playwright "invented" this myth or that, they only argue out of ignorance, as the archaeological discoveries of Troy and Minoan Crete illustrate. It would be strange, then, to think that this man, who made such a profound impression on ancient minds, did *not* exist. The Greeks certainly thought Heracles was a real person. The heroic age, beginning with the establishment of the Greek royal lineages, abutted their era of conventional history, which began in the generations after the Trojan War. Once the Greeks settled on and interrelated the genealogies of the royal families of each power center (Thebes, Argos, Crete, etc), they used them as a synchronic medium to situate the great heroes and their adventures, resulting in the emergence of an amazingly consistent "mythic" history. It is this mythic (or, more properly, legendary) history that I have tried to reconstruct in this work, with Heracles as its foundation.

Historians and mythographers from Herodotus onward had no doubts about Heracles' existence. The earnest Roman writer Diodorus Siculus includes a lengthy biography of Heracles in his monumental *Library of History*, finding it necessary to rationalize its more fantastic elements. The Church Father Eusebius of Caesarea fixed a date for the end of Heracles' Labors in his *Chronicon*, or universal history, preserved and expanded upon by Saint Jerome. Petrarch and Boccaccio, heralding the Renaissance's critical and scholarly interest in antiquity, chronicled his exploits. The ancients also mention other heroes by the name of Heracles existing at different times and in different cultures. Diodorus counted a total of three, with the most ancient one having been an Egyptian, and the other a Cretan Dactyl. Servius reckoned four, Cicero six and the learned Marcus Varro up to forty-four. The Egyptians identified Heracles with their god Shu or Chonsu, whom they worshipped since time immemorial. But all admit, to their credit, that the last and youngest of these heroic incarnations was the Heracles with whom we are concerned: the son of Alcmene, born at the city of Thebes in 1286 B.C.[13] Although I have tried to follow Diodorus in rationalizing as much as possible the life of Heracles, many of his legends are unavoidably replete with the marvelous and romantic; and where the story was in danger of plunging into euhemeristic absurdity, I have retained them. Ater all, who knows if perhaps there were in those bygone days

> *demigods, rustic divinities, nymphs, fauns and satyrs, and*
> *sylvan deities upon the mountain slopes*

—and Heracles really did slay monsters and harrow hell?

The task of reconciling the mass of stories, and effectively interweaving all of the other legends (such as the Argonautic expedition) which intersect, was not without difficulty. There may exist, for example, a number of variants for the same story. In this case, I have either commingled them if appropriate, or else retained the one version that seemed most plausible, taking its age, chronological fit and provenance into account (i.e., general variants generally take precedence over local ones). I have also relied on depictions of Heracles' life in vase paintings, sculptures and other ancient media, but only if they had some narrative basis. Such

---

[13] See the Note on Chronology for the precise date.

sources could hardly be excluded, since Heracles was as popular a figure in ancient art as he was in literature.

The stories of Heracles and the Greek myths in general are so old that that similar characters and themes seem to recur in different ages and cultures as far back as the beginnings of civilization in Mesopotamia. The Greeks of the Archaic and Classical periods reverently preserved these dark age legends, and passed them on in poems, prose, plays and art. Fidelity to tradition was also my guiding purpose. Obviously, as a novelist I have improvised dialog where the original sources are wanting. But every event in the life of Heracles detailed in these pages has a basis in classical authority. Nothing is invented out of whole cloth. I had originally planned to mention the Argonautic expedition, in which Heracles played a small but somewhat interesting role, only in insofar as it impacted the narrative. Then I decided to include the outward journey in detail, up to the episode where Hylas is lost and Heracles is abandoned in Mysia, returning to the Argonauts at the funeral games of Pelias, where Heracles encountered them on his return from the garden of the Hesperides. But when I considered how long it would have taken Heracles to perform this Labor, I thought it fitting to intersperse his world-spanning trip with further episodes of the *Argo*'s voyage to and from Colchis. This, in hindsight, proved appropriate, since Heracles, by invocations and allusions, haunts the Argonauts throughout their remaining and return journey, a convention particularly evident in Valerius Flaccus' 1st century A.D. incomplete and idiosyncratic account. Many scholars, based particularly on Apollonios Rhodios' 3rd century B.C. *Argonautica*, the only complete account that has come to us of the quest for the Golden Fleece[14], have discovered interesting juxtapositions between Jason, the leader of the expedition, and Heracles. Jason is depicted, they say, as the modern opportunistic anti-hero, propelled as much by his virtues as his vices, while Heracles is parodied as a mindless brute and an anachronistic throwback to a vanished heroic age where violence was the answer

---

[14] The tale, however, is ancient. Homer, in the earliest mention, has the goddess-witch Circe tell Odysseus that the *Argo* was "far-famed" (*Odyssey*, xii.69-72*)*. She should know—she was there to greet Jason as well.

to everything. I do not think Apollonios sought to portray Heracles entirely in this way. He, after all, has Heracles refrain from enjoying himself on an island filled with nubile, willing women, and ends up saving the expedition by his dedication to duty. I hope that by putting the Argonautic story in the context of Heracles, rather than vice versa, I have succeeded in countering Apollonios' depiction of the hero, even if, on a second reading, it is not completely irremediable. Apollonios, in deconstructing and reconstructing the Homeric epic, infuses his work with a humanism not found before in poetry, a feature that would come to be exemplified in Vergil. He created the first romantic epic, where romantic love has power to shape events for heroes that, at times, appear all too human. An honest epic about Heracles, had it been conceived by the sensitive mind of Apollonius or Vergil, would have shared the same infusions. Moreover, by including Jason's quest in full, I had the opportunity to deal with Medeia, who I find as fascinating a character as Heracles. She is perhaps the most fleshed-out and psychologically complex character in the whole of classical literature: among females she is rivaled only by the Carthaginian queen Dido, whom Virgil consciously modeled on Medeia's subtle depiction by Apollonios.

I have also felt it necessary to make Theseus and Heracles closer contemporaries. To do this, I had to set Theseus' arrival at Athens before the Argonauts set sail, which prescinded his conflict with the witch Medeia. Whatever witch sought to sway his father Aigeus against him, in this work it could not have been the wife of Jason. Finally, tradition is strong that Achilles was born during Heracles' lifetime since he too was pupiled by the Centaur Cheiron. If Heracles, however, lived a generation or more before the Trojan War, this presents a difficulty for those who consider Achilles still a relatively young man when he sailed with the Greeks.

Heracles enjoyed an extraordinary number of wives and consorts, and produced an even greater number of children. Apart from the fifty daughters of Thespios, Heracles was believed to have bedded ninety other women. Aristotle counted seventy-two sons and one daughter, but other writers catalog up to one hundred and forty-one sons, not including Thespios' fifty grandsons. To present a flavor of his virility, I have managed to preserve many, but not all, of the liaisons and their offspring in this work; unable, at least in this case, to perform as exhaustively as Heracles.

I feel that historical novels should sound historical. There is nothing more jarring—at least to me—than hearing a "modern" voice in such a work. To prevent this misstep, I have constructed the story as if it were a prose translation of an epic poem written around the time of Homer (8th century B.C.), about four centuries after the Trojan War. The characters—and overall narration—are therefore limited to the vocabulary and knowledge of that time. With this in mind, classical purists may take me to task for my use of the terms "Greece" and "Greek" to describe the land of our hero and its inhabitants. It is well known that Homer did not use those names, nor even Hellenes or Hellas, which technically referred only to the realm of Achilles, Phthia, in Thessaly; but instead generally called them Achaians, Argives and Danaans as the meter suited him. As I was not under poetic constraints, and in need of all-purpose terms to describe world of this novel, I hope I can be forgiven by pedantic readers. Along the same lines, the novel depicts a wide diffusion of Greek colonies and settlements beyond the southern Balkans. Although scholars place the colonization of the Black Sea no earlier than the 7th century B.C., Mycenaean culture, the first Greek-speakers as attested by their Linear B writing, had already founded colonies in Asia Minor by the 15th century B.C. In addition, the geographer Strabo mentions, perhaps from a lost passage, that Homer knew the coast of Asia Minor from the Propontis to Colchis. Homer's near contemporary, Hesiod, already knew of the Phasis and Istros (Danube) rivers. The idea that Heracles in the 13th century B.C. seems to encounter Greeks speakers in Asia Minor and beyond is, therefore, not out of question.

Those broadly familiar with the exploits of Heracles will no doubt notice that I have not, apart from some allusions, referred at all to the battle between the Olympians and the Gigantes, in which Heracles was considered to have taken a decisive part. This battle, known to specialists as the *Gigantomachy*, apart from its über-fantastical elements, is quiet problematic from a historical point of view. Not only are the classical writers unsure about where it took place (the Phlegraian plain of Italy or Phlegrai in Pallene), but the chronology is even more suspect, unlike most of Heracles' other exploits. A war of this magnitude, as Diodorus Siculus mentions that the Egyptians pointed out, could have occurred only in a primeval epoch, closer to the time of the general struggle for Olympian preeminence, and not at all within the historical time of Heracles. It is no wonder, therefore, that the classical writers sometimes confuse this war with the *Titanomachy*, the battle between the Olympians and the Titans, which assuredly took place in prehistory, before even the formation of mankind. The omission of this episode from the present work, then, finds support from no less a raconteur as Homer, who likewise fails to mention it.

The reader will not find perfect consistency with the spelling of proper names. This is a challenge faced by any writer translating or presenting classical subjects. I have tried as much as possible to retain the commonly recognized Greek transliterations, although, for aesthetic reasons, I frequently use the hard consonant 'c' instead of 'k', as in the name of our hero. Where names would otherwise be unrecognizable to the modern reader, I have retained the more familiar Latinate or Anglicized spelling.

It is my hope this work revitalizes Heracles for the modern age, where he has been relegated to low-budget movies, cartoons and syndicated buffoonery. The great 17th century English poet John Dryden believed, like his contemporaries, that the great classical epics—such as Virgil's *Aeneid*, which he magisterially translated—could serve as useful models for the cultivation of "heroic virtue" in its readers. In this spirit, I too present my vision of Heracles: a man who early in life decided to take the hard road, and thereafter lived a life of suffering, for his own sins and those of others. In a life of service and self-sacrifice, he overcame evildoers, rid the land of monsters and dangerous beasts, spread order and civilization wherever he went, and even struggled with death itself to bring a woman back to life. Heracles, who bled and wept— although a demigod, he comes across more human than divine— did it all. It is not generally known that only a small number of mortals in the entire canon of Greek myth were ever made immortal. And of these, only Heracles was raised to heaven specifically to join the select company of the Twelve Olympians. As Walter Burkert wrote, Heracles was such a unique figure that he "contained the potential to shatter the limits of Greek religion." He therefore is a model for every man who struggles to tame the world and himself, with the hope that, at the end, such labor is not performed in vain.  Heracles was the quintessential warrior, the supreme athlete, the prototypical philosopher, the Romantic hero, the savior and protector of mankind, to the medieval world an *exemplum virtutis* and, in breaking the terrors of death, the prefigurement of Christ.  He is truly a hero for the ages.

# A NOTE ON CHRONOLOGY

Saint Jerome, in his Chronicon, an expansion of Eusebius' chronological tables in a work by the same name composed around 380 A.D., mentions that Heracles completed his Labors in 1246 B.C. and that he died at the age of fifty-two (although he also records subsequent events completely out of the original scope). He also mentions that Linos became noted as Heracles' music teacher around 1264 B.C. Where Jerome found these figures is not known, but they serve as a useful reference for establishing a chronology of Heracles' life. Eusebius, in his *Preparation for the Gospel*, records Clement of Alexandria as stating that "from the reign of Heracles in Argos to the deification of Heracles himself and of Asclepios there are comprised thirty-eight years, according to Apollodorus the chronicler: and from that point to the deification of Castor and Polydeuces, fifty-three years: and somewhere about this time the capture of Troy." Heracles never actually reigned in Argos; he merely resided at Tyrins while serving Eurystheus. If we accept that the fall of Troy occurred around 1184/1183 B.C. (according to the 3rd century B.C. Greek mathematician Eratosthenes as well as Jerome), which corresponds quite well with the archeological dating for the destruction of Troy VIIA, the main candidate for the legendary city, we come to the year 1275 B.C. as the time Heracles resided in the Argolid. By this time, Heracles had already killed his children. Heracles, therefore, must have lived some time during the first half of the 13th century B.C., a generation or two before the Trojan War.[15] This dating also accords with that of Herodotus, who, citing what was believed

---

[15] To put this time period into perspective: Heracles' life would have coincided with the Biblical Exodus, at least if the "late" date (mid 13th century B.C.) for that event is held.

among his contemporaries, placed Heracles at 900 years before his time.[16]

Although expecting absolute precision when dating legends is clearly futile, we must accord the efforts of these ancient chronographers some respect. Troy, the hinge of this whole timeline, after all, did exist, as each year uncovers more evidence of the truths of the Homeric record. This work, however, requires a tighter framework within which to depict events. Tradition has it that Zeus turned one night into three during Heracles' conception. Like other recorded sons of god, his coming was heralded by a startling astronomical event. According to NASA projections, a total solar eclipse, lasting almost four minutes, was visible in the Mediterranean on February 10, 1286 B.C[17]. Assuming this event inspired the legend of the long night, Heracles would have been born nine months later, or in early November. His birth, however, was delayed due to the machinations of Hera, and so it is possible he was actually born a month later. This conclusion accords with Ovid, who depicts Heracles as born when the sun entered the tenth zodiacal sign (Capricorn)[18]. If Heracles was born in 1286 B.C., then he died fifty-two years later in 1234 B.C., perhaps in July or early August, when the Athenians came to celebrate his festival.

---

[16] *Histories*, ii. 145 (4). Herodotus was active in the mid 5th century B.C.

[17] Others point to another eclipse that occurred on September 7th, 1251 B.C. as marking Heracles' birth, but this seems to me rather late, and the eclipse being annular and not total, a poorer prodigy.

[18] Ovid, *Metamorphosis*, ix. The sun crosses Capricorn from late December to January. A birth at the winter solstice is not uncommon for gods and demigods.

## MAP AND GENEALOGY

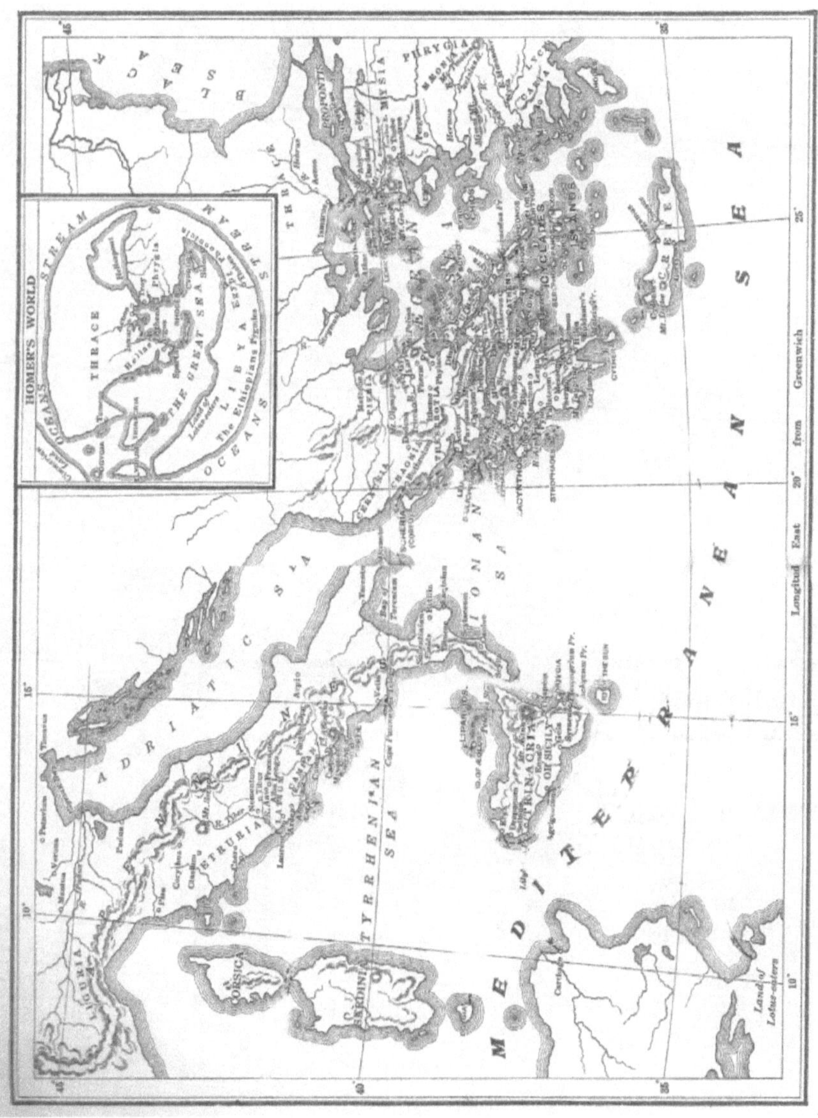

# The Heracliad

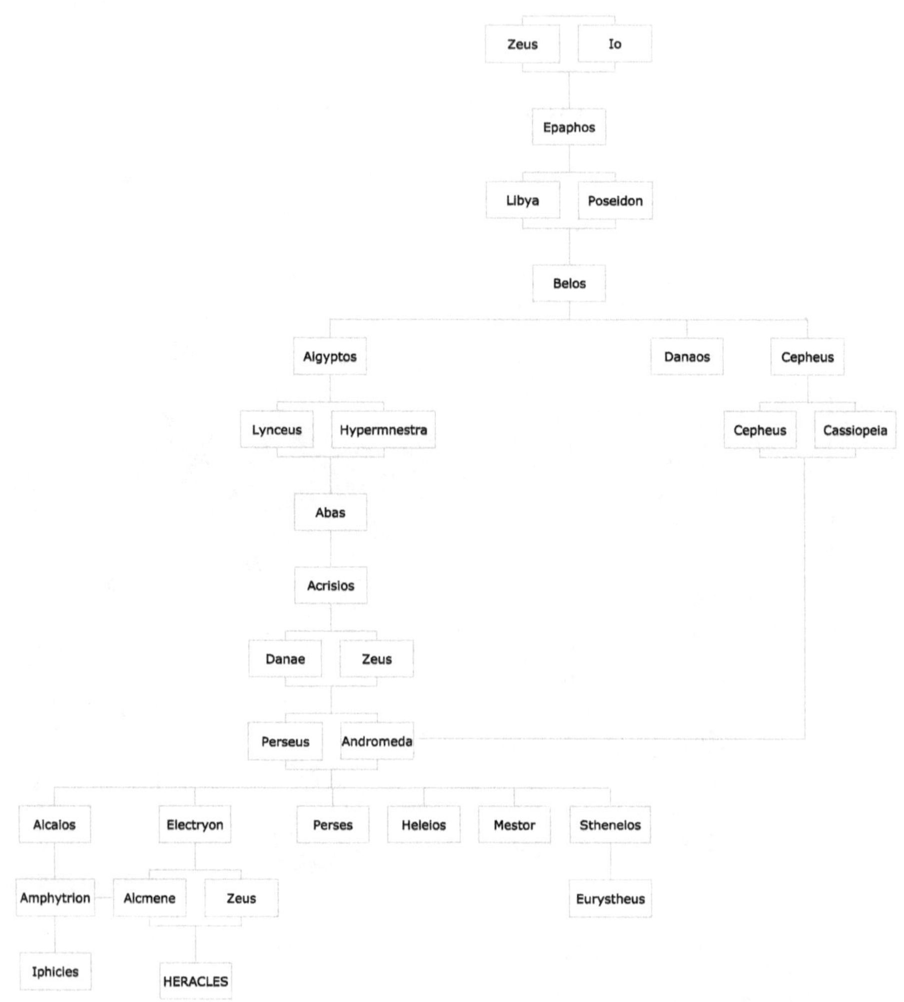

## SOURCES

The number of citations of Heracles in ancient works is vast. I have attempted here to compile a list of the literary sources offering substantial or important references. Entries marked with an asterisk are lost and quoted or merely cited by other authors, or exist only in fragments. There exist also valuable ancient *scholia*, or marginal notes, on the works of Homer, Vergil, Pindar and others.

<u>Primary References</u>

Acusilaus *
Aelian, *De Natura Animalium*
Aelian, *Varia Historia*
Aeschylus, *Alcmene* *
Aeschylus, *Children of Heracles* *
Aeschylus, *Prometheus Bound*
Aeschylus, *Prometheus Unbound* *
Alcaeus *
Alcidamas, *Odysseus*
Alcman, *Partheneion* *
Anacreon *
Antoninus Liberalis, *Metamorphosis*
Apollodorus, *Library*
Appollonius of Rhodes, *Argonautica*
Archilochus *
Aristophanes, *The Birds*
Aristophanes, *The Frogs*
Arrian, *Indica*
Atheneaus, *Deipnosophista*
Aulus Gellius, *Attic Nights*
Bacchylides, *Odes*

Callimachus, *Hymns*
Cicero, *De Natura Deorum*
Cicero, *De Officiis*
Conon, *Narrations*
Creophylus, *Oichalis Halosis* *
Dares Phrygius, *History of the Fall of Troy*
Demodocus, *Heracleia* *
Dercyllus, *Italian History*
Diodorus Siculus, *History*
Dionysius of Halicarnassos, *Roman Antiquities*
Diotimus, *Heracleia* *
Ephorus *
Epimenides *
Erastosthenes, *Catasterismoi*
Euphorion *
Euripides, *Alcestis*
Euripides, *Auge* *
Euripides, *Heracleidae*
Euripides, *Heracles*
Euripides, *Ion*
Euripides, *Merope* *
Euripides, *Syleus* *
Eustathius *
Hecataeus *
Hellanicus *
Herodorus, *Heracleia* *
Herodotus, *History of the Persian Wars*
Hesiod, *Aigimos* *
Hesiod, *Ehoiai* *
Hesiod, *Shield of Heracles* *
Hesiod, *Theogony*
Hesiod, *Wedding of Ceyx* *
Homer, *Illiad*
Homer, *Odyssey*
*Homeric Hymns*
Hyginus, *Astronomie*
Hyginus, *Fabulae*
Isocrates, *Bursiris*
Isocrates, *Panegyricus*

Justin, *Epitome of the History of Pompeius Trogus*
Kinaithon, *Heracleia* *
Lactantius, *Divine Institutes*
Livy, *The History of Rome*
Lucan, *Pharsalia*
Lucian, *Dialogues of the Dead*
Lucian, *Hermotimus*
Lucian, *Preludes*
Lucian, *Dialogues of the Gods*
Lucretius, *De rerum natura*
Lycias, *Funeral Oration*
Lysimachus *
Macrobius, *Saturnalia*
Nepos, *Life of Hannibal*
Nicolas of Damascus *
Oppian, *Cynegetica*
Ovid, *Fasti*
Ovid, *Heroides*
Ovid, *Metamorphoses*
Palaephatos, *On Unbelievable Tales*
Panyassis, *Heracleia* *
Parthenius *
Pausanias, *Guide To Greece*
Peisander, *Heracleia* *
Phaedimus, *Heracleia* *
Pherecydes *
Philochorus *
Philochorus *
Philostratus, *Imagines*
Philostratus, *Life of Apollonius of Tyana* *
Phrynickos, *Alcestis* *
Phrynickos, *Antaios* *
Pindar, *Nemean Odes*
Pindar, *Olympic Odes*
Pindar, *Pythian Odes*
Plautus, *Amphytrio*
Pliny the Elder, *Natural History*
Plutarch, *Greek Questions*
Plutarch, *Moralia*

Plutarch, *On Love*
Plutarch, *Parallel Stories*
Plutarch, *Roman Questions*
Plutarch, *Sertorius*
Pollux, *Onomasticon*
Polyaenus, *Stratagems*
Prodikos, *Minyad*
Propertius, *Elegies*
Ptolemy Hephaestion, *New History*
Seneca, *Hercules Furens*
Seneca, *Hercules Oetaeus*
Seneca, *Hippolytus*
Servius, *Eclogues*
Simonides *
Sophocles, *Ajax*
Sophocles, *Cerberos* *
Sophocles, *Heracles at Tainaron* *
Sophocles, *Philoctetes*
Sophocles, *Trachiniai*
Sosibius *
Statius, *Thebaid*
Stesichoros, *Cerberos* *
Stesichoros, *Cycnos* *
Stesichoros, *Geryoneis* *
Strabo, *Geography*
Tacitus, *Annals*
Theocritos, *Idylls*
Tzetzes, *Chiliades*
Tzetzes, *On Lycophron*
Valerius Flaccus, *Argonautica*
Virgil, *Aeneid*
Virgil, *Eclogues*
Virgil, *Georgics*
Xenophon, *Anabasis*
Xenophon, *Memorabilia*
Zenobios, *Proverbs*

<u>Secondary References</u>

I have included here only focused scholarly treatments of the exploits or significance of Heracles, omitting the well-known popular summaries from Rouse, Hamilton and others.

Blanshard, Alastair. *Hercules: A Heroic Life*. London: Granta, 2007.

Bowden, Hugh & Rawlings, Louis, eds. *Herakles and Hercules*. Swansea: Classical Press of Wales, 2005.

Brommer, Frank. Heracles: *The Twelve Labors of the Hero in Ancient Art and Literature*. New Rochelle, NY: Caratzas, 1986.

Campbell, Joseph. *The Hero with a Thousand Faces*. Berkeley: University of California Press, 1983.

Galinsky, C. Karl. *The Herakles Theme: The Adaptation of the Hero in Literature from Homer to the Twentieth Century*. Oxford: Blackwell, 1972.

Gantz, Timothy. *Early Greek Myth*. Baltimore: Johns Hopkins Press, 1993.

Graves, Robert. *The Greek Myths*. New York: Moyer Bell Limited, 1988.

Hard, Robin. *The Routledge Handbook of Greek Mythology*. New York: Routledge, 2008.

Kerenyi, C. *The Heroes of the Greeks*. London: Thames and Hudson, 1959.

Stafford, Emma: *Herakles*. New York: Routledge, 2012.